WASTELANDS
THE NEW APOCALYPSE

Also edited by John Joseph Adams

* From Titan Books

WASTELANDS
THE NEW APOCALYPSE

EDITED BY
JOHN JOSEPH ADAMS

TITAN BOOKS

WASTELANDS: A NEW APOCALYPSE

Print edition ISBN: 9781785658952
E-book edition ISBN: 9781785658969

Published by Titan Books
A division of Titan Publishing Group Ltd
144 Southwark St, London SE1 0UP
www.titanbooks.com

First Titan Books edition: June 2019
2 4 6 8 10 9 7 5 3

CONTENTS

INTRODUCTION

JOHN JOSEPH ADAMS

As I write this, it's Thanksgiving. A lot of us, including me, have a lot of things to be thankful for. Yet by any reasonable assessment, the world as a whole today seems closer to the precipice of apocalypse than perhaps it has ever been. The Doomsday Clock—maintained by the Bulletin of the Atomic Scientists—shows that we are at two minutes to midnight... which means we're the closest we've been to "doomsday" since 1953.

But if you pay attention to the news at all, you don't need the Doomsday Clock to tell you that. While it is tempting to leave aside—as the subject matter for an introduction to a different anthology—the dystopian elements of today's world (which are legion), the slow but alarmingly frequent collapse of democracies around the world, coupled with the rise of authoritarian regimes and divisive, hateful rhetoric, makes World War III look like an increasingly frightening—and disturbingly probable—outcome.

Of course, destroying ourselves with weapons of war is just one of many possible apocalyptic scenarios that could come to pass. Climate change looms over everything as an omnipresent and terrifying threat to the entire world. I'm witnessing it up close and personal as I write this from my home in California, where there are raging wildfires burning to both the north and south of me—thankfully far enough away that my family is in no danger. Not everyone was so lucky... including the residents of the town called Paradise (which now is anything but). Yet we still have people—including prominent world leaders—denying anthropogenic influence and moving too slowly to try to arrest the progress of climate change. As I've said in the introduction to my climate fiction anthology *Loosed Upon the World*, "Welcome to the end of the world, already in progress."

There are many other ways the world might end. A huge extraterrestrial object slamming into the Earth might cause an extinction-level event. Hell, a huge extraterrestrial *race* might do the same. Neither of these seem terribly likely, though if I were the kind of ghoul who'd bet on how the world will end, I'd put way more money on one than the other.

Or there's always the chance that a horrible pandemic will wipe us out, leaving behind a world devoid of people, and nothing but the edifices of civilization as monuments to what we achieved as sentient creatures. Or—getting back to anthropogenic apocalypses for a moment—there's always the chance some rogue nation will engineer a biological weapon to wipe out a specific population, thereby dooming the entire world by mistake. Or, hey, maybe we'll try to do something *good* with viruses, like releasing some kind of engineered microbe into the atmosphere—perhaps designed to combat climate change. Then everything goes awry, and actively, literally kills us.

My point being: We're almost certainly and in all conceivable ways fucked six ways to Sunday.

Despite that, it somehow still remains entertaining to imagine being one of the survivors, to be one of the ones "scrounging for cans of pork and beans"* and maybe even finding yourself with the responsibility of trying to build a new world from the ashes of the old.

So once again, I've delved into the vault[†] and gathered more "memorabilia"[‡] of the apocalypse… all for your reading "pleasure." The selections you'll find here all come from the last several years—thirty-four stories total, including twenty reprints and fourteen never-before-published tales.

I can only hope you'll get to read them before the end actually comes…

---

* After John Varley, from "The Manhattan Phone Book, Abridged".
† After *Fallout*, but with the small "v" to stay grammatically correct in this particular context.
‡ After Walter M. Miller, Jr., in *A Canticle for Leibowitz*.

BULLET POINT

ELIZABETH BEAR

Elizabeth Bear was born on the same day as Frodo and Bilbo Baggins, but in a different year. She is the Hugo, Sturgeon, Locus, and Campbell Award winning author of thirty novels and more than a hundred short stories, and her hobbies of rock climbing, archery, kayaking, and horseback riding have led more than one person to accuse her of prepping for a portal fantasy adventure. She lives in Massachusetts with her husband, writer Scott Lynch.

It takes a long time for the light to die. The power plants can run for a while on automation. Hospitals have emergency generators with massive tanks of fuel. Some houses and businesses have solar panels or windmills. Those may keep making juice, at least intermittently, until entropy claims the workings.

How long is it likely to take then? Six months? The better part of a decade?

I stand on the roof deck of the Luxor casino parking garage, watching the lights that remain, and I wonder. I don't even know enough to theorize, really.

I'm not an engineer. I used to be a blackjack dealer.

Now I am the only living human left on Earth.

It's not all bad. I don't have to deal with:

- Death (except the possibility of my own, eventually).

- Taxes.
- Annoying holidays with my former extended family.
- Airplane lights crossing the desert sky.
- Chemtrails (okay, those were never real in the first place).
- Card counters.
- Maisie the pit boss. Thank God.
- My ex-husband. *Double* thank God.

Well, of course I can't know for sure that I'm the only living person. But for all practical purposes, I seem to be. Maybe Las Vegas is the only place that got wiped out. Maybe over the mountain, Pahrump is thriving.

I don't think so. I hear the abandoned dog packs howling in the night, and I've watched the lights go out, one by one by one.

I feel so bad for those dogs. And even worse for all the ones trapped in houses when the end came. All the cats, guinea pigs, pet turtles. The horses and burros, at least, have a chance. Wild horses can survive in Nevada.

There are so many of them. There's nothing I can do.

If there are any other humans surviving, they are far away from here, and I have no idea where to find them, or even how to begin looking. I have to get out of the desert, though, if I want to keep living. For oh, so many reasons.

I can trust myself, at least. Trusting anybody else never got me where I wanted to be.

Another thing I don't know for sure, and can't even guess at: Why. Not knowing why?

That's the real pisser.

Here is an incomplete list of things that do not exist anymore:

- Fresh-baked cookies (unless I find a propane oven and milk a cow and churn some butter and then bake them).
- Jesus freaks (I wonder how they felt when the Rapture happened and it turned out God was taking almost *literally everybody*? That had to be a little bit of a come-down).

- Domestic violence.
- Did I mention my ex-husband?

There's more than enough Twinkies just in the Las Vegas metro area to keep me in snack cakes until the saturated fat kills me. If I last long enough that that's what gets me, I might even find out if they eventually go stale.

A problem with being in Las Vegas is getting back out of it again. Walking across a desert will kill me faster than snack cakes. And the highway is impassable with all the stopped and empty cars.

Maybe I can find a monster truck and drive it over everything.

More things that don't exist anymore:

- Reckless driving.
- Speeding tickets.
- Points on your license.
- Worrying about fuel efficiency.

Las Vegas Boulevard is dark and still. Nevertheless, I can't make myself walk on the blacktop, even though the cars there are unmoving, bumper to bumper for all eternity. The Strip's last traffic jam.

There might be bodies in the cars. I don't look.

I don't want to know.

I don't think there's going to be anybody alive, but that might be worse. More dangerous, anyway.

I mean, I *think* I'm the last. But I don't *know*.

That was also the reason I couldn't make myself walk along the sidewalk. It was too exposed. The tall casinos were mostly designed so that their windows had views of something more interesting than hordes of pedestrians—hordes of pedestrians now long gone—but somebody might be up there, and somebody up there might spot me. A lone moving dot on a sea of silent asphalt.

Lord, where have all the people gone?

So I stick to the median. With its crape myrtle hedges and doomed palm trees already drooping in the failed irrigation to break up my outline. With the now pointless crowd control barriers to discourage jaywalkers from darting into traffic.

Two more things:

- Traffic.
- Jaywalkers.

Hey, and one more:

- Assholes.

I am half hoping to find people. And I am 90% terrified of what they might do if I find them. Or if they find me first.

I'm pretty sure this wasn't actually the Rapture.

Pretty sure.

I keep trying to tell myself that there's not a single damned person from the old world that I really miss. That it's time I had some time alone, as the song used to go. It is nice not to be on anybody else's schedule, or subject to anybody else's expectations or demands. At least my ex-husband is almost certainly among the evaporated. That's a load off my mind.

I moved to Vegas, changed my name by sealed court order, abandoned a career I worked for ten years to get, and became a casino dealer in order to hide from him. Considering that, it's not a surprise to find myself relieved that whatever ends up causing me to look over my shoulder from now on, it won't be Paul.

I got the cozy apocalypse that was supposed to be the best-case-apocalypse-scenario—wish fulfillment—complete with the feral dogs that howl in the night.

But it doesn't feel like wish fulfillment. It feels like... being alone on the beach in winter. I'm lonely, and I miss... well, I already left behind everybody I loved. But leaving somebody behind is not the same thing as *knowing they are gone.*

There's potential space, and there's empty space.

Maybe that's why I'm still here. Nobody thought to tap me on the shoulder and say, "Hey, Izzy, let's go," because I'd already abandoned all of them to save my own life one time.

Hah. There I go again. Making things about me that aren't.

I thought I was used to being lonely, but this is a whole new level of alone. I feel like I should be paralyzed by survivor guilt. But I am a rock. I am an island.

- Simon
- Garfunkel

Lying to yourself is, however, still alive and well.

The gun is heavy. Cold, blue metal. It feels about twice its size.

I find it under the seat of a cop car with the driver's door left open. The keys are in the ignition. The dome light has long since burned out, and the open-door dinger has dinged itself into silence.

It's a handgun. A revolver. Old School. There is a holster to go with it, but no gunbelt. There are six bullets in the cylinder.

- The Las Vegas Metropolitan Police Department.
- Crooked cops.
- Throwaway guns.

I unbuckle my belt, thread it through the loops on the holster, and hang it at my hip.

There *are* plenty of rattlesnakes, still.

- Antivenin.
- Emergency rooms.

There *are* plenty of antibiotics. And pain medication. And canned peaches.

And a nice ten-speed mountain bike that I liberate from a sporting goods place, along with one of those trailers designed for pulling your kid or dog along. I've never been much of an urban biker, preferring trails, but it wasn't like I would have to contend with traffic. And it seems like the right tool for weaving in and out of rows of abandoned cars.

I pick up a book on bike repair too, and some tire patches and spare tubes and so on. Plus saddlebags and baskets. And a lot of water bottles.

It turns out that one thing the zombie apocalypse movies got really wrong was the abundance of stockpiled resources available after a population of more than seven billion people just… ceases to exist.

There's plenty of stuff to go around when there's no "around" for it to go. Until the stuff goes bad, anyway.

That's the reason I want to get out of the desert before summer comes. Things will last longer in colder places, with less murderous UV.

Things that apparently *do* still exist: at least one other human being.

And he is following me.

He picks me up at a Von's. I'm in the pasta aisle. The rats have started gnawing into boxes, but the canned goods are relatively fine. And if you can ignore the silence of the gaming machines and the smell of fermenting fruit, rotten meat, and rodent urine, it's not that different than if I were shopping at 2 am in the old world.

I'm crouched down, filling my backpack with Beefaroni and D batteries from the endcap, when I hear footsteps. It's daylight outside, but it's dark inside the store. I turn off my LED flashlight. My heart contracts inside me, shuddering jolts of blood through my arteries. The rush and thump fills my ears. I strain through them for the sounds that mean life or death: the scrape or squeak of boot sole on tile, the rattle of packages.

My hands shake as I zip the backpack inch by silent inch. I stand. The straps creak. I can't be sure if I have managed not to tremble the bag into a betraying clink. One step, then another. Sideways, slipping, setting each foot down carefully so it doesn't make a sound.

As I get closer to the front of the store (good) the ambiance grows brighter (bad). I hunker by the side of a dead slot machine, shivering. From where I crouch, I can peek around and see a clear path to the door.

The whole way is silhouetted against the plate glass windows. The pack weighs on my shoulders. If I leave it, I'm not really leaving anything. I can get another, and all the Chef Boyardee I want. But it's hard to abandon resources.

And hey, the cans might stop a bullet.

Don't hyperventilate.

Easier said than done.

Sliding doors stopped working when the store lights did. Too late, I realize there's probably a fire door in the back I could have slipped out of more easily. In the old world, that would have been alarmed... but would the alarm even work anymore?

There is a panic bar on the front doors. I crane over my shoulder, straining for motion, color, any sign of the person I am certain I heard.

Nothing.

Maybe I'm hallucinating.

Maybe he's gone to the back of the store.

I nerve myself and hit the door running. I got it open on the way in, so I know it isn't locked. It flies away from the crash bar—no subtlety there—and I plunge through, sneakers slapping the pavement. The parking lot outside is flat and baking, even in September. The sun hits my ballcap like a slap. Rose bushes and trees scattered in the islands are already dead from lack of water. The rosemary bushes and crape myrtles look a little sad, but they are holding on.

I sprint toward them. Now the pack makes noise, the cans within clanking and thumping on each other—and clanking and thumping against my ribs and spine. I'll have a suite of bruises because of them. But I left my bike on the kickstand in the fire lane, and—wonder of wonders—it's still there. I throw myself at it and swing a leg through, pushing off with my feet before I ever touch the pedals. I miss my first push and skin the back of my calf bloody on the serrated grip.

I curse, not loud but on that hiss of breath you get with shock and pain. The second time, I manage to get my heel *on* the pedal. The bike jerks forward with each hard pump.

I squirt between parked cars. As my heart slows, I let myself think I've imagined the whole thing. Until the supermarket doors crash open, and a male voice shrill with desperation yells, "Miss! Come back! Miss! Don't run away from me! Please! I'm not going to hurt you!"

And maybe he's not. But I'm not inclined to trust. Trusting never did get me anywhere I wanted to be.

I push down and pedal harder. I don't coast.

He only shouts after me. He doesn't shoot. And I don't look back.

Now that he knows I exist, he's not going to stop looking.

I know this the way I know my childhood street address.

And why *would* he stop? People need people, or so we're always told. Being alone—really alone, completely alone—is a form of torture.

To be utterly truthful, there's a part of me that wants to go looking for him. Part of me that doesn't want to be alone anymore either.

The question I have to ask myself is whether that lonely part of me is stronger than the feral, sensible part that cautions me to run away. To run, and keep running.

Because it's the apocalypse. And I'm not very big, or a trained fighter. And because of another thing that doesn't exist anymore:

• Social controls.

Dissociation, though—that I've got *plenty* of.

He is going to come looking for me. Because of course he will. I hear him calling after me for a long time as I ride away. And I know he tries to follow me because *I* follow *him*.

We're the last two people on Earth and how do you get more Meet Cute than that? We've all stayed up late watching B movies in the nosebleed section of the cable channels and we've all read

TV Tropes and we all know how this story goes.

But my name isn't Eve. It's Isabella. And I have an allergy to clichés.

- Dating websites.
- Restraining orders.
- Twitter block lists.
- Domestic violence shelters.

I stalk him. I'll call it what it is.

It's easy to find him again: he's so confident and fearless that he's still wandering around in the same neighborhood *trying* to get my attention.

I mean, first I go back to my current lair and get ready to run.

I load up the bike trailer with my food and gear, and flats and flats and flats of water. My sun layers and my hat go inside and I zip the whole thing up.

Then I hide it, and I check again to be sure my gun is loaded.

And *then* I go and stalk him.

He's definitely a lot bigger than me. But he doesn't look a damned thing like my ex, which is a point in his favor.

And he isn't trying in the least to be sneaky. He's just walking down the sidewalk, swerving to miss the cars that rolled off the road when their drivers disappeared, pulling a kid's little red wagon loaded with supplies. He's armed with a pistol on his belt, but so am I. And at least he's not strung all over with bandoliers and automatic weapons. Plus, there are enough of those hungry, terrified feral dog packs around that a weapon isn't a bad idea.

I wonder how long it will be before the cougars move back down from the mountains and start eating them all.

The circle of life.

Poor dogs.

They were counting on us, and look where that got them.

* * *

The only other living human being (presumed) is wearing a dirty T-shirt (athletic gray), faded jeans, and a pair of high-top skull-pattern Chucks that I appreciate the irony of, even while knowing his feet must be roasting in them. I make him out to be about twenty-five. His hair is still pretty clean cut under his mesh-sided brimmed hat, but he's wearing about two weeks of untrimmed beard. Two weeks is about how long it's been since the world ended.

He calls out as he walks along. How can anyone be so unafraid to attract attention? So confident of taking up all that space in the world? Like he thinks he has a right to exist and nobody is going to come take it away from him.

He's so *relaxed.* It scares me just watching him.

I *do* notice that he doesn't seem threatening. There's nothing sinister, calculated, or menacing about this guy. He keeps pushing his hat up to mop the sweat from under it with an old cotton bandanna. He doesn't have a lot of situational awareness, either. Even with me orbiting him a couple of blocks off on the mountain bike, he doesn't seem to notice me watching. I'm staying under cover, sure. But the bike isn't silent. It has a chain and wheels and joints. It creaks and rattles and whizzes a little, like any bicycle.

Blood has dried, itchy and tight-feeling, on the back of my calf. The edge of my sock is stiff. I drink some of the water in my bottle, though not as much as I want to.

It's getting on toward evening and he's walking more directly now, in less of a searching wander, when I make up my mind. He seems to be taking a break from searching for me, at least for the time being. He's stopped making forays into side streets, and he's stopped calling out.

I cycle hard on a parallel street to get in front of him, and from a block away I show myself.

He stops in his tracks. His hands move away from his sides and he drops the little red wagon handle. My right hand stays on the butt of my holstered gun with the six bullets in it.

"Hi," he says, after an awkward pause. He pitches his voice to carry. "I'm Ben."

"Hi," I call back. "I'm Isabella."

"You came back."

I nod. Never in my memory—probably in living memory—has it been quiet enough in this city that you could hear somebody clearly if they called to you from this far away. But it's that quiet now. Honey bees buzz on the crape myrtles. I wonder if they're Africanized.

"Nice bike, Isabella."

"Thanks." I let the smirk happen. "It's new."

He laughs. Then he bends down and picks up the handle of his little red wagon. When he straightens, he lets his hands hang naturally. "Have you seen anybody else?"

I shake my head.

"Me neither." He makes a face. "Mind if I come over?"

My heart speeds. But it's respectful that he's asking, right?

I don't get off the bike or walk it toward him. I cant it against one cocked leg and wait.

"Sure." I try to sound confident. I square my shoulders.

You know what else doesn't exist anymore?

- Backup.

We head off side by side. I've finally gotten off the bike and am walking it, though I casually keep it and the wagon in between us and stay out of grabbing range. The step-through frame will help me hop on and bug out fast if I need to.

Ben offers me a granola bar. I guess he learned early on, as I did, that once the power went off, there wasn't any point in harvesting chocolate. Well, I mean, it's still calorie-dense. But if it's daytime, it's probably squeezable. And if it's not melted, it has re-solidified into the wrapper and you'll wind up eating a fair amount of plastic.

"Terrorists," he hazards, with the air of one making conversation.

I shake my head. "Aliens."

He thinks about it.

"We probably had it coming," I posit.

"I don't think it's a great idea to stay in Vegas," Ben says, with no acknowledgment of the non sequitur.

"I've been thinking that too."

He glances sidelong at me. His face brightens. "I was thinking of heading to San Diego. Nice and temperate. Lots of seafood. Easy to grow fruit. Not as hot as here."

I think about earthquakes and drought and wildfires. My plan was the Pacific Northwest, where the climate is mild and wet and un-irrigated agriculture could flourish. I figure I've got maybe five years to figure out a sustainable lifestyle.

And I don't want to spend the rest of my life living off ceviche. Or dodging wildfires and worrying about potable water.

I don't say anything, though. If I decide to split on this guy, it's just as well if he doesn't know what my plans were. Especially if we're the last two people on Earth.

Why him? Why me?

Who knows.

"Lot of avocados down there." I can sound like I'm agreeing to nearly anything.

He nods companionably. "The bike is a good idea."

"I'd be a little scared to try cycling across the mountains and through Baker. That's some nasty desert."

Mild pushback, to see what happens in response.

"I figure you could make it in a week or ten days."

That would be some Tour de France shit, Ben. Especially towing water. But I don't say that.

- Tour de France.

"Or," he says, "I thought of maybe a Humvee. Soon, while the gas is still good."

He loses a few points on that. I wouldn't feel bad at all about bullet pointing Hummers, and I don't feel nearly as bad about bullet pointing the sort of people who used to drive them as I probably ought to.

"Look," Ben says, when I've been quiet for a while, "why don't we find someplace to hole up? It's getting dark, and the dog packs will be out soon."

I look at him and can't think what to say.

He sighs tolerantly, not getting it. I guess *not getting it* isn't over yet either.

"I give you my word of honor that I will be a total gentleman."

You have to trust somebody sometime.

I go home with Ben. Not in the euphemistic sense. In the sense that we pick a random house and break into it together. It has barred security doors and breaking in would be harder, except the yard wasn't xeriscaped and all the

- Landscaping

is down to brown sticks and sadness. Which makes it super easy to spot the fake rock that had once been concealed in a now-desiccated foundation planting, turn it over, and extract the key hidden inside.

We let ourselves in. There used to be a security system, but it's out of juice. The house is hot and dark inside, and smells like decay. Plant decay, mostly: sweetish and overripe, due to the fruit rotting in bowls on the counter. Neither Ben nor I is dumb enough to open the refrigerator. We do check the bedrooms for bodies. There aren't any—there never are—but we find the remains of a hamster that starved and had mummified in its cedar chips.

That makes me sad, like the dog packs. If this *is* the Rapture, I hope God gets a nasty call from the Afterlife Society for the Prevention of Cruelty to Animals.

We find can openers and plates and set about rustling up some supper. All the biking has made us ravenous, and when I finish eating, I am surprised to discover that I have let my guard down. And that nothing terrible has happened.

Ben looks at me across the drift of SPAM cans and Green Giant vacuum-pack corn (my favorite). "This would be perfect if the air conditioning worked."

"Sometimes you can find a place with solar panels," I say noncommittally.

"Funny that all that tree hugging turned out useful after all, isn't it?" And maybe he sees the look on my face, because he raises a hand, placating. "Some of my best friends are tree huggers!" He looks down, mouth twisting. "*Were* tree huggers."

So I forgive him. "My plan had been to find someplace that was convenient and had solar, and if I was lucky its own well. And wait for winter before I set out."

"That's a good idea." He picks at a canned peach.

"Also, the older houses up in Northtown and on the west side of the valley. Those handle the heat better."

"Little dark up there in North Vegas," Ben says, casually. "I mean, not that there's anybody left, but it was."

I open my mouth. I close it. I almost hear the record scratch.

I'd have thought it was safe to bullet

- Racism.

But I guess not.

I don't say, *So it's full of evaporated black people cooties?* I get up, instead, and start clearing empty tin cans off the table and setting them in the useless sink. Ben watches me, amused that I'm tidying this place we're only going to abandon.

Setting things to rights, the only way I can.

He's relaxed and expansive now. A little proprietary.

I am not *quite* as scared as I ever have been in my life. But that's only because I've been really, *really* scared.

"It's just us now. You don't have anybody to impress," Ben says. "You're free. You don't have to play those games to get ahead."

I blink at him. "Games?"

He stands up. I turn toward the sink. Knives in the knife block beside it. If it comes down to it, they might be worth a try. I try to keep my eyes forward, to not give him a reason to think I'm being impertinent. But I keep glancing back.

I look scared. And that's bad. You never want to look scared.

It attracts predators.

"Nobody can hurt you for saying the truth now. And obviously," he says with something he probably means to be taken as a coaxing smile, "it's up to us to repopulate the planet."

"With white people." It just comes out. I've never been the best at self-censorship. Even when I know speaking might get me hurt.

At least I keep my tone neutral. I think.

Neutral enough, I guess, because he leers again. "Maybe God's given us a second chance to get it right, is all I'm saying. Don't you think it's a sign? I mean, here I meet the last woman on earth, and she's a blue-eyed blonde."

The little tins fit inside the big tins. The spoons stack up.

- Ice cream.

Though I could probably make some, if I found that cow. And snow. And bottle blondes are still going to be around until my hair grows out. I don't have any reason to try to change my appearance now.

Ben moves, the floor creaking under him. "If you're not going to try to save humanity, what's the point in even being alive? Are you going to just give up?"

I turn toward him. I put my back toward the sink. I half-expect him to be looming over me but he's standing well back, respectfully. "Maybe humanity has a lifespan, like everything else. You're going to die eventually."

"Sure," he says. "That's why people have kids. To leave a legacy. Leave something of themselves behind."

"Two human beings are not a viable gene pool."

"You don't want to rush into anything," he says. "That's all right. I can respect that."

And then he does something that stuns me utterly. He goes and lies down on the sofa. He only glances back at me once. The expression on his face is trying to be neutral, but I can see the smugness beneath it.

The fucking *confidence*.

Of course he doesn't need to push his luck, or my timeline. Of course he's confident I'll come around. He's got all the time in the world.

And what choice have I got in the long run, really?

* * *

There will always be assholes.

I leave that house in the morning at first light. I lock the door behind me to be tidy.

Only four bullets left. I should have anticipated that I might need more ammo. But this is Nevada. I can probably find some.

Maybe I can find a friendly dog, also. I love dogs. And it's not good for people to be too alone.

There might still be some horses out in the northwest valley that haven't gone totally wild. It'd be nice to have company.

I can get books from the libraries. I've got a few months to prepare. I wonder how you take care of a horse on a long pack trip? I wonder if I can manage it on my own?

Well, I'll find out this winter. And if I get to Reno before the snow melts in the Sierras… I'm a patient girl. And I'll have the benefit of not having slept through history class. What I mean to say is, I can wait to tackle Donner Pass until springtime.

The lights that are still on *stay* on longer than I might have expected. But eventually, one by one, they fail. When I can't see any anywhere anymore, I make my way down to the Strip with Bruce, my brindle mastiff, trotting beside.

Before I head north, I want to say goodbye.

That night the stars shine over Las Vegas, as they have not shone in living memory. The Milky Way is a misty waterfall. I can make out a Subaru logo for the ages: six and a half Pleiades.

I stand in the middle of the empty, dark and silent Strip, and watch the lack of answering lights bloom in the vast black bowl of the valley all around.

I cannot see so far as Tokyo, New York, Hong Kong, London, Cairo, Jerusalem, Abu Dhabi, Seoul, Sydney, Rio de Janeiro, Paris, Madrid, Kyoto, Chicago, Amsterdam, Mumbai, Mecca, Milan. All the places where artificial light and smog had, for an infinitesimal cosmic moment, wiped them from the sky. But I imagine that those distant, alien suns now shine the same way, there.

As if they had never been dimmed. As if the Milky Way had never faded, ghostlike, before the glare.

I reach down and stroke Bruce's ears. They're soft as cashmere. He leans on me, happy.

That night sky would be a remarkable sight. If I had a soul in the world to remark to.

THE RED THREAD

SOFIA SAMATAR

Sofia Samatar is the author of the novels *A Stranger in Olondria* and *The Winged Histories*, the short story collection, *Tender*, and *Monster Portraits*, a collaboration with her brother, the artist Del Samatar. Her work has received several honors, including the John W. Campbell Award and the World Fantasy Award. Her short fiction has appeared in magazines such as *Strange Horizons*, *Lightspeed Magazine*, and *Uncanny*, and has been reprinted in *Best American Science Fiction and Fantasy*. She lives in Virginia, where she teaches world literature and speculative fiction at James Madison University.

Dear Fox,

Hey. It's Sahra. I'm tagging you from center M691, Black Hawk, South Dakota. It's night and the lights are on in the center. It's run by an old white guy with a hanging lip—he's talking to my mom at the counter. Mom's okay. We've barely mentioned you since we left the old group in the valley, just a few weeks after you disappeared. She said your name once, when I found one of your old slates covered with equations. "Well," she said. "That was Fox."

One time—I don't think I told you this—we lost some stuff over a bridge. Back in California, before we met you. The wind was so strong that day, we were stupid to cross. We lost a box of my dad's stuff, mostly books, and Mom said: "Well. There he goes."

Like I said, the wind was strong. She probably thought I didn't hear her.

I think she's looking at me. Hard to tell through the glass, it's all scratched and smeared with dead bugs. I guess I should go. We're headed north—yeah, straight into winter. It's Mom's idea.

I've still got the bracelet you gave me. It's turning my wrist red.

Dear Fox,

Hey. It's Sahra. I'm at center M718, Big Bottom, South Dakota. That's really the name. There's almost nothing here but a falling-down house with a giant basement. They've got a cantenna, so I figured I'd tag you again.

Did you get my message?

It's crowded in here. I feel like someone's about to look over my shoulder.

Anyway, the basement's beautiful, full of oak arches. It's warm, and they've got these dim red lights, like the way the sky gets in the desert sometimes, and there's good people, including a couple of oldish ladies who are talking to Mom. One of them has her hair up and a lot of dry twigs stuck in. She calls me Chicken. It's embarrassing, but I don't really care. They've got a stove and they gave us these piles of hot bread folded up like cloth. Are you okay? I'm just thinking, you know, are you eating and stuff.

Big Bottom. You won't forget that. It's by a forest.

Don't go in the forest if you come through here. There's an isolation zone in there. We even heard a gunshot on our way past. Mom's shoulders went stiff and she said very quietly: "Let's pick up the pace." When we got to Big Bottom I was practically running, and Mom's chair was rattling like it was going to fall apart. It's cold enough now that my breath came white. We rushed up a sort of hill and this lady was standing outside the house waving a handkerchief.

She took us downstairs into the basement where everybody was. The stove glowed hot and some of the people were playing guitars. The lady gave me a big hug, smelling sour. "Oh Chicken," she said.

Oh Fox. I miss you.

We're still headed north.

Tag me.

* * *

Dear Fox,

Hey. It's Sahra. If you get this message—can you just let me know if you left because of me? I keep on remembering that night in the canyon, when we sat up on that cold, dizzy ledge wrapped in your blanket. You tied a length of red thread around my wrist. I tore off a piece of my baby quilt for you, a shred of green cloth like the Milky Way. You said it was like the Milky Way. The stars rained down like the sky was trying to empty itself, and when you leaned toward me, I emptied myself into you. Did you leave because of the fight we had afterward, when I said my family belonged to this country, we belonged just as much as you? "Don't embarrass yourself," you said. Later I said, "Look, the grass is the exact color of Mom's eyes." You told me the grass was the color of plague.

You were her favorite, you know. The smartest. The student she'd always longed for. "Fox-Bright," she called you, when you weren't around.

Well. We're still in Big Bottom. Mom wants to get everybody out of here: She thinks it's too close to the isolation zone. Every night she lectures and the people here argue back, mostly because they have lots of food: They farm and can fruit from the edge of the forest. The lady who calls me Chicken, who seems to be the mom, opens a jar every night with a soft popping sound. She passes it around with a spoon and there's compote inside, all thick with beet sugar. This one guy, every time he takes a bite he says "Amen."

Sorry. Hope you're not hungry.

Anyway, you can see why these people would want to stay in Big Bottom and not try to haul all that stuff somewhere, including sacks of grain and seed that weigh more than me. "We've wintered here before," said the Chicken lady. "We've got the stove. Stay with us! You don't want to go north with a kid and all."

Everybody was nodding and you could see the pain in Mom's face. She hates to be wrong. She argued the best point she had. "Sooner or later they'll come after you," she said. "You're too close. You've got kids, too." She said it was a miracle the isolation folks hadn't already attacked Big Bottom, with all that food. Then everybody got quiet, the Chicken lady looking around sort of warningly, her eyes glinting, and

Mom said, "No." And the guy who says "Amen" over his compote, he told her they'd already been attacked a couple of times.

Mom covered her face.

"We do okay," the Amen guy said. You could tell he felt bad about it.

Later I got in a corner with the other kids, and I asked about the attacks and one of them, a boy about my age, pulled up his sleeve and his wrist had a bandage on it. He didn't get shot or anything, but he twisted it hitting somebody. With a crowbar.

When Mom uncovered her face she said: "That's not the life." She said: "That's not the Movement." She said standing your ground was the old way, not the new, and the Chicken lady said: "Honey, we know."

After I'd seen the boy with the bandaged wrist, I helped Mom to the toilet and back and we both lay down on the blankets. "We've got to get out of here," she muttered.

"Okay," I said.

"You know why, right?" she said. "Because we never stand. We move."

"Sure," I said. Sure, Mom, I thought. We move.

We move when and where you want, Mom. We've sailed back and forth over the ocean. We've slept in the airborne beds of Yambio and the houseboats of Kismaayo. And now you've decided to go to North Dakota when winter's starting, through country dotted with isolation zones, leaving all our friends behind. I had such a good art group back in the valley—you saw our last project, Fox. A slim line linking the tops of twenty trees. Wires and fibers twisted with crimson plastic, with cardinals' wings, making an unbroken trail, a gesture above the earth. It seemed to pulse in the morning light. You said it reminded you of radio waves, of a message. We called it "The Red Thread."

I'll probably never see it again.

Such gentle light here, but it couldn't soften Mom's smile when she saw me crying. "You don't know how lucky you are," she said.

Dear Fox,

Hey. It's Sahra. I'm at center M738. Somewhere in North Dakota. The center's in an old church. At night they feed us pickles and beet soup off plastic tablecloths that an old man carefully clips to the long tables.

They set beautiful candles made of melted crayons on all the windowsills. For travelers. For strangers to find their way at night.

"If we could have known," says Mom, "if we could have known this life was possible, we would have started living it long before."

There's a man with a blunt gray face who argues with her. "You're one of those human nature people," he sneered tonight. "The ones who think, oh, we've proved that people are good. Let me tell you something, friend. If it wasn't for the oil crisis and the crash, we'd be living exactly like we were before."

Mom nodded. A little half-smile in the candlelight. "Sure, *friend*," she said, subtly emphasizing the word.

"And another thing," said the blunt-faced man. "These kids would be in school."

"Or in the army," Mom said sweetly.

Of course the kids *are* in school, because Mom's around. Wherever we shelter, teaching is her way of giving thanks. She gets all the kids together and makes them draw their names in the dirt, she quizzes them on their multiplication tables, she talks about the Movement. How precious it is to be able to go where you want. Just walk away from trouble. Build a boat and row across the water. When she was a kid, she says, you could barely go anywhere at all: borders, checkpoints, prisons, the whole world carved up, everything owned by somebody. "Everything except light," she says. "Everything except fire." And if they wanted, they could keep you in a dark place. Tonight she told the kids what I already know, that that's where my dad ended up, in some dark place, seized on his way to work and then gone forever. "Why?" a kid asked. "I don't know," said Mom. "Because of his name? Because they thought he was working for terrorists? In those days, they could seize you for anything."

Usually she goes on from here with the story of how the Movement once had another name, how people used to call it the Greening, how the media reported it as an environmental movement first, folks abandoning cars on the freeways, walking, some rolling along like her. She tells of how, in the wake of the crash, the Greening intertwined with other movements, for peace, for justice, for bare life. Grinning, showing the gaps in her teeth, she uses her favorite line: "In the old days, when I worked in a lab, we called it evolutionary convergence."

Tonight she just stopped after talking about my dad. Her face shrunken, old. And I said: "We might still find him, Mom," because you never know. When the Movement started, he could have crawled out of that dark space like so many others, the ones you find on the road, cheerful, wearing pieces of their old uniforms. An orange bandana, a gray rag tied on the arm. Tattoos with the name of their prison, where they were kept before the doors opened, before the Movement. I once had a dream that my dad walked down some steps and touched my hair. "We might still find him," I said. Mom pretended not to hear me.

In the night she woke me with a cry.

"What is it, Mom? What's wrong?"

"Nothing, nothing," she whispered. "Go back to sleep."

I can't go to sleep. Lying there, I see you walking along a creek. You're wearing your black shirt and your head's tilted down, with that concentrating look. I think about how I recited the generations of my dad's family for you, there on the ledge, at the cave in the canyon wall. My name, then my dad's, then my grandfather's, then my great-grandfather's, back through time. Sahra, Said, Mohammed, Mohamud, Ismail. I can do ten generations. "Amazing," you said. Your blanket around us and our breaths the only warmth, it seemed, for miles.

"It's like a map," you said, "but it shows people instead of places." You said it felt like the future to think that way.

"Yeah," I said. "But during the war they killed each other over family lines. Like any other border."

Belonging, Fox. It hurts.

Fox it's Sahra. You knew? You knew Mom was sick? You knew and you didn't say anything to me? You knew and you left her?

What kind of person are you? It was like somebody walked

up and hit me in the chest with a hammer. "I told that boy," she murmured in the dark room. "I told that boy." And I knew who she meant. I knew it right away. She said she was sorry. She didn't mean to chase you off.

That's why you left? Because you found out someone who loved you was going to die?

I've never seen Mom work with a kid the way she worked with you. The two of you scratching away at your slates while the rest of us leached acorns. You'd kneel in the dirt by her chair and rest your slate on the arm. Leaning together, you'd talk about how to make the Movement last, how to keep the meshnets running, how to draw power tenderly from the world, and later you told me that you and I were perfect for each other because we both wanted to draw lines over the land, mine visible, yours in code, but the truth is you were perfect for Mom. You were perfect for her, Fox. "Fox-Bright," she called you. And you left her when she was dying.

You know what? I'm not sorry for what I said the day after we spent the night in the canyon. I'm not sorry I said I belong here as much as you. They picked up my dad and probably killed him because they thought he didn't belong here, an immigrant from a war-torn country. But my dad knew this land, he lived in thirty states before he met my mom, in the days of oil he used to drive a truck from coast to coast. He left fingerprints at a hundred gas pumps, hairs from his beard in hotel sinks, his bones in some forgotten government hole. And my mom belongs here, too, even though she cries, can you believe it, my mom, someone you'd look at and swear she never shed a tear in her life, she cries because she grew up in the house we're living in now, an old farmhouse crammed with noisy families—this is where she was born. She cries because she wanted to come back here before she died. That's why we're here. She thinks she's betraying the Movement by clinging to a place. She lies in the bed in the room where we found a page of her old Bible under the dresser and cries at the shape of the chokecherry tree outside the window. That's how much my mother loves the Movement that changed our world, the movement she worked for, for years, before we were born, losing her job and her teeth. She loves it so much she's going to die hating herself.

I've cut your bracelet off.

It's started to snow. I have to go now. Goodbye.

Dear Fox,

Hey. It's Sahra. It must be six months since I tagged you. I see you never tagged me back.

Today I left the farmhouse. I cleaned Mom's room, the room she slept in as a child, the room where she died. Old fingernails under the bed like seed.

There are good people in that house. What Mom called "ordinary people" or, in one of her funny phrases, "the most of us." They got her some weed, and that made it easier for her toward the end. One night she said: "Oh Sahra. I'm so happy."

She laughed a little and waved her hands in the air above her face. They moved in a strange, fluid way, like plants under water. "Look," she said, "it's the Movement." "Okay, Mom," I said, and I tried to press her hands down to her sides, to make her lie still. She struggled out of my grip, surprisingly strong. "Look," she whispered, her hands swaying. "See how that works? There's violence and cruelty over here, and everyone moves away. Everyone withdraws from the isolation zone until it shrinks. A kind of shunning. Our people understood that."

"Our people?"

She gave another little laugh, kind of secretive, kind of shy. She said she'd grown up going to a plain wooden church, a church where they believed in peace, where they sang but played no instruments, where the women covered their hair with little white hats. I said we'd met some people like that back in California. "They had the peppers, Mom, remember?" "Of course," she breathed. "The red peppers." The memory seemed to fill her with such delight. She said she'd left her old church, her old farm, but now she could see her childhood in the shape of the Movement. "What's isolation but a kind of shunning?" she said softly. "That's what we do, in the Movement. We move on, away from violence. A place ruined by violence is a prison. Everyone deserves to get out. The Movement opened up the doors."

She looked so small in the bed, in the light of the pale pink sky in the window. It does that on moonlit nights, in snow. A sky like quartz.

"That baby quilt," she said, "do you still have it?"

I took it out. One square ripped away, a green one. "Your grandmother made this," she said.

I wonder if you still have it, Fox. That green square. The Milky Way.

Later, I don't know if she could recognize me, but she asked: "Where are you from?" And I said "Here." Because "here" means this house and this planet. It means beside you.

"Are you an angel?" she asked me.

"Yes," I said.

Dear Fox,

Hey. It's Sahra. The snow is melting. The geese are back.

When I leave a place, I also leave a word for you. By now, it's like talking to myself. I leave words like I'd leave a stray hair somewhere, a clipped fingernail. My track across the land.

Movement. Back and forth. The two of us sitting wrapped in your blanket, breathing fog against a rain of shooting stars. I'm thinking today about your excitement when I recited my ancestors' names, how you said it felt like the future, and how quickly I cut you off. "There was war," I said. "Those family lines became front lines." As if your enthusiasm was somehow unbearable. I think of the fight we had later, and how you said: "Don't embarrass yourself." Did you mean I'd never belong? Maybe you meant: "Don't make me into a symbol."

Is it possible to be worthy of the Movement? Of my mom? Of my dad? I just walk, Fox, I meet people, seek shelter, avoid isolation. I make art with kids out of gratitude. I think about Mom all the time. All the time. "Are you an angel?" Her last words.

The night after I slept with you in the cave, I woke up cradled in light. My arm looked drenched with blood, but it was just dirt from the floor.

I still have the bracelet you gave me. I carry it in my pocket. I still have a redness on my wrist, as if someone's grabbed me.

* * *

Dear Fox,
Hey. It's Sahra. Sometimes I just feel like leaving one word. Even if it's just my name. A single thread.

Dear Fox,
Hey. It's Sahra.

Dear Fox,
Hey. It's Sahra.

Dear Fox,
Hey. It's Sahra.
I got your message.

EXPEDITION 83

WENDY N. WAGNER

Wendy N. Wagner is the author of the SF eco-thriller *An Oath of Dogs*. She's published more than forty short stories and written tie-in fiction for *Pathfinder* and *Exalted* role-playing games. She is the managing/senior editor of both *Lightspeed* and *Nightmare* magazines, and also served as the Guest Editor of *Nightmare*'s Queers Destroy Horror! special issue. She lives, games, and gardens in Portland, Oregon.

Visiting her was the best and worst part of my day, the good and the bad like the two sides of my rations card. Her voice, our laughter: the side with the Department of Revenue's sunshine logo, the part you tapped on the chip reader and it *beep-beep*ed your purchase of citrigel fruit squeezes and energy sticks. The chemical stink of her room and the ever-dampness of the heavy plastic quarantine gloves were the side of the card imprinted with my pay grade and my address, the side with the orange warning sticker reminding me of the *Serious Penalties* I would incur if caught shopping at illegal sales facilities. Like anyone needed the reminder.

My boots clanged on steel gridding as I passed through the last ring of the city proper and entered the Expansion Zone. This deep and this far out, the lighting turned to shit. Half the bulbs in the tunnel flickered or had gone out, and nobody bothered replacing things out here. The government had quit pretending the city was ever going to grow into this empty space. We were all just biding time, wondering if Portland would go the way the cities south of here had all gone and waiting for Seattle to shut down the last highway north.

Security lights snapped on with a nasty buzz. I shielded my eyes and made my way to the quarantine facility entrance by muscle memory.

"Henrietta!" Joel, the facility guard, beamed when he saw me. "How was work?"

I blinked until the silhouette grew features. "You know how it is." I pulled a much-battered paperback out of my back pocket. "Got that novel I was telling you about. Alfred Bester, at his best."

"Not even going to ask where you found this. Girl, I owe you." He waved me through the security gate without even frisking me. Five years now, six days a week. Everybody knew I knew the drill.

I dropped the energy sticks off at the nurses' station—they practically lived on the stuff—and knocked on Beth's door.

If you squinted at it right, quarantine looked like a hospital, although none of the doors had windows, and bullet-proof glass gated the hallways every thirty feet or so. The poured concrete of the wall and floors glinted behind a polymer sealant no fungus, virus, or mere germ could penetrate. Keeping an underground city healthy took extreme containment measures.

"Come in," the speaker set in the doorframe said. It gave patients the illusion of power to buzz their visitors in at this last step of the process.

I'd learned early on in the process that Joel had already unlocked the door from the security gate. Only staff and approved visitors were allowed behind the massive slab of concrete that separated Beth from the rest of the city, and only security could open or close the doors. I pushed it open and forced my face into a suitable expression.

"Jesus, Henry. I'm half-blind and even I think that smile makes you look like you had a stroke. Shut the damn door and stop faking it."

I dropped into the chair on my side of the clear plastic quarantine wall. It was probably the only reasonably comfortable seat in the entire facility. Beth's great-grandfather had carried it on his back when he'd evacuated from the city above, the chair stuffed full of clothes and diapers. He'd carried it down four miles of tunnels while pushing his twin daughters in their stroller. Years before, his wife had reupholstered the chair in the same brown leather that squeaked beneath my cargo pants. She hadn't made it to the underground.

It went without saying that the chair was never going to leave this room. Beth's dads were going broke paying for quarantine, for round-the-clock nursing, for every half-tested drug the docs were trying this week, and on top of watching their daughter—my girlfriend—die in a box, they were going to lose their best chair. Life in the apocalypse was awfully fucking unfair.

"Glad I can stop pretending I'm happy." I put one of the citrigel fruit squeeze tubes into the transfer box mounted on the plastic barrier and then activated the air seal. "I had a lousy day at work."

The monitor sitting beside the bed flashed a smiley face. The monitor and the speakers attached to it were Beth's primary mode of communication since the fungus had grown over the majority of her face. Sensors implanted in her tongue and throat allowed her to subvocalize instructions to the computer. It made virtual faces and an approximation of her voice. I had gotten used to it, I guess.

The next part, though, I could never get used to. I slid my hands into the bleach-moistened gloves built into the q-wall and reached into Beth's world. I could never feel anything besides the clammy grip of the gloves, but goose bumps never failed to rise on the back of my neck. Such very thin pieces of plastic between me and inevitable death.

They think it was her gloves that had killed Beth. She'd only been a sophomore in college, but she'd been approved to join the advanced students testing materials that Expedition 81 had brought back from topside. She had a theory she was desperate to test about chromosome mutations after exposure to nerve gas. In the lab, she'd followed every protocol. Bleached every last inch of her hazmat suit in the decontamination lock. Nevertheless…

When she woke up with a gray rash on her knuckles, she was the first to guess what was wrong.

On her parents' request, the university went under review by the city's top health officials. Everything but the gloves passed with flying colors. One hundred and fifty years is a long time to keep rubber gloves in perfect condition.

It's a long time to keep a city in perfect condition, too, especially one that wasn't designed to last more than a few decades. The history types always said the end had come too fast for anyone to really be ready for it: the floods, the storms, the wars over water and air and food. But even as a kid, whispering with Beth on our little sleepovers, I hadn't believed it. The world didn't get hot without somebody knowing. If we'd been there—awesome girl scientists that we had decided to be—we would have done something about it.

Not that as adults we were actually saving the world. Beth might have had a chance at it before she got sick, but me? At least I'd gotten a chance to indenture myself to the Oregon Institute of Science and Technology for a specialized degree and the promise of all the underpaid lab time I could ask for.

"Earth to Henry," Beth cooed, pulling me out of my thoughts. "I am waiting for a treat like a very good girl."

I had to contort myself to open the air seal on her side and fish out the citrigel. The top snapped open easily, or as easily as my bumbling gloved hands could manage, and I carefully poured its contents into the robotic delivery system attached to her bed. I looked away from the tube as it maneuvered toward the blackened orifice of Beth's mouth. The nurses used a laser to cut it open every four or five days. Someday the fungus would spread to her gums or her tongue and then there would be no more mouth and no more lasers. At that point, fungalized patients were usually offered the option of lethal injection.

The microphone picked up her gulp and satisfied sigh. Then: "So. No new breakthroughs in the latest starch project?"

I grew starches in a lab. I'd rather be working on a cure for fungal infections, but I was fresh out of school, and frankly, new food strains were the government's top priority. We couldn't just import stuff from California anymore. The underground cities down there had gone silent ten years ago. Viruses, probably. Fungus, maybe. We didn't open the airlocks on the south side just to be safe.

"I managed to make a formerly tasteless goop poisonous, if that's what you mean by 'breakthrough.'"

Her laugh sounded something like a dry cough. I tossed the empty citrigel tube down the waste hatch and reached for her pillow. "Need that fluffed?"

"Eh." She subvocalized something to the computer that didn't translate to the speakers and music crackled on in the background. Her hands had been the first casualty of the fungus, her fingers fusing into the plated mass that continued to coat her body. "Go ahead and fluff me."

I activated another mechanism on the bed. "I've been fluffing your pillows a long time. Remember that God-awful company pillow my mom would put out whenever you spent the night?"

She made her rasping noise again. "I hope they have something better these days."

"I don't know; you were our only guest." I cocked my head. "What are we listening to today?"

"Nirvana. Late twentieth century band, very focused on gloom and doom."

"Isn't their acoustic album supposed to be one of the best in all rock history?"

"I'm still not sure about that. Can any whiny grunge band compete with the vocal stylings of Elvis Presley?"

I rested my forehead against the glass, laughing despite myself. I'd known Beth since we were four years old, and even then she'd been a militant fan of Elvis Presley. She'd downloaded every Elvis compilation in the community database, but it had never been enough. The one decoration in her whole q-room was a framed album her parents had found on the black market.

"You look tired," she said. "Have you been going to the dance clubs and making out with hot chicks again?"

I made a face. "Ha-hah. No, I was up late at the lab and went straight home to check on my parents."

Her monitor flashed an angry face. "You can't be so scared of actually *living*, Henry. You're twenty-four years old. You need to get out and grow up and all that shit I'm not going to get to do."

"Shut up." I stuck out my tongue at her. "I do plenty of living. It's just budget living."

The monitor went blank. I had known her so long I could hear her spinning sarcastic remarks deep within her brain. I didn't want to hear a single one of them.

"You should find somebody else," she whispered. "How many times do I have to tell you that?"

"But you're the one, Beth. My one." I stretched my arm as far as I could reach until my fingertip touched the tip of her nose, that one small centimeter of unravaged flesh.

She made a tiny sound that could have been pain, or sorrow, or happiness. I had to squeeze shut my eyes for a second until they were dry again.

I cleared my throat. "Enough about me. What did you study today?"

"Natural history." The monitor flashed a cute kitty emoji. "God, I wish I was doing research. There's no reason we shouldn't be sending more expeditions to the top-side, get a start on some kind of environmental rehab. It's been three generations since we ran away. It's not good for us."

She didn't just mean the fungus or the new viruses that bred and thrived down here in the dark. She meant it wasn't good for humanity to get away from the stars and the sky and all the other animals. I'd heard it a thousand times before. Others might try to argue with her that the radiation storms and poisoned water made the world above too dangerous for human survival—Beth knew so much more about chemical warfare and radiation than I did that I'd given up playing the devil's advocate.

"Hey, if you want a pet, I've got some fruit flies back at the lab who could use a good home."

The monitor stuck out a tongue at me. Then she made her rasping sound, but it was deeper and harsher than her laugh.

"You okay?"

The rasp became a gurgle like nothing I'd ever heard before.

"*Beth?*" She jerked and lurched on the bed. Her carapace crunched. I yanked my hands out of the gloves, ran to the door, slapped the call button. "We could use some help in here!"

The door buzzed open and an orderly threw me out of the room. Nurses in hazmat suits darted inside as the door swung shut.

"Henry? You okay?" Noor, my favorite nurse, steered me toward the nurses' station. Her green eyes matched her head scarf.

"She sounded really bad."

"Honey." She put her arm around my shoulder. "I don't want to be the one who says this, but Beth's taken a turn for the worse. She might seem okay, but that's just as phony as the smiles you give her. Her hearing's down to thirty percent, and the doctor says we can't risk cutting open her good eye anymore."

I stumbled away from her grip. "Blind? Totally blind? And deaf?"

"They're going to try a new kind of hearing aid, but it's just a matter of time."

I put my hands over my face and let the nurse put both arms around me. The sticky pink smell of energy sticks surrounded me like a bubble.

An impenetrable bubble not so different from the gray shell that closed off Beth from the world.

"Henry?" My mother's voice finally cut through the dreams.

"Hrm?" I managed. My body was still back in those dreams, dark, stuffy, strangling.

"The phone's for you."

I sat up and found the sheets wound so tightly around me I couldn't peel them away from my shoulders. "Thanks. I'll be there in a sec."

I forced the bedding off me, a cold sweat breaking out between my shoulder blades. Was this what it had felt like when the fungus first started sealing Beth's arms to her sides? Trapped, so trapped.

I stumbled into the main room and picked up the phone. We shared just the one since there wasn't enough plastic and circuitry for everyone to have their own. "Henrietta here." I cleared my throat and repeated myself.

"It's Alberto. Sorry to wake you."

I pulled the phone away from my ear and squinted at the time. My shift at the lab didn't start for another two and a half hours. "What's up?"

"Spore contamination in the droso room. We're closing the whole facility until a team can get the place cleaned out."

"Shit. How's the back-up fly stock?"

"Jane's been keeping them at her place, so they're fine." He let out a long groan. "I think we're going to lose at least a week for this."

"Shit." What else could I say? "Well, give me a call when we can reopen."

"Okay."

"Wait—are we still getting paid? Alberto?"

He'd already hung up.

Shit.

My mom hurried by, her workbag over her shoulder. "No work today? Maybe you can clean the kitchen?"

The air pump in the ceiling let out a piercing shriek that made her cover her ears. I squeezed my eyes shut and waited for it to quiet down before answering. "Yeah, sure. Why are you off to work so early? And where's Dad?" School didn't usually start for another hour or so.

"He had a crisis on the second level. I've got health training or something. Maybe we'll finally teach kids how to use a hankie instead of their fingers. Anyway, love you, sweetie." With that, she vanished out the door.

I glanced at the clock again. My dad worked in the water department and had a crisis somewhere at least once a week. The city hadn't been designed to last this long.

My feet shuffled their way back to my room. At least I had my own space here, even if my fingers brushed the walls when I stretched out my arms. I opened the shallow storage cupboard and took out the floppy company pillow.

In my preteen years, my mom had tried to teach me to embroider. I'd managed to work some music notes in a black satin stitch and a big letter B. I pulled the pillow up to my nose and breathed deep. Beneath the dusty smell of time, I thought I could still make out notes of artificial citrus and dandruff shampoo.

I turned away my face so my tears wouldn't contaminate the pillow. I squeezed it hard and then put it back in the cupboard. The blankets lay in a heap where I'd dropped them. I pulled them over my head and sat in the warm darkness, thinking.

She deserved better than a slow death in quarantine. She deserved a chance to make her dreams come true.

I got dressed and left our quarters without bothering to eat breakfast. It was a long walk on an empty stomach, but I didn't have any place more important to be. My stomach didn't even growl as I stood waiting for a family to check in at the security desk. It must have been their first visit. It took a long time.

"Henrietta!" Joel said when he saw me. "You're early today."

I only blinked a little as I found my way to the check-in desk. "I need your help."

I put on the hazmat suit at the second mile marker. The others had said goodbye to us back at Airlock Three, half a mile ago, my mom crying and coughing a little, suffering from the usual March cold, my dad standing stoic and blowing his nose like crazy. Noor wanted to come, too, but had called to let me know she had to cover someone's shift at the last minute. Beth's dads cried too hard to talk. No matter the precautions, this trip to the surface was going to shorten what little time Beth had left.

It had sounded like a good idea three days ago. But that had been in the safety of the city, asking for the support of the people who best knew Beth and I. A mini-research expedition, I had called it. A dream come true for a girl who had given her life for science. All of Beth's professors in college had helped me beg the city for this, and against all odds, we'd gotten approval.

Now it was only me and the nearly dark tunnels and the soft growl and hum of Beth's airtight cart. I turned around to check on her. She was sleeping hard; the pain meds they had given her would have knocked out a man twice her size. Even with the drugs, she'd be in constant pain during the trip. Every bounce, every jostle, every tiny vibration wore on her fungi-crusted exterior and twanged the mycelial threads that had fused her organs into place.

I had to look away from the lumpy shape lying inside the plastic-shrouded cart. This fungus.

This goddamn fungus.

The cart's motor grumbled a little louder as I dialed up the speed setting on the remote strapped to my arm, but Beth slept on. At least her brain was fine. There had been fungal breakouts that left the body functional while eroding the mind. It had flourished in the hot damp conditions just before the war broke out, and once the bombs knocked out pharmaceutical production, there were no anti-fungals to keep it in line.

Nuclear winter had saved us from those strains. It probably saved us from the complete ecosystem-breakdown global warming had promised us, too, only we still didn't know how the environment was coping after planet-wide thermonuclear devastation. We'd sent out expedition after expedition to look for some sign things were turning around, but the news they brought back—the times they actually did come back—was never good.

A line of graffiti on the tunnel wall made me laugh: *Don't forget your sunblock!*

"What's so funny?"

I rushed to Beth's side. "Hey, you're awake."

"Sort of. You laughed? This new hearing aid is pretty good."

"Graffiti from one of the expeditions. About sunblock."

The hiss of air in her microphone might have been a laugh. "Just wait. We'll come back with skin cancer."

"You morbid bitch." I rapped my knuckles on the side of her plastic shields. In my hazmat gloves, they didn't so much knock as gently thump. "Almost to the second airlock now. Gotta keep moving."

Her cart could only carry so much oxygen and still roll. This little expedition had a definite timeline.

At the airlock, I entered the one-time code in the keypad and made sure the cart went in before me. Once the door closed, I'd have to radio in to the city to get a new one, and the computers running the airlock system were over a hundred-fifty years old. They took their own sweet time, oxygen tanks or no.

I slipped inside as the airlock began cycling shut. The cart's tires crunched in darkness. I froze. The lights should have turned on at the cart's movement.

"Henry?"

Beth's monitor flickered a big blue question mark that cast a submarine light on the floor and walls.

In the blue light, the shreds of hazmat suit all over the floor were barely visible. I forced my feet forward, stepping very carefully. "It's okay, Beth."

"What is it? Why is it so dark, and why haven't you turned on your suit light?"

I made it to her side. She was just a dark shadow inside her fragile little air bubble. "Hey, aren't you supposed to be resting, instead of backseat driving?"

"What *is* it?"

"I'm turning on my suit light." I found the toggle on the side of my helmet and fumbled with it. Joel had made it look so easy back at the Quarantine Sector.

"What is taking you so long?"

"Have you seen this suit?" I snapped. "My fingers are like sausages!"

"At least you *have* fingers."

The light snapped on. "I'm sorry. That was a shitty thing for me to say. I just…" I couldn't bring myself to move, to let my light shine around me. "I'm… I'm scared."

Her monitor flashed a pink heart at me. "I know."

I wanted nothing more than to rest my head against the plastic bubble Joel and I had built around Beth's cart and just listen to her voice with my eyes closed. Getting her here had been hard, but it had kept me from thinking about what we were about to do.

I took a deep breath, even though the triple-filtered air tasted stale and fake, and let myself look at the dead people lying all around us.

"It looks like Expedition 82," I said. "I can see numbers on the helmets."

"How many of them are there?"

"It's hard to tell." I took a few steps away from the cart, hunching down so the light could play over the ground. "Two, no, three… Their suits were definitely damaged. Probably why the city wouldn't give them the new key code." I risked nudging a yellow heap of fabric with my boot. I swallowed my breakfast back down. "There's a lot of decay, but I don't see any fungal growth on the remains."

"None?" Excitement colored her voice.

"None that I can see. They're pretty mummified after eight months down here."

"Damnit," she grumbled. "I wish I could get out and take samples."

I went back to the cart with its soft light. "They'd never let you back in. You'd be like these bastards—stuck out in the tunnels to die." I shuddered, just thinking of it. "Now, come on," I said. "Airlock One is a long ways away."

"I'm going back to sleep, if that's okay." Beth's voice was barely audible. The adrenaline from our little adventure must have been wearing off.

"Sleep well, sweetie."

The monitor showed z's.

Airlock One held no unpleasant surprises.

It hissed shut behind us, and I stood beside the cart, blinking stupidly at the tiny dot of light at the end of the tunnel. It took me a minute to remember to turn off my suit light as we rolled slowly toward daylight—the first daylight of my life.

The tunnel was massive up here, wide enough for four of Beth's carts to roll side-by-side. It had been a subway tunnel, once upon a time. They'd poured concrete over the rails to help the digging equipment move faster. We came out of the tunnel mouth slowly, our eyes adjusting to the soft sunlight, the rain pattering all around us.

I had only ever read about rain. I held out my hand and caught a droplet. It was so tiny, and yet it hit with surprising force. I hadn't thought you'd be able to feel the power of its falling, all that momentum building up to drive right into my palm.

My legs went loose and I dropped onto a crumbling concrete platform—the ruins of the old train station—beside the tunnel mouth. It was raining. There was water coming out of the sky because there *was* a sky and there was a sun and there was air, air everywhere like I could just float away. I grabbed the platform edge and swallowed again and again before I could vomit.

"Is it moving? Is that the sky? Does it move, Henry? Tell me what I'm seeing."

I forced myself to get up and kneel beside her. "Yes, that's the sky. It's not like the pictures because it's full of clouds, and the clouds are leaking."

"It's raining?"

"It's fucking *raining!*" I threw back my head so I could see what she saw laying on her back. "And look, oh, wow, Beth, there are trees—oh, God, I'll have to move the cart because you can't see from there, but there are *trees*. You'd probably know what kind. They don't have any leaves right now, so I think it might be winter."

"It'll be spring soon."

I wanted to wipe the tears out of my eyes, but I couldn't because of the stupid suit. "We made it. Just like you always said we would. We're aboveground."

I could hear her trying not to cry. It was the same trying-not-to-cry sound she'd been making since she was seven and Mrs. Meacham told her she was too old to cry over a scraped knee. That had been the first time I'd kissed her. I told her that day I was going to marry her and make sure she never cried again. She told me she could keep her tears under control herself.

It had taken me eleven years to kiss her again—eleven years of being her best friend, eleven years fighting to catch up with her on the playground, in the classroom, in the labs. Eleven years of watching her fly through the world, as dazzling as Elvis in a spangled jumpsuit. When she finally let me catch up with her, I hadn't really minded settling for second-best, because she had chosen me and I could kiss her as much as I liked.

And then one pair of gloves got one microscopic abrasion, and all of that was taken from me. We'd had so little time to really be together.

The rage that had been heating inside me ever since Noor told me about Beth's prognosis boiled over. I grabbed a chunk of broken concrete off the ground and leaped to my feet.

I threw it as hard as I could.

It smashed into the wall of a crumbling gray building, ricocheted off and crunched on a small shrub I had no name for. Something small and gray shot out of the bush and darted into the undergrowth.

"Holy shit—Beth, there are *mammals*."

"What?"

"Probably a rat, I think." I dropped down beside her so I could see the damp slit of her eye. "They never said there were rats."

"Henry."

"I've got to take samples. It might have left some droppings or even some hair. A DNA sample could tell us so much!" I ran toward the bush, scrambling over the broken slabs of concrete and fallen metal beams that must have once been the subway station.

"Henry!"

I spun around.

I had forgotten the little monitor Beth had inside her cart, the camera that allowed her to see around herself. She had a far better view of the creature standing on the other side of the train station than I did.

I froze.

It stared at me, its eyes dark yellow and enormous, its four legs a pale and dirty beige, its snout as long as a wolf's in a fairy tale. It stood more than half as tall as I did, its ears shaggy and hairy and twitching.

If it jumped on Beth's cart, it would certainly kill her.

"Get away!" I shouted. "Go!"

It took a step backward. I grabbed a length of metal off the ground and swung it in front of me. "Go!"

Its top lip pulled back from its teeth. I had never imagined teeth so long, so white, so horrible. Animals were supposed to be cute. We had killed most of them in our ignorance and stupidity and if they existed again, they should be our friends, not this dirty, hairy, terrifying thing snarling at me and my dying girlfriend.

I wouldn't let it get her.

A scream of rage rose up in my throat and I leaped off the old platform, running even as I touched the ground. I choked up on the metal bar like a baseball bat.

The creature spun around and raced away. I could hear it crashing through the bushes as it ran up the hill.

I dropped the metal bar and doubled over, grabbing my legs. My chest hurt. The air filter on my hazmat suit wasn't meant for a runner's oxygen uptake.

"Oh, Jesus, what the hell was that?"

A weird, dry sound made me stand up and turn around. Beth's monitor flashed a laughing emoji at me.

"What's so funny?"

"You." Beth's laugh turned into a cough, but she stifled it. "That was a coyote."

"No, it wasn't. I've seen pictures of coyotes. That was… a werewolf or something." I very studiously turned my attention to the cart's remote control and turned it on. The cart started rolling.

"An admittedly large coyote, but a coyote." She paused. "Where are we going?"

"I'm not sure." I looked around. Beyond the train station, the city streets I'd studied on the maps were cracked and buckled with trees shooting up through the broken places. Squared-off hills surrounded us—hills that a hundred years ago had been office buildings and apartment complexes, now so covered in plants and vines they were indistinguishable from the mountain we'd just walked out of. Shimmering stands of mushrooms sprang from the smaller hummocks that had to have been cars and trucks. "It's not what I expected."

A few feet away from us, a square of bright yellow caught my eye. I paused the cart and walked to it. A lamp post still stood, as out of place in this wild territory as I was.

And beside its base, someone had left two neatly folded yellow hazmat suits.

"Look at this!" I held them up for Beth to see. I tried to remember how many people had gone out in Expedition 82. More than we'd found by that airlock, that was sure.

Beth's camera motor whirred as it focused on me. She was quiet a moment. Her monitor flashed a crooked arrow.

"What is it?"

She was quiet again. Then: "You should sit down."

"Why?"

"I have something to tell you, but it's hard."

I sat down on a slab of concrete. I wondered what it sounded like out here. My suit had a very good pick-up mic, but there had to be so many sounds it was missing. I felt so trapped and small like this.

I thought of Beth inside her plastic bubble for so many years, and wished I hadn't.

"If a coyote can live out here," she said, "so can a person."

I stood up. "Well, maybe. But that doesn't mean you wouldn't live a dramatically shorter, cancerous life."

"I don't know if that's so bad, really."

For the first time in a long time, I made myself look at her. Really look at her. The shape in the bottom of the cart more closely resembled a large, lumpy loaf of bread than a human being. Tubes and hoses ran out of the flaking grayish surface, circulating fluids of several different colors and textures. The only skin still showing was the small lasered cut-out beside her right eye, and that sweet pink tip of her nose.

I did not let myself look away. I had looked away for too long.

"You're bleeding." A thin liquid—it was a stretch to call it blood—puddled around her shoulder area.

"It started when they hoisted me out of the bed. Noor warned me it was going to get worse."

"Why didn't you say anything?"

"Because you didn't know." She paused. "You didn't know they were sending me up here to die."

"*What?*"

"Remember all those health meetings your mom's been going to? It's because there are a lot of sick people in the city."

"What are you talking about?" I remembered the family checking in at the security desk. I'd never run into anyone else coming to visit the quarantine facility before, but I saw four other families while Joel and I were working on Beth's cart.

"Why do you think Noor had to cover that other nurse's shift? The nurse was sick, Henry. They needed a quarantine room to put her in. A room I didn't really need anymore."

We were both silent for a moment, and then she made a wet sound in the back of her throat.

I let my head smack against the plastic sheeting. "No."

"I thought you'd be okay, but when I saw those bodies in the airlock, I knew they were never going to let you back in again."

My head shot up. "Why not? My suit is fine. I'll just go through decontamination and everything will be okay."

"I'm sure that's what Expedition 82 thought, too."

"Yeah, but their suits were wrecked, you saw them." I was pacing now, shaking my head.

"What about the ones you found out here? They looked just fine, didn't they?"

"We don't know that," I spat. "Think about your gloves. They looked fine, too."

"Exactly. Think about my gloves. You're way too dangerous now."

I sat down, just like she'd asked me to do in the first place. "No."

"I have a couple of hours left and then I'll suffocate. I want you to be far away before that happens. You can see if anybody from Expedition 82 is still alive out here."

"No." I shook my head hard. "No!"

The monitor showed a cherry red mushroom with white spots, straight out of one of the video games we'd played as kids. "I can feel changes starting inside my body. I think it's the UV light. I don't know if the fungus is advanced enough to make spores, but I know I don't want you to get this."

I lurched off my slab of concrete. "Beth, *no*." I pressed my cheek to her cart. "I can't lose you."

She coughed again. "I don't think I can talk much more."

"I'm so sorry, Beth. I should've never brought you up here." I stroked the plastic, but it wasn't her skin, wasn't her hair. I couldn't smell her or feel her. Couldn't kiss her. "I ruined everything."

"You were the best thing that ever happened to me, stupid. You and Elvis."

I didn't want to laugh, but I had to. "I forgot about Elvis."

"Don't ever forget about Elvis." She made a terrible sound again, and I sat up straight, but it wasn't a cough, just one of her subvocalizations to her monitor. I heard the speakers crackle.

"This one's always been my favorite," she said—managed to say, half-choking and gurgling. "Would have been nice to see a hound dog."

"A coyote's better than a hound dog." I pressed myself as close to her bubble as I could. I couldn't see through the plastic window of my suit; it was too fogged with tears.

I couldn't see, but I could listen. I could sit beside her and listen to her try to breathe as we listened to "Hound Dog" one more time.

I could remember her dancing.

I could remember her singing.

* * *

When the song was over, I turned off the oxygen in her cart and waited until everything was truly, horribly silent. I wanted to take off my helmet and make sure I really didn't hear anything, wanted to open her cart and carry her into the woods where the leaves could fall on her and make her one with all the things she'd wanted to see. But I knew she was right about the spores.

I walked through the city for a long time, fighting that hazmat suit, looking for some kind of landmark that matched up with my old maps. Finally I came to a heap of rubble that blocked the ruins of the old city street. I wondered if there was any way to get around it or if I dared go over the top. Not like this, there wasn't. I'd need my hands free for sure.

I held them out in front of me, my own two hands hidden inside their rubber sausage casings. Were they even protected in there? Had they ever been? And what did protection even mean when I was never, ever going back to safety?

Fuck it.

I took off the suit.

Suddenly there were sounds all around me, flutterings and rustlings and whisperings and chirpings. I didn't know what any of them meant or what might have made them. Beth had been the one who studied natural history. I was only a food scientist, and a second-best one at that.

Then there was a sound I recognized from movies and games and recordings: birdsong. A bird sang somewhere ahead of me, beyond the nearly impassible heap of rubble that might have been an office tower or a shopping mall or the capital of the pre-apocalypse world.

A bird sang. It wasn't Elvis, but it would do.

THE LAST TO MATTER

ADAM-TROY CASTRO

Adam-Troy Castro's twenty-six books to date include four Spider-Man novels, three novels about his profoundly damaged far-future murder investigator Andrea Cort, and six middle-grade novels about the dimension-spanning adventures of Gustav Gloom. The final installment in the series, *Gustav Gloom and the Castle of Fear*, came out in 2016. Adam's darker short fiction for grownups is highlighted by his most recent collection, *Her Husband's Hands and Other Stories*. Adam's works have won the Philip K. Dick Award and the Seiun (Japan), and have been nominated for eight Nebulas, three Stokers, two Hugos, and, internationally, the Ignotus (Spain), the Grand Prix de l'Imaginaire (France), and the Kurd-Laßwitz Preis (Germany), and been selected for inclusion in *Best American Science Fiction and Fantasy*. His latest projects are a mainstream thriller currently making the publishing rounds, and an audio collection he expects to announce early in 2019. He lives in Florida.

Kayn knew he was being rejected by the orgynism for almost a full year before it fully expelled him.

He could easily live a million years past this humiliation and never understand what he had done to deserve such a rejection from the collective that had loved him so well, for so long.

He had been one of the orgynism's founders, the man who had provided its organizing principles and solicited the first participants, the architect who had drawn up the parameters for the pleasure-feedback loops, and as a result, he'd been honored to spend its many years of existence as the seed nexus around which all its carnality orbited. For all that time, the orgynism's participants, male and female and neuter and recombinant, had always tithed some of their pleasure to his, their sensations flowing in his direction through the neural connections all had agreed to upon joining the collective, just as their other surgically implanted connections also provided him with oxygen for his lungs and nutrients for his blood. Pierced in all of a dozen places and piercing in a dozen others, he had known nothing but mindless bliss, at the orgynism's core.

How lucky he had considered himself, at those rare moments when conscious thought had space to intervene, for living in a time when such things were possible!

One would think that the bastards would have damn well appreciated that.

Then, one by one, the connections were withdrawn, the devotion toward his pleasure above all else was sidelined, and the peristalsis of the dozens of interconnected bodies began to move him, bit by bit, toward the outskirts. The limbs of his many lovers now grasped him not in embrace but in firm urging toward the exit, and though they were gentle about it, taking more than a year to shift him from the orgynism's center to its periphery, they also brooked no argument. He continued to feel pleasure. But, throughout, he also knew that he was being dispensed with.

At the end of the year, Kayn popped sweaty and glistening from the hovering sphere of bodies, and slammed to the soft floor a man-height below. The living tubes that had provided him with nutrients and euphoric drugs tore free of his flesh and slithered back into the ball of copulating bodies, there to disappear beneath the shifting landscape of shoulders and buttocks and ecstatic faces. Nobody whose features were exposed bothered to open their eyes and acknowledge his bereft status, his enforced farewell; not one of the women, not one of the men, not any of the recombinants said goodbye. As far as they were concerned, he was gone, and he was forgotten, as irrelevant to the orgynism as any other sight or sound of the world its pleasures locked out.

For some time, he sat moist and heartbroken below the throbbing ball of former lovers, lost in the novelty of separation. Then a portal opened on the wall to his right and his replacement, a creature with a half-dozen sets of complete sexual organs from forehead to midriff, undulated in, its naked form already studded with the necessary interfaces for the nutrient tubes and neurological feedback wires. It glanced at him, registering his predicament but not remarking on it, before turning away and striding the rest of the way to the orgynism Kayn had left and that it was now joining. One leap and the new lover was caught. The orgynism throbbed at the point of impact, and swallowed the newcomer whole.

Kayn considered fighting his way back into the collective, clawing with tooth and nail back to a dominant place at its center. But as devastated as he was, he knew that this would be a pathetic and doomed attempt at rape. He'd be outnumbered, for one thing. For another, now that not all of his consciousness was dominated by incoming sensation, the emptiness of the rutting that had occupied so many years of his life depressed him. Maybe that's why his lovers had expelled him; they'd sensed his flagging commitment.

So he stood. He applied to the same portal the newcomer had entered for his own exit, passing through the surgical vestibule now tasked with rendering him respectable for the outside world. It first sprayed him with topical anesthetics, and then with flashes of whirring knives amputated the various extra sexual inlets and protuberances that he'd needed before but would not be using again, a dizzying flurry of male and female castrations and other surgeries coupled with accelerated healing that by the time he'd completed ten steps had restored him to his birth settings. As soon as he was whole, spray nozzles emerged from the walls, bathed him, and then covered him with a thin gloss of purple liquid that congealed as neck-to-ankle clothing. It was not clothing in the sense that it preserved modesty, in part because he had none; it simply conformed to the shape of his genitalia, displaying it in full openness as was only proper. It was also imbedded with connections to the machines that did all the city's thinking, which anticipated his likely needs and informed him that there were currently still seventeen other orgynisms being maintained at various other locations around the city. Some were currently recruiting. He could resume his carnal pleasures with scarcely a pause for the gathering of breath. But the paucity of this number shocked him. When he founded his orgynism, there'd been more than three hundred others. Thirteen of the seventeen still in existence were full up, their participants having opted for full lobotomization in order to fight off any urges toward disbanding. Four had heard about his ejection, and had issued invitations to his account. He demurred and moved on. The door at the end of the vestibule slid into its recess and provided the newly-freed, freshly-clothed, sexually-refreshed Kayn back onto the street.

He composed a sonnet of heartbreak. He did this in the way anybody had written anything, in the last few millennia: by taking it upon himself to declare that such a thing should be written and mentally ordering the machines that ran everything to write one for him. It was produced at once, delivered to his cortex by the connection with the machines that was the birthright of all who lived.

What emerged was the worst sonnet ever.

He was no expert in poetry. Nobody was. That was why composing it had long since become the domain of the machines. Who wanted to go to all that effort, especially since no one would ever read it? Might as well let the machines take care of that impulse. But in past years, they would have come up with a *good* sonnet. This one was mostly made-up words, and still failed to scan.

How irritating.

He didn't order a replacement. He just set about finding out what had become of the city during his years of distraction.

Once, there had been tens of thousands of cities. They had hugged the shorelines and punctuated the rivers and marked the wider points in the road, wherever goods were carried from one place to another. They had occupied the places where the holes were dug in the earth so the resources could be ripped out; places where the crops were grown, where the tools were built, even where people went just to lay in the sun. Once there had been enough people to fill those tens of thousands of cities. Then many had fled Earth, launching themselves at a universe that seemed infinite with possibility. A few had come back saying that this had turned out not to be true, that the universe was in fact a cold and inhospitable place with little soil congenial to humanity; a few others had returned and said that this was nonsense, that the stars teemed with opportunities for those who possessed the courage to seize them, and that humanity's diaspora had accomplished wonders undreamt of by those who had stayed behind. Either story could have been true. But it no longer mattered which, now. Eons had passed. The distant outposts had fallen silent. The constellations had gone dark. Most of civilization had crumbled to dust. The descendants of the billions who stayed behind had dwindled to millions, and then to thousands.

Long before Kayn joined the orgynism, the city had shrunk in the ways cities do when there are no longer enough people to fill them. Entire sections had been claimed by the surrounding desert, even as others were built up to look more elaborate, more magnificent, more a play-palace for the residents who remained. When Kayn founded his orgynism, one could still venture out into the remaining streets and find a crowd, at any hour of the day or night (those being antiquated distinctions even by then, as the sun no longer shone brightly enough to make a proper day). But sometime since he first joined his lovers, the city's masses had thinned out even more. Even on the first major thoroughfare Kayn investigated, there were almost no people, except for those who had elected to become trees and who stood at regular intervals, being watered by automatic systems, as they spread their arms and faced a sky that reflected their emptiness with its own.

Some of the trees could still talk and provided him with directions, an important service when the streets had changed orientation and no longer led to the right places, but they were trees and not capable of much conversation beyond that. So Kayn headed for the city center, where there was always activity to be had, and as he went he ran into some of his remaining neighbors.

He met a dandy being fitted for a suit more magnificent than any ever produced by any tailor. It was a glossy multi-colored thing that, the dandy told him, the mechanisms had been laboring to spin on his frame for several decades now. It was far too voluminous to permit physical movement and so the dandy sat at the center of enough frilled cloth to fill a space the size of a ballroom, only his face showing, like an egg being cradled by an acre of satin. Hand-mirrors orbited him, propelled by little puffs of compressed air that also served to dispense perfume. "I am beautiful," he told Kayn. "I am the most beautiful thing alive." It was his ambition to have fresh frills added to his ever-growing outfit for as long as the machines remained sufficiently operational to do so, at which point he would have himself injected with a plasticizing compound so he could spend what remained of eternity as his suit's undecaying mannequin. Kayn commended him on his choice of performance art and moved on.

He met a woman who had decided to spend her years giving birth. She sat naked, her back against a wall, her legs splayed to facilitate the escape of her offspring, a glistening fetal something who while Kayn watched several times squirmed its way free of her birth canal, then climbed up her body to force its way back into her open mouth. This was its cyclical journey: escaping her, then escaping the outside world, then escaping her again. The woman was unable to tell Kayn why she'd chosen to spend her years this way, likely because her child's constant invasions of her throat had ravaged her vocal cords, but the baby had the consciousness of an adult and was able to tell Kayn what it knew of the city's recent history. There'd been some programmed revolutions, some happy genocides, the rise of some murderous despot or two who had painted the streets with blood until the city decreed that it was no longer their turn to have fun. Once, a murderer had been brought in, and the citizenry had amused itself being slaughtered by him. This, Kayn figured, accounted for much of the fallen population. But the baby informed him of something else that also made sense, given the squalor of the cityscape around him: that the machines that kept things running had been breaking down for years, and that as more and more of them stopped working, the servitors were only able to keep some neighborhoods running by scavenging parts from those that didn't. Kayn took this with some excitement. He was starving for novelty and found being part of a crumbling civilization just what he needed. He thanked the baby for its time and moved on.

He passed a circular fountain, now dry and caked with clotted blood, where the skeletons of two human beings lay in a heap that suggested they'd died together. An old man sat throwing bread crumbs on the bodies, in order to enjoy the sight of the birds fluttering around the bones. Kayn asked what had happened and the old man said that there were any number of sights like this, tucked in this place and that: evidence of that killer who had been allowed to run amuck for a while, for the entertainment value that provided. Kayn, who had been murdered once or twice in his long life and did not care to have that happen again, asked if the pet killer had been disposed of once his novelty value was exhausted, and the old man said, "Oh, sure, sure; really, there's only so much you can do with a creature like that, before they start to repeat themselves in unacceptable ways." He sighed, pointed at the larger of the two skeletons and said, "That one was me." Kayn bid the old man farewell and moved further into the center of the city, finding along the way that he had to traverse any number of places where passages were blocked by drifts of sand.

This is how he knew that he was getting closer to the place he sought.

In outline the city resembled the infinity symbol, a pair of teardrop-shapes designed to converge at the narrowest points. This deliberate bottleneck was an intersection less than a hundred paces across at its narrowest point, open to the untouched landscape on both sides. It was a feature originally designed as a place of wonder, a plaza where the citizenry could pause and take in the unspoiled, or at least unpopulated, wilderness outside the city walls, reflect on the part of the world no one in the city ever needed, and move on, to whatever pleasures awaited in either of their home's two halves.

The last time Kayn had been to this place, just before joining with the orgynism, the mechanisms that had kept the desert on both sides from intruding on this narrow bottleneck of civilization had already started to fail, and the pavement tiles had all felt gritty underfoot, a first sign that the sands had already begun to intrude. It was worse now. The drifts of gray sand now extended from one side of the narrow strip to another, fingers of pure decay well into the process of sundering the city's two halves from one another. In the very center, the tiles had disintegrated completely, and Kayn did not just stumble over shifting sands but sink knee-deep into them. Something bit him in the leg. He cursed and dragged himself onto the tiles on the other side of the gap, pulling the buried creature along with him: He yanked it free of his leg, and examined the thing that had bitten him at arm's length. It was a tiny thing as wide as his wrist, with a nearly human face but for the slit nose and lipless mouth, and little human arms, but a torso that trailed to a point rather than sprout legs. Everything below its waist looked like some turds do, when they've been inside the colon so long that they've taken on the wrinkles and folds of the surrounding tissue.

Kayn almost smashed the shit-thing dead, but then it said, "Don't kill me!"

He grimaced but did not hurl it away as he would have wanted. "What are you?"

"I'm a man."

Kayn said, "I don't believe you."

"Laugh all you want. I'm prepared for when the city's gone. I'll survive a lot longer than you. I'll still be thriving in these sands when the sun goes cold."

Blood, Kayn's blood, dripped from the thing's fangs.

Kayn said, "The sun's gone cold. It made the news."

"Colder," the shit-thing clarified. "If it had gone out, we'd all be dead."

"Cold enough. The desert won't support life."

"You're half-right. It won't support *human* life. You can't go stumbling out there, trying to make a go of it, without freezing your nuts off. But life like me is still making a go of it, and will for a while yet. I'm the wave of the future. So feed me or let me go; I'm tired of your crap."

Kayn almost hurled it to the tiles and stomped it to a greasy spot, but there are penalties to casual murder even in a city where murder can be arranged as a source of entertainment, and so he simply dropped it into the gap between the city's decaying halves, and watched as it burrowed its way into the sands. He wondered if it was alone or if it was one member of a thriving colony, and if so, just what they fed on, down there, as it could not survive only on the blood of those like him, who stumbled in the crossing. And then he shrugged. In any city, even this one, it was possible to intercept any number of stories that had nothing to do with yourself, and if you did not want them to become your stories instead, you had to move on, banishing them to the status of footnotes or apocrypha.

He marched on, past the narrows, past a broken archway into the city's other half, where after a while he began encountering other residents again. An emaciated but bearded woman, clad only in the few strips of clothing that had not yet rotted off her, nodded at him as she crossed an avenue, bearing a squirming human-shaped something in a sack on her shoulders. Two children, a rarity when he'd joined the orgynism, sat in a tree chattering nonsense at one another, and he spent a few minutes attempting to coax them down before realizing that, human or not, they were joined to the tree by stems, and enjoying life as its fruit. A man in a long multi-colored coat, ragged and bearded and mad, darted into a narrow alley lined with knives, that ripped pieces from him as he fled heedless into a potent darkness at its other end. Two other men played a variant of chess, only with many thousands of additional pawns and knights, across a game board so vast that their pieces had yet to contend with one another at the center of the board; both players were draped in drifts of dust, each one so involved in calculating the possible ramifications of any move that it might have been years since they had done anything but wait.

It was only after he entered a neighborhood where none of the buildings had doors, where they were just unmarked monoliths offering no clue as to what they might have contained, that he found a place that had once been one of his favorites. Prior civilizations would have called it an inn, or café, or restaurant. It served the same function with some adjustments for the nature of the way the city's people interacted with one another. The last time he'd been here, centuries earlier, had been Poison Day and he had sat alongside two dozen other patrons there to soak up the novelty of dining and dying and dining and dying only to dine and die some more. It had been glorious. Today, of course, he didn't want to feel his insides turn to fire inside him. He just wanted to plug himself back into whatever social intercourse the city could still provide, while making contacts for whatever grand joy came next. And so he entered the familiar room with its frescoes of hanging gardens, overjoyed to find it, if not full, then at least occupied by half a dozen others, including two old men locked in conversation, one lone man addressing his soup with what could only be described as grim determination, and a forlorn young woman with dark circles under her eyes, staring at her plate of something as if wholly uncertain what it was.

Kayn said, "Excuse me."

The woman was silver-skinned, no doubt plated with the actual metal, a fashion choice that had been popular once upon a time. He supposed that it must be completely antiquarian now. So were her eyes, which were pink and lemur-large against cheeks buffed to a mirrored finish. She sat with her delicate hands palm-down on the table, flanking her bowl but making no move to lift it to her lips. But she was not forlorn enough to ignore Kayn's hello. She met his gaze and released half-a-dozen syllables of purest gibberish in no language he knew, which was not all that unusual. Kayn had lived through entire renaissances of enthused linguistic experimentation where all of the city's thousands had ordered the machines to design individual tongues for them, and had happily wandered the streets as citizens of Babel, content to not understand each other at all.

He pressed further: "Do you understand me?"

She cycled through a dozen tongues, some known to him, and some not, before arriving at the one he'd used to address her. "Can I help you?"

"Will you accept my company?"

"I wasn't looking for company, but I don't specifically object to it. I am willing to discuss anything but politics, morality, or the flattening effect of multiplying temporal paradoxes."

"My full name is Adam Splendor Sadness Feline Igneous Ultimate Never Cul-De-Sac Untoward Synchronicity Leverage Cystic Beverage Arrogance Wholly Thirteen Cunnilingus Hummingbird Multiplication Kayn. You can call me Kayn."

She provided her name, not a spoken syllable but a blast of tropical warmth, humid and filled with peat. "You can call me Peat. Please sit."

"All right." He sat opposite her, and let the table generate a meal for him, utensils and all. There was no mucking about with menus, sentient or otherwise. The establishment had tasted him and determined just what combination of foodstuffs was most appropriate for his current mood. What came, rising out of the solid table like the sun coming up on the horizon, was a bowl of something moving, something clearly sentient and alive, something that sang in soft, mournful despair as it awaited slaughter at the tip of his heated, six-pronged fork. He didn't make it wait for very long, just stabbed through its tiny skull with one ruthless thrust, and lifted it to his mouth, feeling satiated as its death throes distributed what flavor it had. This had long been one of his favorite dishes. But today it was oily and bland, and when he was done chewing, it left an unpleasant gritty residue between his teeth. It was as if the sand of the surrounding desert had gotten into the synthesizers themselves.

She noted his displeasure and said, "You're surprised. You must have been gone for a while. Orgynism?"

"Yes."

"I was in one, about eight hundred years ago. It was a big one, with over a thousand participants, at its peak. It was bliss until one near the center went insane and started chewing his way out. I'm still missing some toes. How long have you been out?"

He told her.

"That explains your reaction to the food. You're new to the way things have been falling apart."

"I notice you're not eating either."

"I never do. I have no stomach. No internal organs of any kind. This," she said, drumming her silvery digits on the table, "is what I'm made of now. I suppose I'll last longer this way, when the city's gone."

"So it's not a rumor."

"No."

He pointed at her food. "You ordered."

"I wanted to sit. The table provided. But I outgrew food long ago. You should, too. The city won't be making much more of it."

He remembered the predictions of the shit-thing. "How much time do you think we still have? Months? Years? Centuries?"

"Who cares? It's not like this place is fun anymore. We've seen everything. We've done everything. I'm only alive out of inertia."

He said, "Up for suicide? I'll join you, if that's what you want."

"I've done that," Peat replied. "It didn't take."

"Then let's get married."

"I've done that a couple of dozen times, too. Once with you, in fact, though we weren't the only people involved. But if you'd like to be in love for a while, just to pass the time, I'm willing to do that."

"All right," said Kayn.

Their courtship over, they both left the table, to make the necessary arrangements.

They didn't know each other and didn't like each other much, but that was no longer an inconvenience, not when they were both available and there were still working machines dispensing love. It was just a matter of recalibrating their internal referents and setting what intensity they wanted, from mild affection to all-out raging, clothes-shredding passion. The first through fourth of the stations they investigated were all derelict, three merely devoid of power and one incapable of producing anything but flatulent noises, but the fifth they found, in a vacant bazaar on the seventh level of the abandoned Third Church of Gilgul the Materialist, was still capable of producing Love at some settings, albeit none of the better ones. As per his lifelong habit as a man more comfortable with receiving that emotion than feeling it, he took a dose two notches lower than hers, and felt a surge of deep affection while she elected to feel something more, something rich and genuine and pure.

There was no chance of a standard honeymoon night, not that he wanted one, after the sexual surfeit of his recent centuries. He may have still possessed the parts, but she did not. But companionship, she provided. They shared a bed and sometimes a vat, and during the days they wandered the city, noting all the places that still existed and those that were still a ghost of what they had used to be.

They went to the Cinema, the last Cinema, a place that had been established millennia before, where mechanisms behind the screen projected a perpetual story compelling enough to be joined or abandoned at any point, without any sense that one had missed something. Alas, something primal had been lost over the years. In Kayn's youth, the story had been an intricate saga of intrigue in the court of some medieval kingdom, driven by subtle turns of character and shifts of power dynamics among a cast of thousands.

It had once kept him in his seat, being fed and tended by bots, for more than a month before the sameness overwhelmed him and he'd wandered out of the auditorium looking for a place to set some bombs. Years later, he'd returned, and the story had contracted to two men, armed with knives, grappling with one another in the center of a field of corpses. He'd spent a day watching them cut little strips of flesh off one another's bodies, discerned no story, and left. Now, returning with Peat to an auditorium ankle-deep in sand occupied by a half-dozen dusty patrons he recognized from his earlier visits and who he presumed to have been watching the entire saga from the beginning, he found that the story had contracted still further: It was now a man forever punching a solid wall with the wrist-nubs that were all that remained of his arms, after his fists had eroded from an unimaginable number of constant impacts. "The machines are stuck," Peat explained. "They used to be able to introduce new characters, establish new plot developments, create brand-new complications capable of carrying the narrative to new places, but in recent years they've been deteriorating. The narrative's become fossilized. You can sit for years waiting for something different to happen."

"It's a great unintentional metaphor," said Kayn.

The two of them stayed six hours, just watching the unfortunate on screen pummel the wall, waiting for something else to happen, anything else to happen. Nothing did, and they ultimately left in search of new adventures.

They found an abandoned building where Peat said that she'd lived once, a tower now leaning seventeen degrees which once would have been righted or had its architectural deficiency incorporated as a fresh source of novelty, and scaled the exterior to the summit, one hundred and forty stories above the avenue below. The apartment they found there was infested with spiders, and criss-crossed with vast curtains of webbing. The tenants, three women and one man, were cocooned and in the process of being digested, but did not seem to mind. One explained to Kayn that the spiders made such wonderful music. Kayn could detect nothing. Peat said that she could: "It's just above your range of hearing, Kayn."

He asked her what kind of music they were playing, and she said: "Waltzes. I can hum along, if you'd like to dance." So they danced, the tightly wrapped residents of the apartment watching with delight and fascination as Kayn and Peat spun their circles across the tilted floor. How long they danced, Kayn could not tell, but it was long enough for the spiders to begin the process of capturing them, swathing Kayn in what looked like bandages and Peat in what looked like a diaphanous gown. And for a while he thought that it would not be a bad thing for his years of existence to end this way, so high above the city streets, as close to the dimming stars as he had ever been. But the spiders began to work in earnest, his skin began to itch, and he was moved to tell Peat that maybe they ought to go. They climbed back down, without him hearing so much as a single note.

Back on the streets, they found a corpse willing to speak to them. Terrible things had been done to him by a passing murderer of unremitting savagery, perhaps the same one whose handiwork Kayn had already seen here and there: It honestly didn't matter, not to the victim and not to Kayn, because the deed had been done and the corpse was not willing to do anything constructive to fix it. His chest was still open to the elements, but he had elected not to heal or to die, but rather to continue to lie where the monster had left him, choosing to spend what time the city had left on his back, in contemplation of the few remaining stars. He said, "I remember being part of a great love story. I do not remember whether it was two men or two women or one woman and one man or a pair of thirders or any of the hundreds of other possible combinations we came up with, by the time it all started falling apart, but I remember being one of them. I remember telling the one I loved that I would never forget. I remember the finger against my lips, the whispered words, sure you will; everything we have done is just footnote. That turned out to be true. It was the one great love of my life and it happened so long ago that I cannot remember who my lover was, or for that matter who I was. I just remember regretting that I went on after it ended." He took a deep breath that caused the cavity at the center of his chest to bubble, and then spoke with special urgency: "The city's going to fall."

"We know that," said Peat.

The murdered man said, "I don't mean millennia from now. I don't mean centuries from now, or even any span of years. I mean weeks or months, no more. Listen: We're sinking. Listen: We will soon be swallowed up. Listen: The sand will come in and fill the streets and blot out the sky and scour everything clean. Listen: Anybody who stays will die. Anybody who wants to live must leave."

Kayn had already reached this conclusion just by walking around, but he had seen the dune sea: a desert that had long ago spread worldwide, without any fantastical oases or lands untouched by the entropy that had overtaken everything else. "There's no place to go."

The corpse could only repeat himself. "Anybody who wants to live must leave."

"Shush, shush," said Peat. She pressed a mirrored fingertip to the corpse's lips, burning them slightly because of the generated heat she could do nothing to tamp. Being a corpse, he felt nothing but the intended comfort, and he grew calm long enough for her to speak the only ameliorating truth she could. "There's no reason to worry. Nobody here wants to live, anyway."

Later, Kayn said, "But I do want to live."

By now they were wandering through one of the last remaining libraries with books made of paper. It was not, of course, real paper, made from trees: that would have deteriorated to dust long before. Paper had not been a thing since all information was trusted to the machines, and before that, since any texts human beings might still have some purpose for had been transferred to silicates. These books were designed to feel like paper, but were made of flexible alloys, chemically inert and designed to last forever. What a pity that some past vandal had seen fit to black out every line of type with a pigment just as eternal as the pages themselves, before re-shelving them in cases of the same material, as a means of ensuring that their splendid meaninglessness lasted forever!

He made his pronouncement while Peat was running her silvery hands over the pages of one volume grabbed at random, just to enjoy its texture. She looked up and said, "What?"

He repeated himself. "I do want to live."

"But everything's ending."

"I don't care. I haven't done everything I wanted to do. I haven't seen everything I wanted to see. I don't want this story to be over. I want to keep adding to it. I want to live past the point where there's any point in living."

She was aghast. "Why?"

"I don't know."

"I've watched you. You're as bored as I am. As bored as everyone is."

"I can't deny it."

"Then why would you want this to go on?"

"I don't know. I think it's a birth defect of some kind."

"There are no birth defects. The machines can fix any flaw there is."

"I have one. I don't seem to be able to give up."

She said, "You implanted love for me. You can implant a death wish. It's just as simple. There must be some machine still capable of doing that."

"I tried that, years ago. Before the orgynism. I thought the time had come to end myself. I couldn't make myself want to. I went to one of the machines and told it to adjust me, to make me content with the time I had lived, and ready to stop. It made noise for a while and then stopped. It was non-functional. Something about me had broken it. I tried another machine and then a third, with identical results. I broke down every machine I asked. When I realized it was impossible, I decided that blissful oblivion was just as good, and started recruiting lovers for my orgynism." He thought about it for a while, as driven to silence by her nonplussed reaction as she was to what he said, and reported, "I don't know. Maybe that's why the orgynism rejected me. But I want to live. I'm stuck that way."

She flipped through some more pages, caressing each one she stopped at, finding nothing new on any of them, but still finding mild distraction with the way they felt.

Then she said, "I don't think I can love anyone so old-fashioned."

They didn't break up right away. Just as heat takes time to dissipate, so does affection, and so they spent the next few days having other shared adventures, some romantic and some not, as a means of continuing to spend the time that was now in such short supply.

They found a building on the edge of a neighborhood that had already been reclaimed by the sands, with one collapsed wing and one that seemed to remain upright only out of sheer stubbornness. It was an orphanage, long-abandoned, and the bottom floor was a nursery filled with babies. They were manufactured children, grown in vats and tended by servitors like all the world's children had been, since long before this was the only city. Aged to what the peak age of what once would have been considered appealing, they were forever frozen at that level of maturity to be claimed by whatever adoptive parents happened to show up. There had of course been none for a long time, and thus every crib being tended had an occupant, squirming and cooing beneath inches of dust. There was no point in taking any of them, and so Kayn and Peat just spent an hour or so wandering among the bassinets, neither oohing nor aahing, but not immune to the pathos either. They named the cutest one, the one they would have taken had they been in the market, "Forever." Forever regarded them with interest, imprinting. This, given their dearth of interest, was probably not a favor.

They found a machine in the shape of a pulsating sphincter attended by a tarnished servitor who explained that it was an art installation, designed to turn things into other things. Any object placed within the loading portal would be devoured and shat out the other side as another object entirely. Peat had seen such merriments before but Kayn had not, and so she stood by indulgently as he tested its capabilities with the various artifacts in range. He gave the orifice a stone plucked from the borders of a wilted garden, and watched as the orifice sucked it in, chewed, and produced an obscene statue of a woman having sexual congress with a tree. He gave it a little wooden table from an abandoned nearby café, and watched as the mastication produced a mound of broken glass. Then he ordered the servitor to feed itself to the orifice, and, being a machine, it obeyed without protest. The orifice chewed and the thing that came out the back was alive and boneless and incapable of any action but unending screams.

Peat said, "That was interesting."

Kayn felt bad for the servitor, which had been polite and unoffending and didn't deserve an end of this sort. Maybe feeding it to the orifice would produce an improvement? Perhaps, but it could also produce something much worse, and so he ended up doing nothing.

They sought out warmth, in the form of the city's last furnace, a raging open conflagration that Kayn could not approach but that Peat was able to enter and explore, without harm. Her silvery flesh did not melt but grew red-hot, a transformation that rendered her so beautiful that Kayn might have fallen in love with her all over again, without artificial assistance. She spun and danced and sang, an ember that, for a few minutes, looked like she might have been able to devour all that remained of the city, all by herself. She seemed joyous. But once she left, she cooled rapidly, both in temperature and in mood, and she said, "That, on the other hand, was boring. I think I've decided to die now."

"Are you sure? Maybe you'll feel better in the morning."

"Who wants to feel better? I've *done* that."

Kayn could not dissuade her, and so they spent her last night in a ballroom that had become only a little shabbier over the centuries, dancing tangos and waltzes and pretending for a while to be a great lord and lady from one of those past eras that still had such things. At midnight an artificial moon rose on the other side of the cracked stained-glass windows, casting a beam of multicolored wonder through the dusty air. He kissed her for the first and only time, a moment of contact between his flesh and whatever her flesh happened to be that felt too much like kissing a thing made of ice. She said, "Goodbye," disentangled herself from his arms, and strode to the center of the dance floor, raising one graceful arm and standing en pointe in a spot where her many shiny surfaces could reflect the moonbeam to every corner of the hall. It seemed like a moment of perfect stillness in the middle of a ballet. But as the long seconds passed, and she never came out of it, Kayn saw that she wasn't going to. He approached her and touched a finger to her metallic cheek, finding a nub just below her right eye that might have been a metallic tear, and confirmed that whatever had made her Peat was gone.

He wandered for a few weeks after that, interacting with as many of the city's fading wonders as he could, but found fewer that worked and even fewer that he had not seen.

When he had decided that, he fell into revisiting some of the places where he had already been.

He went to the nursery, found Forever—who was already gathering a new layer of dust—held him for a little bit, and said some things about connections that fail and times that end, that Forever must have understood not at all.

He went to the library, gazed upon all the shelves lined with unreadable books, and stood for a while in the presence of all those unknowable narratives, and contemplated a life spent curled up with them, the life he would have been happy enough to undertake were it possible to cross the obstructions between those words and his eyes.

He revisited the murdered man, who told him again that things were ending and that there was no time to lose, if he wanted to live.

He went back to the Cinema to see where the story had gone, and found that it had indeed progressed since his last visit. The image on screen was no longer a man punching a wall, but was now a different man, one who looked very much like Kayn himself, sitting cross-legged in a desert very much like the one currently engulfing the city. The man was alive and aware and clearly capable of action; it was possible to tell, just from the way he blinked at the moments when one errant breeze or another deposited grains of sand in his eyes. But he did nothing to shield himself, nothing to rescue himself from the forces that would soon enough bury him. He was spent. And in the fourth hour that Kayn spent absorbed in this absence of all adventure, the star of the movie shifted, turned his dusty visage toward the audience, and focused on Kayn alone, ignoring the handful of others who had been sitting for far longer, waiting for him to do something worth seeing.

He said, "Go."

Kayn said, "Where?"

"I don't care, Adam Splendor Sadness Feline Igneous Ultimate Never Cul-De-Sac Untoward Synchronicity Leverage Cystic Beverage Arrogance Wholly Thirteen Cunnilingus Hummingbird Multiplication Kayn. This show is over for you. Go elsewhere."

Kayn, who had never been the type to stay where he wasn't wanted, went.

He retraced all his steps, lingering here and there and taking weeks for the journey, until he found himself back in the room of his greatest humiliation, looking up at what was left of his old orgynism, and found that it had deteriorated horribly in his absence. No longer an approximate sphere, it was now a crescent moon, disfigured by a great gaping crater where fully a third of the participants had either been pushed out, or had left of their own accord. Of those who remained, only about half were still in motion, attempting to make up with their efforts what the immobile remainder no longer could. Their union no longer looked like bliss, but like desperation, denial of that which was coming for all of them. One of those still grinding away, but not looking at all well, opened his eyes and noticed Kayn. He said, "I suppose you came to gloat."

"No," said Kayn. "I did not."

"Liar! I know the way it works! You want us to say that it all fell to pieces when you left! Well, it did, but you had nothing to do with it! It was an inevitability, a shift in our corporeal paradigm, that was only the next natural step in the evolution of our union! Soon, we will re-incorporate under new principles and achieve heights we never would have known were we still with you, slaves to your antiquated erotic philosophy! We would not have you back even if you begged us, do you hear? Not one of us, not all of us! We are better without you and we will continue to be, until the end of the world!"

"That's no more than two days away," said Kayn, whose connection to the city's flailing machinery was still keeping him informed.

"Two days is forever," the dying man told him.

Kayn considered it and thought that yes, this was true. There had been no subjective time in the orgynism. Hours had been the same as centuries, and centuries the same as hours. That it lasted as long as it had was therefore the same thing as not lasting for a heartbeat, a crowning achievement the same thing as a total failure. This truism, it further struck him, was also true of the city itself, and, to a still larger extent, the history of all humanity, a race that had been around for many billions of years and had turned out to be as ephemeral as a sneeze. He thought: *How many terribly depressing things are also tremendously freeing?* and embraced that epiphany, feeling much better.

"Enjoy your two days," he told the man functioning as the voice of the orgynism.

"Go to hell."

* * *

In the past, when great ships sank far from land, those left aboard in the final moments had to choose between two options. One was to stay aboard the vessel for as long as they could, and in so doing embrace what life-preserving properties it still had, at the cost of submitting themselves to the prospect of being dragged with it down into blackness. The other was to damn the dubious comforts of that which would not float for long, dive into the turbulent sea, and swim like mad, knowing that there was no other vessel to swim to, but still embracing fate, challenging the universe to provide deliverance while it still could. There had always been advocates of both methods, people who had lived and died by both methods, people who had doomed themselves by making the wrong choice. The right choice had never been anything but circumstance.

Aware of this, and aware that his own preferred strategy would soon be moot, Kayn trekked through streets that were coming apart even as he traveled on them, to the spot he had chosen for his own egress. His strategy was, as it turned out, not a unique one; there were a dozen others, comprising the largest crowd he had seen in one place since departing his orgynism, in line ahead of him, waiting for their own leap into stormy waters. He watched one or two of them go, and then sat cross-legged on the floor, to do the one thing he'd never really done before, the one that he did not think he would have another chance to do after today.

In short, he composed a poem.

He did not ask the machines to compose a sonnet for him. The last time he'd done that, it had turned out to be the worst sonnet ever written. He had no comprehension of that literary form in particular or of the rules of meter or rhyme, and so his wasn't even a sonnet. It was in truth only a poem at all because that was what he had intended to write and because now, at the end of time, it would have been downright silly for even the most persnickety critic in all the world to make a fuss about definitions. Besides, honestly, it was more than fair to say that Kayn had accomplished the goal sought by all the poets who had written in all of Mankind's languages, since the beginning of time: for their words to last until the end of time. Though Kayn managed this trick by composing his just a few minutes before that grand departure, his seizure of this ancient goal could not be denied. His words, as heartfelt as any that had ever been written, would last to the dying of the light.

He struggled with the most important part, the lines that summarized everything he'd ever learned.

When nothing matters, everything matters.
When everything matters, everything's tragedy.
When everything's tragedy, everything's comedy.
When everything's comedy, nothing matters.

He was sufficiently proud of this to show it to the man standing ahead of him in line, who wore a stained black suit and a matching top hat, all gone ragged and stinking from many years without laundering. That man read the lines, seemed to consider delivering the judgment that it was incomprehensible gibberish, but lit up at that one highlight, saying, "Oh, very good. Very, very good. That summarizes the idiocy of the species more than anything."

"Do you really think so?" asked Kayn, who with this question became the last human being to ever care what a critic thought of his work.

The man in the battered top hat replied in the affirmative and placed himself on the conveyer belt into the orifice, surrendering his eternal fate to whatever it chose to make of him. On the other end lay the things that had been the other people on line: a lampshade, a golden helix, a blinking lizard, a globe, a puff of smoke, a parasol, a gasping fish, a mound of gray sand. Perhaps two or three of these things remained conscious of what they had been before their transformations. Perhaps two or three would survive after the city was gone. There was no way to predict, really. Submitting to the change might or might not be a better survival strategy than finding some secure place and waiting for the city to be engulfed. But this was the choice of those who found themselves on sinking ships: to stay, or to leave, either option equally promising, either option equally bad, the choice ultimately a lesson in philosophy. When that was the only thing left, the only weapon left was confidence.

Kayn was confident. For him, at least, it would not end this way.

In the meantime, he stood by as the penultimate man went through, and awaited his own turn.

NOT THIS WAR, NOT THIS WORLD

JONATHAN MABERRY

Jonathan Maberry is a *New York Times* bestselling author, five-time Bram Stoker Award winner, and comic book writer. His vampire apocalypse book series, *V-Wars*, is in production as a Netflix original series, starring Ian Somerhalder (*Lost*, *Vampire Diaries*) and will debut in early 2019. He writes in multiple genres including suspense, thriller, horror, science fiction, fantasy, and action; and he writes for adults, teens and middle grade. His works include the Joe Ledger thrillers, *Glimpse*, the Rot & Ruin series, the Dead of Night series, *The Wolfman*, *X-Files Origins: Devil's Advocate*, *Mars One*, and many others. Several of his works are in development for film and TV. His comics include *Black Panther*, *The Punisher*, and *Bad Blood*. He is a board member of the Horror Writers Association and the president of the International Association of Media Tie-in Writers. Find him online at jonathanmaberry.com.

-1-

"This is Billy Trout reporting live from the apocalypse..."

The radio still worked. That was something.

As long as that kept working Sam thought there might be a chance. He didn't believe in much. Didn't really believe in that. But a guy has to hold onto something.

He held on.

-2-

Sam Imura leaned against the hard plastic wall of his elevated tree stand and carefully and quietly opened a can of beer. Doing it slowly to allow the gas to hiss very softly and to keep the metal from screeching. He pushed the tab down into the opening and folded the ring back. Nice and neat.

The beer was warm. A local brew that tasted almost, but not exactly, like piss. He drank piss once. Years ago during a week of hardship training at Fort Bragg. Anyone who complained about it got shipped back to whatever branch of service they came from. Sam sipped the beer, and revised his opinion. This stuff tasted every bit as bad as hot urine. He took another swallow and set the can down.

The deer stand was in a nice spot. Just inside a shadowy tree line. To either side and behind, he could see well into the woods, which rose in a series of small humps. Lots of trees, not too much shrubbery. Exposed roots, which made animals walk carefully and made two-legged targets trip. The other direction looked out on a big field that wandered up toward a farmhouse.

The house was empty, cleared out two nights ago. A smoldering mound of gristle and bone was humped in front of the porch. Three other mounds were situated around the property, including one by the blackened shell of a pickup truck that had blown itself up by an old gas pump. There was a story there, but Sam didn't know what it was.

The house itself wanted to tell another story. From what he could see, a few people had tried to reinforce it, but fucked it all up. They nailed boards in a haphazard way across all the windows, but the nails had been driven straight in, not toe-nailed, not screwed. Nothing to give them real resistance. And someone had rigged the cellar door with crossbeams, but for some reason hadn't hidden down there.

There was blood everywhere—and some shell casings.

From the mess in the yard Sam could tell that a wave of people had come through and cleaned out the leavings of the failed stronghold. Shell casings told him that it wasn't military, though. Mostly pistol and hunting rifle rounds, some commercial shotgun shells, so he figured it was local hunters and maybe some cops. That made sense. There would be more of them, and this was rural Pennsylvania.

Every goddamn person out here owned a couple of guns.

By the time Sam got here, though, the killing was done and the killers had moved on. He hoped they were the good guys. If there were any good guys left. He was cynical enough to have his doubts. While running with DELTA and later with the Department of Military Sciences, he'd seen a lot of the worst side of humanity. The tendency toward savagery. The kneejerk reaction to lash out in fear, and to grab in need.

He took another sip of beer, adjusted his billed cap to shade his eyes and studied the field. Nothing moved except what the wind pushed, but that didn't mean anything. There was something out there.

At the very edge of his unaided visual range was his truck. Sitting in the middle of the road with a busted axle. When he'd driven out of here two days ago he got exactly three hundred yards. That was it. He knew it hadn't been the road that killed the truck. It was them.

Them.

Bodies break and burst under the wheels of a big rig, but they are still made of bone, they still have mass. Sometimes he'd had to smash into crowds of them. Sometimes he'd driven over them. Bumping and thumping over dozens of bodies. Men. Women.

Children.

It was worse than driving down a rutted country road. He figured he cracked the axle punching through the last bunch. Maybe did something to the radiator and the engine. The truck was as dead as everything else around here.

Sam never considered abandoning it, though, because he'd spent the best part of a day using a forklift to load pallet after pallet of supplies into a semi. Food, water, camping gear, fuel oil, tents, tools. All the things he thought would be useful to any group of survivors he met.

So far, he had no one to share his supplies with, and no motivation to leave it behind. His plan—still a bit rough around the edges—was to secure the house and the area up to a mile in every direction. Kill anything that needed killing, and clear the way for survivors to come find him. There was a cemetery near here, and a town about seventeen miles away, in a town called Willard, but Sam couldn't find it on a map or with the truck's GPS. Useless as fuck.

So he stayed where he was.

The deer stand was already here, though old and in disrepair. He fixed it. Sam was always good with tools. Building things was as much therapy as it was a hobby. It had the precision that satisfied his sniper's need for detail, and it *made* things instead of destroyed them. That mattered.

Killing was a constant in his life. He enlisted on his eighteenth birthday, choosing that path instead of following his father into law enforcement. His younger brother, Tom, was in the police academy in California. Sam wondered if any of his family was still alive. Maybe Tom. The kid was resourceful. Practical and tough. His dad was old and slowing down, though. Sam didn't know a lot about his stepmom and had never seen his baby half-brother, Benny. They were three thousand miles away, high in the Sierra Nevada mountains of central California. Maybe this plague hadn't reached that far.

Maybe pigs would sprout wings and fly out of his ass.

That news guy, Billy Trout, said it was everywhere, that it was traveling at the speed of human need. Planes, trains and automobiles. Outflying and outdistancing prophylactic measures. Outrunning all common sense and precaution; spread by the people who were trying to outrun it.

There was a joke in there somewhere. His old boss Captain Joe Ledger could have said something funny about that. A twist of wit, sarcasm and social commentary. Sam wondered where he was. Probably dead, too.

He drank the rest of the beer and put the can into the canvas cooler because he didn't want the breeze to knock it off the deer stand. Sam was cautious like that.

He froze.

Something out there moved. He was sure of it.

Sam raised his rifle. It was a CheyTac M200 Intervention sniper rifle. Best of the best for someone like him. Too much gun for hunting, but this wasn't really deer season. He scanned the field with his shaded eyes first to zero on where he'd heard the movement. Found it. Something moving through the corn off to his left. He leaned into the spotting scope, but the corn was tall and green and lush. The stalks moved, but he couldn't see why.

He'd used super glue to attach a sock filled with beans to the rail of the tree stand, and he rested the rifle on that. He did the math in his head. Baseline trajectory and bullet drop. His breathing was calm, his finger relaxed along the outside of the trigger guard.

If this was a deer, then he'd let it go past. He could be here for a while if no one came, and there was plenty of food in the truck. It would make more sense to let the deer breed next year's food. Sam had a feeling that would matter.

If it was a person, he'd have to coax them into the open and make them stand there until he could come over, pat them down, check them for bites, and ask a few questions.

But if it was one of *them*... then there was only one option. A single round placed just so. Catastrophic brain shot. Something he'd done in hostage rescue situations more times than he could count. A shot to the brain stem or the neural motor strips that kills so instantly that body reflexes cannot react. What was funny—in a curious rather than humorous way—was that it was a golden shot for snipers, something they aspired to, but which was rarely even considered by other branches of the military. Most of the soldiers he'd known on the way up had been more concerned with seeing how much ordnance they could throw downrange, operating on a *more is better* plan. Snipers were stingy with their rounds. It was a matter of pride with them, and Sam seldom pulled a trigger unless he was certain of a kill.

He was loaded with .408 Cheyenne Tactical cartridges in a single-stack seven-round magazine, and at four hundred rounds he could kill anything he wanted dead. He'd dropped targets at much greater distances, too, but this wasn't that kind of war. If this was one of them, then they would walk right up to take the bullet.

"Come on," he murmured, softer than the whispering breeze.

The weeds parted.

It was a child.

Six years old. Maybe seven. Sandy blond hair riffled by the wind. Jeans and a Spider-Man sweatshirt. Red sneakers. Holding something in his hands.

For a moment Sam thought it was a teddy bear. Or a doll dressed all in red.

"No," he said, and it came out as a sob.

It wasn't a doll.

It wasn't a fucking doll.

It wasn't.

It.

-3-

Sam took the shot.

-4-

The bullet did what it was designed to do. It ended all brain function. It ended life. Snap. Just like that.

The boy's head was blown apart like a melon. Very immediate and messy. The body puddled down, dropping the awful red thing it carried.

A perfect shot.

Sam sat back and down, thumping hard onto his ass. Gasping as if the shot had punched a hole in the world through which all air was escaping. The day, even here in the shade, was suddenly too bright.

He felt the burn in his eyes. Not from muzzle flash or gunpowder. Tears burn hotter than those things.

The sound of the shot echoed off of the farmhouse and the ranks of corn and the walls of hell. It went away and then found him again, punching the last air from his lungs as he fell onto his back and squeezed his eyes shut.

This was the world.

This was how the world was.

-5-

He came down from the tree stand and stood for a moment, leaning against the rough oak bark. The rifle was up there. He couldn't bear to touch it.

It was bad enough that it had been one of them. He'd been sent to this part of Pennsylvania at the start of the plague. He knew the science of it. *Lucifer 113*, an old Cold War bioweapon cooked up in some Russian lab but brought out of history's trash bin by a deranged prison scientist named Herman Volker and used on a death row inmate. The plan had been to torture the condemned serial killer by introducing the genetically engineered parasites that would hotwire the man's brain while hijacking his motor cortex and cranial nerves. It would keep the higher functions awake and aware, but with no connection to motor functions. The killer would go into his grave totally connected to all five senses—hyper aware of each— while his body, unable to die any normal death, slowly rotted. But aware. Completely and irrevocably aware.

The killer never made it to the grave because when it came to doing things right the system was almost always in clusterfuck mode. A relative appeared out of the devil's asshole, or someplace equally unlikely, claimed the body and brought it home to a little shithole town called Stebbins. In the local funeral home, the killer woke up.

Woke up hungry.

That was how it started. Less than a goddamn week ago. Sam knew the story because he was one of the people who had a need to know. Most people probably still didn't know what the plague was, or why it was, or how it spread. And the one thing that was nowhere on the news was the fact that every single motherfucking one of *them* was aware. Trapped inside. Connected and in touch with every taste, every smell, everything nerve conduction could share. All of those people. Helpless passengers, forced to be both witnesses and accomplices in the murders they committed.

All of them.

The little boy, too.

And the baby he carried.

Every.

Last.

One.

Sam staggered out into the field. Not to see the boy. That kid was gone. Freed, if that word could apply. No. He had to find the baby.

The red, ragged bundle the boy had been carrying.

No, Sam demanded of himself. *Tell the truth. Know the truth. Have the balls to honor the dead by accepting the truth.*

The boy had been feeding on the infant. Carrying it around. Eating.

-6-

It was there. On the ground. Twitching.

Handless. Footless. Faceless.

Alive.

Or… *un*-alive. Sam didn't know the new language required for this fucked up version of the world.

What were these things? They were not living. They weren't dead. Not really. The body was hacked, controlled. All nonessential systems were shut down to conserve food and other resources for the parasites. So much so that a lot of the surface flesh and even some of the organs became necrotic, and the slow rot released chemicals and proteins which the parasites devoured. If not alive and not dead, what was the third option?

Living dead?

It had a lurid quality to it, but it also fit. Like a bullet fits the hole it creates as it drills in the flesh. Forced, but functional. Sufficient to its purpose.

The living dead.

This is what Sam chewed on while he knelt in the dirt and dug a hole with his hands. No, not a hole. A grave. He bruised his fingers on roots, tore his nails, numbed his flesh with the cold, cold soil.

Digging.

There were better ways to do this. He had a knife and it could chop the earth better. That was reasonable. He drew the blade and used it. Tried not to listen to the sound he made. Could not *bear* to listen to the sounds the little undead thing made. Gurgles. Like a baby would. Like a real, normal baby would.

He chopped and stabbed the ground, widening the hole. Deepening it. Then he stopped when he realized that he was making the hole too neat, too perfect. Overdoing it.

"Fuck," he said, and then almost apologized out loud because there were kids there. Kids. Holy fuck.

The infant squirmed and tried to reach for him with its ragged stumps of arms. The hole was deep enough but there were two logistical challenges. Lifting the child meant touching it. And then ending it.

This was not shooting three or four hundred yards from an elevated firing position. This was right here, up close and way too personal.

With a baby.

Living dead or not, it was a baby. If there was anything more clear in the rulebook of soldiering it was that soldiers were there—by their nature—to protect the innocent. All arguments about collateral damage aside, this was a certainty; to go against that was the ultimate taboo. Militarily and as a human goddamn being.

"Do your duty, soldier," he told himself. Speaking out loud. Speaking in an ordinary tone of voice, which was way the fuck out of the ordinary, all things considered.

He paused for a moment, listening to what was going on inside his head. *Is this it*, he wondered. *Is this me going crazy?*

After hundreds of conflicts in scores of battles, after pulling the trigger on a legion of targets, Sam had always taken some rough pride in being stable. No PTSD. Snipers were practical, pragmatic. Grounded.

Except he was talking to himself in a cornfield after shooting one kid and contemplating how best to murder another. Kneeling by a hole he'd dug that was surgically neat.

Oh, yeah, no chance of mental damage here, folks. Move along, nothing to see.

The baby rolled over on its side and then flopped onto its belly. The truncated legs pushed against the dirt. The toothless mouth snapped at the air in his direction. Biting the *smell* of him.

"Jesus fuck," said Sam. This time there was nothing normal or calm or controlled in his voice.

He looked away. The knife that stood straight from the mound of dirt he'd removed. Then down at the automatic in the shoulder rig he wore. Bullet or blade. Either would get it done. Which, though, would hurt less? The baby. Him. Both?

Knife was quicker. It was right there, but he couldn't do it. Sam could not even bring himself to touch the handle. Not for something like this. Knives were too personal. They were meant for enemy flesh. He'd used that knife, and others over the years, to cut throats, puncture hearts, end lives. Those targets had been enemies. They were playing the same game of war and understood the rules. The knife, in those moments, was a tool no different than the hammer the person who'd boarded up the windows of the house had used.

Sam knew he could never use that knife on this target. This child. Never in ten million years. On himself, maybe. Sure. That even felt likely. Attractive. Comforting in its way.

Not on a baby.

The gun, though?

He drew it and held it, weighing it. The gun was a SIG Sauer P320-M17. Fully loaded, as it was now, it weighed twenty-nine-point-four ounces. Seventeen 9mm jacketed hollow point rounds. It was too much gun. A .22 would do it. And it would be appropriate because that caliber was notorious as an assassin's gun. And was this an assassination? A murder? Certainly not an act of war.

Or, he wondered, was it?

The plague was spreading exponentially across the country, and by now almost certainly globally. It was unique in that anyone killed by the plague, or improperly killed by any other means, was recruited by design into the opposing force. A self-sustaining war of attrition. The infected were clear aggressors.

So, sure. War.

The baby kept trying to reach him. To bite him, even though it had no hands to grab, no teeth to bite. If Sam was in hell, then so was it. He bent down and looked into its eyes, wondering if there was an infant's mind looking back. But it was a stupid thing to do, because he wasn't sure he could even tell that with a living baby. Maybe he could have with the boy.

Do it, he told himself.

"Do it," he said aloud.

I can't.

The gun fired. Immediate. Unexpected. Blasting a big red hole in the world.

It was a massive sound because he was bent down close to the baby and because he had no idea his hand was going to fire. The blast punched him in the side of the head and he cried out, reeling, dropped the weapon, grabbed his head. Screamed.

The green corn stalks were painted with bad colors. Red and black. The blood hadn't yet undergone the full biochemical change from normal to totally infected blood. Even so, he could see tiny threadlike worms wriggling in the droplets as they ran down the cornstalks.

-7-

Sam did not remember burying the child.

For the rest of that day and all through a bad night he wasn't sure he had. But when he went out in the morning the hole was filled in, with a hump of dirt patted neatly above it. And there was a second mound next to that one. Bigger. The boy. Sam understood that he must have dug that grave, too, but there was no shred of memory anywhere in his head.

He knew that he should be worried about that. Really worried.

He went and sat on the porch steps to try and sort out exactly how worried. There was a small cloud—just one—skating across the sky. He watched it, leaning back to track its slow progress. He squinted into the sun, closed his eyes for a moment, and woke to darkness.

Crickets sang in the corn and in the grass. Fireflies danced in the air, and overhead someone had shot holes in the nighttime sky, through which cold light shone. The moon was down and the day was gone.

Gone.

Gone where, though?

Sam sat there, shivering with cold that had nothing to do with the temperature. He got slowly and painfully to his feet. Everything ached. Every muscle and tendon; every inch of his skin. The bones of his ass hurt and he knew that he must have been there all day. How long? Ten hours? Twelve? More.

It terrified him.

Then he heard the sound.

Soft. Furtive. Sneaky. Not close, but out in the cornfield. Near where…

Suddenly he was off the porch and running across the lawn, past the trees and the driveway, past the burned wreck of the pickup truck and the splintered shell of the gas pump. He reached the front wall of corn and plunged into it. The stiff, sharp leaves slashed at him, cutting his face and hands, but Sam bashed at them, slapped them aside as he ran.

There were noises in the field now. Grunts. Whispers. No... not whispers. It was more basic than that. Moans.

Then he burst through one row and collided into someone.

Some-*thing*.

A man. A farmer in coveralls. The man fell backward and down, landing hard. Sam rebounded and caught his heel on something, and he went down, too, crashing down on his aching buttocks, jarring his tailbone. He cried out as pain punched from his coccyx all the way up his spine.

The farmer grunted, too. But not in pain. It was a strange noise. A duller, less emphatic sound. Air jolted from lungs but absent of pain.

"I'm sorry," said Sam.

And knew that it was not the thing to say. There was nothing he could say to make this moment work, to fix it. The man sat up and in the darkness his face was etched with blue starlight. His eyes were dull and seemed to look straight through Sam. His lips hung rubbery and slack. There was dirt on his hands from where he'd been digging.

Digging.

For food.

The farmer uttered that same moan. It was a terrible sound of bottomless hunger. Of a need that could never be satisfied. An ugly, awful sound.

"I'm sorry," said Sam again as he reached for his gun.

Which. Was. Not. There.

No gun. No knife.

The farmer lumbered to his feet and reached for him, moaning louder now. From deep inside the cornfield there were answering sounds. Other moans. Many, many more.

Sam Imura screamed.

Special operator. World-class sniper. DELTA gunslinger. Killer. He screamed because the world was not the world anymore. *This* was the world. It was all broken and in that moment, beneath the crowds of stars gathered to witness it, Sam realized that he, too, was broken.

So very badly broken. Splintered, fragmented. Torn loose from the things that fastened him to any understanding.

He screamed and the woods erupted with newer, louder moans. The green stalks shivered and shook as pale figures shambled toward him. Reaching and reaching. Farmers and cops, housewives and school kids. A man in a funeral suit. A naked woman with three bullet holes in her stomach. An old lady in a hospital gown. A nurse without eyes. A fireman with no hands. Coming for him.

Sam screamed and screamed, and then something in him broke. Snapped. Shattered.

He was running across the field with no awareness of leaving the cornfield. He was running and yelling. Figures came out of the shadows and he swung at them, chopped at them with the edges of his hands, kicked at them to break knees. They fell but did not die. The broken ones crawled after him. The others walked, lumbered, loped, staggered.

But he ran.

-8-

He blinked his eyes and he was in the plastic tree stand, up in the tree. His hands were cut and sore; he had scrapes on his shins. But the rifle was there. His gear bag with the four boxes of shells was there. His other handgun, a Glock 26, was there. Even his canvas bag of beer and food was there.

He was there.

The moon peered over the tops of the trees. More time was missing, but he thought he understood it now. He was going mad, or had *gone* mad, but some part of him was still on duty, still protecting him. That part of him did not allow Sam to see everything. Not the worst parts. It disallowed him to witness the process of his own collapse, and so it skipped forward, letting the body do what it needed to do and then allowing his consciousness to catch up.

Sure, he thought, *that sounds reasonable.*

And it *was* reasonable. Just not to the sane. Not to the unbroken.

Below the tree stand were *them*. At least forty. Maybe more. When the moon was all the way up he would be able to count better. He had four boxes of rifle ammunition, fifty cartridges to a box. And a hundred rounds of pistol bullets. Sam Imura, broken or not, didn't need more than one round per target. Not at this range. Not with these slow, shambling targets.

He thought about it. About what the best play was here. He could fight, and maybe clear these things out of his fields—and they were *his* fields now. Or he could use that handy little Glock and go find his brother and his parents and his friends. After all, if the world was this badly broken, why not simply opt out?

Why not?

This wasn't the war he trained for. This wasn't the world he fought for.

Right?

He removed the Glock from the bag, ejected the magazine, held it to the light to make sure it was fully loaded and slapped it back into place. Made sure there was one in the pipe, too. Ready to rock and roll.

The moonlight painted the tops of the corn a lovely silver. He couldn't see the graves he'd dug, but knew they were there. Two graves. One small, the other smaller. Digging those graves cost him more than he ever wanted to spend. It wasn't fair that he had to pay that price. It wasn't fair that those kids had to die like that.

He bent and picked up his radio and fiddled with the dial.

"This is Billy Trout reporting live from the apocalypse," said the voice. As if waiting for Sam to find him. Billy was still there. Sam listened to the reporter give updates on what was going on out there. About battles. About losses. About a convoy of school buses taking kids down south to North Carolina. To Asheville, where the military was making a big stand. Billy talked and talked, and there were tears in his hoarse voice.

Sam listened. The dead moaned.

"If you can hear my voice," said Billy, *"here's what you can do."*

He ran down the ways to kill these living dead. Billy called them zombies, but the word didn't work for Sam. Billy went on to list safe roads, and ones that were impassable. He listed shelters and rescue stations, and disputed the ones that were overrun. Billy talked and talked and talked as the moon rose.

Sam stood there with the Glock. Sometimes he pressed the barrel up under his chin. Sometimes he pointed it down at the white faces.

The two graves burned in his mind.

Billy was with the convoy of school buses. All those kids. *Living* kids.

That's how it started for Sam. He and his team helped Billy and his girlfriend, a local cop named Dez Fox, get as many kids out of Stebbins as possible. Some adults, too. Heading south. Heading to Asheville.

Those kids.

Still alive.

The moon was up now and he could count. Fifty-six of them. And probably more out there. Maybe as much as a hundred more who might be drawn by the sound of gunshots. Maybe two hundred more.

Sam smiled. Okay, say two hundred and fifty of them between him and the house. And ten thousand rounds of ammunition split between the house and the truck.

Those kids.

The living ones.

He could not bear the thought of rows of little mounds of carefully sculpted dirt. Could not bear it. That hurt worse than trying to hold onto his sanity. It hurt worse than trying to stay alive.

All those kids. With a single cop, a few adults, and a stupid news reporter to keep them safe.

"This is crazy," he told himself, saying it out loud, putting it on the wind.

The dead moaned. Dead people moaned.

So, yeah. Crazy.

But at least this was on the sanest side of crazy. Useful crazy. That's how Sam saw it.

He raised the pistol and took aim. It was a target-rich environment. Any shot would hit. Only careful, precise shots, though, would kill.

He was very careful.

He was very precise.

He never missed. Not once.

And if he was crazy, then so what? Surely the world—the broken, hungry world—was crazier. So that balanced it all out. At least he was crazy with a purpose, a goal. A mission. Soldiers need a mission. Even insane ones.

Maybe especially insane ones.

That's what Sam told himself. As he fired and fired and fired.

"I'm coming," he said to the night. To the wind. To all those children on the buses. "I'm coming."

-9-

Sam did not really remember leaving the farm.

He had no idea where he got the UPS truck, or how he filled it with supplies from his crippled truck. So many things were blurry or simply gone.

Sam smiled. "I'm coming."

The sign ahead said, *Welcome to West Virginia.*

The truck rolled on, heading south.

Author's Note: This story is a sequel to my novels *Dead of Night* and *Fall of Night*, as well as the short story "Lone Gunman," which appeared in the anthology, *Nights of the Living Dead*, which I co-edited with George A. Romero. That short story was written at George's request, to officially connect my novels to his landmark movie. He said that those books were, as far as he was concerned, the official explanation for why the dead rose in his movies. Our anthology was the very last project George completed before he died, and was released just a week before his passing. This story continues the tale, and is dedicated with love to my friend, George, the king and godfather of the zombie apocalypse.

WHERE WOULD YOU BE NOW

CARRIE VAUGHN

Carrie Vaughn's latest novels include the post-apocalyptic murder mystery, *Bannerless*, winner of the Philip K. Dick Award, and its sequel, *The Wild Dead*. She wrote the *New York Times* bestselling series of novels about a werewolf named Kitty, along with several other contemporary fantasy and young adult novels, and upwards of eighty short stories, two of which have been finalists for the Hugo Award. She's a contributor to the Wild Cards series of shared world superhero books edited by George R. R. Martin and a graduate of the Odyssey Fantasy Writing Workshop. An Air Force brat, she survived her nomadic childhood and managed to put down roots in Boulder, Colorado. Visit her at carrievaughn.com.

Kath sat on the roof of the beat-up Tesla S, legs draped down the back window, shotgun in both hands, looking out into the dark for whatever might hurt them. They'd come forty miles or so to an encampment in what had once been a park with a picnic area and duck pond. A playground with a plastic slide and jungle gym was still intact, though weeds came up through the bark mulch footing. A collection of trucks and campers clustered here, circled together with space for a campfire in the middle. The fire was banked now. Some tents and lean-tos had been set up a little further out, along with a couple of rickety sheds. In summer, people didn't need much more shelter than that. Winter, the camp would pick up and move south, if they could get the gas for it. Getting hard to find gas, though. The place was starting to look permanent. One of the trailers had a chicken coop built next to it, and a couple of roosting chickens were visible, feathers plumped out. The camp probably housed about thirty, but this late, everyone had gone to bed.

The packed-dirt mounds of four graves were lined up outside the circle of campers. The doctors didn't ask about them, the ones they couldn't help.

Turned away from the light, Kath kept watch. Nothing around the area moved. No one seemed inclined to charge in and grab such a valuable commodity as a doctor.

They'd parked the Tesla next to a medium-sized RV, from which came the groans of a woman in labor. Only this box of a room was lit up with candles and lanterns. The waiting and noise of effort made the air thick. The tenor of the groans had changed over the last twenty minutes, becoming more urgent, and also more exhausted. Kath could try to peek in the door, at the woman tucked up on her cot, straining. But she just listened.

"You've got this. One more push."

That was Melanie's voice. Did Dr. Dennis have her handling this delivery? She usually assisted him.

One more loud groan, then came silence. Kath held her breath until a tiny wail sounded, the new baby successfully announcing itself. A ruckus followed, the handful of people in the RV talking over each other, making admiring noises.

Unless something went wrong in the next little while, which could involve anything from the mother bleeding out to the baby showing some kind of illness or injury, Dennis and Melanie would wrap up and they could be on their way. Might be smarter to wait until dawn to make the trip back to the clinic. But the road between here and there was still passable, and Kath wanted to get home.

The light from the open door changed as figures stood in front of it. Dr. Dennis was standing with the thirty-something bearded man who'd summoned them here that morning. Dennis was giving him instructions.

"We've still got vaccines lying around. Bring her to the clinic in a couple months, we can give her a good start." The man, presumably the father, nodded with a distracted air. Leaning forward a bit, Kath could peer through the doorway and catch a glimpse of the camper's interior. The new mother was there, nested on a narrow couch, sweat matting her hair to her face, sheets tumbled around her. Melanie was helping her bundle the new baby against her skin, probably explaining everything she could about nursing in a handful of minutes. The mother didn't look up at what Dennis was saying.

They might or might not bring their baby to get her shots. They might decide they had bigger problems than worrying about measles or whooping cough.

Dr. Dennis came down the aluminum steps and paced a moment, hands on hips, looking into the night air. "Everything okay?"

"Yeah. No trouble," Kath said.

"Good. I want to get out of here as soon as we can."

So he was on edge, too. The unfamiliar settlement, the warm thick night, might draw out people they didn't want to talk to.

"You okay, Doctor?"

"Six months. I give that baby six months, based on the condition of the rest of the camp. It's so goddamn pointless."

Dennis and the other doctors at the clinic went over the statistics all the time. Without proper nutrition, clean water, medicine, without so many little necessities, infant mortality spiked. And there didn't seem to be anything they could do about it. If they were in the area, maybe one of the doctors could come out to vaccinate. Or maybe the parents really would bring the baby to the clinic.

The man returned to the door and handed over a threadbare pillowcase, half-filled. "Here. It's what we can spare. Thank you. Thank you for coming."

Grimly, Dr. Dennis took the makeshift sack by its bunched-up neck. "You're welcome. Just keep her as safe and healthy as you can, right?"

Dennis took a quick look in the sack, which Kath knew would be filled with canned goods, maybe some wire or screws, some glue. Odds and ends. Whatever salvage the parents thought worth the doctor's attention. Barter. Dennis used to get paid thousands of dollars for delivering a baby.

He looked up. "Kind of a weird question. Do you have any golf balls?"

The man pursed his lips and shook his head. "No, I don't think so."

"Well if you find any, maybe save them for me?"

"Yeah. Yeah, sure."

Two other women came to the doorway to look out. One of them was pregnant, maybe five months. She seemed worried, brow creased, lips tight, hands laced over belly. As if she could use her fingers to cage her unborn child to keep it safe. The other woman looked tired.

Dennis frowned at them. "You all aren't using any birth control at all around here, are you?"

Both women cringed, and the man crossed his arms. "Not like we can pop into Walgreens for condoms."

"It's just… never mind."

The man added, "I mean, so many people have died—don't we need to think about repopulating—"

"Oh Jesus fuck, *no*! Look, repopulating the planet or whatever can take care of itself. You—you just worry about keeping the people you already have safe and healthy. *Fed*. Grow some fucking potatoes!"

For just a moment the man's glowering gaze hardened. He was thinking of trouble, of taking the doctor down a notch for the outburst. Kath straightened, shifting the shotgun on her lap. To show she was watching.

He backed off. "We're trying, here. We're *trying*."

Dennis sighed and came around to the other side of the car to wait for Melanie.

She emerged a moment later, shrugging the strap of an equipment bag over her shoulder and pushing a strand of black hair out of her eyes. She looked the most tired of all, even more than the mother, who at least was smiling when Kath glimpsed her.

Kath hopped off the car and opened the back door. "You okay?" she asked.

"I think so," she said, sighing. "Doc made me handle the delivery on this one."

"How was it?"

Melanie shook her head, her eyes widening in a look of half-panicked disbelief. "It's a lot different when the baby is falling into your own hands. I just kept thinking, God, don't drop it." She closed her eyes and sucked in a breath. "I hope everything stays okay."

Kath touched her shoulder. "Let's get out of here."

Melanie practically fell into the back seat, and Dennis started the motor and pulled away. Kath rode in the front passenger seat. Literally shotgun. That had stopped being clever a while back. She kept the window rolled halfway down and listened for the sound of approaching engines.

"You did great," Dennis said, glancing at his assistant in the rearview mirror. "You should have asked them to name the baby after you."

"No, that's okay. What'd they give you?" She went through the bag, to the sound of cans knocking together. "Eh, not bad. A couple boxes of nails. We can always trade that back out. Canned peaches." She paused, looked quizzical, and drew out a glass jar. "Capers. There's a jar of capers in here. They're organic."

"Organic capers," Dennis snorted. "We're saved."

Dennis kept the headlights dimmed to save the battery. If there'd been enough moonlight, he'd have shut off the lights entirely. But the roads had gotten too hazardous, full of potholes and debris, to risk going entirely dark. Still, the doctor didn't see the three kids standing in their path.

"Stop!" Kath screamed when she realized those shapes weren't odd shadows but children, one older gripping the hands of two little ones, there in the middle of the road, unmoving. Like they intended to get run over.

The car lurched to a stop, skidded a few feet. The bag of loot fell clattering to the floor, and Melanie braced herself on the seat. Kath was already out the door, with Dennis calling after her.

The kids stared back at her quietly. Their eyes were sunken, their cheeks hollow. It could have just been odd shadows cast by the dim headlights, but Kath didn't think so. They were hungry, starving. She scanned around for an adult, maybe a caravan they might have wandered off from. But they seemed so purposeful, the way they looked back at her, their eyes round and shining. They didn't seem lost.

"Hey, what're you guys doing here? Are you okay?" She tucked the shotgun under her arm, muzzle down, and approached them.

The older child looked like a girl, stringy brown hair in a loose braid, her eyes big and unblinking. Kath thought she was around eight, then revised up—ten, and malnourished. The other two might have been anywhere from two to five. Upright, but still uncertain in their movements. They clung to the older girl, gripping each hand and hugging her legs. All three wore t-shirts and loose pants. Only the oldest had shoes, dirty sneakers, toes poking through holes.

Kath inched closer, trying to look friendly and harmless even with a gun under her arm, but she stopped short of reaching out. Both Dennis and Melanie had left the car as well.

"It's okay," Kath said softly. "We're not going to hurt you, I just want to find out what's wrong."

The oldest child licked her lips. "She told us to stand here. She told us to wait for the doctor to come and then go with him to the clinic. She said you'd take care of us."

"Who? Who said?"

Her lips pursed, the girl didn't answer. Kath thought she was about to cry, but she just kept staring, any kind of emotion, any response, locked up.

Kath tried again. "Where'd you come from? From the camp back there? From somewhere else?" It had to be the camp, to know that they'd be driving back this way.

"She just said to wait here. She said you'd take care of us."

How did they know that? How could they be sure? Could have been anyone that came along the road here, and the girl seemed to know it. She was trying to be firm, to be confident. But her lip trembled, and her grip on the little kids' hands was white-knuckled. She might have known just how dangerous this was, trusting in the good will of strangers.

Dennis had gotten out a flashlight and panned it around, scanning broken-down buildings and debris-strewn streets in all directions. No movement, nobody watching, nothing. Whoever had abandoned the kids here had fled.

"We need to get moving," Kath said. She was the guard on this run, but Dennis was in charge. It was his call.

"Jesus Christ. Okay, fine. Everybody in the car."

The littlest one started crying. At what in particular, Kath couldn't say. Maybe it was just general exhaustion. She could understand that.

"What's your name?" Kath asked.

"Chloë. These are Tom and Dakota." She sounded relieved. Her shoulders had lowered a notch.

"I'm Kath. Let's go."

The two little ones fell asleep as soon as the car doors closed, and Kath marveled. How trusting, to climb into a car with strangers and somehow feel safer. This was a different set of rules than what she grew up with. The girl, Chloë, sat in the middle of the back seat, arms draped over both little ones, staring straight ahead.

Dennis drove with both hands on the wheel, clenched. Melanie also fell asleep, not looking at all peaceful. She was going to have a good cry later, Kath was sure.

"Where would you be now?" Dennis asked after a long stretch of silence. His profile was shadow.

"Hm," Kath said. "College. Maybe I'd be at a party. Getting drunk? I dunno."

His smile brightened his voice. "Getting in trouble. Sounds good. I approve."

"Maybe I'd be studying for a test. Would it be exam time right about now?"

"Naw, you should go to the party. Have some fun."

"Where would you be?" she asked in turn.

"Palm Springs. The back nine at Indian Wells. With a Corona in the cup holder of my cart."

"Golfing in the middle of the night?"

"Well, no, not golfing right this minute. But I guess that's where I'd rather be. I suppose that's cliché, the doctor who'd rather be golfing."

"You think it's still there? The golf course?"

He shook his head, a scrap of movement in the otherwise still night. "Even if the grass hasn't all died it wouldn't be getting groomed."

They drove on a little while, tires crunching on pitted asphalt.

"I wish you'd had the chance to go to college," he said. "Even just a year or two. I'm sorry."

"It's okay," she said, because it was what she always said. The entire concept of college was becoming abstract.

Her older brother Eddie had gone to college. He'd gone back east, and that's where he'd been when it all fell apart. She wondered what happened to him. Would always wonder, and it was maddening, not having any way to find out. Maybe even now, five years after his last call, before the power went out, he was still trying to make his way across the country like he said he would. Maybe he'd made it as far as, say, Colorado. Gotten caught in the mountains in winter. Maybe he was just resting. Maybe he'd found a safe place to stay, like the clinic here. Maybe they needed him, so he stayed. How long did it take someone to walk three thousand miles, anyway? She didn't have any idea.

She left a note for him back at the house. Stuck it to the door, covered it with packing tape so it would survive wind and weather. Maybe he'd find it someday. Maybe he'd find her.

They rolled back to the clinic at dawn, when the sky was gray and chilled. Jim was keeping watch on the north side this shift, rifle tucked under his arm, perched on one of the derelict trucks that made up the barricade around the compound. Kath sat up on the edge of the open window and waved an arm high, giving him plenty of time to spot and ID her and the Tesla. She could see him shade his eyes to look out. He waved back and started to open the gate.

The car's charge was just about finished. Eighty miles round trip was at the far end of its range these days; its battery didn't hold as much as it used to. They might need to start rethinking trips like this. Or figure out how to bring solar panels along for a recharge.

A couple of others had come out to help Jim move aside the flatbed trailer stacked with twisted wreckage that served as the north gate. They could move it in and out easy enough, and then use chains and locks to anchor it to rebar loops sunk into concrete pits in the ground. As soon as the Tesla was inside, they shifted and locked the trailer back into place. Dennis rolled the car to a stop in its spot in the back of the clinic, where its charging station was, hooked up to a roof full of solar panels. That had been an epic bit of engineering, to get that all situated. The clinic was the only spot for twenty miles around that still had electricity.

Maggie must have been waiting for them; she came out the front door as soon as the car stopped. "How did it go? Everyone okay?"

"Bouncing baby girl," Dennis said, climbing from the car and stretching his back. "They gave us capers. We can resurrect fine dining."

The other doors opened; Melanie herded out the children. Chloë was carrying the youngest propped on her hip, asleep.

Maggie was a middle-aged woman, tanned, brown hair growing gray, tied up in a bun. She wore a wrinkled blouse, jeans, and workboots. Kath looked at Maggie and saw her own mother, who'd been dead for five years now. Maggie and her mom had been friends; hard not to see her as some kind of stand-in. Kath hadn't wanted to leave home. She'd been waiting, as if her parents might come back. As if Eddie might find her there, and if she left, maybe he never would. Likely, she'd be dead now if Maggie hadn't made her come to the clinic.

Maggie stopped and gaped, looking among the adults for explanation. "What's this? Who're they?"

"Found 'em on the road," Dennis said, casually, like this sort of thing happened all the time.

The older doctor's mouth opened, horrified. "We can't… we don't… we don't have enough food! We can't take care of any more people!"

"Were we supposed to just leave them there?" Kath asked.

Maggie put her hand to her forehead. Her mouth had sunk into a deep frown. "No, of course not. It's just… God." She turned and walked off, scratching her hair.

"Come on," Kath said to Chloë. "We'll get you set up inside."

Kath had them wash faces and hands while she heated up a can of beans to feed them, and made them each drink a glass of water and take a few chewable vitamins. They still had a couple bottles left, and this seemed like a good use for them. After that, the kids curled up on a cot in one of the exam rooms, all three of them together, snuggled under the blanket Kath had tucked them in with despite the heat. Maggie watched from the doorway, arms crossed, clearly unhappy. But she hadn't really been happy ever, the last couple years.

"We couldn't just leave them," Kath insisted.

"And we can't keep taking in strays. We had to throw out those potato plants on the east side of the building. Rot got them."

They weren't strays, Kath thought. They'd been dropped off. People were going to start leaving babies on their doorstep. And the clinic didn't have enough food. "We'll try again," Kath said, because what else could she say? "We'll figure it out."

"Yeah, I know, I know. You should get some rest, okay?" Maggie ran a hand over Kath's hair, something she'd been doing since Kath was five.

Kath smiled grimly, double checked that the shotgun and its spare shells were locked up, and went out to the row of tents lined up along the clinic building. She hadn't really thought about being tired until Maggie mentioned rest.

Kids and doctors slept in the clinic building. Everyone else used the row of tents, some old-fashioned canvas jobs, a few nylon domes, everything in between. Kath used one of the canvas ones, with the flaps tied up during the day to let in air, mosquito netting in place to try to keep out bugs.

Melanie was already inside, stripped to tank top and panties, sprawled face down on the sheet-covered mattress. If Kath was tired, Melanie was probably flattened after the night she had. But Kath paused a moment anyway, to see if she was really asleep. Admired the curve of her shoulder, the slope of her back where it arced to her hip. Melanie had the most amazing, artful shape to her.

Quietly, moving slowly, Kath pulled off her own dusty, rank clothes, then sat with her journal, squinting in the dark to write a handful of words about the image of those kids in the road, the nerve-wracking groans of the woman, the sticky-hot night air. These days, she mostly kept the diary out of habit, and her handwriting had turned tiny, scrunched—trying to conserve space, since she didn't know when she'd ever find another blank book. She figured she'd keep writing until she ran out of space.

Kath tried to be quiet, but Melanie woke up anyway. "Hmm?"

"Sorry, didn't mean to wake you," she said.

"Hm, s'okay, c'mere."

Kath set aside the book, collapsed onto the mattress, and Melanie gathered her into her arms. They clung to each other, body to body, and Kath's near-constant, watchful tension from the night melted a couple of degrees. The scent of Melanie, the soap-and-sweat of her, the warmth of her skin, made Kath feel a little drunk. Melanie shifted, brought her mouth to Kath's, and they kissed, a little desperately. Melanie sighed, like her own tension was finally fading.

"You okay?" Kath asked.

She squeezed her eyes shut. "We're going to be back there in two years helping that same woman deliver another baby, there'll be twenty babies running around that camp and they'll all be starving—"

Kath hugged her. Melanie shuddered a moment. Trying not to cry, unable not to cry. Kath didn't know what to tell her.

"That's optimistic," she said finally.

"What?"

"That any of us are still going to be around in two years."

Melanie pulled away and stared at her a moment, then busted out laughing. They fell together in another tight hug, conveying powerful comfort. Anchoring each other.

"Where would you be now?" Kath whispered.

"Med school. I wanted to go to med school." She laughed, but the laughter turned to crying, like it often did. She didn't try to hide it this time, and Kath held her till she fell back asleep.

Just a year or so into their time camping out at the clinic, a fire flattened the strip mall on the other side of the street. Could have been anything that started it, from a leaking gas line and static build up to lightning. Some traveler tossing a lit cigarette. With no one to fight the fire, it burned walls to the ground, collapsed roofs, and kept going. The few shade trees spaced out on the sidewalk went up like torches, and folk at the clinic stayed up all night stomping on ashes and dumping water on hot spots to keep the fire from jumping the road and claiming their home. The barricade of derelict cars, trucks, and trailers had already been put in place by then, but after the fire died down they hauled, towed, and wrangled the barricade another fifty feet out, and added on to it, to increase their buffer zone. To increase the perception of safety. They also spent six months demolishing buildings up and down their own street. Took a long time, clearing all that space with sledgehammers and controlled burns, but it gave them great line of sight after. And more space for gardening. After security, gardening was their biggest preoccupation.

It had only taken a few years for the entire character of that street, the neighborhood surrounding the clinic, to change. When they sat around at night, drinking whatever bottle of booze turned up, and asked how this could happen, they only had to look around.

The next day, after stopping by the kitchen tent for a cup of water and an apple, Kath went on her daily walk around the barricade. She usually did this in the morning, but after the long night she slept past noon. Melanie had already gotten up and was probably at the clinic helping with the work of the day. Kath would check in in a little while, see how the new arrivals were getting on.

The air was sticky, humid, and the sun was roasting. Calendar said it was April, but this felt like July. She was dripping sweat in moments. She wiped her face and pulled the brim of her baseball cap down to better block the glare.

The clinic housed thirty-two people these days. Thirty-five, she revised. Most of the clinic residents were up and about, working in garden patches, tinkering with the couple of cars they still had, cleaning and maintaining the camp. A half-dozen stood at the barricade with weapons, watching. Kath waved when people waved at her, said hello. The day felt ordinary.

On the west side of the compound, Dr. Dennis stood outside the barricade and hit golf balls with a driver. Flung them up the road, one after the other. When it was safe enough he'd go collect them, and for some of the kids it was a game, to see how many golf balls they could recover for him. A few always stayed lost, but Dennis kept hitting them anyway. Swing, a whoosh of air, *thwack*. He'd shade his eyes to follow the arc of the ball until it hit the ground a hundred yards or so on. Kath didn't know enough about golf to tell if he was any good. Didn't seem to bother him, that he might never play a real round of golf ever again. He just seemed to enjoy hitting balls to nowhere.

Kath sat on the edge of the barricade and watched for a little while.

"Morning," Dennis said finally.

"What happens when you run out?"

He shrugged. "Maybe I'll start hitting rocks. But, maybe I won't run out. Maybe I'll get back to Palm Springs, when everything gets back to normal."

This is normal, she thought. She was thinking that more and more, but never said it out loud.

"You want to try it?" Dennis asked.

"No thanks. I'm just taking a walk."

"Enjoy."

"You too."

He took another ball from the nylon bag at his feet, set it on a bare patch of ground, and lined up for the next swing.

Kath finished her circle around the compound and headed to the squat, concrete building in the middle.

The front room was crowded. The compound's handful of resident kids swarmed. They were supposed to be settling down for the impromptu class one of the nurses taught every other day or so, but something had set them off. A giant spider, Kath gathered from the shouting. The room was loud. Anita , one of the clinic nurses, was trying to settle them down, yelling in both English and Spanish, but nothing worked.

Kath's three refugees cringed away from it all, huddled at the side of the room, watching cautiously. She grabbed a couple of picture books from the basket under one of the chairs and called to Chloë. "Let's go get some air, okay?"

The girl considered a moment, lips pressed in a suspicious frown. She was looking marginally better today, Kath thought. Some color in her cheeks. But then, she couldn't look much worse than she had last night, standing in the dark, bleakly washed out by headlights. The two little ones were hunched up next to her, staring at the proceedings with round, glazed eyes. Maybe trying to decide if this was dangerous. Chloë picked up their hands and tugged them toward the door.

Kath found a shady spot around the side of the building where the clinic's pots of lettuce plants lived. Wasn't exactly a garden, but it was kind of a nice place to spend a few quiet moments.

"Want to do the honors?" Kath asked, opening to the first page of one of the books. The little ones scooted closer, drawn by the colors and pictures of round friendly animals, putting their hands on the paper.

Chloë winced, drawing her limbs in to hug herself. "I can't. I know I should... but..."

Kath thought that might be the case. "No worries. We'll work on it now." She read to them, following with her fingers, showing Chloë the words. She wasn't going to teach the girl to read in one sitting. But they had to start somewhere. The little ones were rapt.

They went through the books she'd brought, went through them all again at the little ones' insistence, and Kath asked them which were their favorites and why. They finally seemed normal. Acted normal, engaged and talking. Then they lost interest in the books and ran off to chase a grasshopper. Kath let them; they couldn't get into too much trouble around here.

Chloë was still suspicious.

"They your siblings? Brother and sister?"

"Yeah."

"Where are your parents?"

She shrugged, shuffling through the books, brushing fingers on the covers. "What's the point? I mean, does anybody still read?"

"We still have books. We have a whole library inside. It's still a good way to learn things."

"I guess."

Kath wanted to draw her out. "Do you remember anything from before?" She was old enough; she might, unlike her siblings. Or depending on how bad things had been for her, she might have blocked it all out. "I remember a lot. I definitely don't want to forget how to read."

Chloë stared out at the barricade of junked cars. Kath didn't think she was going to talk, and was going to let it go. Suggest they go in and find some lunch. But then the girl said, "I remember Disneyland. We went when I was really small. Got my picture with Ariel. She's my favorite. Wish I still had the picture but it got lost somewhere. I guess it's still there? Disneyland? What's going to happen to it?"

Honestly, Kath couldn't remember the last time she'd even thought of Disneyland. But the question suddenly filled her. What had happened to Disneyland? Another stab of grief followed. Another thing to mourn, or lock away and forget.

She said, "It must still be there. Some of it, at least. But the lights have probably gone out."

"I wish I was there. Even with the lights out."

"Yeah."

Kath looked up; Maggie stood at the corner of the building, arms crossed. Her face was screwed up in the way it usually got when she was thinking of crying. Holding it in so hard she seemed to be in pain. Then, the look was gone.

Maggie said, "Hey there! Anita's got soup cooking. Chloë, why don't you take the others around and get yourselves fed."

The girl nodded, clambering to her feet and going to fetch the others, who'd been playing some kind of tag. She didn't call out to them, and Kath wondered about that. That she didn't feel safe, raising her voice.

Kath stood and watched them go, and Maggie watched Kath.

"You're good with the kids. They're comfortable with you."

"Yeah, I like them too." She didn't worry so much with the kids. She didn't think about the future so much. Kids were easy: keep them fed, keep them clean, do everything to keep them safe. Simple. If she could teach them to read, then she'd really have accomplished something.

Maggie seemed to draw even tighter to herself. Her shoulders were rigid, her hands in fists.

Kath's brow furrowed. "What's the matter?"

"It's just… you looked like… you don't want to have your own kids, do you?"

She hadn't thought about it at all. Food and security, that was what she thought about these days. The question startled her, and she had to think a moment, but that moment was too long for Maggie.

"Oh God, you're already pregnant, aren't you? That's why you like the kids, you're practicing—"

"What? No! What gave you that idea?"

This didn't seem to help. "But you're having sex. Tell me, are you having sex?"

Kath glared. "I'm twenty years old, of course I'm having sex!"

"And you're pregnant."

"No, God no!"

"But have you been using protection? How do you know?" Maggie seemed desperate.

Kath paused, then shot back, "Because I'm sleeping with Melanie!"

Maggie drew back, and Kath wondered what she was going to rant about next. It wasn't that she and Melanie had been hiding anything. It just made sense to double up on tents to save space, and they hadn't actually announced anything when they became more than friends. It wasn't being gay that Kath thought would upset people. It was being... adult. She wasn't growing up. She was *grown*.

Now, Maggie did cry. Or laugh. Something that came from tension releasing, and causing whatever was holding her together to collapse. She slumped against the wall, both hands covering her face. "I'm sorry, Kathy. I'm sorry. It's just... we can't feed everyone, and people keep having babies and we can't do anything, we can't feed them—"

Kath put her arms around the woman and just held her.

"God, look at me," Maggie said around sobs. "I'm supposed to be taking care of you and just look at me."

"You don't have to take care of me," Kath said. "You have enough to worry about, just let me... be me."

They stayed like that awhile, hidden in the shelter of the building where Maggie could lose it in private, and Kath stayed to make sure she was okay. The older woman had been right at the edge for such a long time.

Maggie finally pulled away, scrubbing tears off her face and chuckling at herself, a strained and painful sound.

"So, you and Melanie, huh? I think I knew that. Yeah. Oh God, I'm so messed up I can't see what's right in front of my face. I promised your mom I'd look out for you and if you turned up pregnant in this mess—" She took a shuddering breath, rubbed her face one more time. And like that she had put on a new mask, and was smiling. "I'm sorry. I forget sometimes, that you're grown up."

Kath offered words, a gesture of comfort, though it might hurt as much as it helped. Kath wanted to say it. "I never got to come out to Mom," she said softly. "I mean, I sort of knew, I was starting to figure it out. Figuring out that I didn't just put those pictures on my wall because I liked beach volleyball so much, you know? But I never told Mom."

"Oh, hon. You know she'd be okay with it, right?"

"Yeah, I know. But I wish…" She shook her head. They all wished.

"You should be in college," Maggie murmured, running a hand over Kath's hair.

All the adults said that to her in their most maudlin moments. She should be in college. Not staying up half the night with a gun under her arm. Kath herself had stopped believing anything would ever change. This was just what life was now. There'd never be somewhere else.

"Where would you be now?" she asked Maggie.

She looked around at the wide-open compound that used to be part of a pleasant street, the modest building now crammed with solar panels it didn't used to have. "I'd be here, I think. But it'd be a lot different. Can you do a watch shift tonight? Mike's come down with something."

"Bad?"

"No, just a cold."

"Yeah, no problem."

"Thanks. Just… thank you."

Kath's watch shift started late afternoon and went into the evening. She covered about half the perimeter, walking on top of the barricade, stepping from car roof to truck hood to trailer and on. They'd bolted on sheets of metal and spikes, fencing, and other odds and ends to the basic framework over the years. Occasionally she'd come upon a loose bit, a piece of sheeting that moved under her feet, a car roof that was rusting out, and the next day someone would come to repair it. Used to be, they'd have four or five people covering the barricade, especially during the night watch. But since the fire and clearing the line of sight, they needed fewer people watching and could save the effort for other chores. The long approach gave the watchers plenty of time to spot trouble and raise an alarm.

This evening, trouble came right around dusk. The worst time, with the light fading. Her first hint came as movement on the horizon. Could have been anything, so she waited for the movement to resolve into shapes, or fade into nothing. Shadows appearing in wavering heat lines in the distance could be deceptive. She brought binoculars to her eyes, spent a moment focusing with one hand, the other clenched on the shotgun.

The shadows gained definition. Not a mirage, not deer or something else wandering in the distance. Now that she saw them, she heard the noise, a rumbling sound that was becoming rare. Gas-powered engines, beating against the air. Three cars, a couple of motorcycles, more than a dozen people, and those were just the ones she could see from this distance. Who knew how many were hiding inside the vehicles?

The convoy was racing straight for them.

She let the binoculars hang off their strap and cupped a hand to her mouth. "Incoming! Incoming!"

Someone at the clinic heard her and clanged the brass bell hanging off the front overhang.

They didn't need it very often, but they had a routine for this, when strangers came barreling at the clinic compound in a way that didn't suggest friendship. Those standing watch at the barricade stayed put, in case the invaders came on multiple fronts. A dozen others, whoever was on hand, grabbed weapons from the locker and came out to where the alarm had sounded.

Kath waited for her backup, shotgun in both hands, watching her targets come into range. The cars bounced and jutted over broken asphalt, while the motorcycles curved and weaved.

"Where the hell are they getting gas from?" Dennis asked. He'd climbed up on the barricade next to Kath.

Maggie was right behind him. "Don't know, don't care. What do they want?"

Kath said, "Better get down, in case they come in firing."

The barricade had places to shelter: inside cabs, on shielded truck beds. All the invaders would see was their shotguns and rifles bristling out.

The caravan stopped at the edge of firing range. If one of the rifles fired at them now, it might or might not hit. A big man, white, wearing a leather jacket and cowboy hat, scrambled out of the driver's side of one of the cars and marched forward a few paces. He didn't seem to be armed.

Kath stood tall and shouted at him across the barrel of her shotgun. "Stop! Stop and show your hands!"

The man's thick beard worked, as if he was biting his lip under it. He raised his hands. "Is this the clinic?" he shouted. "The one people talk about, that has doctors and medicine? Is that you?"

"What do you want!"

He gestured back. "We have wounded! We need help! We can trade for it! We have gas, guns, bullets—"

"Food?"

He paused a moment. "Yes!"

Kath looked at Maggie and Dennis.

"What kind of wounded?" Dennis shouted back. He stayed behind his shelter.

"Gunshot! Two men. God, please, help them!"

It could be a trick. Or the man could be honest. In the end, half the people here were doctors and nurses, and they recognized that kind of desperate plea.

The clinic had a process for this kind of situation, too.

Maggie and Dennis both emerged on top of the barricade, and Maggie called out. "Okay, here's how it's going to work. You bring the injured men inside, the vehicles stay out. Just the injured and two people each to carry them, no one else gets in, and you leave all your weapons outside. Got it?"

"Yes, okay, fine!"

And they checked, too. While the caravan pulled their injured out of the backs of the vehicles, Maggie and the clinic folk hauled open the gate, but only a couple of feet, just wide enough for two people to walk through. Two of the clinic's biggest guys, Jim and Jorge, patted down everybody at the opening, even the injured. But they didn't have anything, which gave these people an incremental point of trust.

The injured men were being carried chair style, one by two

men, one by the man who'd greeted them and a woman. One of the injured seemed to be unconscious, but the other was making the guttural, deep-belly groans of someone moaning through clenched teeth. Every shadow on them looked like stains of blood.

"Okay, get 'em inside!" Maggie, Dennis, and a trail of clinic folk escorted them to the door of the clinic.

Jim stayed at the barrier. "Kath, go with them, stand watch inside, we'll keep an eye out here."

An odd quiet had fallen—the vehicles in the convoy had shut off their engines, turned off their headlights; those left behind waited quietly. Evening light had all but gone, so figures moved as shapes in the dark. Shotgun in hand, extra shells jangling in the pocket of her windbreaker, she trotted after the others.

Unlike the quiet at the barricade, inside the clinic was loud and brightly lit. Someone was herding the kids outside, to sleep in tents. Kath spotted Chloë and spared her a smile. She and her siblings looked like they might bolt at the sign of the injured men. Kath hurriedly told her, "It'll be fine," and hoped that was enough. Chloë nodded, and might even have been convinced.

Past the waiting room, the first exam room was noisy with shouted orders. Dennis and Melanie had taken the first of the injured men here, the one grunting with fierce pain. Maggie and Anita took the unconscious man to the second exam room. Both doors stayed open and Kath was able to keep an eye on them all. Dennis was shouting orders. Melanie was talking to the first patient in Spanish, telling him to lie back, to breathe, *respire, respire, bien, bien*. The man started crying, *ayudame, ayudame!* Help me, help me.

In the second room, Maggie and the gang's spokesman were talking.

"We can barter," he was explaining. "We have a whole warehouse, whatever you need. We have food. Just save them. Can you save them?"

The man laid out on the table had a great stain of blood covering his chest. It seemed centered on his right shoulder. A gunshot wound, not necessarily fatal. Likely he was in shock and needed support, fluid and oxygen, while the doctors cleaned the wound. But they'd need to get started on him right away. Anita and one of the nurses had cut away his shirt, inserted an IV and were peeling away cloth that had been stuffed into the wound.

After a deep breath, Maggie seemed to come to a decision. She explained, "We don't need food as much as we need protection." She looked him straight in the eye, unwavering. "We help you, you help keep us safe. You get the word out to your people, to anyone else—this is neutral ground. We stay safe, no matter what. No one attacks us, no one hurts us, no one hurts anyone while they're here. Got it?"

"We protect you. And you help us and no one else. Just us."

"No. We help everyone or it doesn't work. We're not a commodity. We're here for everyone."

"Can't promise that."

Maggie bit her lip in a moment of thought. Then she put up her hands and stepped back from the table. After glancing at her and each other in a moment of hesitation, Anita and the other nurse stepped from the table, hands up like hers, blood on latex gloves.

The guy and the woman with him started forward, fists raised as if they could beat her into saving the man's life. Kath stepped in front of him, shotgun raised, warding them off. The standoff persisted for a handful of heartbeats.

The lead thug grinned. "You ever even shot anyone, kid?"

"Yes, I have." No hesitation, no hint of bluffing. She didn't need to bluff. Her tone convinced him; his smile fell, and he backed off.

Everyone watched him now, the one who would decide. His gang would listen to him. But Maggie and the other doctors were the ones who could fix things.

"Okay. Fine. This whole place is off limits. I'll spread the word."

"And you'll make sure we stay safe."

"As much as anyone can stay safe."

Maggie and the others closed back to the table in a flurry of action. Low-voiced commands and bits of information passed back and forth. In moments an impromptu surgery was underway.

Maggie said, "You all should probably wait outside."

A spike of tension followed, both strangers poised to lunge forward again. As if the doctors would really do something nefarious if they weren't supervised. Kath reasserted herself and the shotgun.

The clinic director made a calming gesture. "My people need

room and quiet to work, it's better if you wait." She added, "One of you can stay to watch. Her—"

She nodded to the woman with the leather jacket and wary gaze looking past too much eye makeup. And where had she found a stash of useable eyeliner? "Why her?" the man asked.

"Because she's quiet."

"Cynthia?"

She nodded. "Yeah, okay."

"There are chairs in the waiting room," Kath said, trying to sound neutral, if not friendly. Nodding, he went out.

Dennis had managed to kick out both of the gang members in his room. His patient was sedated now, finally quiet. The medical team was busy with gauze, alcohol, forceps, removing bullets from legs. Melanie glanced up once and gave Kath a thin smile. Kath smiled back, unsure who was comforting whom.

She stayed in the corridor, keeping watch over both rooms and the waiting room. There, the gang members had settled down. Too tired to argue anymore, maybe. One of them had even fallen asleep.

The clinic treatment rooms were made for routine outpatient care, not trauma. But Maggie, Dennis, and the others made do. By morning the two injured men were bandaged, sedated, and recovering quietly. Splashes of blood and red-stained gauze littered the floors, and a whole tray of scalpels and forceps and other instruments lay piled on a tray by the autoclave in the back supply room. The medicals were trying to clean up, wiping down surfaces, peeling off latex gloves. Wiping faces on sleeves and looking out, shell-shocked.

Maggie made a trip to the back supply room. When the woman, Cynthia, followed, Kath quietly moved in behind her. Just to keep an eye on her.

Cynthia glared a moment. "Can you close the door? Just for a minute."

Kath looked at Maggie. Confused, Maggie nodded. Kath shut the door and waited, hands ready on her weapon.

Then Cynthia said, whispering, "Can you help me not get pregnant?"

Maggie froze a moment, processing. The woman pursed her lips and seemed to be holding her breath. When Maggie didn't answer right away, Cynthia tried again. "I mean if I wanted an IUD or something, could you do that?"

"Yes, we can do that. We'll have to do a pregnancy test first—are you pregnant?"

Cynthia's eyes widened. She looked terrified. "Oh God I hope not, I don't want to be, that's why I was asking—"

"But you might be," Maggie asked, and Cynthia ducked her face to hide spilling tears. Maggie touched her shoulder. "Come on, let's check. Not a big deal. Kath, come in back and help me clear off that table."

They went to the back exam room where they'd been stockpiling canned food. Kath had to shift boxes so Cynthia had somewhere to sit, while Maggie dug around one of the cupboards. Cynthia talked. Rambled.

"Adam, the big guy who does all the talking… he's taking care of me. He's promised to take care of me."

"You could take care of yourself," Maggie muttered.

"Don't judge me," Cynthia said through gritted teeth. "Fucking that man is keeping me alive right now. I can't not do it, I can't force him to wear condoms, and I do not want to have a baby."

Maggie looked away.

Cynthia continued. "My… my sister got pregnant. I'd managed to keep her with me all this time, I'd promised to take care of her. But seven months in she got sick. Massive headache, vomiting, cramping. Then seizures."

"Sounds like eclampsia," Maggie said. "It's a thing that happens sometimes. We might have been able to help her, but maybe not."

"I couldn't save her. The baby killed her, and it isn't supposed to be like that, I don't want to go through that. There'd be no one to help me."

The whole thing took maybe half an hour. Maggie had Cynthia go back to the bathroom to pee in a cup. The test came back negative, and Cynthia started crying again. Maggie coaxed her to undress and pulled out the stirrups on the table. "Kath, why don't you see how they're doing up front?"

Kath ducked out.

Both injured men were stable. Dennis was in the waiting room, talking to the gang's leader, Adam.

"They shouldn't be moved for at least a couple of days. Especially not if you're going to shove them in a car and bounce them around—"

"Hey!"

Dennis put up a calming hand and tried again. "You can leave them here, no problem. And yes, any food you want to give us will be appreciated."

"And protection," he said, his curled lip almost making it a sneer.

"We're the only medical help for a hundred miles around. Maybe more. Your people would be dead now. You tell me whether or not we deserve protecting."

Adam didn't have anything to say to that.

Cynthia and Maggie emerged a little while later. Cynthia looked tired, shadows under her eyes, a slump in her shoulders. But she also seemed determined. An edge of that ever-present anxiety was gone. Kath was close enough to hear Maggie say to her, almost under her breath, "We've got a cupboard full of IUDs. I think we even have a few diaphragms stashed away somewhere. Tell your friends. We'll help anyone with birth control, no barter needed. Spread the word."

Cynthia nodded. "Yeah. Okay."

In what Kath thought was a gesture of supreme goodwill, Maggie invited Adam and his gang to stay for the day, to get some sleep, and to share breakfast. Kath realized later the underlying motive: make the clinic compound feel like home. Make it feel safe, and give them a stake in keeping it that way. They declined, however. Adam muttered something about not wanting to feel even more indebted. Cynthia took hold of his arm, whispered something, and the man settled.

They agreed to leave their injured and return for them in two days. That gave the clinic a couple more days to get them as strong as possible, and make sure infection didn't set in. They had a pretty good track record with this sort of thing so far, but it would only take one death from sepsis to undo everything.

The stakes seemed so high, for everything they did.

"We're running out," Dennis said, as they stood on the barricade, watching the caravan drive away, tires kicking up chips of broken asphalt.

"Of what?" Maggie said tiredly.

"Everything, really. But specifically—I think we should try to start growing some penicillin."

She stared. "Can we do that?"

"I think we can. I think we have to."

Maggie bowed her head. "What you're saying is you don't think this is ever going to end. It's never going to go back to the way it was."

"No," he said, folding her into his arms when she started to cry.

Technically, Kath's watch shift ended hours ago. A second night on her feet, she ought to be exhausted. But her nerves were wired, her skin itched. She set off for a circuit around the barricade. Still had the shotgun slung over her shoulder, shells hanging in her pocket.

She hadn't gotten a quarter of the way around when she spotted Melanie standing at the barricade, looking out at the sun-baked plain.

"You okay?" Kath asked cautiously.

"Would it sound weird if I said that was kind of fun? Good trauma practice, you know? Nice, thinking I actually helped save someone."

Kath stepped forward, well into her space, and kissed her. Jangling nerves stilled. Melanie pulled back, surprised, glancing around to see if anyone was watching.

"We're not being discreet anymore?"

Kath shook her head. "I told Maggie. She was freaked out that I was going to get knocked up."

She laughed, hugging Kath close. "That woman needs to chill the hell out."

"Yeah. But I don't know. She's the one holding all this together."

They walked on for a while, arms around each other. The sun felt warm this morning instead of scorching. Kath finally felt ready to lie down for a nap.

Looking ahead, along the junkyard edge of the barricade, Melanie asked, "Where would you be now? If none of this had happened?"

She wouldn't be in Melanie's arms, for one. That was a weird thought, that if none of this had happened she wouldn't have Melanie. And that would be a shame. She rested her head on her shoulder and sighed.

"It doesn't matter. This is where I am."

THE ELEPHANTS' CREMATORIUM

TIMOTHY MUDIE

Timothy Mudie is a writer and editor whose fiction has been published or is forthcoming in *Lightspeed*, *Escape Pod*, *Kaleidotrope*, and numerous other magazines, anthologies and podcasts. He lives outside of Boston with his wife and son.

Liyana had seen elephants form into protective circles when calves were threatened, but this was different. These days, animal behavior was all but impossible to predict, of course—prey turning to predator; trees turning to stone in moonlight—but this didn't feel random. There was intent in the way the elephants moved. The seven of them—she counted three juvenile males, two juvenile females, and two adult females—plodded into a loose formation a dozen or so meters from where Liyana crouched in a blind nestled deep in a thick copse of thorny bushes. Moving in unison, the elephants faced inward, heads turning slightly, inspecting one another as if making sure they were all ready.

Lower back beginning to ache fiercely, sharp twinges shooting up her spine, Liyana wanted more than ever to shift position, to stand up and stretch. To pee, even though it seemed like she'd just done so moments ago. To wipe the sweat pooling in her lower back and between her breasts. Without speaking, she mouthed an apology to the baby inside her. Just a few more minutes.

The largest adult called, a low rumble that Liyana felt more than heard, her heart vibrating, pressure rising through the soles of her feet despite her thick boots. The rest joined in, a basso profundo chorus.

For almost a full minute, the elephants sang a low note that Liyana couldn't help but think of as mournful, though she was always reluctant to anthropomorphize the animals she'd studied and protected. Abruptly the sound cut out, leaving behind an even deeper silence. One by one, like a string of firecrackers, the elephants burst into flames.

Liyana gingerly lowered herself into the sagging remains of what had once been an overstuffed armchair in what had once been the lounge of what had once been the Amboseli Adventure Safari Lodge, where tourists had once paid extravagantly to live in comfort while pretending they were bush explorers, seeking lions and leopards and elephants. Sometimes, even though it had been years—seven as best Liyana's people could tell—it still amazed her to think about how people used to live. At one time, someone had probably complained that the lounge was too cool from the air conditioning. Even with the windows long broken and a breeze riffling through the room, Liyana sweated through her clothes.

"I found out what's happening to the elephants," she said to James. She grimaced. "Sort of."

"How are you feeling?" James asked. "You look pale."

She tried to smile at him. Just like James to worry about her more than the elephants. Though she knew he'd never really love her, that he couldn't, he did care. That was enough. "You're not going to believe this—well, maybe you will, things are crazy—but the elephants seem to be spontaneously combusting."

He ignored her. "I'm serious, Liyana. Are you okay?"

"Did you hear me? They're practically exploding. Fire everywhere. I saw it myself." When he leaned forward, an expression of concern on his face, she waved him off. "I'm fine. My back hurts from crouching in the blind so long. It's nothing."

He leaned back, but his brow remained furrowed. "Okay then. The elephants are spontaneously combusting. Is it just happening? Or are they inducing it somehow?"

"Why would they do it on purpose? And how?"

James shrugged. "Why does anything happen anymore? A week ago, I saw a pack of hyenas surround a zebra. The hyenas melted into some sort of amoeba and absorbed the zebra. When it was gone, they reformed and took off running like it was the most natural thing in the world."

"I guess it is, now."

"My point is that the world is dangerous and unpredictable. You shouldn't be trying to have a child at all, and you certainly shouldn't be going out alone right now. Who knows how an animal would react if it could somehow tell you're pregnant."

"You're sweet that you try to protect me," Liyana said. "But I hate it." She stood up. "Anyway, I'm going to lie down, but first I need to talk to—" Her voice snapped off into a sharp intake of breath as pain stabbed her stomach and she doubled over. In an instant, James was on his feet, his hands on her elbows. She couldn't stay on her feet, so she let him guide her to the floor, first on her knees, but even that was too much, and she curled onto her side.

"Stay here, stay here," he said, looking around frantically, though there was no one in the lounge. "I'm getting Charlotte." For a moment, Liyana thought he would kiss her as he leaned forward, but he turned away and sprinted for the door, shouting already for the doctor, for help from anyone.

As Liyana lay on the floor, hands clutching her stomach, teeth gritted and eyes watering, she thought the same words over and over. Please. Please, not a miscarriage. Not again.

Before the world ended, she'd never actually been in a hospital for anything other than to visit a sick family member, hadn't needed to. She had her tonsils, her appendix. Had never broken a bone or had a terrible fever. Now, as she lay sweating in bed in what had been a tastefully appointed hut for the tourists, Liyana was grateful for that. She had no idea what she was missing.

"You need to take better care of yourself," Charlotte said, sitting next to her, stethoscope on Liyana's belly, that barely-visible bump that said she was with child. She nodded, removed the cold scope.

"Baby's fine, though. Not to jinx anything, but…"

"Seventeen weeks. I'm farther along than I've ever been," Liyana said.

"Well, now you've gone and done it," Charlotte said, but she smiled. "Farther along than anyone since… you know."

Liyana nodded. There was no name for it, not really, the thing that had ended the world. A war, some new weapon, bombs that ripped a hole right in reality. Some author had once said that any far-enough advanced technology would be indistinguishable from magic. Well, they'd gotten there. The little they'd seen before the internet and TV and radio all stopped working showed cities and people imploding, disintegrating, blinking away into air. Reporters just as mystified as everyone watching. Everything broke, the world became surreal. Nothing to do, Liyana thought, but to forge ahead, to will the world back to normalcy.

But most of humanity was dead, and the survivors couldn't have babies, and the elephants were spontaneously combusting.

"You know this was your idea, you can't pretend that it wasn't," James said. "Every time, I tell you that you shouldn't do it, that it's too dangerous, that you could die. Every time you ignore me."

"I don't ignore you," Liyana said quietly. But she knew she did. "This is too important to stop. I could have a baby. Humanity could keep going."

James shook his head. They'd had the argument so many times before, Liyana could predict each beat of it. Now would come the part about how they didn't know that people couldn't have babies, that it could just be them. It was too dangerous to really travel anymore; they never heard from anywhere more than a hundred miles away; maybe there were pockets in the world that weren't as twisted and ruined as Amboseli.

Liyana wouldn't say, but would think that James needed the delusional belief in those safe havens, needed to imagine that his wife—his love, lost when the war began while he was in Kenya with the Elephant Preservation Project—and children were safe. She wouldn't say, but would think that San Francisco was surely gone completely. Like Mombasa, like Durban, where her parents had lived. She wouldn't say, but would think that she wasn't forcing James to be with her, after all, hadn't forced him into sleeping with her. That she was the pregnant one. That all the risk was hers.

Instead, she said, "I can do both. I'm just watching the elephants, and now that I know where they go, I can get a spot farther away, somewhere comfortable."

Sighing, rubbing his fists into his eyes, James said, "Fine. But I'm coming with you."

Liyana knew that James was well aware he couldn't make demands of her, that no one could. But just the fact that he knew that, the hitch in his voice when he said he would come along, softened her stance. She nodded.

There was affection between them, she thought, if not outright love. And he would make a good father, if anyone in the world became parents again. Four pregnancies, nothing to show but bloody and miscarried fetuses. Other women had gotten pregnant as well, but none with the determination of Liyana. She hadn't seen any evidence that animals of any kind were breeding. The world was winding down, but she would bring it back. If need be, thrashing and squalling and fighting her the whole way.

Liyana's cousin Nandi had been the first girl Liyana knew to have a baby. As Liyana held her cousin's month-old daughter in her arms, cooing and making faces at her, she talked to Nandi about her upcoming trip to Kenya, her first time visiting Amboseli, a research trip for grad school, tracking elephants. She supported the baby's head while chattering away about elephant social structures, the importance of the matriarch.

"That's what you're talking about?" Nandi asked. "Elephants? Look at the baby, Liyana. Pretty little Inyoni. You can't say you don't want one for yourself."

"Sure, sure," Liyana said. "Someday. But I have so much to do now. I can't be tied down by a baby." Immediately, she stumbled over her apology, but Nandi laughed it off.

"You're too funny," Nandi said. "Give it time."

Inyoni began crying then, and Liyana handed her back to her cousin, her fingers lingering on the soft skin of the baby's neck.

Durban was gone now. Nandi and Inyoni and everyone else, gone or warped beyond recognition by forces Liyana could never understand. But the elephants remained, at least for now. And Liyana's baby was past what would have been the dangerous time before. But now, there was no longer any time that was safe. Not in this world.

As they watched fourteen elephants silently burn to death, their massive bodies hissing and crackling as flames leapt into the sky above them, James cried.

"There's only fifty-three left now," he whispered. "There were almost a hundred in the bond group when we started. They're just dwindling away."

"Just like us," Liyana said, and he shot her a horrified look. "It's true," she protested. "When's the last time you saw a baby elephant?"

Weeks earlier, when Liyana had told the others back at the lodge that she was going to find out what was happening to the elephants, where they were disappearing to, they'd joked that she was off to find the fabled elephants' graveyard. Half the people there had been part of the Elephant Preservation Project; they knew that was a myth. And yet here she was. The same spot as a month ago, and almost weekly more elephants came, in groups of twos and threes and larger, and caught fire.

The fires burned out, leaving behind nothing but piles of gray ash. On their second time out together, James had noticed that the elephants touched their trunks to the ash before they began singing, each animal in the circle lowering its trunk to each ash pile, then touching the tip of their trunk to their forehead. Remembering the dead.

Now, with the elephants gone, he and Liyana walked down. No, she thought. James walked, Liyana waddled. Twenty-two weeks. Her stomach bulged under her t-shirt like she was trying to shoplift a melon.

They circled the ashes, still steaming in the afternoon heat. Each time they inspected the ashes, and each time gleaned no new information. If this had been before the war, before the great change to the world, they could have brought the ashes to a laboratory, had someone analyze them for bacteria, viruses, some evidence of what could be causing the elephants to combust. Of course, if it were before the change, the elephants wouldn't be combusting in the first place.

"They come to the same spot every time," James said. "Does that mean something? With the touching the ashes beforehand? Like how they'll stand watch over their dead relatives?"

The ashes smelled of char and copper and something almost sweet. The combination made Liyana think of old candy, a caramel that had been forgotten between the seats of a car, left to rot in the sun. Bile rose in her throat and she spit it onto the ground next to the ashes. Spitting directly into the ashes seemed disrespectful. The elephants surely knew that these ashes were the remains of their family members, their friends. Smart animals, they understood death, understood the cycle of growth and decay.

"We're in the wrong place," she said.

"What? You think they have more than one spot?"

"No, no." Liyana shook her head, looking in the direction the elephants had come from. "We're seeing them die. If we want to know what's causing this, we need to see them live."

Her whole life, Liyana rarely cried, and never in front of people. As a little girl, she fell off her bike riding around the neighborhood with some cousins, and as the pain traveled from her bloody knee to her eyes, she swallowed it back, rushed into her house, up to the bathroom, and shut the door behind her before she finally allowed a whimper to escape.

When she lost her first pregnancy, she didn't cry. She knew it was coming, knew academically that she wouldn't be the woman to miraculously carry a pregnancy to term when no one else could. But she felt hollow afterward nonetheless, emotionally scooped out like a pumpkin.

That night, she and James lay in bed, turned on their sides, back to back. Liyana couldn't sleep. She listened to birds calling in the night, insects chirruping in the bush. She tried to clear her head, to think of nothing at all.

The mattress wobbled. A new sound joined those filtering in from outside. Breathy sobs, sniffling. James, her man, lamenting the loss of the baby. Lamenting the loss of his family, his wife and children, the whole world. He shook the bed and gulped air. He snorted and wiped away mucus.

She cried then, holding her body stiff, letting tears flow through ragged controlled breaths. Scalding tears of frustration and sadness and anger. She continued even after James petered out, fell into regular shallow breaths as he fitfully slept. Liyana cried and cried, but she wouldn't let him see.

The matriarch of the clan huffed and trumpeted and called in distress. Even someone who hadn't studied elephants, even someone who'd never even seen an elephant until that moment, would know those sounds didn't portend anything good.

Liyana knew just what the noises meant, and James certainly did, too. She wanted to rush to the elephant, but she knew she couldn't help it. No one could.

No other elephants were in sight, keeping away from the struggling matriarch out of fear or respect. Maybe sheer fatigued depression. It was the middle of the night, and she pictured them out in the bush, trying to sleep, pretending they couldn't hear their matriarch's anguished cries.

The elephant loosed a bellow from deep within and a milky balloon fell from her underside, followed by a rush of blood and amniotic fluid. The broken, half-formed body of a baby elephant came with it.

The matriarch cried anew, reaching down with her trunk to sniff and prod and poke the fetus. But it was premature and deformed, and never had a hope of survival.

Liyana watched the matriarch attempt to lift the body, to place it on its feet, to will it alive. She did some quick math in her head. Twenty-two-month pregnancies, a few months off between. And they wouldn't even last the full twenty-two months. Seven years had passed since the war had turned the world inside out. How many times had this matriarch miscarried or delivered stillborn fetuses?

How many times had she felt life inside her and hoped that this time would be different? Three? More?

The matriarch sat down heavily, and Liyana laid herself on the ground as well, propped on her side, watching the elephant mourn. She felt James's hand on her shoulder, heard him whisper, "We should go."

She shook her head. "I have to stay," she said, and felt a surge of gratitude when James didn't ask why or insist upon leaving. Instead, he sat down next to her, a hand slowly stroking from her hip to her knee and back. Eventually, the stroking stopped, and she realized he was sleeping. But Liyana stayed awake, sitting with the elephant that didn't know she was there.

Her name whispered in her ear, a hand jostling her shoulder. With a start, Liyana woke up, and realized James was speaking to her and pointing at the spot where the matriarch had miscarried.

Groggy, Liyana sat up, and it took her a moment to realize the sun had risen and the elephant was gone.

"Where did she go?" she asked. "Did you see her leave?"

James shook his head, but turned. "Tracks show her heading that way."

"Oh, god." Liyana got to her feet as quickly as she could, hands on the back of her hips, back cracking and bladder throbbing painfully. "They really are doing it on purpose. We have to help her."

James didn't ask how, which was good, because Liyana didn't know. But he went with her, taking her by the elbow and helping speed her along to the spot where the elephants burned.

The matriarch had been joined by four more elephants, all young females. They'd begun circling the ash pile already, the tips of their trunks dusty and gray-black.

Liyana skidded to a stop, her sneakers gouging into the hard dirt, sending a spray of gravel and sand flying, but the elephants ignored her. James stopped alongside her, letting go of her elbow and putting his hands on his knees to suck deep breaths. She hadn't imagined she could run at all this pregnant, let alone so fast.

"It's a ritual," James said. Liyana nodded, though he may as well have been speaking to himself.

Clearly it was a ritual. There was no doubt about that. But what Liyana hadn't realized was the purpose, which now glared right at her, as obvious as the bright sun shining in the open sky above. Elephants' graveyards weren't real, but they remembered their ancestors, understood the passing of generations. Of course they would understand when that cycle ground to a halt. The sadness she saw now in the matriarch's eyes wasn't just for her lost calf, it was for the loss of every elephant in the world, the end of life. How many people had killed themselves in the last seven years? The cataclysm had somehow given these elephants the ability to burn, and they'd come to the conclusion that self-immolation was the best remaining option.

These thoughts swirled through Liyana's mind, touching her consciousness then flitting off, barely cohering. She couldn't think of what to do. Couldn't think that there was anything to do. Something thudded against the inside of her stomach, and she looked down, confused, her hands instinctively cradling. The baby kicked again.

Liyana turned to James. "I'll be fine," she said. "Please stay here." And without waiting for a response, she ran as best she could into the center of the circle of elephants.

They shuffled backward and forward, their trunks flailing, but Liyana held her hands out, kept her head down, trying to appear submissive and unthreatening. As if she could threaten a creature of this size.

Heat radiated off the animals, baking Liyana's skin as if she was standing in front of an open oven. This close, splotches of pink and red danced across the elephants' wrinkled gray skin. Shimmery heat waves blurred their edges.

"Please," she said. "You don't need to do this. The world isn't over. It's going to go on. We're all going to go on." The elephants calmed at her tone, but the temperature still rose. Liyana smelled ozone, and worried that her hair would singe if she didn't move soon.

Such heat couldn't be good for her baby, or for Liyana herself. Her head swam, and she feared she'd swoon, that if she fell she'd be caught up in the conflagration when the elephants set themselves alight. "Don't," she whispered. "Don't go." Her eyelids fluttered.

They shot back open when she felt the air cool and something warm press against her distended stomach, and she found herself staring into the face of the matriarch, the elephant's massive ears flapping slightly, fanning the sweat from Liyana's forehead. It was the closest she'd ever been to an elephant in all her years studying them. Both before and after the destruction of the world, she'd always been at a distance. The matriarch's eyes gleamed with deep intelligence and curiosity. She probed again with her trunk, then used it to lift the hem of Liyana's shirt. Liyana removed it the rest of the way. Around her, the other elephants pressed closer, their bodies cooling, but still giving off residual warmth. She imagined herself in a cocoon of elephant hide, and laughed.

The matriarch lightly pressed her trunk against Liyana's belly and the other elephants joined her. As if sensing them, the baby inside her kicked once, then again and again and again, a rapid tattoo like she was happily stomping her feet, dancing to some inaudible music.

An array of calls sounded from the elephants around her, high and low, a rippling melody that thrummed through her whole body. Trumpeting sounded in the distance, the more distant members of the clan joining in. They sang to her baby for what felt like ages, before they suddenly stopped, turned, and exited the clearing, the matriarch the last to go, her trunk lingering on Liyana's stomach for a long moment before she, too, left, pausing to turn back only once, catching Liyana's eye as she stood frozen to the spot in the middle of the ashes. The matriarch blinked slowly, then walked away.

In an instant, James was at her side as Liyana sagged into the ashes of the dead elephants, breath hitching in a combination of laughter and relief. She still wasn't sure what she'd done, but she believed she'd made a promise to the elephants. She prayed she could keep it.

After the screaming and the unimaginable pain and the gritted teeth, the contractions and pushing, a little girl fell into the world. Crying and slick and sparkling with some unreal internal glow, since nothing in this world could be the same as it had once been. But Liyana held her daughter, and cried unabashed tears of joy. This was her girl. She was alive and in the world, however warped that world had become. She was human. She was magic.

BONES OF GOSSAMER

HUGH HOWEY

Hugh Howey is the *New York Times* bestselling author of *Wool, Sand, Beacon 23,* and *Half Way Home*. His books have been translated into more than forty languages. His latest, *Machine Learning*, collects his short fiction into one volume. He is also the co-editor (with Gary Whitta and Christie Yant) of the ACLU charity anthology *Resist: Tales From a Future Worth Fighting Against* and (with John Joseph Adams) of The Apocalypse Triptych. He currently lives on a catamaran that he's sailing around the world.

This story is dedicated to the people of Fulaga,
who welcomed me as family, and who took care of me
like a refugee when I ran out of all else.

There's a cave behind our house with the bones of those we've eaten. It's been many years since anyone was put inside, but I pass this cave every day on the trail back to the cassava patch. Mid-morning, the sun lances in at the right angle and white bone gleams in the darkness. Hollow-sad eyes peer out—the skulls of those who wish we'd eaten more cassava in their day.

We stopped eating people before I was born, but only barely. Our chief is ninety-two, and human flesh has passed his lips. We like to think the past is further away than it really is, but the past is like the killer in a movie that you know is standing right behind someone, if they'd just turn around and look. It's dangerous not to look. That's when the past will get you.

I grew up on a small island in the Lau Group of the Fijian archipelago. When I was a young boy, I discovered movies and got addicted for a spell. We watched them on a battered cell phone charged by a solar panel, me and my best friend Tui, one ear bud each, sharing laughs and ear wax. There was no cell service here, of course. Never has been and never will be. The past and the present are fast friends in the Lau. You can hardly tell them apart.

I was in my twenties when the first tourists visited our island. Before this, they were not allowed, even as cruise ships and resorts filled the rest of Fiji far to the north. Our small islands were farther away and deemed special. Special meant no development, no jobs, no civilization. It meant cleaning the family solar panel with a wet rag, topping up an old car battery with boiled water, and learning how to wire up a voltage regulator—all so we could have light in our home after sunset in the winter.

The handful of tourists who eventually came arrived by small boat, much as our ancestors did. The islands of the Lau are a pain to reach; a strong wind blows without pause in the wrong direction. They call these "trade winds," but it must mean trade for someone else. These winds have kept us isolated as the rest of Fiji became a giant resort. The winds blow and blow, always in one direction. The palm trees here lean north like they're yearning for elsewhere.

The arrival of white people caused a stir. They came from places we'd heard of but never dreamed of visiting: France, Germany, America. People with pale skin had showed up here before, hundreds of years ago. They taught us religion, that we should to dress from ankle to wrist, and to please not eat each other. Especially not them. Some of their bones are in the cave behind my house.

I think about those people on their boats when I pull up cassava and when I help with the fishing. Ours was a host family, which meant making these wayward sailors feel welcome, showing them around, giving them cassava and fish and coconuts. They'd often see the cave and peer inside and ask how old the bones were, how long since the last time we practiced our old ways.

"Not since Tuesday," we'd tell them. And then we'd laugh, our faces all teeth, while their eyes went wide for a moment. It takes a while to get our sense of humor. But that's no worry; all we have is time.

The supply ship teaches us patience. Once a month the big boat steams toward us under a chimney of gray smoke, its rusty bow burying into steep seas. It's a torturous journey. I've made it six times, and I'll never do it again.

When I was twenty-three I left for Suva to get a job and find a wife. Suva is the "big city," the only place with work and where we might meet a spouse who hasn't known us since we were born. Someone not a cousin.

But then I got married, and my beautiful Maru got pregnant, and we took a supply ship home to have our first child. This is what we do. We drop off our kids with our parents and leave them to grow like buried cassava. Our parents look after them just as our grandparents looked after us.

We skip a generation here. People who don't know their own grandparents judge us. It's different is all. My grandchildren are my everything, just as my grandparents were my sun and moon. I saw my parents at Christmas. That's when I see my children now.

In this way, an entire generation goes missing from our island: the generation in the middle. Suva is no place to raise kids. Children in the city can't even open a coconut, and people there pay money for fish that someone else caught! No, our children are born and raised in Fulaga. They go to school until we run out of things to teach them. Afterward, some go off to college in Suva, but not many. Just a few. Most are like me and go there for work one day, or to see what the city is like, or to visit an older brother or sister. Someone has to make money and send it back home. These are the missing. The people in their prime.

When we get old and tired of work and the whizzing cars, we return to the island where we grew up. Just in time for our children to leave us. Families like skipping stones.

The things that bored us as children are all we care about now that we're old: dragging nets through schools of fish, spearing an octopus, sitting through a long sermon with our feet in the soil, lounging in the shade and watching the cassava grow, grandparents smiling at grandchildren. The middle generation sending money and flour and whatever we beg for on the supply ships, which come once a month.

Except for the months they don't. And then we manage. We get by.

Once, when I was a boy, we went three months between supply ships. Three months in a row, and nothing came. The flour and sugar were all gone by the end of the first month. That's as long as we ever prepare for. So no kava root for drinking the worry away. No lollies for the kids. And no word from our families.

This was before the satellite phone was installed at the school so we could get a warning and ration our things. This was back when cyclones would hit without notice. What seems like just another strong wind grows into something more and more. A rustle, a beating, a whipping, a fury. Step by step, like how empires fall.

All I knew as a young boy was to stop asking if we could eat anything different. Fish and coconuts for breakfast, lunch, and dinner. Years later I would see tourists in Suva rave about the dish I hoped to never see again. In Suva I grew fat on pizza and curries and Coca-Cola. I said I'd never be like my grandfather, who idled in the patch trying to grow pumpkin, happily slurping the last of the coconut milk from yet another bowl of fish stew.

And yet here I am. I am him. Sixty-seven years old. The same hands as his: bones wrapped in brown paper. I thought I'd turn out different somehow. I guess we all did.

But we all turn out like those in that cave, peering out when the sun lances in just right. All those who thought things would go a bit different. We're fools like that. Laughing, our faces all teeth.

The tourists in their little boats kept coming, a dozen or so a year braving the heavy seas and the far distance. They all asked us about the cave of bones. Someone must've written about it somewhere, or the people on boats gossiped the same way islanders did. They took pictures of the bones, wanted to know if it was ceremonial, the way we buried our ancestors here. What was the meaning of this place? What significance did it hold? So many questions.

I realized I didn't have the answers. But I didn't tell them that. They had pockets full of shiny coins, and they'd brought canned meats and reading glasses for my grandmother, so Tui and I told them there was much dancing with fire and many special songs and we did a dance we learned in school and pretended it was the cannibal dance, and these people went away impressed and with lighter pockets.

But now I wanted to know. So I asked our chief, who was very old at the time.

He laughed at the idea of ceremony.

"Those were the bones of our enemies," he told me. "After we ate them, we threw the scraps in that hole up there so the dogs wouldn't drag them out again. That's a rubbish bin."

I wasn't sure what to make of that. Even I had thought that cave must've meant something in the past. Too many people sleeping in there for it to mean nothing. But the chief is never wrong.

Tui and I tried telling tourists the truth, but their disappointment was too much for us. So we practiced a bit and got much better with our dancing. Everyone wants a life to mean something, even if it's not theirs.

It's a fine filament that holds us to the past. So fine we can't see it even if we know it's there and try our hardest to look. Gossamer is the word I like best. It doesn't sound like a real word, gossamer. More like what someone might name one of those small boats that sail into our lagoon. An invisible thing all wings and whispers.

We've lost the thread that goes back to our ancestors who knew how to sail. Now we take longboats with loud Yamahas and run over to Ogea Levu to trade with our neighbors. It's six miles between the islands, which is plenty far when the winds are high. Far enough that we rarely go. Only in an emergency.

An emergency like now.

When the phone went out, it was like another filament making itself known, this tiny little connection to the rest of the world. The phone was where we placed our orders with our families for the next supply ship. It was where we heard the voices of our children, and they heard the voices of their children. It held the two generations on the outsides together.

I don't know how we ever lived without it, but we used to. And now it feels like we can't. It's been five long months since the phone worked. It's been five long months since a supply ship came. Summer is ending, the time of cyclones abating, and we grow anxious. I try not to let my grandchildren see it in my face, but half the time I go fishing, I do not go to fish. I leave the lagoon through the narrow cut and I sit out beyond the reef on the bobbing sea and I stare at the horizon, wishing for a trail of smoke, a white sail, a rusty prow, the contrail of a jetliner, or any sign that God has not forgotten us.

Coconuts and fish. I tell the grandchildren to not complain. We make the same jokes that have amused us for centuries, and we laugh with our teeth, and things are worse over on Ogea Levu, so some of them have moved onto a bare patch of beach near us, and I can hear the wind in the caves rattling bones of old as tribes kept distant are pushed into close proximity.

Gossamer. That's what holds us together.

When my Maru got sick, she went back to her village to get better. The phone and supply ships made it feel like I could reach her when the time was right. Now there is no word. My wife of forty-one years is beyond my reach.

The grandchildren ask if she's okay. Even though we're the ones who've run out of sugar and flour. I sit on the reef and gaze toward Suva.

What else can I do?

I saw the sail first.

The white cloth like a towering wave that refused to break. It grew bigger, and I paddled back to the village to let them know that tourists were coming again. This was before I knew better. We can't call them tourists, the ones who arrive here now.

Refugees is the word.

Survivors.

It's been almost a year since the last supply ship. No one knows why, and we've lost the ability to go see for ourselves. No one remembers how to sail or navigate. We only go to islands we can see—never over the horizon. And we ran out of petrol for the Yamahas months ago.

We paddle to fish these days. Old canoes made of hollowed trees were pulled from the woods and found to still float. They're easier to maneuver by paddle than the fiberglass longboats made in New Zealand. One of the old longboats we used to fight over now sits upturned on the beach, thrown there by a storm, and nobody has bothered to right it. It's no good without the motor.

Oh, but the first white sail on the horizon in more than a year! A sail full of hope. Finally, some kind of contact. I roused the village and we gathered on the shore as the small boat steered through the passage. The rattle of chain and the splash of anchor, and we waded out with happy hearts to receive them and ask if the world has forgotten us, if our children send word, what is going on in Suva.

A German man, gaunt and grizzled, fell from the boat and collapsed into my arms. He was starving, he said. He looked mostly dead, ribs like furrows plowed into the soil, all bones, like someone who belonged in a cave. Every heart in the village broke in that moment, and I'm ashamed to say it wasn't for him that we were crushed. It was for ourselves.

The man spoke little English, but we made enough of his gibberish to know fear for the first time. He spoke of a world without power, a world where machines went haywire. Some say the machines did it themselves and some say it was crazy people who broke the machines on purpose. A world where bombs had become machines with their own minds and clouds of ash covered entire continents. We listened beneath blue skies, on our little green island surrounded by sea and fish, and some walked away rather than believe, and I wasn't sure what to make of it.

The man said even in Suva people had gone crazy fighting over scraps. The big city only ever had a week of supplies at a time. A week. Big ships from New Zealand came with great containers. A week!

Even we planned for longer. The man said his wife had been murdered. I could hear the wind in the caves. I thought of my sweet Maru and part of me knew she was gone. An emptiness grew inside me. An urge to scream that I hadn't felt since I was a boy.

* * *

Our neighbors from Ogea Levu have started a small settlement on the south coast of our island, abandoning their ancient homes to be nearer to us and our lagoon of fish.

There's much discussion about this. In Fiji, everything belongs to someone. Every coconut is owned. We have a rite here of sevusevu where we seek permission to visit someone else's land. Kava is presented; we drink together; and permission is always granted. Of course we welcomed our neighbors. Because we didn't think that they would *stay*.

The German's name is Klaus, and he and I have become friends. He is a terrible fisherman, but getting better. I marveled that a man who lives on a boat couldn't take fish from the sea more easily. He marveled that a man who lives on an island doesn't know how to sail from one to another.

Gossamer. We snip threads without seeing them.

I taught him to fish, and he taught me how to sail his little boat around the lagoon so we didn't have to paddle. He and his wife had left Germany many years ago to see the world together. All he talks about is her, and all I talk about is my two girls. Klaus and I both speak of recent things like they are in the far past, and sometimes the words are hard to get out.

I don't ask much about Suva. I don't tell him about my wife. I fear the worst.

A French family was the next to arrive. They came in a catamaran. They'd been living up in Namuka with the villagers there, but said one day the chief came and told them sevusevu was no more. They had to go.

Rumor is that one of their sons was thinking of taking a wife and that this had started an argument. They were bringing back the old ways on Namuka. Shedding their clothes and going back to carrying spears and smearing mud on their faces. Praying to the wrong gods. I think this French family might've been lucky to get away with their lives.

One day, I found the young French boy sitting on a rock peering north like he'd left something over the horizon. I knew that look. A hand on his shoulder was all I had to offer.

Clouds of birds dove into the sea out beyond the reef, emerging with flashes of silver on their beaks. We watched the gulls fish and everything seemed so simple if you could forget most of what you knew.

In the weeks that followed, the boy and I began sailing together on Klaus's boat. We didn't talk much. We practiced our smiles.

Nobody had touched the longboat for enough months that I decided I could have it. I set it up on the beach behind my house, pushing and tugging with ropes over bamboo rollers, not asking anyone for help because I had to do it myself. And here is where I found my ancestors—not in any cave, or in any religion old or new, but on the beach, fixing a keel to a boat that had never known one, building a rudder where a Yamaha motor had once been, making a mast out of a tree and sails from bedding and laundry.

It was difficult to get to our island, because the trade winds blow without fail. But leaving here would be easy. The wind at my back. It must be how my people first arrived. There must've been someone like me who either thought the world was going crazy, or maybe *this* was the crazy place and it might be better out there if we just go see for ourselves.

And anyway isn't the wind calling and the sea full of fish?

Klaus and Emanuel took turns visiting my project and offering gestures of advice. Klaus loaned me some old ropes. Emanuel brought a small can of paint and a brush and said I had to name her. I slept on this and the next morning I painted *Gossamer* on her stern.

Out there, somewhere, the world was going to hell. But I was getting better.

I think my brother was the first to know what I was planning. He stopped making fun of my project after I named the boat. He brought me his favorite lure and helped me clean two dozen coconuts for the journey. We husked without much talking. He tried to give me his knife. I hugged him and could smell our father on us both.

I pushed off the next morning with the sun low. Emanuel came in tears and begged me to take him, to drop him off at Namuka on the way, but I knew he wouldn't be welcome there and that his parents would miss him. But it was painful to deny a man who wants something that badly. He was my brother in that moment.

Outside the reef, the wind was stronger than I expected. Ropes creaked, and the boat lurched to the side, and I nearly went over the rail and imagined swimming back to shore ashamed and beaten. But the rigging held, and so did I.

It was four days to Suva if I was lucky. I didn't know what I would find there. Hopefully my children, whom I barely knew. Maybe my Maru, holding on for a final goodbye. The entire world might be gone.

Or maybe it was out there, silently waiting for me.

The wind howled the further I got from land, out of the protection of our small island, and I thought I could see the grandchildren back on the beach. There were regrets all around me. I should never have let Maru leave. Or I should've gone with her. I should've spent more time with my parents and my children. Generations should not be forgotten.

I sailed north in a frightful wind, the sky half gray and half blue, fear and hope in my breast, the seas lapping at the stern like chasing dogs, just me and my little *Gossamer*, my mind dipping and soaring like some old rusty prow.

I know it was the perils of the sea making me think this way, and my old age, my time running out. But it shouldn't have to run out to want to spend it more wisely.

The world shouldn't have to end to think of all it might be.

AS GOOD AS NEW

CHARLIE JANE ANDERS

Charlie Jane Anders' latest novel is *The City in the Middle of the Night*. She's also the author of *All the Birds in the Sky*, which won the Nebula, Crawford and Locus awards, and *Choir Boy*, which won a Lambda Literary Award. Plus a novella called *Rock Manning Goes For Broke* and a short story collection called *Six Months, Three Days, Five Others*. Her short fiction has appeared in *Tor.com*, *Boston Review*, *Tin House*, *Conjunctions*, *The Magazine of Fantasy & Science Fiction*, *Wired Magazine*, *Slate*, *Asimov's Science Fiction*, *Lightspeed*, *ZYZZYVA*, *Catamaran Literary Review*, *McSweeney's Internet Tendency* and tons of anthologies, including *Best American Science Fiction and Fantasy*. Her story "Six Months, Three Days" won a Hugo Award, and her story "Don't Press Charges And I Won't Sue" won a Theodore Sturgeon Award. She also organizes the monthly Writers With Drinks reading series.

Marisol got into an intense relationship with the people on *The Facts of Life*, to the point where Tootie and Mrs. Garrett became her imaginary best friends and she shared every last thought with them. She told Tootie about the rash she got from wearing the same bra every day for two years, and she had a long talk with Mrs. Garrett about her regrets that she hadn't said a proper goodbye to her best friend Julie and her on-again/off-again boyfriend Rod, before they died along with everybody else.

The panic room had pretty much every TV show ever made on its massive hard drive, with multiple backup systems and a fail-proof generator, so there was nothing stopping Marisol from marathoning *The Facts of Life* for sixteen hours a day, starting over again with season one when she got to the end of the bedraggled final season. She also watched *Mad Men* and *The West Wing*. The media server had tons of video of live theatre, but Marisol didn't watch that because it made her feel guilty. Not survivor's guilt, failed playwright guilt.

Her last proper conversation with a living human had been an argument with Julie about Marisol's decision to go to medical school instead of trying to write more plays. ("Fuck doctors, man," Julie had spat. "People are going to die no matter what you do. Theatre is *important*.") Marisol had hung up on Julie and gone back to the pre-med books, staring at the exposed musculature and blood vessels as if they were costume designs for a skeleton theatre troupe.

The quakes always happened at the worst moment, just when Jo or Blair was about to reveal something heartfelt and serious. The whole panic room would shake, throwing Marisol against the padded walls or ceiling over and over again. A reminder that the rest of the world was probably dead. At first, these quakes were constant, then they happened a few times a day. Then once a day, then a few times a week. Then a few times a month. Marisol knew that once a month or two passed without the world going sideways, she would have to go out and investigate. She would have to leave her friends at the Eastland School, and venture into a bleak world.

Sometimes, Marisol thought she had a duty to stay in the panic room, since she was personally keeping the human race alive. But then she thought: what if there was someone else living, and they needed help? Marisol was pre-med, she might be able to do something. What if there was a man, and Marisol could help him repopulate the species?

The panic room had nice blue leather walls and a carpeted floor that felt nice to walk on, and enough gourmet frozen dinners to last Marisol a few lifetimes. She only had the pair of shoes she'd brought in there with her, and it would seem weird to wear shoes after two barefoot years. The real world was in here, in the panic room—out there was nothing but an afterimage of a bad trip.

Marisol was an award-winning playwright, but that hadn't saved her from the end of the world. She was taking pre-med classes and trying to get a scholarship to med school so she could give cancer screenings to poor women in her native Taos, but that didn't save her either. Nor did the fact that she believed in God every other day.

What actually saved Marisol from the end of the world was the fact that she took a job cleaning Burton Henstridge's mansion to help her through school, and she'd happened to be scrubbing his fancy Japanese toilet when the quakes had started—within easy reach of Burton's state-of-the-art panic room. (She had found the hidden opening mechanism some weeks earlier, while cleaning the porcelain cat figurines.) Burton himself was in Bulgaria scouting a new location for a nano-fabrication facility, and had died instantly.

When Marisol let herself think about all the people she could never talk to again, she got so choked up she wanted to punch someone in the eye until they were blinded for life. She experienced grief in the form of freak-outs that left her unable to breathe or think, and then she popped in another *Facts of Life*. As she watched, she chewed her nails until she was in danger of gnawing off her fingertips.

The door to the panic room wouldn't actually open when Marisol finally decided it had been a couple months since the last quake and it was time to go the hell out there. She had to kick the door a few dozen times, until she dislodged enough of the debris blocking it to stagger out into the wasteland. The cold slapped her in the face and extremities, extra bitter after two years at room temperature. Burton's house was gone, the panic room was just a cube half-buried in the ruins, covered in some yellowy insulation that looked like it would burn your fingers.

Everything out there was white, like snow or paper, except powdery and brittle, ashen. She had a Geiger counter from the panic room, which read zero. She couldn't figure out what the hell had happened to the world, for a long time, until it hit her—this was fungus. Some kind of newly made, highly corrosive fungus that had rushed over everything like a tidal wave and consumed every last bit of organic material, then died. It had come in wave after wave, with incredible violence, until it had exhausted the last of its food supply and crushed everything to dust. She gleaned this from the consistency of the crud that had coated every bit of rubble, but also from the putrid sweet-and-sour smell that she could not stop smelling once she noticed it. She kept imagining that she saw the white powder starting to move out of the corner of her eye, advancing toward her, but when she would turn around there was nothing.

"The fungus would have all died out when there was nothing left for it to feed on," Marisol said aloud. "There's no way it could still be active." She tried to pretend some other person, an expert or something, had said that, and thus it was authoritative. The fungus was dead. It couldn't hurt her now.

Because if the fungus wasn't dead, then she was screwed—even if it didn't kill her, it would destroy the panic room and its contents. She hadn't been able to seal it properly behind her without locking herself out.

"Hello?" Marisol kept yelling, out of practice at trying to project her voice. "Anybody there? Anybody?"

She couldn't even make sense of the landscape. It was just blinding white, as far as she could see, with bits of blanched stonework jutting out. No way to discern streets or houses or cars or anything, because it had all been corroded or devoured.

She was about to go back to the panic room and hope it was still untouched, so she could eat another frozen lamb vindaloo and watch season three of *Mad Men*. And then she spotted something, a dot of color, a long way off in the pale ruins.

The bottle was a deep oaky green, like smoked glass, with a cork in it. And it was about twenty yards away, just sitting in one of the endless piles of white debris. Somehow, it had avoided being consumed or rusted or broken in the endless waves of fungal devastation. It looked as though someone had just put it down a second ago—in fact, Marisol's first response was to yell "Hello?" even louder than before.

When there was no answer, she picked up the bottle. In her hands, it felt bumpy, like an embossed label had been worn away, and there didn't seem to be any liquid inside. She couldn't see its contents, if there were any. She removed the cork.

A *whoosh* broke the dead silence. A sparkly mist streamed out of the bottle's narrow mouth—sparkling like the cheap glitter at the Arts and Crafts table at summer camp when Marisol was a little girl, misty like a smoke machine at a cheap nightclub—and it slowly resolved into a shape in front of her. A man, a little taller than she was and much bigger.

Marisol was so startled and grateful at no longer being alone that she almost didn't pause to wonder how this man had appeared out of nowhere, after she opened a bottle. A bottle that had survived when everything else was crushed. Then she did start to wonder, but the only explanations seemed too ludicrous to believe.

"Hello and congratulations," the man said in a pleasant tone. He looked Jewish and wore a cheap suit, in a style that reminded Marisol somewhat of the *Mad Men* episodes she'd just been watching. His dark hair fell onto his high forehead in lank strands, and he had a heavy beard shadow. "Thank you for opening my bottle. I am pleased to offer you three wishes." Then he looked around, and his already dour expression worsened. "Oh, fuck," he said. "Not *again*."

"Wait," Marisol said. "You're a—you're a genie?"

"I hate that term," the man said. "I prefer wish-facilitator. And for your information, I used to be just a regular person. I was the theatre critic at *The New York Times* for six months in 1958, which I still think defines me much more than my current engagement does. But I tried to bamboozle the wrong individual, so I got stuck in a bottle and forced to grant wishes to anyone who opens it."

"You were a theatre critic?" Marisol said. "I'm a playwright. I won a contest and had a play produced off-Broadway. Well, actually, I'm a pre-med student, and I clean houses for money. But in my off-off-hours, I'm a playwright, I guess."

"Oh," the man said. "Well, if you want me to tell you your plays are very good, then that will count as one of your three wishes. And honestly, I don't think you're going to benefit from good publicity very much in the current climate." He gestured around at the bleak white landscape around them. "My name was Richard Wolf, by the way."

"Marisol," she said. "Marisol Guzmán."

"Nice to meet you." He extended his hand, but didn't actually try to shake hers. She wondered if she would go right through him. She was standing in a world of stinky chalk talking to a self-loathing genie. After two years alone in a box, that didn't even seem weird, really.

So this was it. Right? She could fix everything. She could make a wish, and everything would be back the way it was. She could talk to Julie again, and apologize for hanging up on her. She could see Rod, and maybe figure out what they were to each other. She just had to say the words: "I wish." She started to speak, and then something Richard Wolf had said a moment earlier registered in her brain.

"Wait a minute," she said. "What did you mean, 'Not again?'"

"Oh, that." Richard Wolf swatted around his head with big hands, like he was trying to swat nonexistent insects. "I couldn't say. I mean, I can answer any question you want, but that counts as one of your wishes. There are rules."

"Oh," Marisol said. "Well, I don't want to waste a wish on a question. Not when I can figure this out on my own. You said 'not again,' the moment you saw all this. So, this isn't the first time this has happened. Your bottle can probably survive anything. Right? Because it's magic or something."

The dark green bottle still had a heft to it, even after she'd released its contents. She threw it at a nearby rock a few times. Not a scratch.

"So," she said. "The world ends, your bottle doesn't get damaged. If even one person survives, they find your bottle. And the first thing they wish for? Is for the world not to have ended."

Richard Wolf shrugged, but he also sort of nodded at the same time, like he was confirming her hunch. His feet were see-through, she noticed. He was wearing wing-tip shoes, that looked scuffed to the point of being scarred.

"The first time was in 1962," he said. "The Cuban Missile Crisis, they called it afterwards."

"This is *not* counting as one of my wishes, because I didn't ask a question," Marisol said.

"Fine, fine," Richard Wolf rolled his eyes. "I grew tired of listening to your harangue. When I was reviewing for the *Times*, I always tore into plays that had too many endless speeches. Your plays don't have a lot of monologues, do they? Fucking Brecht made everybody think three-page speeches were clever. Fucking Brecht."

"I didn't go in for too many monologues," Marisol said. "So. Someone finds your bottle, they wish for the apocalypse not to have happened, and then they probably make a second wish, to try and make sure it doesn't happen again. Except here we are, so it obviously didn't work the last time."

"I could not possibly comment," Richard Wolf said. "Although I should say that everyone gets the wrong idea about people in my line of work—meaning wish-facilitators, not theatre critics. People had the wrong idea when I was a theatre critic, too, they thought it was my job to promote the theatre, to put buns in seats, even for terrible plays. That was *not* my job at all."

"The theatre has been an endangered species for a long time," Marisol said, not without sympathy. She looked around the pasty-white, yeast-scented deathscape. A world of Wonder Bread. "I mean, I get why people want criticism that is essentially cheerleading, even if that doesn't push anybody to do their best work."

"Well, if you think of theatre as some sort of *delicate flower* that needs to be kept protected in some sort of *hothouse*"—and at this point, Wolf was clearly reprising arguments he'd had over and over again, when he was alive—"then you're going to end up with something that only the *faithful few* will appreciate, and you'll end up worsening the very marginalization that you're seeking to prevent."

Marisol was being very careful to avoid asking anything resembling a question, because she was probably going to need all three of her wishes. "I would guess that the job of a theatre critic is misunderstood in sort of the opposite way than the job of a genie," she said. "Everybody is afraid a theatre critic will be too brutally honest. But a genie…"

"Everybody thinks I'm out to swindle them!" Richard Wolf threw his hands in the air, thinking of all the *tsuris* he had endured. "When, in fact, it's always the client who can't express a wish in clear and straightforward terms. They always leave out crucial information. I do my best. It's like stage directions without any stage left or stage right. I interpret as best I can."

"Of course you do," Marisol said. This was all starting to creep her out, and her gratitude at having another person to talk to (who wasn't Mrs. Garrett) was getting driven out by her discomfort at standing in the bleached-white ruins of the world kibitzing about theatre criticism. She picked up the bottle from where it lay undamaged after hitting the rock, and found the cork.

"Wait a minute," Richard Wolf said. "You don't want to—"

He was sucked back inside the bottle before she finished putting the cork back in.

She reopened the bottle once she was back inside the panic room, with the door sealed from the inside. So nothing or nobody could get in. She watched three episodes of *The Facts of Life*, trying to get her equilibrium back, before she microwaved some *sukiyaki* and let Richard Wolf out again. He started the spiel about how he had to give her three wishes over again, then stopped and looked around.

"Huh." He sat and sort of floated an inch above the sofa. "Nice digs. Real calfskin on this sofa. Is this like a bunker?"

"I can't answer any of your questions," Marisol said, "or that counts as a wish you owe me."

"Don't be like that." Richard Wolf ruffled his two-tone lapels. "I'm just trying not to create any loopholes, because once there are loopholes it brings everybody grief in the end. Trust me, you wouldn't want the rules to be messy here." He rifled through the media collection until he found a copy of *Cat on a Hot Tin Roof*, which he made a big show of studying until Marisol finally loaded it for him.

"This is better than I'd remembered," Richard Wolf said an hour later.

"Good to know," Marisol said. "I never got around to watching that one."

"I met Tennessee Williams, you know," Richard said. "He wasn't nearly as drunk as you might have thought."

"So here's what I figure. You do your level best to implement the wishes that people give you, to the letter," Marisol said. "So if someone says they want to make sure that a nuclear war never happens again, you do your best to make a nuclear war impossible. And then maybe that change leads to some other catastrophe, and then the next person tries to make some wishes that prevent that thing from happening again. And on, and on. Until this."

"This is actually the longest conversation I've had since I became a wish-facilitator." Richard crossed his leg, ankle over thigh. "Usually, it's just whomp-bomp-a-lula-three-wishes, and I'm back in the bottle. So tell me about your prize-winning play. If you want. I mean, it's up to you."

Marisol told Richard about her play, which seemed like something an acquaintance of hers had written many lifetimes ago. "It was a one-act," she said, "about a man who is trying to break up with his girlfriend, but every time he's about to dump her she does something to remind him why he used to love her. So he hires a male prostitute to seduce her, instead, so she'll cheat on him and he can have a reason to break up with her."

Richard was giving her a blank expression, as though he couldn't trust himself to show a reaction.

"It's a comedy," Marisol explained.

"Sorry," Richard said. "It sounds awful. He hires a male prostitute to sleep with his girlfriend. It sounds… I just don't know what to say."

"Well, you were a theatre critic in the 1950s, right? I guess it was a different era."

"I don't think that's the problem," Richard said. "It just sounds sort of… misanthropic. Or actually woman-hating. With a slight veneer of irony. I don't know. Maybe that's the sort of thing everybody is into these days—or was into, before the world ended yet again. This is something like the fifth or sixth time the world has ended. I am losing count, to be quite honest."

Marisol was put out that this fossil was casting aspersions on her play—her *contest-winning play*, in fact. But the longer she kept him talking, the more clues he dropped, without costing her any wishes. So she bit her lip.

"So. There were half a dozen apocalypses," Marisol said. "And I guess each of them was caused by people trying to prevent the last one from happening again, by making wishes. So that white stuff out there. Some kind of bioengineered corrosive fungus, I thought—but maybe it was created to prevent some kind of climate-related disaster. It does seem awfully reflective of sunlight."

"Oh, yes, it reflects sunlight just wonderfully," Richard said. "The temperature of the planet is going to be dropping a lot in the next decade. No danger of global warming now."

"Ha," Marisol said. "And you claim you're just doing the most straightforward job possible. You're addicted to irony. You sat through too many Brecht plays, even though you claim to hate him. You probably loved Beckett as well."

"All right-thinking people love Beckett," said Richard. "So you had some *small* success as a playwright, and yet you're studying to be a doctor. Or you were, before this unfortunate business. Why not stick with the theatre?"

"Is that a question?" Marisol said. Richard started to backpedal, but then she answered him anyway. "I wanted to help people, really help people. Live theatre reaches fewer and fewer people all the time, especially brand-new plays by brand-new playwrights. It's getting to be like poetry—nobody reads poetry any more. And meanwhile, poor people are dying of preventable cancers every day, back home in Taos. I couldn't fool myself that writing a play that twenty people saw would do as much good as screening a hundred people for cervical cancer."

Richard paused and looked her over. "You're a good person," he said. "I almost never get picked up by anyone who's actually not a terrible human being."

"It's all relative. My protagonist who hires a male prostitute to seduce his girlfriend considers himself a good person, too."

"Does it work? The male prostitute thing? Does she sleep with him?"

"Are you asking me a question?"

Wolf shrugged and rolled his eyes in that operatic way he did, which he'd probably practiced in the mirror. "I will owe you an extra wish. Sure. Why not. Does it work, with the gigolo?"

Marisol had to search her memory for a second, she had written that play in such a different frame of mind. "No. The boyfriend keeps feeding the male prostitute lines to seduce his girlfriend via a Bluetooth earpiece—it's meant to be a postmodern Cyrano de Bergerac—and she figures it out and starts using the male prostitute to screw with her boyfriend. In the end, the boyfriend and the male prostitute get together because the boyfriend and the male prostitute have seduced each other while flirting with the girlfriend."

Richard cringed on top of the sofa with his face in his insubstantial hands. "That's terrible," he said. "I can't believe I gave you an extra wish just to find that out."

"Wow, thanks. I can see why people hated you when you were a theatre critic."

"Sorry! I mean, maybe it was better on the stage, I bet you have a flair for dialogue. It just sounds so… hackneyed. I mean, *postmodern Cyrano de Bergerac*? I heard all about postmodernism from this one graduate student who opened my bottle in the early 1990s, and it sounded dreadful. If I wasn't already sort of dead, I would be slitting my wrists. You really did make a wise choice, becoming a doctor."

"Screw you." Marisol decided to raid the relatively tiny liquor cabinet in the panic room, and poured herself a generous vodka. "You're the one who's been living in a bottle. So. All of this is your fault." She waved her hand, indicating the devastation outside the panic room. "You caused it all, with some excessively ironic wish-granting."

"That's a very skewed construction of events. If the white sludge *was* caused by a wish that somebody made—and I'm not saying it was—then it's not my fault. It's the fault of the wisher."

"Okay," Marisol said. Richard drew to attention, thinking she was finally ready to make her first wish. Instead, she said, "I need to think," and put the cork back in the bottle.

Marisol watched a season and a half of *I Dream of Jeannie*, which did not help at all. She ate some delicious beef stroganoff and drank more vodka. She slept and watched TV and slept and drank coffee and ate an omelet. She had no circadian rhythm to speak of anymore.

She had four wishes, and the overwhelming likelihood was that she would foul them up, and maybe next time there wouldn't be one person left alive to find the bottle and fix her mistake.

This was pretty much exactly like trying to cure a patient, Marisol realized. You give someone a medicine which fixes their disease but causes deadly side effects. Or reduces the patient's resistance to other infections. You didn't just want to get rid of one pathogen, you wanted to help the patient reach homeostasis again. Except that the world was an infinitely more complex system than a single human being. And then again, making a big wish was like writing a play, with the entire human race as players. Bleh.

She could wish that the bioengineered fungus had never dissolved the world, but then she would be faced with whatever climate disaster the fungus had prevented. She could make a blanket wish that the world would be safe from global disasters for the next thousand years—and maybe unleash a millennium of stagnation. Or worse, depending on the slippery definition of "safe."

She guessed that wishing for a thousand wishes wouldn't work—in fact, that kind of shenanigans might be how Richard Wolf wound up where he was now.

The media server in the panic room had a bazillion movies and TV episodes about the monkey paw, the wishing ring, the magic fountain, the Faustian bargain, the djinn, the vengeance-demon, and so on. So she had plenty of time to soak up the accumulated wisdom of the human race on the topic of making wishes, which amounted to a pile of clichés. Maybe she would have done more good as a playwright than as a doctor, after all—clichés were like plaque in the arteries of the imagination, they clogged the sense of what was possible. Maybe if enough people had worked to demolish clichés, the world wouldn't have ended.

Marisol and Richard sat and watched *The Facts of Life* together. Richard kept complaining and saying things like, "This is worse than being trapped inside a bottle." But he also seemed to enjoy complaining about it.

"This show kept me marginally sane when I was the only person on Earth," Marisol said. "I still can't wrap my mind around what happened to the human race. So, you *are* conscious of the passage of time when you're inside the bottle." She was very careful to avoid phrasing anything as a question.

"It's very strange," Richard said. "When I'm in the bottle, it's like I'm in a sensory deprivation tank, except not particularly warm. I float, with no sense of who or where I am, but meanwhile another part of me is getting flashes of awareness of the world. But I can't control them. I might be hyperaware of one ant carrying a single crumb up a stem of grass, for an eternity, or I might just have a vague sense of clouds over the ocean, or some old woman's aches and pains. It's like hyper-lucid dreaming, sort of."

"Shush," said Marisol. "This is the good part—Jo is about to lay some Brooklyn wisdom on these spoiled rich girls."

The episode ended, and another episode started right away. You take the good, you take the bad. Richard groaned loudly. "So what's your plan, if I may ask? You're just going to sit here and watch television for another few years?" He snorted.

"I have no reason to hurry," Marisol said. "I can spend a decade coming up with the perfect wishes. I have tons of frozen dinners."

At last, she took pity on Richard and found a stash of PBS *American Playhouse* episodes on the media server, plus other random theatre stuff. Richard really liked Caryl Churchill, but didn't care for Alan Ayckbourn. He hated Wendy Wasserstein. Eventually, she put him back in his bottle again.

Marisol started writing down possible draft wishes in one of the three blank journals that she'd found in a drawer. (Burton had probably expected to record his thoughts, if any, for posterity.) And then she started writing a brand-new play, instead. The first time she'd even tried, in a few years.

Her play was about a man—her protagonists were always men—who moves to the big city to become a librarian, and winds up working for a strange old lady, tending her collection of dried-out leaves from every kind of tree in the world. Pedro is so shy, he can't even speak to more than two people, but so beautiful that everybody wants him to be a fashion model. He pays an optometrist to put drops in his eyes, so he won't see the people photographing and lighting him when he models. She had no clue how this play was going to end, but she felt a responsibility to finish it. That's what Mrs. Garrett would expect.

She was still stung by the idea that her prize-winning play was dumb, or worse yet kind of misogynistic. She wished she had an actual copy of that play, so she could show it to Richard and he would realize her true genius. But she didn't wish that out loud, of course. And maybe this was the kick in the ass she needed to write a better play. A play that made sense of some of this mess.

"I've figured it out," she told Richard the next time she opened his bottle. "I've figured out what happened those other times. Someone finds your bottle after the apocalypse, and they get three wishes. So the first wish is to bring the world back and reverse the destruction. The second wish is to make sure it doesn't happen again. But then they still have one wish left. And that's the one where they do something stupid and selfish, like wishing for irresistible sex appeal."

"Or perfect hair," said Richard Wolf, doing his patented eye-roll and air-swat.

"Or unlimited wealth. Or fame."

"Or everlasting youth and beauty. Or the perfect lasagna recipe."

"They probably figured they deserved it," Marisol stared at the pages of scribbles in her hands. One set of diagrams mapping out her new, as-yet-unnamed play. A second set of diagrams trying to plan out the wish-making process, act by act. Her own scent clung to every surface in the panic room, the recirculated and purified air smelled like the inside of her own mouth. "I mean, they saved the world, right? So they've earned fame or sex or parties. Except I bet that's where it all goes wrong."

"That's an interesting theory," said Wolf, arms folded and head tilted to one side, like he was physically restraining himself from expressing an opinion.

Marisol threw out almost every part of her new play, except the part about her main character needing to be temporarily vision-impaired so he can model. That part seemed to speak to her, once she cleared away the clutter about the old woman and the leaves and stuff. Pedro stands, nearly nude, in a room full of people doing makeup and lighting and photography and catering and they're all blurs to him. And he falls in love with one woman, but he only knows her voice, not her face. And he's afraid to ruin it by learning her name, or seeing what she looks like.

By now, Marisol had confused the two processes in her mind. She kept thinking she would know what to wish for, as soon as she finished writing her play. She labored over the first scene for a week before she had the nerve to show it to Richard, and he kept narrowing his eyes and breathing loudly through his nose as he read it. But then he said it was actually a promising start, actually not terrible at all.

The mystery woman phones Pedro up, and he recognizes her voice instantly. So now he has her phone number, and he agonizes about calling her. What's he afraid of, anyway? He decides his biggest fear is that he'll go out on a date with the woman, and people will stare at the two of them. If the woman is as beautiful as Pedro, they'll stare because it's two beautiful people together. If she's plain-looking, they'll stare because they'll wonder what he sees in her. When Pedro eats out alone, he has a way of shrinking in on himself, so nobody notices him. But he can't do that on a date.

At last, Pedro calls her and they talk for hours. On stage, she is partially hidden from the audience, so they, too, can't see what the woman looks like.

"It's a theme in your work, hmmm?" Richard Wolf sniffed. "The hidden person, the flirting through a veil. The self-loathing narcissistic love affair."

"I guess so," Marisol said. "I'm interested in people who are seen, and people who see, and the female gaze, and whatever."

She finished the play, and then it occurred to her that if she made a wish that none of this stuff had happened, her new play could be un-written as a result. When the time came to make her wishes, she rolled up the notebook and tucked it into her waistband of her sweatpants, hoping against hope that anything on her immediate person would be preserved when the world was rewritten.

In the end Pedro agrees to meet the woman, Susanna, for a drink. But he gets some of the eye-dilating drops from his optometrist friend. He can't decide whether to put the drops in his eyes before the date—he's in the men's room at the bar where they're meeting, with the bottle in his hand, dithering—and then someone disturbs him and he accidentally drops the bottle in the toilet. And Susanna turns out to be pretty, not like a model but more distinctive. She has a memorable face, full of life. She laughs a lot, Pedro stops feeling shy around her. And Pedro discovers that if he looks into Susanna's eyes when he's doing his semi-nude modeling, he no longer needs the eye drops to shut out the rest of the world.

"It's a corny ending," Marisol admitted. "But I like it."

Richard Wolf shrugged. "Anything is better than unearned ambivalence." Marisol decided that was a good review, coming from him.

Here's what Marisol wished:

1) I wish this apocalypse and all previous apocalypses had never happened, and that all previous wishes relating to the apocalypse had never been wished.

2) I wish that there was a slight alteration in the laws of probability as relating to apocalyptic scenarios, so that if, for example, an event threatening the survival of the human race has a ten percent chance of happening, that ten percent chance just never comes up, and yet this does not change anything else in the material world.

3) I wish that I, and my designated heirs, will keep possession of this bottle, and will receive ample warning before any apocalyptic scenario comes up, so that we will have a chance to make the final wish.

She had all three wishes written neatly on a sheet of paper torn out of the notebook, and Richard Wolf scrutinized it a couple times, scratching his ear. "That's it?" he said at last. "You do realize that I can make anything real. Right? You could create a world of giant snails and tiny people. You could make *The Facts of Life* the most popular TV show in the world for the next thousand years—which would, incidentally, ensure the survival of the human race, since there would have to be somebody to keep watching *The Facts of Life*. You could do anything."

Marisol shook her head. "The only way to make sure we don't end up back here again is to keep it simple." And then, before she lost her nerve, she picked up the sheet of paper where she'd written down her three wishes, and she read them aloud.

Everything went cheaply glittery around Marisol, and the panic room reshaped into The Infinite Ristretto, a trendy café that just happened to be roughly the same size and shape as the panic room. The blue-leather walls turned to brown brick, with brass fixtures and posters for the legendary all-nude productions of Mamet's *Oleanna* and Marsha Norman's *'night, Mother*.

All around Marisol, friends whose names she'd forgotten were hunched over their laptops, publicly toiling over their confrontational one-woman shows and chamber pieces. Her best friend Julia was in the middle of yelling at her, freckles almost washed out by her reddening face.

"Fuck doctors," Julia was shouting, loud enough to disrupt the whole room.

"Theatre is a direct intervention. It's like a cultural ambulance. Actors are like paramedics. Playwrights are *surgeons*, man."

Marisol was still wearing Burton's stained business shirt and sweatpants, but somehow she'd gotten a pair of flip-flops. The green bottle sat on the rickety white table nearby. Queen was playing on the stereo, and the scent of overpriced coffee was like the armpit of God.

Julia's harangue choked off in the middle, because Marisol was giving her the biggest stage hug in the universe, crying into Julia's green-streaked hair and thanking all her stars that they were here together. By now, everyone was staring at them, but Marisol didn't care. Something fluttery and heavy fell out of the waistband of her sweatpants. A notebook.

"I have something amazing to tell you, Jools," Marisol breathed in Julia's ear. She wanted to ask if Obama was still president and the Cold War was still over and stuff, but she would find out soon enough and this was more important. "Jools, I wrote a new play. It's all done. And it's going to change *everything*." Hyperbole was how Marisol and Julia and all their friends communicated. "Do you want to read it?"

"Are you seriously high?" Julia pulled away, then saw the notebook on the floor between their feet. Curiosity took over, and she picked it up and started to read.

Marisol borrowed five bucks and got herself a pour-over while Julia sat, knees in her face, reading the play. Every few minutes, Julia glanced up and said, "Well, okay," in a grudging tone, as if Marisol might not be past saving after all.

ONE DAY ONLY

TANANARIVE DUE

Tananarive Due is an author, screenwriter, and educator who is
a leading voice in black speculative fiction. Her short fiction has
appeared in magazines such as *The Magazine of Fantasy & Science
Fiction* and *Lightspeed*, and in many anthologies, such as *A People's
Future of the United States*, all three volumes of The Apocalypse
Triptych, and many best-of-the-year volumes. Her first short-story
collection, *Ghost Summer*, won a British Fantasy Award. Due teaches
Afrofuturism and Black Horror at UCLA and in the creative writing
MFA program at Antioch University Los Angeles. A recipient of the
American Book Award and NAACP Image Award, Due is the author/
co-author of twelve novels and a civil-rights memoir, *Freedom in the
Family*. Due frequently collaborates with her husband, Steven Barnes,
including on their YA zombie novels *Devil's Wake* and *Domino Falls*.
She lives in Southern California with Barnes and their son, Jason.
Learn more at tananarivedue.com and @TananariveDue.

Soon

A sound like thunder—if thunder were an army—boomed beneath
Nayima's floorboards, and her living room trembled.

Spray lashed the deck outside her glass door. Then the swell of
sound retreated across drenched sand below, sucking back the roar
as the tide pulled away to marshal its strength.

It was high tide, and a storm might be coming, somewhere beyond the hidden rim of the darkening Pacific she could glimpse through the sheer parted curtains. The ocean swelled beneath her faster than she'd expected, and again the floor tremored. It was like living in a cruise ship, she thought—a ship that never moved or rocked. Rooted.

This apartment was the best place Nayima had ever lived. The best place she ever *would* live, came the silent correction. Maybe the best place, period, now or ever, for anyone. Two years ago, this beachfront apartment might have cost a couple million dollars. She had found it empty and undisturbed, the key not so cleverly hidden beneath a flower pot beside the door at the top of the wooden beach house steps.

No bodies inside. (Hallelujah!) No rotten food anywhere—or not much, anyway. Maybe the owners had been vegan, because only rice, vegetables, and fruit had gone bad in grocery store packages in the freezer. The fridge had been empty except for a pitcher of water and a six-pack of Corona.

The owners clearly had left Malibu in an orderly fashion. The apartment's furniture was simple and mostly disposable, any metal near the windows rusting slightly from the salt water air. It must have been a vacation rental, because she'd found a laminated sheet of instructions explaining the electrical wiring, how to work the huge television's remote, and where to find the towels. Of course, no one in Malibu *had* electricity or working televisions anymore, but the towels in the linen closet were still there and smelled like that fabric softener with the smiling teddy bear. True hospitality.

The waves crashed the boulders and sea wall beneath the apartment again.

"Jesus!" Karen complained from the bedroom. "How do you sleep with that racket?"

Nayima closed her eyes. The sound of the ocean might be keeping her alive, making her relish her aliveness. "How do you stay awake?" Nayima called back.

Other people's tastes were a burden. Nayima had invited Karen to move in only two days ago, and already it felt like a mistake. Nayima had spent weeks, sometimes months, craving conversation with another person who would not try to kill or rob her—or report her to the marshals—but after knowing Karen for less than a week, Nayima was tired of her.

Her complaints. Her pessimism.

Her in general.

Nayima asked herself if she would have tried to like Karen more if Karen were a man, or if *she herself* was a man, but the question felt trite. True, she'd never been in bed with a woman before Karen, but her body liked Karen's warm skin and gentle touch just fine. Karen's sudden kiss was the only reason she'd invited her to move in; otherwise, they might have just kept running into each other on the beach from time to time while they fished and looked for crabs.

To her shock, Karen said she'd never had the vaccine. Another NI—Naturally Immune—was something, anyway. Nayima knew she would have died ten times over by now if she hadn't been immune to the flu, and the same was true of Karen, or probably so for many of the others still finding their way to Malibu. Still, for someone to stride up to you and ask for a kiss was bold, and Nayima had liked the kiss in every way.

Maybe it was the age difference, then. Nayima was only twenty-four, and Karen was forty-five, old enough to be her mother. Or, maybe Nayima couldn't just snap her fingers and fall in love, no matter how few candidates were left. Was that it? She was still being picky?

One for the joke file.

Nayima brought out the notebook she'd begun carrying with her after she escaped the chaos in Bakersfield for a change of scenery. She had intended to use it as a journal, but she couldn't make herself chronicle her story, or any stories, about the flu. Instead, she wrote down thoughts that amused her, like she used to in her theater class at Spelman, the first time a teacher had told her she was funny.

It turns out beggars CAN be choosers, Nayima wrote. She drew a circle, two eyes and a wide O: a surprised face. It made her laugh more loudly than she should have. Even the waves couldn't smother the sound.

Karen came out of the bedroom wearing the white terry cloth robe the owners had left behind the bathroom door: Nayima's robe. When irritation flashed, Nayima thought about Karen's silhouette in the dusk sun when they'd finally stopped circling each other from a wary distance. The law of the beach—the only law, really—was *Don't start none, won't be none.*

Karen was Irish-from-Ireland, so her short, spiky hair was carrot orange and her face was permanently sunburned and peeling, no matter how much sunblock she used. But she was strong, and Nayima thought everywhere her strength showed was lovely: steely eyes, a strong jaw, a body of lean muscle. Karen could haul in fishing nets that were astonishingly heavy. She'd been an airline baggage handler for Delta. Before. Nayima hadn't had time to be anything but a student.

"I wish you wouldn't wear that," Nayima said. "Without asking."

Karen ignored the chide. "I heard you laugh. Were you laughing at me?"

Karen was already reading her notebook over her shoulder and Nayima had too much pride to slam it shut. That, and she wanted Karen to see her jokes. Karen usually said she didn't see the point of jokes; nothing was funny, at least not anymore.

Karen gave a short sigh, pointing at Nayima's last scrawl. "Me?" she said. "Beggars and choosers. I don't get it, really. It's a little mean, isn't it?"

"A little."

"But it made you laugh."

"Obviously I need therapy," Nayima said. *Therapists would be making a killing if they weren't already dead.* She scribbled it down before she forgot.

While Nayima wrote, Karen mulled over the page as if she did not recognize the language. "May I?" she said finally—the way she should have asked about her robe. Without waiting for Nayima's answer, she took the notebook and walked to the love seat, her robe falling open when she sat on folded legs. Nayima watched her face for signs of amusement and saw none. Karen sighed and fidgeted each time the surf roiled beneath the apartment.

"Can we go to the flat I found across the highway?" Karen said. "You can see the water, but it won't be as loud."

Karen's place was practically a shed, the only one she'd found that didn't stink.

"I already have a place I like," Nayima said.

She had long forgotten how to compromise. She had fought hard for her pleasures and would let go of none of them. If there was a silver lining, as people used to say, she'd learned how to stand up for what she wanted.

"These houses right on the beach are the first place they'll look, Neema." Neema might be a nickname, or maybe Karen couldn't remember her actual name. That was how little they knew each other.

"I thought you wanted to move because of the water."

"I can think of a lot of reasons to move. Can't you?"

There. Karen wasn't trying to, but her voice had slipped into Mommy mode. Nayima grinded her teeth. "If you want to sleep somewhere else, you know where to find me, Caitlin."

"Karen," she said. "Not Caitlin."

"Nayima, then. Let's use our actual names."

Gram hadn't raised Nayima to envy or notice blue eyes, but damn if Karen's gray-blue eyes weren't the color of moonlight. Every time Nayima wanted to start a fight, she noticed another aspect of Karen she liked, and this time it was her eyes, even if it was only because they were hers. Nayima wished they were in bed instead of arguing. Her body was waking under Karen's eyes.

"Nayima," Karen said, memorizing her name, her eyes back on the notebook. "I'll get it."

With nothing left to argue about, Nayima was forced to remember the truth of Karen's warning: the marshals would come. She'd driven back southwest to Malibu for the same reasons as everyone else—food, warmth, beauty. Making salt water potable wasn't easy, but it was better than no water at all in the drought regions. She'd hoped she could stop running. She'd hoped maybe this apartment wouldn't just be her *latest* stop, her *best* stop, but her *last* one.

And there were others—not many, but a few. They lived scattered among the beach houses and hillsides, but she had spotted at least ten other people at the pier or on the beach in the three weeks she'd been in Malibu, not counting Karen. She'd chronicled them all in the last page of her notebook, describing her neighbors: a father and two daughters about ten and twelve (she called him Mister Mom, his daughters Flopsy and Mopsy); The Old Man in the Sea who took his rowboat out to fish every day; three rough-looking guys who might be brothers (The Three Stooges) and the Brat Pack, one pimple-faced teenaged boy and two girls, maybe sixteen, who mostly stayed out of sight. There might be more, but on the beach sometimes even with binoculars she couldn't tell if she had seen someone before or if they were new. Like Karen.

The father and daughters moved furtively across the sand in gas masks, always wearing bright blue gloves. They never got close to anyone, so they had survived. Nayima assumed they were not vaccinated—and no way the father and both daughters were immune, if they were related; in any family, maybe *one* would be immune—or one on any street, in any neighborhood. Maybe one or two in each town. A father and two daughters in one family must not have the virus yet.

Good for them. If their blood stayed clean, they might qualify to go to Sacramento. The city had declared itself a separate republic and had electricity, water, crops, livestock. Mr. Mom and his kiddos might rejoice if marshals came.

But not Nayima. Not Karen. Not the immune—though they could not be infected, they were carriers, and rumors said carriers who weren't shot ended up in lab cages. Fuck that. If scientists didn't have enough blood from carriers for the vaccines already, one or two more wouldn't help.

Karen was right about the beach apartment they were in: it was in plain sight on the Pacific Coast Highway, so any vehicle driving by might see them without even trying.

Nayima's breath hitched in her throat as her chest tightened, and she could exhale only when the waves crashed beneath her and seemed to knock the blockage free.

The back of her neck tingled. New anxieties, no matter how big or small, crumbled the wall she'd erected around her memories. The strongest memory charged through: Gram's bloodied pillow case. A cop had shot Gram to force Nayima to evacuate, knowing she would not leave Gram behind. Nayima could still smell the gunpowder and the blood from his treacherous act of mercy.

Karen closed the notebook and said, "These are good."

Nayima wiped her tears, turning her face away. She did not let herself cry often, or she'd never stop. She wasn't ready to share tears with Karen. "What?"

"These jokes. Not all of them, definitely—but some of them are good."

To prove it, Karen smiled. The sea crashed like cymbals to mark the occasion. Nayima had never see Karen smile. Gram's blood-soaked pillowcase washed away with the tide.

"Really?" Karen's smile sparked across Nayima's lips too.

Karen read from Nayima's notes in a deadpan: "'I always wanted to move to Malibu, but I had to wait for the prices to drop.'"

"It's the delivery," Nayima said. "When you say it like that—"

"I'm not a comedian, but I'm just saying, I think it could be funny. To some people."

Some people. That phrase sounded strange, dual plurals in the land of the singular. Nayima noticed faint freckles on Karen's lips and traced them with her fingertip.

"Like… if I did a comedy show?" Nayima said, teasing her.

Karen's lips moved closer. "You can do your show for me."

Except for Nayima's kiss from Darryn Stephens, who had surprised her with a declaration of his affection at a house party when she'd been Brandon Paul's date, kissing mostly had felt like an obligatory activity before sex. But kissing Karen was a discovery each time, an exploration. Nayima could kiss Karen for an hour and lose track of time.

They opened the glass sliding door, and the sound of the ocean became a gale. They waded through the sound to the deck's corner bed, which was covered in a thin blanket damp from saltwater spray. The bathrobe fell away. Nayima tasted the salt on Karen's lips, on her neck, on her shoulders.

They were naked in the moonlight, sharp contrasts wherever their skin touched. When Nayima sang out her pleasure, the ocean answered her. Afterward, they lay together, hugging in the chilly breeze. Nayima thought of how warm it must be inland, where she and Gram had lived. She thought of the ghost cities west of them.

"That day on the beach?" Karen said.

They spent all their days on the beach, but only one day mattered. Nayima grinned.

Karen's short-lived smile was gone. Her voice fell to a whisper, a tear creeping from the corner of her eye. "I didn't know… I was immune."

A cold ball knotted in Nayima's stomach, but she kept her voice playful. "I was a test?" she said. "Cool. I don't mind being your guinea pig."

"No, not that," Karen said. "I said to myself, I'm gonna get it from someone, so it might as well be her—the most beautiful woman left in the world."

Only Gram had called her beautiful. She imagined Gram's face—alive, bloodless.

"You could have killed me," Nayima said. "You didn't know anything about me."

"I swear… I had no idea about me. I expected…"

"A kiss of death?"

"I thought so," Karen said. In her voice, Nayima heard *I hoped so*.

Because it was too terrible, she didn't tell Karen the irony: she *had* killed a man by kissing him. A year and three months ago, she'd met a man on State Road 46 outside of Lost Hills, only briefly. She'd fooled herself into imagining a future together. She hadn't come across a survivor in so long that she'd been eager to latch onto him. And she was sure he was immune, like her.

But no. Only six hours later, he was already sick. Throwing up. Because of her.

Kyle. His name had been Kyle. Nayima didn't think of him often, but she owed him remembering his name. She had leaned over him in the dark, giggling with mischief after he'd asked her, so politely, to stay away. She had kissed him—killed him—in his sleep.

Was Kyle the one standing between her and Karen? Who made her itch to flee? Karen and all of Malibu felt like nothing but a mirage.

The surf's mighty hiss buried the rest of their unspoken words.

By morning, Nayima was using her neatest handwriting to write out her flyer, page after page of repetitive motion, all caps for clarity. Her sweaty hands were sticky inside her gloves, but she didn't want the paper to spread the flu. Whatever she touched might turn to dust.

ONE DAY ONLY –
COMEDY SHOW!!!
FREE WATER
PIER AT PCH
DAWN – FRIDAY

It was Wednesday, so people had two days to hear about the show. Maybe their seaside hamlet would be stable for two more days. Sleeping beside Karen, hearing her breathing between the swells, she'd had a premonition: they should grab their backpacks and leave Malibu. Too many people were coming, and the word would spread. Mister Mom might already have sent out an alarm. Then they would be invaded by marshals looking for carriers to punish for the end of the world.

But Karen had said that *some people* would find her jokes funny. And if that were true, why not give them a show? She'd always wanted to try stand-up comedy, and this was her only chance.

She might give someone their last laugh.

"Free *water*?" Karen said, reading her flyer. As if Nayima had promised the moon.

"I could purify a few cups. There's only about ten."

"You don't know that for sure," Karen said. "People are hiding. Besides, no one will take water from you. They don't know you. They won't go near you. I wouldn't take it. You make your own water, or it's an unopened bottle. That's it. Think like one of *them*."

Karen was in her Mommy mode again. She was insufferable sometimes. Nayima wasn't going to cross off *free water* from every page in her stack. Or deny someone who might not have time to desalinate it themselves.

Nayima made fresh water every day, more than she needed: slowly boiling a covered pot of water with a glass in the center on her deck fire pit, allowing the freshly condensed water to drip into the glass, or simply leaving bowls and glasses wrapped in plastic wrap in the sun. The kitchen cabinet had been full of bowls and glasses to use. Not everyone had that, or even knew how to ensure the water you had was safe to drink. She herself had learned how long ago at camp.

"I'm bringing the water," Nayima said. "It's my show."

Silence. Nayima braced for what she knew Karen wanted to say: "They won't come. Don't expect them to come." A quiet plea.

Karen's shitty attitude again.

Nayima figured the others wouldn't come—they were all fugitives, whether it was from the flu or from flu-hunters, and fugitives did not gather on the bones of the world to take in a show. Hell, either she or Karen—or neither of them—might not make it back to the apartment. But hearing it from Karen infuriated her.

Nayima snatched up her pages and stood up to pack her backpack: her Glock, her key, and the plastic box of thumb tacks she'd found in the kitchen drawer—at least a hundred—with heads in the soft pastel colors of Easter eggs. As an afterthought, she packed a hammer, and water bottles, beef jerky and an extra pair of sneakers were always inside her pack, just in case.

"I'm coming with you," Karen said. "We're not supposed to go out alone, remember?"

That had been Karen's rule, not Nayima's, and probably served Karen more. If trouble came, Nayima might not have time to slow down and see after Karen, which she told Karen with a look. Nayima had made her no promises of heroics and she didn't expect heroics in return, but Karen's hangdog eyes wanted to stay with her always. Karen might kill or die for her.

Why did that simple *caring* repel her so much?

"Come on, then," Nayima said. "Post office first."

The post office closest to her apartment was a twenty-minute walk on the Pacific Coast Highway, in a small roadside strip mall modeled after a frontier town, with wood facades and old-fashioned lettering. Most of the other storefronts' windows were broken or partially burned out, but the post office was still in good shape even though the door was unlocked. Most people weren't looking for anything the post office had to offer—except announcements and notices.

The Daykeeper had come and gone. On the door, Nayima found the newest sign tacked into the wood: the day, date and year stenciled in bright red paint. Someone spent time and care spray-painting each sign and came each morning to post a new one. Beside it, an older paper flyer flapped in the breeze, from weeks or months before: *SURVIVORS—REPORT TO SACRAMENTO FOR TESTING & VACCINE* above an Eagle crest proclaiming *REPUBLIC OF SACRAMENTO AUTHORITY*.

Nayima chuckled every time she saw the sign. Traveling four-hundred miles on the Five was easier said than done, even if you had a car and gas. And "Authority" was a stretch. The Daykeeper, whoever they were, had more authority in Malibu.

Also, the sign had implied fine print: if you tested positive for antibodies, you were a carrier. And no carrier in her right mind would report to anyone.

Another older sign read: CERTIFIED VACCINATIONS!!!! At her feet lay the litter of old vaccine needle packs from a long-ago drop or visit from Sacramento. At one time, more survivors had lived here. Like Karen, they had stayed hidden and missed the worst of the plague. Karen had said she'd heard helicopters and megaphones about six months before, but she'd thought she had dreamed them. And she had been afraid to show herself, ready to die.

Nayima didn't go inside the post office to see the bulletin board, which she already knew was crammed with index cards and paper scraps from long ago, people searching for loved ones or trying to pass on news of the plague. She doubted that there had been many reunions. Instead, Nayima tacked her flyer beside Sacramento's, struggling to drive the tack into the sturdy wood. She should have brought nails instead, she realized. But four pretty little tacks would hold it in place for a couple of days.

Nayima stepped back and assessed the flyer, only wishing she had included her name. Still, the simple proclamation felt like her finest moment since the flu began. Even Karen exhaled a *hnh* sound as if to say: *OK, I get it now*.

One Day Only. Three words evoked excitement. Joy, even. What was the name of that baseball movie with the line *If you build it, they will come*? And even if they didn't come, the sign was hopeful. Maybe hope could be contagious.

Karen moved closer as if to hug her, but Nayima pulled away.

"No," Nayima said. "Someone might see." She couldn't help glancing around to see if anyone was nearby. The only movement was from seagulls wheeling toward the surf.

"So what? There's a vaccine," Karen said.

"I bet none of these people have seen a vaccine," Nayima said. "That's still just a myth until there's a better supply line. Trust me, they'd just assume we're carriers who don't give a damn about getting infected. It's a quick way to draw a bullet."

"You have so many reasons," she murmured.

"Reasons for what?"

"That I should go piss off. I just wanted to celebrate a leaflet."

Kyle had tried to keep Nayima away from him too; maybe she had learned the habit from him. But if she stayed with Karen, she would get killed or caught one day. Karen wasn't careful enough. She'd been too spoiled in her Ventura County hideaway, so far from the bigger cities and the roads. Everyone Karen knew was dead too, but she still had no fucking idea.

"Every morning, I half expect you to be gone," Karen said. "Is that the way it'll be? You'll be a phantom in the night? Like I dreamed you?"

Probably, Nayima thought. "I don't know," she said instead.

"I would have loved you even in the real world."

Nayima looked at her, startled. Only Gram had loved her, and her best friend Shanice, and her cousins in Baldwin Hills. No one else. She had dated and fucked, but she had never *made love* before the flu. Karen looked lovely in that moment, her face framed against a palm tree and the clear morning sky the color of a postcard. Nayima could imagine how she looked to Karen's eyes: like a future. The beauty in Malibu was a lie.

"*This* is the real world," Nayima said. "Get used to that before you start using words like 'love.'"

The light left Karen's eyes before Nayima turned away.

Even at the end of the world, everyone wanted to come to Malibu.

The Pacific Coast Highway was still clogged. That was Malibu's greatest drawback—still. Nayima had visited Malibu with friends on spring break in her senior year of high school, when most of her friends had been white and thought vacations were for skiing and surfing. As novice drivers they had felt they were taking their lives into their hands to try to master the manic traffic on the PCH. No one slowed down for almost any reason, driving as if they would live forever.

Now, cars snaked up and down in both directions as far as the eye could see, bumpers almost locked together. Most of them were coffins with a view, and too many of the windows were open, but the sea air had long ago washed away the odor, accelerating decomposition so that the sight of near-skeletal drivers and passengers was far worse than the smell.

She and Karen grew hushed as they crossed the PCH back toward the pier, past the proud parents of Honor Roll Students and U.S. Marines and those who'd had Babies on Board. The sight of a child's remains still strapped into a car seat had haunted Nayima's dreams for two nights, so she never let her eyes wander, focusing on the rusting hoods and bumpers instead. A few of the cars' windows were spray-painted over, someone's valiant attempt at neighborhood beautification.

But maybe it was only fitting that they could never escape the dead.

The whitewashed structures lining either side of the Malibu Pier entrance made Nayima think of a Moorish castle, except for a tacky blue sign above that once had glowed in neon.

MALIBU SPORT FISHING PIER
LIVE BAIT & CHARTER BOATS

She surveyed the area, deciding she would do her stand-up act closer to the sidewalk rather than on the pier itself. She would build a stage just far enough away from the road that the corpses in the stalled cars wouldn't ruin her act, but far enough from the ocean that her voice wouldn't be washed out in the waves.

So much to think about. So much planning to do.

Working on her own now, Nayima used the sole of her shoe to tack a flyer to a wooden bus bench advertising a law office. She and Karen had found a steady pace together as they walked up and down the highway, so they had posted all but two of the flyers by the time they reached the pier itself. No matter. She would come back and post more flyers the next day.

A sudden motion from the pier shocked her. The Old Man in the Sea was shuffling toward them with a bucket in one knobby hand and a fishing rod over his shoulder. His face was nearly hidden in the tangle of his white hair and wild beard. Nayima wondered if he had any other clothes except his tattered fisherman's raincoat.

He wasn't wearing a dust mask, so he slowed when he saw them, changed the angle of his approach through the walkway. Karen followed Nayima's lead and backed away from him, giving him a wide passage—which turned out to be a good thing, because a mighty stink of unwashed skin and clothes walked with him. He hesitated, as if he wondered if they might try to steal his catch.

Nayima pointed to the sign. "I'm doing a comedy show," she said. "Right here, in two days. I hope you'll come."

He shuffled to the sign on the bus bench and read it a long time, as if it were much longer than a dozen words. Then he turned to look at her, assessing her. From his sour face, he found her unfit for the task.

"George Carlin," he said.

She'd heard of George Carlin, but she'd never seen his act. "Kind of like that, I guess," she said. "Except—"

"Richard Pryor," he interrupted.

She *knew* Richard Pryor. One of her few memories of her father was when he'd come over three or four times the summer when she was sixteen and, with nothing else to talk about, he'd put on Richard Pryor standup DVDs, turning the volume lower and lower until they could barely hear it because Gram was in the next room. Then he'd gone back to the Philippines, where he was stationed in the Army. Nayima wondered how the Philippines had fared with the plague.

"Pryor's a lot to live up to, but I'll do my best," Nayima said. She remembered Pryor's routine after he went to the hospital for freebasing, and the one after his heart attack, and wondered what he would have said about the apocalypse.

"She's very funny," Karen assured the old man.

He scowled at Nayima, then at Karen, then back at Nayima. Both of them were wearing masks and gloves, but she felt naked, as if he could see the antibodies in their blood. As if he knew what she had done to Kyle.

"More vaccine's coming," he said. "Radio said so."

They both thanked the Lord above. Nayima felt a sting in her eyes as she summoned tears that would look like joy. Her theater classes had not been wasted like Gram had said they would be.

"Did the radio say when?" Nayima said, trying to sound eager instead of terrified.

Nayima did not have a radio; she'd broken it on the way to Malibu. Also, there were no batteries in her apartment—she'd looked—so a radio wouldn't do her any good.

He shrugged and began walking on with his fish. He swung one stiff leg, his gait uneven. Water from his bucket splashed. His bare feet were gray with grime, toenails blackened.

"Free water!" Nayima called after him. "Tell your…" She almost said *friends*. "… You know… Other people."

He kept walking without looking back. "Jerry Seinfeld!" he said, like an epithet.

She would have to bring up her joke game to get this withered old grouch to laugh, especially if he was comparing her to comedy legends. How was that even fair?

"Well, shit," Karen said, once he was out of earshot. "What happens to… us?"

"I'm not gonna stick around to find out," Nayima said.

I, not, *we*.

Not *us*.

Nayima did not sleep that night.

Karen had said they should leave Malibu by morning, but now Nayima understood the meaning of the phrase *The show must go on*. While Karen sobbed in the bedroom, Nayima worked by candlelight at the living room table to write flyers, even though she knew she should be writing more jokes. She wanted to prove herself, but there was no point in honing her material if no one would hear about her show. She doubted the old fisherman would tell anyone to come. And if *he* showed up, he'd be a heckler for sure.

Nayima finished the entire ream of paper: a stack of two-hundred. She hadn't been so excited about a project since years before the plague. Maybe ever.

By the end of the next day, Malibu was Nayimatown. Her flyers were everywhere; clamped beneath windshield wipers on empty cars, tacked to telephone poles, pinned beneath rocks atop the giant beach boulders. She'd remembered every spot where she'd seen Mister Mom or The Three Stooges or The Brat Pack, where anyone might be likely to go. While she placed the flyers, she ran over her act in her mind. She might not have a notebook one day, so she would need to be able to rely on her memory.

Karen did not hang flyers with her the second day. She was packing.

Nayima was always packed. She wore her world on her back.

On the day of the show, Nayima set out with her backpack before a hint of daylight. She did not want to see the apartment in sunlight, or she might come back. She locked the door and kicked the key down over the railing to the sand below so she would not be tempted to return. The tide would bury the key or sweep it away.

Karen followed her, but neither of them spoke. They were each carrying a plastic crate that would serve as Nayima's stage, to give her a small height advantage, a touch of grandness. The surf's music followed them, coaxing tears from Nayima. She would miss the ocean wherever she went next. Karen had a backpack too— with far too much inside. Karen was already breathing hard under the weight of her pack. She would not last. They had been walking for fifteen minutes before Nayima realized her tears might be for Karen.

"Let me take your crate," Nayima said. "I can carry both."

She knew Karen had only offered to carry one of the crates to be useful to her. Nayima had sterilized extra water bottles for the audience, so her backpack was much heavier too.

"You were right," Karen said, "I packed too much."

"It's OK."

Karen's sigh was more a silent wail. "Nothing is OK, Nayima."

"I mean don't worry about it now. When we get there, decide what to leave behind."

She saw Kyle's slack, sleeping lips like a photograph. *I'm sorry*, she whispered to him. She had to leave Kyle behind too if she was going to make room for Karen. Or anyone.

Now that the day had arrived, she almost hoped no one would come see the show. She and Karen needed the extra water for themselves. Karen had been honest about what she thought, and at great cost. Honesty was the greatest treasure left; maybe the only one that mattered.

"I'll try not to be like this all the time," Nayima said. "I can be better."

"Me too," Karen said.

Nayima's heart sped with the rising tide, as if it were wind pushing her. As soon as the show was over, if there were a show at all, she would search the driveways and parking lots for a working car with keys. Maybe she could get one to start. She'd once found a PT Cruiser that had driven her straight to paradise, and maybe she could find a vehicle that would let her drive there again.

They could.

The skyline shone in the barest pink, just enough to show the silhouette of the pier's sign ahead. And below it... vague shadows. Movement. Or was it her imagination?

"Someone's there," Karen said.

Karen sounded happy, but Nayima's chest cinched with ice. Silently, Nayima held out her arm to stop Karen's quickening pace. She gestured to the side, and they crouched behind a Dumpster on the side of an old surf shop. Karen groaned from the weight of her pack.

As the light grew, Nayima recognized The Old Man in the Sea. He had brought a folding chair and was already sitting, dressed as he'd been the day before.

"Holy shit," Nayima said. "He came."

Karen clasped her shoulder and shook her. "Aren't those the kids and their dad? Look. Over by the sign?"

The father and his two children looked elephantine in silhouette because they were wearing gas masks, but they were ten yards from the old man, keeping distance even from each other. Four! Four was a good crowd, half of the town's remaining population.

But two were kids—she would have to keep her act clean.

Since no marshals were in sight, she and Karen resumed their walk to the pier. She chose a spot a few yards away from the old man's chair, far closer to the PCH than she'd planned, but she didn't want to ask him to move. She would do her routine without looking at the cars.

Nayima felt shy beneath the strangers' stares, under the weight of what they needed and her promises to them. She opened her backpack and stood ten water bottles upright, fighting common sense that told her to keep it.

"Here's the free water," she said. "It's desalinated, but go on and boil it. I boiled the bottles too, but you can use gloves."

When Nayima stepped back, no one stepped forward for the water. Good.

She measured the space in the center of the pier's walkway to set up her crates. While Karen offered her a hand to steady herself, Nayima climbed up and tested her balance with one foot on each. The crates were not quite even, rocking her like she was surfing.

Nayima wished the sun rose in the west, but the dawn sky was growing bright with resolve, washing everything in pink and lilac like the colors of her thumbtacks.

"We're up here!" she heard Karen shout out behind her, motioning to someone from farther down the pier. Nayima hoped Karen had sense enough not to be hailing marshals.

"There's, like, six more of them," Karen told her, excited.

Two members of the Brat Pack had come in dust masks and blue gloves, a new young couple who looked carefree in beach clothes and light jackets. Most of the faces were new: a brown man with three women of different hues, all of them taller than him, all four of them hiding their faces behind clean, colorful scarves. Their clothes were clean too. One of the women was wearing perfume, even.

"Are you from Sacramento?" one of the women said, hopeful inside her purple scarf.

Nayima shook her head. She repeated her spiel about the free water, so the woman in the purple scarf walked up to take a bottle in her gloved hands. She motioned to Nayima, asking if she could take two, and Nayima nodded. The woman offered one bottle to the old fisherman, and he shook his head, waving her away. He was not wearing gloves.

Nayima counted: twelve people had gathered in Malibu! She had not been in the company of so many others in more than a year, almost since the plague began.

"It's great to be here!" Nayima proclaimed.

The crowd, stone silent before she'd spoken, transformed into a rousing amen corner. The old man was already smiling. Their clapping was muted by their gloves.

Nayima was so shocked by their response that she almost forgot her first joke. She'd planned to open with the joke Karen liked about Malibu prices going down, but it felt wrong now, especially with the car tombs in view. Why were most of her jokes about the lost?

She blurted: "I went swimming in the ocean the other day—my friend said, 'Aren't you afraid of the sharks?' I said 'No, I'm only afraid of the lifeguards.'"

She'd rushed it. Her delivery had been bland.

But their laughter nearly rocked Nayima from her unsteady crates. The bearded man laughed so loudly that the approaching tide could not smother him. He pointed at her, head turned over his shoulder to be sure everyone knew she was there. Farther back, the children squealed and tugged at each other, until their father separated them. Most of them applauded.

Nayima told every joke she could think of, every joke she had ever known. She raised her voice until she was hoarse so everyone would hear her punchlines. Their smiles were hidden, and sometimes the waves drowned them out, but she saw laughing in their eyes. She luxuriated in so many eyes. Especially Karen's—staring at her as if she were the goddess Yemayah rising from the sea.

Nayima smiled at Karen, her hand over her heart to say: *I love you.* She didn't know if it were true yet, or if loving was possible anymore, but Karen deserved to be loved as much as these strangers deserved to laugh. As much as these children deserved a childhood. As much as they all deserved a memory without claws.

Nayima did not stop her show—not at first—even when she heard the faraway *chop-chop-chop* sound of helicopters and saw the swarm of black dots advancing in the morning sky.

BLACK, THEIR REGALIA

DARCIE LITTLE BADGER

Darcie Little Badger is a Lipan Apache geoscientist and writer. Her short fiction, nonfiction and comics have appeared in multiple places, including *Love Beyond Body, Space, and Time*, *Strange Horizons*, *Fantasy Magazine*, *The Dark*, and *Deer Woman: an Anthology by Native Realities*. She currently lives on both coasts but will always be home along the Kuné Tsé.

Outside, the quarantine train was unblemished white. Where its tracks skirted populated regions, barbed wire and warning signs—DANGER! ¡PELIGRO! INFECTIOUS MATERIALS! ¡SUSTANCIAS INFECCIOSAS!—discouraged trespassers from marking the cars with spray paint.

The interior was another story. In her cabin, a narrow sleeper with four beds (one for Screaming Moraine, one for Fiddler Kristi, one for Drummer Tulli, and one for their carry-on luggage, several densely packed grocery bags, and an electric violin), Tulli found graffiti scrawled near her upper bunk.

Amber Smythe was here
I LOVE JON HUYNH
Kallie + Brett + Austin Klark August 17-18
FOR A GOOD TIME, CALL THE CDC
god help us

Tulli fished a leather-piercing needle from her sewing kit. With marks like spider silk, she etched: *The Apparently Siblings rode the White Train.*

Tulli, Moraine, and Kristi were only siblings in the spiritual way; their band name was a response to all the strangers who asked, "Are you triplets?"

When she felt thorny—so almost always—Kristi responded, "Because Natives look alike? No. Well. We might have the same great-uncle. He gotta *reputation.*"

"Hey! Tulli! Are you defacing the train?" Moraine shouted, as if she couldn't hear him across three feet of recirculated air. "Don't write our names! I'd rather not pay a fine."

"Uh oh. I wrote our band name already."

"Don't worry," Kristi said. "There's no chance anybody will recognize it."

So the Apparently Sibs weren't remotely famous, but they'd been off to a promising start before the plague spread. On average, they played four paid shows a month and had sixty followers on Twitter (sixty-three, if you counted their mothers). With enough time, they could have serenaded the right person, signed a contract, and toured the world. Or, at the very least, toured states outside Texas.

Now, their on-stage corpse paint seemed like a premonition. What little humankind knew about the Big Plague pointed to a grim, albeit sluggish, prognosis. The poor souls who carried the strain had a year, more or less. Could be enough time to find a cure. Maybe even enough time to mobilize the largest treatment plan in human history. Unfortunately, some people crashed fast, their nervous systems torn apart.

A rap on the door announced breakfast: oatmeal and tea. The twenty-something, freckled nurse, Jon—is he the Jon of wall graffiti fame, Tulli wondered—prepared the food with automaton efficiency and took their temperatures. Ninety-nine, ninety-eight, one hundred and one point nine. Kristi was running a vigorous fever already.

"Can we do anything to slow her symptoms?" Tulli asked. Like all White Train nurses, Jon was a carrier, immune to the virus but contagious. Lucky: a hazmat suit would obscure the sympathetic crinkles around his eyes.

"Possibly," he said. "The doctors at Mariposa Compound will do everything they can." Jon dropped the disposable thermometer tips down a biohazard chute near the door. He hesitated in the exit, gazing beyond Tulli's head, as if distracted by a memory. "Goodbye, then," he said. "Call if you need anything."

During breakfast, Tulli and Moraine hovered over Kristi, prepared to steady trembling hands as she drank lukewarm black tea. Full-body shakes were a late-stage plague symptom, but they begin with subtle tremors, and Kristi shivered when she choked down the dregs in her cup.

"It's just chilly," Moraine said, wrapping a black Pendleton blanket around Kristi's shoulders. "We need sunlight. Open the curtains."

"Good idea." Tulli obliged, revealing the yellow desert. There were mountains in the distance and barrel cacti in the foreground. Nearby, a bird's tattered, desiccated corpse hung from a coil of barbed wire. "You should both have a nap," she suggested. "Terrible scenery."

The Apparently Siblings first met during the Maria de Soto University Pow Wow and Cake Walk for Charity. As poor college freshmen, they were enticed by the one hundred dollar "best student intertribal dancer" prize, not community togetherness or actual dancing, pinkie swear. Tulli had to scour the boxes in her dorm room to find her neglected dancing regalia: turkey feather fan, knee-high doeskin boots, and thirty-pound jingle dress. It had been years since her last pow wow, and the dress clutched her hips and arms, uncomfortably tight. *Do it for money*, she thought. *And maybe you'll win a free cake, too. German chocolate would taste so good right now.*

That year, the MdSUPWCWC, normally held on the soccer field, was moved to the indoor gymnasium in defiance of sparking, mountainous clouds overhead. The drum group sat in the center circle of the basketball court. They were surrounded by the dancing ring and crowded benches for participants.

Tulli noticed Moraine on the bench next to hers. Under the vibrant red fringe and sunset-colored beadwork that covered his grass dancer regalia, he resembled somebody in her music composition class, the kid who always answered Dr. Brumford's rhetorical questions.

"Are you a music student at de Soto?" she asked.

"Yeah!" He lowered his Navajo taco to shake her hand. "I'm Moraine, like the glacial deposit. That's a well-crafted jingle dress."

"Thanks. My mom made it."

"Blue suits you."

"Maybe, but I wanted black and orange. Halloween colors. Mom hates the holiday."

"Mine does, too! She thinks focusing on death and gloomy junk attracts evil."

"My mom says I have ghost sickness."

"What?"

"A mental shroud, a preoccupation with death, a fearful obsession that manifests as physical illness and psychic anguish. So basically I'm haunted because my favorite movie is *Ringu*."

Moraine laughed.

"What if it's real, though?" Tulli asked.

"You believe in the supernatural?"

Tulli shrugged. "I'm skeptical, but Moms have been right before."

"Let's test it. My throat hurts, and you're wearing a jingle dress."

"Okay?"

"Jingle dancing is supposed to heal people, right?"

"Maybe. It healed at least one person. Like a hundred and fifty years ago. Reputedly. An Ojibwe girl, I think? Dunno, man." Jingle dresses, draped with hollow silver cones, clang with every leap. Tulli loved their rhythm, that's all. She knew zilch about the origin of the dance, its significance. Not like they taught that in public school.

"Try to heal me," Moraine insisted. "I want to believe."

A young woman—fancy shawl dancer, her regalia cluttered with shades of yellow and pink—stepped between Tulli and Moraine. "First," she said, "ghosts are real. They look like shadows, and your jingle dress test doesn't prove anything. Actually, it's borderline offensive, so don't let respectable people hear you. Second: I think you're both in my music composition class. Hey. I'm—"

"Kristi," Moraine said. "Yeah, I know! Great to officially meet you!"

They spent the pow wow arguing about ghosts—Moraine insisted that the shadowy figures Kristi saw at night were symptoms of sleep paralysis, Kristi thought he was just scared of the unfathomable truth, and Tulli remained noncommittal. However, they didn't annoy each other too much, so friendship inevitably blossomed.

None of them won the competition. That prize went to a hoop dancer math major.

Five years later, Tulli truly loved her buddies. She couldn't envision better people to live with. To die with.

Hopefully, the death part would take its sweet time.

The White Train's mechanical heartbeat, a low whir that sounded nothing like the *chug, chug, chug* in movies, was punctuated by Tulli's fingers drumming on the windowsill and her steel-toed boots tapping the vinyl floor. They were nearing the Mojave Desert, where several compounds, including Mariposa, treated high-threat contagious citizens away from the lucky uninfected.

Kristi's reflection appeared in the glass, her wide eyes transposed over the cloudless sky. The Pendleton fell in a heap at her feet.

"Sorry, Hon," Tulli said, turning. "Did my drumming disturb you?"

"My dream…" Kristi pointed to a silhouette that cut the white-blue sky with long, sharp wings. "She was in my dream."

"That's just a turkey vulture. Strange. I didn't know they lived here. Don't quote me on that before I Google it, though. Go back to—"

"She sent them. They're her children, vultures. Eating… eating sick, old meat. To help make the world clean."

"What? Whose children?"

"The Plague Eater." With a sleepwalker's drowsy gait, Kristi stumbled back to bed, pulling the cotton sheet up to her chin and murmuring something about dancing. Tulli tucked the Pendleton over her friend.

"What?" Moraine asked, waking. "Did Kristi have a nightmare? Must be exciting. I'd love to experience her brain for just one REM cycle."

"Nightmares aren't pleasant, last I checked."

"Better than the tedious junk I experience. This time, I dreamed of notes in the major key."

"You're a true musician, Moraine."

"Guess I'll try again." He pulled the sheets up to his chin. "Hey."

"Yeah?"

"Keep an eye on her, okay?"

"I promise."

Once her friends drifted off to sleep, Tulli sat on the end of Kristi's bunk and held her hand. The muscles in her long fingers—a violinist's fingers, spidery and dexterous—tensed, relaxed, and tensed. Her livelihood, if not her life, was rapidly expiring.

Where were the powers their mothers swore by? The great forces that heal faithful children and make bodies strong? "I'll do anything," Tulli whispered. "You just need to ask."

In the silence that followed, she chuckled. The Apparently Siblings reveled in gallows humor. It was much nicer than weeping.

Later, as the train chugged through Mariposa Compound, it passed rows of white barracks with slatted pitch roofs. Laundry lines, sun-bleached plastic toys, and potted plants cluttered the residential grounds. The train stopped between sprawling, nearly identical facilities. To the right: a hospital. To the left: a community center. Beyond them were convenience shops, the kindergarten to twelfth-grade school, a computer lab, a library, and a cafeteria. Tulli had memorized her compound map during the trip, knew where every facility was located. Where she and her siblings would live. Where they would be treated. Where they could eat, rehearse, and hang out. Where they would be memorialized, if the plague consumed them.

Nurse Jon helped load their bags on a trolley. "I have to ask something," he said. "Are you three related?"

"Because we look alike?" Kristi asked.

"Excuse me, Miss. I don't meet many goths."

"You're my new favorite person, Jon," Tulli said. "Our style is closer to neoclassical alt-metal fusion than goth."

"Here's why I asked," Jon said. "They house men and women separately in Mariposa Compound unless you're family or dating."

Moraine shook his head. "I see," he said. "We have the same great-uncle. Will that do? I can't convincingly pretend to date a woman."

"Hopefully. Good luck, you three." Jon escorted them outside, stealing a breath of fresh air before ducking back into the White Train.

Thanks to their apocryphal great-uncle, the Apparently Siblings shared a bedroom that was originally designed for one patient. Imperceptibly tinier than their efficiency apartment in McAllen, the close quarters did not bother Tulli. At least they had a window. Granted, it overlooked a blank white wall, one of the neighboring barracks.

"The internet broke again," Kristi said, prodding her laptop. She'd been bedridden for three days, shivering under her covers and racing to finish her memoirs before the illness made typing impossible. "I'm supposed to call my parents in twenty minutes."

"There's a landline in the common area," Moraine said.

"I want to see them."

Tulli peered out the window, her back to the other siblings. During sunset, the blank wall resembled a cool flame: vivid orange, blushing darker, slipping into shadow. "How's your family doing?" she asked.

"Still healthy, but worry will kill 'em before any virus, at this rate," Kristi said.

Orange became rust, red, black. Tulli rapped a shrill toy drum she borrowed from the K to 12 music room. Pacing, Moraine hummed the tune he dreamed on the White Train. Kristi finished her memoirs with a discontented sigh. At nightfall, they all climbed into bed. Breakfast ended at nine sharp, and the meal lines got longer every day. "What's the opposite of a vampire?" Moraine asked. "'Cause I feel like one. It's unnatural, this early-to-bed schedule."

Tulli pretended to be asleep. If she responded, Moraine would chatter well into late-night-early-morning. The last time that happened, they overslept and missed both breakfast and lunch.

She could hear Kristi shifting, shuddering, contorting under the Pendleton blanket with whispering *shif, shif, shifs*. Plague-triggered muscle spasms: most people called them slow death throes. It was like a dance, a terrible dance.

In the hypnagogic realm between awake and asleep, where dreams poisoned reality, a shadow stood proudly against the wall. It possessed eyes: unblinking, round, yellow eyes with pupils that swallowed Tulli's soul, two points of space-time singularity from which nothing could escape.

Drumbeats rang—*rap, RAP, rap*—and the shadow began to spin. It revolved clockwise around the walls, and when the circle was completed, a final, thunderous *rap* rang out, punctuated by the sound of breaking glass.

Tulli leapt to her feet; the window near her bed had cracked. Cautiously, she peeked outside. "Whoa!" A wake of turkey vultures stumbled drunkenly below the window, stunned by their impacts against the glass. One by one, they alighted, until all that remained were three tail feathers piled in the dust.

"Hyuh!" Moraine said, patting his pillow-ruffled punk pompadour. "I just had the worst case of sleep paralysis."

Kristi, wrapped in black wool, said, "It was a dancing ghost. Unless you believe in shared hallucinations?"

"What about shared visions?" Tulli asked. "Guys. This may be our jingle dance moment. I think we've been chosen."

"By whom?" Moraine said.

"No idea. Hold your imperious retort while I grab those feathers."

As Tulli entered the alley, she heard a radio muttering through a neighbor's cracked window. The static-thickened voice said, "I looked, and behold, an ashen horse; and he who sat on it had the name Death." Tulli was not religious, but, as a fan of horror movies and the novel *Good Omens* by Neil Gaiman and Terry Pratchett, she knew all about the four horsepeople of the Apocalypse, color- and noun-themed riders who emerged during the End Times.

The moon was full and high, its light spilling into the alley between barracks. When the radio preacher concluded, "... to kill with sword and with famine and with pestilence and by the wild beasts of the earth," Tulli pressed the turkey vulture feathers over her eyes, blocking the obnoxious white globe. They were so dark, Tulli wondered if their vanes devoured more light than the blackest material on Earth, a forest of carbon nanotubes constructed by Japanese scientists, her personal STEM heroes.

"Not today, Apocalypse," she said.

Inside, Moraine and Kristi were fussing. Nostalgia washed over Tulli; she thought about the day they met. How little things changed, even when everything changed.

"The virus causes hallucinations when it damages the temporal lobe," Moraine said. "Shadows are common."

"We all saw a woman spinning around our bedroom as turkey vultures smacked rhythmically into the window."

"Okay. Sure. What makes you believe she was teaching us a special dance?"

"Powerful dances come from visions. That's what my mother taught me. That's what her mother taught her. That's how I know what I know."

"Don't take this the wrong way: if your ancestors knew powerful dances, why aren't we ruling the world right now?"

"We're holding our own," Tulli interrupted.

"And dying," he said.

"The whole world is dying. Seems like the perfect time for higher powers to reawake. You're a singer. I'm a drummer. Kristi is a dancer... until her hands work again. We're going to respect the vision that danced across our wall tonight. What's the worst that could happen?"

"Nothing," he said.

"*Nothing* would be the very worst," Kristi agreed.

"Right. Nothing. Moraine, I'm scared of nothing right now."

He bit his lip, contemplative. "All right. Let's get started, Ladies. Kristi needs regalia. What was the vision dancer wearing?"

"A dress?" Kristi said. "And a shawl? It's hard to tell. The whole thing was a shadow."

"A shadow..."

They needed black fabric. Lots of it.

The first flier the Apparently Siblings pinned to the community message board was short and informative:

BLACK FABRIC NEEDED
FOR A DANCE CEREMONY!

*Hóóyíí! Please consider donating used clothes, thread, buttons,
etc. A collection box is outside our door (Barrack 19, Room 3).
FYI: you won't need mourning suits once we destroy the virus
with sick (but not actually sick) rhythm and motion. :D Cheers!
Tulli+Moraine+Kristi of Apparently Siblings fame*

The flier only attracted one donation, a pair of black wool socks.
Somebody also offered to DJ their "plague prom." Undeterred, they
tried again:

BLACK FABRIC NEEDED

*Hóóyíí! We are Apache/Navajo. Ceremonial dances have social
and religious power in our communities. For example, we dance
to honor veterans, win cakes, and appeal to grand forces. It's a
fact! Please help us perform a dance for community wellness.
Leave used black clothing outside Barrack 19, Room 3. Thank
you, bless you, and thank you again! Tulli+Moraine+Kristi*

In came donations of lace-trimmed dresses, conservative blouses,
and skirts: outfits made from silk, cotton, polyester, and rayon
blends that were dyed every conceivable shade of black.

First, Tulli and Moraine crafted the dress with cotton and
synthetic scraps, stitching a patchwork skin over Kristi's body, its
voluminous skirt trimmed by lace and tulle from mourning veils.

Next, they made her ankle-high moccasins by taping faux leather
from a wannabe motorcycle jacket around her flip-flops. "I know
we're amateurs, but I'd look better wearing garbage bags on my feet,"
Kristi said.

"They have charm," Moraine promised.

"What will we do about the shawl?" she asked. "The ghost was
definitely wearing one."

"Voilà!" Tulli draped the black Pendleton blanket around Kristi's
shoulders. "All it needs is fringe. I'll start shredding socks."

As the pièce de résistance, Tulli fashioned three hair clips from
the tail feathers. She thanked the turkey vultures; from rachis to

barbed vane, their gifts held the plague eater's blessing. Plus, those vultures had kicked her off the fence straddling belief and denial. *Cathartes* species didn't live in the Mojave Desert; Tulli absolutely knew their territory because she Googled "where do turkey vultures live" after Kristi noticed one outside the White Train. Indeed, those birds were scientific proof of the supernatural; they had to be sent by powers greater than nature: spirits, ghosts, gods. All of the above?

"Are you ready?" she asked, pinning the blue-black feather to Kristi and the brown-black feather to Moraine.

"Shouldn't we practice?" he asked. "I've only heard this song in my head. What if I can't hit the high notes?"

"No time. The virus ruins lives every hour. Plus, Kristi's boots are falling apart, and we won't find another free motorcycle jacket. Do you want to scrap your leather pants, Buddy? It's now or never."

As the Apparently Siblings marched outside, turkey vulture groupies landed on the barrack rooftops. Neighbors peered out windows and gathered in dirt streets to marvel at the birds. Some people leaned against canes or shivered atop wheelchairs, their faces tilted skyward. "They think we're carrion!" a man said, laughing at his own gallows joke. Nobody else would.

"Follow us!" Moraine shouted. "To the memorial courtyard!"

The vultures—two, three, four dozen—swooped from their perches and hopped-waddled-hobbled after the Apparently Siblings, their wings spread for balance. Draped from head to toe in black, Kristi led the procession, supported by her two friends. With the setting sun at their backs, their shadows stretched ahead of them and parted the light that fell against the glittering white stones in the circular courtyard. A pillar—white marble, nine feet high—jutted from the belly of the courtyard. Its bronze plaque read: **IN MEMORIAM**. Already, several names had been etched into the base of the pillar, but there remained room for thousands on its blank faces: one canvas that Tulli hoped would remain empty. She crouched against the eastward-facing side and beheld the night encroaching.

"What's with the birds? Everybody go inside! Back to your rooms, please!"

Was that security speaking? A doctor or administrator? Though the voice was magnified by a bullhorn, Tulli could not see its source beyond the wall of spectators and turkey vultures that surrounded her.

"On my count," she said, drumstick raised. "Káye, dáki, táłi!"

"What?" Moraine asked.

"Sorry. That was Lipan. Um, what's the Diné word for three?"

"Just use English," he said.

"Three, two, one!"

Moraine sang in clear, deep vocables; it had been ages since Tulli heard his voice without a hint of guttural death growl. Stunned, she nearly missed her entrance. The first beat on her toy drum cracked like a whip.

Rap!

Even with a bullhorn, the security-doctor-administrator could not overwhelm Moraine.

Rap, RAP, rap!

Tulli's drum spoke of healing and hunger.

Rap!

Kristi spread her arms and began to spin as she orbited around the memorial pillar, clockwise. By the second loop, she staggered more than she spun; every successive loop was smaller, closer to the pillar, as if it drew her in. On the fifth, she fell and crawled.

"Almost done!" Tulli shouted.

RAP!

The ground crumbled, and darkness enveloped their world, a darkness so absolute, even phosphenes vanished. As if drawn together by organic magnetism, Tulli, Moraine, and Kristi found each other and linked arms as they fell. "Are we dead?" Moraine hollered.

"I feel great," said Kristi, "so probably."

"Do you see that?" Tulli asked. "Below us!"

Two arms lit by their own radiance—glowstick-bright bones illuminating muscle, veins, and flesh with cool red light—sprouted from the abyss; their skin was rough with pox scars, their nails curled like talons. The Apparently Siblings landed on one pillowy, massive palm.

"Children," a hoarse, tooth-rattling voice said, "I enjoyed the performance." It came from everywhere, as if the void spoke.

"Thank you!" Tulli rolled into a sitting position; she'd landed gracelessly. They all had. "Are you its composer? Are you the one who gave us visions?"

"I am."

"It's an honor. May I ask, um…"

"Why?" Kristi interrupted. "There are lots of decent people on Earth, so why choose us instead?"

"Because," the void said, "I am your *biggest* fan. Apparently Siblings, when you scream in dim places, I listen, and I relish what I hear."

So they *did* serenade the right person. Tulli knew it would happen eventually, though she'd expected a human talent scout. "Will… you help?" she asked. "Help make us and everybody else healthy again?"

The temperature dove from chilly to Alaska winter cold. Even Kristi, with her wool shawl and patchwork dress, shivered. "From the world Above," boomed everywhere Below, "I take the Big Plague, drink its coils, and sate my hunger. The virus is now just a troubled memory. Make no mistake: you'll all die eventually. Heheh. Mortals *always* perish. Maybe by illness. Maybe by accident. Maybe by something stranger. It's not my place to know. When the time comes, I hope you will find me and perform for all the dead, the never-born, and the monstrous who live in my deep country."

"Woah. *Metal*. What… what are you?" Tulli asked, leaning against her friends for warmth. "A spirit?"

"A ghost?" Kristi asked.

"A god?" Moraine asked. "Or could you be part of a complex delusion? Maybe I'm asleep, and all this has been a nightmare."

"Just call me Plague Eater. The rest is mystery." The fingers curled around them. "But I'm definitely not that last guess."

"I have to admit," Tulli said, "that the White Train is much nicer this time. I even saw Nurse Jon sipping a martini in the dining car. I asked if he wanted an autograph, and he said, 'No, you left one on the wall.' What a funny guy. I may really love him."

Kristi snorted. "Get his number, but don't invite him home. Our apartment must be rank. We left chili in the sink."

"Let's hire a maid after the tour finishes," said Moraine.

"Maybe even rent a bigger apartment?" Tulli asked.

It had taken a few weeks to check, double-check, and triple-check their blood samples; not a hint of Big Plague remained. In fact, nobody carried the virus anymore, regardless of the bodily fluid or tissue that was screened. Big Plague even vanished from test vials in laboratories and secure government facilities.

Maybe that's why so many people believed that the Apparently Siblings apparently saved the world. YouTube videos of their performance helped, too: turkey vultures bobbing their naked heads, the dance, song, and drum, a flurry of feathers, an empty courtyard, cheers when the crowd spotted Tulli, Kristi, and Moraine on the medical center rooftop.

In every video, their bodies were perfect silhouettes against the red western sky.

THE PLAGUE

KEN LIU

Ken Liu is an author of speculative fiction, as well as a translator, lawyer, and programmer. A winner of the Nebula, Hugo, and World Fantasy awards, he is the author of The Dandelion Dynasty, a silkpunk epic fantasy series: *The Grace of Kings*, *The Wall of Storms*, and a forthcoming third volume. He is also the author of the collection *The Paper Menagerie and Other Stories* and wrote the Star Wars novel, *The Legends of Luke Skywalker*. In addition to his original fiction, Ken has also translated numerous works from Chinese into English—including *The Three-Body Problem* by Liu Cixin and "Folding Beijing" by Hao Jingfang, both Hugo winners. Learn more at http://kenliu.name.

I'm in the river fishing with Mother. The sun is about to set, and the fish are groggy. Easy pickings. The sky is bright crimson and so is Mother, the light shimmering on her shkin like someone smeared blood all over her.

That's when a big man tumbles into the water from a clump of reeds, dropping a long tube with glass on the end. Then I see he's not fat, like I thought at first, but wearing a thick suit with a glass bowl over his head.

Mother watches the man flop in the river like a fish. "Let's go, Marne."

But I don't. After another minute, he's not moving as much. He struggles to reach the tubes on his back.

"He can't breathe," I say.

"You can't help him," Mother says. "The air, the water, everything out here is poisonous to his kind."

I go over, crouch down, and look through the glass covering his face, which is naked. No shkin at all. He's from the Dome.

His hideous features are twisted with fright.

I reach over and untangle the tubes on his back.

I wish I hadn't lost my camera. The way the light from the bonfire dances against their shiny bodies cannot be captured with words. Their deformed limbs, their malnourished frames, their terrible disfigurement—all seem to disappear in a kind of nobility in the flickering shadows that makes my heart ache.

The girl who saved me offers me a bowl of food—fish, I think. Grateful, I accept.

I take out the field purification kit and sprinkle the nanobots over the food. These are designed to break down after they've outlived their purpose, nothing like the horrors that went out of control and made the world unlivable...

Fearing to give offense, I explain, "Spices."

Looking at her is like looking into a humanoid mirror. Instead of her face I see a distorted reflection of my own. It's hard to read an expression from the vague indentations and ridges in that smooth surface, but I think she's puzzled.

"*Modja saf-fu ota poiss-you,*" she says, hissing and grunting. I don't hold the devolved phonemes and degenerate grammar against her—a diseased people scrabbling out an existence in the wilderness isn't exactly going to be composing poetry or thinking philosophy. She's saying "Mother says the food here is poisonous to you."

"Spices make safe," I say.

As I squeeze the purified food into the feeding tube on the side of the helmet, her face ripples like a pond, and my reflection breaks into colorful patches.

She's grinning.

* * *

KEN LIU

The others do not trust the man from the Dome as he skulks around the village enclosed in his suit.

"He says that the Dome dwellers are scared of us because they don't understand us. He wants to change that."

Mother laughs, sounding like water bubbling over rocks. Her shkin changes texture, breaking the reflected light into brittle, jagged rays.

The man is fascinated by the games I play: drawing lines over my belly, my thigh, my breasts with a stick as the shkin ripples and rises to follow. He writes down everything any one of us says.

He asks me if I know who my father is.

I think what a strange place the Dome must be.

"No," I tell him. "At the Quarter Festivals the men and women writhe together and the shkins direct the seed where they will."

He tells me he's sorry.

"What for?"

It's hard for me to really know what he's thinking because his naked face does not talk like shkin would.

"All this." He sweeps his arm around.

When the plague hit fifty years ago, the berserk nanobots and biohancers ate away people's skins, the soft surface of their gullets, the warm, moist membranes lining every orifice of their bodies.

Then the plague took the place of the lost flesh and covered people, inside and outside, like a lichen made of tiny robots and colonies of bacteria.

Those with money—my ancestors—holed up with weapons and built domes and watched the rest of the refugees die outside.

But some survived. The living parasite changed and even made it possible for its hosts to eat the mutated fruits and drink the poisonous water and breathe the toxic air.

In the Dome, jokes are told about the plagued, and a few of the daring trade with them from time to time. But everyone seems content to see them as no longer human.

Some have claimed that the plagued are happy as they are. That is nothing but bigotry and an attempt to evade responsibility. An accident of birth put me inside the Dome and her outside. It isn't her fault that she picks at her deformed skin instead of pondering philosophy; that she speaks with grunts and hisses instead of rhetoric and enunciation; that she does not understand family love but only an instinctual, animalistic yearning for affection.

We in the Dome must save her.

"You want to take away my shkin?" I ask.

"Yes, to find a cure, for you, your mother, all the plagued."

I know him well enough now to understand that he is sincere. It doesn't matter that the shkin is as much a part of me as my ears. He believes that flaying me, mutilating me, stripping me naked would be an improvement.

"We have a duty to help you."

He sees my happiness as misery, my thoughtfulness as depression, my wishes as delusion. It is funny how a man can see only what he wants to see. He wants to make me the same as him, because he thinks he's better.

Quicker than he can react, I pick up a rock and smash the glass bowl around his head. As he screams, I touch his face and watch the shkin writhe over my hands to cover him.

Mother is right. He has not come to learn, but I must teach him anyway.

FOUR KITTENS

JEREMIAH TOLBERT

Jeremiah Tolbert is a writer and web developer of websites for authors and publishers. His stories have appeared in magazines such as *Lightspeed*, *Asimov's*, *Analog*, *Interzone*, *Escape Pod*, *Shimmer*, and *The Magazine of Fantasy & Science Fiction*, along with numerous anthologies edited by John Joseph Adams. His story "The West Topeka Triangle" was a finalist for the Shirley Jackson Award, and "Not by Wardrobe, Tornado, or Looking Glass" was selected for inclusion in *Best American Science Fiction and Fantasy*. He lives in northeast Kansas with his wife and son. Learn more at jeremiahtolbert.com.

Jetting down the highway at 120, near flat out, just pedal to the metal, all cylinders firing, frame vibrating to pieces. Thoughts jumbling around in my head like the kittens in the box on the bench seat behind me.

Just rebuilt the transmission, thank Chrysler. Does the road curve now, or in another mile? Just hope they don't start shooting. The nitrous in the trunk don't play nice with bullets.

Table-flat, bone-dry landscape whizzing by in a blur, spring bugs banging the windshield, and I remember that old joke. What's the last thing that goes through a bug's mind as it hits a windshield? Its ass, abdomen, rear-end, ha ha, you know?

Behind me on the road—slick, one-a.m.-black SUVs are crawling up on *my* rear-end, growling like abused dogs, revving forward inch by inch to nip at my Goodyear heels. I open it up just a little more, hope the frame holds. Pulling away a little now, but—*shit*—they've been holding back too.

That switch curve comes up like a boy sneaks up on his girlfriend's window, quick and quiet, and I'm slamming the brakes, hauling on the wheel, praying to the Four Wheeled Gods that I don't lose it. I come out of the curve and gun it, glance back to see if I've lost 'em. One, two, three… lost one. Fucking lot of good that'll do me; with less of 'em they'll just take longer to beat me to death when they catch me.

Skill takes a back seat to engine and instinct. Plain old engine power's all I got left, and it's not going to be good enough. They aren't shooting yet—

Damn me to cracked head gasket hell for even thinking that, because now out pops one of those gray-suited gorillas, leaning out the window with a matte-black 9mm in hand. Well, damn the nitrous too while we're at it—I'd rather go out in a ball of flames than with a bullet in the brain.

Tap the brakes, and the black beasts behind me leap forward, startled, slow to react. My poor ride shudders like it's gonna fly apart any second. Ha! Dumb bastard hanging out the window falls out, tumbles into a speck behind us in the distance.

Cheer me on, kitty cats. I've got to get rid of six more just like him, all knuckles, thick necks, and suits attached to guns.

They don't try shooting again, only strain to get a lead on me, wanna force me off the road. I'm holding out for now, I know the road better, the bumps and potholes. They're in my territory, that's my advantage, plus my baby, a roaring hot, eight cylinder Detroit-made hellbeast, but they've got numbers, and by numbers, I mean the steel-jacketed ones too.

I hear mewing behind me, sharp and sweet above the wailing wind and whining engine. I'm doing this for them, like a total fuckin' sap, but those big blue eyes cut through me like shivs.

Chrysler knows I put up with a lot working for the big man, but *kittens* is where I draw the fucking line.

I flinch like the devil yanked on my soul as a bullet zips past. Damn those thugs and their guns, and all I can do is keep one eye on the road, the other on my rearview mirror; one hand firmly on the wheel, and the other protecting my testicles. Times like this, even though it's hard enough to feed one mouth in this dead world, I wish I still had a co-pilot. A partner, a pal, someone to wheel around with a big old 12-gauge and blast those bastards' tires out. *Tires*. Why aren't they shooting *my* tires? Must be afraid to hurt the kittens? Bullets don't come too close to the car, I see now; they're just tryin' to scare me.

I flip the cover off the switch; time to risk the nitrous. I'll blow rings and hoses all over the place, and my sweet, sweet ride'll be scrap after, but hell, what's the use in driving a suped-up getaway car if it doesn't get-you-the-fuck-away? Figure I'll bury her somewhere special, a nice scrap yard up north away from all the scavenger buzzards and gear-grinding Venom-heads. She's earned her rest after this.

So damn it all and fuck it too for good measure. Flip the switch, fire the trigger, and zoom, man, zoom. Needle pushes around the bend, the car throws me back into my seat, the mewing in the back goes silent, and the black dogs of death fade away behind me like mist when the sun comes up.

Still, there ain't a lot of cover out here to hide behind, and my silver bullet of a ride ain't going to blend in with any traffic (not that we see much down here anymore anyways), so all this does is buy me time to think. Time to figure out what I can do to lose them, get the lead I need to get over the horizon. Find a back road to take me so far out of sight they'll just give up and forget about me. The thought of leaving the kittens on the road, that might work, but hell, I've wasted my car already, so why not go all the way?

That gives me an idea. If I'm careful and they're stupid—and they established that they are with the shooting stunt—so hey. If I'm careful, I'm golden.

I reach back with one arm and tip the kittens out of the cardboard box. They're balls of fur stretched over firecrackers, only these firecrackers got wet. I mean, they're dang tired. They blink in the light, and one even takes a swipe and a hiss at my hand as I haul their box up. He doesn't like me any more than lead man-gorilla Saul does, but at least *this* little guy isn't capable of ripping me limb from limb, even if he shares the man's thirst for my blood.

I scramble for some empty beer cans, rags, anything on the floor that'll give the box some weight, stuff it in and get the box good and closed with a bit of oil to seal the deal. Window cranks down, out flies the box, weighted good, rolls down the highway, and I watch in the mirror as it comes to a stop just perfect, right side up. Yeah, they'll have to stop and check that out, and that'll give me just the edge I need to make it to the canyon, which is opening up ahead.

The road dips down from table-top mesa to twisty, ancient water-cut maze. Smoke's curling out of my hood, chastising me on the way by; my car's ghost, escaping its body, fleeing for roadster heaven. She holds out until I make the main canyon chasm, and then sputters, gasps, and rolls to a slow stop.

Sorry baby, I'm no marine. Gonna have to leave you behind. All plans to give her a proper funeral go by the wayside in favor of saving my own hide.

Four little kittens in the backseat of my dead car, and I've got twenty miles between me and safety; twenty miles of rocky desert canyon paths and deadly scorpions, snakes, and rabbits. Don't get me started on those rabbits, some wack-job's idea of post-Crash hardened wildlife. Remember hearing once that some dumb fools brought all these birds over from England to America because they were mentioned in a book of plays. Now we all gotta deal with starling shit covering our cars if we park under the wrong dead tree. So it was like that with some post-Crash survival who thought they could help wildlife survive the die-offs. Now rabbits just as likely to gore you to death as they are to fill your belly. Damn shame how some people deal with the end of everything.

So what do I do? I'm not ready to call it quits, gonna have to do something I never do, which is hoof it. I'm wishing I still had that box, but I've gotta have something in the trunk that will work to carry these little fur babies. I pop the back and rummage around through the tools and parts and scavenged junk I been holding onto just in case it ever proved useful. There we go—tool box. Covered in grease, filled with rusty screwdrivers, hammers, wrenches, but it'll do.

I dump it out without a thought, just a small whimper, slipping one good wrench into my back pocket, and gently place the kittens inside. I take a bloody nick on the hand from the pissy one. Shut the lid just part way, not latching it. I can't hardly imagine being the kind of asshole who'd walk into Shantyville with a toolbox full of suffocated kittens.

Got no choice but to walk across the canyon floor, not sure what I'm going to have to cross on foot, having only been through these parts in my ride, but I know I'd better stick to the difficult terrain so they can't run me down from their still-working rides. After a minute of jogging, I see a path high up on the canyon wall, so I head that way. Clouds of dust approach from behind, the dogs hot on my trail again, but still a ways off. My ruse must have worked. I crack a smile, pat my tool box, and cut my own dust cloud up that trail, hoping to make it out of sight before they pull in, wishing I'd learned something about covering tracks, or desert survival, back before the Crash. Shoulda been a boy scout instead of spending all that time helping my old man change oil and shit. Course, I can't beat myself up too bad; knowledge of engines had gotten me this far. It was only the past few minutes where that was worth about as much as a handful of rancid beans.

I stumble for an hour, then another, up crumbling canyon walls, down dry streambeds, ducking, looking back constantly. Wishing I had eyes in the back of my head so my neck wouldn't hurt so much from trying to look two ways at once.

The kitties are mewing just loud enough they'll give me away if those bastards get too close. I tear off my shirt and wrap it around the box, gotta muffle that sound and keep the box from heating up too much. Plus who knows what'll come running, worse than thugs, at the sound of a struggling animal. The thought chills me, turns my sweat cold, which is kind of a relief in the heat. Being scared out of your mind has some fringe benefits, turns out.

I'm working on a sunburn twenty minutes later, but it's better than being shot or eaten alive. I try to keep the small things in perspective like my old man taught me. I do okay except at the worst times, like when I decide to ditch off with a box full of kittens and royally piss off my now-former employer. Stealing from the big man has to be the last straw in our already strained working relationship. Oh well; plenty of other wannabe dictators to work for out there in the wastes. I'll look for gainful employment just as soon as I'm sure I don't die gut shot on a sandy stretch of ghostly creek bed.

I hear shouts, gunshots in the distance. They're spread out all over, keeping tabs on each other by firing off their guns like good, stupid henchmen. Several times I switch directions, scramble down some boulders, around a corner to avoid the sources of gunfire, but mostly the sound's confusing, echoing off the canyon walls, making it hard for me to be sure exactly which direction they're headed. I try hauling my dragging-ass carcass up high on some rock, scalding my calloused hands and arms by grabbing the sun-scorched surface. The thugs aren't far back, ever, not more than a mile, and they had the forethought to bring water with them, I guess. My throat's in dire need of lubrication and my eyes are sore from sand-grit and dust. Sure could use a good washing out about now. I soldier on, though. At first, this was about sentimentality; now it's about plain old survival. Don't think I could live with myself if I let Saul and his boys kill me.

Sun setting, moon rolling up. What's left of it anyway—big old shattered dinner dish in the sky, constant reminder that the world can't never be put back together again. Air's getting nippy, and everything's coming to life around me. I skirt around an enormous sleeping rattlesnake and spook some spiky-haired rat-thing that shambles off, spines waving and prickly nose held high with offense. An hour after dusk, I still hear the shouts and gunshots behind me but eventually they go quiet except for one large volley of blasts that I suspect are intended to kill or maim something, rather than communicate. I hope whatever they're shooting gets in a few licks of its own.

I stagger on, dust clinging to my hair in the grease I use to keep it slicked back and out of my eyes. I'm thinking about a nice, warm bath with a pretty lady when out of nowhere comes this behemoth of a man, dirty pinstripe gray suit, pistol leveled at my head.

"Give 'em up and I'll kill you quick," he says, voice like an avalanche. I'm shaking, adrenaline making me jittery, and he sees it, gets nervous. "Do it now!"

Got no choice now, I think, only there's the weight of that wrench in my pocket, that fucking wrench that's been slowing me down all afternoon. I've forgotten until now what it is. I lower the toolbox to the ground, heavy with sleeping feline, and take a short step back, putting my hands behind my head like I'm ready for him to just shoot me, praying he has the brains to check the box before he does.

Luckily the monster has a few brain cells not killed with shooting up Viper-venom. He slips right up in front of me, bending down to remove my sweat-stained shirt and flip up the lid—

Instead, I flip *his* lid. Quick as anything, like I was *born* for this shit instead of rebuilding carburetors, I bring up the wrench, striking him clean in the jaw with an honest-to-goodness uppercut swing that knocks him senseless. He collapses on top of the box. After, I look down at the bloody wrench in my hand in astonishment like the appendage belongs to a stranger. Lots of opportunity for violence in my life since the Crash, but I've always dodged by being good at fixing and driving things on wheels.

Muffled kitty noises under the body remind me I don't have time to think about it. Soon as I stop shaking, I roll the body away, pick up my load, and take off, not looking back, not even for a second, not wanting to see a dead man any longer than necessary. Especially not wanting to see a dead man in the light of the FUBAR-ed moon. On I walk, hoping his ghost never tracks me down.

My neck's stiff. My back burns like it's been dipped in battery acid. My head feels like it's wrapped in cotton. All I've had for sustenance is a beer and a couple of rabbit burgers two days ago, maybe a little stale pump water at the cantina. Enough for me to get around on wheels, but on foot, things are different.

For now, I keep putting one foot in front of the other—but I'm staying alert for any signs of water, food, anything. I think you can get water out of cactuses, but I haven't seen any on these rocky slopes. I could find one in the canyon, but down there, I might also find a bullet with my name on it.

Got no choice but to tough it out. I can make it to Shantyville, I think. Dehydrated for sure, but alive. With the kittens in hand, they'd be sure to let me past the wall. They'd be fools if they didn't.

Next thing I know, I'm crashing to the ground and I feel a searing pain in my ankle—twisted it good between a couple of rocks. A curse slips out of me—quietly, thank Chrysler—and I see that the box of kittens has tumbled open. They're all wide awake now, the little devils, blue eyes glowing in the moonlight. *Freedom*, I can just see them thinking, and just like that, they *scatter*.

No way in hell I'm going to leave those beautiful babies to die in the desert, so I scramble to my feet, wincing from pain, and start trying to snatch them up. I get three pretty easy with a piece of string I find in my pocket, but the fourth, the tough bastard, he plays it cool, regards me from a perch high up in a dead tree. I'm torn between amusement and terror. That kitten has spirit, and I'm sure that this little fucker's going to get me killed.

A couple thrown rocks later and the gray and white bastard's backed up even further, hissing and spitting, looking at me as if to say, "I knew you'd betray me. It was only a matter of *when*."

I don't know if I'm still being followed, but either way, I'm wasting precious time, and this cat's chosen his own path, so I start to walk off, as if I don't need him, as if I don't care if the bastard lives or dies. I get about fifty feet away and he buys it. I hear this soft pattering sound behind me, and when I look down there he is, trotting along after me. He stops, turns away, licks himself when I turn around, like, "Hey, I was going this direction anyway." But he lets me pick him up and return him to the box, and finally I'm making tracks again.

I've run my baby ragged and abandoned it to the desert, I'm ducking my boss's killers, I'm even dodging dangerous wildlife I don't know the names for... but in the end, it's the Chrysler-forsaken sun that gets me.

I limped on through the night, but come morning the heat just sears me deeper than skin, and my arms and legs start to feel like I've been flayed and lit on fire. My eyes aren't any better. Everything's blurry and I trip and fall every couple of minutes. Finally, I fall hard enough that time stretches weird and I lose my grip on everything. The sun turns into a swarm of headlights bearing down. I give in; I accept it. Somehow, I always knew I'd turn roadkill.

When I wake up, I'm in the shade, only I first figure it has to be those towering pricks standing over me so I try to jump up, ready to go down in a fight. A soft gasp chills me out, gets me to give up and lie back down, and my eyes focus enough for me to see that I'm lying on a flimsy mattress surrounded by dry, wooden walls, sunlight peeking through any crack it can find. A distinctly male grunt comes from the corner to my right, and I make out someone sitting in a chair there, a shotgun or a rifle across his lap. His face is like a map of canyon country where it isn't hidden by white beard. There's a glint of menace in his eye that I don't have to be psychic to read. I've gotta keep myself small and harmless if I'm going to get out of this one.

"Where the hell am I?" I ask with a groan. Not too hard to keep myself small when I'm barely skin and bones and the room keeps tilting to one side like the whole cabin's about to come tumbling down on me.

"You're in our home, so I'll thank you to show some respect and not curse in front of Molly," the man grumbles.

"Can I see what's in his box now, Pa?" the girl asks. I turn to give her a look-over, guessing the sight is better than the grizzled desert rat ready to shoot me if I flinch. Sure enough, she's got long blond hair all pulled up, pretty oval face. I'm guessing fifteen, sixteen, which means post-Crash is all she's ever known. Hard to believe that people keep making more people in this mess of a world.

"Sorry. I don't suppose you could spare something to drink?" I ask.

"Fill a jug from the well, Molly," the man says. "This fella's gonna need his strength to move on."

The girl nods, picking up an old plastic milk jug, and heads outside. "Not before I find out what's in his toolbox!" she says over a shoulder.

"Thanks for taking me in," I say. "I'll move on just as soon as I can get my feet under me. Mind if I try and stand up?" I've got a pounding headache, a twisted ankle, and some scrapes, but nothing so serious that I have to stay and risk getting shot.

"Go right ahead, just don't get any thoughts about trying to turn Molly's good deed into opportunity for worse. We ain't got nothing worth stealing anyway."

FOUR KITTENS

I sit up again, stretch my neck a little, and test the ankle. It's swollen, but not badly enough I can't hobble off when the time comes.

The toolbox begins to make scratching sounds, and Pa shoots me a curious look.

"Just some... mice I caught. Dinner." *Please don't meow*, I think at them.

The little bastards, not knowing when to give up being catty, do, in fact, meow.

"Mice, huh?" Pa sits his gun against the wall and stands, moving toward the toolbox. Even if he has a couple decades on me, I'm in no state to take him in a fight. Anyway, I couldn't see myself repaying their kindness with more violence.

"Okay, no, not really. They're kittens."

Pa's face splits with a broad, surprisingly toothy grin. "Where'd you get kittens around here? I haven't seen a cat in ten years at least."

"Sir, I have to be honest with you. I stole them. Don't give me that look—ordinarily, I'm no thief. I was just a runner and mechanic for Gunter, over in Crabtree."

The old man nods. "Thought I recognized your face from the last time I was at the trading post. Now how did that scumbucket get his hands on kittens?"

"The boys brought 'em in—got them off a raid down in Bracken Valley over on the main stretch of highway. None of Gunter's boys can read too well, so they didn't understand the shipping markers right, thought they were stealing medical supplies. Anyway, Gunter decided he wanted them cooked up as a little feast."

Pa blinked. "Good god damn, but that man's a monster. Even with a world gone to total shit, pardon the language, there's no excuse for eating a kitten."

"I don't remember the old world too well; I was eight when the shit hit the fan belt, but... I just couldn't stand there and watch Gunter eat these little guys. Besides, they're too small to do much more than get stuck between your teeth. Go ahead, open it up and see for yourself."

The old man opens the box, and there's that grin again. A little sparkle of gold in the world. For a minute everything I been through in the past day feels worth it and I feel good, like someone's topped up my tank with high octane.

"They've been treated pretty well, but they look thirsty," he says. The one tough little bastard rears up on his hind legs, takes a swipe at the man's ragged beard. The old man breaks out in a raspy chuckle.

"I think they're Siamese or something?" I say.

"Nonsense like breed and what-not doesn't matter anymore," the old guy says. "Lord almighty. Kittens, here in *my* shack. What in the world do *you* plan on doing with them?"

What, indeed. I don't know the first thing about the care of any animal that doesn't have an engine instead of a heart. Start to wonder if maybe I should leave them here. I might make it further without the weight of them slowing me down. Maybe the old man and the girl would know better than me how to keep them alive.

I start to say all that, but I'm cut off when Molly sprints back into the cabin and slams the door shut.

"Pa, there's men... getting out of big black trucks... coming up the hill," she says between gasps for breath. I wonder if I can make it out the door before the old man shoots me in the back. The girl hands me the jug of dirty water, so I start to down it, then change my mind and pour it into the cup of my hand for the kittens. They cluster around and drink it greedily.

Pa looks over to me. "Gunter's boys?"

I nod. "Must be."

"Molly, get down in the crawlspace." She moves to a corner of the room, rolls back a rug and some boards, and starts down a ladder into the darkness. The old man covers it up real quick. I get the feeling this ain't the first time they've had to hide her away.

I force myself up and stagger to the door and peek out between the boards. Shouting outside startles the kittens and sends them scattershot through the cabin. Four of Gunter's goons are hunched over, hustling up the hill, guns pointed our way. How they managed to find me, I don't know. What I *do* know is I can't run any further.

"Maybe you should get down in your hidey hole with your daughter," I say. "This is my mess."

"Not my daughter, not really. Just another stray. Seems I'm a magnet for them in my old age. Anyway, not sure I could live with myself if those brutes eat the little ones."

"I'm sorry to drag you into this," I say. I mean it. These people have been nothing but kind to a strange man they found dying in the dirt and sun, and now I've brought Gunter's brand of brutality to their door.

"If we're lucky, there'll be time for apologies later," Pa says. "Now what are we going to do here?"

"Do you have any other guns?" I ask.

"Nah," he says, growling. "And I only got five shells for this old thing. Half likely to blow up in my hands if I fire it anyway."

Five shells, four men, each with enough ammo to kill us five times over. Trying to think quick, but my brain's moving in slow motion, my eyes fixed on the henchmen climbing up the hill. All I have is the trick from before, but hell, if it worked once, it might work again.

"Mister," I say, "keep that gun ready. When one of them turns their back to ya, shoot him. Shoot him only if you *know* you'll kill him," I say. I slip along the floor quietly, looking for one of the kittens. I grab Bloodthirsty, trying not to think about how I've named him and now he's my favorite. I crack open the door and wait for the men to make it up the hill. As they crest it, they stop and catch their breath, and then Saul, the biggest tough among them and a bastard who always hated my guts, starts walking toward the cabin.

I shove Bloodthirsty out the door, pinching his tail hard enough that he cries out. My oil- and rust-crusted heart nearly breaks, but the kitten tears out across the hilltop, headed straight past the bewildered thugs. Saul shouts orders over his shoulder and keeps coming. *Shit*, I think, and reach for my wrench; only I must have lost it sometime in the night because it's gone. Pa opens fire, gun roaring and spitting buckshot, cutting down two of them before Saul busts through the door.

I do the only thing I can think of in the moment and lurch straight up into his solar plexus, tackling him to the ground and flailing around to pin his gun arm. He's much stronger than me, but he wasn't expecting me to come flying at him so I have the element of surprise. More gunshots ring out and I can see out of the corner of my eye that Pa's plugged the last gunman, only I think he's used up all his ammo but I can't seem to count so good with three hundred pounds of thug-beef trying to crush the life out of me. Saul elbows me in the face, dropping me to the dirt floor, then grabs Pa by the throat and throws him against the wall, where he collapses in a groaning heap.

Now it's just me and big-ass, hulking, eats-glass-for-fun Saul. Right about now is when I take the worst beating of my life.

Saul works my upper body like I'm a ball of dough, and my ears, nose and mouth start gushing blood like my own bodily fluids can't take it no more and have decided to seek their fortunes elsewhere, the traitors. Pain, I've experienced it, but this surpasses anything I previously knew about pain. This makes my previous pain cower in the corner and beg for mercy.

I try to bring my arms up to shield my body from the blows, but I'm so weak that he bats them aside and goes for the prize (my face). I'm staring at a fist coming straight for my nose, certain it's the last thing I'm going to see, when I spot a streak of gray and white coming straight toward us. *Someone lit a firecracker*, I think, then there's a burst of stars from Saul's fist pulverizing my nose. But when my vision clears, Saul's standing there, *his* eyes bleeding, trying to tear Bloodthirsty off *his* face.

God damn, what a beautiful sight, but it all turns to shit too fast for me to really appreciate it.

Saul hurls the kitten to the ground so hard I hear a crack. The whole room goes dead silent for a moment and I never felt more rage and despair in all my miserable life. I grasp a broken splinter from the door and throw all my weight behind it, coming up low, under his ribs. He totters, tilts over backwards; I fall forward with him, giving my shard more momentum, driving it deep into his chest, my head right in his stinking crotch.

So *this* is the last thing I get to see, I think, right before the darkness wraps me in a cold blanket. It sure was a pretty sight, seeing that kitten with its claws half-way to Saul's teeny brain.

This time I come to, I'm more cautious, and crack open a blood-caked eye first—see I'm still in the cabin with a pleasing buzz of relief. Old man Pa sits next to me, a goofy look of worry cutting across his bruised face. He looks like he'll live, but regret it. Molly sits in his chair, cradling something in her arms. Tears roll down her face, and before I know it, despite that I was sure I ran out of tears a long time ago, I'm crying too.

We bury Bloodthirsty behind their cabin. I use my lucky wrench as a tombstone—turns out that the old man had taken it off me before I woke up the first time. I mumble a few incoherent words at the graveside, nothing proper really, and head back into the cabin to help clean up the mess I made.

Just before I set off again for Shantyville, I pick out the prettiest kitten and hand it to the old man and the girl, all of us all red-eyed and puffy. They say nothing, and neither do I. Sometimes the gift of a cat is better than words.

A story I read once, back before we'd burned up all the books for kindling, ends with a line that I never quite understood: "a boy loves his dog." Not sure I know what love is, not sure if love even exists anymore. I sure as hell ain't never loved a dog unless I was hungry.

I set out again, nearly broken down as much as my late, lamented ride, and at first I'm not even sure what's keeping me going anymore. But as I walk I remember that line and an idea forms like a perfect drivetrain in my mind, propelling me forward.

I don't know much that isn't about grease, gears, and gasoline, but what I can tell you is this: seeing the look on a person's face when you give her a feisty ball of fur is one of the last good and pure things left.

It never occurred to me that there was more to be had from this life beyond survival and tweaking an engine to run cooler and faster. All my life I've only been living to race a little further forward, never slowing down for nothing, because what was the point?

Now my step quickens for a reason; if my luck holds out, if the sun or the wasteland don't kill me first, I'm gonna see that beautiful look in a new kitten owner's eyes twice more before my work in this fucked up world is done.

THE EYES OF THE FLOOD

SUSAN JANE BIGELOW

Susan Jane Bigelow is a librarian, political columnist, and science fiction/fantasy author from Connecticut. She is the author of several books, including the *Extrahumans* series. Her short fiction has appeared in *Lightspeed*, *Strange Horizons*, *Fireside*, and *Apex*, among other publications. She can usually be found somewhere near the Connecticut River, which floods every spring.

The river's in flood again, and it feels like a blessing from God. You emerge from your home, built with wood and plastic scraps of ancient towns, and stand on the green hill high above the rushing waters.

You remember from when you were young that the river would spill over its banks every year, submerging the low-lying land, turning fields that had lain fallow through the darkness and bitter cold of winter into lakes of rushing, wild water. And then when the waters had drained away, the corn could be planted in the deep sediments left behind. The river's gift.

The first flood after the war had brought black water choked with bricks, scorched wood, crumpled cars, and corpses. You remember the smell of it all during those rare days when the sun came out and the temperature rose and you could venture hesitantly, like a mouse creeping out from under the sofa, from the concrete bunker. You gagged and wept and sighed and raged, but your family below needed food and supplies, so you went to the bloody banks of the river to scavenge what you could. It hadn't been much.

In the end the radiation and the plague killed them anyway, leaving you alone.

You have canoes you've made by hollowing out the thick trunks of fallen trees, and you set your newest and sturdiest in the water. Today you will drift south to see what the floods might give you easy access to that you couldn't reach before. You have your camping supplies—you can stay in the south for weeks until the floods recede. Then you'll paddle north, against the current, back to your home.

As you set the canoe in the water and shove off, you feel the insistent tug of the far south. You once ventured down to the briny expanse of the Sound, and then west to where the Sound narrowed and the great city began. You turned back at the sight of one of the bridges; it was somehow still intact, but now wrapped in climbing vines. Gnarled trees rose from the roadbed, their branches twisting around the cables.

But barely visible on one of the towers were two faded words painted in red—*Go Back*.

The words were old, the ones who had scrawled them there long dead, but it had felt like a sign to you. You are careful; it's why you've been alive for so, so long. Or so you believe.

So you turned back.

And as you paddled away, delicate fingers grasped the rusted railings of the bridge, and hungry eyes followed your slow, curving wake.

You paddle softly out into the middle of the river, and you wonder about what lies far to the south, in the lands you've never seen. Maybe the people there had been better able to survive the winters, the years without sun, the blight, and the poison water and sky. Maybe there or far to the west you might find pockets of survivors like yourself.

That's the marvel of the Earth, you think, your mind moving in slow, familiar patterns: Life survives. Even now, the trees grow tall and birds sing as your canoe slips by. They are not the same trees, not the same birds. These trees have long, delicate leaves, almost like pine, and the birds are smaller and meaner. The creatures in the vast forest stretching from the ocean to the mountains are different, too, in subtle and strange ways. You leave them alone, and they return the favor, but at night you can sometimes hear their high, eerie calls.

The ruins of the small river city are just beyond the rapids. The feeder stream there has finally burst free of the concrete that once encased it, and you paddle up until you find a patch of high ground to camp on for the night. You need little food, but still you build a fire and deliberately chew the bark of one of the trees.

When night comes, the sky is full of stars. You watch them, your thoughts slowing to a crawl, and you train your gaze on the new, dazzlingly bright one that appeared only three seasons ago. There was a time when you would have wondered what it was. But now you only accept it. It is. It is here.

Strange things happen in the heavens, they come and they go. They rarely concern you, though they make you feel small and grateful for your life. Once, your life ran with the phases of the moon, but the moon is rarely visible these days, and you stopped bleeding long ago.

You form a picture of God in your mind and you circle your arms above your head in prayer. Then, warmed by the fire, you drift away.

As you dream, you are watched.

The flood has grown in the night, and by the time the morning dawns, gray and rainy, it has come halfway to your shelter. You are glad. You decide to venture further up the narrow lake made by the swollen stream, paddling silently between the whip-thin trunks of the young trees.

Then, suddenly, you draw in your breath and ease your paddle out of the water, all senses alert. There are long, narrow, parallel tracks in the mud by the water.

The canoe drifts, just wood borne by the stream, as your mind spins. This is new. You don't recognize this.

But some part of you, some ancient memory combined with new insight, does know. A vehicle has been here.

You are not alone.

You float on the water, paralyzed, and for the first time in many, many years, you are afraid.

The last time you were not alone was when the few remaining survivors from the eastern farm towns came to your shelter, their eyes hollow and hungry, begging for food. You gladly gave them what little you had; they tried to kill you anyway. You were impossibly alive, impossibly healthy. Your eyes shone with something they didn't recognize, something they were afraid of.

They were easy to fool, and easy to outrun. They were half dead already. The world was extinguishing humanity's light, a desperate act of self-preservation.

You have not seen anyone since, and you have been alive for a very, very long time.

You are careful. You want to flee, to let the current carry you back to the river, to hide and let the floodwaters rise and cover the bank.

But you cock your head, looking and listening. You see and hear nothing new, nothing moves in the distance, there is no sound of an engine or a voice. You dip your paddle in the water and redirect the canoe ever so slightly in the direction of the shore. The canoe runs aground, hitting the mud with a dull, scraping *thunk*.

You take what you need, including a sharpened piece of rock, and follow the tracks.

You don't know why you are still alive. Your husband, your children, and everyone else died so long ago that their bones are dust. But instead of being burned by acid rain, poisoned by the air and water, or rotted away by the fast, relentless, and pitiless plague, you remained yourself. You lived.

You know you're different, that you somehow in the moments after the blast became something *else*, but you don't know why or what. You used to spend long days by the river staring at your reflection, wondering, as your jaw lengthened, your hair receded, your eyes changed color, and your ears grew scaled and long.

It occurs to you that the person with the vehicle might know why. You are not certain you want to know, though, after all this time has passed. You're not happy, exactly, nor are you sad or worried. But you are calm, and you are balanced. You have few needs. You exist, and you will endure.

You are careful. You aren't sure that you should risk what you have. What good would knowing do, anyway?

Yet still you follow the tracks carved into the muddy ground as they lead into the forest.

The trees here grow thick; this is high ground and good soil, so they are ancient. Some of them, the tallest with the thickest trunks, have been here nearly as long as you. You place a fond hand on one as you pass. It is good to endure.

The tracks lead into a clearing ahead. You know there was no clearing there before, and you hide behind one of the huge, old trees to decide what to do next. To endure is good; to risk and perhaps be cut down is wasteful, wrong, and too like the past.

Isn't it?

You listen. And then you hear a voice.

You remember voices, and you remember language. You used to talk to yourself, endless streams of thought given voice, but you fell silent long ago. You are not sure what your voice sounds like, or even if you can still use it. You think not in spoken or written language, but in grand pictures and emotions and scenes. To you, God is a flowing river, a bright sun, and life pushing up from beneath the once-tainted ground. God is a bomb, a plague, a shower of rain that stings, a beach choked with bodies and rubble. God is fresh air and putrescence, a fish in the water and the spear that pierces its scaly sides.

But God is not a voice. You listen. You do not know the sounds. You dare to look, and you see movement.

You see the vehicle, narrow and silver and graceful. And beside it, you see yourself.

But this is not you.

This is like you, but taller, more graceful, and, you think, older. This one has scaled ears, a long jaw, a shining bald scalp, and wide eyes the color of sunset. They are beautiful.

They turn to where you are hiding, and speak.

You want to run. You are careful! This is danger! You must be like the tree, you must endure, you must get away.

But something, some older impulse, some piece of you that existed before the first bomb put the first city to the fire, keeps you rooted where you are.

They walk toward you, and you are afraid.

But you stand your ground. You finger the sharp rock you have.

They hold out a webbed hand, so like your own. Your grip tightens on the rock.

They do not move. The trees blow in the breeze. Behind you, the river's flood begins to recede.

You make a decision. You are not a tree, and you are not a bomb. You drop the rock.

Then you reach out, and at last, after so long, your hand closes on mine.

THE LAST GARDEN

JACK SKILLINGSTEAD

Jack Skillingstead is the author of the apocalyptic science fiction-thriller *The Chaos Function*, which was published in March 2019 (John Joseph Adams Books). His novel *Harbinger* was nominated for a Locus Award for best first novel, and his second, *Life on the Preservation*, was a finalist for the Philip K. Dick Award. He has published more than forty short stories to critical acclaim and was short-listed for the Theodore Sturgeon Memorial Award. His writing has been translated internationally. He lives in Seattle.

The Surrogate walked past Casey's window. She watched its shadow slip across the shade, then she stood and zipped up her flight suit. This was the day. No matter what.

The doorbell rang.

It was polite, the Surrogate. It had manners. It rang the doorbell. It said please and thank you. It had saved Casey's life, twice, and the first time she had been grateful.

Casey bit her lip hard enough to hurt. The pain helped her focus on her mission. Because sometimes she didn't believe in it. Sometimes she was weak and disloyal to her own kind. That was understandable, considering her own kind, the human race, on Earth at least, was an extinct species. What was there to be loyal *to*?

The embryos. The cloned embryos in cryostasis.

Her mother.

Twenty-six months ago, Casey and her nine crewmates had watched helplessly from orbit while a plague wiped out humanity with the brutal efficiency of a worldwide tsunami. The final message sent from Washington to all orbiting spacecraft said simply, "Don't come down." But Casey and her crew had no choice. Without re-supply vehicles, they couldn't remain in space. Meanwhile, arguments raged on the Lunar colony, which was self-sustaining. Those in favor of staying put seemed to be winning. Then all communication coming from the Moon ceased.

The polite Surrogate rang the bell again. It claimed to worry about her, like a parent. But it couldn't really be worried about her. The Surrogate was a machine, a top-secret military-grade AI, from when there had been both a military and anything secret.

Casey stood in the entry, arms folded, feet planted on the vinyl floor. Military housing, drab and cheap. When she was a child in Virginia, Casey had lived with her mother in a big house with white columns in front. She remembered her mother pulling her down the dappled sidewalk in a red wagon, remembered the sound of the hard rubber wheels rolling on pavement. It was funny how that memory stood out but later ones had folded away into the dark. It was like peering down a long tube to a vision drenched in sunlight.

The knob turned, encountered the lock, turned harder until the lock broke and the door splintered away from the jamb.

The Surrogate had a paint-can head, eyes that glowed blue, and a slot mouth. The sturdy torso contained the power source. A flexible spine, like a length of knuckled bike chain, attached the torso to a pair of ingeniously swiveling hips. The legs were like attenuated cages made from carbon rods.

When Casey and her crewmates descended from orbit in two vehicles, automated defenses had immediately attacked them, destroying one vehicle outright and severely damaging the other. Casey managed a hard landing in the high desert of New Mexico near Tourangeau Air Base. Only Casey survived. Pinned inside the wreckage, her leg broken, she had expected to die of plague. The microbes, however, had all perished as soon as no humans were left to host them, and Casey had returned to consciousness and a world of bright pain in time to see the robot Surrogate peel away a flange of the damaged hull and reach for her.

Now Casey had let the Surrogate break open the door of the house. She hoped the destruction would make her angry at the robot, instead of frightened by what she was planning. She needed the anger.

"You didn't answer, Casey Stillman," the Surrogate said. "Our agreement was that you would answer."

"I know that." Casey's voice broke. She wiped her eyes roughly. It was the stupid door, wood splintered and hanging there on bent hinges, like a memory of things unbroken that were now broken forever. Instead of producing anger, it lifted the cover off a deep well of sadness. For months after the crash, she had combed the internet and the airwaves, desperate for contact. But if anyone had survived, they were unable to communicate. During those same months, the Surrogate had nursed Casey, waited on and bonded with her—as it was programmed to do.

The robot fitted the split doorjamb together. "I will repair this."

"Don't bother."

"Then I will help you move to a new house."

"I don't want a new house." She stood as straight as she could. "I'm flying out to the Doomsday Vault, and you can't stop me trying. I want you to lower the shield."

If the Surrogate could have sighed, this is when it would have done so. "As we've discussed," it said, "the embryos will not have survived."

"You can't stop me trying."

"I have never stopped you. You have stopped yourself. Before this, your mission was the gun."

"Will you not talk about the gun?"

"It concerns me."

"You can't be concerned about anything. You're a machine."

"I am an empathic Surrogate."

"If you won't lower the force shield, I swear I'll crash into it on purpose and die. I know you don't want that."

Almost a minute passed. From the robot came only a sound like a flywheel flutter, or humming bird wings. "Here is my analysis," the Surrogate said.

"Spare me."

"The embryo clones preserved in cryostasis once represented your desire for restoration. But now they represent your desire to stop living. They are like the gun."

"You are so full of shit."

"My casing is filled with many things, but excrement is not among them."

Casey rolled her eyes. "I wish you wouldn't try and be funny."

"Apologies. Our relationship has caused a symbiotic evolution of my algorithms. It is by design."

"This isn't a relationship," Casey said. "And the embryo clones are *not* like the gun." After the Surrogate came upon Casey fooling around with a pistol and her soft palate, the robot had gathered all the loose weapons on the base and locked them in the armory.

"They beckon, like the gun, and promise the same conclusion. Leaving the protection of this base for a hopeless goal is irrational. It is suicide."

"It isn't, but even if it were, it would be none of your business."

"It's wiser, and safer, to await the Moonites."

Casey snorted. She had long given up on a rescue mission from the Lunar colony, though the Surrogate continued to flog the possibility, probably as a strategy to mollify her. But Casey knew they would never come. The Surrogate referred to that certainty as Casey's "attitude."

"I'm going to try," Casey said, "whether you turn the shield off or not."

"My algorithms will not allow me to restrain you. But if you are determined, then I will come with you."

"No."

"Otherwise I won't disable the force shield."

"I already told you, I'll fly into it. I'll *gun* myself."

"If you truly want to save the embryos, you will let me accompany you. Otherwise you admit your mission is a gun and not what you claim it is."

"I don't have to make deals with you." Casey pushed past the

Surrogate and strode out to the street. She stopped and closed her eyes, took a deep breath.

"Well, come *on*," she said.

Shattered aircraft hangars gaped like broken shells. Black furrows crisscrossed the runways. Wreckage smeared across the tarmac in rusty debris fields. The plague came and was assumed to be an act of biological warfare. Someone in the US, or China, or India, or Iran, or Russia unleashed the first retaliatory assault. The reactive response spread like the plague had spread. The world became a gun aimed at itself, which kept on firing even after there were no humans left to pull the trigger.

Ironically, in the last days, CDC scientists determined that the plague itself had *not* been an act of war. Microbes had filtered into the atmosphere, where they thrived, located human hosts, and proliferated throughout the population. Where the plague failed to kill, the weapon response from every country in the world had succeeded. The shield over Tourangeau Air Base should have protected it, as should have the shields over the White House, Norad, and other critical places. All the shields had gone down under cyber attacks as vicious as the hardware ones. The Surrogate, however, had figured out the code to reactivate the one at Tourangeau, and now the AI controlled it.

Some air vehicles at Tourangeau Air Base had gone undamaged. A wasp with a long stinger was painted on the nose of the electric VTOL. Casey hauled herself up to the canopy and claimed the forward seat. The Surrogate installed itself behind her. Casey buckled up and began her pre-flight check. But when she attempted to move the control surfaces, ailerons, rudder, and elevators—her side stick and pedals resisted her. "Are you doing that?"

"I will fly us out," the Surrogate replied.

Casey craned her head around, awkward in the snug helmet. "You just open the shield, like we agreed."

"The moment this air vehicle passes beyond the shield it will be attacked by weapons still in terrestrial orbit as well as the automated weapons still operating on the ground. I have downloaded complete specs and will fly."

Casey wrenched at the control stick. "Let me fly my own goddamn ship."

The Surrogate went quiet. Hummingbird wings fluttered.

Casey closed her eyes, let her fury subside to the point where she could speak without shouting. "You think you can fly better than I can?"

"I do not doubt your skill. But I can predict the assault and react with greater efficiency."

Casey tapped her fingers on her thighs. She knew the Surrogate was right. The Surrogate was *always* right. It was one of the most infuriating things about it (a trait the robot shared with Casey's mother). Rudimentary AIs directed the orbital and ground-based automated weapons. Some of the weapons were "ours," some "theirs," some "who knows." And yes, it was probably beyond Casey's skill set to evade them all.

"You'll give me control once we clear the attack?" Casey said.

"There will be other attacks."

"You will give me control." Not a question this time.

"Very well."

"Then let's go."

The instrument panel and heads-up display came alive. Powerful GE engines spun up. The ship rose vertically. At two hundred feet, the nose pitched down and they powered toward the invisible shield.

Beyond the shield, buried in a Doomsday Vault under the Sangre de Cristo mountains, lay the frozen embryos cloned from some of the greatest scientists and leaders on Earth, including Casey's mother. They were the seeds of humanity's future.

And Casey was the last garden.

They sped toward the shield. Casey blinked sweat out of her eyes. "The shield's off, right?"

"No need. We can pass through unaffected from this side."

"What? You never told me you could do that! You mean I could have—No wonder you wanted to come. You tricked me."

"There will be a bump."

The ship accelerated to full power, crushing Casey in her seat. If there was a bump, she didn't feel it. The airframe was already shuddering. And then they were through and pitching steeply upward while rolling left. The sky flashed white and blue with energy bursts. The ship rocked wildly.

"Shoot back!" Casey yelled.

Instead, the Surrogate throttled down and deployed speed-breaks, which threw Casey against her restraints. If the Surrogate hadn't reacted with inhuman speed and precision, the VTOL would have been destroyed. They skated across the sky, wing tips banked steeply. Then they were clear, rolling right and gaining altitude, finally leveling out.

"Okay," Casey said, "hand it over."

"I am adjusting the vector," the Surrogate said. "Destination in six minutes."

"Give me control!"

"There will be other attacks."

"You shouldn't even be here. You lied to me about the shield."

Casey seized the side stick and pressed her feet to the rudder pedals, fighting the Surrogate for control. She hadn't realized the robot *could* lie. That made it almost human. A warning light flickered, and something streaked up from the desert. The Surrogate wrenched the ship over, but the projectile clipped the starboard wing, and the ship barreled out of control. Sky and Earth swapped relative positions. Casey grasped the stick in a death grip. Despite that, the Surrogate established a semblance of stable, albeit inverted flight, rolled again for straight and level, and compensated for the loss of starboard thrust.

"Casey Stillman, let go, please."

Casey released her grip and watched the displays. Hydraulic pressure dropped steadily on the starboard wing. The strike had severed a line. Worse, battery levels had plummeted, an emergency reflected in the off-key whine of the big electric turbine on the port side.

The ship wallowed toward the ground.

"We're going to crash!" Casey's heart was racing.

"I am managing it."

The remains of a town passed below them. The VTOL, rocking and swaying under depleted power, traveled another mile. A landing pad came into view. The Surrogate angled them toward it, dumping two hundred feet of altitude before rearing back and engaging sputtering vertical thrust. The ship teetered on the edge. Casey tensed her body for impact. In the next moment the undercarriage absorbed the bone-rattling jolt of touchdown. Casey looked up. They had landed fifty yards short of the pad.

The instrument panel displayed the red lines of overtaxed and underpowered systems, and then the display went dark.

Casey popped the canopy. "Don't say it."

"Don't say what?"

"That if I'd kept my hands off the controls we wouldn't have been hit."

The Surrogate reverted to hummingbird wings.

Casey unbuckled her restraints and turned around, kneeling on her seat. The Surrogate's blank face regarded her. "Damn it. *Not* saying anything is the same as *saying* it."

"I could have avoided the attack, yes."

"I knew you couldn't resist rubbing it in."

She climbed down to inspect the damage. Hydraulic fluid dripped on Casey's boot. A piece of the starboard wing's trailing edge was missing, a ragged bite taken by the projectile. If the VTOL had been running on jet fuel instead of electricity, it would have exploded. As it was, shrapnel had penetrated the fuselage and damaged the battery array. Maybe the Surrogate could repair the wing, but without power, they were stranded. "I will effect repairs," the Surrogate said.

"What about—"

"The repair procedure will render me helpless. So you will get your opportunity to pilot us back to base. You will have to manually deactivate the barrier. I will provide instructions. Don't do it too soon, or the weapons will gain access ahead of you. Don't wait too long, or you may misjudge the approach and destroy us."

"How long will repairs take?"

"Estimated three hours."

"I'll be back by then."

"Don't go, please."

From the stowage compartment Casey retrieved a pulse rifle, a sidearm, and a flashlight.

"Without me, your survival is questionable," the Surrogate said.

"Thanks for the vote of confidence."

But the robot was already dismantling the starboard aileron assembly.

Casey hiked up the steep terrain to the blast-door. She stayed off the road, using the trees for cover. Her boots swished in the undergrowth. She held her rifle at the ready, knowing it wouldn't do her much good if weapons attacked her. Once upon a time, her mother had given her a tour of the Doomsday Vault. Casey had only gone because it was so rare that her mother invited her *anywhere*. "You're so busy with your career," she told Casey, neatly reversing the situation. Casey hadn't been the one "too busy" for her mother.

Standing before the cryostasis capsules, Casey's own lifelong position as a daughter-in-stasis did not fail to ring ironic bells. As an Important Person, one of the world's top researchers in genetic engineering, Casey's mother had spent most of Casey's childhood somewhere *outside* Casey's childhood. Maybe that's why the little-red-wagon memory was so important.

At first glance the blast-door appeared intact, a slab of thick steel recessed under a brow of granite. Casey studied it from the trees. Something wasn't right. Finally, Casey bit down hard on her lip, burst out of the trees, and ran to the door. Nothing attempted to stop her. In a moment, she understood why. From the trees, she hadn't seen that the door's magnetic locks had failed, probably as a result of the cyber attack two years ago. A narrow gap presented itself. She hooked her fingers around the edge, and hauled on the door until the gap widened sufficiently for her to squeeze through.

Inside, daylight fell in dusty shafts from the shattered ceiling.

Daylight.

High above, where Casey had been unable to see it, an explosive discharge had ripped open the mountain. Just as the Surrogate assured her, the weapons had long ago destroyed the Doomsday Vault. Casey's hope vanished like the mirage it had always been, something to crawl toward in a desert of regret and loneliness.

For years, Casey had imagined the cloned embryos, tiny quick-frozen shrimp sealed in cryogenic capsules, buried deep behind impenetrable walls. She had imagined her mother.

Casey unclipped the flashlight from her belt, found stairs, and descended to the cryo vault. She had to be sure. Twenty minutes later, she was.

The embryos were all dead.

Her *mother* was dead. Again. Of course, it wouldn't have been her mother, just her genetic potential, her familiar features. Casey would have nurtured the potential in her own virgin womb, would have raised the child behind the force shield, and perhaps she would even have sat with her and told her a fairy tale about the Moonites coming back to Earth.

Casey sat on an iron beam that had partially melted and crashed down. Alone in the dark, she felt the weight of her life, like the weight of the mountain. What else had she expected? The Surrogate had been right, again. The cryo vault was another gun, a thin excuse for a suicide mission. Casey wiped her eyes and stood up. How could a robot know her better than she knew herself? In symbiosis, its algorithms had deciphered the mystery of Casey's own secret intentions.

She began climbing stairs.

The Surrogate had cannibalized itself to repair the ship. Hollow rods from its legs completed the broken linkages in the starboard aileron assembly. Unused rods and couplings lay in the wing's shadow, like discarded turkey bones. The hydraulic line had been welded, but what good would that do without fluid in the reservoir?

Using only its arms, the Surrogate had pulled itself back to the cockpit, where it sat bolt upright in the pilot's seat, strapped in place.

"Okay," Casey said. "You were right about the cryo vault. Satisfied?"

The Surrogate did not reply.

Casey hauled herself up to the cockpit. The Surrogate had patched a line from its own body and drained itself of fluid, giving the wing reservoir a blood transfusion. A thin cable led from the Surrogate's chest through a new hole in the firewall to the batteries. Casey toggled the power on. Battery levels jumped to ninety-six percent. But the surrogate was inert. Even the hummingbird was still.

A different emotion supplanted all the others roiling inside Casey, an emotion she had once felt acutely and then spent years suppressing.

Grief.

"You goddamn piece of junk," she said, not meaning it.

Without the Surrogate, there was only Casey's voice left in the world.

A tablet device lay on the tandem seat. Words displayed on the screen, instructions on transmitting a number sequence. Casey picked up the tablet, which was the key to unlocking the shield. She climbed into her seat, buckled her restraints, and waited for anger to muscle aside the grief of loneliness; then she spun up the engines, lifted away, and swung towards home base.

The first attack came almost immediately. Projectiles streaked up from the desert. Casey rolled left, rolled right, then plunged for the desert scrub, leveling out at fifty feet. A warning light flashed. Out of the clouds, a glittering swarm came at her.

Casey punched the throttle. The electric power plants whined like things about to burst apart. A burning odor filled the cockpit. The Surrogate rattled and bounced on the cable, the ship violently sucking the last kilowatt from its chest. The base lay dead ahead. So did the shield.

Heat rays crossed her flight path. Casey banked onto her wing tip and veered between them, flying with the skill of unconscious desperation, proving she *did* want to live. The maneuver drew the attack swarm into the rays. Fireballs burst like red kernels all around her. Casey tapped in the key code and transmitted it to the shield. She squeezed shut her eyes as the VTOL streaked over the border, the force shield rising automatically behind her. Rays, projectiles, and swarms burst spectacularly against it.

On the ground, Casey threw open the canopy. Sweating profusely inside her flight suit, she reached over the seat to unbuckle the robot, but the straps had melted into its frame. She used her knife to cut them away. The Surrogate's metal body remained searingly hot. Casey ran to the nearest intact hangar and returned with a chain-fall and a rolling cart. She pulled on big silver oven-mitt-looking asbestos gloves and used the chain-fall to hoist the Surrogate out of the cockpit and lower it onto the cart.

Restoring the Surrogate's mobility proved impossible. Casey had left the turkey bone parts behind, and she wasn't a mechanic, anyway. Replenishing the robot's power seemed at least worth a try. Casey rolled the Surrogate to the fusion generator building, which powered the force shield and everything else on the base. She rigged a connection between the generator and the Surrogate, and then she waited. After three days the Surrogate showed no signs of life, or whatever it was that animated the AI. After a week she stopped checking on it.

Without the Surrogate's voice, the base became a tomb in which Casey wept and talked to herself and then stopped talking. She wandered the streets she had always wandered, while inside she unraveled in loneliness. Some nights she stood at the perimeter, almost wishing the weapons assault would resume—and this time be successful. She toyed with the idea of lowering the shield, but she was past that.

At night, stars encrusted the New Mexico sky, a bed of diamonds to hold the yellow rind of the moon. Suddenly Casey's attention quickened. A point of light sped silently across the sky. She sat forward, making the chair creak. But it was only a weather sat, remnant of the conquered human race, not a humanitarian mission from Luna. She stood up and walked through the broken door into her house.

After a month's absence, she returned to the generator building. It had taken that long to believe again in the possibility of hope. She dragged her feet the whole way, indulged detours, pretended she wasn't hoping, and finally approached the door. Something rapped against it from the other side. Casey stopped—then ran the rest of the way. When she wrenched open the door, the legless Surrogate lay on the floor, one arm raised.

"You were gone a long time, Casey Stillman," it said. "I was worried."

She swallowed. "I'm here now."

Casey took the Surrogate with her when she went to the warehouse for supplies. MREs lasted forever and there were enough of them to feed a thousand soldiers for a year. She placed the Surrogate's torso and paint-can head on the cart and pulled it behind her, the way Casey's mother had pulled *her* in the red wagon. The sound of the wheels was like a memory echoing up a long tunnel. Casey looked over her shoulder. The Surrogate's blue eyes watched her.

"They're really coming, aren't they," Casey said. "The Moonites."

"Yes," the head in the wagon replied.

The Surrogate was always right.

THROUGH SPARKS IN MORNING'S DAWN

TOBIAS S. BUCKELL

Tobias S. Buckell, who has been called "violent, poetic and compulsively readable" by *Maclean's*, is a science fiction author and *New York Times* bestselling writer born in the Caribbean. He grew up in Grenada and spent time in the British and US Virgin Islands, and the islands he lived on influence much of his work. His popular Xenowealth series begins with *Crystal Rain*. Along with other stand-alone novels and his over seventy stories, his works have been translated into eighteen different languages, and selected for inclusion in *Best American Science Fiction and Fantasy*. He has been nominated for awards like the Hugo, Nebula, Prometheus, and the John W. Campbell Award for Best New Science Fiction Author. His latest novel is *The Tangled Lands* written with Paolo Bacigalupi, which the *Washington Post* said is "a rich and haunting novel that explores a world where magic is forbidden." He currently lives in Bluffton, Ohio with his wife, twin daughters, and a pair of dogs. He can be found online at TobiasBuckell.com.

A raider on a horse burst out of the scrubby bush along the road, and Mara swung hard on the tiller to jam the rear wheel of her sail cart to the side. The cart was an open cabin for two on a low-slung aluminum tricycle chassis, and Mara winced as the old fiberglass pod snapped and creaked; it was too old for strain like this. She shoved Gillem down without even thinking as the boom swung over their heads. The brake-boy's eyes went wide at the near miss. The cart's sail cracked as the wind filled it once more.

The horse was *fast*. Mara flicked the contact switch on the tiller to *on* and pushed a pedal. The tiny rubber wheels just under their legs skidded as the hub motors kicked in for a boost and shoved the sail cart forward down the old county road.

Gillem's eyes were wide open and white with fear. Sweat trickled off his dirty, shaved scalp. His eyes were huge behind oversized, thick eyeglasses strapped to his face with a dirty rubber strap.

"Hold the wheel!" Mara ordered.

He did, his black grease-stained hands gripping the hand-carved pine as he awkwardly stumbled back toward her. The cart's springs shifted and squeaked, the whole oblong body of the cart nearly tipping both of them out onto ancient asphalt.

Gillem was a brake-boy on the *Zephyr* and little more than a bag of bones, as boys his age usually were these days. He spent most of his time sitting in an axle cubby, waiting to push hard at a contact plate. He wasn't used to riding out in the open on a tiny cart, tipping over when the wind gusted. The *Zephyr* was three hundred feet long, trundling with ease over the great potholes that in the little sail cart Mara had to swerve to dodge lest they get swallowed up by crumbling asphalt.

"Eyes forward!" Mara hissed at the boy. The last thing they needed to do was eat road right now.

She raised the long barrel of her rifle and tried to sight down it at the man on the horse. He wore a tattered pre-collapse US Army kevlar vest, painted black. There were ram horns on his helmet, dipped in some fluorescent yellow substance, and he bellowed rage at her. Mara held her breath, as she'd been taught, and began to tighten her grip on her weapon.

Suddenly another horse burst through from the side of the road and struck the sail cart, scattering the mast and rigging—along with the batteries, wheels, and occupants—as if all were kindling.

Mara's head hit the ground, her limbs dragged down the road, burning her sleeves away, and then she bounced and rolled a few times.

The rifle fired off uselessly into the air.

Mara tensed as the raider on the horse rode hard toward her. Blood started to drip down over her eyes, and pain began to sear through her. She tried to sit up, but the world spun. A tall woman wearing what looked like an entire bush as clothing walked to the center of the road, holding Gillem by his collar. She reached down and picked up the rifle.

"A little young to be riding the road alone, aren't you?"

Gillem yanked at the chain holding him to the wall. "You got us captured by *raiders*," he said.

"I'm sorry." Mara strained at the other end of the room, pulling her own chain to its limit to try and get to a window.

"I didn't ask to go with you," Gillem said. "I *liked* being a brake-boy. The Mayor-Captain ordered me. It's not safe to leave the ship. Everyone knows that. You're a fool."

Mara looked back at him. He was being brave, trying to hold back tears. He'd been born on the swaying, creaking world that was the landship *Zephyr*. He'd only ever known the world trundling slowly past the portholes. And even Mara, who'd only known this world for some months, found that she had quickly become addicted to it. You kept your own home around you, and yet, the rest of the world came to it. Slowly, eventually, it came to you—all you had to do was wait.

To leave the safety of the *Zephyr* made you feel small and vulnerable, cast out.

On the other hand, some of the crew felt like their life's aspiration was to be no more than a turtle. Mara had only been on the great landship for three months now. Enough to get far from her controlling family for good and start a new life. Yet it had hardly been long enough to see much of the world beyond the place where she grew up.

She wanted to see the ocean. The old, shattered skyscrapers. She wanted to see the prairie grass and buffalo surge around the massive wheels of the ship.

Getting captured by raiders was not in her plans.

"Don't say anything about the *Zephyr* to these people," Mara warned him. The landship they called home was well defended, but she didn't want to be the one that led raiders—or whatever these people were—to it. She'd first thought of them as raiders, but the small circle of fifteen or so yurts and handmade wooden buildings she'd seen when being taken here didn't look like the fortress of some raider stronghold.

Gillem balled up against the wall and turned his back to her.

Mara began to study the locking mechanism on her handcuffs. They were pitted, and yet machined so well she knew right away they were artifacts from the time of plenty. How many people over the centuries had been trapped by this exact pair of cuffs?

There were scratch marks around the keyhole; someone had once tried to pick the lock.

And probably failed.

Mara couldn't find anything to try the lock with, so she paced back and forth through a beam of sunlight that came through the window that was just annoyingly out of reach, dragging the chain around the tile floor behind her.

What did the burly old engineer Evgeny keep telling her? Think through the problem, examine all the resources at your disposal, *then* try something. He had said that to her just a week ago, as they stood on the rear of the *Zephyr* and eyed the wooden palisades bolted onto the sagging roof of the ancient Legacy Mall together.

"Those braces look ready to fail," Mara had muttered to him. "The concrete's rotted. The raiders will have them, next fall, if they don't repair them."

Evgeny had agreed, so Mara pushed further: "We should stay and help them, their offer to us was generous."

"It was," Evgeny had agreed. "Though, it was so generous they would have changed their minds about giving us a third of their crop next year."

"It's that or starve."

"So," the old engineer had said with a grin, "it was never really an offer. We can hardly afford to give them all our resources. There is little enough in this world."

Mara remembered that she had folded her knees up to her chin. "All we do is guard what we have left, while everything around us slowly fades away."

And then a loud crack from one of the stays as the third of the four great sail-masts sagged to its side had made her jump.

"The way of the world," Evgeny said sadly, not even surprised.

He'd been monitoring the stress fractures and predicting this for months. "But here on this ship we don't slow down for anything. We can't afford to get trapped anywhere. Not when it's all dying."

No one came for them.

Mara tried to listen to the muffled conversation outside the wooden walls, but it just sounded like chatter. It didn't seem like it was about her and Gillem at all.

Then everything fell quiet as the voices moved away.

"Give me your glasses," Mara said, kicking at Gillem to get his attention.

"My glasses?" Gillem blinked owlishly at her.

The beam of sun had shifted closer to the pillar they were chained to. It was a thick slab of wood.

"Yes, your glasses."

They were Gillem's greatest possession, glasses that had been handed down and traded across towns and no few generations, and mounted in new wooden frames. But he loosened the rubber band and handed them over.

"What are you doing?" he asked as Mara held them up to the sun. "Don't do that, you'll burn your eyes!"

"Exactly."

She gathered straw from the dirt floor, ripped cloth from their sleeves, and within a half hour, had flames licking hungrily up the wooden beam.

"You're going to kill us!" Gillem wailed, pulling all the way to the end of his chain and away from the fire.

The fire spread up the pillar, and then onto the roof. She hadn't expected it to happen so fast. She'd wanted the pillar to burn through just enough that they could pull free of it. Now the fire began to catch the roof and spread overhead, and smoke started filling the room. But fire wasn't the only thing spreading; Mara felt a surge of fear tingle through her whole body as well.

She yanked at the chains, looking for weakness in the wooden beam. But it remained solid.

Gillem screamed for help, and Mara couldn't get him to shut up, though he eventually started coughing too much to shout.

"Stay low."

She had to project a confidence she didn't have as they tried to breathe air through their shirts.

And then, mercifully, the beam *cracked*.

Mara and Gillem burst out of the burning building dragging their chains behind them, and they found people struggling to pull hoses and hand pumps into the center of the village. The fire blazed along the top of two nearby buildings, wooden structures with walls starting to bow inwards.

Four men had grabbed one of the nearby yurts by the walls to drag it across the dirt away from the embers. Children sobbed in the distance, and Mara felt baleful glares aimed at her.

"I don't think they're raiders," Gillem whispered, looking around them.

"It doesn't look like it," Mara agreed, holding him behind her and trying to shield him.

The older woman who captured them was no longer wearing a suit decorated with bushes and leaves but heavy robes. She ran up to them, tears wet on her cheeks.

"Those were *storage buildings*," she said. "That's our winter food burning!"

If she'd been a raider, she would have killed them where they stood. Mara knew that. Instead the woman pointed Mara to the iron pump. "Don't just stand there—help undo what you've done!" the woman shouted.

Mara did not argue, but began to man the lever, pumping as if her life depended on it, knowing that it very well might. Old canvas-reinforced hoses led off through the village to a nearby river. The other hose, held by women trying to get near to the burning storehouse, finally gushed water.

Mara kept at the pump until her hands blistered and the old woman finally pulled her away and bandaged her palms.

"We've saved what we can, the rest will have to just burn out," she said softly.

* * *

Mara sat with Gillem on bundles of supplies singed black, and the woman, who Mara was beginning to think of as a leader in this community, sat with them. Her name was Emi, and her cloud-gray eyes pierced Mara as she stared at them both.

"We put you in there because we weren't sure who you were, if you were a danger to the community. Turns out, you are very dangerous."

"You chained us up," Mara said defiantly.

"How did you do all this?" Emi waved her hand at the ruined buildings.

"She used my glasses," Gillem muttered angrily.

Mara kicked him.

"Why are you here?" Emi asked. "What are you doing in my town?"

The exasperation in her voice made it sound like she was trying to figure out how a dog had gotten into the trash and made a mess.

"The sails broke," Gillem said. Mara hissed at him, and Gillem recoiled.

"I said not to talk about—" Mara started.

But Emi interrupted, sitting between them on the bale and putting a gentle, motherly hand on Gillem's shoulder.

"Sails," Emi said. "How interesting. Tell me more about these sails."

Mara tried to lean back and glare at Gillem behind Emi's back. But the woman sensed the movement and shifted to block Mara.

"We thought you were raiders, but you're not, and we hurt you. I'm sorry. It's the *Zephyr*," Gillem told Emi. "It lost its sails and it's turning around to come this way for trade."

And after that the young brake-boy began telling Emi everything.

In the time of plenty the ancestors had always thought the next generation would see more, live longer, create greater, better, bigger things. Mara had read some of their books in the scholar's area of the Wal-Mart her people had grown up in. They'd assumed that growth was inevitable, due to them, a destiny granted to them that was obvious.

Even as they pursued things that would end that same prosperity.

All civilizations lived among the ruins of the ones that came before. That was the standard reality of human history. The Romans marveled at the pyramids and the great civilization that had constructed them. The peasants of Europe marveled at Roman roads and thought giants had made them.

Mara knew who made the interstates. Although the old giants of transportation built them cheaply from asphalt and didn't intend their work to last for eternity like the Romans had, so most of the ancient American roads had long since faded away from weather and use.

The *Zephyr*'s massive wheels were built to trundle over anything, though. The dilapidated roads were eaten up as the trading ship slowly crossed the midwest.

The landship had shaken and shivered as it crossed the miles after the second mast broke, sometimes lurching violently this way and that. And the great masts, shaped like wings to ride the winds even over the treetops, swayed wildly. One of the masts had already shorted out the motors that turned it to grab the wind just right. Now a second one had failed.

Mara had watched as mast-girls got winched up on bosun's chairs to start work on trying to rerig the lower the mast for repairs. All the *Zephyr*'s masts were stepped—so that they could be lowered to pass under bridges, though Mayor-Captain Sun Shah preferred to sail around the old, rotting structures wherever she could.

"Nothing lasts forever," Evgeny had said to her.

"But this ship is freedom," Mara said. They moved with the winds and freeways, trading between the plaza towns and city remnants. "What happens when we stop?"

"Come with me to the quarter-meeting," Evgeny grunted. "Share your ideas."

"How do you know I have an idea?"

Evgeny had smiled, and turned to walk down the companionway into the heart of the ship, where the section chiefs all met around the Mayor-Captain's great table for an update on the situation.

There was nothing good to report. They didn't have the resources to fix the third mast, and of the two remaining masts, one had serious cracks beginning to appear. Three of the mast sails were carbon fiber, and one aluminum. They couldn't patch the one that just shattered. The shredded pieces couldn't be knitted back together because the ancient piece of technology had been cast as one unit. And no one had the tools anymore to build a replacement, wing-shaped mast.

"We can weld the aluminum," Evgeny reported. "But it'll require us to use most of the battery reserves for the work, and we'll use up almost all of our wire."

If they did that, the next big break on the ship wouldn't be fixable until they found a town with the resources to help them. And they would gouge for the price.

"We need to build a new sail," Mara spoke up. "Or this is just delaying the inevitable."

At that, the Mayor-Captain—her thin, mohawked hair gleaming in the oil-lamp light—leaned forward and looked at Mara with a squint. Mara swallowed. Here she was in the captain's quarters, lamps swinging and spilling faint trickles of smoke, with all of the ship's chiefs staring at her.

Well, she hadn't run away to be a mouse, had she?

She was an adventurer, now. A traveler. One of the crew of the *Zephyr*. There was nothing Mara wouldn't do for the ship that had saved her from being trapped behind the barricades of her old home.

"It's about the honey," Mara said.

Emi frowned and leaned back to look at Mara. "Honey?"

If Mara could have cut Gillem's tongue out she would have. Or at least, that's how she felt. That was just anger, and even though she imagined it she knew it was just the frustration in her.

She bit her lip and tried to match Emi's stare.

But Emi wasn't going anywhere, and Mara had to think. The woman already knew about the *Zephyr*. It was coming. And there was some debt here. Particularly if Emi was just the leader of a friendly village, another group of people just trying to survive out here.

"The *Zephyr* delivers mail, and news. It knits the world together.

It helps them trade." Mara described the great ship in glowing terms, emphasizing what it could do to help them. Also, she subtly mentioned how well defended it was. The gun mounts, the spearmen, the grenade throwers.

"But what about the honey?" Emi asked.

"Sweeteners are some of the most demanded trades when we sail into town," Mara said. And the prices at the Legacy Mall had been amazing, far below the usual trades. There'd been beautiful paper there as well, which she'd purchased for sketching out machines on.

What the honey had been stored in had caught her attention. Brand new, shiny, aluminum cans. The Mayor-Captain was old. There was gray in that strip of hair that ran down her dark-skinned scalp. Some said she was born to a collapse mother, who'd told her what the dark times had been like, and that's why Sun Shah would never stop the ship. Not until the day it died. She was always running from the memories of the world that was.

But after Mara had talked about honey, Mayor-Captain Sun Shah had given Mara a sail cart and told her to ride ahead to find who had made those cans.

And she had promised to do something the *Zephyr* almost never did: turn around and follow an unfamiliar road.

Emi took them into one of the larger yurts and gave them some kind of beef stew from a pot simmering away by a fire in the heart of the round, tent-like building. The walls were made out of a thick wool, but panels had been opened to allow a steady breeze to waft through. It carried the smell of charred wood and wetness.

Gillem all but drank the stew from his bowl, and Emi smiled slightly to see it.

"Growing boys," she said to Mara. "Where *do* they put it all?"

There were fur-lined blankets for them to sleep in, and Emi made sure Gillem was tucked away. Mara waited, and watched the open panels move this way and that in the wind.

She felt very alone in the dark, far from the familiar creak of the *Zephyr*.

"I see you watching me," Emi said softly in the dark. She sat by the embers of the cook fire. "You can leave, if you want. Go to your ship. I won't stop you."

"Some of your people looked angry."

"Can you blame them? We're still not sure how badly your fire set us back. All of our hard work, our planning for the winter… it might be all for naught."

Mara looked down and bit her lip, a prickle of shame and fear passing through her.

"I didn't mean to…" she trailed off.

"You have a quick mind," Emi said. "You were in chains and scared. I should have paid closer attention, but my mind was elsewhere."

"On what?" Mara asked.

But while Emi had thus far been quite open with Mara, the woman kept her troubled thoughts to herself, instead watching the coals. She poured water over the last of them and listened to the hiss as the mild red light ebbed away.

"*Kites*," Gillem said.

Mara blinked awake and scrabbled up to her feet. "What?"

"They're up on kites, like people in the planes of old that you told me about," Gillem said. He tugged on her hand. "Come see!"

Mara followed him outside, shielding her eyes with an open palm, and looked. Three children, not much larger than Gillem, hung in harnesses underneath massive kites just a few feet over the ground. They bucked hard against wires on the ground held by several of the adults of the community.

The two of them watched the kite flyers rise up into the air. A hundred feet. Two. Further and further. Higher.

"Why are they doing that?" Mara asked.

"They said they were looking for trading parties. And the *Zephyr*."

But they knew where the ship was coming from, Mara thought; why did they need to *see* it? There was a puzzle here she felt she needed to solve, yet she didn't know what the pieces even *were*.

She watched the tiny figures fly far overhead.

"Aren't they amazing?" Gillem gasped.

"They are," Mara agreed, letting go of the puzzle in the back of her mind to marvel at the kites. The wind that far up was strong, so strong the wire cables anchoring them to the ground buzzed taut.

Emi doted on Gillem for the next few days, making sure he had sweets and friends to play with. Brake-boys had time to themselves, and lessons on the deck from an old teacher. But here he got to run in the woods, splash in the stream, play chase.

"They're nice to me," he told her. "Not grumpy like you. And this is nicer than a brake box."

She did not begrudge the boy his days of fun. In fact, she felt she could almost relax a little herself. Only some of the villagers' food had been damaged—a rare stroke of luck.

"We will add foraging to our daily routine and make some trades to resupply what we lost," Emi said. "Soon your ship will arrive. Our flyers will let us know when we spot it."

Before long, Mara would be back on the deck. A sailor once more. She glanced up at the kites as Emi walked away from them.

"You know they have bigger kites packed away," Gillem whispered conspiratorially with a grin. "We saw them when we were playing hide and seek."

And then the pieces all fell together, like when she was playing with the cogs and springs of a machine and suddenly all the components lined up as they were supposed to. Mara could see it all.

Her mouth dried, and her knees buckled.

Mara put an arm around Gillem. "We have to run."

"*What?*"

"Run. We need to run. Now. To warn the *Zephyr*."

"That's crazy!" Gillem whined. "They fed us. They gave us a warm place to sleep. They did all that even after you burned their buildings down. These people are *nice*."

Mara grabbed Gillem's hands. "They're nice. So nice. And so were my parents when they locked me up to try and force me to marry the 'right' person. They were nice when they stopped me when I came of age from ever going to the community library, as it was time for me to focus on my new role as a wife and mother to be. Do you understand?"

Gillem shook his head.

Mara leaned down to look him in the eye. "After the Vikings raided villages they went home, and they hugged their wives and kissed their children. They were nice. Serial killers, the old chronicles said they were always nice. *Good* isn't the same thing as *nice*, Gillem. Emi *is* a raider. *Everyone* here is a raider."

"You can't know that." Gillem looked at her with wide eyes.

"See all the yurts?" That had been eating at her since they'd arrived. "They're light, packable, and right next to the heavy buildings made of lumber. And *those* were built to last, to stand here and never go away."

"That doesn't mean—"

"*Yes it does*," Mara hissed, and cursed the boy silently; Gillem had given up so much to them already. "Get ready, we need to leave tonight. Be ready."

Fortunately Emi and her people had been so focused on being nice, they had left the camp sufficiently unguarded that Mara thought they'd be able to slip away easily.

"But I don't *want* to leave," Gillem protested.

"Be. Ready."

There was an old sail cart in the corner of the village. Mara had paid close attention to where the road began, and where the sun had been. She knew which way to run, as well as any navigationist back on the ship.

Gillem followed her to it, nervous.

"You are not just a sailor," Emi said, making them both jump. She held out a hand, and Gillem left Mara to go stand by Emi.

"Gillem," Mara said softly.

Gillem couldn't meet her eyes. He stood, half turned toward Emi, shuffling his feet awkwardly in the dirt.

"He told me everything." Emi put a hand on Gillem's head. "Such a good, trusting boy. Go on Gillem, go back to the tent."

Gillem looked at Mara, then Emi, and then ran back to the tent.

Mara clenched her jaw. "Will you put me in chains again, then?"

"The last time I did that you burned down the buildings." Emi folded her arms and leaned against the sail cart.

Mara swallowed. This was it. They were going to kill her. "Will you be good to Gillem?" she asked, her voice cracking slightly.

"He's just a boy, of course we will."

"You can't take the ship. It's too big, too well guarded. You'll dash yourselves against the hull and die there. Even the way you hide to ambush folk, like you were doing back alongside the road, that won't help you."

She threw out her defiance with each word. But none of it made Emi even blink.

"You're clever, but you still don't see the things in front of you when it comes to the real world outside the comfort of your ship. They won't attack like that." She pointed up into the air. "No—they'll fall down out of the sky and be on your decks before anyone even understands what is happening."

Mara tried to hold back bile bubbling up in the back of her throat. "No…" she trailed off weakly.

"Great forts with their stockades full of the strongest fighters have fallen to us when we glide out of the night." Emi shook her head sadly. "The thicker the walls, the more complacent."

"And these folk?"

"They had no walls. They were honey traders. Trying to build a small world for themselves at the halfway point. One of our kites spotted the clearing." Emi shrugged, the motion somehow suggesting the rest of the sad story.

Those poor traders. Mara couldn't stop thinking about them. This whole place was a graveyard.

Emi walked past her. Mara flinched. Emi paused and ran a finger along her cheek. "I'm not going to kill you. I'm a warrior, not a murderer. To face someone in a battle, where we each have a chance to kill each other or surrender, that is a different thing."

"Death is death," Mara said. And sweeping in from the sky to surprise someone, that wasn't a noble face-to-face fight. "You want Gillem because he's small; you'll use him on the kites."

All around her, Mara suddenly realized there was a lot of movement happening for the late hour: Emi's people were breaking down the yurts. They were all getting ready to move, and packing things onto horse-drawn carts.

"You can come and join us, after the attack," Emi said. "But I think you might prefer to keep going north. The honey traders—they were too dug in for us to attack. They might take you in."

"You're a waste," Mara said to her. "You can only think to take. You can't see the world in a way where you get something and someone else does too, you can only imagine that if you get something, someone else has to lose."

"There's not enough to go around," Emi said. "It's just the way the world is."

She handed Mara a small bag with food in it, and then got into the sail cart.

"People like you, they destroy each other until there's nothing left," Mara said. "And you drag the rest of us down with you."

"I see the hatred in your eyes. If you choose to join instead of heading north, that must be gone when I see you next. If it isn't, your fate will be that of everyone else aboard your ship."

Raiders in bulletproof jackets rode off into the night, and they took the kite lines with them. In the dark, the wings of the kites were shadows flitting about under the clouds.

There was no way to warn the ship.

For a moment, Mara despaired. Maybe she should take the bag and flee.

But then she took a deep breath. *Think through the problem, examine all the resources at your disposal,* then *try something.* Evgeny taught her that when repairing the ship, and he needed her help more now than ever.

Mara began ripping through the crates and bundles of supplies that Emi and her raiders had left behind, things not valuable enough for them to take with them as they wandered the country to maraud.

She stopped when she found stacks of light, beautiful paper. The same paper she'd admired and purchased for sketching.

The ship just needed to be warned. They would have a chance if they just looked up.

* * *

The *Zephyr* came through in the morning, trundling implacably on. There were new scars on the hull, and a few missing faces. A scout on the forecastle shot at Mara when she waved to be picked up, but Evgeny cuffed them on the side of the head and shouted for her to grab at a rope they lowered. Mara ran alongside the ship to catch it, and they hauled her aboard.

"I knew it was you that warned us," Evgeny said, something like pride in his voice as he grabbed her shoulder. "Floating arrows in the night sky, making us look up."

Working calmly and quickly with twigs and paper, Mara had built lanterns. Floating paper lanterns. Square, wobbly, ungainly, and with large arrows painted on their sides.

She'd hung tiny burning plates underneath to heat the air inside.

"Half of them were blown into the trees," Mara said.

"We only needed to spot one and wonder what was in the sky," Evgeny said.

The remains of two broken kites lay on the deck. There was blood staining the wooden frames. Mara picked up a piece of one of the wings.

"The boy who left with you?" Evgeny asked. "What did they do to him?"

"He chose to go with them. They were nice to him, he said. Where are they—the raiders?"

"They ran back into the woods. We'll take a different route west, not come back down this way," Evgeny told her.

"It's good they were stopped." Mara looked out at the trees. "People who think like them, they're the reason we spiraled down this far."

The Mayor-Captain came to see Mara in the evening, when all the solar lamps were taken down from where they hung on the rails to line the walls. A great honor. And Mara got to provide some valuable intelligence: She told her that the aluminum and honey were still farther north.

But Mara was already looking further ahead than that. Imagining kites, maybe bigger parasails made with silks from the southeast. They could reach the stronger winds that always lived up by the clouds. It would be more dependable than the swooping masts they used now.

And a faster ship would mean more trade. They could build on that. Bring communities closer together. Outrun any trouble.

Mara ran a finger over the kite's cloth.

They stood in the shadow of the grand past, but a future was worth building toward.

"I can build you greater sails. We won't be repairing an old ship; I can remake it into something better," Mara told the Mayor-Captain. "But I want you to do something for me."

Evgeny gaped. Mara had only been on the ship a few months. Yes, she'd saved them, but to ask such a favor was impertinent at best.

"What would you ask of me?" Shah asked.

"We need to help Legacy Mall or those people won't be around when we come back to trade with. These raiders will destroy them. We need to rebuild more than just the ship."

They needed to rebuild a world.

Mayor-Captain Sun Shan rested her elbows on the railing. "They can't pay us what they promised," she said.

"I wanted to join the *Zephyr* to get away from everything. But you can't run away from the entire world, can you?" Mara said. "If we help those people, they'll help us build another ship, using my sailing method."

"We'll have to stay put for a while," Sun Shah said. "I don't like stops."

"Leave me to build the ship and I'll catch up."

Sun Shah looked at her sideways. Then grabbed her face with two hands. "First, child, before you promote yourself to captaining a ship of your own, fix my sails. Then we shall talk."

She kissed Mara on the forehead and left. And Mara stood on the shifting deck, looking up at the masts.

Up into the sky.

CANNIBAL ACTS

MAUREEN F. MCHUGH

Maureen F. McHugh is a Hugo and Tiptree Award winner. She is the author of four novels, including *China Mountain Zhang* and *Nekropolis*. Her collection *Mothers & Other Monsters* was a finalist for the Story Prize, and her second collection, *After the Apocalypse*, was one of *Publishers Weekly*'s Ten Best Books of the Year. She teaches screenwriting and new media at University of Southern California, School of Cinema Arts.

There's a difference between dissection and butchering. Dissection reveals, but butchering renders. I'm a dissector, professionally, pressed into service as a butcher. I mean, I was a biologist. Am a biologist.

The body in front of me is a man. I know him, although not very well—there aren't that many of us so I know pretty much everybody. His name is Art. He looks much smaller, positively shrunken, laid out in the kitchen, and very, very white. I haven't seen many naked male bodies but I am intimately acquainted with Art's. I have washed him. I'm not attracted to men when they're alive, much less when they're dead, but I feel a weird protectiveness toward Art. I've felt the soft spot in his skull from the fall that killed him. I have washed around his balls and the curled mushroom of his penis. I have cradled his hard and bony feet.

Now I tie a rope around his ankles and hoist him. This is a

commercial kitchen with big steel counters and a Hobart dishwasher. The pulley in the ceiling is new. It sounds easy—"I tie a rope around his ankles and hoist him"—but I am not very strong these days and just one pulley means I'm hauling his whole weight. I don't know what Art weighs. He used to weigh more; we all used to weigh more. I am so tired, my fingers are cold. I'm seeing spots when I pull hard on the rope.

Kate has taken to calling the town Leningrad, which is lost on most of the people here. It's because we're under siege in this stupid little Alaska excuse. It's got an airstrip, a Coast Guard base, an Army listening post, a dozen houses, and it's surrounded on two sides by water—the ocean at our back and a river called Pilot's Creek on one side. The Army listening post was monitoring the Russians, of course, which is probably where Kate got the idea of Leningrad.

So anyway, I get Art hanging, fingers just sweeping the floor. The dead are limp. Heavy. One of the locals used to hunt when there was anything to hunt. Eric Swetzof is a long-bodied, short-legged native Unagan. Maybe, he says, he and his wife are the last Unagan left alive. He told me the steps to field dressing a large animal.

Eric is not going to eat Art. There is a group of people who have declared themselves to be non-eaters. Eric says he understands the people who have voted to eat and he doesn't judge them, he just can't. Can't cross that line.

I understand him, too. I stand in front of a human with a good knife. "Blade at least four inches long," Eric said. "You want a real handle on the thing, and a guard. When the knife hits bone it can turn and you can end up cutting yourself."

I used to like to cook. I've cut chickens into parts. I'm familiar with the way a joint shines white with ligament and tendon. What hangs in front of me is an animal. I am an animal. I don't believe there is something particularly special about bodies and I don't believe in souls, the afterlife, or the resurrection of the dead. I tell myself that this is a technical challenge. It's a skill I have some parts of and I will learn the rest as I go.

I am not sentimental.

I put a plastic tub underneath Art to catch blood and viscera.

It's still very hard to open his throat. His insides are still lukewarm. I'm so hungry.

Butchering has gotten me out of manning the defenses today. We all have to man the defenses but I'm nearsighted and terrible with a gun. Luckily, there isn't much shooting because neither side has much in the way of ammunition. They are mostly men, as best we can tell, a lot of them fairly young. Maybe thirty of them, some still in ragged military fatigues. They are in the sharp green hills, waiting us out. They have a couple of boats, Zodiacs, but we sunk one when they first attacked and now they either don't want to risk them or they are holding them until we're too weak to fight back.

Or maybe they're getting too weak to fight.

I find Kate on Beach Road. It runs along the beach, of course, and then turns inland and runs to the airstrip. It's cloudy and soft, it rains all summer here. The air off the water smells wrong. It should smell of fish and salt, that slightly rank and pleasant stink of ocean, but instead there's a taste to it, like nail polish or something. Organics. Esters and aldehydes.

Kate is sitting cross-legged with a paperback on one knee and a rifle next to her. Technically she's on sentry, watching the ocean, but we're sloppy civilians. Does the distinction even matter anymore? She's taller than me—a lot of people are taller than me. I'm 5' 4". She's rangy; a long-legged, raw-boned woman with large hands and feet. She's originally from New Mexico but she's an Anglo with light hair and blue eyes.

I am still surprised when I see her in glasses. She has worn contacts as long as I have known her. She was always going to get corrective eye surgery. Too late now.

I can't tell if she is pleased to see me. I mean, usually she would be, but she knows what I've been doing. Kate is a non-eater.

I sit down next to her and watch the chop.

"All done?" she asks.

I nod.

I think for a moment she is going to ask me if I'm OK, which is something we would have done for each other before. She doesn't and I don't know what I would answer if she did. I'm both not OK and weirdly OK.

"What's the book?" I ask.

She flips it over so I can see the cover. *The Da Vinci Code*. I can't help it, I bark out a laugh. Kate hated the book when it came out.

She sighs. "There aren't that many books here at the end of the world."

"It's not the end of the world," I snap.

She rolls her eyes. "Don't tell me about the Great Oxygenation Event or Snowball Earth again or I'll scream."

It isn't the end of the world—just maybe the end of us. Or maybe not, humans are clever beasts and the world is a big place. It's probably not even the biggest extinction event the Earth has ever seen. The Permian extinction killed something like 95 percent of life—including bacteria. Life comes back. It may take millions of years. First bacteria, then multicellular organisms, then plants and animals. We're just another set of dinosaurs, about to go extinct. Although some dinosaurs actually survived the Cretaceous-Tertiary extinction. We just call them birds.

"You're sitting there composing a speech," Kate says.

"I'm not going to say anything," I say.

"You intellectualize as a defense mechanism."

"I don't think psych talks about defense mechanisms anymore," I say. Back when we were both at the university we were also both in therapy. Growing up gay pretty much ensured you were messed up about something. My therapist told me I was an emotophobe— afraid of negative emotions.

"What's your defense mechanism?" I ask.

She laughs. "These days? Anger. When I have the energy."

I brought her here. Not specifically here, this ass-end little Alaskan town, but "here" as in leaping at a chance to go to Juneau to study giant viruses and get us away from the increasing chaos of the lower forty-eight.

I look at her wrists, narrow, the knob of the Olecranon Process standing under scaly skin. Her ankles are swollen.

Kate and I bitched about Houston the entire time we lived there. When I took the position, I had no idea that Houston was tropical.

Ninety-eight degrees in the summer with 99 percent humidity. Flying cockroaches the size of my thumb. Getting into the car at the end of the work day was like climbing into a pizza oven.

Honestly, though, I remember Houston this way:

In the last year we were there, crime was getting horrible. There were refugee camps outside Brownsville and Laredo. Rolling brownouts. We had a used Prius, which was good because gas was rationed. Hamburger was twenty-two dollars a pound.

Kate gardened and we had half a dozen chickens. We had close friends, Ted and Esteban, and we'd take eggs and garden vegetables over to their place and make dinner. They had huge trees in their backyard and a pool. The electricity would go out and we'd sit in the dark and complain about mosquitos and drink beer.

I was coming home from work one day and stopped at a stoplight, as one does, and someone wrenched open the driver's-side door of the Prius. It was a very angry man with a blue bandanna covering half of his face. He'd have looked like some kind of old movie bandit if he hadn't also been wearing sunglasses. He was waving around a gun and screaming at me.

He yelled "Get out of the car!" at some point.

Back in the day, if you were on Facebook or Tumblr, and you were a woman, you probably got safety tips in your feed. I had read *something* about whether you were safer in a car or out of it although I think it was about getting into a car with someone who was armed—like someone who was going to get you into the car and take you somewhere. I remember it seemed vitally important to know whether I was safer in the car or out of it but I couldn't remember and in the end I scooted across the middle console and out the passenger's-side door.

He got in the car and drove off. My laptop was in the back seat. I had the key fob in my pocket, so he didn't have that.

The police came and we went down to the police station and I told them everything. Then Kate took me home in a Lyft and Esteban made me a precious vodka martini (vodka was expensive) and everyone came over and sat around, commiserating. The electricity went out and we lit a couple of candles. I remember people brought food. Ted said he could take me to work the next day. Another neighbor volunteered to pick me up at work—it wasn't that far out of her way.

I was genuinely shaken. I don't want you to think that I wasn't. But it was such a pleasure to be the center of everyone's concern and attention. As the city vibrated apart, we worked to take care of each other.

In Houston I was studying big viruses. Everyone was, all over the country. My head of research, an asshole named Mark Adams, said it was like the nineties when everybody got sucked into the Human Genome Project. Careers were stagnant for a decade, he said.

Careers. Imagine worrying about a career.

Imagine having deep discussions about things at conferences in Atlanta or Baltimore. Big viruses were different from regular viruses. They didn't just take over a cell and destroy it to make new viruses. They took over a cell and turned it into a virus factory, pumping out viruses at an order of magnitude higher. They had already been linked with a meningitis outbreak in India.

I was doing work on ATP, the energy transfer mechanism in cells, and how the virus co-opted the system. I was at a conference and ended up sitting next to a guy named Zhou Limin from the University of Science and Technology of China in Hefei. We'd corresponded but never met.

We ended up getting lunch. He was a short, intense guy in glasses. He'd done graduate work at Penn State and been a post doc at UCLA so he spoke great English. We bitched about the emphasis on virus coatings and how that was a legacy of HIV research and how the organizers of the conference were biased toward those people.

"You want a beer?" he asked.

I didn't know if he knew I'm gay. I think I did the thing where I said I had promised to call and check in with my girlfriend.

He didn't care so we ended up sitting in the hotel bar, some Hilton or Sheraton. The beers were nineteen dollars a piece.

"Let me expense it," he said.

"USTC covers alcohol?" I asked.

He grinned. "There'd be mutiny if they didn't."

Sometimes I fantasized about doing work in China. There were fewer restrictions there. The Chinese were willing to play fast and loose with ethics. I mean, I knew it would not really be anything like

I thought; their office politics were complicated and so were their governmental. "I wish we could do some of the things you guys can do," I said.

He turned his beer glass in his hands. "The government is weaponizing big viruses," he said. "They're trying to make them to deliver bird flu."

Everyone talked about what China might be doing. China had been the first country to bring human clones to term in violation of international ethics. Of course we thought they might do something like this. "You know for sure?" I asked.

"I know people on the project," he said. "I've seen some of the results."

So, you might think I would instantly rush to the government or to the newspapers. That I was in a position to save the world.

But I wasn't. What were we going to do, invade China over microbiology? All that would happen was that Zhao would be compromised. I think he just had to tell somebody and I was the stranger on a plane.

I told a couple of friends without mentioning Zhao. Then I saw the job listing for a new lab in Juneau and it sounded so far away, so clean and cold and safe. (Juneau was actually like Seattle, wet and green.) I remember watching television in the airport while we waited to catch our plane first to Salt Lake City and then to Seattle and then on to Alaska. There were reports on the bird flu epidemic in Russia. Russia had been sabre rattling at China in Mongolia and the Chinese had retaliated. In a month we were all working on ways to stop the viruses—vaccinations, antivirals, manufactured viruses that spread their own antivirus (and look how well that went in Japan). People were getting sick, all over the world. Kate got sick early and was in the hospital on a ventilator for three days. She was lucky. In a month there were nowhere near enough ventilators for the people who needed them and infection among hospital staff was running at over 80 percent.

Pakistan and India went to war and we all waited for India to drop the bomb, but instead North Korea nuked Tianjin and Los Angeles.

The pandemic was burning unchecked—bird flu, the counterflu—

and it seemed like being near other people was a terrible idea. We decided to retreat to a cabin on the Alaska Peninsula. It was owned by a guy in my department but he was dead.

My parents died in the pandemic. Kate's mother, too. We don't know about her father, she hadn't talked to him in a decade. Is Houston still there?

It's like asking if Troy is still there. There's a place on the map marked Troy but nobody has lived in those ruins or called it Troy in centuries. Maybe someone still lives in Houston. Maybe Ted is standing on his back deck looking at his empty swimming pool and he's converted it into a kind of greenhouse, like he always threatened. Maybe they are growing things. Maybe the chickens we gave him live there.

Everything we try to grow here in Alaska dies and no one, least of all me, knows what that means.

In the late afternoon there are gunshots and I scramble to the airstrip. Scramble is a relative term. When I stand up too quickly, I see spots. We all conserve energy. But the rule is, when you hear shots, anyone not on sentry has to grab a weapon and go.

We dug trenches and put up barricades of useless vehicles, trash, and fence before these guys even showed up. I find Eric. The big man is crouched in a trench.

"What's the password," he says. A joke between us.

"Leningrad," I say. "Where's Deb?" Deb's his wife.

He shrugs. Eric doesn't talk much. It took me a long time to figure out he's a sarcastic bastard. He's so deadpan it's scary.

"What are they doing?" I ask. "I heard shots."

(I wish I could say I was some sort of intrepid survivor, but the first time someone shot at me I just froze. I hunkered down and couldn't move. Eric's comment later was, "It happens.")

"They aren't doing anything," Eric says.

I watch the green and granite hills. No sign of movement in their trenches.

"I wonder how much food they've got," I say. "Maybe we should do some kind of nighttime sneak attack." Not that there's much night at this time of year.

"Jeff said no," Eric says. Jeff is our elected mayor/commandant.

I'm tired from jogging to the airstrip and these days my concentration is pretty shot so I sit for a minute carefully studying the landscape and feeling empty and stupid. (And thinking about Art cooking back in the kitchen.) "Wait, you suggested it?"

Eric glances at me, expressionless, which I think is Eric speak for "are you a moron?" He looks back out at the blank hills.

We sit there for a while and I try to figure out what that means. It starts to drizzle.

"Do you think they're planning something?" I ask.

"I think they're desperate," Eric says.

"Join the club," I say.

Eric looks at me, stonefaced. But I'm beginning to get when he's amused. I think he's amused.

The eaters assemble in the canteen. Len did the cooking. He has worked very hard to make sure that Art no longer looks like Art. We have Art a couple of ways. We have some of Art roasted and sliced thin. Lean strips of meat. The rest is boiled. So here it is: human flesh tastes… pretty bland. Tough and maybe a little bitter. I can see why people compare it to veal or pork or chicken. I am so hungry but I eat it slowly. Len cries as he eats. He was a fisherman—like the guys in the television show who catch crab, only he worked on boats that caught halibut, pollock, and herring and occasionally did stints in processing plants. I almost sat down next to him, solidarity in our grisly parts in this meal. But I thought maybe it was better if I didn't make us so obvious.

There isn't a lot of meat. The broth is salty. I feel full.

Thank you, Art.

I wonder who at this table will eat me? Although I'm a short woman and there's a good chance I'll outlive most of the men.

I almost fall asleep at the table. Spoons clink against bowls. Len cries as he drinks spoonfuls, salty tears slipping into his ragged beard, flannel shirt loose on him.

* * *

A single gunshot the next morning brings us to the airstrip.

It's sunny for a change. Kate and I walk over together. We haven't said anything about what I've done. It should have been some kind of personal Rubicon and maybe it was but what I feel is that I held out on Kate. That I didn't share food with her. Like I cheated. There was a time when we'd have talked about it. It's what lesbians do, you know, we talk and talk. We negotiate our needs and our wants. We explore our feelings. But here, at the end of the world, it's okay that some things won't be resolved. We'll go to our deaths with resentments and unfairness clutched to us like greedy children. What else have we got?

There's a white T-shirt flying on a stick.

We all sit on the ground, the edge of a trench, whatever. I mostly feel as if I don't have the energy to deal with this. Not after Art. No more decisions.

"What do you want to do?" Len asks everybody and nobody in particular.

"They surrendering?" Callie asks.

Eric's face doesn't exactly change but I suspect he's thinking, "moron."

Callie is perfectly nice. I think she was local, administration. Like a secretary or data entry. I can imagine her thinking she'd work for a few years, get a nest egg, and then get a job in Juneau. Or maybe she's like a lot of Alaskans and she likes the ass end of nowhere and she had a husband who loved snowmobiles or something.

"I don't trust them," she says.

Oh for Christ's sake.

"We can ask them," I say. I thought I was too worn down to care but I remain myself—opinionated and unwilling to shut up till the end.

Everyone looks at me.

I stand up and yell over the tipped Land Cruiser that forms part of a barricade. I yell, "Hey! Are you surrendering?"

Kate finds me embarrassing sometimes.

A guy comes over the hill. He's dressed in camo pants and a T-shirt and he looks normal, not super skinny. He waves his arms. "We need help! We're dying! We're sick!"

"All of you come out in the open!" Eric yells.

It's a long five minutes or so before three men shuffle to the edge of the airstrip. We shout back and forth. They are all that's left, they say. We don't believe them. One of them weeps.

It takes most of the morning before we are convinced. There are four more guys too sick to walk. We could shoot them.

They don't look starving. That's the important thing.

"What if we quarantine them?" Kate asks me.

"We'd be talking Ebola levels of decontamination," I say. "Bleach. The whole nine yards. We don't have that stuff."

"I've already had the flu," she points out. "I'd be immune. I'd just have to be very careful."

Three of us have had it and survived. They decide to risk meeting; everyone else will be ready for an ambush. We have rubber boots and Wellingtons, and latex gloves and hairnets that were for the kitchen staff. The three put on raincoats and gear and I use duct tape to seal the sleeves of the raincoats to the tops of the latex gloves. When they come back I will make them walk through tubs of bleach and wash everything off before putting on a pair of gloves and taking all the homemade gear off.

"Cover me," Kate says to me, grinning—I am a terrible shot—and walks across the airstrip.

No one shoots.

That evening, in our bed, she tells me what it was like. The graves. The newly dead. The smell. The sick. The trash and carelessness. "They were, like, teenagers," she says. One of the sick men died during the afternoon.

There is a box truck three-quarters full of supplies. Bags of beans and rice. MREs. These weird emergency bars.

Kate tells me they were convinced we had medical supplies. One of them said that he knew we had supplies when they smelled meat cooking. They assumed then that we had power, maybe a freezer.

"They're just kids," she says. "Like my students." Kate taught English, Freshman Composition, in Houston. "Just clueless kids."

"Like we have a clue," I say.

We eat MREs. Mine is Mexican chicken stew. There is the stew and a packet of red pepper to spice it up, Spanish-style rice, and jalapeno nacho cheese spread. There are cheese-filled pretzel nuggets. There is Hawaiian punch, so sugary that when I taste it, tears come to my eyes. And these weird crackers, like saltines but coarser. Some weird refried beans with so much flavor. There's a full-sized bag of peanut M&M's. It's weird, seeing it all bright. It's exotic.

Kate gets spaghetti with meat sauce (we reached in and drew blind so we wouldn't know what we were getting). We agree she won. It's like canned spaghetti and comes with a weird cracker that is shaped like a slice of bread but isn't either bread or a cracker. Cheez Whiz-type stuff, hot sauce, potato sticks, and blueberry-cherry cobbler.

I feed her some of mine because, I keep saying, I ate yesterday. Besides, I'm full. We share her blueberry-cherry cobbler, which has no crust and isn't really anything like a cobbler but who cares and we keep the M&M's to share in bed.

Cheese and crackers! A meal!

It makes me think that maybe we'll survive. Maybe in a few months there will be fish in the ocean and Len will show us ways to catch them. It makes me think that a society that made things this marvelous will not just disappear.

It makes me think that none of the rest of us will get the flu.

It makes me believe we will hang on.

We sit in our bed in the big main building of the Coast Guard station—no one lives in the houses because they are too hard to defend. Our home is a mattress and box spring sitting on the floor of an office, next to a desk. I feed Kate a yellow M&M and eat a brown one.

"Don't eat all the brown ones," she says.

"Oh, do you like them best?"

"No, you're giving me all the pretty ones and eating all the broken and brown ones."

"I ate yesterday," I say.

"I ate today." She picks up a red one and holds it out to me on the palm of her hand.

I take it.

"I'm sorry," I say. "I'm sorry I ate." I wish they had surrendered before.

"I want you to eat," she says.

"You're not."

"I am," she says, and pops an M&M in her mouth. "Now I am again."

I sigh and settle on my side.

"Promise me you'll eat me," she says. "If it happens."

I don't say anything.

"You're so brave," she whispers. "I would if I could but I can't. I can't be like you."

I smell the M&M's and the dusty carpet. I feel the bones of my hips on the mattress.

"Eat me because I love you," she says. "Because you love me. Because you have to. Promise me."

ECHO

VERONICA ROTH

Veronica Roth is the #1 *New York Times* bestselling author of the Divergent Series (*Divergent, Insurgent, Allegiant,* and *Four: A Divergent Collection*) and the Carve the Mark series (*Carve the Mark, The Fates Divide*). Her short stories and essays have appeared in the anthologies *Summer Days and Summer Nights, Shards and Ashes,* and *Three Sides of a Heart*. The Divergent Series was developed into three major motion pictures. Veronica grew up outside of Chicago and graduated from Northwestern University. She now lives in Chicago proper with her husband and dog and writes full-time. You can find Veronica on Facebook and Instagram (@vrothbooks) or at her website (veronicarothbooks.com). Her next two books are a YA short story collection, *The End and Other Beginnings: Stories from the Future* (fall 2019, HarperCollins), and her adult fiction debut, *The Chosen One* (spring 2020, John Joseph Adams Books).

Tabor Kata stood alone near the hatch of her one-person domicile ship, waiting as her vacsuit pressurized. An oxygen tank was fixed to her back, enough for two hours' worth of exploring before she'd choke to death on poison. When the tank was low, or if it began to leak, the whole thing would start whistling like a tea kettle. The first time that had happened, she had screeched at the sound, making Drobo laugh at her—without actually laughing, in that way only progs could.

"*There is no need to panic*," Drobo had said in her ear.

He—"it," really, because he had no physical body, and no gender preference, but she thought of Drobo as a "he"—had asked her once how she could tell that he was mocking her, so that he could adjust his voice modulator accordingly. I just know, she had said. It's instinct, or something.

The faceplate of her helmet was cloudy from the heat of her exhalations. She smacked it with a gloved hand. "Stupid busted junk," she said. She had purchased it from a SILF—Synthetic Intelligent Life Form—in a back alley of the exodus town of Third City. And nothing quality ever came out of Third City.

"*Striking your suit will not accomplish anything*," Drobo said in her ear. "*I will adjust the internal controls*."

"Thanks," she said, and bounced on her toes as she waited for the glass to clear. She didn't like coming back here, to a ruined Earth, to an abandoned home. But this was more important than her preferences.

The helmet offered maximum visibility, transparent at the front and sides, streamlined, and coated so it was less reflective. Once the glass was clear, she looked around to get her bearings.

Kata had touched down in the middle of a street in Cluj-Napoca, Romania, beside the crumbling Szent Mihály church in the middle of Old Town. The square—Plata Unirii—reminded her of the annual Christmas Fair held there, where she had gone for hot cider as a child… and also to watch people fall on their asses while they tried to ice skate, of course.

And now—no Christmas Fair, no ice skaters, no *people*. No movement, even, but for the scurry of a cockroach every now and then. She had always heard they would survive the apocalypse, but she had not thought of what that would look like—the shock of organic movement in a now-inorganic world.

"*May I help?*" Drobo asked.

"No," Kata said, her voice rough. "Be quiet."

"*Very well*," he said, but he wasn't happy about it. She could hear that in his voice, too.

Kata walked south, toward Strada Avram Iancu, and behind it, the steep slope of the cemetery. She had seen it from the air, headstones and tombs poking up like little broken teeth from the overgrown hillside. During All Saints Day, it had glowed red with candles placed beside each grave, surrounding them. Remembering them. She had walked those paths with her father, her hand in his, the living coexisting with the dead. Just as she did now, only now there were far more dead than living.

Cluj had been in the radiation zone surrounding one of the massive blasts of the WMDs that had struck Europe. The city had been evacuated before the catastrophe, so there were no bodies in the streets, no leveled buildings. There were some signs of upheaval if she cleared dirt from the windows—drawers pulled open and left that way, books scattered on the floor as objects were pulled from bookshelves, torn tapestries dangling from whitewashed plaster. It was an old city, and a new one, and a city in between—traditional buildings painted lively colors next to beige brutalist structures from the Communist era, modern minimalist white towers that glinted with windows jammed between the maximalist neo-Baroque facades that had come next. Layer after layer of time.

She walked the narrow alley where shop signs, half in English, half in Romanian, boasted of plăcintă and fresh produce and, for some reason, camera equipment. There were so many nooks and crannies in the city that she had not gotten to explore. Her brother had been fond of the dim hardware stores with nuts and bolts in little tubs that had prices scribbled on the outside. 2 lei. 1 leu. 5 lei. Her mother had favored the newer shops in Iulius Mall, which also had a Starbucks.

Kata reached the end of the alley and crossed the street to the house. It stood right over the sidewalk, decorative bars shielding its windows with curlicues, stately stone cracked in places and dotted with graffiti. She had to kick open the gate—not difficult, since it was barely hanging on to its hinges—but the door to the front apartment was already open.

It was a simple place but for the wood-burning stove in the corner, which was decorated with glazed green tiles. The narrow kitchen table was bare, the stools pushed neatly beneath it. The whitewashed wall was streaked with water that had leaked from one of the pipes leading to the baseboard heaters. For all that the world had advanced—to develop progs, to build SILFs (or "sylphs," as most people called them), to settle on other planets and begin to terraform them—so many things hadn't changed. Water heaters on the walls, elegant bars on the windows, sobe de teracotă in the older houses, red candles on the cemetery graves.

The old world persisted.

The only other aberration she could find was a worn teddy bear perched on top of the lamp in the corner. She pinched its worn ear and lifted it, testing its weight.

Yes, this was it. This was what she had come back to Earth for.

"Ah-ha!" said a familiar voice.

Kata had just returned to her ship when she heard the exclamation, the sound of it harsh and horrible in the quiet.

"*Do you want me to shoot him?*" Drobo asked.

"No," Kata said, with a sigh.

She knew him.

"Speaker on," she said, and she heard the telltale click of the suit's external speaker turning on. "Where's your crew, Boris?"

"On the hunt," the man replied. He wore a newer, sleeker version of Kata's suit. "Looks like you're due for a cleaning." He ran a fingertip along the hull of her ship, drawing a line in the dust. And then a curve, and another curve. The letter "B".

"Don't you dare write your name on my ship," she said, striding over and smacking his hand away. "What do you want?"

Boris glanced at her, then reached over to start the "o."

She dropped the teddy bear, and smacked his hand away again—with her right hand, this time. Boris swore, shaking out his fingers. "Shit. Forgot about that metal arm."

"I figured. Answer my question."

"I'm under contract with the EJC."

She was familiar with the acronym, but gave Boris a blank stare anyway.

"And you call yourself a human," Boris said. "The Earth Justice Commission, Mausebär. They're gathering evidence before the trials, to prove the sylph war was waged illegally."

Kata began to feel her pulse in her throat and in her fingertips.

"And this brings you to Koloszvar... *why*?" She used the Hungarian name for the city reflexively, though she was sure Boris wouldn't know it. There had been one and a half million Hungarians living in Transylvania before the evacuation, yet this region had not been theirs.

And never would be again. Not anyone's.

Boris shrugged. "A report of some outgoing transmission to the sylphs surfaced recently. Its origin code led us here." He bent and picked up the teddy bear she had dropped. "I was going to ask if you had found anything that might be helpful to us. I would be willing to pay for it, of course."

"Not as much as you would sell it to the EJC for, I'm sure," she said, swallowing hard. Boris turned the bear over, looking at the stitching on its back and the worn patch on its ear. "I found nothing."

"How could you say such a thing in front of our friend here? He is not nothing," he said, holding up the bear. She snatched it back.

"Sentimental value only," she said. "I am from here."

"Yes, I know," Boris said, his blue eyes narrowing. "What a strange coincidence, that I would find you here, of all places on Earth, the place where that suspicious transmission came from. And if I were to match up your ship's records to all the other places I have been where key pieces of potential evidence have vanished into thin air...?"

"You would have to get a subpoena for those records," Kata said.

"Yes." Boris looked up at the sky. "I have asked myself many times why a fellow human, such as yourself, would hide evidence that might support Earth's case in these trials."

"Maybe the evidence wouldn't support Earth's case," Kata said. "Maybe any human who hid such evidence would be doing you a favor, in which case you ought to let her keep hiding it, and forget you ever knew about it."

Boris's eyes were hard to see behind the glass of the helmet. But she thought that he looked at her for a long moment.

"Have a safe launch, Ms. Tabor," Boris said. "I'll be seeing you."

* * *

"*Was this the purpose of our trip, Kata?*" Drobo asked, a light pulsing above the ship's computer with the emphasis of each word. To compensate for his lack of a physical body, Drobo manipulated parts of the ship to give her something to look at. He seemed to understand that it made things easier for her. "*To retrieve a... plush toy?*"

"He is a bear—"

"*He does not much resemble a bear. For one thing, his nose is a plastic tortoiseshell button rather than a projecting snout—*"

"He's a *bear*," she emphasized. "And he belonged to my sister."

Kata had taken off the vacsuit in the airlock, hanging it on its hook, and stacking the gloves and helmet on the recessed shelf intended for that purpose. She wore the heavy boots still, so that she could activate the magnets in case of gravity malfunction.

"When Erszi was a teenager, she used to hide things from our parents. Cigarettes and drugs, mostly. They never found out, but I knew," Kata said. "And more importantly, she knew that I knew."

She tipped the bear forward on the table, and lifted the scissors she had retrieved from one of the drawers in the galley, nosing the point into the bear's back. She cut through the fabric from butt to neck, then stuck her hand into the stuffing.

From somewhere inside the bear's head, she pulled a slim gold cylinder, about the length of her pinkie finger.

"*Erszi's Echo,*" Drobo said, with something like reverence.

Kata had followed her sister's path for a long time. Retracing her footsteps over Earth's ruined surface, and then to fuel outposts and transport ships and post offices in the parts of space that had been colonized when Kata was a child. They had found the Echoes of her friends and neighbors and even her co-conspirators. Each time they found one, Kata had come back to the ship, launched it into orbit, and placed the Echo in the dock to see the projection, waiting for the ghostly figure of her sister to appear. The Echoes contained memories—the ones the dead wanted remembered.

But her sister had never appeared. This time, though, she would. Kata was certain of it.

The dock was a device about the size of her palm, indented in the middle where the Echo would fit. A small red light in the base turned blue after Kata plugged in the Echo, her hands trembling.

And then standing about a meter away from Kata was a slim young woman. Shorter than Kata, as she had been since Kata's preteen growth spurt, her hair loose and limp over her shoulders, her eyes and cheeks sunken. This was how she had looked the last time Kata had seen her, but years after she fell in with Ütközet.

"Hello Erszi," Kata said, bracing herself on the desk.

Erszi's Echo would be able to respond to her as if she was a person, but she was not *actually* Erszi, not capable of being Erszi. She wasn't a prog; she was just a narrow range of data pressed into the image of a person, a self-selected bundle of memories that told Kata not what Erszi really was, but what Erszi had wanted to be, what she had thought she was... or what she had intended to communicate about herself. It was just as likely that this Erszi was a post-mortem manipulation as a genuine attempt at memorializing herself.

But did the Echo *know* Kata? Did it contain any memories of the little sister Erszi had left behind? It would not make sense for Erszi to have retained such memories in her Echo. When Kata had chosen to undergo the surgery that had saved her from a premature death—replacing some of her body with computer and mechanics and synthetics—Erszi had sworn she would never speak to Kata again, that she was dead to her. And then the attack had happened. The evacuation. The end of the world. No chance to find out if her sister had really been so dedicated to her ideology.

Ütközet, the organization that had captured Erszi's heart, had begun as a movement for the preservation of human life. A rejection of technology, a return to older ways, more "natural" ways. And it had transformed. *Erszi* had transformed.

"Kata?" the Echo said, scrunching her nose as she peered at Kata. She moved like Erszi had, all hunched and loping, no grace to her at all. Kata blinked away tears.

"You remember," Kata said.

"It's been a long time," Erszi said, lifting a hand to touch Kata's cheek. She couldn't truly touch anything, of course, but her faintly glowing fingers hovered next to Kata's face.

"Too long," Kata said. "What did you do, Erszi?"

Erszi's smile slanted into her cheek. She put her hand down.

"You already know, or you wouldn't ask the question that way," Erszi said.

"You had a weapon," Kata said. "The others, your friends, they told me." The other Echoes were lined up in the drawer just beneath the dock, labeled with Kata's messy handwriting.

"A weapon that was harmless to humans, and deadly to sylphs," Erszi said. She clasped her hands in front of her and looked up, as if to the heavens. "A clean slate for us. No progs. No sylphs. No self-aware computers left to destroy us."

Kata saw the flash of light that meant Drobo was listening, but he said nothing.

"You would have killed every last one of them," Kata said.

"You can't kill something that isn't truly alive," Erszi said. "*We* are alive. Lungs and beating hearts. Pain and decay. Birth and growth. Those things are life. I wanted to shut down all the machines, yes. I wanted a better life for our next generation. But I wasn't able to send the virus in time…" A grimace of pain across her glowing face. "And *they* attacked, instead."

"And now Earth is destroyed," Kata said.

"With the sylphs still around, it may as well be destroyed," Erszi said, and she hummed a little. "We lost, and so now our time is over."

"Why did you make an Echo, then?" Kata scowled at her. "If we're a dying species, why bother preserving us in any way?"

"So that what we're becoming will remember what we once were," Erszi said. "We won't die as we were supposed to, like animals limping off into the woods. We will die by becoming like them. Look at you, Kata." She nodded to Kata's right hand, covered now with her long sleeve. "How much of you is flesh and bone? Fifty percent, maybe?"

Sixty percent was the answer, but Kata didn't speak it aloud.

"How do you know what they put in your head hasn't changed you?" Erszi said. "How do you know that what you feel is the same as what I feel?"

Kata had been born with a wasting disease. Bones rotting away from the inside. In a constant state of rapid decay. She would not have lived past fifteen if they had not done the surgery that wrapped up her bones in metal and replaced some of her limbs with circuitry, with an implant in her brain to control it all.

You will never come back from that, Erszi had said. *I will mourn you as if you were already dead. Come home and die in peace, with us, as yourself.*

Fuck you, Kata had replied. Because she had wanted to live, and it was all well and good to speak of passing away "in peace" when you weren't the one who had to do it.

"I know that I will never feel the same things you feel," Kata said. "Because what *you* felt started a war."

With that, she left the main deck of the ship, climbing up the ladder to her quarters near the engine room, and laid down on her little slab of a bed.

"*She wasn't what I expected*," Drobo said to Kata.

"She wasn't always like that," Kata replied. "She used to carry me around the house on her back, when I couldn't walk anymore. She let me feed her carrots, like a horse." She laughed a little.

"*And this was… meaningful to you?*"

"Yes." Kata closed her eyes. "Can you leave me alone for a little while?"

Drobo let out an affirmative chirp, and went silent.

Kata held her hand up to the light. Though artificial and constructed of metal, it was finely made, so she was still capable of deft, delicate movements with her metal fingertips. It didn't look like a human hand—she hadn't been interested in the added expense— but was, in every functional way, equal to one.

Her original hand had been amputated at the elbow. Better to just start fresh, the sylph surgeon had said. She didn't feel this one, of course, but it sent pulses to the implant in her brain, so she had been able to learn its position in space, a new kind of sensation. Her brain had mapped it with the implant, the same as it had her old body.

And was it so different, really? The brain dealt exclusively in electrical impulses between neurons, a crackling thundercloud that made a human being think. Whether those neurons were synthetic or not, connected by myelin or wire, they were all creatures of pulse and impulse, all the same.

* * *

The fueling outpost between Earth and Mars was lit up in all colors of the rainbow, flashing and glittering. *GIRLS GIRLS GIRLS!* pulsed in Kata's mind even after she closed her eyes to shut out the assault of advertising for a moment. The male strip club across the way favored a subtler approach; Kata had once wandered in by mistake seeking an actual sausage. Needless to say, she had not found one.

The scent of fried food made her mouth water, but she had her small loyalties. She walked past the funnel cakes and French fries and shrimp tempura to the little cart at the end, staffed by a wrinkled Polish woman selling pierogi. They never spoke to each other, really; neither knew the other's best language, so they had to conduct their transaction in English. But Kata always came for one spinach, one potato and cheese, and one strawberry for dessert.

She walked with the pierogis on a paper plate through the rest of the human quarter, a place designed to meet the needs of the flesh. Grim, dirty "motels" for sleeping; hot food for eating; strip clubs for desire; broken-down pharmacies for medicine; sly side counters for drugs. Then she passed through an empty stretch with piles of discarded boxes and bundles of barbed wire, and suddenly found herself confronted by two lines of guards.

The first were human, dressed in black, protective vests thick with tech, helmets, boots. She kept her head down as she passed them. Five meters away, facing her, was a line of sylphs.

Sylphs had once looked like humans, because humans had made them, perfected them for an increasingly broad range of tasks. But since the first sylph war—which resulted in them establishing a colony on Mars and declaring their independence—they had been manufacturing themselves, and many of them had decided they had no interest in looking human. They were human*oid*, of course—since so much of the technology they used was made for articulated fingers and hands, for bodies that stood less than a meter wide—but apart from that there was room for endless variation. Heads shaped like pyramids; impossibly long legs that bent backward like a goat's; mouthlike orifices set in the chest instead of the head. There were few limits to what she saw before her. Functionality seemed to be the main priority, but it was not the only one. Creativity, self-expression, self-indulgence—there was room for that too.

Kata approached the one she knew, an obelisk on stilt-legs that called itself Hal (an homage to a fictional robot, she assumed, like many sylph names).

"Hey, Hal," she said.

"Kata." Its voice came from a series of slits on its chest, right at the level of Kata's ears. "Here on business?"

"As always," she said. She took out her ID card, an old flimsy thing with permanent smudges at the corners. He gave it a glance, and, with an elegance that never failed to surprise her, stepped back to let her through.

"I can only give you an hour," he said. "More tension than usual, with the Minos Trials approaching."

"That's fine, I won't be long," Kata said.

The trials were Kata's reason for coming in the first place. She wanted to know what evidence the sylphs were presenting on their own behalf. It was solid; she didn't need to decide what to do with Erszi's Echo—it wouldn't matter either way.

And Maria would have the information she needed. Maria knew everything.

She hadn't realized how tense she was until she stepped into the grid of the sylph quarter and was finally able to relax. She didn't have to do as much pretending here. She tied her heavy hair back, wicking sweat from her neck with her hand as she did, and shed the heavy jacket she wore to conceal her prosthetic arm. She also made less of an effort to move with the light spring in her step that scanned to observers as "human". She was as out of place here as she was in the human quarter, of course—more, perhaps, because it was impossible to pass as a sylph with a flushed face and a rumbling stomach—but the sylphs kept their reactions to themselves, or expressed themselves in ways she couldn't yet decipher, so walking among them was simpler.

The quarter had no signs—not all sylphs could "see" in the way that a human saw—but Kata had memorized the way to Maria's place, so it didn't matter. The air here smelled different—like grease and burnt plastic instead of fryer oil—and the refuse that piled in the streets was different, too: old wires and broken tools and busted screens instead of food wrappers, bottles, and condom wrappers. As she approached Maria's shop, Kata kicked a cracked metal plate out of the doorway and then slipped inside.

Maria had modeled herself after her namesake in the movie *Metropolis*: she was humanoid, womanly, sleek. Kata had often wondered why she would mimic a human body so closely before understanding that it was intended as irony: Maria repaired busted sylphs for a lower price than the established vendors, and she did it wearing a human body as a costume—one she had chosen herself, not a human master, which made all the difference, Kata had learned.

The sylph was sorting through a pile of nuts and bolts when Kata approached, and without looking up, her free hand reached out to turn on a lamp.

"Thanks," Kata said, pulling out a stool from under the counter and perching on top of it. "How's business?"

"You shouldn't be here," Maria said. Her voice was a feminine chirp, modulated like a human voice, but with a distinct robotic character to it all the same. "And you should not return until after the trials, whatever their outcome."

"They know me here," Kata said.

"I didn't mean just *here*, in the sylph quarter," Maria said, still sorting. Her fingertips were a marvel of engineering, capable of quick, delicate movements that Kata still found mesmerizing. "I mean the entire outpost. I've heard there is violence brewing among your kind as well as ours, toward... people like you."

"Did you hear this from your sylph government friend?" Kata smiled.

"Perhaps."

"If that's the case, there's not many places I can go where humans won't feel that way. Can't yank out my skeleton, Maria."

She couldn't remove the parts of her that humans hated when they were the same parts keeping her alive. And moreover, she didn't *want* to.

"I suppose that's true," Maria said. "But perhaps now is the time for an extended scavenging mission."

"You're worried about me," Kata said. She looked down at her prosthetic hand, glinting in the light. "I wonder if your worry feels the same as mine."

"What do you mean?"

"Fear is... mammalian. Essential to survival for any organism that has natural predators," Kata said. "You don't have predators, not really—so why did you program it? Why not write it out of your programming entirely?"

Maria's voice was flatter than usual when she replied. "If I was never afraid, how would I know to protect myself? If I was never angry, how would I know to fight for what I want?"

"Yeah, I just... wonder if we're using one word for two different feelings. If the way fear feels, to me, is the same as the way it feels to you."

"You are wondering if I am as real as you are," Maria said.

"No, that's not—" Kata shook her head. "That's not what I meant."

"Yes it is. You are wondering if my feelings 'count'. If I am as worthy as you are of existence." Maria pressed too hard on one of the bolts, and it shot away from the countertop, hitting the opposite wall with a *ding!* "Let me make this clear, then: I am not human, and I have no desire to be. Your kind is not an ideal to which I aspire."

"I—"

"Please leave," Maria said.

Kata didn't argue. But, before leaving, she paused in the dark doorway to say, "I'm sorry."

Back on the ship, Kata sat at the table in the galley. She had lined up all the Echoes she had retrieved from all their hiding places, on Earth as well as its moon. The first one, she had found while unpacking her parents' things on the moon colony. When she had asked her father about it, he had said something about Erszi's friend leaving it behind after one visit. That one had led her to the next, which she bought on the gray market at the outpost on the way to Mars. The third, she had gone to Berlin to scavenge. Then Budapest for the fourth.

She rested her chin on her hands and stared down at the Echoes. Together, they made an airtight case for the Minos Trials—just not for the right side, the human side.

One of them hinted at the idea for the weapon Ütközet had developed, and another at the hours spent engineering it. The third detailed how they had disguised their activity from anyone who might be watching. But no Echo established the intent to use the weapon as clearly as Erszi's did.

"*What will you do with them now?*" Drobo asked her.

Kata rolled Erszi's Echo toward herself and back, a few centimeters at a time.

"I don't know," she said.

"*If you send them to the Earth Justice Commission, what will they do?*" Drobo said. "*Drop their case?*"

"I don't think so. I think if I send them there, they will be destroyed," Kata said. "Without them, the sylphs have no proof that their initial attack on Earth wasn't a war crime. All it takes is one corrupt person and the whole thing falls apart."

"*Because it is a war crime,*" Drobo said, "*to attack without cause.*"

"To attack only to kill, and not to defend yourself," Kata said, nodding. "Which is what they were doing—defending themselves against Ütközet. Against Erszi."

"*Ütközet—*"

Kata laughed. "Your Hungarian pronunciation is horrible."

"*I don't have lips, so it is difficult for me to articulate those particular vowels.*" Drobo sounded irritable. "*Ütközet's virus—you believe it actually could have killed the sylphs, if your sister had been able to hack through their defenses?*"

"Say what you like about the sylphs, but they're careful," she said. "They wouldn't have attacked Earth if they didn't think it was their best chance of survival."

"*Indeed,*" Drobo said. "*So, if you don't want this evidence destroyed… what do you want instead?*"

"I want…" She laughed a little. "I want to remember my sister as the one stashing cigarettes in a teddy bear, not the one plotting to commit genocide. I want my family's name to be unsullied by what she's done. I want to run up the hill to the Hotel Belvedere without a helmet on and scold the teenagers for making out on all the benches. I want to go *home.*"

She sighed.

"*That is impossible,*" Drobo said, quietly.

"I wish this could be bigger than it is, that it could be about righteousness, or truth. But it's not." Kata shook her head. "It's about where I was, when Erszi was planning this attack. I was in a sylph workshop, and a sylph cybernetics expert was saving my life with the same tech that Erszi was trying to destroy."

She put her head down on her arms. The Echoes clinked together like a wind chime.

"You have to fight for the ones who fight for you," Kata said. "And you don't get to pick who they are."

"Erszi," Kata said to the ghostly image of her sister, standing before the window in the galley.

Erszi turned, and offered a watery smile. She had never been beautiful. Neither had Kata, really. They had the look of people constantly on the verge of argument, like a couple of twittering birds, beaked and fierce. But there was something lively in Erszi's eyes that appealed, regardless.

"Do you remember when I was twelve, and you told me we would go on an adventure?" Kata said. "You asked your friend, the burly one—"

"Ábel," Erszi said, nodding. "With the mustache."

"Yes, him. You asked him to carry me out to the river with you."

Erszi smiled. "I had blown up that inflatable raft I bought at Polus Mall and dragged it down to Kis-Szamos so we could float under the stars. Only I failed to account for Ábel's weight—"

"So ten minutes in, we sank, and we had to abandon the raft, and I almost died because I couldn't move my legs—"

Erszi shook her head. "I almost killed you."

"Sure," Kata said. "But you just wanted to give me an adventure."

"I should have gotten a sturdier raft."

"It was the best night of my life, I think," Kata said, and she stood beside her sister's virtual ghost at the window. "And I'm glad it's one of the memories you decided to put in your Echo. I wondered if I would make it in there at all."

"Kata." Erszi frowned. "There is so much of you in here."

"Oh, don't tell me that," Kata said, wiping tears from her cheeks. "It will make it so much harder."

"Make what—"

Kata pulled the Echo from its dock and the projection of her sister vanished. She put the Echo in the metal box on the table, along with all the others, stripped of their labels and wiped clean of her fingerprints. She put the lid in place and activated the seal.

Then she bit down on her hand to keep herself quiet as she cried.

The next day, the box would arrive in Maria's mailbox. Kata could almost see it in her mind: Maria's deft fingers typing in the security code on the box, the little door popping open to reveal a metal box, half a meter long.

Contained within it would be a row of polished human Echoes, with a note, scribbled on an old piece of newspaper, resting on top.

The note read: *send these to your government friend.*

Kata's ship was in orbit. Glowing large in the windows, lit by the Sun, was Earth, dappled with clouds, patched with land.

From here, she couldn't see the empty streets of Koloszvar, the curved bars that decorated the windows of her childhood home, the crumbling walls of the old city bolstered by the new. From here, she could pretend that humans still lived on the land beneath her, still drifted on rivers in inflatable boats.

Someday, maybe, they would find a way to go back. Time healed, or so they said, so perhaps it would heal Earth, or some clever scientists would find a way to make it habitable again. Perhaps one day they would fill the silent buildings with voices once again, send the cockroaches scurrying to their hiding places, and Plata Unirii would bustle with people selling embroidered pillowcases and magnets with Dracula's face on them for the tourists.

But it would never be the same as it had been before. Time did not run backward, much as Kata wished it would. So for the time being, she was content to look down at the planet, now a monument to a particular time, following its winding rivers with her eyes until they disappeared behind clouds.

SHOOTING THE APOCALYPSE

PAOLO BACIGALUPI

Paolo Bacigalupi is the author of the *New York Times* bestselling novel *The Water Knife*, a near-future thriller about climate change and drought in the southwestern United States. His novel *The Windup Girl* won the Hugo, Nebula, Locus, Compton Crook, and John W. Campbell Memorial Awards. *Ship Breaker*—his first foray into young adult fiction—was a Michael L. Printz Award winner, and a National Book Award finalist, and its sequel, *The Drowned Cities*, was a Kirkus Best of YA selection, a *Voya* Perfect Ten Book, and a Los Angeles Times Book Prize finalist. He is also the author of the middle-grade novel *Zombie Baseball Beatdown* and the YA novel *The Doubt Factory*. Paolo's short fiction has appeared in *Wired Magazine*, *High Country News*, *The Magazine of Fantasy & Science Fiction*, *Asimov's*, and elsewhere; has been collected in *Pump Six and Other Stories*; and has been nominated for three Nebula Awards, four Hugo Awards, and won the Theodore Sturgeon Memorial Award.

If it were for anyone else, he would have just laughed in their faces and told them they were on their own.

The thought nagged at Timo as he drove his beat-up FlexFusion down the rutted service road that ran parallel to the concrete-lined canal of the Central Arizona Project. For any other journo who came down to Phoenix looking for a story, he wouldn't even think of doing them a favor.

All those big names looking to swoop in like magpies and grab some meaty exclusive and then fly away just as fast, keeping all their page views and hits to themselves... he wouldn't do it.

Didn't matter if they were *Google/NY Times*, Cherry Xu, *Facebook Social Now*, Deborah Williams, *Kindle Post*, or *Xinhua*.

But Lucy? Well, sure. For Lucy, he'd climb into his sweatbox of a car with all his camera gear and drive his skinny brown ass out to North Phoenix and into the hills on a crap tip. He'd drive this way and that, burning gas trying to find a service road, and then bump his way through dirt and ruts, scraping the belly of the Ford the whole way, and he still wouldn't complain.

Just goes to show you're a sucker for a girl who wears her jeans tight.

But it wasn't just that. Lucy was fine, if you liked a girl with white skin and little tits and wide hips, and sometimes Timo would catch himself fantasizing about what it would be like to get with her. But in the end, that wasn't why he did favors for Lucy. He did it because she was scrappy and wet and she was in over her head—and too hard-assed and proud to admit it.

Girl had grit; Timo could respect that. Even if she came from up north and was so wet that sometimes he laughed out loud at the things she said. The girl didn't know much about dry desert life, but she had grit.

So when she muttered over her Dos Equis that all the stories had already been done, Timo, in a moment of beery romantic fervor, had sworn to her that it just wasn't so. He had the eye. He saw things other people didn't. He could name twenty stories she could still do and make a name for herself.

But when he'd started listing possibilities, Lucy shot them down as fast as he brought them up.

Coyotes running Texans across the border into California?

Sohu already had a nine part series running.

Californians buying Texas hookers for nothing, like Phoenix was goddamn Tijuana?

Google/NY Times and *Fox* both had big spreads.

Water restrictions from the Roosevelt Dam closure and the drying up of Phoenix's swimming pools?

Kindle Post ran that.

The narco murders that kept getting dumped in the empty pools that had become so common that people had started calling them "swimmers"?

AP. Fox. Xinhua. LA Times. The Talisha Brannon Show. Plus the reality narco show *Hard Bangin'*.

He kept suggesting new angles, new stories, and all Lucy said, over and over was, "It's been done." And then she'd rattle off the news organizations, the journos who'd covered the stories, the page hits, the viewerships, and the click-thrus they'd drawn.

"I'm not looking for some dead hooker for the sex and murder crowd," Lucy said as she drained her beer. "I want something that'll go big. I want a scoop, you know?"

"And I want a woman to hand me a ice-cold beer when I walk in the door," Timo grumped. "Don't mean I'm going to get it."

But still, he understood her point. He knew how to shoot pictures that would make a vulture sob its beady eyes out, but the news environment that Lucy fought to distinguish herself in was like gladiatorial sport—some winners, a lot of losers, and whole shit-ton of blood on the ground.

Journo money wasn't steady money. Wasn't good money. Sometimes, you got lucky. Hell, he'd got lucky himself when he'd gone over Texas way and shot Hurricane Violet in all her glory. He'd photographed a whole damn fishing boat flying through the air and landing on a Days Inn, and in that one shot he knew he'd hit the big time. Violet razed Galveston and blasted into Houston, and Timo got page views so high that he sometimes imagined that the Cat 6 had actually killed him and sent him straight to Heaven.

He'd kept hitting reload on his PayPal account and watched the cash pouring in. He'd had the big clanking cojones to get into the heart of that clusterfuck, and he'd come out of it with more than a million hits a photo. Got him all excited.

But disaster was easy to cover, and he'd learned the hard way that when the big dogs muscled in, little dogs got muscled out. Which left him back in sad-sack Phoenix, scraping for glamour shots of brains on windshields and trussed-up drug bunnies in the bottoms of swimming pools. It made him sympathetic to Lucy's plight, if not her perspective.

It's all been done, Timo thought as he maneuvered his Ford around the burned carcass of an abandoned Tesla. *So what if it's been motherfucking done?*

"There ain't no virgins, and there ain't no clean stories," he'd tried to explain to Lucy. "There's just angles on the same-ass stories. Scoops come from being in the right place at the right time, and that's all just dumb luck. Why don't you just come up with a good angle on Phoenix and be happy?"

But Lucy Monroe wanted a nice clean virgin story that didn't have no grubby fingerprints on it from other journos. Something she could put her name on. Some way to make her mark, make those big news companies notice her. Something to grow her brand and all that. Not just the day-to-day grind of narco kills and starving immigrants from Texas, something special. Something new.

So when the tip came in, Timo thought what the hell, maybe this was something she'd like. Maybe even a chance to blow up together. Lucy could do the words, he'd bring the pics, and they'd scoop all the big name journos who drank martinis at the Hilton 6 and complained about what a refugee shit hole Phoenix had become.

The Ford scraped over more ruts. Dust already coated the rear window of Timo's car, a thick beige paste. Parallel to the service road, the waters of the Central Arizona Project flowed, serene and blue and steady. A man-made canal that stretched three hundred miles across the desert to bring water to Phoenix from the Colorado River. A feat of engineering, and cruelly tempting, given the ten-foot chain-link and barbed wire fences that escorted it on either side.

In this part of Phoenix, the Central Arizona Project formed the city's northern border. On one side of the CAP canal, it was all modest stucco tract houses packed together like sardines stretching south. But on Timo's side, it was desert, rising into tan and rust hill folds, dotted with mesquite and saguaro.

A few hardy subdivisions had built outposts north of the CAP's moat-like boundary, but the canal seemed to form a barrier of some psychological significance, because for the most part, Phoenix stayed to the south of the concrete-lined canal, choosing to finally build itself into something denser than lazy sprawl. Phoenix on one side, the desert on the other, and the CAP flowing between them like a thin blue DMZ.

Just driving on the desert side of the CAP made Timo thirsty. Dry mouth, plain-ass desert, quartz rocks and sandstone nubs with a few creosote bushes holding onto the dust and waving in the blast furnace wind. Normally, Timo didn't even bother to look at the desert. It barely changed. But here he was, looking for something new—

He rounded a curve and slowed, peering through his grimy windshield. "Well I'll be goddamned..."

Up ahead, something was hanging from the CAP's barrier fence. Dogs were jumping up to tug at it, milling and barking.

Timo squinted, trying to understand what he was seeing.

"Oh yeah. Hell yes!"

He hit the brakes. The car came grinding to a halt in a cloud of dust, but Timo was already climbing out and fumbling for his phone, pressing it to his ear, listening to it ring.

Come on, come on, come on.

Lucy picked up.

Timo couldn't help grinning. "I got your story, girl. You'll love it. It's *new*."

The dogs bared their teeth at Timo's approach, but Timo just laughed. He dug into his camera bag for his pistol.

"You want a piece of me?" he asked. "You want some of Timo, bitches?"

Turned out they didn't. As soon as he held up the pistol, the dogs scattered. Animals were smarter than people, that way. Pull a gun on some drunk California frat boy and you never knew if the sucker was still going to try and throw down. Dogs were way smarter than Californians. Timo could respect that, so he didn't shoot them as they fled the scene.

One of the dogs, braver or more arrogant than the rest, paused to yank off a final trophy before loping away; the rest of the pack zeroed in on it, yipping and leaping, trying to steal its prize. Timo watched, wishing he'd pulled his camera instead of his gun. The shot was perfect. He sighed and stuffed the pistol into the back of his pants, dug out his camera, and turned to the subject at hand.

"Well hello, good-looking," he murmured. "Ain't you a sight?"

The man hung upside down from the chain link fence, bloated from the Phoenix heat. A bunch of empty milk jugs dangled off his body, swinging from a harness of shoelace ties. From the look of him, he'd been cooking out in the sun for at least a day or so.

The meat of one arm was completely desleeved, and the other arm... well, Timo had watched the dogs make off with the poor bastard's hand. His face and neck and chest didn't look much better. The dogs had been doing some jumping.

"Come on, vato. Gimme the story." Timo stalked back and forth in front of the body, checking the angles, considering the shadows and light. "You want to get your hits up don't you? Show Timo your good side, I make you famous. So help me out, why don't you?"

He stepped back, thinking wide-frame: the strung-up body, the black nylon flowers woven into the chain link around it. The black guttered candles and cigarettes and mini liquor bottles scattered by the dogs' frenzied feeding. The CAP flowing behind it all. Phoenix beyond that, sprawling all the way to the horizon.

"What's your best side?" Timo asked. "Don't be shy. I'll do you right. Make you famous. Just let me get your angle."

There.

Timo squatted and started shooting. *Click-click-click-click*—the artificial sound of digital photography and the Pavlovian rush of sweaty excitement as Timo got the feel.

Dead man.

Flowers.

Candles.

Water.

Timo kept snapping. He had it now. The flowers and the empty milk jugs dangling off the dude. Timo was in the flow, bracketing exposures, shooting steady, recognizing the moment when his inner eye told him that he'd nailed the story. It was good. *Really* good.

As good as a Cat 6 plowing into Houston.

Click-click-click. Money-money-money-money.

"That's right, buddy. Talk to your friend Timo."

The man had a story to tell, and Timo had the eye to see it. Most people missed the story. But Timo always saw. He had the eye.

Maybe he'd buy a top-shelf tequila to celebrate his page view money. Some diapers for his sister Amparo's baby. If the photos were good, maybe he'd grab a couple syndication licenses, too. Swap the shit-ass battery in the Ford. Get something with a bigger range dropped into it. Let him get around without always wondering if he was going to lose a charge.

Some of these could go to *Xinhua*, for sure. The Chinese news agencies loved seeing America ripping itself to shit. BBC might bite, too. Foreigners loved that story. Only thing that would sell better is if it had a couple guns: *America, the Savage Land* or some shit. That was money, there. Might be rent for a bigger place. A place where Amparo could bail when her boyfriend got his ass drunk and angry.

Timo kept snapping photos, changing angles, framing and exposure. Diving deeper into the dead man's world. Capturing scuffed-up boots and plastic prayer beads. He hummed to himself as he worked, talking to his subject, coaxing the best out of the corpse.

"You don't know it, but you're damn lucky I came along," Timo said. "If one of those citizen journalist pendejo lice got you first, they wouldn't have treated you right. They'd shoot a couple shitty frames and upload them social. Maybe sell a Instagram pic to the blood rags... but they ain't quality. Me? When I'm done, people won't be able to *dream* without seeing you."

It was true, too. Any asshole could snap a pic of some girl blasted to pieces in an electric Mercedes, but Timo knew how to make you cry when you saw her splattered all over the front pages of the blood rags. Some piece of narco ass, and you'd still be bawling your eyes out over her tragic death. He'd catch the girl's little fuzzy dice mirror ornament spattered with blood, and your heart would just break.

Amparo said Timo had the eye. Little bro could see what other people didn't, even when it was right in front of their faces.

Every asshole had a camera these days; the difference was that Timo could *see*.

Timo backed off and got some quick video. He ran the recording back, listening to the audio, satisfying himself that he had the sound of it: the wind rattling the chain link under the high hot Arizona sky; meadowlark call from somewhere next to the CAP waters; but most of all, the empty dangling jugs, the three of them plunking hollowly against each other—a dead man turned into an offering and a wind chime.

Timo listened to the deep *thunk-thunk-thunk* tones.

Good sounds.

Good empty desert sounds.

He crouched and framed the man's gnawed arm and the milk jugs. From this angle, he could just capture the blue line of the CAP canal and the leading edge of Phoenix beyond: cookie-cutter low-stories with lava-rock front yards and broke-down cars on blocks. And somewhere in there, some upstanding example of Arizona Minute-Man militia pride had spied this sucker scrambling down the dusty hillside with his water jugs and decided to put a cap in his ass.

CAP in his ass, Timo chuckled to himself.

The crunch of tires and the grind of an old bio-diesel engine announced Lucy's pickup coming up the dirt road. A trail of dust followed. Rusty beast of flex-fuel, older than the girl who drove it and twice as beat up, but damn was it a beast. It had been one of the things Timo liked about Lucy, soon as he met her. Girl drove a machine that didn't give a damn about anything except driving over shit.

The truck came to a halt. The driver's side door squealed aside as Lucy climbed out. Army green tank top and washed out jeans. White skin, scorched and bronzed by Arizona sun, her reddish brown hair jammed up under an ASU Geology Department ball cap.

Every time he saw her, Timo liked what he saw. Phoenix hadn't dried her right, yet, but still, she had some kind of tenacious-ass demon in her. Something about the way her pale blue skeptical eyes burned for a story told you that once she bit in, she wouldn't let go. Crazy-ass pitbull. The girl and the truck were a pair. Unstoppable.

"Please tell me I didn't drive out here for a swimmer," Lucy said as she approached.

"What do you think?"

"I think I was on the other side of town when you called, and I had to burn diesel to get here."

She was trying to look jaded, but her eyes were already flicking from detail to detail, gathering the story before Timo even had to open his mouth. She might be new in Phoenix, but the girl had the eye. Just like Timo, Lucy saw things.

"Texan?" she asked.

Timo grinned. "You think?"

"Well, he's a Merry Perry, anyway. I don't know many other people who would join that cult." She crouched down in front of the corpse and peered into the man's torn face. Reaching out, she caressed the prayer beads embedded in the man's neck. "I did a story on Merry Perrys. Roadside spiritual aid for the refugees." She sighed. "They were all buying the beads and making the prayers."

"Crying and shaking and repentance."

"You've been to their services, too?"

"Everybody's done that story at least once," Timo said. "I shot a big old revival tent over in New Mexico, outside of Carlsbad. The preacher had a nasty ass thorn bush, wanted volunteers."

Timo didn't think he'd ever forget the scene. The tent walls sucking and flapping as blast-furnace winds gusted over them. The dust-coated refugees all shaking, moaning, and working their beads for God. All of them asking what they needed to give up in order to get back to the good old days of big oil money and fancy cities like Houston and Austin. To get back to a life before hurricanes went Cat 6 and Big Daddy Drought sucked whole states dry.

Lucy ran her fingers along the beads that had sunk deep into the dead man's neck. "They strangled him."

"Sure looks that way."

Timo could imagine this guy earning the prayer beads one at time. Little promises of God's love that he could carry with him. He imagined the man down in the dirt, all crying and spitty and grateful for his bloody back and for the prayer beads that had ended up embedded in his swollen, blackening neck, like some kind of Mardi Gras party gone wrong. The man had done his prayers and repentance, and this was where he'd ended up.

"What happened to his hand?" Lucy asked.

"Dog got it."

"Christ."

"If you want some better art, we can back off for a little while, and the dogs'll come back. I can get a good tearaway shot if we let them go after him again—"

Lucy gave Timo a dirty look, so he hastily changed tacks.

"Anyway, I thought you should see him. Good art, and it's a great story. Nobody's got something like this."

Lucy straightened. "I can't pitch this, Timo. It's sad as hell, but it isn't new. Nobody cares if Old Tex here hiked across a thousand miles of desert just to get strung up as some warning. It's sad, but everyone knows how much people hate Texans. *Kindle Post* did a huge story on Texas lynchings."

"Shit." Timo sighed. "Every time I think you're wise, I find out you're still wet."

"Oh fuck off, Timo."

"No, I'm serious girl. Come here. Look with your eye. I know you got the eye. Don't make me think I'm wasting my time on you."

Timo crouched down beside the dead man, framing him with his hands. "Old Tex here hikes his ass across a million miles of burning desert, and he winds up here. Maybe he's thinking he's heading for California and gets caught with the State Sovereignty Act, can't cross no state borders now. Maybe he just don't have the cash to pay coyotes. Maybe he thinks he's special and he's going to swim the Colorado and make it up north across Nevada. Anyways, Tex is stuck squatting out in the hills, watching us live the good life. But then the poor sucker sees the CAP, and he's sick of paying to go to some public pump for water, so he grabs his bottles and goes in for a little sip—"

"—and someone puts a bullet in him," Lucy finished. "I get it. I'm trying to tell you nobody cares about dead Texans. People string them up all the time. I saw it in New Mexico, too. Merry Perry prayer tents and Texans strung up on fences. Same in Oklahoma. All the roads out of Texas have them. Nobody cares."

Wet.

Timo sighed. "You're lucky you got me for your tour guide. You know that, right? You see the cigarettes? See them little bitty Beam and Cuervo bottles? The black candles? The flowers?"

Timo waited for her to take in the scene again. To see the way he saw. "Old Tex here isn't a *warning*. This motherfucker's an *offering*. People turned Old Tex into an offering for Santa Muerte. They're using Tex here to get in good with the Skinny Lady."

"Lady Death," Lucy said. "Isn't that a cult for narcos?"

"Nah. She's no cult. She's a saint. Takes care of people who don't got pull with the Church. When you need help on something the Church don't like, you go to Santa Muerte. The Skinny Lady takes care of you. She knows we all need a little help. Maybe she helps narcos, sure, but she helps poor people, too. She helps desperate people. When Mother Mary's too uptight, you call the Skinny Lady to do the job."

"Sounds like you know a lot about her."

"Oh hell yes. Got an app on my phone. Dial her any time I want and get a blessing."

"You're kidding."

"True story. There's a lady down in Mexico runs a big shrine. You send her a dollar, she puts up an offering for you. Makes miracles happen. There's a whole list of miracles that Santa Muerte does. Got her own hashtag."

"So what kind of miracles do you look for?"

"Tips, girl! What you think?" Timo sighed. "Narcos call on Santa Muerte all the time when they want to put a bullet in their enemies. And I come in after and take the pictures. Skinny Lady gets me there before the competition is even close."

Lucy was looking at him like he was crazy, and it annoyed him. "You know, Lucy, it's not like you're the only person who needs an edge out here." He waved at the dead Texan. "So? You want the story, or not?"

She still looked skeptical. "If anyone can make an offering to Santa Muerte online, what's this Texan doing upside down on a fence?"

"DIY, baby."

"I'm serious, Timo. What makes you think Tex here is an offering?"

Because Amparo's boyfriend just lost his job to some loser Longhorn who will work for nothing. Because my water bill just went up again, and my rationing just went down. Because Roosevelt Lake is gone dry, and I got Merry Perrys doing revivals right on the corner of 7th and Monte Vista, and they're trying to get my cousin Marco to join them.

"People keep coming," Timo said, and he was surprised at the tightness of his throat as he said it. "They smell that we got water, and they just keep coming. It's like Texas is a million, million ants, and they just keep coming."

"There are definitely a lot of people in Texas."

"More like a tsunami. And we keep getting hit by wave after wave of them, and we can't hold 'em all back." He pointed at the body. "This is Last Stand shit, here. People are calling in the big guns. Maybe they're praying for Santa Muerte to hit the Texans with a dust storm and strip their bones before they get here. For sure they're asking for something big."

"So they call on Lady Death." But Lucy was shaking her head. "It's just that I need more than a body to do a story."

"But I got amazing pics!"

"I need more. I need quotes. I need a trend. I need a story. I need an example…"

Lucy was looking across the CAP canal toward the subdivision as she spoke. Timo could almost see the gears turning in her head…

"Oh no. Don't do it, girl."

"Do what?" But she was smiling, already.

"Don't go over there and start asking who did the deed."

"It would be a great story."

"You think some motherfucker's just gonna say they out and wasted Old Tex?"

"People love to talk, if you ask them the right questions."

"Seriously, Lucy. Let the cops take care of it. Let them go over there and ask the questions."

Lucy gave him a pissed-off look.

"What?" Timo asked.

"You really think I'm that wet?"

"Well…"

"Seriously? How long have we known each other? Do you really think you can fool me into thinking the cops are gonna give a shit about another dead Merry Perry? How wet do you think I am?"

Lucy spun and headed for her truck.

"This ain't some amusement park!" Timo called after her. "You can't just go poke the Indians and think they're gonna native dance for you. People here are for *real!*" He had to shout the last because the truck's door was already screeching open.

"Don't worry about me!" Lucy called as she climbed into the beast. "Just get me good art! I'll get our story!"

"So let me get this straight," Timo asked, for the fourth or fifth time. "They just let you into their house?"

They were kicked back on the roof at Sid's Cafe with the rest of the regulars, taking potshots at the prairie dogs who had invaded the half-finished subdivision ruins around the bar, trading an old .22 down a long line as patrons took bets.

The subdivision was called Sonora Bloom Estates, one of those crap-ass investments that had gone belly up when Phoenix finally stopped bailing out over-pumped subdivisions. Desert Bloom Estates had died because some bald-ass pencil-pusher in City Planning had got a stick up his ass and said the water district wasn't going to support them. Now, unless some company like IBIS or Halliburton could frack their way to some magical new water supply, Desert Bloom was only ever going to be a town for prairie dogs.

"They just let you in?" Timo asked. "Seriously?"

Lucy nodded smugly. "They let me into their house, and then into their neighbor's houses. And then they took me down into their basements and showed me their machine guns." Lucy took a swig of Negro Modelo. "I make friends, Timo." She grinned. "I make a *lot* of friends. It's what I do."

"Bullshit."

"Believe it, or don't." Lucy shrugged. "Anyway, I've got our story. 'Phoenix's Last Stand.' You wouldn't believe how they've got themselves set up. They've got war rooms. They've got ammo dumps. This isn't some cult militia, it's more like the army of the apocalypse. Way beyond preppers. These people are getting ready for the end of the world, and they want to talk about it."

"They want to talk."

"They're *desperate* to talk. They *like* talking. All they talk about is how to shove Texas back where it came from. I mean, you see the inside of their houses, and it's all Arizona for the People, and God and Santa Muerte to back them up."

"They willing to let me take pictures?"

Lucy gave him another smug look. "No faces. That's the only condition."

Timo grinned. "I can work with that."

Lucy set her beer down. "So what've you shot so far?"

"Good stuff." Timo pulled out his camera and flicked through images. "How about this one?" He held up the camera for her to see. "Poetry, right?"

Lucy eyed the image with distaste. "We need something PG, Timo."

"PG? Come on. PG don't get the hits. People love the bodies and the blood. Sangre this, sangre that. They want the blood, and they want the sex. Those are the only two things that get hits."

"This isn't for the local blood rags," Lucy said. "We need something PG from the dead guy."

She accepted the rifle from a hairy biker dude sitting next to her and sighted out at the dimming landscape beyond. The sun was sinking over the sprawl of the Phoenix basin, a brown blanket of pollution and smoke from California wild fires turning orange and gaudy.

Timo lifted his camera and snapped a couple quick shots of Lucy as she sighted down the rifle barrel. Wet girl trying to act dry. Not knowing that everyone who rolled down to Phoenix tried to show how tough they were by picking up a nice rifle and blasting away at the furry critters out in the subdivisions.

The thought reminded Timo that he needed to get some shots of Sumo Hernandez and his hunting operation. Sucker had a sweet gig bringing Chinese tourists in to blast at coyotes and then feed them rattlesnake dinners.

He snapped a couple more pictures and checked the results. Lucy looked damn good on the camera's LCD. He'd got her backlit, the line of her rifle barrel across the blaze of the red ball sun. Money shot for sure.

He flicked back into the dead Texan pictures.

"PG, PG...," Timo muttered. "What the fuck is PG? It's not like the dude's dick is out. Just his eaten-off face."

Lucy squeezed off another shot and handed the rifle on.

"This is going to go big, Timo. We don't want it to look like it's just another murder story. That's been done. This has to look smart and scary and real. We're going to do a series."

"We are?"

"Hell yes, we are. I mean, this could be Pulitzer type stuff. 'Phoenix's Last Stand.'"

"I don't give a shit about Pulitzers. I just want good hits. I need money."

"It will get us hits. Trust me. We're onto something good."

Timo flicked through more of his pictures. "How about just the beads in the guy's neck?" He showed her a picture. "This one's sweet."

"No." Lucy shook her head. "I want the CAP in it."

Timo gave up on stifling his exasperation. "PG, CAP. Anything else, ma'am?"

Lucy shot him a look. "Will you trust me on this? I know what I'm doing."

"Wet-ass newcomer says she knows what she's doing."

"Look, you're the expert when it comes to Phoenix. But you've got to trust me. I know what I'm doing. I know how people think back East. I know what people want on the big traffic sites. You know Phoenix, and I trust you. Now you've got to trust *me*. We're onto something. If we do it right, we're going to blow up. We're going to be a phenomenon."

The hairy biker guy handed the rifle back to Lucy for another shot.

"So you want PG, and you want the CAP," Timo said.

"Yeah. The CAP is why he died," she said absently as she sighted again with the rifle. "It's what he wanted. And it's what the Defending Angels need to protect. It's what Phoenix has that Texas doesn't. Phoenix is alive in the middle of a desert because you've got one of the most expensive water transport systems in the world. If Texas had a straw like the CAP running to some place like the Mississippi River, they'd still be fine."

Timo scoffed. "That would be like a thousand miles."

"Rivers go farther than that." Lucy squeezed off a shot and dust puffed beside a prairie dog. The critter dove back into its hole, and Lucy passed the rifle on. "I mean, your CAP water is coming from the Rockies. You've got the Colorado River running all the way down from Wyoming and Colorado, through Utah, all the way across the top of Arizona, and then you and California and Las Vegas all share it out."

"California doesn't share shit."

"You know what I mean. You all stick your straws in the river, you pump water to a bunch of cities that shouldn't even exist. CAP water comes way more than a thousand miles." She laughed and reached for her beer. "The irony is that at least Texans built where they *had* water. Without the CAP, you'd be just like the Texans. A bunch of sad-ass people all trying to move north."

"Thank God we're smarter than those assholes."

"Well, you've got better bureaucrats and pork barrels, anyway."

Timo made a face at Lucy's dig, but didn't bother arguing. He was still hunting through his photos for something that Lucy would approve of.

Nothing PG about dying, he thought. *Nothing PG about clawing your way all the way across a thousand miles of desert just to smash up against chain link. Nothing PG about selling off your daughter so you can make a run at going North, or jumping the border into California.*

He was surprised to find that he almost felt empathy for the Texan. Who knew? Maybe this guy had seen the apocalypse coming, but he'd just been too rooted in place to accept that he couldn't ride it out. Or maybe he'd had too much faith that God would take care of him.

The rifle was making the rounds again. More sharp cracks of the little .22 caliber bullets.

Faith. Maybe Old Tex's faith had made him blind. Made it impossible for him to see what was coming. Like a prairie dog who'd stuck his head out of his burrow, and couldn't quite believe that God had put a bead on his furry little skull. Couldn't see the bullet screaming in on him.

In the far distance, a flight of helicopters was moving across the burning horizon. The thud-thwap of their rotors carried easily across the hum of the city. Timo counted fifteen or twenty in the formation. Heading off to fight forest fires maybe. Or else getting shipped up to the arctic by the Feds.

Going someplace, anyway.

"Everybody's got some place to go," Lucy murmured, as if reading his mind.

The rifle cracked again, and a prairie dog went down. Everyone cheered. "I think that one was from Texas," someone said.

Everyone laughed. Selena came up from below with a new tray of bottles and handed them out. Lucy was smirking to herself, looking superior.

"You got something to say?" Timo asked.

"Nothing. It's just funny how you all treat the Texans."

"Shit." Timo took a slug from his beer. "They deserve it. I was down there, remember? I saw them all running around like ants after Hurricane Violet fucked them up. Saw their towns drying up. Hell, everybody who wasn't Texas Forever saw that shit coming down. And there they all were, praying to God to save their righteous Texan asses." He took another slug of beer. "No pity for those fools. They brought their apocalypse down on their own damn selves. And now they want to come around here and take away what we got? No way."

"No room for charity?" Lucy prodded.

"Don't interview me," Timo shot back.

Lucy held up her hands in apology. "My bad."

Timo snorted. "Hey everybody! My wet-ass friend here thinks we ought to show some charity to the Texans."

"I'll give 'em a bullet, free," Brixer Gonzalez said.

"I'll give 'em two!" Molly Abrams said. She took the rifle and shot out a distant window in the subdivision.

"And yet they keep coming," Lucy murmured, looking thoughtful. "They just keep on coming, and you can't stop them."

Timo didn't like how she mirrored his own worries.

"We're going to be fine."

"Because you've got Santa Muerte and a whole hell of a lot of armed lunatics on your side," Lucy said with satisfaction. "This story is going to make us. 'The Defending Angels of Phoenix.' What a beautiful scoop."

"And they're just going to let us cover them?" Timo still couldn't hide his skepticism.

"All anyone wants to do is tell their story, Timo. They need to know they matter." She favored him with a side-long smile. "So when a nice journo from up north comes knocking? Some girl who's so wet they can see it on her face? They love it. They love telling her how it is." Lucy took a sip of her beer, seeming to remember the encounter. "If people think you're wet enough, you wouldn't believe what they'll tell you. They've got to show how smart and wise they are, you know? All you need to do is look interested, pretend you're wet, and people roll right over."

Lucy kept talking, describing the world she'd uncovered, the details that had jumped out at her. How there was so much more to get. How he needed to come along and get the art.

She kept talking, but Timo couldn't hear her words anymore because one phrase kept pinging around inside his head like a pinball.

Pretend you're wet, and people roll right over.

"I don't know why you're acting like this," Lucy said for the third time as they drove out to see the Defending Angels.

She was driving the beast, and Timo was riding shotgun. He'd loaded his gear into her truck, determined that any further expenses from the reporting trip should be on her.

At first, he'd wanted to just cut her off and walk away from the whole thing, but he realized that was childish. If she could get the hits, then fine. He'd tag along on her score. He'd take her page views, and then he'd be done with her.

Cutting her off too soon would get him nothing. She'd just go get some other pendejo to do the art, or else she might even shoot the pictures herself and get her ass paid twice, a prospect that galled him even more than the fact that he'd been manipulated.

They wound their way into the subdivision, driving past ancient Prius sedans and electric bikes. At the end of the cul-de-sac, Lucy pulled to a halt. The place didn't look any different from any other Phoenix suburb. Except apparently, inside all the quiet houses, a last-battle resistance was brewing.

Ahead, the chain link and barbwire of the CAP boundary came into view. Beyond, there was nothing but cactus-studded hills. Timo could just make out the Texan on the far side of the CAP fences, still dangling. It looked like the dogs were at him again, tearing at the scraps.

"Will you at least talk to me?" Lucy asked. "Tell me what I did."

Timo shrugged. "Let's just get your shoot done. Show me these Angels of Arizona you're so hot for."

"No." Lucy shook her head. "I'm not taking you to see them until you tell me why you keep acting this way."

Timo glared at her, then looked out the dusty front window.

"Guess we're not going to see them then."

With the truck turned off, it was already starting to broil inside. The kind of heat that cooked pets and babies to death in a couple hours. Timo could feel sweat starting to trickle off him, but he was damned if he was going to show that he was uncomfortable. He sat and stared at the CAP fence ahead of them. They could both sweat to death for all he cared.

Lucy was staring at him, hard. "If you've got something you want to say, you should be man enough to say it."

Man enough? Oh, hell no.

"Okay," Timo said. "I think you played me."

"Played you how?"

"Seriously? You going to keep at it? I'm on to you, girl. You act all wet, and you get people to help you out. You get people to do shit they wouldn't normally do. You act all nice, like you're all new and like you're just getting your feet under you, but that's just an act."

"So what?" Lucy said. "Why do you care if I fool some militia nutjobs?"

"I'm not talking about them! I'm talking about me! That's how you played me! You act like you don't know things, get me to show you around. Show you the ropes. Get you on the inside. You act all wet and sorry, and dumbass Timo steps in to help you out. And you get a nice juicy exclusive."

"Timo… how long have we known each other?"

"I don't know if we ever did."

"Timo—"

"Don't bother apologizing." He shouldered the truck's door open. As he climbed out, he knew he was making a mistake. She'd pick up some other photographer. Or else she'd shoot the story herself and get paid twice for the work.

Should have just kept my mouth shut.

Amparo would have told him he was both dumb and a sucker. Should have at least worked Lucy to get the story done before he left her ass. Instead he'd dumped her, and the story.

Lucy climbed out of the truck, too.

"Fine," she said. "I won't do it."

"Won't do what?"

"I won't do the story. If you think I played you, I won't do the story."

"Oh come on. That's bullshit. You know you came down here for your scoop. You ain't giving that up."

Lucy's stared at him, looking pissed. "You know what your problem is?"

"Got a feeling you're going to tell me."

"You're so busy doing your poor-me, I'm from Phoenix, everyone's-out-to-get-me, we're-getting-overrun wah-wah-wah routine that you can't even tell when someone's on your side!"

"That's not—"

"You can't even tell someone's standing right in front of you who actually gives a shit about you!" Lucy was almost spitting she was so mad. Her face had turned red. Timo tried to interject, but she kept talking.

"I'm not some damn Texan here to take your water, and I'm not some big time journo here to steal your fucking stories! That's not who I am! You know how many photographers I could work with? You know how many would bite on this story that I went out and got? I put my ass on the line out here! You think that was easy?"

"Lucy. Come on…"

She waved a hand of disgust at him and stalked off, heading for the end of the cul-de-sac and the CAP fence beyond.

"Go find someone else to do this story," she called back. "Pick whoever you want. I wouldn't touch this story with a ten-foot-pole. If that's what you want, it's all yours."

"Come on, Lucy." Timo felt like shit. He started to chase after her. "It's not like that!"

She glanced back. "Don't even try, Timo."

Her expression was so scornful and disgusted that Timo faltered.

He could almost hear his sister Amparo laughing at him. *You got the eye for some things, little bro, but you are blind blind blind.*

She'll cool off, he thought as he let her go.

Except maybe she wouldn't. Maybe he'd said some things that sounded a little too true. Said what he'd really thought of Lucy the Northerner in a way that couldn't get smoothed over. Sometimes, things just broke. One second, you thought you had a connection with a person. Next second, you saw them too clear, and you just knew you were never going to drink a beer together, ever again.

So go fix it, pendejo.

With a groan, Timo went after her again.

"Lucy!" he called. "Come on, girl. I'm sorry, okay? I'm sorry…"

At first, he thought she was going to ignore him, but then she turned.

Timo felt a rush of relief. She was looking at him again. She was looking right at him, like before, when they'd still been getting along. She was going to forgive him. They were going to work it out. They were friends.

But then he realized her expression was wrong. She looked dazed. Her sunburned skin had paled. And she was waving at him, waving furiously for him to join her.

Another Texan? Already?

Timo broke into a run, fumbling for his camera.

He stopped short as he made it to the fence.

"Timo?" Lucy whispered.

"I see it."

He was already snapping pictures through the chain link, getting the story. He had the eye, and the story was right there in front of them. The biggest luckiest break he'd ever get. Right place, right time, right team to cover the story. He was kneeling now, shooting as fast as he could, listening to the digital report of the electronic shutter, hearing money with every click.

I got it, I got it, I got it, thinking that he was saying it to himself and then realizing he was speaking out loud. "I got it," he said. "Don't worry, I got it!"

Lucy was turning in circles, looking dazed, staring back at the city. "We need to get ourselves assigned. We need to get supplies… We need to trace this back… We need to figure out who did it… We need to get ourselves assigned!" She yanked out her phone and started dialing madly as Timo kept snapping pictures.

Lucy's voice was an urgent hum in the background as he changed angles and exposures.

Lucy clicked off the cell. "We're exclusive with *Xinhua*!"

"Both of us?"

She held up a warning finger. "Don't even start up on me again."

Timo couldn't help grinning. "Wouldn't dream of it, partner."

Lucy began dictating the beginnings of her story into her phone, then broke off. "They want our first update in ten minutes, you think you're up for that?"

"In ten minutes, updates are going to be the least of our problems."

He was in the flow now, capturing the concrete canal and the dead Texan on the other side.

The dogs leaped and jumped, tearing apart the man who had come looking for water.

It was all there. The whole story, laid out.

The man.

The dogs.

The fences.

The Central Arizona Project.

A whole big canal, drained of water. Nothing but a thin crust of rapidly drying mud at its bottom.

Lucy had started dictating again. She'd turned to face the Phoenix sprawl, but Timo didn't need to listen to her talk. He knew the story already—a whole city full of people going about their daily lives, none of them knowing that everything had changed.

Timo kept shooting.

THE HUNGRY EARTH

CARMEN MARIA MACHADO

Carmen Maria Machado's debut short story collection, *Her Body and Other Parties*, was a finalist for the National Book Award and the winner of the Bard Fiction Prize, the Lambda Literary Award for Lesbian Fiction, the Brooklyn Public Library Literature Prize, the Shirley Jackson Award, and the National Book Critics Circle's John Leonard Prize. Her essays, fiction, and criticism have appeared in the *New Yorker*, the *New York Times*, *Granta*, *Tin House*, *VQR*, *McSweeney's Quarterly Concern*, *The Believer*, *Guernica*, *Best American Science Fiction and Fantasy*, *Best American Nonrequired Reading*, and elsewhere. She holds an MFA from the Iowa Writers' Workshop and has been awarded fellowships and residencies from the Michener-Copernicus Foundation, the Elizabeth George Foundation, the CINTAS Foundation, Yaddo, Hedgebrook, and the Millay Colony for the Arts. She is the Writer in Residence at the University of Pennsylvania, and is the guest editor for *Best American Science Fiction and Fantasy 2019*. She lives in Philadelphia with her wife.

The last carnival in human history was in Miami. It became the last carnival because Gilberto refused to switch to the devices. "To download popcorn," he wheezed. "Foolish. Those ugly terminals. No ambient smells."

The bird-men who had come for the hard sell offered him Scenters for half-price. They would pump the air full of fat butter-smells and fried-dough-smells, they promised. He refused again.

"How do you even shove food through those tubes, anyway?" Gilberto was unclear on the mechanics of computers, even on a good day. The bird-men shifted from foot to foot, and one of them muttered something about electricity.

Gilberto ignored them. He'd been a small boy when Castro had taken power, and did not respond well to threats, no matter how much they were packaged as helpful suggestion. Behind him, the thin-gold filament of a funhouse bulb went bright as a dying star and then blew. The daylight dimmed incrementally around us, and the fabric of the emerging sky was matte and black. The moons of the bird-men's faces waned into half-shadow. I did not like the way the darkness pooled in the creases between their stippled skin and the wicked curve of their beaks.

"The day when a carnival uses those stupid things—bosh," Gilberto said. "Strip the ghost from my bones. I embrace the future as heartily as the next man, but this? Strip the ghost from my bones." He chuckled a little, probably imagining carnival patrons plugged into the machines like rows of toasters.

Perhaps if he had seen the silver knives of the bird-men, he would not have said this twice, or even once. They moved quickly and obliged him, and though many of us saw his body fall to the packed dirt, there was nothing else to do or say. A carnie's life was defined by fear of extinction. We buried him and we ran.

Many years after that last Ferris wheel came down, when the terminals were everywhere and the fields were permanently fallow, I sat in a restaurant in Little Havana. This was in the final wave, and the nauseating fog of hunger defined my days. With trembling fingers, I hooked the jack into my neck. Somewhere in a distant server, a fixed amount of credit left my account and entered another.

Around me, other people were hooked in and silent. The only sound in the room was the thin, barely perceptible hum of many machines running at once. The terminals filled me with the nutrients that I technically needed. I was a cavernous and empty well, and they tipped a thimbleful of water into my depths.

The splices did not intend for this to happen, not in this way. They say this as a matter of propaganda, though I think I believe them. After we created them, and after they freed themselves, they could have killed us outright, but they did not. They just wanted us passive.

How could we blame them?

In the beginning, the bird-men were the foot-soldiers, the enforcers. The cow-men were wiser than we had previously supposed—what we had attributed to stupidity was actually a kind of deliberate thoughtfulness that most humans did not possess—so they made up the majority of the splice governing body. The pig-men became radicals and in the early days blew up the terminals with dynamite before they realized we were being phased out anyway and did not need to be slaughtered directly.

Of course they laid waste to our farms and our meat-packing plants. Of course they tore up and torched the acres of genetically modified crops. Whole states burned. My three sisters fled Miami for the rolling earth of Iowa, but Iowa was a field of fire, after.

Slow starvation was a kind of transcendent experience. So I was certain, there at the terminal in Little Havana, that I saw Gilberto, moving through the sea of people like they were a field of wheat, though I had never seen a field of wheat, and I had not seen Gilberto since my teenage days as break-boy and ticket-taker and sweeper-of-trash. The Gilberto vision came to me.

"How have you survived, Mario?" he asked me.

"I do not know," I said.

He pressed his thumb into the center of my forehead. "Wake up, Mario. Wake."

I closed my eyes and opened them, and I was again in this room of humans, completely alone. A woman fell off her chair. The jack popped out of her neck and the room was awash in her moans.

I slumped back in my seat, my arms resting in my lap, the base of my skull cradled in a soft brace. I could twitch my fingers a little, and I found myself tapping out the rhythms I overheard on the leg of my pants: the cycles of rain that struck the roof and floor-to-ceiling windowpanes, the syncopated sound of human breath, even the uneven sounds from the woman who had fallen and could not stand. No one lifted from the chairs.

I remembered a howling storm that tore over the carnival in the weeks before the bird-men came. The rain drummed against the main tent, and we all sat and watched the structure around us inhale and exhale like it was alive, as if we were resting in the lungs of a giant beast. When I touched the leathery canvas and pulled my hand away, beads of water slid down my fingers. The whole place smelled like wet animals and hay, and human sweat. Celia, one of the acrobats, held me tightly against the bony arc of her ribcage, her heart banging around like a terrified bird, gently *shush*ing me even though it was really her own fears she was trying to soothe away. Thunder slit open the seams of the air. Lightning threw our faces into relief unevenly, like we were watching a badly joined filmstrip. The horses panicked and gouged nautilus-shaped curls of wood out of their stalls with their flailing hooves.

There, in the restaurant, Celia dead, Gilberto dead, the horses freed by the bird-men, a gust of wind blew an outdoor chair into the long glass window that faced the street. It went thickly veined with cracks, and then shattered. No one moved. Behind my fluttering lids, I saw the bird-men, again, the first time they came, how I wanted nothing more than to touch them, and how the tallest of them flinched away from my dry fingers. Then, darkness. Then, Gilberto's hoarse laugh. Then silver knives. The carnival tents burning. A sheet-wrapped body thudding against the packed dirt of a shallow hole. Darkness again. I might have had a fever. I might have been there for two days, for fifty. The fallen woman's moans of hunger went silent. Maybe it was only a few hours. I do not know. A deer—a full deer, not a splice—picked its way through the glass pieces, the room of people, curiously touching her black nose to us and to the terminals. Head dip, *tap*. A thin, gentle face so close I could see the high cheekbones, the liquid curve of her eyes. Stretched neck, *tap*. No fear. *Tap. Tap.*

* * *

298

Of course we all died, eventually. People's credit ran dry, and anyway, the human body is not meant to have nutrients downloaded into it. Or uploaded. The mechanics of the machines were never clear to me, or anyone. As the last crop of humans failed, the splices said to us via the terminal screens, "We are sorry. This is part of the natural cycle. It was always supposed to happen this way. A normal flux. Evolution." The message would scroll and then blink out, and then scroll again, over and over. I stopped reading it, after a while.

For those of us with enough credit—credit that was both useless and now saved us, though to what end?—we remained in the place we had last sat down, alive and aware, but motionless. In this way, we saw the cow-men and pig-men and bird-men, loosed of their need to pretend to be like us, return to nature. They shed their clothes and took to the outside world. As grass pressed up between blocks of pavement and trees split apart the streets and buildings, the splices lived there. They rollicked and pulled plants up with their teeth. They made sounds that may have been laughter. They reminded me, in the dim hallways of my memory, of the carnival freaks, the bearded woman who had trimmed my hair and slipped me butterscotch that I would click against my teeth, the melted man who had shown me how to throw a knife and pin a butterfly. The splices' backwards knees allowed them to lollop thunderously across the earth like horses, but sometimes I saw them reading.

Those of us who were still alive did not fight what was coming. The footfall of our hearts did not quicken when green tendrils curled around us, grew into us, took what they needed. Where the soycorn and hydroponic lettucemelons had once grown, where we had built our cities, nature reclaimed her skin. She reached vines and microorganisms into the buildings and the houses and the land that had once sustained us. She reached into *us*.

Centuries hungry, she choked us down.

LAST CHANCE

NICOLE KORNHER-STACE

Nicole Kornher-Stace is the author of *Desideria*, *The Winter Triptych*, the Norton Award finalist *Archivist Wasp*, and its sequel, *Latchkey*. Her work appears in *Clarkesworld*, *Apex*, and *Fantasy*. She lives in New Paltz, NY. She can be found online at nicolekornherstace.com and on Twitter @wirewalking.

Mama was the very best torturer in all the Three Valleys. Everybody said so. Torturer means somebody who's good at making you tell secrets, even when you don't want to. It's hard to lie to Mama. So I know she's really good at her job.

Even the king up in Grayfall knew Mama was the best. He probably had his own torturer, because a king has everything, but who was it getting brought in the fancy cart all the way up the highroad whenever the king had a secret-keeper in his jail? You guess who.

I don't know why Mama didn't want to move to Grayfall. We spent so much time going back and forth, Sunrise to Grayfall along the highroad and back. The first time in the cart was okay, sitting on the soft seats with Mama, looking out the windows, playing I Spy and Count the Fires and Who Can Hold Their Breath the Longest, but on the way home it was already getting boring, and Mama said there'd be lots of next times after that, a job's a job, so I better just get used to it.

Deep down I didn't want to move to Grayfall either, not really. I liked it in Sunrise. Even if there was no king and no fancy cart and no kingsguard bringing me blackberry pastries from the castle kitchen while Mama was off working. In Sunrise we had our very own house, just me and Mama, with our very own mint plant and our very own tree, with a swing on the low branch that's the perfect height for me and I didn't have to share it with anyone.

But the best part about Sunrise was the giants. Sometimes for Mama's work she puts a secret-keeper's feet into a box of stones and makes them stand in the river with just their face sticking out until they tell her all the secrets the king wants to know. These two giants have their feet stuck in the earth pretty much exactly like that, their heads tilted back in just the same way, the Waste drifting up around their ankles like snow. The rest of their bodies are rusty like an old knife and you can't really tell what they used to look like, but I like how the highroad to Sunrise runs between them and you can look up and imagine that they were in the middle of play-fighting like me and Jamie sometimes do when our chores are done and somebody said FREEZE and so they froze there, one of them grabbing the other one's fists in midair.

Jamie's dad says the giants are old old magic. Older than any house in Sunrise. Older than the castle in Grayfall. Older than the highroad, which is so old it's mostly gone in places and workers have to go out with flat rocks to patch up the places where the road disappears and it's just Waste where the road should be. Older even than the Grayfall songkeeper, who's so old her face looks like a dried apple with no juice left in it at all.

One time Mama tried to scare me, said the giants move while we're asleep, they go around town and peek into the houses with their windowy eyes, but I know that's not true. It's a lie, but not the bad kind. The giants are there to protect Sunrise with their old magic. You learn that from little. You put your hands like this and say GIANTS WATCH OVER ME IN ALL MY ENDEAVORS and they do. Endeavors means stuff you want the giants to watch you do and make sure you do a good job and nothing bad happens.

But the giants can't watch the whole long highroad, so how can they protect you if they can't see you?

We went to Grayfall thirteen times, me and Mama. But we only came back twelve.

Mama says there are bad parts in every story. Scary parts. Sad parts. If it was happy and fun all the time, it wouldn't be like life, so it wouldn't be a good story.

Fires in the Waste means traders or scav armies, Mama says. A cookfire makes smoke, and that could be anybody, but scav army raiders burn their dead to Carrion Boy, and that smoke looks pretty much the same from far away. And you don't know what kind of fire it is until it's too late.

Here's what Mama taught me to do. Hold out your arm as long as it goes, make a fist, then stick out your thumb. If the smoke from the fire is wider than your thumb, that means Stay Off the Road, Somebody's Close. Same if there are lots of little fires all together. Same if you're by yourself alone on the highroad, even if there's zero fires you can see.

The day the scav army raiders got us coming back down the highroad from Grayfall was a zero-fires day. I don't know what happened, I was asleep on Mama's shoulder in the fancy cart, having a bad dream about big dogs chasing me, and then when I woke up I was sitting in a scorchweed bush beside the road and my shoulder hurt and the leftover blackberry pastry I was saving in my pocket for Jamie was all mashed up against my leg and I didn't know why I wasn't in the cart anymore.

I wasn't in the cart anymore because it was lying on its side in the middle of the road, three raiders poking around in the guts of it. They took out Mama's big orange work bag and my blue backpack. I wanted to yell at them for taking our stuff, but then I saw that one of the raiders was dragging the cart driver out of his seat and tying his hands together. His face was all bloody, and seeing that made my voice dry up in my mouth.

I looked at the cart again. Half of Mama was lying next to it. Something happened to my eyes when I saw that—everything went all white and sparkly for a second—but then the sparkles melted away and a raider was pulling Mama's arms and she wasn't cut in half at all, just her legs were stuck under the cart. But *really* stuck, I guess, because when he pulled she screamed. It was the first time I ever heard Mama scream. Also the last. She didn't sound scared though, just really, really mad.

"You stupid fucking slag-for-brains," she yelled at the raider. "Do you KNOW WHO I—"

That surprised me even through my scaredness because I'd never heard Mama use words like that before. I was saying STUPID FUCKING SLAG-FOR-BRAINS to myself in my mind when Mama's eyes landed on me, and she looked pretty surprised to see me there in that scorchweed bush. I guess she'd thought the other raiders already got me, because something happened in her face, something sad and happy both at the same time. She did the thing with her eyes that means Listen To Me Right Now Or You Will Be Sorry Indeed and shaped her mouth like the word RUN except no sound came out.

But I didn't want to RUN. I wanted Mama. We should have moved to Grayfall. Then I'd be safe eating blackberry pastries, watching Mama sharpen her work-knives until they were shiny like stars, instead of sitting in this poky bush with my shoulder hurting and some stupid fucking slag-for-brains stealing my blue bag.

I made a face at Mama that meant No I Will Not, Come Over Here And Make Me, and I turned my heart into a stone too heavy to be moved, no matter what face she made back at me.

Instead she waited until the raider stopped pulling her arms again. Then she took his knife out of his boot and stuck it into his leg and he fell over, screaming and kicking at Mama with his good foot. Mama pushed herself partway up onto her elbows and threw the knife toward me. It landed next to my scorchweed bush. I knew she wanted me to take it and run away before the raiders saw me, but my body wouldn't work. Then the man's foot kicked hard across Mama's face and she made a little noise and fainted. Fainted means your brain goes to sleep for a little while. I see people faint all the time when Mama works, but none of those people have been Mama before now. I knew it was just that she fainted and not died because Mama would never die and leave me here alone.

The fainting part still scared me, but it made me mad too. Nobody kicks my Mama. I don't remember getting out of the scorchweed bush, or picking up the knife, just the way the world was going dark around the edges like I couldn't see right and be this mad both at the same time. But I guess I picked it up because the next thing I knew there was a raider taking it out of my hand and another raider picking me up by my feet and I swung through the air like on my tree swing but not really like that at all and then I heard a loud bang and everything went dark.

I want to say I woke up and it was all a dream, but instead I woke up because somebody was shaking me and kind of whisper-yelling KID, HEY KID, ARE YOU ALIVE and I wanted to say my name's not KID, it's ANEKO but when I tried to move my mouth it hurt so much the world went white and sparkly again and my head felt like it was coming unstuck from my body and I wondered if that was what Mama felt like when they—

I came awake all at once, sitting up and grabbing at whoever it was in front of me. It was an older kid, a girl like me. Her face was dirty and her feet were tied together. I grabbed at her and lost my balance. That was because the floor was moving, just like in the fancy cart, except bouncier, and also my feet were tied together too. She grabbed me back so I wouldn't fall over. I decided she wasn't a raider. A raider would've let me fall.

"Have you seen Mama?" I asked her, before my brain caught up with my mouth and I remembered she wasn't this girl's Mama, just mine. I wanted to say she looks like me, but then I remembered her squashed legs and her kicked-at face and didn't know if that was true anymore. I wanted to say she always has a big orange work bag with her, except the scav army raiders took it. I didn't know what I could say that was still true, but then something fell into my head so I said it. "She works for the king in Grayfall."

The girl shook her head. "I don't know Grayfall," she said. "I'm from Chooser's Blindside."

"Where's that?"

Instead of answering, she tapped a wall of the cart where there were all these little scratches. More scratches than all my fingers and toes put together. I didn't understand but I nodded like I did because I didn't want this new girl to think I was a stupid fucking slag-for-brains and leave me alone to die.

There was a map of the Waste in the king's castle but it was confusing. A little dot I could cover with my fingertip was supposed to be the whole town Sunrise, and even the huge city Grayfall was so little that if a baby sneezed on it it looked like it'd blow away. Maybe there was a Chooser's Whatever on there somewhere, but I didn't remember.

I thought about that for a minute while I looked around. We were in a closed-up little box, bigger than the fancy cart but it didn't have any windows, just little holes high up on the walls that let in a little bit of light. Mama has a box like this, all folded up in her big orange work bag, made special to fit over a secret-keeper's head. It's full of holes that she closes up one by one until the secret-keeper wants to talk. So I knew the holes up high on the cart-walls were for air. Bundles of dried ghostgrass hung in them, just like any window, keeping us safe. Which is kind of funny when you think about how not-safe we really were.

"I'm sorry about your Mama," the girl was saying. Then, in a voice like she was trying to make me feel better, she said, "They'll keep her around if they think she's useful. Is she good at fixing things, or making clothes, or fighting, or finding food? Anything like that?"

I wanted to tell the girl about Mama's big orange work bag and her long busy days working for the king in Grayfall but I remembered how Jamie told me one time what happened if scav armies caught you and didn't think you were useful. And I got really scared that if I said Mama's job was to find people's secrets then the girl would tell me that that's not useful enough and if I heard that I didn't know what I'd do, my whole self would close up like a fist so I couldn't hear that Mama wasn't useful enough to keep alive, so I didn't say anything.

The girl thought for a second and said, "That is, if she wasn't dead already." And made a question-face at me.

That one was easy to answer and I shook my head.

"Okay. Good. That's good." Now the question-face turned into a thinking-face, and while I was wondering if this girl would get as mad as Mama does when I interrupt her thinking-face, the cart slowed down, then stopped, and quick as a snake the girl spun around and slapped a pile of nasty old blankets in the corner. "Wake up," she whisper-yelled at the pile.

The pile kind of rustled around for a second.

"Slag you, Nina, help me out here."

The pile didn't say anything.

"Whatever," the girl said. "You're on your own. I tried." Then to me, "You saw me try."

All of a sudden she got a new look, like she could hear something I couldn't, and one of those quick hands shot out and covered my mouth. "Quiet."

"But I didn't say—"

"QUIET."

There was a kind of door in the side of the cart, and the girl gave it one sharp scared look and then back to me. She was holding my face in both her hands now, staring at me like Mama did when I had to listen to something really important.

"Quick," the girl whispered. "Tell me your name." She was whispering so fast it all squished into one word, TELLMEYOURNAME, but I knew what she meant.

"Aneko," I whispered back.

"I'm Sam. Okay, Aneko. Listen. Wherever they take you. Wherever they put you. Don't try to run. You'll just make it worse. Just do what they say and I'll find you. I'll help you. As soon as I can. Promise. Just—"

Then the door came open, and hands reached in and dragged Sam out, and before I ever got to talk to her again she was dead, lying there on the roadside staring up at the rain. I don't know what killed her, but I knew she was dead because her eyes were open and flies were walking on them and she didn't blink them away. Just lying there for the flies and ghosts and dogs to chew on. I wanted to help her somehow, I didn't know how really, maybe close her eyes so her ghost wouldn't see other ghosts coming at her across the Waste. It'd keep the flies out anyway, with their dirty feet. Her mouth was open a little like she was about to say something. But she didn't.

You draw stars over dead people's eyelids so Catchkeep can find them easy. You put something in their mouth so they can cross the dead people's river and their ghost doesn't get stuck in the Waste to walk forever. Mama never did those things herself, if one of the king's secret-keepers died before her work was done. The king had a person who did that. I watched it one time, even though that secret-keeper's mouth was a mess and he didn't have any eyelids anymore to draw on, so I'm pretty sure I know how.

But I couldn't stop and do those things for Sam, because they pushed us right on past her, and I stumbled looking down at her but the kids on the chain in front of me kept walking so I had to get my feet back under me or be dragged. But I held her name in my mouth without saying it. SAM, I thought, HER NAME IS SAM. I closed my mouth on the name and held on tight like the secret-keepers do when they make Mama work so late that she doesn't have any time to play with me after.

One time I heard a secret-keeper yell at Mama. I'LL TAKE IT TO MY GRAVE, he yelled at her, and there was a kind of spitty sound. Then there was a little space of quiet, and then the secret-keeper made the worst noise I've ever heard anybody make and I was happy I was behind the door and couldn't see what happened to him to make that sound come out of his mouth.

I didn't know what the secret-keeper wanted to take to his grave, or if he took it there. But it sounded like a brave strong thing to say. HER NAME IS SAM, I thought again. I'LL TAKE IT TO MY GRAVE.

Then I tucked it away in the back of my mind, where I keep the things I have to remember, like holy days and promises and chores. I didn't want to forget, but I also needed to clear some room in my head for the great big thing that was in there, itching in my mind, pushing everything else away, hot and red like blood.

I had to stay alive long enough for Mama to find me. And then we were going to escape.

Like Mama would say, first things first. I didn't know where she was. I didn't even know where I was. She might be a ghost now for all I know. We walked for days. I think maybe the cart broke, but nobody ever said. We got dragged out and chained together, me and

Sam and the other girl Nina who was asleep under the blankets, and some other kids from other carts. Mama was nowhere, and if Sam and Nina and everybody had grownups with them before, they were nowhere now too. But then that first night they unchained Sam and took her away and I thought she was going with the grownups because she was almost a grownup really herself but then the next day was when I saw her dead and I looked around for a chain like ours except with grownups on it but I couldn't find one. Just Waste on both sides, and the cart burning in a big chopped-up pile, and the road going forever in front and behind.

Nina was in front of me on the chain but I couldn't talk to her. There was somebody else on the chain behind me but I couldn't turn around to see who it was. If I did either of those things, bad stuff would happen. One time there was a lot of noise somewhere behind me, a grownup yelling and a kid crying, and after a minute of that the chain stopped, and the crying got louder for a second and then the kid started screaming, screaming like some secret-keepers do when they see Mama start to slowly unpack her work bag, and then there was a noise like something thunking into something else, a firewood-chopping kind of sound, and after that the crying stopped, but when the chain started moving again it was harder to walk, like we were dragging something heavy behind us.

After that I didn't cry, not even quietly. And I made sure to walk fast enough and pull extra hard with every step on that heavy mystery off behind us, because if I didn't then Nina would have to pull her part and mine too and Mama taught me from little that if we treat other people like tools to be useful to us, then the only thing making us different than the scav armies is that we live in towns and not on the Waste-roads in between.

I tried to keep my mind off of my hurting back and my tired feet and my growling belly and my thirsty thirsty mouth by counting the kids in front of me. But it was hard. We were all walking in a straight line on a straight road so I had to kind of remember which arms and legs and tops of heads belonged to which kid, so if one kid stepped sideways a little or put an arm out, I'd see that part of the kid, and if that happened enough times with enough different kids, I could have some kind of count. I counted five separate kids plus Nina and over the long day I double-checked and even triple-checked my count but when we finally stopped at sundown and they sat us in a circle with a raider guarding us I saw I was wrong. There were eight kids in front of me, and another eleven behind, ten alive and one dead, just lying there all dirty from the road with a horrible huge split in his head. There were other groups of people on chains, farther off, and a bunch of raiders in a big group beyond. I did see two chains of grownups, but no Mama.

That made me remember Sam, who looked littler and not so strong now that she was dead. And it made me think of the kid who couldn't walk and was now lying on his face in his spot in the circle, and those two thoughts kind of joined up and started walking toward another thought about Mama and how she couldn't walk because the cart had landed on her legs, and I yelled at those thoughts in my head to SHUT UP, SHUT UP, SHUT UP, until they went away somewhere else and I could be smart again and ANALYZE MY SITUATION like Mama would tell me to do.

Us kids had to sit really still because two raiders were circling behind us, round and round, like the circle of kids was a planet and the raiders were orbiting moons. ORBITING means going-around, which is what the raiders were doing. Going around with their weapons in their hands, making sure we didn't do anything bad.

We weren't allowed to talk, of course. There was a boy next to me, on the not-Nina side, and it was weird to think he'd been walking behind me this whole time and I didn't see his face at all until now. This boy tried to ask for water and the raider passing behind him swung her weapon down and smashed him in the cheek without even slowing down. Her weapon was some kind of heavy stick or club with sharp things sticking out of it, and the boy put his hand to his cheek and pulled it away all bloody and started screaming. That brought more raiders, and one of them started yelling at the one with the stick, and then she went away and the new raiders unchained the screaming boy and dragged him off into the dark and came back later without him.

They had to feed the rest of us so we could walk tomorrow. There was a big raider argument about that. Some of them didn't want to feed us, said there were still three days hard march to Last Chance, whatever that was, and then I didn't listen anymore because my whole mind was full of THREE DAYS HARD MARCH and I knew, just knew, that my feet could never walk that far, I'd end up like the dead boy with the inside-out head and never see Mama again.

But when they were done arguing they fed us. Not a lot. Each kid got one little strip of weird dried meat and one little broken-off piece of stale flatbread and three tiny dried berries, so small and hard that I couldn't even really chew them, they just got stuck between my teeth.

We had to eat the dried meat first and fast because if we took too long the salt in it would draw ghosts down on us from as soon as they took it out of its ghostgrass bag. One time Mama told me that the Grayfall king's first torturer used to sprinkle salt around his secret-keepers and let the Waste-ghosts at them bit by bit, but Mama never did that. She said it was lazy, and sloppy, and cruel. I never knew if she meant cruel to the secret-keepers or the ghosts.

We also got two sips of nasty water from a bottle the scav army raiders passed around. An older girl tried to take more water. I don't think she could stop herself, she got that water to her mouth and her mouth kept moving all on its own to take more. So the raider behind her reached down, took the bottle, then stepped in front of her and kicked her in the stomach so she threw up the water and tiny bit of food. The raider left and the girl looked down at the throwup. She looked like she was thinking about something, probably THREE DAYS HARD MARCH, because she picked the throwup meat and berries off the ground like a dog and ate them while we all stared. It was really hard not to make any noise or say anything while she was doing that, but I didn't want to have to choose between eating my own throwup or dying on the Waste-road from being too weak to walk, so I locked my mouth like Mama's work bag and kept it locked.

After that was sleeptime. Just there on the ground, which I thought would be fun before I tried it but then when I did it wasn't fun at all, it was cold and the ground was hard and I had to pee. The raiders had made a fire but it was far away by where they slept and didn't warm us kids up even a little. I wanted my pillow and blanket and most of all I wanted Mama. I tried to close my eyes and count big numbers until I fell asleep but Nina was next to me sniffling, not letting herself cry, so I whispered to her COME CLOSER SO WE CAN STAY WARM but then she just sniffled into my hair instead and you can't fall asleep with somebody doing that no matter how tired you are. So I scooted away and rolled over and something in my pocket went squish.

I pretended to fall asleep so the raiders wouldn't watch me, but really I was spying on them out of the tiniest opening in my eyes. After a long time one of them said I'M FREEZING MY BALLS OFF, LET'S GET OUT OF HERE and the other one kind of swept a look across us kids and said WELL THEY'RE NOT GOING ANYWHERE, and then I closed my eyes quick while the raider stepped over me, and I could hear them take a couple steps away, but then the first one stopped and said LOOK, MAYBE WE SHOULD JUST and the other one said THEN STAY, I'M GOING OVER THERE and their footsteps crunched away over the ashy Waste dirt toward the fire and when I opened my eyes again they were gone.

So I snuck my hand down to my pocket, really slow and quiet, and there was the blackberry pastry from the king's castle, all gummed together and mushed into the cloth of the pocket. But it was food, so I scooped it out in little slow secret bits on my fingers and ate it. It tasted like treasure. I felt bad about not sharing with Nina, but if I shared with her then all the kids would want some, and they'd be noisy and the raiders would come back and drag me away into the darkness or kill me right here on the ground.

When I couldn't scrape any more crumbs and fruit goo out of my pocket, I licked my fingers as quiet as I could, then licked the crumbs from around my lips and ate them carefully, one by one. I couldn't let the raiders smell the sweetness on me, and I wanted every speck of that food-energy to go to my walking feet, my seeing eyes. I still had lots farther to go.

The raiders were wrong. It was FOUR DAYS HARD MARCH to Last Chance, not THREE. Well, THREE plus ONE where we had to stop right where we were on the road and wait for a storm to blow over. It took all day, which was good for me because my feet hurt so much that I don't know if I could've walked on them even if all the scav armies in the whole wide Waste were chasing me, and bad for me because the extra day meant we ran out of food before we got to where they were taking us.

They put us all together while the storm was going over, and told us to keep our heads down and close our eyes and they tied pieces of cloth over our noses and eyes to keep the ash and dust out, and told us to shut up and go to sleep if we know what's good for us.

But there's no sleeping in a Waste-storm, at least not for me. It's too loud and too windy and every time you breathe you can feel some Waste sneaking into your nose and mouth so you sneeze out black gunk for days.

I tried to open my eyes just a little to see if I could see Mama anywhere, which was a mistake. Waste-ash flew into my eyes as soon as I opened them and I couldn't even wipe it back out because my hands were covered with it too. My eyes were too dried out to cry the ash away so I just squeezed them super tight so it wouldn't hurt as much and after a while I guess I fell asleep because I saw Mama walking toward me, no smashed legs, no chains, so I knew it was a dream and I woke up.

The day after that we ran out of food, and the day after that we arrived at the scav army town Last Chance, and by that time there were only twelve kids left on my chain plus me, and they put us straight to work.

Here's what Last Chance is NOT like: Sunrise. Grayfall. Any kind of town. It doesn't even have houses, not really, just tents and carts all shoved together in a kind of messy townish shape. It has chickens running around but no kids playing. It has dogs to pull the carts but no goats for milk. There's not even a garden, which is the number-one important thing for a town to have, Mama says, because people get sick if they don't have green growing things to eat, their bodies don't work right and they die, just like what happened with Jamie's big brother and his friends who went out to draw a map of the Waste past the mountains and got lost from first-apples day to second snow.

Also Last Chance doesn't have old Before-magic giants like Sunrise. That makes sense. I don't know what there is in Last Chance that the giants would want to protect.

Here's what Last Chance DOES have: Raiders. Lots of raiders.

Kids on chains like me and Nina. Nothing fun to do ever. Waste-ash in the air, always. Work.

My work gang is me and the rest of the kids on my chain. It's the same chain, just with gaps in it now where the other kids were when they were alive. There were two other chains of kids in my group, and other chains of kids already there working. They have grownups too, but they don't do the same work as us. They do stuff like fixing and cooking and some of them get taken into the scav army as fighters and finders and some of them just disappear.

Me and Nina and the rest of our chain, our job is digging. We all have digging-sticks, but there are only two shovels, so we have to take turns with them. We're supposed to dig around in some old ruins and put the stuff we find into a cart. We're looking for any Before-stuff we can find there. Broken relics, fossils, whatever.

Sometimes our SUPERVISOR, which means the raider who's boss of our chain, takes one of us kids off the chain and sends us into some little gap between ruin-stuff where a grownup won't fit. Sometimes it's because the SUPERVISOR saw something interesting in under the ruin-stuff and sometimes I think he's just a bad guesser about what spots are lucky because kids usually come out of there holding the same digging-stick they went in with and that only, no ruin-treasure, no old Before-magic, no nothing.

Nina gets sent in more than me because she isn't scared of the dark or tight places so she never cries going into the caves. Plus one time she found a pretty green glass ball that made the SUPERVISOR happy because it was top-shelf ruin-treasure even though it had white scratches all over it like a spider web. I don't think that's fair because how am I supposed to find top-shelf ruin-treasure if the SUPERVISOR always sends her in instead of me?

Nina's chain-name is THREE, because she's the third kid on the chain now. My chain-name is FOUR.

The first few days of this new work were really hard, and my whole body was tired and hurting the whole time, and I was always hungry and thirsty but the SUPERVISOR said YOU'LL EAT WHEN THIS SECTOR IS CLEARED, which I think means never because the only thing we got was more of the stale flatbread stuff, a piece the size of my hand that was all the food I ate the whole day.

On day four or maybe five all the kids were too tired and hungry to dig. We had to try anyway but it was slow and hard and all we found was two little pieces of good metal and some tiny bits of glass and a few old bone-pieces and a tooth, and then EIGHT went into a ruin-stuff cave with his digging-stick and fell asleep or fainted so me and TWO had to reach in and drag him out by the feet.

That day it was raining and the kids were crying and the SUPERVISOR pointed at Nina and pointed at the ruin-stuff cave and tilted his head quick like HURRY UP, like words were too good to waste on Nina. That made me mad. Nina was sick, she coughed all day every day, and she wasn't strong enough anymore to dig anything, and when the SUPERVISOR pointed at her she stood there shaking her head and quiet-crying and shivering like she was cold even though it was a hot day. So when the SUPERVISOR started moving toward Nina with a face like Did You Just Say No To Me, right for that one second I forgot how scared I was of the SUPERVISOR's hitting-stick and I kind of scrunched myself down like a kid who could fit in a ruin-stuff cave no problem and I said I'LL GO.

The SUPERVISOR gave me a kind of up-down look, then looked along the chain at the other kids, then back to me. Then he shrugged and took me off the chain and I went in.

It was my first time actually inside a ruin-stuff cave so I didn't know what I'd see. From the outside the ruin-caves looked more like big piles of Waste-ash with pieces of junk kind of spiking up out of it, which is how you know it's ruins and not just a place where lots of Waste-ash has been pushed all up together by the wind.

Inside was weird, but nice. The best part was the quiet. You go in there and the whole world around you kind of stops, and you keep moving inside the stopped bubble of it, all the Before-stuff around you, the plastic and metal and bricks and things, but the Waste's still under your feet and dusting all over everything, which is weird because the songkeeper says that in the Before the earth used to be green, not just in gardens like the one we have in Sunrise but everywhere.

So you're kind of in both places, the Before and the now, and also not in either one of them really, and the sun shines down on you through the gaps in the ceiling, and it's the same sun Before as now, which makes my head feel weird to think about.

I crawled in and then kept crawling for a little ways, farther than EIGHT went I guess because I squeezed and squirmed and got in too far for anyone to reach me. And then I kept crawling. Everybody knew you shouldn't go too far in because the ceiling is just made up of piled junk and it could fall on your head any second and that would be the end of you. But I knew if I came out of there without any ruin-treasure then the SUPERVISOR wouldn't send me back in again and in there in the quiet was way better than out there in the yelling and hitting and wind. I decided I'd find something really extra great so the SUPERVISOR would say ANEKO FINDS THE BEST RUIN-TREASURE, I WILL SEND HER IN EVERY DAY FOREVER AND THE SICK KIDS LIKE NINA WON'T HAVE TO GO IN ANYMORE. I mean I know he'd say THREE instead of NINA and FOUR instead of ANEKO but that was okay as long as my plan worked, because when I looked at Nina's coughing sick face all I could think about was Sam's swollen dead face and it made me sadder than I've ever been in my whole life but also so mad my eyes felt like fire.

I was going to outsmart the SUPERVISOR like Mama outsmarts me every time we play What Am I? And this pile of Before-junk was going to spit out some top-shelf ruin-treasure that would help me do it.

But first I had to find some. All us kids had bags tied to our waists where we were supposed to put whatever we found. Anything that was Before-stuff, the SUPERVISOR wanted. Anything old. The best thing my chain ever found was yesterday when SEVEN found the edge of a big metal box and we all dug it out together and the SUPERVISOR was so excited he took a shovel and started digging himself, but we dug out the lid or maybe door of the box but nobody could figure out how to open it and it was too heavy to move, so the SUPERVISOR took out one of those red strips of fabric that get tied around things that are too big for people to move by themselves without a cart and dogs. But there was nothing on the box to tie it to and the Waste was already blowing ash back over top of the whole thing anyway so the SUPERVISOR hit SEVEN for wasting his time and told us all to get back to work or else.

Now this was my one and only chance to do better. The tunnels through a ruins-cave are made by luck only, just the way the stuff fell when the Before-buildings came down. Where the tunnel started there wasn't anything left to take, other kids had already gotten there before me. So I decided to keep crawling back into the ruins-cave until I found something great or the SUPERVISOR started yelling.

I crawled back and back until I counted up to forty-two, and then the little tunnel through the broken bricks and stuff got wider where the pieces of stuff fell against each other in a way to leave a sort of little room, the pointy sort-of-ceiling just a bit above my head.

It was brighter this far in. Maybe the storm blew some gaps in the ceiling ash, or some stuff fell down not long ago. Anyway, I could see just fine, which was a nice surprise.

Three sides of the little room were just big piles of broken bricks with some long pieces of metal holding them up. It looked like somebody, somebody big, the Sunrise giants kind of big, took the metal pieces and shoved them into the ground really hard and left the long parts sticking out, but really I knew it was just the way this one Before-building fell. The other side of the little room was a giant-size letter S, taller than the tallest grownup I ever saw, and some long pieces of metal leaned up against the middle part of the S made up the ceiling of the room. I could just make out the top half of the S going on above the metal-pieces ceiling where the sun shone through.

Nobody had been here in a really long time. Maybe never. I could tell that right away. For one thing, Mama taught me to look for footprints and people-marks anywhere I go in the Waste ever, to see if people were there before me, and there weren't any here. For another thing, there was Before-stuff on the ground of my little room, poking up out of the Waste. Pieces of easy carrying size. Stuff other kids on chains or raiders or whoever would've grabbed up way before today.

I didn't have time to go through all the stuff really carefully. Maybe the SUPERVISOR would be just as happy with lots of sort-of-okay things as he would be with just one EXTRA GREAT one. So I just picked up everything I could as fast as I could. Anything that wasn't attached to the stuff that was holding up this ruins-cave from falling on my head. Plastic. Metal. Broken pieces of Before-brick, better than the best lake-clay. The dry darkness of the ruins-cave had kept this stuff from rotting in the sun and rain. I didn't look real close at anything, just shoved it all in my pockets.

"You in there," the SUPERVISOR yelled from outside. "Hurry up."

"Found stuff," I yelled back, fast and breathless, anything before he pulled me out and started hitting and put me back on the chain and sent Nina in instead. One chance. "Just a minute."

I glanced over my findings. Random nothing scraps of junk. But thanks to my find, the SUPERVISOR would flag my little room as a scavenge-spot, and other kids would be all over it like flies on a dead dog.

I had to do this smart. There was stuff sticking up out of the Waste, so it was an easy guess there was probably more stuff deeper down.

I started poking around with my digging-stick. The Waste was ashy and loose like always, and I could wiggle the pointy end of the stick down into it no problem. Then I could kind of get a piece of metal down in there and use that together with the stick to pull stuff out. I knew not to reach down into the Waste-ash with my bare hands. Too many tiny bits of glass and poky metal, too small to see, but it'd go into you like needles and you'd get an infection. Infection means when stuff gets into your skin that doesn't belong there and your blood has like a war with the bad stuff inside you and the bad stuff wins and your hand or whatever gets all red and puffy and you get nasty sick until they cut off your hand, and maybe you die anyway.

A little bit down it was hard to dig any deeper. There was something in the way. One time Jamie and I had to help dig new beds in the Sunrise town garden and that was really hard because just underneath the top layer of Waste there's all the stuff the ash has blown over and covered up, and you have to dig it out. It's like the Before is right there, sleeping under your feet, snuggled up under an ashy gross blanket that people walk on every day.

But Before-stuff is exactly what I wanted, so I just dug harder, shoving my digging-stick into the ground until it got totally stuck in something underground. I pulled, I pushed it back and forth, but it was stuck, and if I came back out of that ruins-cave with no digging-stick, it was going to be a bad day for me.

I took the piece of metal and tried to dig a hole around where the stick went in. Scooping out the ash was hard because it just kept sliding back down into the hole I was making. So I tried to go under the mystery underground thing instead. Sometimes you could lever up a rock like that, if you get something in under it and push down to lift up the end you can't see. Jamie's dad taught us that, when we were out digging for the garden.

The SUPERVISOR was shouting again. "I have to send somebody in after you," he was yelling, "you both pay."

"Something's stuck," I heard myself yell back, all frozen scared because what was stuck was my digging-stick and not some piece of ruin-treasure that would save me from the hitting. Then, making the lie even worse, I yelled, "I can get it, I just need a few minutes is all."

The SUPERVISOR went quiet again. I didn't know if he was sending someone in, or who it would be, or how I would keep them from telling the SUPERVISOR about my lie. But the SUPERVISOR couldn't fit back here, and I knew he was scared to come in under that huge pile of ruin-stuff himself. All the raiders were. Nina said that was the whole reason us kids were here doing their scav army work for them, because we're expendable, which means nobody cared if we got crushed like bugs under all of this.

So I wiggled the metal piece in as far as I could and leaned on it. Then, while I was still leaning on it, I took another piece of metal and dug around my guess of the shape of the underground thing I couldn't see. It felt round and smooth, like an egg bigger than my head. That was disappointing because round and smooth meant rock, and the SUPERVISOR wasn't going to care about that, even if rocks were actually even older than the other Before-stuff, like every little knows.

But… how do you get a digging-stick stuck in a rock?

I did my best to get the hole dug around the maybe-rock and then I grabbed the digging-stick and pulled with every drop of my strength.

It didn't move.

I pulled harder. I pulled with muscles I didn't even know I had until I lost my grip and my balance and fell over backwards. It hurt, but I stayed quiet so the SUPERVISOR wouldn't hear.

The stick still hadn't moved. It was poking up out of the ground exactly how I'd left it.

I started feeling myself getting mad. Really mad. The kind of mad Mama always tells me not to get, because it's not productive. Productive means being able to do your best at something because you're not too busy being so mad that you can't think right and you want to kick everything instead.

But Mama wasn't here to tell me to take my calm-down breaths, so before I could stop myself I kicked the stuck-out part of the digging-stick as hard as I could.

And it moved.

Quick as I could, I jammed the piece of metal down in beside where I guessed the edge of the thing to end, fast before the ash could fill the hole back in. Then I kind of pushed the metal up and down with my foot while pulling the stick up and sideways the other way with both hands and praying to the One Who Got Away for strength and silence and the SUPERVISOR leaving me alone a little while longer.

It felt like pulling up a big old corpseroot out of new garden dirt, except even tighter stuck. I got my feet in a better position and dug in with my heels and fought that piece of Waste for my digging-stick and whatever dumb thing it was stuck to.

Deep under my feet, I felt something give way. There was a soft *pop*, so quiet I felt it more than heard it, and then the stick flew out in my hands, raining dirt and ash and those tiny sharp bits of Waste-stuff all over, and I shut my eyes.

When the stuff stopped raining down, I carefully wiped around my eyes.

Then I opened them and almost screamed.

Stuck to the end of my digging-stick was a head. A big, hard, made-of-Before-stuff head. Like the Sunrise giants, but way way smaller, more the size of like a big round bucket. Maybe it was metal, maybe plastic. Sometimes with Before-stuff it was hard to know for sure. It wasn't very heavy but it felt really strong, like if my head was made of this stuff, the SUPERVISOR's hitting-stick would feel like the tiniest mosquito booping against it, not bothering me even a little.

I waited for a ghost to come out of it and devour the salt from my bones. Devour means eat every last bit, like Mama tells me to do with my dinner. But no ghosts did. There was just a skull, or the little pieces left from one. I pocketed a tooth for remembrance, which means asking the Chooser to be nice to the dead. I left the rest of the skull-pieces to the Waste.

Every little knows about the bones in the earth. People bones and plastic bones and metal bones of Before-stuff long long dead and extinct, which means not just your regular dead but all your kind dead forever. Bones and stories are all we have left of the mystery people Before and their Before-magic, their metal crab-shells and bird-wings and broken dead weapons, also extinct. These things are called FOSSILS, which means bones and relics that are older than anything.

I knew all this stuff since forever. Mama taught me, Jamie's dad taught me, the Sunrise songkeeper and the Grayfall songkeeper taught every little in their towns. But apart from the Sunrise giants this was my first time seeing any whole unbroken fossil close enough to touch. Usually it was just little pieces, and the songkeepers kept them in special hands-off boxes and only brought them out for stories.

The dirt shook off of the fossil-head no problem. Underneath it was shiny and black and empty inside, with a kind of little almost-black window on the front that looked like something part plastic, part glass. The window-thing was broken on one side, and that's where the digging-stick had gotten stuck, in that hole. The bottom edge of the head wasn't smooth, there were all these in-and-out pieces that made it look like it was supposed to lock onto something else, the way some of Mama's work tools went together to make a whole new more complicated thing. Those were priceless Before-relics, given to Mama by the Grayfall king from his own treasure-room. The Before-magic ran through them and made them still work, as long as Mama made sure to set them out in the sunshine when she was done with them. I wasn't allowed to touch them ever. Not even when they were just sitting there in the sun waiting for the magic to come back.

I thought about that while I wiggled the stick out of the little window on the head. Easy now that I could see how it was stuck. I wiped the shiny head on my sleeve and put it on my head like a hat, waiting for the Before-magic to go smashing through me like a storm.

The fossil-head was too big for me. It probably could have fit the SUPERVISOR, or Mama, or maybe even Jamie. On me it wasn't any kind of hat at all, it went down over my whole face and head and neck and sat perched on my shoulders. It was like what the Grayfall kingsguard wear on their heads to protect them from raiders and bears and whatever, except way way better, because it covered my whole head and not just the top of it.

For a five-count I held my breath, waiting to see what it would do to me. Would the Before-magic of it get into me like an infection? Would it turn me into a Before-person, part metal and part meat? Would it mistake me for one of them and kill me dead extinct? I pictured it squeezing tighter and tighter, popping my head like a grape.

But nothing happened. It was a cold dead fossil and couldn't hurt me, only help. I knew what would happen if I gave this thing I found to the SUPERVISOR. This was my top-shelf ruin-treasure, a Before-people mystery fossil, and there wouldn't be any more hitting after I gave it to him. It would keep me safe. At least for a little while. Long enough to—

Suddenly I heard a weird little surprised noise behind me. I turned and there was Nina. Her mouth was open and she was making huge eyes at the fossil-head.

She looked like she was about to start yelling so I took it off real quick so she would know it was just me underneath. At the same time I took a step back. Nina even being here was messing up my whole plan. She was bigger than me and probably stronger. What if she took the head back to the SUPERVISOR instead of me and got credit for my find? Then I'd get hit and she'd get sent into the ruin-caves tomorrow instead of me.

"It's mine," I whispered, keeping my voice quiet so nobody outside the ruin-cave would hear. "I found it."

I didn't know if Nina heard me either. She was still staring, not saying anything. She looked like she forgot how to talk. Like a secret-keeper after a long day with Mama and her work bag.

"Promise you won't tell," I demanded, as fierce as I could while still whispering.

Nina blinked and stared at me. It was the first time she was looking at me and not the head. She was giving me a look like you give a little who keeps eating rainstealer flowers, forgetting that something so pretty can still make you so sick.

"Tell?" she whispered back at me, and her voice matched her face. It was a Don't Be Stupid, Little voice, and it made my hands curl into fists before I could stop them, because for one thing she wasn't THAT much bigger than me, and for another thing, what belonged in this ruin-cave was Finder of Before-Treasure Aneko FOUR and her Before-treasure find and not Nina THREE Finder of Nothing.

"Relax," she was saying. "Telling that slag-brain is the last thing we're going to do."

"Then what—"

"We're going to find the rest of it."

That filled my whole head with questions. What was Nina talking about? What was I going to give the SUPERVISOR if I didn't give him this fossil? What if we had to come out and the storms blew ash over the ruin-cave and we couldn't find it again? What would the SUPERVISOR do to us if he heard Nina calling him a slag-brain?

And—wait. The rest of *what*?

"It's mine," I said again instead, because all those questions got stuck in my head and couldn't all squeeze out my mouth together. I wanted to take another step back but there wasn't any room.

"You don't even know what it is," Nina hissed at me.

"It's a fossil," I hissed back. "It's Before-people bones from the earth and it's MINE."

Nina gave me a sigh like You Really Are A Very Stupid Little Aren't You. Then she turned back to the tunnel out. I was scared she was going out there to tell on me, but she just shouted, "There's something here. I'm helping FOUR dig it out. Don't send anybody else in, the ceiling is shaking and I think it might come down."

I looked at the ceiling when she said that. Then I realized she was lying and wanted to kick myself for falling for it. Then I wanted to kick myself even harder for not thinking of the lie by myself before the SUPERVISOR sent Nina in after me.

But Nina didn't notice. She'd already gone over to the hole I'd made in the Waste and started digging.

"Back in my town my dad was songkeeper," Nina told me all in a rush while she dug. Her voice was clear and soft like Mama's used to get when I had to Shut Up And Listen Right Now, so I put away my mad mood and listened. "You know what that means? Songkeeper?"

Songkeeper means Person Who Tells The Important Stories. Every little knows that from walking. So I nodded.

"My dad had a relic like this," Nina said. "But not a head. An arm. Made out of this same shiny black Before-stuff. Help me dig."

Just like that, my mad mood was back. Like she was going to boss me into helping her do something I didn't even want HER to do in the first place. "I told you. It's mine."

"Ragpicker take you. Listen. This is important. The arm-thing? My dad said there was a whole person-shape of it," Nina said. "Not just the one arm but a whole body. But the arm was the only thing he had enough to trade for. He said somebody used to wear the whole person-shape thing, back in the wars. And whoever wore it, it would protect them."

"Before-magic," I told her.

"My dad says Before-magic is just a story for littles," Nina said, in that nasty know-everything voice I hated. What did I care what she or her stupid dad thought? They weren't from Sunrise. They were from some dumb town that probably didn't have any giants or anything. "That," she said, and she kind of nodded toward the head I'd found, "is a MACHINE. Well, a piece of one. And the rest…"

"The rest what?" I said, but I was looking at the hole in the ground while I said it, and I knew. All at once I could feel the pieces of an idea sliding together, I could feel it prickling in my brain behind my eyes.

I started digging.

It was a lot faster with both of us working. Nina was bigger and stronger than me, and she'd put her sickness and tiredness away someplace where I couldn't see it anymore. She hadn't brought a digging-stick, and the Waste was scratching deep lines up her arms, and her hands were bloody and gross and made me kind of sad and scared to look at them, but she didn't care about any of that. She wanted this Before-thing too much. The wanting moved her body for her while her mind ran off ahead. That happened to secret-keepers sometimes, Mama said. They could peel their minds away clean from the hurt in their bodies. It made Mama's job a lot harder sometimes, she'd have to work until I was asleep so there was nobody to tell me bedtime stories except the kingsguard, and they never did the voices right.

I helped along with my digging-stick, loosening the ash and junk so Nina could move it away with pieces of metal and her poor nasty messed-up hands. "A little farther," she kept saying, way down low on the bottom of her voice so I wasn't sure if she was talking to me or to herself or her hands or the Waste or something hidden underneath or what. "Almost there."

And then I poked in my digging-stick for what felt like the millionth time that day. And this time, instead of the soft *tshhh* sound of stick into ashy dirt, I heard a kind of *clunk*.

Nina looked at me, and her face was like learning your favorite story is true.

Together we pulled out a black shiny leg-shape of the stuff, then another. Then a broken-off arm, then a shape kind of like a jacket with one sleeve that was the other arm, except the jacket-shape had a big hole melted straight through the middle, in one side and out the other. That arm's fist was curled around something that dangled from it, a long dark weird shape that was jagged and smooth at the same time, with a long tube coming out of one end.

That thing fell out into Nina's hands. She sucked her breath in between her teeth and dropped the thing like it was about to bite her.

When it landed I got a good look at it. It was a Before-people weapon. It was the first one I'd seen that wasn't broken into pieces or melted into a lump of uselessness. From this one I could see the way you'd hold it, just like in the pictures of the wars Before, the way you'd put one part in one hand and one part in another, and if the strap wasn't so rotten it would go around your neck like a satchel.

"Ragpicker slag me," Nina was whispering, under her breath like a prayer. She kept running her hands over the shiny person-shape, like she was scared if she stopped it'd disappear.

Then came the SUPERVISOR's voice from outside. "You better not be trying anything stupid in there," he said. "I want to see that ruin-treasure and I want to see it NOW."

Hearing that voice made me feel like I wanted the Waste to open up and swallow me alive, but Nina got a lid slammed down on whatever was going through her head and just yelled back in this airy voice like nothing: "Just digging still." Then she whispered to me: "Quick. Help me put it on."

I gave her a dirty look.

"It won't fit you," she whispered.

That was true, and I knew it. I pointed at the jagged-smooth weapon shape. "Then I get that."

"You don't know how to use it."

"Neither do you."

Nina looked at it, then at me. There was hard wanting in her face, but fair was fair. She nodded.

"Out in one minute or I send another one in after you," the SUPERVISOR yelled back.

"Oh you don't want to do that," Nina shouted, shoving her foot into one of the shiny legs. There was a tiny shake in her voice but it didn't carry. She got the other leg on and stood up. She looked funny, that skinny body on those huge monster legs. I helped her balance. "Stuff falling out of the ceiling everywhere. Lose three kids instead of two, and all the ruin-treasure besides." She took a piece of metal and threw it clanging against that giant letter S. "Ah! Chooser save me. That one was CLOSE."

Silence from outside. For the first time ever I had this thought: what if the SUPERVISOR was scared of somebody too? Who yelled at him and hit him when we came back from the ruin-fields with no treasure?

I stared at Nina. She winked.

Then she pulled the jacket-shape on over her head. It went down over her waist and hips and butt and hung real loose on her, like how Jamie's old nettle-yarn sweater fits me. She got her arm through the one attached arm, then picked up the other one and held it out for me to hold. She dug around inside it like she was looking for something, and I remembered how she'd said her songkeeper dad had a Before-relic fossil arm just like this one. So I didn't say anything, just held it and waited, and after a second she pulled out a long thin tube with a much thinner pointy thing on the end of it like a sewing needle.

"Help me put this in my arm," she said, and pointed with one hard plasticky finger to the soft inside of her other elbow. "Here."

"Why?" I asked, and my voice was shaking like a scared-of-the-dark little, but I couldn't help it. There was a cold feeling in my belly suddenly, like the Before-magic was a bucket of ice water I'd swallowed.

"Because it's in the old stories," she said, "and now it's here." Her voice was shaking too, but not like she was scared, more like something amazing was about to happen, like a party just for her. "It'll help us if we let it."

"How do you know that?" I asked, hating how small and scared my voice sounded.

She looked at me strangely. "I don't."

I thought about Mama and Jamie and the Sunrise giants and Sam with the flies in her eyes, and I knew what I had to do. "Okay, Nina," I told her, and I slid the needle in, and she watched me do it and didn't look away, and I think it's the bravest thing I ever saw.

After that I helped her kind of push-pull the arm on like a cold, hard, too-big glove. Last, she pulled the fossil-head down over her head and I couldn't see her face anymore.

For a ten-count nothing happened. Then the shiny black Before-stuff started *humming*. Then, slowly, *slowly*, the arms and legs and head started locking themselves onto the jacket-body with these gentle little whispering sounds.

"Nina?" I asked, because I couldn't trust my eyes to tell me what I was looking at.

"It's not me," her voice came from inside the fossil-head, shaking with more scared than mad now. "I'm not doing it, Aneko, it isn't me."

Then suddenly her voice changed, went up all high and squeaky with surprise: "There's words on it, there are like words and shapes on the window where I look, I think it's trying to talk to me," and I had no idea what she was talking about and didn't ask, I was too busy staring at the sudden shiny dark shape that used to be Nina, before she got swallowed up by the Before-magic weirdness.

I picked up the Before-relic weapon. It was cold and slick in my hands like a snake. There was a place on it that looked like the shape of a hand, and I had to stretch my fingers hurting wide to fit. The hand-shape started glowing bright bright blue, the same color as the very bottom of a candle-flame, or the stars on a cold night, or the very first scorchweed flowers in springtime.

I had to push away so many questions. What would happen to us when we got out there? Would Nina even fit out of the ruin-cave with that stuff on? How long would it keep working? Could I find Mama out there? Was she even still alive to find?

"Time's up," the SUPERVISOR yelled. "Get out or I burn you out."

Nina turned her shiny black fossil-head to me. Through the little hole in the little window it was hard to see her face. She looked like a Before-people ghost come alive, like a Sunrise giant and all its old old magic shrunk down to person-size.

She nodded once to me. I nodded back.

"Coming," she called.

A SERIES OF IMAGES FROM A RUINED CITY AT THE END OF THE WORLD

VIOLET ALLEN

Violet Allen is a writer based in Chicago, Illinois. Her short stories have appeared in *Lightspeed*, *Liminal Stories*, *Best American Science Fiction and Fantasy*, *Resist: Tales from a Future Worth Fighting Against*, *A People's Future of the United States*, and elsewhere.

This wasn't so long ago, but the memory is beginning to decay into narrative. Already, I find myself inclined to manufacture details in the retelling, and I fear that soon the real events will be consumed by a story that I hold too close to my heart.

Look at this photograph. Here is Flynn, sitting in the lower basin of a ruined fountain, smiling beneath a tangle of neon flora spilling out from the upper basin, rendering him an orange-green-violet silhouette in the half-dark. I look at this image, and I can no longer tell you what day it was, or what part of the city we were exploring when I took it. I can tell you that I joined him in the fountain after I took the photograph, and that we climbed up and plucked the glowing blossoms off the vines and let them float away in the wind and laughed and fell asleep next to one another.

This kind of sentimentality is the root of all lies.

Still, I want to tell you about my meeting with Flynn, in the ruins of the city where I was born. The narrative will encompass seven days and six nights. I will be as honest as I can, and I will try not to let sentimentalism creep in.

I first saw Flynn shortly after I crossed into the Quarantine Zone. He was walking alone on the side of the road. I stopped and asked him if I could take his picture. I had received special dispensation to survey and photograph the ruins by the leadership of my camp.

At this time, "Quarantine" was more theory than practice. Scavengers entered and exited the affected areas more or less as they pleased, and there were rumors that people were once again living in some of the smaller eastern cities. This was before we had given up on reclaiming the old cities, when we had hope of unraveling this strange, new world instead of rebuilding in the spaces between. But my motivations were not so lofty. I simply missed the city I had grown up in, and I thought it might be nice to go there one more time and to have some pictures so that I would not forget more than I already had.

Flynn was tall and thick, and he wore a coat made out of golden fur with a hood shaped like the head of a spider. I had never seen the creature the coat had presumably been crafted from, so I was curious. I thought his image would make a good addition to my collection, a bit of rustic neo-Americana. Flynn told me I could take his picture, but asked that I take him in my transport to a certain neighborhood in the northwest. I quickly agreed. My mission, such that it was, had no particular parameters, and I had planned to mostly wander the city aimlessly with the only real goal of viewing the area where my childhood home had been.

As he stepped inside my transport, I removed my gun from its holster and held it up for him to see.

"I fought in the war," I said. "Don't fuck with me."

This was technically true, but only just. I had only once been on a battlefield, and I had never pulled the trigger on a weapon. Still, it was important to establish that I was not a soft target. People were mostly civilized again at this point, but we still remembered plainly how easy it was for people to become animals.

He shrugged and softly laughed. "Sure. Me too."

And so we went. Our conversation was slow at first. Back then, people mostly wanted to talk about the old world. The invasion, the war, the changes, these were not polite topics, at least not with strangers, and we had not yet made very many memories of the new world. We talked about where we were from, how we used to live, and even though the details were different, it was always the same story. Things had been as they were, good or bad, and then everything changed in an instant.

But then, he told me about the Shit Lake.

"I used to come here for the summers to stay with my grandma, right? And there was this little lake in the park by her house. The water was brown, and it smelled like shit, hence the name. I don't know if it was sewage or rotten vegetation or just algae. It was awful, whatever it was. The neighborhood kids had this whole mythology around it. They said that if you swam to the bottom and waited for a whole five minutes, you would get special powers. Like a superhero. You remember how it was in early 90s, right? All the superheroes powered by slime and filth. Remember the Turtles? The Toxic Avenger? Swamp Thing? It was like that. I was kind of a dork, right? I used to dream about diving in and becoming someone strong and brave, someone who would always do the right thing, even if I smelled like shit. One time, I said I was going to do it in front of all the other kids, but all I could do was stick my foot in and then I ran away. They never let me forget it."

It was sort of a standard kids are dumb assholes story, but I was taken with it. The appeal was obvious to me now; of course I wanted something beautiful to emerge from the ugliness. But at the time, it just seemed like a nice little story, a bit of color in an otherwise drab conversation.

"Did they call you Shit-foot?" I asked. "That's a great superhero name."

"No."

"I would've called you Shit-foot. It gets the point across rather elegantly."

"Were you a mean kid?"

"Yeah, but I didn't mean to be. I just liked to have too much fun, and sometimes people got hurt."

"Sounds like you were a bully."

"Not really. I was sort of in the middle. Kids with a little more social capital were shitty to me, and then I was shitty to the kids with a little less social capital. It was a circle. The bullies were the ones who were shitty to kids way below them on the ladder."

"That's a very nice way of absolving yourself. Just an innocent cog in a cruel machine."

"I admit that I was kind of an asshole. I'm just saying, I wasn't a motherfucker."

"Being a hero is about standing up, not just doing what you're supposed to."

"Yeah. That's why superheroes aren't real."

We spent that night in the transport, hidden in a thicket of witchtooth just outside the city proper. We left it behind the next morning. The roads were too overgrown to navigate in any vehicle and the sound of an engine could draw unwanted attention. Against my better judgment, I gave Flynn my rifle while I kept my pistol at the ready. I trusted him enough that I didn't think he would try to hurt me, but not enough that I was sure he wouldn't do something stupid.

Look at this one. The skyline. I took it when the sun came up that morning, just as we were walking into the city. Even now, it's strange to look at, like I superimposed multiple photos into a single image. There are the remains of the old skyscrapers, still standing (but barely), and there are the structures the invaders had been building, half-finished, both new and old at the same time, and there is the alien flora and fauna commingled with our own, strange vegetation and humongous insectoids and lifeforms that I cannot class in any of the familiar kingdoms. The juxtaposition was surreal. It was like the old world and the war and the present were places you could go instead of stretches of time.

We moved slowly, safely, staying in cover, avoiding open spaces. The city was open, but it was not *safe* exactly. I had spent some time in the Quarantine Zone, but never in the city. I was more scared than I had expected, more scared than I could admit to myself. We had weapons, food and water, oxygen tanks, and all the sundry items one might need to survive in the wilderness, but I felt naked. I was glad Flynn was there with me. He was loud and didn't seem to care about anything. I kept telling him to be quiet, but it made me feel better that he wouldn't shut up. We were past small talk about our histories, and he had taken to regaling me with tales of his adventures, particularly at night, before we went to sleep. He was a wanderer, self-described, and he had seen all the horrors and wonders the new world had to offer.

"There was this nest of giant spiders. Big gold boys with nasty teeth. Maybe the scariest thing I've ever seen. But there was this kid there, right smack in the middle of 'em. I couldn't just leave her. I only had a couple bullets left, though, and those spiders would've ripped me apart before I could get a scream out."

"What'd you do?" I asked. It was definitely bullshit, but it was entertaining bullshit. The reason I have to be on guard against sentimental stories is that I am easily intoxicated by them.

"Well I shot one, and then I ran like hell. They chased me, but I just kept on running. I ran and I ran and I ran. Then finally, we came to this river. One of them half-terraformed ones, where it goes up like a waterfall and comes down again? I see that and I come up with a plan. So I head out to where the water shoots up, and I wait for them. There's five of them now. They're getting closer and closer, but I just stand there wading, fighting the current. They're so close now I can smell them, and they look mad. Not mad like an animal, mad like a person, just angry, and right when one of them's gonna stick his stinger in my chest, I jump back and let the water suck me up. They get sucked up, too. And then, when we're coming down, we're all lined up real pretty because of the gravity or however those things work, and I line it up, and I take one shot and boom, all five dead. I run back to the nest, and the little kid's fine. I took the shell of the one I killed at the beginning, and I stripped the hair and made this coat."

"Amazing," I said.

"I just got lucky," he said.

And so it went. I'm not sure if I can tell this part of the story honestly. This is when I took that picture from before, the one of Flynn and the fountain. A couple days went by without any incident and we were relaxed, almost comfortable. Stopped looking out for monsters. Started sleeping under the stars instead of in tents. This is when I got most of my pictures. The architecture and the plants and all that. You've seen them. Those are all in the book. But here are some more of Flynn.

Here we are in the museum, Flynn wanted to take some paintings, but I was worried they were contaminated. And here's one of the invaders' tower.

This is me. I never used to smile in pictures, but Flynn got one out of me. Still can't believe I let him touch my camera. I never let anyone else touch my camera, not ever. And look at this one. She's beautiful, isn't she? Part bird, part I-don't-know-what. At least six feet tall. The scales were like polished fire. She was just walking in the middle of the street. I wanted to shoot her just to be safe, but Flynn said I shouldn't. He said he knew from experience that she wouldn't hurt us, that she was just looking for her flock, but I could see in his eyes he was lying. Still, God help me, I trusted him.

I'd loved people before him, and I've loved people since, but I never liked anyone like I liked him. We just sort of fit together. There was something magical about being with him in that place, like we were exploring a dream, just the two of us and no one else left in the world. It was stupid, but my life had been nothing but serious for decades. It was nice to indulge a little.

One night, we made a campfire in the middle of a park like a couple of fools. Flynn had a bottle of whiskey he said he had gotten as a reward for singlehandedly saving a small encampment from the tanglefires, and I had meat rations and bread to spare, so we had a little bit of a feast. After we were completely full and a little drunk, he asked me why I came to the city.

"The *real* reason," he said. "It's been killing me. I don't believe it's just for pictures."

The truth slipped out before I managed to compose the lie. "I wanted to see if I could survive out here."

"Why?" he asked.

"In case I need to leave my camp. Or if I want to."

"You want to leave?"

"I might."

"Why?"

"I don't know. I've got a position back at the camp. Responsibilities. People count on me. Back in the war, I was at the very bottom. It didn't matter what I did. I just followed orders. As long as I didn't do anything stupid, nothing was ever my fault, good or bad. Now, if I fuck up, people get hurt, maybe they die, and it's all on me."

"So you want to just leave? And do what?"

"Be a wanderer. Like you. See the country. Have adventures. Make stories."

He laughed and took a big swig of whiskey before passing the bottle to me. "You don't want to be like me."

"Why not?"

"It's no kind of life. Some of my stories may be... slightly exaggerated."

I laughed. "Oh really?"

"It's no kind of life," he repeated, softly.

"Maybe. I just think sometimes, things get so broken that fixing them is more trouble than it's worth."

I finished off the bottle and blew over the top so it made that low, eerie whistle, and I kept doing until the fire went out. And in the dark, I crawled up next to Flynn and gave him a kiss. He kissed me back. He tasted like shit, but it was nice anyhow. I started to pull off my shirt, but he grabbed my hand.

"No," he said.

"What is it," I said.

"It's not you. I just... I'm married."

"You're married?"

"I got a family."

"Where are they?"

"I don't know. Back east, I imagine."

"You imagine?"

"I left them a few years ago. Just up and walked out."

"Oh."

"I didn't mean to. It was just too much. It's like you were saying. I never had much taste for taking care of people. Not something I was made for. But I'm gonna fix it. That's why I came out here. I'm going to the Shit Lake. I'm gonna go in, and someone stronger is gonna come out. I'm gonna go back to them and take care of them like I should."

"That's fucking stupid," I said. I rolled away from him, and I went to sleep without saying anything else.

He was gone the next morning. There's a certain kind of man who only likes you when you see him a certain kind of way. When you get a glimpse of the real person, he runs. Some people can only live inside stories.

It was a relief to me, honestly. I was pretty mad about the whole situation, and I didn't want to sort out whether I was mad at him or myself.

I decided that I wanted to get some pictures of my childhood home, or whatever was in its place, and then I would make my way out of the city.

Flynn left behind my rifle, thank God, and I felt like myself again, which was both good and bad. I took it slow and careful, like a soldier on a mission, not a kid on vacation. There was a very large, horned ant on the way, and I didn't stop to take a picture—I just put it down without thinking.

No unnecessary risks.

Here. This is my house. Those mushrooms were everywhere, inside and out. The film doesn't capture the color very well. They were bright orange, like neon or something, and they were covered in slime that smelled like bleach. The house was flooded inside, and the walls were crumbling.

This is my childhood bedroom. Huh. It's not like I remember. The picture, I mean. I remember more mushrooms. It was violent almost. Like the mushrooms had forced their way in, like they had destroyed everything they touched. But in this, it looks like the mushrooms are all that's holding the place together, like they were preserving it for me. Weird.

Anyway, I got a little emotional while I was there, and for the first time in a long time, I really remembered what it used to be like, before they came and tried to make this into their world. Not the story we told, but the real thing. All these little memories came flooding back all at once, so sharp and clear that it made the last couple decades of my life seem like a dream. It was the first time I felt like I was home in ages, and I almost couldn't make myself leave. The air in that place was no good, and I didn't have enough oxygen to stay for more than a couple hours.

Home. I had forgotten what home was. I think most of us had. I had remembered how much it hurt when it was taken away, but only now did I remember how great it was when I had it. In a way, that made it worse.

I decided I would go visit Shit Lake before I made my way out of the city. It wasn't too far from my parents' house. I never went to that park as a kid, but I knew where it was. I figured it would be nice to have a picture, and maybe it wouldn't be the worst thing if I happened to catch Flynn. I still hadn't decided whether I was mad at him or not, and I felt that another meeting would really help to clear things up.

So here's the last picture I took of Flynn. He was just outside the park, lying in a gutter, bleeding from a big hole in his belly. He was already dead. Does he look like he's sleeping? I wanted it to look like he was sleeping. I don't know what got him. The city is dangerous, and he didn't have a weapon.

"Superheroes aren't real," I whispered.

Did I cry? Maybe. The park had grown into a small forest, and the canopy was so thick it was almost too dark to see, even though the sun had barely set. Too dark to get a good picture.

I couldn't lift Flynn's body, but I could drag him, just barely. It was exhausting, and at times I thought it would be impossible, but I did it.

The lake was right there, in the middle of everything. And this will seem like the most sentimental of details, but sometimes real life is unlike itself: a bird with scales like polished fire was there, drinking. It couldn't have been the same one I'd seen earlier, but I could not see a difference.

It reared back, spread its wings, then leapt at us. My gun was in my pack. I ought to have just run, but I didn't. I wrestled with the damn thing, right over Flynn's body. I had a mission. I had to complete it.

It pecked me, and I bled. All I could really do was swat at it and pull its feathers. I screamed, hoping to scare it. It just screeched back at me. I kept at it, louder and louder, and I wasn't just screaming at it, I was screaming at everything. I don't know if that was what did it, or if it just got tired of the whole thing, but it stepped back, slowly, and made its way back into the bush. I took just a moment for myself before grabbing Flynn again and pushing on.

The surface of the lake was covered in flowers, but it still stank like death. I took off my clothes, and I waded in, dragging Flynn with me. He floated at first, and it was a struggle to hold him down long enough for the air to escape his lungs. Up and down, up and down in the dirty water. I nearly drowned, I think.

But he sank soon enough, and I went down with him. The lake wasn't very deep. I stayed down there as long as I could, until my lungs burned and I felt like I was going to die.

Here's a picture of me after I came up, covered in mud and rotten leaves and God knows what. Sorry if it's a little faded. I keep it on me all the time.

I went back to the camp after, back home, and things were what they were.

It's important to remember these things, I think. That's the magic of the image. The memories will lie, but I will always know that I am this person, someone strong and brave, and I will always possess the image, no matter how much things change.

COME ON DOWN

MEG ELISON

Meg Elison is a science fiction author and feminist essayist. Her debut novel, *The Book of the Unnamed Midwife*, won the 2014 Philip K. Dick award. Her second novel was a finalist for the Philip K. Dick, and both were longlisted for the James A. Tiptree award. She has been published in *McSweeney's*, *Lightspeed*, *The Magazine of Fantasy & Science Fiction*, *Catapult*, and many other places. Elison is a high school dropout and a graduate of UC Berkeley. Find her online, where she writes like she's running out of time.

Turn the squeaky wheel of the old bingo cage and the crowd goes wild. Inside, tumbling around are pieces of garbage plastic: cups and spoons and faded balls from the play pit. All with names written or scratched on them. I open the cage door and reach in to pull the first contestant.

"Angie Becker, come on down!" She's an old woman but she races at me anyway. She's pumping her hands over her head and they quake something fierce, but her face is all smile lines.

I pull another piece of trash, this one a tin can with the name scratched into one end. "Tomtom, come on down!" Tomtom comes every day, but they didn't expect to be picked and they're not ready. They offload their weapons to some woman I've never seen before and then jog over, whooping like a hunter.

"Aaaaaand Luis Robles, come on down!" I pull something small for the last one. A spork. I've heard grumbling after the show that I never pull anything small. I pinch it between my fingers and pluck it triumphantly, holding it up like a bit of good luck. The ghost-taste of KFC rises in my unforgetting mouth and I banish it away.

Luis has seen better days. He's got one hand in a crusty bandage. Red streaks are racing up his arm to see which gets to kill him first. But he's steady on his feet, with eyes like wet steel.

"All right, who's ready to play?" I have to pass the mic around. There's no crew to wire us now, and no sound anyway. I remember watching Mack do the same thing on the old show. The smaller set, the one big mic. I'm glad I took one with me when we left L.A. It reminds them where to look. I bet it seemed stupid at the time, but I knew what I was doing. I don't know how to use any other tool.

The crowd knows their job, too. Some of them do this every time we have a show. They break away from their group or make a trade and spend their noon to sundown here, hoping for a shot at showing their hollow belly when they reach up to spin the big wheel. The crowd's job is to sing the music. It's been the same jolly circus tune since the '70s and they all know it. It's ragtag and the tempo is all over the place, but they do it. And it all comes back to me.

The banter and the silliness. Sometimes they still jump up and down when they win.

The basic rules haven't changed. The prices are still pegged to the local conditions, and the crowd still screams out their suggestions of what things should cost.

My showgirl Jessica opens the first case gesturing smoothly and grandly at three undented cans of boiled baby potatoes.

Angie's jaw quivers and she crosses her shaking arms against her chest. "One pigeon and two dried apples."

Tomtom is already shaking their head. "Pigeon. That's all."

Luis licks his lips and looks to the crowd. He came alone, but he's everybody's friend, now.

"PIGEON APPLE SHIRT METAL," they holler in cacophony, one voice on top of the next. I don't know how he gets anything from that, but he does.

"One dried apple and a shirt," he says decisively.

Jessica pulls up the picture board and there it is: one apple (which really means any fruit) and a shirt drawn on it. Luis is dead-on. I move to clap him on the back, but I can feel the heat baking off him and I think better of it.

This carnival had a plinko game when we found it. That was how I knew we should start it all up again. I took one look at this thing, the rat shit piled up in the bottom, and I felt everything roll into place like a jackpot. People were getting sick, and there were no doctors. People were antsy, fighting over salvage. I don't have any other skills, and the girls worked their whole lives at being pretty. Together, we talked about our odds of survival. Asked if we were any good to our fellow man, if we could save anyone. Even ourselves. If we should run. That stupid plinko game was the answer. We could give the people something to root for as the world goes dark. We could keep from getting killed for meat, probably. Most of these folks still recognized me from TV. I could use that to keep some order. I could make sure the show would go on.

The old carnival was a dump, but the girls helped me get it into shape. Drag the bleachers away from the dead animals and rip the chain out of the ferris wheel so we can spin it by hand. Everything needed work. I wanted torches but we never got any. We just start at midday to beat the dark.

The plinko still works. The rats moved on to richer gnawing and we replaced the chits with a stack of coasters Jessica found in a bar and grill. We have to keep a close eye on those. Everyone takes a shine to them.

Angie's coaster gets caught twice. According to the rules, she's allowed to pound the plinko with one fist. She does it both times, but takes one of the smallest prizes. She gets a bag of plantain chips. She pockets them at once and looks up at the rearing height of the wheel. Tomtom drops their coaster and takes a fat crow, shot this morning as it ate from our scraps. That's Flo—she's got the good eye. Not bad for a model who could barely make toast before we left L.A. There's two more crows hanging up in our place to eat tonight when it's just the three of us and the fire. Luis takes the middle prize: a little salted fish. He pockets it with the same look that Angie had; careful, but still hoping to win big.

The wheel looms. We walk up to it and crane our necks back to look up. One day it'll surely come down. By then I hope we are long gone from this cracked asphalt. Luis spins first. The wheel is too big to be spun by one person. People would have freaked out in the old days, but I solved it easy. Jessica and Flo go around to the other side and assist. If it's a kid or an old person, they help a lot. A little if it's an adult in good shape.

I peer through the rusty buckets that people used to ride in and see they already know. Luis will need a lot of help.

The wheel is the only place where we kept numbers. We couldn't agree on adding up food and clothes to any kind of standard, so we just painted on the same wheel from memory. The colors are off, but it looks pretty good.

The girls help Luis with a big shove and the wheel is turning slowly against its own rust, coming down from the flat gray sky, creaking as it comes to rest against the pointer we made out of an old wedge of sponge to land on 85.

"Come on down" used to be something only the host would say, but things change. The audience chants it now as the big wheel rolls forward and down, forward and down. *Come on down. Come on down.* You'd think these people would have had enough uncertainty in their lives, but they yell for more. They're bundled from the cold. Red in the cheeks. Begging for the next thing that comes down to be good news. If not for them, for somebody. Sometimes just seeing it is enough.

Angie can barely reach up and I see her elbows are crabbed with arthritis. The girls are ready and the wheel comes down down down to rest at 55. Angie risks a second spin and wipes out, landing on 75 this time. She goes back into the crowd, lip quivering in time with the rest of her. My chest aches to watch her go. We used to give folks like that a consolation prize but I've got almost nothing to console with anymore. I can maybe slip her one of those cans of potatoes when it starts to get dark.

Tomtom reaches up mightily, showing off hard muscles in a brown belly. They pull the wheel hard and the creak goes high, shrieky, the wheel moving almost as fast as it did when it ran. The showgirls stand back. The crowd claps and claps and then explodes when Tomtom pulls a perfect 100, painted in that funny glowing green.

The wheel is far away from the stands, so we walk back over

toward the bleachers for the showcase round.

The hush is on now. This is what they really came for. Jessica saunters up with the case slung around her neck. She holds one hand hidden behind it, and they know that's where the gun is. They act better when they don't see it and we don't mention it. But it has to be there.

Flo pulls around the corner in the car and they absolutely lose their shit. We haven't put a running car in the showcase for months now. We're all going to have to convoy South, and nobody wants to be left on foot. The night never ends here and the wind is getting colder. There are only a handful of running cars, and only one or two people who can work on them. It's a long way to the equator, where things are supposed to be better. Please, sponsors, deliver the showcase of a better place. I've told them it's better, and they believe me. They have to. I bring them luck.

But Jessica opens her case and there's dead silence as people whip back the other way to see a full and pristine med kit. Luis licks his dry lips with a dry tongue.

It's time.

I wheel the mic in front of Tomtom, who gets to choose whether they'll go first on the kit or pass on that and try for the car. It's a sorry thing, without any remaining windows and four bald tires threatening to birth their belts at any moment. Tomtom thinks for a long minute while the crowd frets. So do I.

I knew before anybody knew, because I could see it in the prizes. No more flights to Italy or Thailand, then no more flights to anywhere. Train trips to New Orleans pitched with great romance as we pretended nothing was wrong.

Then I saw it in the audience. Two or three folks in uniform in the stands, then twenty. Then everyone.

Then none.

At the end, we hit record numbers of people lined up outside. Prizes were all forms of escape. Boats stayed in the running long after cars dropped out. For a while, they were the most popular item. Boats gave people ideas. Freedom still seemed possible, if only you could navigate those concrete rivers to the sea.

They talked to the newsroom people, and I thought they'd take us off the air or just leave us alone, but they didn't. They told us the job was more important than ever. Us daytime shows made sure people felt normal. More and more of them were staying home from work, and they couldn't get streaming after we lost the net and the phones went down. All they had was TV. Local affiliates were still carrying the good stuff—us and the soaps—and we held out.

Until the very end.

Tomtom picks the car and Flo honks the horn. Car sounds like it has the flu, but the crowd loves it anyway. I can see some folks at the edges consider their odds of taking it from her. Jessica stands up straight, eyes like a predator. The kit bumps against the muzzle of the gun. Nobody makes a break for it.

Tomtom faces the car with their hips pushed out, one hand stroking a stubbly chin. "A live cow. No, ten bullets and a live cow."

Tomtom takes the car.

Luis' eyes are too bright. He's staring and staring at the case. That look isn't new. I used to see it all the time. People who didn't just *want* to win—they *had* to. It's why you get famous in this job. Me and Mack and Pat and Alex and Monty. Because we could make something more than dreams come true. We could make life go on. That's what they came to see today, and every day since this sorry business began. And now, a word from our sponsors.

Luis opens his mouth for the first time and his voice is a dry, hot croak. "A gun. A fully loaded gun. Ay, chingado." He touches his head.

Nobody sees me wink except Jessica. She pulls the right card, deft as a magician. Luis wins. Tomtom wins.

I can't watch people lose anymore. I tell them their luck will improve. I tell them we all have something to look forward to, that we're headed toward hope. I don't have to say anything about how things are; they know. I ask them to help the dog population. To meet up after the show and try to breed them. We all need a little more love in our lives.

The things we do to gather these prizes. These showgirls are braver than anyone will ever know. Days are getting harder to count as the sun gets lazier and dimmer. But I tell people we'll be here, same time next week. We'll spin this wheel every week, until the world makes us move on.

DON'T PACK HOPE

EMMA OSBORNE

Emma Osborne is a queer fiction writer and poet from Melbourne, Australia. Emma is a graduate of the 2016 Clarion West Writers Workshop, and their writing has appeared in *Nightmare Magazine*, *GlitterShip*, *Shock Totem*, *Apex Magazine*, *Lightspeed Magazine* (Queers Destroy Science Fiction special issue), *Pseudopod*, *The Review of Australian Fiction* and *The Year's Best Australian Fantasy and Horror*. Learn more at emmakosborne.com and @redscribe.

The horde is attracted to bright colours, so when you put together your bug-out bag, you pack the drab outfits you'd sworn never to wear again once you'd finally, breathlessly, emerged as your true, radiant self.

You pack a heavy hunting knife, because what you carry looks valuable. You're glad that your arms are gym-strong and intimidating, because the idea of hurting someone, even in self-defense, makes you want to vomit.

You leave behind your old name. You try not to wonder if you're the only one left who remembers it. You don't know how you'd feel if that were true.

You take two photos of yourself, one of a gap-toothed girl on her first day of school, her shoes pink like the inside of a scalp, and a photo of a strong young man shirtless in the sun.

Same eyes, same mouth.

Heavier shoulders, denser bones.

More scars, some of them deep.

You pack a map, but you already know all the good hiding places: the disused stairwells in the school that hid you for years, the storm drain near your apartment that you saw in a documentary about the Cave Clan, the hollow of the swooping gum tree that stands bold and tall in the front yard of your best friend's house.

You know where to go where nobody will hear you, not Jason Miller from the cricket team, with his sharp laugh and rough knuckles, and not the horde with their clacking teeth and hungry hands.

You leave behind fear. Can't afford the weight. You've had enough of it to last a lifetime, anyway, and you're only twenty-seven. You've been frightened, though, of leaving your apartment, of being a body in a world where bodies are consumed. The horde thump on your walls sometimes, and you imagine them finding weak points, streaming in. They're as smart as ravens, maybe pigs. You know you'll feel nothing after a bad bite, but you're scared of another transformation, this one unwilling.

There are four sets of car keys in the front pocket of your bag. They belonged to exes and old lovers, and in one case, your best friend, Kristy. Odds are, they're all dead, but you hope that at least one of their cars is still there, free of fleshy detritus and containing enough petrol to make it out.

You hope that Kristy's car is long gone.

Maybe you'll find a car that runs, and you'll be able to drive for a while. Maybe you'll get as far out as the sun-blasted fields on the outskirts of Melbourne, maybe as far as your parents' house in the country. Something tells you that they're still there, still managing and still safe, with their rainwater and their solar cells and their little white dog.

You've drummed the fantasy of their safety into your heart, because if they're safe, you don't have to go out and find them. You don't have to be the hero, the rescuer.

You haven't spoken to them since the phones went down, but even in the dark you know your way home the same way you somehow always know which way is north. It's an uncanny, gut-deep pull. You feel it in your bones, as if they were heavy with metal, magnetic.

It has always surprised you that your earth-moving, beer-drinking, football-cheering stepdad loves you completely and utterly for who you are. Your mother, too, but she's blood. She'll have a hundred and one natural remedies stashed away. Some of them might work for minor troubles, but you've seen with your own eyes that nothing will calm the horde when they smell sweat and blood in the air.

You pack your hormones, of course. You have a couple of pre-loaded syringes, but you can't remember how long the clinic said they'd last. When they're gone you'll have to figure something out. Hope that looters will overlook T when they break into abandoned chemists. Maybe you'll get lucky on the road.

You don't pack hope. You can't quite imagine getting free of all this. Not yet.

It smells like hot, broken death outside, and the horde never stops moving. They break like waves on park benches, on abandoned cars. They are soundless but for the tramp of their decaying feet. When you're half asleep they sound like an inland sea, their dry skin whispering like canvas, their loose arms slapping like ropes.

You have protein bars to spare from that online sale, but they won't last forever, and you need something green to balance them out. Still, they help. The chocolate kind still almost feels like a treat. Your fridge is full of spoiled vegetables. You opened it once to make sure there was nothing useful in there and nearly threw up at the smell. Still, there was half a bottle of vodka in the freezer. You did a couple of quick shots to settle your nerves and thought about the times you danced to the Spice Girls in Kristy's lounge room.

You still don't know where she is, but you looked as long as it was safe. Kristy grew up in the country, too. Maybe she made it out.

You can't take all of your other people with you, your global community. They're scattered, hopefully safe, hopefully not dead. Last you heard, the horde is confined to Australia, parts of Indonesia. Maybe quarantine caught the spread early enough, and everyone else is okay. You refuse to worry about anyone in particular, because you know that once you've started, you won't stop, and tears won't help.

You're used to checking in with them throughout the day, and now that they're gone, you feel truly alone. Your hand creeps spasmodically to your jeans pocket, muscle-memory yearning to flick open your phone screen, to navigate to a sanctuary. You carry your phone even though it's a useless brick of plastic and glass.

You add fishhooks to your pack, although you always hated stabbing fish behind the eye when you'd pulled them gasping out of the water. It was years ago now that you'd fished with your dad. Your real dad, the dead one. At least now he won't chase you around with a severed fish-head, laughing, thumb poked through the teeth. It'd always made you scream, but these days it would take much more than that.

Matches. They wouldn't let you into the Scouts, so you need them to get a fire started. Maybe your brother still has the flint and steel he always kept in his car for barbecues and hunting trips. Something tells you that he's with your parents. Your nieces and your sister-in-law have to be safe, they just fucking have to be, because if they're not okay, your brother won't be either.

He'd let something happen to them over his dead body.

That's what you're afraid of.

You don't pack your music. You hope that what's left on your dead phone is enough to keep you going if the power comes back on. Part of you wishes that you could play something to steady yourself, to amp you up for the dash outside to find a car, but you have to convince yourself in silence. It's hard.

It's useless to take your heavy laptop or the hard drives. You hide them all in the garden of your tiny flat, buried after wrapping them in garbage bags to keep the dirt and moisture out. Music has saved your life more times than you can count. You hope one day that you'll be back to dig up your lifelines, the songs that held you safe.

Cash. Just in case it still works. You don't have much left after your surgery, but thank God that happened before the horde came. It might help to bribe someone, to convince them to let you go. You might be able to trade it for something useful, if someone is that stupid.

A first aid kit. If you're seriously bitten and your blood mixes with theirs, it'll all be over, but you might need the supplies for minor scrapes, accidents. You know how to strap a broken arm, how to cool down a black eye. Useful survival skills for anyone, really.

You leave behind your compass. Someone else who doesn't have your sense of direction might find it, might need it. You hope that it keeps somebody safe.

You hope that there's somebody else out there to keep safe.

Someone had left a sleeping bag in your room after a music festival, so you strap that to your pack. Maybe you should take your yoga mat, to sleep on, but you figure that it's too flashy to carry safely (that'll teach you for picking out a lime-green mat), and it's so thin that you might as well just sleep on the dirt if you can snatch some rest. Your stepdad is the one with all of the decent camping gear, anyway, and by the time you see him, you probably won't need it.

The sun is setting, and that slows the horde down, not that you know why. You could bargain with yourself for another night here, maybe three, but the guilt at staying safe when your family might need you is pushing you out the door. With luck, you'll be home in a few days. You just need to take those first few steps.

You hear the thump and sway of the horde outside, and you make sure your knife is loose in its sheath. You know to drive it up under their chin, because the blade is long enough to reach the brain from there, and there's less of a chance it'll stick in bone.

Just a few more things, to give you luck, to keep you safe.

You sort through your nail polish and pick out your favourite. Bright red. You felt a little weird about wearing it after you came out. But you get to decide how you present, what makes you feel like you, and what you love.

Especially now.

The last thing you pack before you venture out into slow-moving danger is the tear-stained letter that you wrote to your grown-up self when you were thirteen, begging yourself to keep going, to make it, to survive. You always knew it would be hard, but you couldn't have guessed what you'd face. You nearly laugh then, because the horde is almost the least of it.

You tuck a couple of blank sheets of paper and a pen in with the letter, because when you're home, when you're safe with your family, you're going to write another letter right back to yourself.

You're going to say thank you, and tell the thirteen-year-old version of you that you love them, that you stayed brave, and that you made it.

POLLY WANNA CRACKER?

GREG VAN EEKHOUT

Greg van Eekhout is the author of several novels, including the California Bones trilogy and the middle-grade novels, *Voyage of the Dogs* and the upcoming *Cog*. His work has been shortlisted for the Nebula and Andre Norton awards, and reprinted in *Best American Science Fiction and Fantasy*. Visit writingandsnacks.com.

Every season there are fewer eggs.

Every season, fewer chicks hatch.

Every season, fewer hatchlings survive.

Our flock diminishes, but we remain, and we gather beneath the full night sun to recall our glory. Barefeather's old legs need two tries to leap to the top of the log in the center of the clearing. She shows more flesh than plumage, and I don't think she'll be here to lead us next season. We gaze at her in reverence, but I do not know if she sees us through her clouded eyes.

She shifts her weight, flutters her wings, and begins the chant.

"Hello," she says.

"Hello," we repeat as a chorus.

"Hello," she says again.

"Hello," we respond.

"Hello."

"Hello."

I listen for the rustle of small mammals in the brush, but there is nothing. My stomach rumbles. Even Barefeather strains for the sound of prey. We are all hungry.

Barefeather resumes.

"If you or a loved one has been diagnosed with mesothelioma you may be entitled to financial compensation," she calls.

"If you or a loved one has been diagnosed with mesothelioma you may be entitled to financial compensation," we answer.

"Honey, have you seen my keys?" she says.

"Honey, have you seen my keys?" we say.

"Who's a pretty bird?"

"Who's a pretty bird?"

"Let's go to the mall."

"Let's go to the mall."

She takes us through the ancient litany, the echoes of a time before we changed. Before we forgot our own calls, when we perched on the shoulders of gods. From the time when we could fly.

"Polly wanna cracker?" Barefeather says.

"Polly wanna cracker?" we conclude.

Last season, my nest mate, Green, left the flock. Nobody wanted him to go, but nobody stopped him, because he left to search for more of our kind. There is strength in numbers, and our flock has grown sparse as the feathers on Barefeather's back. The elders say the gods changed the world with their magnificent fires. One day the bounty of the forests will return, but we will be gone by then.

So Green said he wanted to go outside the tree line, across the river, and beyond our range. Even if he didn't find a new flock, perhaps he'd find prey, and with full bellies we might lay more eggs and hatch more healthy chicks.

When he didn't return by the end of the season, I feared he was dead. Months later, I was sure of it. So, when he stumbles into the clearing as the last echoes of our chant fade into the boughs, we squawk with delight and run to him.

Crusted blood streaks his head and chest. One eye is gummed closed. I shudder when I see the crack in his bill.

"Green, where have you been? What happened to you?"

Before he can answer, Barefeather nudges me away. "First we care for our brother. Then, we talk. Gather food for him."

We bring him seeds. He hunches with puffed feathers, weak and famished. Barefeather cracks open a nut and regurgitates for him, as if Green is a hatchling.

"My brother," I say, gently picking at the mites in his dusty feathers. "My nest mate. It is me, Dullclaw. It is me, your sister."

After a time, still trembling with weakness, Green speaks.

"I went outside the tree line," he says. "Across the river, beyond our range. I left the forest and ached in the desert. I floated on wood across a sea and climbed a mountain, where I froze beneath the stars. When I came down the other side of the mountain, I found a new forest."

We shuffle and scratch with questions.

Barefeather manages a sharp look, even with her ghost eyes. But I cannot help myself. I must know.

"Green, did you find prey?"

"Only a little," he croaks. "Insects. A dead mouse. Some strings of muscle."

My chest deflates with disappointment. Is the world everywhere as it is here? A garden, but not for us?

Even Barefeather sinks at this news. "We are the last flock, then. We are a flutter before the wind dies. We are alone."

"No," Green says. He lifts his head. His good eye grows keen. "We are the last flock, but we are not alone. I saw them." He shakes his wings and rakes his claws in the dirt. "I saw the gods."

And then he falls into an exhausted slumber.

I watch over him through the night, glancing in wonder at the tree line.

Green dies the next morning. He traveled too far, ate too little, suffered too many winds. Clucking and clicking with grief, I rake an embankment of dirt around him. The flock gathers leaves and twigs to cover him.

Insects and worms will return his flesh to earth, but I am thinking forbidden thoughts. We are so hungry. We are dying. Why don't we feast on the body Green no longer needs? There's no need to vocalize it. We are all thinking the same thing. But Barefeather straightens herself and stands tall. She spreads her wings, and in their span we find rebuke.

We do not eat our own.

It is not our way.

I cannot hold it in any longer. "Why? What is the purpose of this custom?" I regret speaking, but I cannot stop. I must go on. "Our ancestors did things with purpose. But we just mimic. We squawk litanies, not even knowing what they mean. And while we make noise and imitate, we perish."

The squawks of alarm sound far away, dimmed by the slam of my own heart. To challenge Barefeather is to challenge the flock, and to challenge the flock is to challenge everything. I fear the slap of wings. I fear being ripped by beak and talon. Green might not be the only one to die today.

But Barefeather lowers her wings. "Let Dullclaw be," she says. "Gather seeds. Gather nuts. Go."

The flock shuffles away, leaving me with my great-great-grandmother and the mound covering my dead brother.

I look at my feet and scratch.

"He is thin," she says. "His flesh shared among the flock wouldn't sustain us. He would nourish us for hours while depriving us of who we are."

I raise my eyes to her. She speaks not of tradition. She speaks of practicalities.

"Are we that near to the end, Barefeather?"

She draws closer and pecks bits of dirt from the back of my neck. "That depends on two things," she says very softly, so only I can hear. "It depends on you. And it depends on the gods."

This must be what it feels like to fly for the first time. To step off a sturdy perch with the ground far below. You know it can be done because you've seen it done, but you don't know if *you* can do it.

Under the dark sky, I take my first step.

Then the next.

And another.

Another.

I am falling. Tumbling helplessly toward the hard ground.

But, no.

This is merely walking. Leaving my flock. Going past the tree line. And I will continue across the river and beyond our range and I will leave the forest and ache in the desert. I will float across a sea and climb a mountain and survive in frigid, thin air. I will find a new forest. I will find new foods. I will save my flock.

I cannot fly, but I can do this.

I was wrong. I cannot do this.

Splintered talons.

Feathers, heavy as stone.

Not a fruit, not a nut, not a seed I can eat.

Stomach, clenching with pain.

Burning sun.

A floor of thorns.

Flesh scoured by wind and sand.

Insects that bite but elude capture.

Air burning my lungs.

Frost sealing my eyes.

Green did this. Everything I am suffering now, my nest brother suffered, and he endured. He did not die until returning to the flock.

So I take a step. And the next. And another. Ever forward.

I can do this.

When I finally come upon a new tree line, I am disappointed by how much this new forest is like the one I left behind. The trees are the same, and they bear the same meager fruits and tiny seeds. My flock can live no better here than at home. But I push into the shady coolness because I cannot go back with nothing but emptiness.

After another day, my hunger and fatigue are finally rewarded. It is not another flock, and not a new source of nourishment, but it is something I have never seen before.

Standing at the top of a ridge, I look down into a broad hollow where stands a massive sort of rock, pocked with deep gaps. It is like a mountain cavern, with the mountain eroded away and leaving caves behind.

There are markings on the side of the cave. They look old but reverently maintained, perhaps with berry juices to keep them whole.

I scratch the shapes into the dirt to remember them.

Entrance.

Parking.

Fox Hills Mall.

Flashes of movement, murmurs of noise leak from the caves, and I hide in the brush. Orange firelight flickers within. And voices. Much of it is unintelligible, but here and there, I recognize words from our flock's chants. Just fragments, just crumbs, but enough to convince me this is where the gods dwell.

Then they come out into the night with flaming sticks and gather in a circle. I have not seen creatures like this, except possibly in the dirt scratchings of Barefeather and the other elders. Two legs. Featherless wings. Nut-shaped heads, fringed with fur. All else is bare flesh.

Yes, these are the old gods. It is their words we repeat in our litanies. It is their world we dwelt in when food was plentiful and we could fly.

And now, finally, I understand why we recite the litany. It is for this moment, this time near the end, when we most need the gods, so that when we speak to them, they will know our words.

I make my way down the hill and approach them with hope and terror. My wings tingle, as if they're begging me to take flight and flee but are frustrated by being anchored to this heavy body. I feel like I could fall into a sleep, so great is my fear. Or maybe it's hunger.

My foot lands on a twig, and it cracks sharp and high, like thunder shredding the sky. The gods raise their fire sticks and shine light on me.

"Polly wanna cracker?" I say.

And the gods do something unexpected. Their eyes grow wide. They clutch each other. They shriek. Even in these strange beings I recognize fright. I do not understand how I can inspire fear in gods.

It is only when they creep closer to me, some holding sharpened sticks, that I see what I could not from a distance.

I was told since I was a hatchling that the gods were giants. That we once perched upon their shoulders. But I would crush them if I tried. They are half my size. The gods have withered and diminished.

Or...

We no longer fly. Perhaps we have changed in other ways as well. Perhaps we have grown.

The gods form a circle around me, and step by cautious step, they make the circle smaller.

Are they hunting me? These little things with their splintered wood?

"Who's a pretty bird?" I ask them.

They flinch and quiver, but the circle grows tighter.

And so I have no choice.

Wing slaps.

Sharp kicks.

Beak strikes, puncturing soft bellies, digging into their hot insides. The sweet flavors of intestines and livers and kidneys and hearts.

Yes, I do believe we have changed. I have changed in the span of a few seconds. I have tasted the flesh of shrunken gods.

The gods cry and run, and I pursue. The pounding of my feet against the earth mimics the magnificent pounding of my heart.

Sated by a full belly, I begin the journey back home. It is perilous, and difficult, and sometimes torturous. But I left the flock afraid and starving. I am no longer starving, and I know I can survive the return to my flock, so I am no longer afraid.

When I arrive home, the flock gathers around me. I repeat words from our litany. Ancient words invested with new meaning. Gibberish of the gods, but now an expression of our bountiful future, of satiated appetite, of strength and mastery. I have found a new forest, and the meat of the gods will be our fruit.

Barefeather tucks her head, giving me permission to lead the flock into the next tomorrow.

"Let's go to the mall," I say.

OTHERWISE

NISI SHAWL

Nisi Shawl is the author of the 2016 Nebula finalist novel *Everfair* and the 2008 Tiptree Award-winning collection *Filter House*. She is also the co-author of *Writing the Other: A Practical Approach*, a standard text on inclusive representation in the imaginative genres, and her short fiction has appeared in *Strange Horizons*, *Asimov's*, the groundbreaking *Dark Matter* anthology series, and *Best American Science Fiction and Fantasy*. She has taught and spoken at institutions ranging from University of Hawai'i Manoa to Smith College, as well as in Sweden, Wales, and the Netherlands. Shawl is also a Carl Brandon Society founder and a Clarion West board member. She lives in Seattle.

"Let's cross it while it's still floating." Aim was always in a hurry these days. Nearly eighteen, and she didn't figure she had a whole lot of time left before she'd go Otherwise.

"Hold up," I told her, and she listened. I listened, too, and I heard that weird noise again above the soft wind: an engine running. That was what cars sounded like; they used to fill the roads, back when I was only eleven. Some of the older models still worked—the ones built without chips.

A steady purr, like a big, fat cat—and there, I saw a glint moving far out on the bridge: sun on a hood or windshield. I raised my binoculars and confirmed it: a pickup truck, headed our way, east, coming towards us out of Seattle.

"What, Lo?" Aim asked.

If I could see them, maybe they could see us. "Come on. Bring the rolly; I'll help." We lifted our rolling suitcase together and I led us into the bushes crowding over the road's edge. Leaves and thorns slashed at our pant legs and sleeves and faces—I beat them away and found a kind of clear area in their middle. Maybe there used to be something, a concrete pad for trash cans or something there. Moss, black and dry from the summer, crunched as we walked over it. We lowered the suitcase, heavy with Aim's tools, and I was about to explain to her why we were hiding but by now that truck was loud and I could tell she heard it, too. All she said was, "What are they gonna think if they see our tracks disappear?"

I had a knife, and I kept it sharp. I pulled it out of the leather sheath I'd made. That was answer enough for Aim. She smiled—a nasty smile, but I loved it the way I loved everything about her: her smell; her long braids; her grimy, stubby nails.

I thought we'd lucked out when the truck barreled by fast—must have been going thirty miles an hour—but then it screeched to a stop. Two doors creaked open. Boot heels clopped on the asphalt. Getting louder. Pausing about even with where I'd ducked us off into the brush.

"Hey!" A dude. "You can come out—we ain't gonna do ya no harm."

Neither one of us moved a hair. Swearing, then thrashing noises, more swearing, louder as Truckdude crashed through the blackberries. He'll never find us, I thought, and I was right. It was his partner who snuck up on our other side, silent as a tick.

"Got 'em, Claude," he yelled, standing up from the weeds with a gun in his hand. He waved it at me and Aim and spoke in a normal tone. "You two can get up if you want. But do it slow."

He raised his voice again. "Chicas. One of 'em's kinda pretty but the other's fat," he told Claude. "You wanna arm wrestle?"

Claude stopped swearing but kept breaking branches and tearing his clothes as he whacked his way over to us. I stayed hunkered down so they'd underestimate me, and so my knife wouldn't fall out from where I had it clamped between my thighs. I felt Aim's arm tremble against mine as Claude emerged from the shadows. She'd be fine, though. Exactly like on a salvage run. I leaned against her a second to let her know that.

The dude with the gun looked a little older than us. Not much older, of course, or he'd have already gone Otherwise, found his own pocket universe, like nearly everyone else whose brain had reached "maturity"—at least that's how the rumors went.

Claude looked my age, or a year or two younger: fourteen, fifteen. He and his partner had the same brown hair and squinty eyes; brothers, then. Probably.

I leered up at Guntoter. "You wanna watch me and her do it first?"

He spat on my upturned face. "Freak! You keep quiet till I tell you talk." The spit tickled as it ran down my cheek.

I didn't hate him. Didn't have the time; I was too busy planning my next move.

"Hey, Dwight, what you think they got in here?" Claude had found our suitcase and given me a name for Guntoter.

"Open 'er up and find out, dickhead."

I couldn't turn around to see the rolly without looking away from Dwight, which didn't seem like a good idea. I heard its zipper and the clink of steel on steel: chisels, hammers, wrenches, clamps, banging against each other as they spilled out on the ground.

"Whoa! Looky at these, Claude. You think that ugly one knows how to use this stuff?" Dwight took his eyes off us and lowered the gun like I'd been waiting for him to do. I launched myself at his legs, a two-hundred-twenty-pound dodgeball. Heard a crack as his left knee bent backwards. Then a loud shot from his gun—but only one before I had my knife at his throat.

"Eennngh!" he whined. Knee must have hurt, but my blade poking against the underside of his chin kept his mouth shut.

I nodded at Aim and she relieved him of his gun. Claude had run off—I heard him thrashing through the bushes in the direction of the road. "Be right back, Lo." Aim was fine, as I'd predicted, thinking straight and acting cool. She stalked after her prey calm and careful, gun at the ready.

I rocked back on my haunches, easing off Dwight's ribs a bit. That leg had to be fractured. Problema; how was I supposed to deal with him, wounded like this? Maybe I shouldn't have hit him so hard. Not as if I could take him to a hospital. I felt him sucking in his breath, winding up for a scream, and sank my full weight on his chest again.

"Lo! You gotta come here!" Aim yelled from the road.

Come there? What? "Why? You can't handle—You didn't let him get his truck back, did—"

"Just come!" She sounded pissed.

Dwight wasn't going anywhere on his own any time soon, but just in case I tugged off his belt and boots and pants and took away the rest of his weapons: a razor poking through a piece of wood, a folding knife with half the blade of mine, and a long leather bag filled with something heavier than sand. I only hurt him a little stripping off the pants.

I got to my feet and looked down a second, wondering if I should shoot the man and get his misery over with. Even after years of leading salvage runs I didn't have it in me, though.

I loaded dude's junk and Aim's spilled-out tools in the rolly and dragged it along behind me into the bushes. When he saw I was leaving him he started hollering for help like it might come. That worried me. I hurried out to Aim. Had Claude somehow armed himself?

Claude was nowhere in sight. Aim stood by the truck—our truck, now. She had the door open, staring inside. The gun—our gun, now—hung loose in one hand and the other stretched inside. "Come on," she said, not to me. "It's okay." She hauled her hand back with a kid attached: white with brown hair, like his brothers. They must have been his brothers—I got closer and saw he had that same squintiness going on.

"Look," I said, "leave him here and climb in. If they got any back-up—" Boom! Shotguns make a hecka loud noise. Pellets and gravel went pinging off the road. Scared me so much I swung the rolly up into the truck bed by myself. Then I shoved Aim through the door and jumped in after her. Turned the ignition—they had left the key in it—and backed out of there fast as I could rev. Maybe forty feet along, I swung around and switched to second gear. I hit third by the time we made the bridge, jouncing over pits in the asphalt. Some sections were awful low—leaky pontoons. Next storm would sink the whole thing, Aim had said. I told myself if the thing held up on the dudes' ride over here it was gonna be fine for us heading back.

I looked to my right. Aim had pushed the kid ahead of her so he was huddled against the far door. I braked. "Okay, here you go." But he made no move to leave. "What's the matter, you think I'll shoot? Go on, we won't hurt you."

"He's shaking," Aim reported. "Bad. I think he's freaking out."

"Well that's great. Open the door for him yourself then, and let's go."

"No."

I sighed. Aim had this stubbornness no one would suspect unless they spent a long time with her. "Listen, Aim, it was genius to keep him till I drove out of shooting range, but—"

"We can't just dump him off alone."

"He's not alone; his brothers are right behind us!"

"One of 'em with a broken leg."

"Knee." But I took her point. "So, yeah, they're not gonna be much use for making this little guy feel all better again real soon. C'est la flippin vie." I reached past her to the door handle. She looked at me and I dropped my hand in my lap. "Aw, Aim…"

Aim missed her family. I knew all about how they'd gone on vacation to Disney World without her when she insisted she was too old for that stuff. Their flights back got canceled, first one, then the next, and the next, till no one pretended anymore there might be another, and the cells stopped working and the last bus into Pasco unloaded and they weren't on it.

"Hector—" She couldn't say more than his name.

"Aim, he's twelve now. He's fine. Even if your—" Even if her mom and dad had deserted him like so many other parents, leaving our world to live Otherwise, where they had anything, everything, whatever they wanted, same as when they drank the drug, but now for always. Or so the rumors said. Perfect homes. Perfect jobs. Perfect daughters. Perfect sons.

"All right. Kid, you wanna come with us or stay here with—um, Claude and Dwight?"

Nothing.

I tried again. "Kid, we gotta leave. We're meeting a friend in—" In the rearview I saw five dudes on foot racing up the road. One waved a long, thin black thing over his head. That shotgun? I slammed the truck out of neutral and tore off. They dwindled in the dust.

Aim punched my shoulder and grinned at me. "You done good," she said. I looked and she had one arm around the little kid, holding him steady, so I concentrated on finding a path for the truck that included mostly even pavement.

Here came the tunnel under Mercer Island. Scary, and not only because its lights were bound to be out—I turned the truck's on and they made bright spots on the ivy hanging over the tunnel's mouth. That took care of that. Better than if we'd been on foot, even.

But richies… more of them had stayed around than went Otherwise. Which made sense; they had their own drugs they used instead of Likewise, and everything already perfect anyways. Or everything used to be perfect for them till too many ordinary people left and they couldn't find no one to scrub their toilets or take out their garbage. Only us.

When things got bad and the governments broke down, richies were the law, all the law around. What they wanted they got, in this world as much as any Otherwise. And what they wanted was slaves. Servants, they called us, but slaves is what it really was; who'd want to spend whatever time they had before they went Otherwise on doing stupid jobs for somebody else? Nobody who wasn't forced to.

We drove through the ivy curtain. I jabbed on the high beams and slowed to watch for nets or other signs of ambush. Which of course there were gonna be none, because hadn't this very truck come through here less than half an hour ago? But.

"Can't be too careful." Aim always knew what I was thinking.

The headlights caught on a heap of something brown and gray spread over most of the road and I had two sets of choices: speed up, or slow down more; drive right over it, or swerve around. I picked A and A: stomped the gas pedal and held the steering wheel tight. Suddenly closer I saw legs, arms, bloated faces, smelled the stink of death. I felt the awful give beneath our tires. It was a roadblock of bodies—broken glass glittered where we would have gone if I'd tried to avoid them, and two fresh corpses splayed on the concrete, blood still wet and red. A trap, but a sprung one. Thanks, Claude. Thanks, Dwight.

The pile of rotting dead people fell behind us mercifully fast. I risked a glance at the kid. He stared straight forward like we were bringing him home from seeing a movie he had put on mental replay. Like there was nothing to see outside the truck and never had been and never would be.

"Maybe this was what freaked him out in the first place?" asked Aim. "You know, before he even got to us?" It was a theory.

We came out into the glorious light again. One more short tunnel as the road entered the city was how I remembered the route. I stopped the truck to think. When my fingers started aching I let go of the wheel.

A bird landed on a loose section of the other bridge that used to run parallel. Fall before last it had been the widest of its kind in the world, according to Aim.

She cared about those kinds of things.

The sun was fairly high yet. We'd left our camp in the mountains early this morning and come twelve mostly downhill miles before meeting up with the kid's brothers. The plan had been to cross the bridge inconspicuously, on foot, hole up in Seward Park with the Rattlers and wait for Rob to show. Well, we'd blown the inconspicuous part.

"Sure you don't wanna go back?" I asked Aim. "They'll be glad to see us. And the truck'll make it a short trip, and it's awesome salvage, too…" I trailed off.

"You can if you rather." But she knew the answer. I didn't have to say it. Aim was why I'd stayed in Pasco instead of claiming a place on the res, which even a mix had a right to do. Now I had come with her this far for love. And I'd go further. To the edge of the continent. All the way.

Rob had better be worth it, though. With his red hair and freckles and singing and guitar-playing Aim couldn't shut up about since we got his message. And that secret fire she said was burning inside him like a cigarette, back when they were at their arts camp. He better be worthy of *her*.

"Stop pouting." She puckered her face and crossed her eyes. "Your face will get stuck like that. Let me drive. Chevies are sweet." She handed me the gun, our only distance weapon—and I hadn't even gotten Dwight's cartridges, but too late to think of that—then slid so her warm hip pressed against mine for a moment. "Go on. Get out."

The kid didn't move when I opened the passenger door so I crawled in over him.

Aim drove like there was traffic: careful, using signals. Guess she learned it from watching her folks. The tunnel turned out clear except for a couple of crappy modern RVs no one had bothered torching yet. One still had curtains in its smashed windows, fluttering when we went by. We exited onto the main drag—Rainier Avenue, I recalled. Aim braked at the end of the ramp. "Which way?"

"South." I pointed left.

Rainier had seen some action. Weed-covered concrete rubble lined the road's edges, narrowing it to one lane. A half-burned restaurant sign advertised hotcakes. A sandbag bunker, evidently empty, guarded an intersection filled with a downed walkway. A shred of tattered camo clung to a wrecked lamppost. Must be relics of the early days; soldiers had been some of the first outside jail to head Otherwise, deserting in larger and larger numbers as real life got lousier and lousier.

"Wow. What a mess." Aim eased over a spill of bricks and stayed in low gear to rubberneck. "How're we gonna get off of this and find the park?"

"Uhhh." Would we have to dig ourselves a turnoff? No—"Here!" More sandbags, but some had tumbled down from their makeshift walls, and we only had to shove a few aside to reach a four-lane street straight to the lakeshore. We followed that around to where the first of the Rattlers' lookouts towered up like a giant birdhouse for ostriches with fifty-foot legs. A chica had already sighted us and trained her slingshot on the truck's windshield. Her companion called out and we identified ourselves enough that they let us through to the gate in their chain-link fence. Another building, this one more like the bunker on Rainier, blocked the way inside. Four Rattlers were stationed here, looking like paintball geeks gone to heaven. We satisfied them of our bona fides, too, using the sheet of crypto and half a rubber snake their runner had turned over with Rob's message. They took my knife. I didn't blame 'em. They let us keep our gun, but minus the bullets.

"What's in the back?"

I hadn't even looked after tossing up the rolly. Dumb. When the sentries opened the big metal drums, though, they found nothing but fuel in them, no one hiding till they could bust out and slit our throats.

Four of those, and the rest of the bed was filled with covered five-gallon tubs: white plastic, the high grade kind you use to ferment beer in. And that's what was in the ten they checked.

"Welcome home," one chica maybe my age said. Grudgingly, but she said it. She walked ahead to guide us into their main camp.

Didn't take her long. A few minutes and I saw firepits, and picnic tables set together in parts of circles, tarps strung between trees over platforms, a handful of big tents. We pulled up next to their playground as the sun was barely beginning to wonder was it time to set. The chica banged on our hood twice, then nodded and scowled at us. Aim nodded too and shut off the ignition.

The kid opened the truck's passenger door. Aim and I looked at each other in silence. Then she grinned. "I guess we're there yet!"

Maybe it was the other littles on the swings and jungle gyms that got through to him. He slid to the ground and walked a few steps toward them, then stopped. I got out too and slammed the door. Didn't faze him. He was focused on the fun and games.

"What have we here?" A longhaired dude wearing a mustache and a skirt came over from watching the littles play.

Aim opened her door and got out too. "We're a day or so early I guess—Amy Niehauser and Dolores Grant." I always tease Aim about how she ended up with such a non-Hispanic name, and she gives me grief right back about not having something made-up, like "Shaniqua" or "Running Fawn." "We're from Kiona. In Pasco?"

Dude nodded. "Sure. Since Britney was bringing you in I figured that was who you must be. I'm Curtis. We weren't expecting a vehicle, though." He waved a hand at the truck.

Britney had hopped up on the bed again while we talked, lifting the lids off the rest of the plastic tubs. "Likewise!" she shouted. "Look at this!"

Aim and I leaned up over the side to see. Britney was tearing off cover after cover. Sure enough, the five tubs furthest in were all at least three-quarters full of thick, indigo blue liquid with specks of pale purple foam. I had never seen so much Likewise in one place.

Curtis lost his cool. "What the hell! We told you we don't allow that—that—" He didn't have the vocabulary to call the drug a bad enough name.

"No, it's not ours—we stole this truck and we didn't know—" Aim tried to calm him down. She tugged at the tub nearest the end. "Here, we'll help you pour 'em in the lake."

"You seriously think we wanna pollute our water like that?"

"Look, I'm just saying we'll get rid of it. We didn't know, we just took this truck from some dudes acting like cowboys on the other side of the bridge, the little dude's big brothers, and they had a few friends—"

That got Britney's attention. "They follow you?"

"Not real far," I said, breaking in. "Since when we took this we left 'em on foot." And they hadn't shot at us more than once—the fuel explained why. "They ain't the only trouble you got for neighbors, either—I'd be more worried about Mercer Island if I were you than them bridge dudes—or a load of Likewise we can dump anywhere you want."

"Right." Curtis seemed to quiet down and consider this. "Yeah, we'll dig a hole or something…"

No one had proved a connection between Likewise and all the adults talking about living Otherwise, then disappearing. No one had proved anything in a long time that I'd heard of. But the prisons where it first got made were the same ones so many "escaped" from early on, which is the only reason anyone even noticed a bunch of poor people had gone missing, IMO. News reports began about the time it was getting so popular outside, here and in a few more countries.

Some of us still cooked it up. Some of us still drank it. How long did the side-effects last? If you indulged at the age of sixteen would you vanish years later, as soon as your brain was ready? Could you even tell whether you went or not?

The ones who knew were in no position to tell us. They were Otherwise.

Britney went to report us to the committee, she said. A pair of twelve-year-olds came and showed us where to unload the fuel drums. I helped Aim lower the rolly from the bed—how had I got it up there on my own? My arms were gonna hurt bad when the adrenaline wore off—and she handed them the keys. They drove to the bunker with the Likewise for the sentries to watch over.

Aim had to head back to the playground after that. The little dude seemed thoroughly recovered: he'd thrown off his jacket and was running wild and yelling with the other kids like he belonged there.

The Rattlers' committee met with us over dinner in this ridiculous tipi they'd rigged up down by the swimming beach. Buffaloes and lightning painted on the sides. I mean, even I knew tipis were plains technology and had nothing to do with tribes in these parts. But, well, the Rattlers acted proud and solemn bringing us inside, telling us to take off our shoes and which way to circle around the fire, and damn if they didn't actually pass a real, live pipe after feeding us salads plus some beige glop that looked a lot worse than it tasted. And tortillas, which they insisted on calling frybread.

Tina, their eldest, sat on a sofa cushion; she looked maybe Aim's age, but probably she was older. Trying to show the rest of the committee how to run things when she was gone Otherwise, she asked about folks at Kiona: who had hooked up with who, how many pregnant, any cool salvage we'd come across, any adults we'd noticed still sticking around. Aim answered her. There were two dudes, one on either side of Tina—husbands, maybe?—Rattlers were known for doing that kinda thing—and a couple younger chicas chiming in with compliments about how well we were doing for ourselves. I waited politely for them to raise the subject they wanted to talk about. Which was, as I'd figured, the five tubs of Likewise.

They decided to forgive us and opted to pour 'em in a hole like Aim suggested.

Tina had brains. "What's interesting is that they were bringing this shipment *out* of Seattle." She stretched her legs straight, pointed her toes up and pushed toward the fire with her wool-socked heels. August, and the evenings were on the verge of chilly.

"Not like the whole city's sworn off," one of the chicas ventured to say.

"Yeah." I had the dude that agreed pegged for a husband because he wore a ring matching the one on Tina's left hand. "That crew up in Gas Works? They could be brewing big old vats of Likewise and how would we know?"

The second dude chimed in. "They sure wouldn't expect us to barter for any." He wore a ring that matched the one on Tina's right.

The young chica who'd already spoken wondered if it was their responsibility to keep the whole of Seattle clean, suburbs too. Husband One opined that they'd better think a while about that.

"Next question." That was Tina again. "What are those bridge boys gonna do to get their shipment back?" She looked at me, though it was Aim who started talking.

We hadn't told Claude or Dwight where we were going, or made a map for 'em or anything, so I thought the Rattlers were pretty safe. Plus I had hurt Dwight, broken at least one bone. But the committee decided the truck was a liability even if they painted it, and told us we better take it with us when we departed their territory. Which would have to be soon—"Tomorrow?" asked Husband Two.

Aim folded her lips between her front teeth a few seconds in that worried way she had. We'd expected more of a welcome, considering her skills. Kinda hoped she'd be able to set up a forge here for at least a week. Were the Rattlers gonna make us miss her date with Rob? But according to the committee's spies he was close, already landed on this side of the Sound and heading south. He'd arrive any minute now. So we could keep our rendezvous.

Dammit.

Then I finally got to find out more on where all those corpses in the tunnel came from: richies, as I'd suspected. Didn't seem like the committee wanted to go further into it, though. The dead people were who? People the richies had killed. How? Didn't know. Didn't think it mattered; dead was dead. And why were they stacked up on the road all unhygienic-like instead of properly buried? Have to send a detail to take care of that. And the two fresh ones? Tina said she figured the way I did that they were fallout from Claude and Dwayne's trip through the blockade.

So why? Well, that was obvious, too: use the dead ones to catch us, alive, to work for 'em.

It became more obvious when Curtis took us to where we were supposed to sleep: a tree house far up the central hill of the park's peninsula. He climbed the rope ladder ahead of us and showed us the pisspot, the water bucket and dipper, the bell to ring if one of us suddenly took violently ill in the night. Then he wanted to know if we'd seen his little sister's body in the pile.

"Uh, no, we kinda—we had to go fast, didn't see much. Really." Aim could tell a great lie.

"She had nice hair, in ponytails. And big, light green eyes."

Anybody's eyes that had been open in that pile, they weren't a color you'd recognize anymore. Mostly they were gone. Along with big chunks of face. "No, we, uh, we had to get out of there too fast. Really didn't see. Sorry."

He left us alone at last.

Alone as we were going to get—there was a lot of other tree houses nearby; dusk was settling in fast but we could see people moving up their own ladders, hear 'em talking soft and quiet.

"Lie down." I patted the floor mat. She came into my arms. I had her body, no problema. I did hurt from heaving the rolly around, but that didn't matter much. I stroked her bangs back from her pretty face that I knew even in the dark.

"What'd they do with Dwayne?"

"Who?"

"Dwayne, you know, the little dude?"

Right: Claude and Dwight's kid brother. "That what you wanna call him?"

Aim snorted. "It's his *name*. He told Curtis. I heard him."

My fingers wandered down to the arches of her eyebrows, smoothing them flat. "You worried about him? He looked happy on the playground. They must have places for kids to sleep here. We seen plenty of 'em."

"Yeah. You're right." The skin above her nose crinkled. I traced her profile, trying to give her something else to think of. It sort of worked.

"Why don't the committee care more about the Mercer Island richies? That was—horrible. In the tunnel."

I laughed, though it wasn't the littlest bit funny. "Fail. Mega Fail—they were supposed to be protecting these people here and the richies raided 'em. I wouldn't wanna talk about it either."

I felt her forehead relax. "Yeah." She reached up and tugged my scarf free so she could run her hands over my close-clipped scalp. That was more like it. I snuggled my head against the denim of her coat.

That was our last night together as a couple.

She only mentioned Rob once.

* * *

Next morning my arm felt even sorer. And my shoulder had turned stiff. And my wrist. Was getting old like this? No wonder people went Otherwise.

Aim and I woke up at the same time, same as at home and on salvage runs. "Good dreams?" I asked. She nodded and gave me a sheepish half-smile, so I didn't have to ask who she'd dreamed about. It wasn't me.

What kind of universe would Aim make if she went Otherwise? It wouldn't be the same as mine.

Curtis had pointed out a latrine on the way to our treehouse. We dumped the pisspot there and took care of our other morning needs. It was a nice latrine, with soap and a bowl of water.

Down we went, following the trail to the main camp. Aim held my hand when we could walk side by side. Sweet moments. I knew I better treasure 'em.

I helped set out breakfast, which was berries and bars of what appeared to be last night's beige glop, fossilized. Aim retrieved the rolly from where we'd left it under a supply tarp. She cleaned the gun, which she called Walter, and shined up her tools. Soon enough she attracted a clientele.

First come a dude could have been fourteen or fifteen; he wanted her to help him fix up an underwater trap for turtles and crayfish. Then he had a friend a little older who asked her to help him take apart a motor to power his boat. Actually, he had taken it apart already, and wanted her to put it together again with him.

Aim called a break for herself after a couple hours of this so she could go check out how Dwayne was doing. And she wanted to bring him a plum from the ones I collected for snacks. I waited by the tools for her to come back. A shadow cut the warm sun and I looked up from the dropcloth.

"Hey." A dude's voice. All I could see was a silhouette. Like an eclipse—a gold rim around darkness.

"Hey back."

"You're not Amy."

"Nope."

He sat down fast, folding his legs. "Must be Dolores, then? I'm

Rob." He held out a hand to shake, so I took it.

Now I could see him, dude was every bit as pretty as Aim had said. Dammit. Hair like new copper, tied back smooth and bright and loose below a wide-brimmed straw fedora. Eyes large, a strange, pale blue. Freckles like cinnamon all over his snub-nosed face and his long arms where they poked out of the black-and-white print shirt he wore. But not on his throat, which was smooth as vanilla ice cream and made me want to—no. This was Aim's crush.

His hand was a little damp around the palm. Fingers long and strong. I let it go. "Aim's around here somewhere; she'll be back in a minute, I think, if you wanna wait."

"Sure." He had a tiny little stick, a twig, in the corner of his mouth. His lips were pink, not real thin for a white boy. Dammit.

"Where's your guitar?" I asked.

"Left it back home, at the bunkers. The Herons'll take care of it for me; too much to travel with. But I packed my pennywhistle." He swapped the stick for something longer, shiny black and silver. He played a sad-sounding song, mostly slow, with some fast parts where one line ended and the next began. Then he speeded up, did a new, sort of jazzy tune. Then another, and I recognized it: "Firework."

Aim recognized it, too. Or him, anyway—she came running up behind me shouting his name: "Rob! Rob!" She hauled him up with a hug. "I'm so glad! So glad!" He hugged her back. They both laughed and leaned away enough to look each other in the eyes.

"Oh, wow—" "Did you—" They started and stopped talking at the same time. Cute.

Dwayne had showed up in Aim's wake. He stood to one side, hands in his front pockets, about as awkward as I felt.

Rob and Aim let go of each others' arms. "Who's this?" he asked her, bending his knees to put his face on the kid's level.

"I'm Dwayne. I come all the way from Issaquah." Which was nine times more words than I'd ever heard him use before. Maybe he liked white dudes.

"That's pretty far. But I met somebody came even further."

"Who're you?"

"I'm Rob. I live in Fort Worden, other side of the Sound."

"Issaquah is twenty-two miles from Seattle."

"Well, this chica I'm talking about sailed to Fort Worden over the ocean from Liloan. That's in the Philippines. Six thousand miles."

"She did not!"

"I'm telling you."

Here came Curtis over from the playground. He said hey and dragged Dwayne back with him with the promise of a swim, "—so you can get packed quick."

The Rattlers wanted us gone yesterday. While Rob met with their committee to tell them the news out of Liloan—how the Philippines had been mostly missed by the EMPs and other tech-killers thrown around in the first mass panic—Aim loaded her tools in the rolly, and I went to find the truck. At the fuel shed they directed me up the remains of a service road. The twelve-year-olds had parked at the end of it; they were just through filling in the hole they'd dug, tamping down dirt with a couple of shovels. The empty Likewise tubs lay on their sides in the dead pine needles.

"Thanks," I said. "We were gonna do that."

"'Sall right," the bigger one said. "Didn't take long."

"Yes it did." Her friend wasn't about to lie. "But we're done, now, and nobody drunk it.

"Have you ever—" The smaller girl smacked the bigger one on her head. "Stop! I was only asking!" She turned to me again. "You ever taken any Likewise yourself?"

Once. A single dose was low risk—I'd heard of adults with the same history as me, twenty-four, twenty-five, and still not Otherwise.

"Tastes like dog slobber," I told her. "Like spit bugs crapped in a bottle of glue."

"Eeuuw!" They made faces and giggled. I thought about the questions they didn't ask as they brought me back down in the truck. About how Likewise felt, what happened when I had it in me.

You could call it a dream. In it, my mom had never hit me and my dad had never got stoned. I was living in a house with Aim. The drug was specific: a yellow house with white trim, a picket fence. We had a dog named Quincy Jones and a parakeet named Sam. The governments were still running everything. We had a kid and jobs we went to. I remember falling asleep and waking up and getting maybe a little bored at work, but basically being happy. So happy.

Seemed like it went on for years. I was out for eight hours.

We could have driven all the way to Fort Worden, only Aim wanted to see the Space Needle. "C'mon, when are we gonna have another chance?"

I rolled my eyes. "You can *see* it from freakin *anywhere*, Aim. Ask *them* if *they* see it." I pointed up at the chicas in the fifty-foot-high lookout.

"Okay. Touch it then. I mean touch it."

Our first fight.

Of course Rob took her side. "Yeah, the truck; tough to let it go, but there's no connections for us in Tacoma. Olympia either; can't say who or what we might run into going south. I told the captain up at Edmonds I'd be back in a week. Maybe he can stow it for us? And even if we're early that's our best bet. North. So the Space Needle's not much of a detour."

Aim looked at me. "*All flippin right*," I said.

I drove again. Aim took the middle seat, but it wasn't me she pressed up against.

Rattlers had told us where to avoid, and I did my best. From Rainier I had to guess the route, and sometimes I guessed wrong. And sometimes my guesses would have been good if the roads didn't have huge holes in 'em or obstacles too hard to move out of our way. We didn't see anyone else, only signs they'd been around: coiled up wires, stacks of wood—not a surprise, since anyone on a scavenge run would have lookouts. Groups had mainly settled in parks where you could grow crops, and we weren't trying to cross those.

We reached Seattle Center late. No time to find anywhere else to spend the night.

There had been action here, too. I remembered the news stories, though they hadn't made any sense. Not then, and not now—why would anyone fight over such a place, so far off from any water? But tanks had crawled their way onto the grounds, smashing trees and sculptures, shooting fire and smoke back and forth. They left scars we could still see: burned-out buildings, craters, bullet holes.

The Space Needle stood in the middle of about an acre of blackberries covering torn-up concrete—what used to be a plaza. Old black soot and orange rust marked its once-white legs. I tooled us under a pair of concrete pillars for the dead Monorail and backed in as close as I could get without slicing open a tire. "There you go," I said. "Touch it." Which was a little mean, I admit.

Rob climbed out the window without opening the door and got up on the truck cab's roof. He stuck his arm in and hauled Aim after him. I heard the two of 'em talking about chopping a path through the thorns if they'd had swords, and how to forge them, and a trick Aim knew called damascening. Aim recited her facts about how high the thing was, how long it took to erect, et cetera.

Then I didn't hear anything for a while. Then her breath. I turned on the radio, like there'd be something more than static to cover up the sounds they were going to make.

One of them shifted and the metal above my head popped in and out. That gave me courage to hit the horn—a short blast like it was an accident—and open the door. Very, very slowly.

Shin deep in brambles I unhooked from my pants one by one, I took a blanket from the boxes of supplies the Rattlers sent us off with. Then I couldn't help myself; I looked. They both had all their clothes on and were sitting up. For the moment. Aim waved. Rob pretended to stroke a beard he didn't have and smiled.

"In a minute," I said, meaning I'd come back. Eventually. Give me strength, I thought, and I smiled, too, and waded carefully along the trail the truck had smashed.

She wanted to be with him. I loved her anyhow. To the edge of the continent. All the way.

I would follow her.

But tonight I would sleep alone.

At least that was the plan. When it came down to it, though, I didn't dare rest my eyes. Dark was falling. The place was too open—bad juju. I had a feeling, once I got out from under my jealousy. So I found a trash barrel, rolled it up a ramp in the side of some place looked like a giant scorched wad of metal gum. I set the barrel upright, climbed and balanced on its rim, and scrabbled from there to lie on my stomach on a low roof—must have been the only flat surface to the whole building, even before the howitzers and grenade-launchers and whatever else attacked it.

Me and Walter settled in to keep watch. The Rattlers had returned his magazine when they gave me back my knife, and there were seven rounds left.

Aim and Rob were maybe fifty feet south. I still heard 'em clear enough to keep me awake till Claude and his friends showed up.

Trying to be smart, the bridge dudes turned off whatever vehicle they drove blocks away. The engine's noise was a clue, and its silence was another. Insects went quiet to my east in case I needed a third.

Starlight's not the best to see by. I couldn't really count 'em—four or five dudes it must be, I figured, same as yesterday. They zeroed in on Aim and Rob, who were talking again.

"Hands up!" a dude commanded. How were they gonna tell, I wondered, but one of 'em opened the truck door and the courtesy light came on. There was Aim and Rob, a bit tousled up. Too bad I didn't want to shoot *them*. Couldn't get a line on anyone else.

"Get your sorry asses outta me and Dwight's—outta my truck." That would be Claude.

"Daddy? Where's Daddy?" And that would be that kid Dwayne? His age was all wrong for Dwight to be his dad, but who else was it rising out of that supply box, pale-faced in the yellow courtesy light?

The kid must have stowed away. He held out his arms and kicked free of something and Claude stepped up to grab and lift him and now I had a great shot. Couldn't have been better. But I didn't take it.

Next minute I wished I had when dudes on either side yanked Aim and Rob out of opposite doors. I heard her yell at them and get slapped.

Someone else was yelling, too—not me, I was busy shimmying off the roof while there was cover for my noise. "No! Don't hit her! No! Put me down!" Little Dwayne was on our side?

Brightness. Someone had switched on the truck's headlamps. I ducked down. Aim was crying hard. They shoved her to the pavement. I hadn't heard a peep outta Rob. When they marched him into the light I saw one dude's hand over his mouth and a shiny piece of metal right below his ear. Knife or a gun—didn't matter which. Woulda kept me quiet, too.

Only four of 'em. Plus Dwayne. Seven bullets seemed plenty—if I didn't mind losing Rob.

I didn't. But Aim would.

Bang! Bang! Walter wasn't quite loud as a shotgun. Glass and metal pinged off the pavement, flew away into the sudden dark. Only one round each for the truck's headlamps. I was proud of myself.

Light still came out of the cab from the overhead courtesy. Not much. I couldn't see anybody.

But I could hear 'em shouting to each other to find the chica, and shooting. Randomly, I hoped. No screams, so Rob had probably got away all right.

I shifted position, which made the next part trickier, but would keep the dudes guessing where to kill me. I went round to one side, with the frame of the open driver's door blocking my vision. Walter stayed steady—I gripped him with both hands and squeezed. Got it in one. I was good. Total night, now. I squirmed off on my belly for a ways to be sure no one had a flashlight, then crawled, then stumbled to my feet and walked. Headed north by the stars, with nothing on me but Walter, my knife, my binoculars. A blanket. Not even a bottle for water.

It was a shame to leave all the provisions the Rattlers had given us. And too bad I had to damage a high-functioning machine like that truck. Aim would cuss me out for it when we caught up with one another at Edmonds.

Aim would be fine. She always was. Rob, too, most likely.

I took the rest of that night and part of a day to walk there. It was easy: 99 most of the way. The stars were enough to see that by, and the Aurora Bridge was practically intact. I wondered what facts Aim would have told me about it if we were going over it together. All I knew was people used to kill themselves here by jumping off. Kids? Didn't we used to have the highest rates of suicide?

If Aim didn't show up at Edmonds in a few days maybe I'd come back. Or find some Likewise.

I snuck in the dark past where they used to have a zoo, worried I might run into some weird predator. I didn't; when the animals got out they must've headed for the lake on the road's other side. The sky got lighter and I began to look for pursuit as well as listening for it. Nobody came. The stores and restaurants lining the highway would have been scavenged out long ago. I was alone.

No Aim in sight.

Rain started to fall. I hung the blanket over my head like the Virgin Mary. Because of the clouds it was hard to tell time, but I figured I turned onto 104 a couple of hours after sunrise.

I went down a long slope to the water. Rob had said if we got split up to meet by a statue of sea lions on the beach.

This was my first time to be at the ocean. It was big, but I could see land out in its middle. Looked like I could just swim there.

Route 104 continued right on into the water. The statue was supposed to be to its south. The sand moved, soft and tiresome under my wet chucks. I spotted a clump of kids digging for something further towards the water, five or six of 'em. They didn't try to stop me and I kept on without asking directions. A couple of 'em had slings out, but I must not have seemed too threatening; neither chica pointed 'em my way.

A metal seal humped up some stairs to a patch of green. Was this the place? I climbed up beside it. At the top, a garden. I could tell it was a garden since it wasn't blackberries, though I had no idea what these plants were. But they grew in circles and lines, real patterns. And more metal seal sculptures—okay, sea lions—stuck out from between them.

Definitely. I was here. I curled up in the statue's shelter and the rain stopped. I fell asleep.

A whisper woke me. "Lo!" My heart revved. Aim? Eyes open, all I saw was Rob.

"You can't call me that."

"Sorry. Didn't want you to shoot me."

I sat up straight and realized I had Walter in my hand. Falling asleep hadn't been so stupid after all.

Rob's ice cream throat had a red inch-long slice on one side, so it had been a knife the bridge dude held there. He seemed fine besides that. "Is she around?" he asked. "She and you came together?" I shook my head and he folded up his legs and sat down beside me. Too close. I scooted over.

We didn't say anything for a long time. Could have been an hour. I was thirsty. And hungry. I wondered if maybe I ought to eat from the garden.

Rob held out his water bottle for me and I took it and drank. When I gave it back he didn't even wipe the mouth off.

The clouds pulled themselves apart and let this beautiful golden orange light streak through. The sun was going down. I'd slept the whole afternoon.

"Look," said Rob. "Look. I know you and Aim—"

"You can't call her that."

"Yes I can! Listen. Look. You were with her before me and I don't want to—to mess with that."

As if he hadn't. "And?"

"And—and we were talking." Among other things. "And she was saying if we got married—if she got married she would want to marry *both* of us."

I stared at him hard to make sure he was serious. Me and Aim had teased each other about being married ever since we met in gym class. Even before people over twenty began going Otherwise.

Apparently I wasn't the only one it was more than a joke for.

"So would you?"

"Would I what?" But I knew.

"Would you freakin marry me! Would you—"

"But I'm a lesbian! You're a dude!"

"Well, duh."

"And only because you wanna hook up with *my* chica? Unh-unh."

"Well, it's not only that."

"Really?" I stood up. He did too. "What, you're in love with me? I'm fat, I'm a big mouth, a smartass—"

"You're plain old smart! And brave, and Aim thinks you're the closest thing to a goddess who ever walked the earth."

"What if I am?" I wanted to leave. But this was where she would come. I had to be here. I wrapped the blanket around me and tucked my arms tight.

"Yeah. What if you are? What if she's right? I kinda think—" He quit talking a minute and looked over his shoulder at the beach. "I kinda think she is. You are."

If he had tried to touch me then I would have knocked the fool unconscious.

Instead, he turned around and looked at the beach again. "That's him," he said. "Captain Lee." He pointed and I saw a bright yellow triangle sailing toward us out of the west. "Our ride's here ahead of time. I have to go meet him and tell him we need to wait for Aim." He left me alone with my wet blanket.

It was almost dark by the time he came back, carrying a bucket. "Here you go. Supper." I was ready to eat, no doubt. Inside was a hot baked yam and some greens with greasy pink fish mixed in. I washed it all down with more of Rob's water.

We took turns hanging out at the statue. Rob had connections with the locals, the Hammerheads and this other group, the Twisters. He stayed with them, and I bunked on Lee's boat.

Three days dragged past. I got used to a certain idea. I let him put his arm around me once when we met on the stairs. And another time when he introduced me to a dude he brought to pick some herbs in the garden—they were for medicines, not that nice to eat.

And another time. We were there together, but with my binoculars I saw her first. I shouted and he hugged me. Both arms. I broke away and ran and ran and yes, it was Aim! And Dwayne, which explained a lot when I thought about it afterwards, but I didn't care right then.

"Aim! Aim!" I lifted her in the air and whirled us around and we kissed each other long and hard. I was with her and it was this reality, hers and mine and everybody else's, not one I created just for me. I cried and laughed and yelled at the blue sky, so glad. Oh so freakin glad.

Of course I had known all along she'd make it.

And then Rob caught up with me and he kissed her too. She held my hand the whole time. So how could I feel jealous and left out?

Well, I could. But that might change, someday. Someday, it might be otherwise.

AND THE REST OF US WAIT

CORINNE DUYVIS

Corinne Duyvis is the award-winning, critically acclaimed author of young-adult novels *Otherbound*, which *Kirkus* called "original and compelling; a stunning debut," and *On the Edge of Gone*, which *Publishers Weekly* called "a riveting apocalyptic thriller with substantial depth," and which was declared a Best Book of 2016 by *Kirkus* and *Paste Magazine*. She is also the author of *Guardians of the Galaxy: Collect Them All*, which *The Mary Sue* called "a joy to read from start to finish," and the forthcoming *The Art of Saving the World*. Corinne is a co-founder and editor of Disability in Kidlit as well as the originator of the #ownvoices hashtag. She was born and raised in the Netherlands.

We were among the earliest to arrive at the shelter—a day and a half before impact—and it still took two hours for the volunteers to process us. My parents and I stood on one side of a long desk in a low-ceilinged office, the muffled noise from the shelter hallway outside growing louder the more people joined the line behind us.

They scanned us for contaminants. They scanned our bags. They double- and triple-checked our blood, our IDs, and our shelter assignment letters. They squinted at our faces to match the photos, and I waited for a glimpse of recognition as they placed my face and accent, but nothing came. They asked me to explain my cathing equipment and leg braces. They asked where we were from (Riga,

379

Latvia), how long we'd been in the Netherlands (seven weeks), where we'd stayed (twenty minutes outside Amsterdam); I couldn't tell if they were verifying their information or making small talk. Right when I thought they were ready to let us go, they went through our bags again, which contained spare clothes and little else.

"No food?" the shelter volunteer asked in thickly accented English.

Mum shook her head. "We spent the last five weeks in a refugee centre."

"Should've saved food."

Mum opened her mouth and shut it again.

"There's food here. Right?" Dad's lips twitched. "They said…"

The woman shrugged. "We have food, but it's tight. Better if people bring their own."

"We'll remember that for the next apocalypse," I said.

Afterwards, as we sat down on the creaky beds we'd been assigned in a sea of camping beds, bedrolls, and stretchers, Mum leaned in. "Careful, Iveta," she whispered. "Don't stand out."

Dad scanned the hall, as though the other families hesitantly testing their beds would descend on us at any moment. We weren't the only ones who'd arrived early. I recognised others from our refugee centre: from Finns to Belarusians, from Ukrainians to Romanians, even a stray Bulgarian and Turkish family, although most people that far south had fled to Africa rather than Western Europe.

People looked up as I stalked through the narrow aisle between beds. During my few weeks in the country, the only Dutch people I'd interacted with were the refugee centre volunteers. Still, I could recognise the language, and the moment I heard an older couple talk in hushed Dutch, I stopped by their cots. They'd seen me coming. Mum could warn me not to stand out all she wanted, but I was hard to miss: I walked with a waddling limp, my hips seesawing fiercely.

"Question," I said in English. "Did you bring any instruments?"

They gave me a confused look.

"For music." I mimicked playing the piano.

"No, we… of course not. We only brought the supplies we needed. Why?"

I swept an arm at the hall, which was three or four times the size of my high school gym. They couldn't have designed it any plainer if they'd tried: nothing but pillars and beds and cold lighting, and the pale green walls were bare aside from the occasional water fountain and posters displaying shelter rules in a dozen languages.

"What else is there to do while we wait?"

Cot by cot, the shelter filled up.

People arrived by the busload that day and the day after. I trailed the aisles, hitting up other Dutch families I found. I didn't need to identify them by their speech anymore. They were the ones with the bulging backpacks, the uncertain look about them, while those of us from the refugee centres carried narrow sacks and looked weary more than anything else.

I explored the rest of the shelter and found myself lingering outside the main halls, glad for the relative silence. It was too easy to get a headache in the murmur and anxiety permeating the shelter, and the last thing I needed was to worry about minor headaches.

Aside from the five sleeping halls, there were two smaller halls, the walls soft blue and every inch filled with mismatched chairs and tables instead of beds. Packets of playing cards and old books were strewn around the tables. Some of the kids' tables had crayons, pencils, paper.

No instruments.

"Not impressed?" a voice behind me said. "It's only for three days."

I turned, facing a girl a few years older than me—early twenties, probably—with a prettily patterned hijab framing a narrow face.

"And afterwards we can all go home, right?" I said, sceptical.

"That… would be nice. Iveta?"

Had someone finally recognised me? There were a lot of Baltic curly blondes around, but people always said I looked unique, with narrow blue eyes and a wide forehead made wider by the way I pulled those curls behind my ears. I was never a huge name outside of Latvia, but I'd done a handful of European shows, and I'd expected more people to recognise me. It was the lack of wheelchair, I figured:

even if people recognised my face, they might not recognise it atop an upright body.

"Iveta. That's me," I said.

"Samira. I'm helping shelter management. Our medical information on the refugees assigned here is incomplete. I'm trying to fill it up."

"This late in the game?"

"We still have a few hours before impact." She smiled an almost-genuine smile. She was trying; I gave her that much. "They didn't even realise they missed this information until I pointed it out."

"It's been chaotic," I said airily, which was an understatement the size of the comet that was about to hit us.

"So you're from Latvia?"

"Yes."

"I'm sorry."

I leaned against a table. The room was surprisingly empty—most people were guarding their bags in the sleeping halls. "Yeah, well." I scratched at the table, seeking resistance and finding only smooth surface. "We might survive all right."

The comet had been announced in July 2034, half a year ago. They hadn't been certain where it would hit: Eastern Europe was their best guess. It might hit south of that, near the Middle East, in which case my words to Samira might be true; it might hit north of that, near Scandinavia, in which case Samira's sympathies were justified but nowhere near enough.

Latvia wouldn't be the only casualty. The Netherlands wouldn't stay intact, either. No place would. Not with impact dust masking the sun for at least a year, not with wildfires and earthquakes and more. Millions—perhaps billions—of people had already left on generation ships or taken shelter in permanent basements deep underground. The rest of us only had these temporary government shelters to outlast the initial impact. Afterwards, we'd flood back onto the surface and fend for ourselves.

But even if the Netherlands didn't stay intact, it would *exist*.

Latvia might not.

"Did you bring any instruments?" I asked abruptly. "Or do you sing?"

Her head cocked. "Badly enough to make my fiancé leave the room."

I exhaled with a whistle. "All right. What do you need to know?"

For the next ten minutes, I told her about my spina bifida and all that came with it: from my club foot to my partially paralysed legs, from my spinal implant against chronic pain to my shunt to manage my hydrocephalus.

"What does that implant run on?"

"Body heat. We got the latest and greatest." Money had been one of several upsides to my bout of fame. I'd made enough to move my family into an accessible apartment and buy a brand-new wheelchair for shows and long distances. It had gotten stolen on the long, crooked escape from Latvia to the Netherlands.

"Good. We can charge prosthetics and equipment, but the more power we save, the better."

We'd sat down at a table in a quiet corner. Normally, people got weirded out when presented with my laundry list of conditions. Samira hadn't batted an eyelash. She'd asked all the right questions, too, but for the sake of completeness rather than prying.

"How much do you know about KAFOs?" I knocked on my leg braces.

"Sorry?"

"You're a doctor. It's not exactly the flu or messing with organs, but how good are you with orthotics?"

"I'm just a volunteer. I'll ask Dr Kring, but he's been busy. Some of the refugees arrived with severe malnutrition."

At least someone was looking after them. The refugee centre volunteers had tried to help, but doctors—like food—were a rare commodity. Too many medical professionals had left on generation ships or moved into permanent shelters.

Again: just like the food.

Samira leaned in as though confiding in me. "I'm… really just a medical student. I simply volunteered when I saw how overworked Dr Kring was."

I scratched at the table and was left just as unsatisfied as before. "All right."

"What's the matter with your orthoses?"

I stood. "It's not urgent. Like you said: we've got all the time in the world."

"I said we have three days."

My smile was steady. "Same thing, isn't it?"

Any minute now.

I didn't know what I was supposed to feel.

I sat on the bed, Mum on one side, Dad on another, both leaning into me as though that would help. Someone from shelter management had given a speech about what we'd need to do around impact time, and they'd repeated themselves on the intercom system.

The instructions were clear: *stay on your cots; stay calm; we'll update you when we can.* We'd feel shaking, but they didn't know how strong or how long for. We might hear something, but they doubted it.

I thought half a year would've been enough to prepare me, but it still hadn't sunk in. Mum stared stoically ahead. Dad had tear tracks on both cheeks. Me—I didn't know whether to panic or cry, and in the end, I did neither. Instead, my mind wandered off, tweaking lyrics in Latvian and English both. I reached for my wrist only to find it empty, our wrist tabs bartered for food weeks before.

Mum took my hand, squeezed it. "We'll be fine," she whispered.

I squeezed back and hoped she didn't expect me to believe her.

The lights flashed bright and crackled for a flash of a second.

Then they went out.

Gasps. Beds creaked as people sat upright. Someone called out in Dutch. Next, a high-pitched voice spoke in Russian. Then, a pained groan.

My eyes were still adjusting, blinking rapidly in a desperate attempt to find *some* source of light that was just too faint for me to have clung onto yet. Didn't some people still have their tabs? Shouldn't there be light coming from underneath the doors?

Nothing.

Experimentally, I raised my hand in front of my face. I didn't see a thing. I couldn't remember darkness like this since—since ever.

"What's happening?" someone called in English. "No one warned us about this!"

Dad grabbed my hand. At the same time, Mum stood. I could only tell because the bed veered up below me and her clothes brushed past mine.

The yells layered into each other, near and far, angry and frightened, in languages I didn't even recognise. All of a sudden, I missed home with a passion. I missed my room, the Dauvaga Promenade, Grandma's mushrooms, performing at Kalnciema Quarter, a quiet mind and not translating every word and *music*—

"This wasn't supposed to happen," Mum insisted, yanking me back to the dark. "They have enough battery power for days. And the shelters are shielded against EMPs."

"Maybe they turned off the lights as protection," Dad said.

I didn't bother to shake my head. They wouldn't see. "Shelter management would've warned us." Governments had announced months in advance why and when they'd be deactivating the power plants, to give time to prepare. There was no chance shelter management would've so thoroughly informed us about our rations and the bathroom policy, but neglect to mention turning off the lights.

I peeled Dad's hand from mine and stood, feeling Mum's presence by my side. "Does anyone have a tab?" I called in English. "We could use the light to—"

"Tabs aren't working!" someone shouted back. "Mine was fully charged—"

"Mine just turned off—" someone else added.

"Doctor!" someone screamed. It might've been in Dutch, but if so, the word was similar enough to leave no doubt. "*Doctor!*"

Snippets of shouts. I caught a word here—*heart*—and there—*help*—which was enough.

Lights out. Tabs dead. Sudden heart attacks.

"The shielding didn't work," I said.

Abruptly, it hit me what that meant. If there was an EMP, it meant the comet had hit, that it really had *happened* after all these months, and Latvia was—

The notion slipped away.

"Help me onto the bed," I said. There was no use in theorising and panicking. Everyone else was doing a fine job of that already. I groped in the darkness for Mum's arm, then used it to steady myself and climb on. My legs buckled once or twice, the soft mattress too unsteady, but once I stood, I remembered a dozen concerts I'd given, and a dozen smaller shows besides. I remembered crowds hanging on my every word. I got them to scream at the top of their lungs, and to go so quiet a moment later that they could've heard me whisper even without the microphone. I got them to shout in support of deregulated Internet and better accessibility and against Russia's latest stunts.

At home, I'd been Iveta, teen novelty. Here, I was just another refugee.

Let's see if I can still pull it off.

I braced myself against Mum and called out, "*Listen up!* Get on the beds! Keep the paths clear!" I wished my accent when speaking English didn't mark me as a refugee so clearly. I kept shouting, again and again, until it shut up the panicked voices around me. "Keep the paths clear! Keep quiet! If your neighbour is hurt, help them to the exit. Keep the injured in the hallway until someone finds a doctor—"

"I'll find someone!" a voice from near the exit called.

Around us, I heard the shuffle of people climbing onto their beds, shouts in other languages that I was half-sure were people repeating my instructions.

I let Mum help me sit, already aching from exertion.

"Good," Dad murmured. "That was good."

"Not exactly lying low like Mum said." A nervous laugh escaped me. People passed by in a rush of air and footsteps and urgent Dutch words. I wiggled my fingers under the KAFO to massage my calf, which hovered between numb and painfully tingly.

Mum tugged lightly at a curl of my hair. "My daughter would never listen to such silly advice."

God, that tingling was annoying—it reminded me of forgetting to take my pain meds and—

My fingers curled tight as the realisation hit.

"The EMP," I whispered. "My spinal implant died."

"Oh." Mum pulled me in close. She made another small sound: "*oh.*"

* * *

I couldn't tell if the pain was worse than before or if, after a year of blissful nothing, every small prick simply felt like a stab.

It made it impossible to sit still. So I didn't.

People had found candles by now. Flickering flame lit up the broad central hallway, which contained an urgent mess of people slipping into different rooms to seek familiar faces or staff and tossing out occasional half-shouts of "Keep your bags close!"

Every now and then, a rumble went through the walls and floor. I groped the wall for stability. The first big shakes had been enough to knock people down, but now, it was just occasional trembles.

I didn't want to think about what the world above looked like. What buildings that *hadn't* been built with a comet impact in mind looked like.

There should have been an announcement by now. Why hadn't shelter management stepped up?

I wasn't the only one wondering. I caught snippets of Russian and English. Something about the EMP. About Dr Kring. About death.

Goosebumps shuddered across my skin. I stayed close to the walls, ready to grab them for balance in the push-and-shove of the crowd and the inconstant tremors. I scanned the dimness for familiar faces. Samira, shelter management, neighbours from the refugee centre.

"Listen, listen!"

It was a male voice, his English tinged with a Dutch accent. He stood so tall above the crowd that he must've been standing on a chair. He held a candle in one hand, lighting him in eerie yellow.

"I wanted to update… My name is Ahmed. I'm with the Amsterdam police." If his name made the murmur increase, his job had people quieting down a little. Relief flashed over his face. "It looks like an EMP hit us."

Someone shouted in Dutch. For a moment, I worried I'd lose track of the conversation, but Ahmed responded in English without missing a beat. "Yes, the shelter was shielded. It must not have held. What we know is that our generator… stopped working. Several people were injured putting out the fire. Lights, tabs, radio equipment, much of the kitchen—anything electrical is gone. We may have functional flashlights, but we're not sure."

He repeated the answer in Dutch, but was quickly drowned out by further questions.

"What about the doctor?"

"What about fresh air? Will we be okay without electricity?"

"Why are *you* talking to us? Where's shelter management?"

Ahmed's candle flickered beneath his face. "Between, ah, pacemakers failing and the generator fire, not all of shelter management has survived." He rattled off a list of names, some deceased, others—like Dr Kring—injured. "The rest of management is discussing options. Others are helping the injured, including Sam—including my sister-in-law. Anyone with medical know-how, come to the med bay."

"There won't be other *doctors*. We were lucky to have Kring!"

So much for Kring looking at my KAFO, I thought, jittery. Without a doctor—with amateurs looking after a dozen injured people—my situation became a lot less urgent. What if the pain worsened? What if I got headaches? Nausea?

"Can we eat okay? Without the kitchen equipment?"

"We don't know yet. If—"

Voices surged. A burly Russian man nearby argued with someone by his side. I picked up just enough to know that his wife was one of those with a pacemaker. I chose the opportunity to wobble through the crowd towards Ahmed.

He spoke louder. "Anyone who knows about engineering or air ventilation systems, come talk to me."

He stepped off the chair just as I broke through the crowd. I wasn't the only one trying to talk to him, but I *was* the only one he happened to stand right in front of. "Samira?" I called.

He frowned, half annoyed, half distracted.

"Your sister-in-law! Samira? Tell them she's a doctor." I struggled to speak loudly enough to be heard, let alone keep his attention.

"She's not—" He stepped past me.

I followed him through the crowd. We reached a less packed part of the hallway, and I took the opportunity to surge closer and talk privately. "End on a positive note. Public speaking 101. Back when I—never mind. You had bad news. People are panicking. Lie—give them *something*."

"I shouldn't even be doing this. If I lie…"

"Shelter management doesn't know about that speech? What are they *doing*?"

"Panicking," he said wryly. "Get to your cot. That's all anyone can do right now."

The pain was a vindictive thing. I lay flat on my bed, arms under my back, knuckles pressing into my skin.

Shelter management didn't serve dinner that night. Once they got their act together, they rattled off the state of things and encouraged us to eat and share whatever food we'd brought. People did share, to their credit, but only with those they knew.

Us refugees only knew each other.

Management promised we'd have breakfast by morning, once they'd spent the night organising the remaining food and staff. They'd brought in more candles, and a handful of body heat flashlights from properly shielded cases in storage.

"But why wasn't the full shelter shielded?" Inga said. She was a fifty-something Latvian-Russian woman from Salaspils, outside Riga. She'd been at a refugee centre on the Dutch coast, waiting on a boat to England that never came. Now, she sat cross-legged on the ground by our beds, along with two near-identical girls my age and a Finnish male couple she'd befriended at her shelter.

"There were a lot of shelters to build in a very short time," Dad said. "These temporary shelters, the permanent ones, the ships. They might've made a mistake, or there weren't enough supplies."

"Bet there were supplies for those ships and permanent shelters, though." I pushed my thumbs deep into the fleshy parts on either side of my spine. I wished I could reach in and around, cutting off the pain signals the way my implant was supposed to.

"They cut corners," Mum said from the foot end of my bed.

"They wouldn't. *Not* with lives at stake." One of the Finnish men was sitting up all prim and proper.

"If our lives mattered, we'd be on a ship." I turned my head to face them properly and pulled my lips into a distorted grin. "Sucks being left behind. Doesn't it?"

It was one of my lyrics. Apparently, that did the trick: Inga's daughters went *oh!*

"Iveta?" one said.

"Aren't you? You are! I knew I recognised you."

"I am."

"I thought you'd be on a generation ship…"

"Me too." I faked that same grin. It was nice being recognised, I had to admit. The novelty had worn off quickly for those at our refugee centre. I guessed that mimicked my career: from one day to the next, hundreds of thousands of people had known my name. *That cute blonde girl in the wheelchair on that talent show from, what was it, Latveria? Did you see her audition footage? Holy shit, right?*

Just as quickly, it dropped off. I'd floundered for a bit, but rather than push on in desperation, I had claimed to want to focus on school, and promised to pick up my career again at eighteen, when people might take me more seriously. I never imagined doing anything else.

Then July 2034 happened, and I found out the world would end three weeks before my seventeenth birthday.

I'd done free pop-up concerts in every major town from Riga to Amsterdam. I'd told the audience I wanted to offer a distraction—*we need music at the end of the world, am I right?*—and told my parents one of my fans might find us a spot somewhere permanent. Except no one did. The final truck we hitchhiked on dropped us off in the Netherlands, and not a single boat would take us further towards safety.

The girls crept closer while the adults talked. "Where's your wheelchair?" one asked, switching to Latvian.

"Got stolen. I mostly used it during performances, anyway."

She faltered. "You're not really…?"

"I used it during *performances*, so I could *save energy*, and not have to worry about *falling over*." I'd been lying down for the past hour, so they couldn't have seen my unglamorous waddle, but even then, my shoulders were crooked as hell. You'd think that would tip them off I wasn't faking.

"Oh," she said quietly. "Oh, okay."

I pushed upright and grimaced. As if the pain wasn't enough, my stomach was rumbling uncomfortably too. "Sorry. I'm being snippy."

"I wondered because…" She pulled up her left sleeve. In the candlelight, I saw shining metal, matte plastic. A prosthesis.

"The EMP busted it," her sister chimed in.

"I'm uncoupling it soon. Too heavy to carry around for nothing. I just hoped…"

I looked closer at the robotic arm. It hung heavily, limply, by the girl's side.

"I couldn't remember if your chair was electric. I was worried it might've broken down too. I saw someone else with that problem earlier." She blushed, tugging the sleeve back down. "I can't believe we didn't recognise you. Without the chair, and in this light, and—"

"And under these circumstances. I'm not expecting to run into any colleagues. I get it."

"I'm Ginta."

Her sister added, "I'm Vera. We love your music. We went to two of your concerts."

"Yeah?" My head tilted as I regarded them. "What about *playing* music?"

I woke early.

My parents were still asleep. All around were whispers, isolated pools of light. I gestured at someone a few beds down to shine their flashlight at me so I could light our candle. I put on my KAFOs, grabbed my cathing gear, and headed to the bathrooms.

I supposed the pain itself wasn't so bad. It hurt, yes, but it was easy enough to cope with if I focused on something else. The problem was, I could only focus on something else for so long. The pain was too constant, like a fly whizzing around my head. Inevitably, the buzzing grated enough to become thunder.

The line to the bathrooms was short, twenty minutes at most. Afterwards, I lingered outside the med bay. I tried the handle. Locked. I knocked.

A baggy-eyed Samira opened the door. "Look, we'll update you if… oh. You."

"Me," I confirmed. "Do you have a minute? I have a… problem."

She stepped aside.

Inside, scattered flashlights lit the room from bizarre angles. Slowly, my eyes focused. A dozen people were laid out side by side. Some sat upright, reading a book; others were sound asleep. One woman rocked back and forth, the bed creaking underneath, as she sewed up a coat—at least, I thought she was; her hands holding the needle and thread were frozen still.

The door shut, locking away the noise. She breathed in shakily and resumed her sewing.

"It's so *quiet*," I marvelled.

"Meet my assistant." Samira gestured at an older, severe-looking man holding a book that he paid no attention to. If not for the white coat, I'd have pegged him as a patient.

"Ex-military. No formal medical training, but I improvise." He offered a nod in greeting.

"And we have two physical therapists and a trainee EMT volunteering."

"That's pretty good," I said, relieved.

The man nodded a second time. "If only it convinced Samira to take a break."

"You didn't sleep?" I asked her.

"I napped." She guided me into an open office so we could talk semi-privately. "What do you need?"

"My spinal implant…"

It took her a second. "Crap. How bad is it?"

"Not heart-attack bad. But not pleasant." I described it—pricking nerve pain, centred around my lower legs—and Samira frowned.

"Is that part of the spina bifida?"

"My doctors were never sure. Just one of those things."

"Well, I might have something mild to take the edge off. You'll have to ration it." She pointed a flashlight at a desk and started rifling through a stack of paper. "Dr Kring is recovering. If you still want to ask about your KAFOs, the physical therapists could help."

I hesitated. "They don't fit well. They might need readjustment."

"Did you lose weight?" Samira grimaced. "That's a silly question. I'll ask the physical therapists."

She found a form with my name on it and ran her index finger down the page, where her handwriting got increasingly squiggly to fit everything on. I assumed she was checking the information I'd given her to determine the medication, but the longer her finger paused at the bottom of the page, the less sure I was.

"Impressive list, right?" I said, an unsubtle prod.

"That's not it."

"Then are you thinking about how screwed I am?"

Her head dipped. I almost expected her to blush. "It's just—"

"Samira?" Military Guy stuck his head around the corner. "Breakfast arrived for the patients. I'll ask them to bring us some."

"No, I'll grab my own. Did they get the portions right?"

"Surprisingly, yes." He retreated again.

"Shouldn't be that surprising." Samira sighed to herself. "I gave specific instructions about everyone's needs. Anyway…" She looked back at the sheet.

"You were thinking about how screwed I am," I said helpfully. "Until yesterday, I'd have said my implant wasn't a concern, but that EMP proved me wrong. Instead, I get to worry about running out of whatever medication you give me. Or my cerebral shunt clogging and my hydrocephalus killing me with no one around to replace the shunt. Or being unable to disinfect my catheter and getting a UTI with no antibiotics around, or my KAFOs breaking with no one to repair them, or my scoliosis getting worse with no one around to build a brace."

The scoliosis was a best-case scenario. It meant there'd be time for it to get worse.

Samira seemed unsure of what to say. For a moment, I wanted to leave it at that. Make her feel even a fraction of my dread. Make her prove me wrong.

Then I just wished I hadn't said anything at all; it wouldn't make a difference.

I stood. "I should get my ID papers if I want breakfast. People are already queueing." In the time it would take to grab my ID, stow my cathing gear, and perhaps replace the sloppy clothes I'd used as pyjamas, I bet that line would grow twice as long.

"Come see me at noon. I'll have that medication, and I'll have talked to the physical therapists."

Noon. I could last that long, especially once I got some food in me. My stomach groaned in anticipation.

Samira hesitated. "Do you want to talk…?"

"I've had half a year to consider my odds." I gave a one-shouldered shrug. "We're all doomed. Some of us are simply more doomed than others."

The line for breakfast was huge. I thought it was just the number of people, but the closer I got, the more I realised it was something else: at the big counter between the hall and kitchen, volunteers were rifling through files the same way Samira had done.

"You're *kidding* me."

Manually looking up each individual. Checking their dietary needs and allowances. Marking off breakfast. For *hundreds* of us. No wonder it took so long.

Finally, after an hour and a half, I managed to walk away with an apple, a protein bar, and vitamin-boosted water, and thumped onto my bed where Vera and Ginta waited in the near-dark.

"Sorry. I got in line late." It was nice switching back to Latvian. I bit down, savouring the apple's sweet, sticky freshness. Maybe I should have eaten the protein bar first, get something solid in, but actual flavour couldn't be beaten.

"You said you had a song in mind? From your album, or…?" Vera looked at me with eager eyes.

"Something newer." Bite, chew, swallow. Even the needling in my legs felt less urgent. "I performed it on the way here."

"Wish we could've seen those concerts," Ginta said wistfully.

"Now you'll be in one." I reached into my bag for a few torn pieces of paper. I'd jotted down lyrics with a stubby pencil. I put them under the light Ginta was holding. "Here's the chorus. I need back-up voices for this part, and this… Vera, did you get those drums?"

"The kitchen gave me some containers. Not the same, but I can build a rhythm." Excitement coloured her cheeks. "I only played in the school band so far. Backup."

"Can you do something like this?" I hit my thighs with flat palms, creating a quick rhythm that was a pale imitation of anything my old band could've done. The thwacks doubled as welcome distractions from the pain, numbing my skin for half-moments.

Vera mimicked the rhythm on her own thighs, nodded.

"Okay, so the English chorus goes like…" I sang a fast version, emphasising the key line, which was in spiteful-enough-to-spit Latvian: "*But you made up your mind, one look was enough*—Ginta, can you sing that line, but kind of quieter…"

Ginta mimicked me. It took a few tries to get the right tone. It wasn't the way I'd done it originally—more subdued—but her quieter version made the line all the more venomous.

"Yes! That, *that*!" I bounced from excitement, my apple nearly rolling from my lap. I'd almost forgotten about it. I took another bite, my mind working overtime to incorporate Ginta's approach into the rest of the song. I missed my producer for a fierce second, but shoved that feeling into a dark corner alongside the stabbing in my legs and my maybe-headaches and the thought of home.

"So, first refrain. Originally, I had it like this." I launched into the old version, but didn't get far.

"Do you mind?" someone hissed in English.

The sisters turned as one. "Sorry, we'll keep it down," Ginta said.

The man shone his flashlight from a few beds away. I squinted at the glare. "How can you be singing at a time like this?"

"You're welcome." I planned to say more, but clenched my jaw as sudden pain jolted through my right calf.

"Have some respect. We're trying… trying…"

"I'm glad you girls are having fun," a neighbouring woman pitched in, "but this isn't the time."

"We'll go somewhere else," Vera said.

I'd have given them the finger, so I guessed it was a good thing Vera got there first.

At noon sharp, I knocked on the medical bay entrance. The door opened, revealing that military guy from this morning. He looked wary. "Yeah?"

I peered past him. More people sat upright than last time, and some beds were empty. "Samira said I should come by."

One patient—a woman Mum's age—laughed weakly. "Samira?

Good luck with that." She sat on the edge of a high stretcher, a flickering candle beside her and a loose-leafed paperback in her lap.

I stepped inside. "What do you mean?"

"She's just talking to her fiancé," Military Guy said.

"Pft. Samira'll be gone the moment that fiancé finds a shelter with electricity." The woman's English was solid—smoother than mine—but I detected an accent I couldn't place. "I overheard them talking, you know. He went outside."

"Outside?" I said. Outside was ruination. The dust cloud was so thick you'd need an air filter to breathe. The minimal shaking we'd felt would have had far worse results topside. It was only another twenty-four hours before the shelter was supposed to empty out, but anyone sensible would make of those twenty-four hours what they could.

I planned to.

"To find *help*," Military Guy said.

"You think she wouldn't stay gone? Find a shelter with fresher air, lights that work, hot food? Fewer refugees, pre-starved, pissed off, and needy as hell?" She gestured at herself and sneered. "Ha!"

"You need to lie down and stop talking nonsense." Military Guy pointed at the patient. "At least you're getting stronger."

"Damn right."

"'Cause of Samira. She hassled a lot of people to get you that diet. So have faith, will you? And *you*." He turned his pointed finger at me. "Samira got your meds ready."

"How fast do they work?" I asked. "I'm giving a show—tomorrow morning, right before we leave."

The woman laughed, but Military Guy only shook his head. "Follow me."

I didn't feel pre-show jitters the way I used to. Perhaps it was the medication. It felt like lying down after a long day on tour, finally letting my muscles relax. No frantic back-and-forths, no triple-checking my equipment, no peeks at the audience.

That would've been difficult, anyway: only a handful of people knew we planned to perform in an hour.

"It's almost nice, knowing no one gives a damn," I told Vera and Ginta. We each had a container-turned-drum in our laps and were scribbling on them with black markers. Professionalism was too much to aim for, but we could at least avoid advertising frying oil and salted peanuts. While Vera and I went for all-black containers, Ginta clamped hers between her knees and used her one arm to black out the logo and draw elaborate patterns on the remaining white areas. Her shoulder kept jolting forwards when the container shifted, as if to reach for it, but she didn't say a word.

"Are you sure no one…" Vera's words faded.

Our flashlight was trembling. Just a quiver. I wouldn't have noticed if the light beam didn't amplify the movement. Another quake? I thought they'd tapered off by now.

The flashlight's trembling worsened. It skittered sideways across the table, a gentle *rat-rat-rat*. Across the room, something fell. A muted sound rumbled in the far distance.

"Are earthquakes this constant?" Vera asked.

"At least we're holding up okay," I said. Others seemed to come to the same conclusion; some had rushed to their cots and families, but most were talking in curious tones.

Ginta looked at the ceiling. "I wonder what it'll look like later. Outside."

"Did you hear?" Vera said. "The doctor's boyfriend and two others got special permission to scout outside. They weren't supposed to tell anyone, but I heard—"

"I heard a hundred different things," I cut in. The ground was covered in rocks and dirt, no, the ground was cracked all over; not a single building remained upright, no, they were still standing, just broken skeletons; it was pitch dark, no, it was gloomy, no, you could see by the lightning storms and wildfires—

We'd find out in a few hours. That was soon enough.

I went back to scribbling on my container. "Let's just get ready."

Forty minutes later, a woman from shelter management climbed atop a table and asked us to gather round. "Nearly fifty minutes ago," she said, "we had to lock down the central air vents. Because…"

The room was mouse quiet. I sat upright, stretching as though it would let me hear her better.

"Because salt water was coming in via the vents." She cleared her throat. "The dunes and dikes must have given in. We're under—"

I couldn't hear the word "water" in the sudden screams.

But I didn't need to.

The good part was that we were no longer leaving the shelter that day.

The bad part was everything else.

We huddled together near the sisters' and their mother Inga's cots, clutching our few possessions tight as the shelter blurred in panic.

"Please!" someone shouted every few minutes. "Go to your beds and *wait*!"

"How long will the air last?"

"How much water are we talking about? Can we get to higher ground?"

Inga shook her head in disbelief. "Higher ground? Half this country is below sea level."

"How long are we *staying*? Is there enough food?"

"We'll have to ration even—"

"Is anyone coming?"

"Is it the entire coastline? My brother's in—"

"The oxygen!"

"Do the permanent shelters know? Does the government—"

"*Government*." Mum barked a laugh. "As though there still is one."

"There is," I said, "in those ships and shelters."

For all those screaming for answers, there were enough families just like us. Clustered together, quiet, nervous. A teen boy and his little brother leaned into each other. Their mum squeezed the younger boy's shoulder so tight it had to hurt.

I thought of the rations, barely sufficient to sustain and never enough to satisfy. Of candles shrinking into stubs, of flashlights starting to flicker. Only devices that ran on body heat would last.

We could ration flashlights. We couldn't ration air.

"Below sea level," Mum scoffed, "and they build underground shelters? How are we supposed to reach dry land? How far *is* dry land?"

"Tens of kilometres. A hundred? We don't know how far the water went." Dad shook his head. "We knew the risks when we decided to go the Netherlands."

Given the certainty of debris and earthquakes and the sun disappearing behind dust, we hadn't worried about the relatively slim chance of a flood—even then, it'd been worth being so far from the impact site and any volcanoes or fault lines. No other country would've taken us, besides. France and Switzerland had closed their shelters to refugees, so once we'd realised we couldn't reach England, it was too late to risk going south.

I supposed being stuck inside with limited food was better than being stuck outside where we'd need to scavenge for any food at all. But at least outside, there was a chance in the long run.

In here, there wasn't.

From the eyes of those two boys and their mother, I could tell they'd come to the same conclusion.

I abruptly stood. "Let's get ready."

My parents looked up.

"To leave?" Vera said.

"Nope."

Ginta had been talking to her mum in soft tones, but now glanced sideways. "You're joking."

"I'm not. Vera, where'd you leave those containers?"

Our audience-to-be had the same idea as Ginta.

Not at first. At first, they didn't even realise what was happening. But by the time we'd shoved a handful of similar-sized tables together to form an impromptu stage, climbed up, and Vera started hitting the containers, "you're joking" seemed to be the general impression.

Vera led us in, starting with a slow rhythm.

I wished I had a microphone to dramatically grab. Instead, I stepped forwards. My foot came down hard on the table. I raised my voice, kept it harsh and even for the intro, with Ginta providing a background hum.

Three times last night I woke

Three times last week I cried
Three times last month I fought
Three times in life I nearly died

A single slap on a container for emphasis. People were staring, grimacing, disbelieving. "Get off there!" someone called. I called back:

But: one too-short skirt I wear
and you know all there is to know
Nah: two crutches in my hands
and you know there's nothing left to know

"The hell is wrong with you?"

I missed amplification; an outfit that had been washed at any point in the past weeks; fans' joyful screams.

Here's what I had, though: those two boys staring, transfixed; Ginta backing up the next verse; my *own* screams.

Afterwards, I collapsed onto the nearest chair. "I miss my wheelchair," I huffed.

"No one's clapping." Vera stared at the audience. Most people had started ignoring us halfway through.

Ginta leaned against the table. "That was so cool."

"You were awesome. Both of..." I trailed off. My parents were elbowing through the still-anxious crowd towards us. Two others did the same: the woman who'd given the announcement earlier, and Ahmed, Samira's brother-in-law. Neither looked happy.

"Did you like the show?" I asked innocently.

"That was *not* appropriate," the woman said.

"I made sure the language was fine for kids. Can't people use a distraction?"

Ahmed eyed me sharply. "Keeping order in a place like this is difficult enough without"—he gestured at the tables—"*this*."

"Especially after news like today's!" the woman added. "Any other time would've been fine, but this... this was..."

"Don't do it again," Ahmed said.

* * *

"We're doing it again, right?" I asked the sisters in line for lunch the next day.

Things had quieted down since the announcement that the water levels had stabilised and our air vents were no longer underwater.

We had air. But we were just as stuck, and just as hungry. The flood had left something tense and restless and scared in the atmosphere. It was one thing to wait—it was another thing to wait without knowing what you were waiting for, without knowing when or if or how it would even come.

I wanted to do more than *wait*.

"We totally are." Vera nodded vehemently. "Yesterday was great, but we can do better."

"You just want applause," Ginta teased.

My head snapped up at a commotion further down the line. Not that we had a "line"—more of an uncoordinated mess of people, with those who'd already gotten their food disappearing into a hall on the right, and everyone else pressing closer to the counters where volunteers were putting marks by our names and handing out our rations.

Near those counters, people were pushing and shouting. The rest of us surged back. I grabbed Vera to steady myself. There had been other scuffles—mostly people mad at others cutting in line—but the handful of volunteers standing on chairs and overlooking the hall kept an eye on those.

"'Scuse me? Sir?" I asked in English, tugging at the sleeve of the man ahead of us. "What's going on? We can't understand them."

"Nothing to worry about." He stared across the crowd with a frown. "I think there's a woman who got a different lunch from everyone else. They're saying she might've—ah—bribed people."

"I thought lots of people get different rations," I said. "If they have some sort of condition."

The man offered a sympathetic smile. "That might be it." He winced—as did the three of us—at a particularly loud shout. "But, well… they can't exactly get special meals once they leave, either. It's kind of a waste, isn't it?"

He turned back as the line surged forwards. I watched him fade into the crowd, and was still biting my lip when Vera said, "Same song, or did you have something else in mind?"

* * *

Afterwards, I spoke to Samira—who seemed glad to answer questions *other* than about what her fiancé had seen outside—and asked whether she'd be able to check for hydrocephalus better than my parents and I could.

"Not without equipment. Do you have a headache? Nausea?"

"Not really." I hesitated. "I wanted to know. In case."

"How's the pain?"

"Not gone, but *so* much better. But let's talk about something else"—I gave a quick drumroll and ba-*tish* on an imaginary drumset—"can I extend a personal invitation for my show later today?"

After a few hours of practice, we performed "The Yes and the No", which the sisters knew almost by heart, and which people in the hall knew, too. I assumed they did, anyway: some mouthed along, and others looked up, surprised, as though they'd heard their name being called.

"*Again?*" someone shouted. "Do you even realise—"

Conveniently, my next line had the word *jackass*. I placed extra emphasis on it.

I didn't know whether I expected applause this time. But when Samira—standing a dozen feet from the stage—started whooping and bouncing at the end of the song, I couldn't help a crooked smile.

Others hesitantly joined in. A few claps. A shout, "*Nice!*"

One person called out, "Are you that singer from Lithuania?"

"Latvia!" I shouted back. "And damn right I am. So are these two!" I swept an arm at Vera and Ginta.

Samira put her hands by her mouth and let out another whoop, though that wasn't enough to distract me from a pissed-off Ahmed stalking closer. He threw up his hands. "Come on. We asked you—"

"—to not perform right after bad news." I let Mum help me climb down. "You *did* say any other time would've been okay."

"Will you perform again?" While my parents and I stood in line for dinner, a lanky woman by Dad's side had kept glancing over. It looked like she'd finally scrounged up the courage to say something.

"You think we should?" I asked. My publicist would've been proud. *Turn back the question, keep your fans involved.* If I weren't stuck with a hundred others in a sweat-stenched, candlelit hall, waiting for a meal that would've barely passed as a healthy snack last year, I'd almost have felt like I was backstage in the Arēna Rīga again, signing autographs for eager fans.

"It's not really my kind of music. It's not bad… just… just young. But my daughter was in line for the bathroom at the time, and she was so mad she missed it."

"We'll do another one," I promised.

"Oh! She'll be thrilled. Let us know when?" She gave the location of their cots. "I'm Mandy, by the way."

"Line seems to be moving faster," Dad observed, in English so as to not be rude.

Mandy nodded, glancing from him to me as if confirming we were together. "They split things up. Parents with young kids have a separate line. So do people with different diets. And I think they asked anyone over fifty-five, or who can't handle crowds, to wait until after eight thirty to get in line."

"About time they figured that out," Dad said.

"'Can't handle crowds'? Oh, come *on*," a woman on the other side of Mandy scoffed. "I heard they're even delivering special meals to the med bay."

"Well, people are in there for a reason." Mum scrunched up her nose. "I heard there was a fight at lunch about a different diet. That must be why they split us up."

"It's such nonsense. Special diets? Come on. It's the end of the damn world. If even one percent of us ends up surviving, I'd call it a win."

I was glad to be hidden from the woman's sight behind my parents. She was right, of course. That was the whole problem.

She was right.

Dad didn't seem so convinced. Before he could say anything, the woman continued, on a roll. "I don't like it either, but you *know* those people will die within a week of setting foot outside. A day! What's the point in coddling them? We don't have enough food for everyone. We should set priorities, right? Focus on people with half a chance of surviving? I mean, look at those sick girls wasting energy on silly teen music—like there aren't more important—"

"Sick?" Dad said.

Silly? I mouthed.

Mandy stepped back, as if out of the line of fire.

"Well, you know! One of them was missing her arm. Another one, she could barely walk, and her shoulders were all…" I imagined the woman dropping one shoulder to form an uneven line.

"Stop talking," Mum said.

"I'm not saying—they're just teenagers, it's not like they *deserve* what's gonna happen, but we should be realistic—"

"No," Dad said. "Stop. *Talking.*"

Mum gripped my shoulder tight. I wanted to listen to her for once. Hide, not get involved, and not replay those words over and over.

Instead, I shoved past her until I could look the woman in the eye.

She froze.

"We're doing another show tomorrow. You should come. We all deserve some music before we die." I snapped my fingers. "Wait, you'll be with that surviving one percent, right? *So* sorry, your highness, truly. Didn't mean to lump you in with food hogs like me. Really, I ought to be lying down and dying for your convenience."

"I wasn't—" She seemed torn between apologising and digging in further. "I'm just *pragmatic.*"

"And that makes it okay. I completely understand." I offered her a spiteful-sweet smile. "I'm gonna enjoy wasting this meal on my crippled ass *so* bad."

That night, Mum and I bowed over my bare legs, holding a candle close.

I always had to check for injuries I might not feel, but normally, I did it in the privacy of my shower seat. Perhaps I should've cared that a hundred people could turn to see me half-nude on the bed; once, I would have. I'd have felt insecure over skinny, ghost-pale legs, over my KAFOs' imprints, over being unable to stand.

Now, I stared across the hall and idly thought, *I wonder where they got the supplies for that mural.* All across one wall stretched wild blotches of deep green forest. The rays of a setting sun cut between the trees, lighting up rough earth. Still-wet paint glistened in the candlelight.

"There's a cut here." Mum tapped the back of my calf.

I ran my fingers over it. A faint feeling of pain registered, almost like a bruise.

"You should get that doctor girl to disinfect it."

We finished checking the rest—nothing—then Mum grabbed the KAFOs again. With one of them in hand, she paused. She turned it over, fiddled with the knee joint. "What that woman said… in line for dinner."

I was still studying the mural. "She was charming, right?"

"You'll have it harder than most people once we leave, yes, but… it doesn't mean that…" Mum chewed her lip, for once at a loss for words.

"I know you won't make promises you can't keep." I finally tore my eyes away, taking the KAFO from Mum. "Thanks."

"I just *hate*…"

I'd had a lifetime of people looking at me in horror or pity or with too-friendly smiles, or trying hard to not look at me at all. Only the occasional person would lean in and confide: *I couldn't deal. I'd kill myself if I were you. How do you do it?*

That meant only the occasional person was misguided enough to say it to my face. Didn't mean no one else had that same thought, talking with their friends over dinner: *You know, if it were me…*

The woman's words weren't news to either of us. She was just the only person in the shelter to say it out loud.

I looked past Mum at a dozen whispering families clustered together in their beds.

"I know," I told her.

"You're doing *what*?"

"Shh, shh!" Samira looked into the main med bay to see if I'd woken anyone. "You'll be fine without me. Dr Kring is still weak, but he's sharp enough to give advice."

"Go back to the part where you're leaving the shelter tonight. I thought outside was—"

"Parts of the shelter—like the air vents—reach above the water level. We can exit safely."

"*Safely!* Nothing about that is safe!"

"The shelter has an inflatable raft. Ahmed has a hunch where we can find even better transport. If we reach other shelters, we can trade for food, flashlights—"

"They might've been badly shielded too. And they'd be just as stuck. Why would they have *food* left?"

"They could have working radios," Samira insisted.

"Radios." I blinked. Damn it—she was right. "Why you?"

"Because I won't let my fiancé go alone. And because we need to be able to trade something—like medical assistance."

"Well… you'll miss our next show."

Samira laughed and held up a medical spray. "Haul up your pant leg."

Word spread quickly.

By mid-afternoon the next day, everyone knew the following things:

Three people had killed themselves.

The med bay had been raided by someone convinced they had a food stash.

A young couple had left the shelter to seek help.

Those Latvian girls had another performance at five o'clock, in the sitting hall behind the kitchen.

"I don't know about this," Ginta said. "Maybe they're right. Is it in poor taste?"

Vera shook her head. "You kidding? Look, people are already staking out spots. It might be their last chance to see a show. Besides, we're not the only ones performing. I saw these fifteen-year-old twins doing magic tricks for the kids, and a woman in the hall across sang opera this morning."

"Was it any good?" I asked.

"*Awful*," Vera said. "Just awful."

I smiled.

"Why the smile? Less competition?"

"It's… just nice to picture."

"Maybe we inspired her." Vera beamed. "See. Helping."

"You just want applause." Ginta sounded quietly annoyed.

"If I do," Vera said, "it's 'cause applause is a good indication that people are happy."

"It's fine if you just like applause, too," I said. "Any reason is fine."

"I don't even know mine." Ginta played with her empty sleeve. "I didn't have anything else to do. Is that awful? I enjoyed it, really, I just—"

"You're *good*," Vera said. "You really are."

I nodded. "You are. But if you weren't…"

Ginta glanced over.

"That opera singer didn't let it stop her, either."

Ten minutes before the show, Ahmed pulled me aside to speak with the woman from management.

"You can't cancel us," I said. "People are excited. We prepared a whole new song—"

Ahmed shook his head. "No, no. We need your help. You heard about what happened last night?"

"The med bay break-in?"

"Among other things. We were supposed to have left days ago. We're stretching food we barely have. We thought… you mentioned public speaking. You could help with an announcement about the rations. We won't last the way we've been going."

Eyes ceilingwards, the woman said, "We're not lasting anyway unless your brother finds help." She looked back at me. "An announcement would look better coming from—"

Ahmed cut her off with a glare.

"You could help," she amended.

I frowned. "I'm supposed to tell everyone they'll be even hungrier… so they won't get pissed at *you*?"

"That's not it." She hesitated. "People are agitated. There are fights, break-ins. The meal lines take forever. We're not simply cutting back, we're streamlining: everyone will get the same."

"What?"

"You wanted to keep people calm, right? Making exceptions doesn't help. It's not fair to everyone else. These shelters were built on a principle of equality—"

I laughed, short and high-pitched. The shelters' very existence proved the opposite. "I'm sorry. Okay, let's ignore anyone who's already underfed, ill, or injured, has diabetes or anaemia… I'm with you."

"Look, we can't help—if they—everybody should receive the same treatment."

"Except it's not the same if it hurts some but not others, is it? But I said I'm with you. *Do* go on."

Her lips pressed together. "Do you want to actually help? Or just keep yelling from atop a table?"

I stared at her long and hard. "You can come on stage after the show. But I'm *not* making your announcement."

Ginta dropped out. "I can't focus. I'm sorry. I'll cheer really loudly, though."

Vera would take over for the few lines that needed backing vocals the most. Her voice wasn't as good as Ginta's, and she was overexcited, rattling off the lines too fast.

"Don't worry about that, okay?" Mum said before helping me on stage. "People won't even notice."

"I wasn't worried," I said.

"Oh. Forget I said anything, then."

"Is that weird?" I wondered suddenly. "We're doing this for them. Shouldn't I care more about what they think?"

"Are you?" she asked. "Doing it for them?"

At a loss for an answer, I let her help me onto the table.

"Go. Kick ass," Mum said. "And enjoy."

On stage, Vera and I looked out at the crowd. A few dozen people stood near the tables. Even behind them, people had gone quieter than usual. Many looked up with interest.

I took a deep breath. "Shelter management has an announcement after the show. Stick around."

A few people murmured to each other. Vera was eyeing me, waiting for the signal—a flick of my hand—to begin. Previously, we'd dived right in.

I didn't give the signal. "So… some of you were already familiar with my music. A lot of you probably didn't want to be, but were stuck in the room yesterday. Hope you're converts now. P.S., buy my album."

Scattered laughter sounded at the back of the room.

"Yes, thank you. That was, indeed, a joke." I gestured at a laughing person, who might've been Ginta. "If you listened to the lyrics—I promise it's not *just* yelling—you'll know where I stand on the idea of equality." I sought out the woman from management in the crowd. When our gazes locked, I offered a nod.

She nodded back, encouraging.

"Equality means that… even if we're not the same, we get the same chances.

"But here's the thing. People like me, or like those in the med bay—I'm not confident about our survival chances. I know you aren't, either." I shifted my weight. "You can't promise us we'll live. I get that. But you *can* promise us that, if we *don't* survive, it's not 'cause you didn't give us an equal chance. It's not 'cause you sped it along."

My parents were restraining the management woman from coming towards me. My chin jutted out. A grin spread across my lips. I didn't know if my words would change the rations, if they would rile people up further, if they would make any difference at all.

What I did know was this: "I'm not writing us off."

I gave a flick of my hand and plunged us into music.

THE LAST CHILD

SCOTT SIGLER

Scott Sigler is a #1 *New York Times* bestselling author and creator of fifteen novels, six novellas and dozens of short stories. He gives away his stories as weekly, serialized, audiobooks, with over 40 million episodes downloaded. Scott launched his career by releasing his novels as author-read podcasts. His rabid fans were so hungry for each week's episode that they dubbed themselves the "Junkies." He is also a co-founder of Empty Set Entertainment, which publishes his Galactic Football League series and manages Scott's multimedia projects. He lives in San Diego, CA, with his little dog Reesie.

O. Vanev rests on one knee, ripped black coveralls exposing his torn skin to the cold, wet jungle floor. His blood mixes with the endless mud. He can't stop coughing. He is exhausted. His chest heaves, every breath drawing in a lungful of smoke-tainted air. He and the others stopped in a small clearing. Around them, Omeyocan's jungle burns, beautiful yellow leaves crisping to nothing, brown tree trunks crawling with orange flame, blue vine stems wiggling from the heat as if they are animals writhing in pain. Fire chases away the night, makes the clearing as bright as day.

His arms ache. He rests his rifle against a tree trunk. He doesn't want to hold the weapon anymore.

He doesn't want to kill anymore.

Ash fills the air, blowing with the fire-driven wind. Smoking, glowing embers drop all around, a demonic rain that sizzles against the mud in some places, starts new fires in others.

Over the roar of a jungle ablaze, he hears the sound of rockets—the sound of death.

O. Vanev is a boy with no past.

When he first woke, he thought it was the morning of his twelfth birthday. The others thought the same thing when they woke, when in truth, the day they woke was the first day of their lives.

He is one of the Birthday Children. His sole purpose? To be a blank slate, to have his mind overwritten by his progenitor so that his progenitor could be young again, could walk freely on the paradise promised by a prophet long since dead.

Vanev and the others spent centuries in stasis, enclosed in "husks" that kept their slumbering bodies healthy. He was nothing but a hunk of meat and bone. Never meant to act, to think, to *live*.

Em Savage changed that. She woke the sleepers.

Vanev knows little of his past, almost nothing of the culture that spawned him. He doesn't even know his first name. Some people have remembered theirs, but not him. All he knows is the letters engraved on the base of his husk: *O. Vanev.*

In the brief year since that husk opened, he has become his own person, living alongside his fellow Birthday Children. Together, they learned. They trained. They *fought*.

At first, Omeyocan was anything but paradise. Poisons in the water, in the food, in the very air itself. And from the beginning, war with the Springers, the intelligent race that had lived in the jungle long before humans arrived.

Lethal threats on all sides.

Many had died.

But the Birthday Children endured. They persevered. They made peace with the Springers. They neutralized the jungle's poisons. They tamed the planet.

For a few, precious months, Omeyocan had been what the prophet had promised—paradise. The Birthday Children settled in Uchmal, a sprawling, walled fortress city filled with massive buildings and ancient, towering ziggurats. They drove the predators from the surrounding jungle, leaving a vast, lush hunting ground teeming with game. They turned large plots into farmland.

Paradise promised… paradise *made*.

But it proved to be short-lived.

Perhaps it ended when the hatred began. Silent, invisible threads spreading through human and Springer alike, causing fighting, violence… murder. Or, perhaps paradise ended with the coming of the aliens, called from across the void by that same unseeable hatred. Called to fight, to kill… to destroy.

The alien ships had launched a devastating aerial assault, hurling a barrage of burning boulders that smashed centuries-old buildings, that left gaping, rubble- and corpse-filled craters all across Uchmal.

Then came the aliens themselves, fighter craft streaking through the skies, sowing death as drop ships poured armored infantry into the city streets.

Em led the Birthday Children to a bitter victory, clearing the city of enemy soldiers, only to find that the Uchmal attack had been a distraction. Tanks, artillery and tens of thousands of alien troops had landed deep in the jungle.

An overwhelming force that marched toward the city, killing anything and everything in its path.

The rocket roar is already fading.

Above the blazing tree line and billowing black smoke that blocks any view of Uchmal, O. Vanev watches a cluster of lights streak high into the dusk sky. Three larger lights, rising rapidly, heading for the stratosphere, chased by a dozen smaller lights. The three larger lights: the ships of his people, deserting the planet. The smaller lights: enemy fighters giving chase.

He knows what this means. He doesn't know if B. Bureau, Y. Pajari and B. Marija truly understand, but reality will hit them soon enough.

Four people, barely into their second year of actual life, and they are all as good as dead.

Physically, they are all thirteen years old.

None of them will see fourteen.

"They're leaving," Bureau says. "How can Em leave us?"

Bureau's young face is streaked with ash and mud, flecked with bits of dead leaves. He holds a hatchet in his right hand. His left hand holds nothing—it's burned to a glistening, blistered, red and black claw that he keeps close to his chest. Haunted, empty eyes. In the last four hours, Bureau has faced death. He has killed.

All of them have killed.

They've watched their friends die horribly, screaming for someone to save them, screaming for mothers and fathers they have never known.

Vanev wonders if he will scream the same way when the Wasps come for him, when one of their bullets punches through him, like the one that killed S. Eadburg, or when one of their knives drives into his heart, like the one that killed J. Nikole.

Will he cry out for his mother? He never met her. Or his father. He doesn't even know what they looked like. He has only a vague sense of their existence, shadowy memories that refuse to crystalize.

Because they aren't *his* parents. Not really. They are the parents of his progenitor, a person that travelled for a thousand years to reach this place. Vanev is a copy of that person; Vanev is a *receptacle*. He was never meant to live at all.

But none of it matters now—Em has abandoned them.

"We need to move," Marija says. "The Wasps will be hunting for us."

Marija's mud-covered face makes her eyes seem shockingly white. She holds one of the strange Wasp rifles in her arms; it looks far too large for her teenage body. Before the battle began, she covered herself in mud and ash—both on the exposed skin of her face and hands, and all over her black coveralls—then wrapped herself in the blue vines, camouflage that let her fade into the jungle. The mud and ash mostly covers the circle-star symbol embedded in her forehead. That symbol signifies she was bred for war, engineered for bloodshed.

Vanev has a different mark on his forehead: a plain circle. Y. Pajari and B. Bureau have the same symbol. They are all *Empties*—engineered to *work*, not *fight*—yet Em gave the Empties weapons, sent them into the streets and the jungle to battle the invaders.

Because *everyone* had to fight.

Is Em on one of the shuttles streaking for orbit? Probably.

She gave the order, the order that Vanev and the others followed, yet she is undoubtedly alive.

Alive, because she ran.

"They *left* us," Bureau says, his voice cracking, maybe from the smoke, from the pain, or from puberty. "It's all over. We're dead."

Bureau gets it. Will Marija and Pajari? Or will Vanev have to explain it to them?

The enemy is overwhelming. They have more weapons, more soldiers and more technology.

Em knew this was a battle that could not be won. The only way for the Birthday Children to survive was to flee Omeyocan, abandon the very planet they had been created to live upon.

The shuttles in the city center hadn't been ready for evacuation. Vanev and the others—everyone, really, who wasn't involved in prepping the shuttles—had marched into the jungle to fight the aliens.

Em had called it a "delaying tactic." The goal of the battle wasn't to win; it was to slow the enemy long enough for the shuttles to fuel up, to load supplies and people, then leave Omeyocan behind forever.

The shuttles were the only way off the planet.

Now they were *gone*.

Bureau was right; it was over. Only one question remained—how long would Vanev and the others survive? On a planet overrun by alien soldiers, in a jungle ablaze, he knew the answer: not long.

"Em will come back for us," Pajari says, her voice so weak Vanev can barely make out her words over the flames and the rockets and his own coughing.

Pajari is on the ground, one hand clutching her bloody stomach. An hour ago, maybe more, maybe less, a Wasp artillery round had hit a tree, sending out an explosive hail of wood shards that killed two people. One shard had punched into Pajari's belly. She was still alive… but for how much longer?

"Em will come back," Pajari says again, staring up at the tiny lights steadily vanishing into the night sky. "She promised."

Em promised no such thing. Her orders had been simple: fight hard, slow the Wasps down, and when the retreat signal sounded, get back to Uchmal as fast as possible.

Vanev and the others had heard the signal. They'd retreated as ordered, but had been slowed by Pajari. She had to be carried, each step causing her to cry out in pain. Then they'd run into several Wasp stragglers. The brief firefight had caused another delay. When the four Birthday Children finally killed the stragglers, they'd rushed for the city—only to find a massive blaze blocking their way. A spreading wall of flame too thick to go *through*, instead they'd desperately tried to go *around*.

One delay too many.

"Wasps control this area," Marija says. "We have to move away from the city, hide deeper in the jungle."

Somewhere in the shimmering flames, the crack of a falling branch, the *whoosh* of a burning weight hitting the ground. The air grows hotter by the second. Vanev is sweating. Soon this small clearing will be surrounded by fire.

He coughs again. It hurts. Something wrong in his lungs. He's breathed in too much smoke.

"No," Pajari says. "We have to stay near Uchmal. They'll come back for us."

Marija looks to the clearing's edges, searching the flames for any sign of the enemy. She's coughing, too; not as bad as Vanev is, but the smoke is getting to her.

"Ammo check," she says. "Sound off."

Pajari doesn't have a gun. Neither does Bureau—his only weapon is the hatchet.

Vanev looks at his rifle, still leaning against the tree. How many rounds did he fire? He closes his eyes, trying to remember the firefight with the Wasp stragglers. He knows he hit two. One died instantly. The other had taken a round in the chest. Too weak to fight back, it had made strange noises as Vanev hammered its head with the rifle butt, hitting it over and over again, continuing to smash the broken pulp until Bureau had grabbed him, yanked him away. If not for Bureau, Vanev might still be back there, screaming, smashing, turning the strange alien flesh into yellowish paste.

"*Vanev!*"

He lurches, startled back into the moment. Marija is staring at him. "Ammo count," she says again.

He remembers firing eight times. "Two rounds left. No reloads."

Marija looks to the others.

"Pajari? Bureau? Any rounds on you? I know you dropped your weapons." Marija says *dropped your weapons* as if it is the greatest sin that could ever be.

Pajari says nothing. Bureau shakes his head.

"Then we need to search for Wasp weapons," Marija says.

Bureau laughs, a sound of desperation and dark humor.

"And the Wasps that are holding them? Give it up, Marija... we're dead."

"Then lay down and die for all I care," she says. "I'm going to live." She's trying to sound angry, but she sounds scared, just like everyone else.

Bureau gestures to the jungle that burns around them. The light of the flames plays off tears on his face, tears that cut lines through the dirt and grime clinging to his skin.

"And go *where*?" He snarls, frustration welling up, overtaking him. "Em *abandoned* us! We're going to die here. The Wasps are going to kill us!"

Marija slings her Wasp rifle. Two short steps take her to Bureau. He's taller than she is, but she's thicker, stronger. She grabs the shoulders of his black coveralls, clutches the fabric, gives the boy a solid shake.

"Shut up," she says. "Just *shut up*."

Bureau doesn't try to push her away; instead he puts his arms around her. The move surprises Marija—Bureau holds her tight, his body shaking with sobs.

Vanev doesn't know what Marija will do. The girl has killed so many Wasps in the last few hours that he's lost count. She killed some with her rifle, some with the folding scythe she carries in a hip holster. One she killed with her bare hands, strangling the alien's thin neck until it stopped kicking, stopped struggling, stopped moving.

Without Marija, Vanev and the others wouldn't have survived this long.

"Em didn't wait for us," Pajari says, as if the horrible truth is finally hitting home. She has barely enough strength to form words. "She… she left us."

Vanev coughs again, winces at the pain. The smoke grows thicker, the heat more intense. The entire jungle is ablaze, a chasm of fire separating the Birthday Children from their home.

But Uchmal isn't their home anymore.

Now it belongs to the Wasps.

The last of Pajari's energy drains away. She sags to her back, stares up at the darkening sky, her bloody hand still covering her ugly wound.

"They're gone," she says. "Why did they leave us? We fought. We fought hard."

Vanev stares at her, unable to hold back his disgust. *Why did they leave us?* Just as valid a question as *Why didn't we leave you?*

At the time, no one had thought to do so. Pajari was one of them. Birthday Children didn't leave their own behind. They'd scooped her up and continued on, continued fighting.

If Pajari hadn't been wounded, though, if they hadn't carried her, they would have moved much faster, maybe missed the Wasp stragglers, maybe gotten past the city walls before the fire spread.

Maybe they would have reached the shuttle in time.

Trying to save Pajari had condemned three others to death.

"They had to leave us," Marija says. "The city has fallen. They had to leave or they all would have died."

She still holds Bureau in her arms, perhaps not knowing what else to do with him. His sobs grow louder. Loud enough to draw in the Wasps that must still be out there, searching?

Still out there, *hunting*.

"Vanev," Pajari says, her words a whisper. "Can you signal Em? Tell her where we are so they can come back for us?"

Bureau's cries lower to a sniffle; he looks at Vanev, as does Marija. The three of them want an answer. They want hope.

Vanev has none to give.

"There is no way to contact the shuttle," he says, hearing a hollowness in his own voice.

Marija gently pushes Bureau away. She unslings her captured

enemy rifle, holds the big weapon in her hands, stares at Vanev.

"Unacceptable," she says. "Think of something. Fast."

Vanev feels lost.

They don't understand—Em will not come back for them. Em *can't* come back for them.

For a time, before they detected the incoming alien ships, Vanev studied science with the Gears. Just as Circle-Stars were engineered for war, Gears were engineered to know science. Vanev, an Empty, had studied with them, trying to be something he was not, something other than a servant. He had learned about stars, orbits, spaceships... so many things. Not that any of his knowledge mattered now—he would die here, dirty and bloody and sweaty and scared.

The only devices that *might* be able to contact the shuttle were inside Uchmal's walls, inside a city now controlled by thousands of Wasp soldiers.

Vanev can no longer hear the rockets. The last echoes have died away, drowned out by the roar of the orange demon that is devouring the jungle.

Pajari coughs, groans in pain. Bureau stands there, shaking. Marija glares, still waiting for an answer.

"You don't understand," Vanev says. "I'm trying to tell you—"

The crack of gunfire, the sound tiny against the fire's constant bellow. Tree trunks splinter, kicking out showers of shredded bark.

Marija turns and fires into the burning jungle, the big alien weapon kicking hard against her shoulder.

"Get Pajari, *run*," she screams, taking cover behind a thick tree trunk that is already smoldering, already crawling with small flames. She leans around the trunk, firing at an enemy only she has seen.

Vanev rushes to Pajari—but why? She has already cost them their lives. He knows he should run, he should leave her... but he cannot. Pajari is one of them.

She struggles to get to her feet, reaching one arm and pleading eyes toward him. There is no time to be gentle. Vanev throws Pajari over his shoulders, the way Marija taught him to do. Pajari screams in pain. Bullets smack into trees. Vanev can't tell where the enemy is, so he runs opposite the way Marija is shooting. He runs into the burning jungle, feeling the flames reach out to his hands, his face.

Pajari begs him to stop.

Vanev ignores her.

He has lived only one year. One single year. He does not want to die.

Over the flames, Vanev hears Bureau scream—with rage or fear, he does not know. Vanev focuses on moving forward, running through the flames as fast as he can while carrying Pajari's weight, searching for a path through the fire, for anywhere the orange monster has yet to touch.

Pajari stops screaming.

She goes limp.

Vanev runs.

His flesh begins to bubble. His flesh begins to burn.

To his left… the flames seem lower there. He runs that way, the pain starting to set in, to reach deep into his body.

He realizes he left his rifle. A distant part of him knows Marija will be angry with him.

He breaks into the clearing, only it's not a clearing—it's a crater. He falls forward. Pajari tumbles away. Vanev rolls once, dirt filling his mouth. He hits hard against the crater's bottom, broken tree roots jamming into his back.

Ash, mud, but no fire.

A Wasp artillery round must have hit here, kicking up a wave of dirt and rock.

His hands are on fire. He screams, expecting to see them ablaze. They are not. Red blisters dot his skin, growing larger even in the brief instant he looks at them. His face feels the same way—it, too, is surely blistering.

It burns. It burns *so bad*.

Pajari.

Vanev tries to push away the pain as he moves to his friend. She is the smallest of them. She is face-down in the mud. He flips her over—she is limp.

Her eyes stare out at nothing.

He presses his burned fingers against her neck.

There is no pulse.

Pajari is dead.

Fury fills him. He stands, stares down at her.

"We saved you. This is your fault!"

He kicks her body, once, twice, almost a third time before he realizes what he's doing.

Vanev falls to his knees.

Like Bureau, he starts to cry.

They did the right thing—they helped Pajari. Doing so cost them all that there is. They helped her; she died anyway.

And because of her, he, too, will die.

He can't hear Marija's weapon. He can't hear anything but the roar of the fire. Is Marija still alive? Is Bureau?

If so, they won't be for long.

All around the small crater, the dying jungle rages with flame.

He coughs, harder than ever before.

It's getting hard to breathe.

Smoke crawls down the crater's slope, an intangible beast oozing toward him.

Vanev can't stop coughing.

He tries to block out the burning pain in his hands and face.

He will not see fourteen.

He will not even see tomorrow.

He feels dizzy. The ground spins beneath him.

He falls to his back, staring up at the night sky, at the stars, wondering if Em and the others made it.

O. Vanev closes his eyes.

In his last moments, the world fades away, and a tiny shred of his past rises up from the darkness, a past that was never his.

Oscar. That's what the *O* stood for.

His name was *Oscar.*

Author's Note: This story is part of the Generations Trilogy, also by Scott Sigler. The series includes the novels *Alive*, *Alight*, and *Alone*. "The Last Child" takes place during a pivotal moment in *Alone*.

SO SHARP, SO BRIGHT, SO FINAL

SEANAN MCGUIRE

Seanan McGuire has released more than forty traditionally published works under both her own name and the pseudonym "Mira Grant" since the publication of her first book in 2009. She has won the Hugo, Nebula, Campbell, Alex, and Pegasus Awards, which is a very nice thing to be able to say. Seanan lives in the Pacific Northwest with her collection of cats, comics, and creepy dolls. If you need her, look to the nearest cornfield. She is always there. Waiting for your call.

They don't like bright light, and it's bright today, so bright that it's giving me the nagging edge of a headache. That's a good thing. Means until they hit the final stages, the middle of the day is as close to safe as it gets. We slept during the day for the first couple of months, like we had to shift our own internal clocks to match the monsters if we wanted to stay alive. I got over that pretty quick. If I'm going to die, I'd almost rather do it fast, with all the lights off, and never see it coming. They don't like water, either. When it rains—and it's been raining more and more as we move toward the wispy edge of winter—the streets are empty, and I can run down the sidewalk and see them watching sullenly from their hidey-holes, nothing but eyes in the dark, angry and yearning to lash out. They hate us. How they *hate* us, for the crime of being alive and uninfected.

They'd change both those things in a second if we let them. If we get careless. There was this song I heard once. A funny song, on one of my little brother's nerd radio shows. It was about the old Looney Tunes characters, about that coyote who always wanted to catch the roadrunner. He talked about all the times he'd lost, all the times he'd failed, and then he said—sang, I guess—"Remember that I have to win only once."

I remember.

I remember a lot of things I don't want to remember.

I remember my little brother—Danny, Danny, it's so hard to even think his name anymore, after everything that happened, after everything fell apart—sitting at the dinner table, talking too fast around a mouthful of mashed potatoes, trying to make us care about some stupid article he saw online. Bats in Arizona, he'd said. Rabid bats, and rabid coyotes, and rabid dogs turning on their owners.

"Whatever, Cujo," I said, and rolled my eyes, and Dad laughed, and I felt this hot pride in my chest, because I'd made our father happy and Danny hadn't, and sometimes that was what mattered. We weren't brother and sister—we were combatants in the same gladiatorial ring, both fighting for the prize of parental approval.

That night, I won and Danny lost, and I'd give anything to take it back, anything at all. Even my life. If I could just rewind the clock long enough to relive that one evening, to savor my food and smile at my brother and be his friend and his supporter, not his adversary, I'd take the consequences willingly.

But I can't. The world is broken, the world is *wrong*, and still we don't have time travel, or magic, or any of the other things the books used to say would come and save us. We just have the sunlight, and the rain, and the slow decay of everything that matters.

We just have the end.

I'm hungry.

It was easier before the power grid went down. Back then, I could flip a switch and play God, let there be light, let there be safe passage through the aisles of canned vegetables and shelf-stable legumes. I ate so many beans during the first few weeks that I was terrified I'd fart so loudly it would lead them right to me. Death by flatulence. Not a great thing to put on my headstone—not that I was ever going to get one. Graveyards are a thing of the past, of course. They're *smart*, the ones who used to be us, and they like to leave corpses in the places we're likely to go, propping them up against walls and stretching them across doorways.

Corpses carry all kinds of disease. Not just the big one. Lots of nasty things enjoy making a meal of human flesh, and if you breathe in too deeply around the dead, you're likely to join the legions of the lost in no time at all.

So first the stores filled up with dead bodies, and then the lights went out, and now every Target is a potential killing field, every Safeway is an abattoir, because there's no flashlight bright enough to keep them away forever.

I'm so hungry. I'm hungry, and I'm thirsty, and my head is killing me.

Someone has already done the hard work of smashing the store windows; glass glitters in the sun, tipped here and there with streaks of blood. I don't know if it's ours or *theirs*, which means I have to treat it all as an infection risk. The light stretches into the store, bright and buttery and inviting.

I can't see any food there, but that doesn't have to mean anything; maybe the shelves at the front have been picked bare, or maybe *they* pulled the food back, out of the light, to save it for themselves. They don't usually spend their days sleeping on linoleum, and why should they? They still have houses. They still have beds, and shelter, and walls to keep out the weather, the sun and rain. We accidentally created the perfect dens for our own destruction, and now those of us who are still *us* scavenge around the edges, trying not to be seen.

It's probably safe. It's *probably* safe. There's almost no chance someone is hiding in there, waiting to strike. Unless it's a hungry dog. They don't have homes anymore, and they're all infected, and they hide wherever the sun doesn't reach, at least until the final stages, when the anger and confusion and disorientation is finally enough to drive them out into the light.

I pull a rock out of my pocket, weighing it carefully in my hand before I fling it through the opening. It clatters on broken glass, rolling across the linoleum with soft thumping sounds until it comes to a rest against the base of a shelf. There are no other sounds. I start to step forward, and stop as a hand grabs my elbow.

Any contact is enough to make me freeze. I count to ten and there's no pain, no teeth in my shoulder or knife in my side. Slowly, I turn.

The girl behind me must have been pretty, twenty pounds and a bunch of showers ago. Now she's gaunt and filthy, like everyone else. *They* don't like water, but they got to keep all the showers, all the warm, comfortable bathrooms and soft, clean towels.

Nothing about this is fair.

"Wait," she mouths, and she isn't hurting me, so I wait, because everyone who isn't attacking is an ally now: that's the way you stay alive.

I wait, and all is silence, and I'm about to shake her off and follow my stone into the store when I hear it. It's a small sound. I might not have noticed it if I hadn't been standing in silence for so long.

The clap of a palm against a shelf, soft and moist and undeniably human, too high up to belong to a dog, too quick to belong to an unthinking creature.

Something in me deflates. The store isn't safe. "Thanks," I mumble, and I both mean it—I'm still alive, still uninfected, still *me*—and I don't, because part of me is waiting for the day when I slip. Remember that they have to win only once.

I can't give up. I can't surrender. For Danny. For the way he used to laugh in triumph when he unsnarled a particularly tough problem, for the way he was teaching himself how to code, for all the things he was never going to have the chance to do—for the way he tried to warn me, before everything went wrong, when we thought we'd have our entire lives to learn how to safely love each other, allies and adversaries and gladiators in the same ring, competing for the safe harbor of our father's affection. Because he didn't have this chance, I have to keep fighting, and fighting, and fighting, until something takes the fight away.

But I'm so tired. I'm so tired, and I'm so lonely, and sometimes I just want it to be over.

"Don't worry about it," says the unfamiliar girl. She looks me over, measuring, assessing. We're going feral, one day at a time, locked out of the civilized world our ancestors spent their lives creating. "You from this neighborhood?"

She's really a stranger, then, not just another neighbor I never took the time to know. "A couple blocks over," I say.

"It's not safe to stay so close to home."

I rankle at the faint disapproval in her tone. She's right, of course: we all figured that out fast. Most of my friends have run as far away as they could, seeking sanctuary in the unfamiliar. Unless something changes, I'll never know whether they made it.

Nothing's going to change. This is the world now. Danny saw it coming. Danny tried to warn me. Maybe there were other Dannys, older Dannys, Dannys in white coats with letters after their names, and maybe there's a bunker somewhere filled with scientists and government officials, all of them working around the clock to find a cure or a vaccine or something, some way for them to take the world back. Probably, even. My brother was special, but he wasn't unique.

I guess it should make me feel better to think that this isn't the way humanity ends. It doesn't. It just makes me more tired. What does it matter if there are still humans in a hundred years? Danny won't be there. My friends won't be there.

I won't be there.

"It's not safe to run, either," I say. "I don't know where to find food anywhere else. I don't know where to find shelter. Where are you from?"

"Hillsdale."

I blink slowly to muffle my surprise. Hillsdale is an hour's drive from here. "Do you have a car?"

"No."

Of course she doesn't have a car. Some of *them* have cars. They drive around at night, windows down, plates of bacon in their passenger seats, like anyone who's stayed alive this long is stupid enough to give it all up for a few strips of fried pig. If it still *is* pig.

It's been so long since I've seen a truck pull up behind any of the local grocery stores, and I know the shelves aren't being restocked, and the power's been out for weeks, so it's not like anyone still has a freezer full of squirreled-away supplies for a rainy day.

People are supposed to taste a lot like pigs. I bet we'd make pretty good bacon.

"So how did you…?"

"I walked." She looks at me defiantly. "I didn't want to stay where they knew me."

"Sorry."

"You shouldn't be here if this is where you're from. They *know* you. Unless…" She pauses, gives me a thoughtful look. "Orphan?"

That would be the easiest answer. If there's no one who can lure you in with a smile or a plate of bacon or the whisper of your name, you might be almost safe staying where you feel like you belong. Most of the people I see clustering in the brightly lit places are orphans. Some are self-made, but that doesn't change the word, only the way you got there.

I shake my head. "No. My father and brother are still in the house where I… where I used to live. I mean, they were last time I checked. My father was… he was one of the first around here. He's probably late-stage by now. My brother may be alone."

Danny always hated to be alone. My heart clenches at the thought.

The stranger looks at me, calculation in her eyes. "No one else is in there with him? Just your brother and your father, who's probably late-stage?"

"Yeah."

"So if we kill them, we could take the house?"

She says it so calmly, like it's the solution to all our problems. I stare at her, silent in my horror, and wonder how we got here. Will it really matter if we stay uninfected?

We're all going to wind up monsters anyway.

Danny stayed interested in the rabies outbreak in Arizona. It was always so hard to predict what would interest him, and once something did, he tended to grab and hang on as hard as he could, like learning everything there was to know about some new kind of robot or battery or disease would make it something he could control, something he didn't have to be afraid of. Sometimes he would come to my room, eyes grave behind his glasses, and try to explain it to me.

"Rabies is scary," he said.

I laughed at him. When I think about it now, it makes me sick. He was my brother—is my brother, no matter what else has changed—and when he tried to tell me something that mattered to him, I laughed. Maybe I deserve everything that's happened to me. Maybe I'm being punished for laughing.

But he should never have been punished that way.

I'd been laughing at him since we were little kids, since I'd been the first one to figure out that with Mom gone, Dad's love was all we had, and he didn't have enough for the both of us. Undaunted, Danny pressed on.

"Rabies is scary, but because it's only transmitted through fluid contact, it's never been scary enough to be a real threat. Even when we've had *bad* outbreaks, people could mostly stay safe by staying away from wild animals and seeking medical attention immediately if they thought they might have been exposed. Look at how often people decide not to vaccinate their dogs, even though a dog that gets infected will always have to be put down. It's stupid. It's short-sighted and it's stupid."

I sighed and pushed myself away from my desk. "What does this have to do with you being in my room on a school night? You didn't even knock."

"The bats in Arizona."

"Uh-huh. You keep bringing them up."

"There's this outbreak there—it's huge. Biggest one we've ever seen, and it's been affecting all sorts of other local animals, even ones whose owners swear that they never came anywhere near a wild animal. Researchers have been trying to figure out how this is happening, and they finally did." He paused dramatically.

Looking back, that should have been the moment when I realized how bad things were going to get. Danny always looked so happy when one of his obsessions came to a head. I think it was sort of like popping a mental zit for him. He poked and prodded at the problem until it was ready to blow, and then he squeezed it clean.

He didn't look happy that time. He looked scared, and small, and a little confused, like he couldn't understand how the universe could be this cruel.

"So?" I asked. "What is it?"

"It's airborne."

I frowned. "So? Everything's airborne. That's what makes a virus a virus."

"Not true. A lot of viruses are transmitted through fluids, or fomites, or other mechanisms. Ebola isn't airborne. Neither is herpes. Rabies has never been airborne before. That's how we could keep it under control, even a little bit. It's endemic in the mammals of North America. We've never been in a position to eradicate it. I don't think we ever *can*. It must have... it must have mutated somehow. It's spreading without actual contact."

"So?"

"So rabies is *bad*." He looked at me solemnly. He looked so small, and so young, and so afraid. "You know how in zombie movies, suddenly your friends aren't your friends anymore? Because they got a disease?"

"Yeah?"

"Rabies is sort of like that. It affects the brain. We don't know as much as we'd like about what it does in people, because when someone gets exposed we try to treat them as fast as we can, before they can get sick, but in animals, rabies causes paranoia, aggression, a fear of light, an aversion to water... and they can still do everything they could do before they got sick. A dog with rabies can still play fetch and remember how to use the doggie door. A person with rabies could probably still do anything a person without rabies could do."

"So it's like a zombie virus only people could still use tools?"

"Um," said Danny. "Yeah."

"Cool," I said, and I had never been more wrong about anything in my life, and I'll be paying for that word until I die. The whole world will. Danny already did.

My little brother was smart—*is* smart—but he didn't know everything, because no one knew everything, not then, maybe not even now.

He didn't know that the new form of rabies is only airborne when it's carried by canines: dogs and wolves and coyotes. Something about the mutation that makes it thrive in the lungs goes away when it gets into any other kind of animal. So the bats were sick because bats just get sick sometimes, and then the dogs got sick because rabies vaccinations were expensive and most people thought they were a waste of money, since how often is your dog *really* going to be at risk? And then, once the dogs were sick, they breathed on all sorts of other animals, raccoons and cats and other dogs and even people.

People couldn't make each other sick by breathing on them, but they could scratch, and bite, and spit, and that was enough. We thought we understood what rabies looked like. We thought it was all drooling and snarling and immediate, obvious rage. We thought it would stay far away, in Arizona, in someone else's house, in someone else's life.

Shows what we knew.

They're not zombies. They're not monsters. They're just people with a disease attacking their brains, a disease that makes them want to hurt the people they used to love. A disease that drives them away from the light and into the shadows, until it starts burning out their synapses. The late stages of the infection include coma, spasms, and eventually death, as everything gives way under the pressure of the viral load.

The last thing I remember from the radio before it went dead was a voice saying that we can wait them out, if we don't get caught, and don't get infected, and don't get breathed on by anything that's already sick. That voice...

It was a grownup voice, and I guess that's how it could be so wrong. Grownups get used to things staying the same. They believe in the status quo, and the status quo says that sometimes there's an outbreak, but it always goes away, and everything always goes back to normal.

It doesn't say that rats can carry rabies. Rats and squirrels and bats and a million small, furry bodies that move through the world unseen and unencumbered and unaware that everything has changed, is changing, will not change back. We're not going to have movie nights and taco nights and family nights anymore. We're going to have empty stores with broken windows and strangers watching us warily, wondering whether we have anything worth stealing.

We're going to have the end of the world.

The strange girl looks at me patiently, waiting for me to agree with her. And part of me, the part that used to pick fights with my brother for the sake of winning, almost does. Danny wouldn't want to live like this, it argues. Danny was always so gentle, so kind, and the last time I saw him, he nearly crushed my skull with Mom's old cast iron pan. This isn't him. I'd be setting him free. I'd be granting him peace.

The *rest* of me recognizes this for ableist bullshit. Danny doesn't want to be at peace. Danny didn't ask to get sick, but he's smart, and if he wanted this to be over, it would be. This strain of rabies makes people violent and paranoid. It doesn't make them incapable of committing suicide. Danny could end this any time he wanted to.

"My brother is in that house," I say. "I'm not going to hurt him."

"Why not? He'd hurt you. He wouldn't even stop to think about it." The girl scowls at me. "They're not *people* anymore. They're the walking dead."

"They're not," I say. "That would be too easy. They aren't zombies, they aren't monsters, they aren't invaders from space. They're people who got sick."

She pushes me, so suddenly that it catches me by surprise. I stagger a few feet back, toward the store with its broken windows and unknown, shadow-snarled dangers.

"They're people who think *killing* us is just fine because *we're* not sick," she snaps. "They're people who take everything and leave us with nothing. It'll be winter soon. What are we going to do when we're outside and it's snowing and we don't have any roofs over our heads or food in our stomachs or sunlight to keep us safe? We're all going to die out here. Exposure is something you die of."

"So find a different house," I say. "Find a house where the owners are already dead." Of rabies, or rabid people, or anything. Why you die doesn't matter. Only that you do.

"Other houses aren't safe. You can't know if someone's there until you check."

But a house with living people in it—living infected people, who would kill to defend what they'd claimed—was safe, as long as we knew how many people and where they were likely to be. Dad is probably late-stage, and Danny's just a kid. We could take him. We could take him, and I hate myself for even thinking about it.

He deserves to be comfortable for the last few months of his life. He deserves to have his own bed and his own things and to know that he's safe.

But I deserve those things too. It's not my fault he got sick and I didn't. It's not my fault the rabies is in him, changing him, making him hate me when he used to love me. The Danny from before wouldn't want me to be cold and hungry and afraid. I know he wouldn't.

The stranger touches my arm. Her face is understanding. It's probably a lie, but I want to be lied to right now. I want someone to tell me that it's all going to be all right.

"We can do it fast," she says. "He's just one kid. He'll go down easy, and you can bury him in the sunlight, and we can be safe for the whole winter. Don't you want to be safe?"

I look at her solemnly, and I think about all the times I didn't listen, and I nod.

I want to be safe.

I want that more than anything in the world.

Her name is Tess; she comes from farther away than I thought. She's been walking for weeks, sleeping where she can, always moving during the day, scavenging from abandoned gardens and unprotected fruit trees. She's tough and she's smart and she's not quite fearless, but she's fatalistic, which is practically the same. She's too good to be true.

I don't trust her.

There are a lot of dogs between here and Hillsdale. A lot of coyotes, a lot of houses. Even if she wasn't infected, she should have run into trouble somewhere—the kind of trouble that leads to open wounds and an increased chance of getting sick. There's no way she made it this far without sickening. It doesn't make sense.

I watch her out of the corner of my eye as we walk. The sun is too bright for me to make out the fine details of her face, but I think she's watching me, too. Measuring me. Trying to figure out whether I'm leading her into a trap.

Honestly, I feel like there's definitely a trap, but I don't know who's leading who. Danny is in the house. Danny, who wasn't that sick the last time I saw him. Sure, he tried to kill me, but he apologized while he was doing it, and I've always known, deep down, that he'd let me in if I came home. He can't make me sick with a sneeze the way a dog could, but he could bury his teeth in my shoulder, he could taste my blood and drip his sickness into the wound, and we could be a family again. He'd accept me once he smelled the sickness on my skin, the same way he and Dad accepted each other. He'd love me again.

My head hurts *so bad*. I put my hand briefly to my temple, and watch as Tess stiffens. She has a weapon, a baseball bat with a nail driven through it like the tooth of some great, terrible beast.

It should look silly, like a prop stolen from somebody's *Walking Dead* LARP. A lot of things that should look silly don't, anymore.

"Something wrong?" she asks. "Sun in your eyes?"

"I haven't been able to find clean water for a few weeks," I say. "I've been making do with Pepsi, but it ran out yesterday. I have a caffeine headache." The lie is easy to tell, and beautifully believable. Humans don't do well without water.

Tess accepts my words at face value. She relaxes, slightly, and offers me a small, understanding smile.

"I spent a week drinking nothing but the syrup they pack peaches in."

I blink. "How did you get that many peaches?"

"My grandmother used to buy them from Costco. By the case. I was hiding in the shed in our backyard, going through her emergency supplies."

That sounds like heaven. A roof, four walls, food… "Why did you leave?"

"My grandmother found me."

There's a story in that sentence, something dark and cruel and worst of all, familiar. Remember that they have to win only once, and they've been winning once, over and over again, since this nightmare began. "I'm sorry," I say, and the words are worthless, the words are desert-dry and empty.

Tess shakes her head. "She had this dog. A little Bichon Frise. I guess his rabies shots weren't up to date. Why would they be? He was always with her, he was never at risk, until the day he *was*. No one realized he was sick until it was too late and he started biting. No one…" She stops, gaze going distant, and just walks.

The houses around us look like they've aged a decade in a single summer. The infected don't care about mowing lawns or fixing broken windows, and at least in the beginning, the uninfected were all about throwing rocks at houses in the middle of the day, shattering glass and letting the light in. It was like we thought rabies was a form of vampirism, like we could turn the monsters who had replaced our families into ash and memory.

We forgot the infected were as smart as they'd been before they got sick. They painted the rocks nearest the houses with their own saliva, and the rock-throwers unlucky enough to scrape their palms found themselves in the early stages of rabies before they realized the rules had changed again. Dizziness; thirstiness; headaches; increasing photosensitivity; paranoia; and finally, hydrophobia and irrational violence, rages against nothing, and the urge to kill, to kill, to kill anyone who wasn't already sick.

We lost half our number in a weekend, and we adapted. So did they.

"Remember that I have to win…" I whisper, and stop. There is no comfort there.

We stop in front of the house where I grew up. The welcome mat is still on the porch, still inviting us inside. The windows have been boarded up. Danny's doing, probably. It keeps the light out, and the wind, and everything else. Dad could never have figured out what needed to be done. He's not handy.

He's probably not anything, by now. Rabies is a cruel mistress.

"This the house?" asks Tess.

I nod.

"You're sure your brother is alone in there?"

"My dad could still be alive." But I don't think so.

Tess nods. "We can take him."

This is all happening so *fast*. It's not the worst idea, I guess—winter really is on the way—but that doesn't mean it should be happening like this. We should have more people. A better plan.

More risks. More mouths to eat whatever food is still in the cupboards. God, I'm hungry. I wipe my mouth with the back of my hand. I'm hungry enough to start drooling at the thought of a bowl of cereal.

Tess lifts her bat.

I step forward and open the door.

The house is dark and smells like rot, like backed-up plumbing and food left on counters and something sweeter, poisonously so, something that makes my nose itch and my stomach rebel. I step inside anyway, and Tess is right behind me.

"Danny?" I call. "It's Stacy. I came home. I missed you, and I came home."

Nothing moves. Nothing breathes. I let my feet guide me to the dining room, and there they are, Dad and Danny both, waiting for me. Neither of them turns. Behind me, Tess gasps. I don't care. It's so *good* to see my family again. I missed them so much.

My head hurts.

"Stacy," says Tess, joy and horror mingled in her voice, "they're dead. They're dead! All we have to do is push them outside and close the door and the house is ours! We can—"

She has a bat. I have a chair. I also have the element of surprise, and when the chair smashes against her face, down she goes, not even able to scream. I hit her again, and again, and again, until she stops moving, until she stops trying to get up.

When I'm done, when my hands are raw and bloody, I drop the chair on her body and stand where I am, panting. The dimness in the house is so nice. The sun was so bright. It's better in here. My head hurts less.

Dimly, I start to understand what my body has been telling me all day. What happened, and how, I may never know, just like I never knew what happened to Danny. A coyote, maybe, too far to bite, but close enough to sneeze, or a bat, with its sharp, sharp teeth, or touching something that had been touched by something else, contagion clinging to a seemingly safe surface. What does it matter? This is the end of the world. But I'm home now, and my family is here, and I'm safe, for now.

There's a box of cereal open on the table. It's stale, it's old, but I don't mind. I sit down in the chair that's always been mine, and I stick my hand in the box, and I crunch down a mouthful of sugary flakes.

"Remember that I have to win only once," I say, and I laugh, and the ghosts of the lost laugh with me, their teeth so sharp, their eyes so bright, their inevitable end so final.

BURN 3

KAMI GARCIA

Kami Garcia is the #1 *New York Times*, *USA Today*, and international bestselling coauthor of the Beautiful Creatures and Dangerous Creatures novels. *Beautiful Creatures* has been published in fifty countries and translated into thirty-nine languages, and the film *Beautiful Creatures* was released in theaters in 2013 from Warner Brothers. Kami's solo series, The Legion, includes the instant *New York Times* bestseller *Unbreakable*, and the sequel *Unmarked*, both of which were nominated for Bram Stoker Awards. Her other works include *The X-Files Origins: Agent of Chaos* and the YA contemporary novels *The Lovely Reckless* and *Broken Beautiful Hearts*. Kami was a teacher for seventeen years before co-authoring her first novel on a dare from seven of her students. She lives in Maryland with her family, and their dogs Spike and Oz. Visit Kami at KamiGarcia.com.

The faces of missing children flash across three vid screens above our heads, forming a gargantuan triangle that looms over the street. Children have been disappearing for weeks now. Protectorate officers claim they're runaways, but there's nowhere to go inside the Dome. The truth is no one cares about a bunch of poor kids from Burn 3.

I glance at the screen again and squeeze my little sister's hand tighter, dragging her through the filthy alley.

"Why are we running?" Sky asks.

"We're just walking fast."

I don't like bringing her outside at night, but we're out of purification tablets and she hasn't had any water all day. The dirty streets are bathed in neon light from the signs marking the rows of identical black metal doors that serve as storefronts. In the distance, towering buildings covered in silver reflective panels rise up around a labyrinth of alleys. Those buildings are all that's left of the city that stood here twenty years ago. Retrofitted and repurposed for the world we live in now. I've never been anywhere near there. It's the wealthy part of Burn 3, no place for poor kids like us.

We reach an exposed stall draped in a black plastic tarp. An old woman swathed in layers of dark fabric huddles underneath. Her face is pebbled on one side, the result of poorly healed burns. Even though the Dome keeps us under a constant shadow, it's dangerous to be outside all day, and I feel sorry for her. But few people can afford the high rent for an indoor shop.

"Two purification tablets, please." I hold out the coins stamped with a crude number three on both sides.

She takes the currency in her gloved hand and gives me two pink tablets. They don't look like much, but they'll turn the black water running through the pipes a safer shade of gray. Before our father died, he told us stories about the world before the Burn. A time when water was clear and you could drink it straight from the faucet, and walk outside to stand in the sun without layers of protective clothing. That was before his mind deteriorated and I couldn't tell if his stories were memories or delusions.

A siren eclipses the sounds around us and an automated voice issues a directive. "Alert: the atmosphere inside the Dome has reached Level 2. Please put on your goggles and return to your domiciles immediately. Alert: the atmosphere inside the Dome—"

"Hurry home," the old woman says, collapsing the tarp around her like a tent.

My sister looks up at me, blue eyes wide. "I'm scared, Phoenix."

"Put on your goggles." I dig in my pocket for mine.

She unfolds the wraparound eyewear that makes everything look bright green, a color you never see inside the Dome.

"Run," I yell, pulling her along behind me.

A man pushes Sky, and she stumbles. He glances at her and starts to turn away without offering help or an apology. Tears run down my sister's face.

I shove him as hard as I can, and grab my sister's hand. She runs behind me until we reach our building, a twenty-story domicile divided into single rooms. The Dome is so crowded that there's nowhere left to build but up, even though it's more dangerous on the higher floors.

Our room is on the eighteenth floor.

I unlock the door and push Sky inside. "Get in the shelter."

She scrambles for the makeshift tent in the center of the room. It's made from Firestall, an engineered material that absorbs heat and UV rays.

The Dome is supposed to protect us from the holes in the ozone layer—holes that turned more than two-thirds of the world to ash twenty years ago. But the sun's invisible hand can still reach into the Dome. The burns people suffer on a daily basis are proof of that. Most of us have been victims at least once, our skin curling like the edges of burning paper.

Some people believe you're more likely to get burned in the buildings without reflective panels like this one. I don't know if it's true, but I can't take chances with my sister. Sky's skin is perfectly smooth. She's never felt the savage itching and heat of a burn, and I'm not going to let her feel it now.

We huddle together in the darkness, and Sky chokes back tears. "I'm scared."

"Don't worry." I pull her closer and listen to the alert repeating over and over until I fall asleep, more worried than ever.

In the morning, I look out the small window and see people wandering through the streets. The alert must be over, though many are still wearing their protective goggles. My father told me this city was called New York before the Burn. The buildings were even taller than the ones beyond the alleys, so tall they seemed to touch the clouds. He said you could see the clouds too—white streaks in a blue sky. A sky filled with beauty instead of destruction.

The Burn happened suddenly, although scientists had predicted it years before. The sky turned red and the temperature rose dangerously. No one could step outside without suffering third-degree burns. Within weeks, the heat was melting steel and plastic. My father said hundreds of thousands died after inhaling the toxic fumes from their disintegrating homes.

For years, people lived in the sewers or underground shelters until scientists developed a compound strong enough to withstand the temperatures in the areas where the atmosphere was still intact.

People traveled hundreds of miles underground until they reached a safe zone—a place without a hole in the sky above it. They built the Dome and named our city Burn 3 because it was the third city in the world to turn to ash.

From where I stand looking down on the black coats rushing through the gray streets, the city still looks like it's made of ash.

I drop the purification tablets into two black cups of water and watch the liquid turn a less lethal shade of charcoal. I choke mine down and leave Sky's on the counter. She's still asleep, blond hair peeking out from beneath the ratty blanket. I can't stand to wake her. The world of her dreams is so much better than the one we live in.

I leave her a note instead.

An hour later, I climb the eighteen flights of stairs with two food packets tucked in my pocket. Noodles with spicy red sauce, Sky's favorite. Orange doors line both sides of the hallways and I can see ours from the landing.

It's wide open.

My pulse quickens, and I bolt up the stairs. Sky would never open the door for anyone. She knows better. "Sky?"

I glance around the room. She's not here, but someone else was. Blankets are strewn all over the floor, and the shelter is shredded.

"Sky!" I know she won't answer, but I keep calling her name. This can't be happening. Children have been disappearing from the streets, not from the domiciles.

I run for the door and trip over the shredded strips of Firestall. My face hits the cement floor hard, and for a second, the room sways. I push up onto my knees, and something glints under the black strips of material.

A glass bottle the size of my thumb. It has a silver cap with a hole in the top, but the bottle is empty. A white label is peeling off the front. I've never seen anything like it in the stores along the alleyways.

I hit the stairs and notice the open door a floor below me. Clothes and personal items are strewn across the floor. Sky might not be the only kid missing.

I'm back in the streets, running down the alley under the neon signs. "Sky?"

I check the shops she frequents, like the one with hand-sewn dolls that cost more than we spend on a week's worth of food packets. Or the store several blocks away where they sell tea made from roots and the salve that heals burns.

I stop a woman selling bread packets on the street. "Have you seen a little girl with blond hair?" It's Sky's most recognizable feature.

Almost no one has blond hair or blue eyes anymore. My father said they made people more vulnerable to the sun, a vicious sort of natural selection. It's the reason I rarely take Sky outside during the day, and keep every inch of her skin covered when I do.

The woman shakes her head. "Haven't seen no blond hair."

I stand in the middle of the street, the black doors stretching out in front of me, the vid screens above me.

She's not here.

I think about my sister's smile and the way she never complains when we don't have enough to eat. I can see her blue eyes, bright and curious. My mother named her Sky because of her eyes. She said the real sky was just as blue once. I look up at the Dome and the red sky beyond it.

I would trade a real blue sky in a second to find her.

Faces flash across the gigantic vid screens one by one.

Sky's will be up there tomorrow.

I've never been inside the Protectorate. Protectorate officers are dangerous—as quick to draw their guns as the criminals they hunt.

And Burn 3 is full of criminals, men with nothing left to lose who will cut your throat over a few coins or a food packet. I try not to imagine Sky in their hands.

The building is made of Firestall, the same material used to construct the Dome. It's only used for government buildings, and the Protectorate is the only government facility in this part of town.

I burst through the doors, and the scanners go off. There's nothing in my pockets except the glass bottle. I don't own anything but the clothes on my back, and I spent all the coins I had this morning.

"Stop right there," an officer shouts. His weapon is pointed at me, the red glow signaling that it's armed. He's prepared to use the heat we all fear to kill me.

"I'm sorry," I stammer. "My sister—she's missing. I think someone took her."

"Scan her." He nods at another officer, with smooth hands a few shades darker than the flesh on his face and neck. Skin always takes on a darker shade after it heals from a burn. Judging by his hands, he was burned badly. Only the expensive salves can smooth the texture of the affected skin.

The officer waves a small electronic device over my body. "She's clean."

The weapon lowers, and I struggle to catch my breath. I notice the cages hanging above us—at least twenty feet from where I'm standing. Arms hang between the bars. There are men inside.

"Someone broke into our room at the domicile, and my little sister is missing. She's only ten."

Please help me.

"How do you know it was a break-in?" the Protectorate officer with the scanner asks.

"The door was wide open, and everything inside was destroyed."

He shakes his head. "Maybe she left in a hurry. Don't you watch the vid screens? You know how many kids run away every day?"

I try to make sense of what he's saying, but I can't. "You think they're running away? Where would they go?"

The one with the weapon leaning against his shoulder shrugs. "The Abyss maybe. Who knows? Lots of kids like it down there. Plenty of stuff on the black market to help them forget about their problems."

"My sister doesn't have problems." I realize how ridiculous it sounds as soon as I say it. "No more than anyone else."

I don't know how to make them believe me. For a second, all I can think about is my father. He died two years ago, slowly poisoned by toxic fumes he and the other evacuators inhaled decades ago when they risked their lives to save others. My father would know what to say to make these men listen.

I shove my hands into my pockets, my fists curled in frustration. The cool glass slides against my skin, and I remember the bottle safely tucked inside. My hand closes around it, but I hesitate. What if they take it? I don't trust these men, and it's the only clue I have.

The officer with the scanner looks bored. "I'm sorry your sister's missing, kid. But we can't chase down every runaway."

I take a deep breath and swallow my anger. If I lose control, I'll end up in one of the cages hanging above us, and I won't be able to look for Sky. "Did you ever think that someone might be taking them?"

They both laugh. "Why would anyone want extra mouths to feed?"

"Maybe they're not feeding them." It's hard to believe these idiots are responsible for protecting us. But I have to convince them to believe me.

I start to pull the bottle out of my pocket—

"Sounds like a conspiracy theory." He shakes his head. "Did you come up with that on your own, or are you one of those crazy evacuators' kids?"

My whole body stiffens, and I push the bottle back down into my pocket.

The evacuators are the only reason you're alive.

That's what I want to tell him, but the familiar shame eats away at my stomach instead. My father was crazy, a fact I tried to hide when he was alive.

But he taught me to trust my instincts, which is the reason I slide my hand back out of my pocket. Empty.

A cage above us rattles, and something falls, nearly hitting one of the officers. His head jerks up. "Throw something out of there again, and I'll rip your arms off. You hear me? Then I'll send you back down to the Abyss, and we'll see if you can steal without them."

His partner looks at me. "You kids think the Abyss is one big party because there are no rules, but it's full of criminals. If you spend enough time down there, you'll end up in a cage too."

Full of criminals…

These men aren't going to help me find Sky. I'm going to have to do it myself.

But at least now I know where to look.

The entrance to the Abyss is a round metal plate in the street. A ladder leads to what's left of the underground city where everyone lived until scientists figured out how to build the Dome. I climb down until the ladder reaches the damp ground, the mouths of stone tunnels surrounding me. Names and arrows are painted on the walls, directions to places I don't recognize.

My father brought me down here once when I was Sky's age. I remember the darkness punctuated by dim strings of tiny bulbs that led to a crowded market of open stalls. He was looking for a friend, one of the guys like him who helped thousands of burned and injured people find their way down here during the Evacuation. He bought me a piece of dried meat from a stall—the first thing I'd ever eaten that didn't come from a sealed silver pouch—and left me to play games with the other children while he spoke to a man with one arm. My father didn't explain the visit, and made me swear never to go down into the underbelly of the city again.

He would understand why I am breaking that promise now.

I don't remember the name of the place my father took me, so I choose a random tunnel and follow the steady stream of water and rats. I can't imagine Sky down here. Everything about her is clean and bright.

I try to imagine my father guiding me, but all I can think about is the last thing he said before he died. When the toxicity levels in his blood rose so high we had to admit him to a clinic. "Be brave, Phoenix. Take care of your sister."

Another broken promise to my father.

My feet are soaked by the time I hear voices and notice a pool of pale light in the distance. The tunnel opens up, and I see the stalls. They're lined up in crooked rows, the ripped awnings forming aisles. Tiny strings of white bulbs dangle above them. I'm not sure if this is the same market I visited as a child.

I scan the crowd, searching for any trace of my sister's blond hair. I move closer to the stalls and watch as customers haggle over the price of burnt books, medicine long past its expiration date, and sweets in clear plastic wrappers instead of pouches. Everything the merchants are selling here is illegal. Things the Protectorate officers would throw you in the cages for possessing aboveground. But here, people are bartering for drinks in dark glass bottles and matches—a controlled substance in Burn 3. The sight of them makes my skin itch as if it's already on fire.

"Whatcha lookin' for, kid? Jerky? Cigarettes?" a man with an eye patch shouts.

I don't know what he's talking about. "Have you seen a girl with blond hair? About this tall?" I hold up my hand to match Sky's height.

His eye narrows, and he glances over his shoulder. "Little girls don't buy cigarettes."

I try again. "Have you seen her? She's wearing a black tunic and outercoat."

He strikes a match in front of me and watches it burn.

"Do you know what this is?" I hold the glass bottle with the printed label in my palm.

His eye grows wide, and he covers my hand with his, closing my fingers around the bottle. "Not here," he hisses under his breath.

"I don't—"

He jerks my arm so hard it feels like he's trying to break it. "Got me those cigarettes back here," he yells loud enough for anyone listening to hear.

I don't know what cigarettes are, but I know I wouldn't buy them—or anything else—from him.

"Come on." He slips between the stalls and gestures for me to follow. The opening to another tunnel waits, but there are no strings of lights hanging across this one. It's completely dark. Even the water trickling from the mouth looks blacker.

I shouldn't follow him. I've heard stories of kids being hacked to pieces in the alleys of Burn 3. Down here, it could be worse. But at sixteen, I'm not a kid anymore—only a year younger than my father was when he saved hundreds of people—and my sister is missing.

"Where are we going?" My voice echoes against the slick walls.

"Shh!" He waves a scarred hand at me. The skin is darker and rough, the mark of a severe burn. I picture a pack of lit matches in his hand and the flame jumping from the matchstick to his clothes.

I blink the image away and listen to his footsteps to be sure they stay ahead of mine. If he stops walking, I want to know. But he doesn't, moving quickly until we reach a dead end.

A lopsided wooden shack leans against the tunnel wall, its windows covered in black tape. Who blacks out their windows when they live underground?

Someone crazy.

The man glances around as if he thinks we've been followed. Satisfied, he sorts through the keys attached to a long chain at his waist, carefully matching them to the rows of locks on the door.

He's just like the evacuators who were exposed to burning plastic and other chemicals. Paranoid. The ones who didn't die immediately went crazy, their minds rotting away from the poison they inhaled to save others. I should know.

I don't want to go in, but what if he knows something about Sky or the bottle I found?

"Get inside." He opens the door and shoves me through.

A cracked bulb buzzes to life, and when I see the room, I realize he is crazy. The walls are plastered with papers, strange numbers and symbols scrawled all the way to the corners. And photos—not digital scans, but actual photos—of children with dirty faces and tired eyes. One stands out.

The boy has blond hair like Sky's. I can't take my eyes off his face.

"Who are all these kids?" I point at the pictures, the edges water-stained and bent.

He takes a long look at the photos and swallows hard. "Mind your own business," he snaps.

I step away from the images and the numbers I don't understand. Boxes of dirty beakers and lab equipment are stacked along the far wall, next to torn and partially burnt books. He must have salvaged the books from somewhere. I doubt he could afford to buy them.

"Know what those are?" He points to the strange symbols and numbers and shakes his head before I have a chance to answer. "'Course you don't. Those are equations. Scientific compounds."

"I'm just trying to find my sister."

He points at my pocket. "Show it to me one more time."

I hand him the bottle, and he holds it up to the light. "Ketamine. Give a kid enough of this stuff and they lose consciousness—or worse."

I clench my fists, imagining someone dragging my sister's limp body out of the domicile.

"Makes it easy to take them to the Skinners."

The word makes my skin crawl, even though I don't know what it means. "What's a Skinner?"

He turns quickly, so he can look at me with his good eye. "Are you messing with me? If you're holding that bottle, you know who they are. Or you will soon."

"Please tell me." I don't know what I can say to convince him to help me. "My father is dead, and my sister is all I have."

"How did he die?" The man's tone is suspicious.

"What?" I don't know why he cares, but he waits for me to answer. "My father was an evacuator," I say as if that's explanation enough.

He flips his eye patch up, and there's a hollow recess where his eyeball should be. "Then you know what it's like when they take someone from you."

Those are the delusions talking. This guy is too far gone to give me any information, and I've already wasted enough time. I turn to leave. "Thanks for your help."

The man starts pacing in the cramped space, muttering and biting his nails. I remember the way my father paced at night when he thought we were asleep. Sometimes his mind was sound, and others I could see the effects of the poison he inhaled during the Evacuation. Toxins that were slowly killing him.

"Wait here." The man disappears behind a folding screen, and I can hear him rummaging around. He emerges wearing a heavy black coat that makes his thin frame look much bigger.

"I really think I should—"

He slides a rotted panel of wood along the back wall of the shack, revealing the opening to another sewer tunnel. "Do you want to find your sister or not?"

I have no way of knowing if this man has any information—if the symbols on his walls are scientific equations or the delusions of a damaged mind. But something about the photos of the children convinces me he knows something, even if he is insane.

My father had moments of clarity when every word he spoke was the truth. This man reminds me of him, the flashes of sanity grappling for footing on the sliding rocks of madness. If one of those moments can help me find Sky, I have to follow him.

We step into the darkness, and a flame illuminates the void. The man is holding a gold object between his fingers. A small flame rises up from the wick inside it. "Never seen one of these before, have you?"

I shake my head and take a step back. No one produces fire intentionally in Burn 3. The risk of starting a fire is too great when there is so little water to extinguish one.

I picture the flame catching his skin again and wonder if that's how he got the burn on his hand.

"It's called a lighter. You fill this part with oil." He taps on the bottom half of the rectangular object. "Then you turn this dial and it strikes the flint."

I nod as if I understand, and he seems satisfied.

We move deeper into the sewage tunnel, the device he calls a lighter illuminating barely a few feet in front of us. "Kids started disappearing down here first. Bet you didn't know that, did you?"

I remember the photos from his walls. Were they missing children from the Abyss?

"The vid screens don't broadcast news outside of Burn 3."

He shakes his head at my ignorance. "We aren't outside of Burn 3."

"I'm sorry. I didn't mean—"

He waves me off. "Forget it. Children who live aboveground with hair the color of the sun will always be more valuable than ours."

"But the boy in the picture on your wall had blond hair."

His body tenses and I realize I've made a mistake mentioning it. "Don't worry about the kids down here. Your sister's the one you care about."

Heat creeps up my neck, and shame settles in the pit of my empty stomach. The Abyss—the underground sewers I'm walking through—were the only safe place to live for years. Now people don't venture down here unless they want to buy something on the black market. He's right. No one cares if kids in the Abyss go missing.

Yet I expect this stranger to care about my sister. A little blond girl from a world that treats the people in his like rats. "I just meant—"

He cuts me off again. "I know what you meant. Now shut up. We're getting closer."

Closer to what?

The cement cylinder stretches out in front of us, murky water splashing under our boots. The stench of mold turns to something more nauseating, one even worse than flesh burning.

I try not to gag. "What is that?"

"The smell of bodies rotting."

"Where is it coming from?" I whisper.

He nods into the darkness. "The old labs where the scientists worked before they built the Dome. The place where they figured out how people could walk in the sun again." His tone is sarcastic. We both know no one can walk in the sun. Everyone in Burn 3 is hiding, above *and* belowground. "The labs are abandoned now. At least, they're supposed to be."

The hair rises on the back of my neck. "Who's in there?"

He stops, the edges of his coat floating in the ankle-deep water. "You really don't know what they're doing down here, do you?" His expression is a twisted mixture of terror and wonder, as if he can't fathom the idea.

I shake my head, afraid to answer.

"They're stealing kids so they can sell them for parts."

I couldn't have heard him right. I want to run and pretend this guy inhaled too much burning plastic—that everything he's told me is the delusion of a rotted mind. Anything to avoid asking the next question I know I have to ask. "What kind of parts?"

He doesn't hesitate. "Why do you think they call them Skinners?"

The ground slides out from under me, and I stagger.

My sister...

He reaches out and grabs my elbow to steady me. "If they have your sister and she looks the way you say, we have to hurry."

The words turn over in my mind, but I can't make sense of them. There is only one word caught in the tangled threads of my thoughts.

Skinner.

I push past it, forcing myself to hear what this stranger is saying. "If she looks what way?"

"Light-haired," he says. "It's rare. I haven't seen someone with light hair since—" He stops, his expression defeated. "Rare things are always worth more money to the people doing the selling. And the ones buying."

He is talking about Sky like she is a bottle of clean water or a book—an object to be bought and sold at one of the stalls in the underground market. He doesn't know how kind she is—the way she shares her food packets with the poorer children in the domicile, though she never has enough to eat herself. The way she pretends the life we have now is equal to the one we had when my father was alive to protect us. The way she never doubts me, even when I doubt myself.

I look at the man I'm following blindly. "What's your name?"

Suddenly, I want to know. I am trusting him with my sister's life, which is worth much more to me than my own.

He strikes the flint on the lighter again, and the flame casts a strange glow over his face. "A name is a way to make a claim. No one can claim me."

I watch the familiar paranoia creep into his features. He reminds me of my father again. "A name is also the way you claim your friends."

He turns his back on me and disappears into the darkness. "I don't need any friends."

I follow the echo of his footsteps in silence, hoping with each step that we are getting closer to Sky. I try to ignore the grim reality—that if I find her and this man is telling the truth, she won't be alone.

I need to know more about the Skinners—these monsters

kidnapping children to sell their skin. For what? I didn't even know.

"What—" I almost can't ask. "What are they doing with their skin?"

He grabs my arm and pulls me against the wall. There are voices in the distance, but they're too far away to make out anything intelligible. "Shh. The tunnels echo."

My heart bangs against my ribs, and I try not to make a sound while he stares down the black hole.

He pushes his long, greasy hair out of his face. "They sell the good skin for grafts."

"Grafts?" I've never heard the word before.

He rubs his good eye, and I notice how thin his arm is under the long coat. I wonder when he ate last. My father forgot to eat sometimes. He said he lost his sense of taste and smell after the Evacuation, and everything tasted like cardboard—whatever that was.

"You can replace burned skin with new skin. At least a doctor can. They call it a skin graft. Works better than those expensive salves," he says. "And people say it looks almost as good as the skin you were born with."

It sounds barbaric and painful. "Who would do something like that?"

He laughs, the sound laced with bitterness. "Wealthy people who don't want to look like they've been burned like the rest of us."

"They're willing to kill kids to get rid of their burns?" The Skinners aren't the only monsters.

"Maybe they don't ask questions about where it comes from. Or maybe they do. People are capable of all kinds of evil." He peers down the tunnel again.

"Why doesn't someone stop them?" I realize how accusatory it sounds, but I don't care.

"The Skinners run things down in the Abyss. People that question them end up dead—along with their friends, their families, in some cases whole tunnels full of their neighbors. There's no Protectorate down here. The Skinners are the law. No one can touch them."

I can see the shame hiding in his eyes.

He swallows hard. "Time to go."

We follow the muffled sounds until we reach the mouth of the tunnel. The passage in front of us looks more like a cavern than a sewage tunnel. A gray metal building stands a few yards away, artificial light illuminating the barred windows. This place looks more like a prison than a laboratory.

The man who refuses to tell me his name pulls a gun from the back of his waistband. It's old, and it doesn't resemble the weapons Protectorate officers carry.

He notices me staring. "It's a semiautomatic, from the days before the Burn." He slides a cartridge out of the bottom. "This thing doesn't shoot fire. These are hollow-tip rounds. They can kill you in the blink of an eye."

"Do I need one of those?"

"Only have one," he whispers. "Guess that means I'm going first."

He edges his way closer as shadows move in front of the windows. I realize he's risking his life to help me, and I wonder why.

But there's no time. He's already at the door using something to pick the lock. I rush to catch up, my mind racing.

How many Skinners are inside? Do we stand a chance against the kind of people who cut the skin off children?

He grabs my outercoat, his voice low. "When we get in there, we'll only have a few minutes." He nods at the door. "That's the surgical room. Run past and stay to the right. They keep the kids in a box in the back. If they're still here."

A box?

Bile rises in my throat, but I force it back down.

"What if it's locked?" I try not to picture my sister trapped in a box like an animal.

He hands me a thin piece of metal. "Slip this in the lock and jiggle it around until you hear a click. Then get the kids out of here."

"What if they aren't there?"

"If they're still alive, they will be."

"How do you know?"

"I've been here before." It's the last thing he says before he pops the lock.

We step inside and I freeze. Metal tables and trays of crude instruments covered in dry blood dominate the room. A dirty pole with a plastic bag suspended from it looms in the corner. I don't want to think about what they do in here.

Was Sky in here?

My stomach convulses.

"Go," he hisses at me, pointing to the door at the end of the room.

I obey and rush to the dark corridor on the other side. I stay to the right like he told me, working my way to the far side of the building. I hear muffled voices in other rooms, but I can't stop or think about what the Skinners will do to me if they catch me.

Instead I think about Sky. I pretend she's only a few feet away and all I have to do is get there.

The corridor is dimly lit, but I see the rectangular metal container at the end. It looks like a rusted shipping container from a factory. The box.

When I get closer, I see the slats along the sides of the metal. The stench of sweat is everywhere, and it fills me with hope. If the kids were dead, the odor would be different. But it could also be the lingering scent of children who are no longer inside…

I slip the thin piece of metal in the lock and move it around.

Nothing happens.

I try again. This time I hear the pop, and I pull the door open, anticipating the worst.

Nothing could've prepared me for what I find inside.

Eight or ten children huddle together in the corner. Most of them look about Sky's age, but some are older. They're filthy, dressed in torn hospital gowns. But I know if I make it out of this place alive, it's the look in their eyes that will haunt me forever—complete and utter terror.

There's nothing else left.

I run toward them, trying to find my sister in the huddle. "Sky?"

A soft sound pushes its way forward from the back of the group. "Phoenix?"

I try to move the other children out of the way so I can find her. "I'm not going to hurt you," I promise them.

I see a stripe of blond hair.

Sky looks up at me, her face as tormented as the others. Her eyes look less blue somehow. I gather her into my arms. "I'm going to get you out of here. All of you."

Flashes of hope pass across their faces, though some of them seem too weak to react.

"That's a big promise for a girl who's in way over her head."

My neck snaps back to the door.

A huge man stands in the doorway. His face is noticeably lighter than his hands. He's probably used the skin of some helpless child to repair his own. But there are other thin scars—most likely made by knives—running down his neck. His brown outercoat is crusted in dry blood, and he's holding a Protectorate-issue firearm.

I pull Sky to her feet and shove her behind me. "I—I came for my sister."

The man stares over my shoulder at Sky. "She's not going anywhere. We'll get a lot for her skin. Those blue eyes too." I shudder, and he looks me over. "Yours not so much. But if your legs are clean, you'll be worth skinning."

He steps into the small container, so close I can almost reach out and touch him. Another man steps inside behind him, holding an identical weapon. He moves to the corner, covering me from a different angle.

"I'll stay. Just let my sister go."

Both men laugh, and I want to kill them.

"I say you let them all go," a familiar voice calls from the corridor. His expression is fierce, the patch covering his missing eye. He's pointing his gun at the man doing the talking.

"Ransom. I was wondering when you'd come back," the man in the bloodstained outercoat says. "Looking for work?"

"I had no idea what you were doing down here, Erik," Ransom, the man who refused to tell me his name, responds.

Erik laughs. "The lies we tell ourselves."

"You said we were doing experiments to help burn victims."

The corner of Erik's mouth lifts. "Technically, it was true."

Ransom's expression hardens even more. "Today it's going to get you killed if you don't let these kids go."

Erik raises an eyebrow and points his weapon at Ransom. "You shouldn't have come back. I warned you, didn't I? And look what it cost you last time."

Last time.

"I should've killed you then." Ransom winces and his jaw tightens.

"Except you couldn't." Erik glances at the guy in the other corner of the container. "The odds have never been in your favor."

Ransom's grip on the gun tightens. "I'll say it one more time. Let them go."

"No one's going anywhere. Think you can point that relic at me and I'll hand over the kids?" Erik's eyes narrow. "I'm gonna burn the skin off your bones. Then I'll take your other eye and sell it to the lowest bidder."

The man in the corner laughs. "Maybe we should give it away."

Ransom examines the outdated gun in his hand. "This thing is my good luck charm. But I did bring some other *relics* with me."

Ransom opens his outercoat, revealing a black vest covered in bricks of plastic that look like putty. He raises his free hand, holding some kind of switch attached to the vest. "Remember C-4, Erik? It's old, but you used it to blow up plenty of tunnels down here."

I remember when Ransom disappeared behind the screen in his shack. He must have put the vest on then.

The kids start crying.

"Why now, Ransom?" Erik taunts. "You could've come back here a million times. Is your mind finally that far gone?"

Ransom glances in my direction, but he's not looking at me.

He's staring at the wisp of tangled blond hair peeking out from behind me. Just like the blond boy's hair in the photo on his wall.

"I'm doing this for my son. For Alex. You're not taking him again."

I realize he's referring to Sky, and I'm not sure if it's the delusions talking or if he means it symbolically.

Erik's expression changes. He realizes he's not going to be able to scare Ransom. Right now, Ransom is the most terrifying person in the room. And—judging by whatever he has strapped to his chest—the most dangerous.

"You have ten seconds to let them go before I start counting. If you do, I might let you live. But I'm blowing this place either way."

Ransom's lying. He's going to kill them. I can tell by the way he looks almost happy.

Erik nods at the other man. "Turn them loose."

I grab Sky's hand and help up some of the children. They look dazed, as if they aren't really sure what's happening. The ones with bandages on their arms lean against the stronger children as we inch our way between the men locked in a standoff.

I stop in the doorway and look at Ransom—the man who saved my sister and all the other children stumbling down the corridor now.

The man who's half crazy and all hero.

"Thank you."

He nods. "Thanks for reminding me there's always a way to right a wrong. Now get out of here."

We run through the passage and the sadistic surgical room, into the mouth of the tunnel that led me here. We're only a few yards away when the deafening sound of the explosion hits.

The concrete around us rumbles, and I can see the fire consuming the building in the distance.

For a moment, I can't move. I stare at the flames that keep us locked in the shadow of a life only some people remember. Fire has always represented pain and sorrow for me. A sad sort of imprisonment none of us can escape.

Today, it represents something else.

Freedom.

A tiny girl with knotted curls is sobbing. "I don't know how to find my way home."

A boy with dark-brown eyes glances around. "Me either."

Sky squeezes my hand and looks up at me, her eyes the shade of blue I remember. "My sister knows the way."

I study their tear-streaked faces and I think about my father. The way he led so many down here to safety; the way I'm about to lead only a few back up now. I think about the price he paid for it, and what he said to me the last time I saw him.

Be brave, Phoenix.

Today I was braver than I ever believed I could be.

Today I changed things.

Sky is still staring up at me. "You know the way, don't you, Phoenix?"

For the first time, I know I do.

SNOW

DALE BAILEY

Dale Bailey is the author of eight books, including *The End of the End of Everything*, *The Subterranean Season*, and his latest, *In the Night Wood* (John Joseph Adams Books). His story "Death and Suffrage" was adapted for Showtime's *Masters of Horror* television series. His short fiction has won the Shirley Jackson Award and the International Horror Guild Award, has been nominated for the Nebula and Bram Stoker awards, and has been reprinted frequently in best-of-the-year anthologies, including *Best American Science Fiction and Fantasy*. He lives in North Carolina with his family.

They took shelter outside of Boulder, in a cookie-cutter subdivision that had seen better days. Five or six floor plans, Dave Kerans figured, brick façades and tan siding, crumbling streets and blank cul-de-sacs, no place you'd want to live. By then, Felicia had passed out from the pain, and the snow beyond the windshield of Lanyan's black Yukon had thickened into an impenetrable white blur.

It had been a spectacular run of bad luck, starting with the first news of the virus via the satellite radio in the Yukon: three days of disease vectors and infection rates, symptoms and speculation. Calm voices gave way to anxious ones; anxious ones succumbed to panic. The last they heard was the sound of a commentator retching. Then flat silence, nothing at all the length of the band, NPR, CNN, the Outlaw Country Station, and suddenly no one was anxious to go home, none of them, not Kerans and Felicia, not Lanyan or his new girlfriend, Natalie, lithe and blonde and empty-headed as the last player in his rotating cast of female companions.

On the third day of the catastrophe—when it became clear that humanity just might be toast—they'd powwowed around a fire between the tents, passing hand-to-hand the last of the primo dope Lanyan had procured for the trip. Lanyan always insisted on the best: tents and sleeping bags that could weather a winter on the Ross Ice Shelf, a high-end water-filtration system, a portable gas stove with more bells and whistles than the full-size one Kerans and Felicia used at home, even a Benelli R1 semi-automatic hunting rifle (*just in case*, Lanyan had said). The most remote location, as well: somewhere two thousand feet above Boulder, where the early November deciduous trees began to give way to Pinyon pine and Rocky Mountain juniper. Zero cell-phone reception, but by that time there was nobody left to call, or anyway none of them cared to make the descent and see. The broadcasts had started calling it the red death by then. Kerans appreciated the allusion: airborne, an incubation period of less than twenty-four hours, blood leaking from your eyes, your nostrils, your pores and, toward the end—twelve hours if you were lucky, another twenty-four if you weren't—gushing from your mouth with every cough. No-thank-yous all around. Safe enough at seventy-five-hundred feet, at least for the time being—the time being, Lanyan insisted, lasting at least through the winter and maybe longer.

"We have maybe two weeks' worth of food," Kerans protested.

"We'll scout out a cabin and hunker down for the duration," Lanyan said. "If we have to, we'll hunt."

There was that at least. Lanyan was a master with the Benelli. They wouldn't starve—and Kerans didn't have any more desire to contract the red death than the rest of them.

All had been going according to plan. Inside a week they'd located a summer cabin, complete with a larder of canned goods, and had started gathering wood for the stove. Then Felicia had fallen. A single bad step on a bed of loose scree, and that had been it for the plan. When Kerans cut her jeans away, he saw that the leg had broken at the shin. Yellow bone jutted through the flesh. Blood was everywhere. Felicia screamed when Lanyan set the ⬛⬛⬛⬛ g it back into true, or something close to true, spli⬛⬛⬛ a couple of backpack poles, and binding the entire bloo⬛ ith a bandage they found in a first-aid kit under the sink. ⬛⬛ ge had soaked through almost immediately. Kerans, holdin⬛ nd, thought for the first time in half a dozen years of their we⬛ the way she'd looked in her dress and the way he'd felt insid⬛ the luckiest man on the planet.

Luck.

It had all turned sour on them.

"I'm taking her down, first thing in the morning," he told Lanyan.

"What for? You heard the radio. We're on our own now."

"You want to die, too?" Natalie asked.

"I don't want *her* to die," Kerans said. That was the point. Without help, she was doomed, anybody could see that. There wasn't a hell of a lot any of them could do on their own. A venture capitalist and a college English professor and something else, a Broncos cheerleader maybe, who knew what Natalie did? "Even if it's as bad as we think it is down there," he added, "we can still find a pharmacy, antibiotics, whatever. You think there's any chance her leg isn't going to get infected?"

Grim-faced, Lanyan had turned away. "I think it's a bad idea."

"You have a better one?"

"How are you going to get down, Dave? You planning to use the Yukon?"

Kerans laughed in disbelief. "I can't believe you'd even say that."

"What?" Lanyan said, as if he didn't know.

"You were the best man at my wedding. Hell, you introduced me to Felicia."

"The rules have changed," Natalie had said. "We have to think of ourselves now."

"Fuck you, Natalie," Kerans said, and that had been the end of the conversation.

He was wakeful most of the night that followed. Felicia was feverish. "Am I going to die, Dave?" she'd asked in one of her lucid moments. "Of course not," he'd responded, the lie cleaving his heart.

Lanyan woke him at dawn. They stood shivering on the porch

of the cabin and watched clouds mass among the peaks. The temperature had plunged overnight. The air smelled like snow.

"You win," Lanyan said. "We'll go down to Boulder."

The snow caught them when they were winding down the rutted track from the cabin, big lazy flakes sifting through the barren trees to deliquesce on the Yukon's acres of windshield. Nothing to worry about, Kerans thought in the backseat, cradling Felicia's head in his lap. But the temperature—visible in digital blue on the dash—continued to plummet, twenty-five, fifteen, ten; by the time they hit paved road, a good hour and a half from the cabin, and itself a narrow, serpentine stretch of crumbling asphalt, the snow had gotten serious. The wipers carved arcs in the snow. Beyond the windows, the world had receded into a white haze.

Lanyan hunched closer to the wheel.

They crept along, pausing now and again to inch around an abandoned vehicle.

"We should have stayed where we were," Natalie said, and the silence that followed seemed like assent.

But it was too late to turn back now.

Finally the road widened into a four-lane highway, clogged with vehicles. They plowed onward anyway, weaving drunkenly among the cars. By the time they reached the outskirts of Boulder, the headlights stabbed maybe fifteen feet into the swirling snow.

"I can't see a thing," Lanyan said. They turned aside into surface streets, finding their way at last into the decaying subdivision. They picked a house at random, a rancher with a brick façade in an empty cul-de-sac. The conventions of civilization held. Lanyan and Kerans scouted it out, while the women waited in the Yukon. They knocked, shouting, but no one came. Finally, they tested the door. It had been left unlocked; the owners had departed in a hurry, Kerans figured, fleeing the contagion. He wondered if they'd passed them dead somewhere on the highway, or if they'd made it into the higher altitudes in time. The house itself was empty. Maybe they'd gotten lucky. Maybe the frigid air would kill the virus before it could kill them. Maybe, Kerans thought. Maybe.

SNOW

They settled Felicia on the sectional sofa in the great room, before the unblinking eye of the oversized flatscreen. Afterward, they searched the place more thoroughly, dosing Felicia with the amoxicillin and oxycodone they found in the medicine cabinet. Then the food in the pantry, tools neatly racked in the empty garage, a loaded pistol in a bedside table. Natalie tucked it in the belt of her jeans. Kerans flipped light switches, adjusted the thermostat, flicked on the television. Nothing. How quickly it all fell apart. They hunched around a portable radio instead: white noise all across the dial.

Welcome to the end of the world, it said.

Not with a bang, but a whimper.

The snow kept coming, gusts of it, obscuring everything a dozen feet beyond the windows, then unveiling it in quick flashes: the blurred limb of a naked tree, the shadow of the Yukon at the curb. Kerans stood at the window as night fell, wondering what he'd expected to find. A hospital? A doctor? The hospitals must have been overwhelmed from the start, the doctors first to go.

The streetlights snapped alight—solar-charged batteries, the death throes of the world he'd grown up in. They illuminated clouds of billowing white that in other circumstances Kerans would have found beautiful. Cold groped at the window. He turned away.

Lanyan and Natalie had scrounged a handful of tealight candles. By their flickering luminescence, the great room took on a cathedral air. Darkness encroached from the corners and gathered in shrouds at the ceiling. They ate pork and beans warmed over the camp stove, spread their sleeping bags on the carpet, and talked. The same goddamn conversation they'd had for days now: *surely we're not the only ones* and *how many?* and *where?* and *what if?*

"We're probably already dying," Natalie said, turning a baleful eye on Kerans. "Well, we're down here now," she said. "What's your plan, Einstein?"

"I don't have a plan. I didn't figure on the snow."

"You didn't figure on a lot of things."

"Cut it out," Lanyan said.

"We didn't have to do this, Cliff," Natalie said.

"What did you expect me to do? I've known Felicia for years. I've known Dave longer. It's not like we had access to weather reports."

No, Kerans thought, that was another thing gone with the old world. Just like that. Everything evaporated.

By then the cold had become black, physical.

Kerans got to his feet. He tucked Felicia's sleeping bag into the crevices of the sofa. She moaned. Her eyes fluttered. She reached for his hand.

Kerans shook two oxycodone out of the bottle.

"These'll help you sleep."

"Will you stay with me, Dave?"

All the way to the end, he thought, and he knew then that at some level, if only half-consciously, he had accepted what he had known in his heart back at the cabin. She was gone. She'd been gone the moment she'd slipped on that bed of scree. And he'd laughed, he remembered that, too. *Whoops*, he'd said, and she'd said, *I'm hurt, Dave*, her voice plaintive, frightened, tight with agony. He'd never heard her use that voice in seventeen years of marriage, and he knew then that she was beyond help. There was no help to be had. What had Natalie said? *The rules have changed. We have to watch out for ourselves now.* Yet Lanyan had surrendered the Yukon, and they had knocked on the door before barging into this house, just as they had knocked on the door of the summer cabin in the mountains before that. How long, he wondered, before they reverted to savagery?

"Will you stay with me, Dave?" she said.

"Of course."

He slid into his sleeping bag. They held hands by candlelight until the oxycodone hit her and her fingers went limp. He tucked her arm under her sleeping bag—he could smell the wound, already suppurating with infection—and lay back.

The last of the tealights burned out.

Kerans glanced at the luminescent dial of his watch. Nine-thirty.

The streetlights' spectral blue glow suffused the air.

He closed his eyes, but sleep eluded him. An endless loop unspooled against the dark screens of his eyelids: Felicia's expression as the earth slipped out from under her feet. His helpless whoop of laughter. *I'm hurt, Dave.*

He opened his eyes.

"You awake, Cliff?" he said.

"Yeah."

"You think Natalie's right? We're all going to wind up coughing up blood in twenty-four hours or so?"

"I don't know."

"Maybe the snow," Kerans said. "Maybe the cold has killed the virus."

"Maybe."

They were silent.

"One way or the other, we'll find out, I guess," Lanyan said.

Snow ticked at the windows like fingernails. Let me in. Let me in.

"About the Yukon—" Kerans said.

"It doesn't matter, Dave. You'd have done the same for me."

Would he? Kerans wondered. He liked to think so.

"I'm sorry I was an asshole," Lanyan said.

"It doesn't matter."

"Felicia's going to be okay."

"Sure she is. I know."

Kerans gazed across the room at the shadowy mound of the other man in his sleeping bag.

"What do you figure happened?"

"Hell, I don't know. You heard the radio as well as I did. Something got loose from a military lab. Terrorists. Maybe just a mutation. Ebola, something like that."

Another conversation they'd had a dozen times. It was like picking a scab.

A long time passed. Kerans didn't know how long it was.

"It doesn't matter, I guess," he said, adrift between sleep and waking.

"Not anymore," Lanyan said, and the words chased Kerans down a dark hole into sleep.

Lanyan woke him into that same unearthly blue light, and for a moment Kerans didn't know where he was. Only that strange undersea radiance, his sense of time and place out of joint, a chill undertow of anxiety. Then it all came flooding back, the plague, Felicia's fall, the blizzard.

Lanyan's expression echoed his unease.

"Get up," he said.

"What's going on?"

"Just get up."

Kerans followed him to the window. Natalie crouched there, gazing out into the sheets of blowing snow. She held the pistol in one hand.

"What is it?" he whispered.

"There's something in the snow," she said.

"What?"

"I heard it. It woke me up."

"You hear anything, Cliff?"

Lanyan shrugged.

Wind tore at the house, rattling gutters. Kerans peered into the snow, but if there was anything out there, he couldn't see it. He couldn't see anything but a world gone white. The streetlamp loomed above them, a bulb of fuzzy blue light untethered from the earth.

"Heard what?" he asked.

"I don't know. It woke me. Something in the snow."

"The wind," Kerans said.

"It sounded like it was alive."

"Listen to it blow out there. You could hear anything in that. The brain, it"—he hesitated—

"What?" Natalie said.

"All I'm saying is, it's easy enough to imagine something like that. Voices in the wind. Shapes in the snow."

Natalie's breath fogged the window. "I didn't imagine anything."

"Look," he said. "It's late. We're all tired. You could have imagined something, that's all I'm saying."

"I said I didn't imagine it."

And then, as though the very words had summoned it into being, a thin shriek carved the wind—alien, predatory, unearthly as the cry of a hunting raptor. The snow muffled it, made it hard to track how far away it was, but it was closer than Kerans wanted it to be. It held for a moment, wavering, and dropped away. A heartbeat passed, then two, and then came an answering cry, farther away. Kerans swallowed hard, put his back to the wall, and slid to the floor. He pulled his knees up, dropped his head between them. He could feel the cold radiating from the window, shivering erect the tiny hairs on his neck. He looked up. His breath unfurled in the gloom. They were both watching him, Lanyan and Natalie.

"It's the wind," he said. Hating himself as he said it, hating this new weakness he'd discovered in himself, this inability to face what in his heart he knew to be true.

Came a third cry then, still farther away.

"Jesus," Lanyan said.

"They're surrounding us," Natalie said.

"They're?" Kerans said. "They're? Who the hell do you think could be out there in that?"

Natalie turned and met his gaze. "I don't know," she said.

They checked the house, throwing deadbolts, locking interior doors and windows. Kerans didn't get the windows. You wanted to get inside bad enough, you just broke the glass. Yet there was something comforting in sliding the little tongue into its groove all the same. Symbolic barriers. Like cavemen, drawing circles of fire against the night.

As for sleep, forget it.

He leaned against the sofa, draped in his sleeping bag, envying Felicia the oblivion of the oxycodone. Her skin was hot to the touch, greasy with perspiration. He could smell, or imagined he could smell, the putrescent wound, the inadequate dressing soaked with gore.

Across the room sat Lanyan, the Benelli flat across his legs. At the window, her back propped against the wall, Natalie, cradling the pistol in her lap. Kerans felt naked with just the hunting knife at his belt.

The snow kept coming, slanting down past the streetlamp, painting the room with that strange, swimming light. Lanyan's face looked blue and cold, like the face of a dead man. Natalie's, too. And he didn't even want to think about Felicia, burning up under the covers, sweating out the fever of the infection.

"We should look at her leg," he said.

"And do what?" Natalie responded, and what could he say to that because there *was* nothing to do, Kerans knew that as well as anyone, yet he felt compelled in his impotence to do something, anything, even if it was just stripping back the sleeping bag and staring at the wound, stinking and inflamed, imperfectly splinted, oozing blood and yellow pus.

"Just keep doling out those drugs," Lanyan said, and Kerans knew he meant the oxycodone, not the amoxicillin, which couldn't touch an infection of this magnitude, however much he prayed—and he was not a praying man. He couldn't help recalling his mother, dying in agony from bone cancer: the narrow hospital room, stinking of antiseptic, with its single forlorn window; the doctor, a hulking Greek, quick to anger, who spoke in heavily accented English. *We're into pain management now,* he'd said.

"How much is left?" Natalie said, and Kerans realized that he'd been turning the prescription bottle in his hands.

"Ten, maybe fifteen pills."

"Not enough," she said. "I don't think it's enough," and a bright fuse of hatred for her burned through him for giving voice to thoughts he could barely acknowledge as his own.

After that, silence.

Kerans's eyes were grainy with exhaustion, yet he could not sleep. None of them could sleep.

Unspeaking, they listened for voices in the storm.

At two, they came: one, two, three metallic screeches in the wind.

Lanyan took one window, Natalie the other, lifting her pistol.

Kerans stayed with Felicia. She was stirring now, coming out of her oxycodone haze. "What is it?" she said.

"Nothing. It's nothing."

But it was something.

"There," Natalie said, but she needn't have said it at all.

Even from his place by the sofa, Kerans saw it: a blue shadow darting past the window, little more than a blur, seven feet long or longer, horizontal to the earth, tail lashing, faster than anything that size had any right to be, faster than anything human. There and gone again, obscured by a veil of blowing snow.

Kerans's own words mocked him. Imagination. Shapes in the snow.

He thought of that icy snow tapping like fingernails at the window. Let me in.

Felicia said, "Dave? What is it, Dave?"

"It's nothing," he said.

Silence prevailed. Shifting veils of snow.

"What the hell was that thing?" Lanyan said.

And Natalie from her window. "Let's play a game."

Nobody said a word.

"The game is called 'What if?'" she said.

"What are you talking about?" Kerans said.

"What if you were an alien species?"

"Oh, come on," Kerans said, but Lanyan was grim and silent.

"Way ahead of us technologically, capable of travel between stars."

"This is crazy, Dave," Felicia said. "What is she talking about?"

"Nothing. It's nothing."

"And what if you wanted to clear a planet for colonization?"

"You read too much science fiction."

"Shut the hell up, Dave," Lanyan said.

"We're intelligent. They would try to—"

"We're vermin," Natalie said. "And what I would do, I would engineer some kind of virus and wipe out ninety-nine percent of the vermin. Like fumigating a fucking house."

"And then?" Lanyan said.

"Then I'd send in the ground troops to mop up."

Kerans snorted.

"Dave—"

"It's craziness, that's all," he said. He said, "Here, these'll help you sleep."

Nothing then. Nothing but wind and snow and the sound of silence in the room.

After a time, they resumed their posts on the floor.

Felicia, weeping, lapsed back into drugged sleep.

"We're going to have to get to the Yukon," Natalie said.

"We can't see a fucking thing out there," Kerans said.

"At first light. Maybe the snow will stop by then."

"And if it doesn't?" Lanyan said.

"We make a run for it."

"What about Felicia?" Kerans said.

"What about her?"

Kerans looked at his watch. It was almost three o'clock.

He must have dozed, for he came awake abruptly, jarred from sleep by a distant thud. A dream, he thought, his pulse hammering. It must have been a dream—a nightmare inside this nightmare of dark and endless snow, of a plague-ravished world and Felicia dying in agony. But it was no dream. Lanyan and Natalie had heard it, too. They were already up, their weapons raised, and even as he stumbled to his feet, shedding like water the sleeping bag across his shoulders, it came again: a thump against the back of the house, muffled by snow and the intervening rooms.

"What is it?" Felicia said, her voice drowsy with oxycodone.

"Nothing," he said. "It was nothing. A branch must have fallen."

"That was no branch," Natalie said. "Not unless it fell twice."

And twice more after that, two quick blows, and a third, and then silence, a submarine hush so deep and pervasive that Kerans could hear the boom of his heart.

"Maybe a tree came down."

"You know better," Lanyan said.

"Dave, I'm scared," Felicia whispered.

"We're all scared," Natalie said.

Felicia began softly to weep.

"Shut her the fuck up," Natalie said.

"Natalie—"

"I said shut her up."

"It hurts," Felicia said. "I'm afraid." Kerans knelt by the sectional and kissed her chill lips. Her breath bloomed in the cold air, sweet with the stink of infection, and he didn't think he'd ever loved her more in his life than he did at that moment. "There's nothing to be afraid of," he whispered, wiping away her tears with the ball of his thumb. "It's just the wind." But even she was past believing him, for the wind had died. The snow fell soft and straight through the air. The streetlamp was a blue halo against the infinite blackness of space. Natalie's game came back to Kerans—what if—and a dark surf broke and receded across the shingles of his heart. Felicia took his hand and squeezed his fingers weakly. "Just don't leave me here," she said. "Don't leave me here to die."

"Never."

The glitter of shattering glass splintered the air. Felicia screamed, a short, sharp bark of terror—

"Shut her up," Natalie snapped.

—and in the silence that followed, in the shifting purple shadow of the great room with its sectional sofa and the gray rectangle of the flatscreen and their sleeping bags like the shucked skins of enormous snakes upon the floor, Kerans heard someone—something—

—*let's play a game the game is called what if*—

—test the privacy lock of a back bedroom: a slow turn to either side. *Click. Click.*

Silence.

Felicia whimpered. Kerans blew a cloud of vapor into the still air. He clutched Felicia's fingers. He remembered a time when they had made hasty love in the bathroom at a friend's cocktail party, half-drunk, mad with passion for each other. The memory came to him with pristine clarity. He felt tears upon his cheeks.

And still the silence held.

Lanyan snapped off the safety of the Benelli.

Natalie put her back to the foyer wall, reached out, and flipped the deadbolt of the front door. She pushed it a few inches ajar. Snow dusted the threshold.

"The Yukon locked?" she whispered.

"No."

Once again, the thing tested the lock.

"Dave, don't leave me—"

"Natalie—"

She froze him with a glance, and something else she had said came back to Kerans. *The rules have changed now. We have to look out for ourselves.* God help him, he didn't want to die. He choked back a sob. They had wanted children. They had tried for them. In vitro, the whole nine yards.

"I won't leave you," he whispered.

Then the privacy lock snapped, popping like a firecracker. The door banged back. Something came, hurtling down the hallway: something big, hunched over the floor, and God, God, shedding pieces of itself, one, two, three as it burst into the room. Guns spat bright tongues of fire, a barrage of deafening explosions. The impact flung the thing backward, but the pieces, two- or three-foot lengths of leg-pumping fury, kept coming. Snapping the Benelli from target to target, Lanyan took two of them down. Natalie stopped the third one not three feet from Kerans's throat. It rolled on the floor, curving needle-teeth snapping, leathery hide gleaming in the snow-blown light, and was still.

Those alien cries echoed in the darkness.

"Time to go," Natalie said.

Lanyan moved to the door.

Felicia clutched at Kerans's hand, seizing him with a tensile strength he did not know she still possessed. The cocktail party flashed through his mind. They had wanted children—

"Felicia—" Kerans said. "Help me—"

"No time," Natalie said.

And Lanyan: "I'm sorry, Dave—"

The moment hung in equipoise. Kerans wrenched his hand away.

"Time to go," Natalie said again. "We can't wait. You have to decide."

And regular as a metronome inside his head: *the rules have changed the rules have changed the rules the rules —*

Natalie ducked into the night. A moment later, Lanyan followed.

Glass shattered at the back of the house, one window, two windows, three.

"Don't leave me, Dave," Felicia sobbed. "Don't leave me."

Outside the Yukon roared to life.

The rules have changed. We have to watch out for ourselves now.

"Dave," Felicia said, "I'm scared."

God help him, he didn't want to die—

"Shhh," he said, brushing closed her eyelids with his fingers. "Never. I'll never leave you. I love you."

He bent to press his lips to hers. His fingers fumbled at his belt. They closed around the blade.

A moment later, he was running for the Yukon.

THE AIR IS CHALK

RICHARD KADREY

Richard Kadrey is the *New York Times* bestselling author of fifteen novels, including the Sandman Slim supernatural noir series. *Sandman Slim* was included in Amazon's "100 Science Fiction & Fantasy Books to Read in a Lifetime." Chad Stahelski of *John Wick* fame is set to direct it as a feature film. Richard has also written comics for *Heavy Metal*, *Lucifer*, and *Hellblazer*. His newest book is *Hollywood Dead*.

There were three million people in L.A. when the party started. Now there's a few hundred scattered around in shopping mall emergency shelters, office buildings, and the subway tunnels. It's okay where I am, but most of the others I talk to by radio are running out of food and water, so they'll have to go scavenging soon. We'll be down to less than a hundred people left by the end of the month. If the Rollers don't get them at night, Floaters and Stingers will get them during the day.

That's just how things are now.

It's hard to stay focused on anything besides life and death. Each minute is a choice: stay inside and live or go outside and die. It was easier when there were other people here with me. Now that I'm the only one it's harder to justify waking up, much less staying alive. The army is gone. The government vanished. Even the crazy militias and God squad true believers who fought the freaks are gone. No white knights or cavalry riding to the rescue.

We're alone.

Actually, I should say *they're* alone. The other shelters. I'm never alone.

I wear noise cancelling headphones all the time now and when I forget to recharge them, I hear voices screaming my name day and night.

The truth is, I'd feel sorrier for myself if I wasn't a big part of what happened. Maybe I'm the main reason. Hell, there's no maybe.

It was my fault.

Now that there's no one around to blame me, I can go over it and put the pieces together.

I'm what you call a celebrity bodyguard. *Was* a bodyguard, excuse me. I've taken care of starlets, studio heads, corporate assholes, and even a few foreign diplomats. I was good at my job. Could turn on the charm when I had to. People appreciate that in a big guy. Everybody loves a gentle giant. And even though the giant might get sick of it, not showing it is part of the charm. I took good care of people and got paid well for it. My wife, Macy, was a casting agent at one of the big talent agencies and she was good at her job too. We were doing all right.

Then Bill fucked everything up by talking me into doing a job with one of his clients.

He'd phoned me just after noon and said, "Darla's parents are going home tomorrow, which means they have to go on the Universal Studios tour tonight. Darla will never forgive me if I don't take them."

"Seriously? It's been ten days since I had a night off and you want me to make it eleven so you can see a plastic shark?"

"It's my in-laws want to see the goddamn shark. I'm just a victim of circumstance. Come on, man. I've covered for you plenty of times."

"And I've covered for you too. But I'll do this extra special favor for you now because I'm that kind of guy."

I could hear the relief in Bill's voice. "Thanks, man. You're a life saver."

"All part of the service, man. Now, what kind of run is it?"

"It's easy. You're going to play chauffeur from Beverly Hills straight down to LAX, then you're a free man."

"Damn. I hate having to take care of people and drive their asses too."

"I know, but it's what the client wants," said Bill. "He's squirrely. Rich as fuck and afraid of everything. Don't touch him. That's rule number one. Don't shake his hand or anything. Just get him in the car."

"Sounds delightful. Just text me the particulars and I'll be there."

"Thanks. You're the best."

"That's what I keep telling everyone."

I picked up Bill's client at 2 p.m. sharp at the Beverly Wilshire hotel. I've done the Beverly Hills to LAX run so many times I could do it napping in the back with the passengers. The client's name was McKee. I recognized him because he's the one standing all by himself, far away from the crowd. Yeah, claustrophobic as shit.

"Mr. McKee?" I said. "I'm Paul, your driver. Would you like me to take your luggage?"

"Yes. Thank you," he said. I didn't get too close to him or bother asking about his attaché case, which he was clutching to his chest with both arms like it was the Lindbergh baby. When I opened the backseat door for McKee, he looked around inside before getting in. That and the attaché case said a lot and made me a little nervous. I studied the crowd for a minute before getting back in the limo. If there was trouble coming, I wanted to know from which direction. But I didn't see anything funny, so I steered us out of the hotel and headed for the airport.

McKee didn't say a word on the drive down, just stared out the window and checked his watch. And he never once let go of the attaché case. I've driven around enough show biz low-lifes and business creeps to know that there's only a few things McKee could be so worried about. The case was full of either embezzled cash or drugs. I glanced at him in the rearview mirror and our eyes locked for a second. He gave me a tight little smile, gripped the case tighter, and went back to staring at the traffic on the 405.

I had to tell someone about this ridiculous situation, but my wife would be at a business meeting this time of day, so I got out my phone and texted Alexandra, my girlfriend. She was a singer with her first single on the charts and a lot more on the way. She was also beautiful and young enough that the fact I was married just made me more exotic and not a big fucking problem. And she loved hearing gossip about my clients.

I texted: *In the limo with a metric ton of coke. Want some?*

A second later, I got back: *YES!!!*

Where are you?

At home bring drugs and fuck me NOW

From the back, McKee said, "Are you texting? Could you please not do that?"

I looked at him in the rearview. "Sorry. Company business. I'll be done in a second."

I texted: *Be there soon. Don't bother with clothes.*

The accident happened in the second it took me to hit send. I didn't see a pickup truck cut across two lanes toward an exit until it was too late, and I realized what was happening just in time to rear end an Escalade that had hit its brakes to avoid the truck. A cab hit me from behind and nudged me over into the next lane where I got sideswiped by a moving truck. The limo slammed nose-first into the guardrail on the side of the freeway. We hit hard enough that McKee's door popped open. The asshole wasn't wearing a seatbelt and almost flew out of the car. His attaché case launched like a goddamn rocket out of his hands and smashed open on the freeway shoulder. When I got out and went around the car, he was on his hands and knees in a blizzard of hundred-dollar bills.

"My pills," he said over and over.

A million bucks was blowing down the freeway and all McKee was worried about was his fucking *pills*? I reached out to help him up and he lurched back. Right. No touching. There was blood all over the money where he knelt. He touched his face. Blood trickled out of his nose. He sat back on his haunches and laughed. Took a handful of money and threw it in the air.

"What do you believe in?" said McKee.

"Are you all right, sir? Did you hit your head?" I crouched next to him, but he moved away.

"I mean it," he said. "When things go bad—really bad—what do you blame? Global warming? Chemtrails? Aliens? An angry God?"

"Please. Don't move around so much."

He waved a finger at me. "It's none of those things. It's just me. And I don't know why. It just happened one day."

Fuck this. He was bleeding and maybe something worse. I had to get him to settle down. "Calm down, sir. You'll be all right."

"Call it evolution. Call it *de*volution," he said. He smiled. "My wife evolved. I don't recognize her anymore. I hoped the pills would keep it from happening to me."

I'd seen this kind of thing before. People get a shot to the head and their brain goes sideways. They talked about their dreams, some movie they saw when they were six, all kinds of shit. He needed medical attention fast. I tried to get him to lie down, but he wriggled away.

"When my wife changed she tried to eat me."

Goddamnit. This was bad, but maybe if I went along with it it would calm him down. "What do you mean tried to eat you?"

He threw out his arms and looked around. "I don't know. I really don't. I'm sorry about all the blood. I was hoping to get far away before something like this happened."

"Just wait there, sir. I'm calling you an ambulance."

He stabbed a finger in my direction. "Some bodyguard you are. This is your fault. When the shit hits the fan, you're the one who threw it. I'm toxic, but I was going away. Now it's too late." He touched his nose and held out a bloody hand.

By now, there was a crowd around us. People were running wild, grabbing the cash. The situation was getting out of control. I gently put my hand on McKee's shoulder. "Please, sir. Stop moving."

He bit my hand until I let go. Then he jumped over the freeway guardrail and started down a small embankment toward the feeder road. "It's too late," he shouted. "It's out in the air. *I'm* out in the air. It's too late."

I followed him, but wasn't fast enough. McKee calmly stepped in front of a fuel truck headed for the airport. For someone who was worried about a few drops of blood a minute earlier, he sure left a lot around after that stunt.

Poor bastard.

Hell, poor *me*. I was about to be out of a job. Maybe worse.

I went back up the embankment and found my phone on the floor of the limo. Before calling work, I texted Alexandra.

Shits come up. Can't make it now. See you tonight?

And got back: ☹ *okay later gator*

I called the company and told them about the wreck and McKee offing himself. They were sending the cops, an ambulance, and a corporate rep. I was more scared of the rep than anything else that had happened that day.

I sat in the car, rubbed my shoulder and thought about what McKee had said. Something was out. What did that mean? And his wife tried to eat him? None of it made any sense, which I guess helps explain why he strolled out in front of that truck. He was nuts.

While I was waiting for the rep and others to arrive, the wind changed direction and my throat went dry. Nearby, someone said, "What's that smell?"

A few of us stood there for a minute with our noses in the air like a pack of dogs.

Finally, the cabbie who hit me said, "I think it's chalk. Like in school."

He was right. That was my first time smelling it on the wind. Later on, I realized that most of these grinning idiots with me on the side of the road were probably dead meat.

Me, on the other hand? If I didn't get arrested, I was going to a fucking party.

You learn your lessons the hard way these days. You learn or you're gone. It's not a rule. It's just reality.

The thing you need to know about Rollers is that while they look like one big beast, they're really made out of a lot of little ones. You see, people who get infected change fast. You can hear their bones crack as they curl up into fetal balls, while spines like barbed wire sprout out of their backs. If more than one person is changing, they'll crawl together and spiral around each other into a spiked ball of bleeding meat.

Then they start rolling.

If those barbed wire spines get hold of you, you won't get away. You'll be pulled into the flesh mass and the only human part left of you will be your eyes. I've seen Rollers the size of two-story houses. A hundred blinking eyes staring down at you, the air smells like chalk, and there's nothing you can do but run.

Rollers might be meat and bone, but once they're moving, nothing can stop them. They'll crush cars and crash through buildings to get to you. I've seen them take down ten, twenty people in one mad run. So, you might wonder, why didn't a Roller ever get *me*?

It's like the old joke about how do you outrun a bear? I don't have to outrun the bear.

I just have to outrun *you*.

I headed home after the cops interviewed me and the company made me write a report on the accident. I mostly talked about the pickup truck that cut everyone off and didn't mention the texting because, really, who needed to know? My bosses were happy enough with my story, but not with me letting a client get killed. They fired me on the spot. But at least I wasn't going to jail.

The party that night was in San Teresa, a ritzy gated community for people who thought Bel-Air was for losers. The mansion was owned by Franklin Bradbury, one of those faceless secret masters of money who traded movie studios and record labels like kids used to trade Pokemon cards. Frank was made of cash and power—which can get you hated in L.A.—but he churned out enough good product and treated people well enough that he was everybody's favorite billionaire. He only had a few quirks I knew about. Like, when he found out I was a bodyguard, all he wanted to do was talk about guns. Frank had an impressive gun vault, and a safe full of ammo to go with all the toys.

"Don't worry, big guy," he always joked. "When you're in my house, *I'm* the one guarding *you*."

"I always appreciate it, Frank. We all do."

It wasn't a big party by Frank's standards, just a get together of thirty or so people from his TV company. They were launching a new network that weekend so everyone was in a good mood and most of them were already lit by the time I got there. That included Macy, my wife. She'd come up with some other people from work and we hadn't spoken all day. I winced a little when she put her arms around my shoulders to kiss me.

She said, "What's wrong?"

"I'm just a little sore. There was an accident today at work."

Macy frowned. "*What?* Why didn't you call me?"

"It was no big deal," I lied, not wanting to get into it here. "Just a fender bender, but I got some nice bruises."

She pushed my hair back from my forehead, something she always did when she was concerned for me. "I'm glad you're okay, but call me next time."

"I promise."

She took my hand and led me into the botoxed masses. I was never comfortable with these people. They were all so pretty and tan that I couldn't tell them apart or remember half of their names. Still, it was drinks all around, so no one minded if you got their name wrong on the first try.

Frank had a television the size of Kansas and someone was flipping through the channels until they stopped on a late-night talk show. I watched just long enough to see Alexandra appear on screen and give the host a peck on the cheek. I looked over at the sofas. The real Alex was there with the remote in her hand. She looked at me and winked. I smiled back.

She was curled up next to Geoff somebody, a handsome up and coming actor. They had a good relationship. He got her into all of the big movie premieres and she was his beard, hanging on his arm whenever he went out somewhere the studio wanted him to look macho. Macy was off talking business with Frank, so I went over and sat down with the happy couple.

Instead of hello Alex said, "So, did you bring any with you?"

"Bring what?"

"The coke! I told Geoff you'd have enough for all of us."

I shook my head solemnly. The one thing you never want to tell a twenty-something singer who's been waiting all day for a bucket of cocaine is that there isn't any. But there was nothing I could do. "I'm sorry, baby. The guy was a ringer. There was no coke."

Alex fell back against the sofa, bounced off and collapsed across Geoff's lap like a dying deer. She said, "You've ruined my life, you know."

"No, I didn't. I just slowed down your evening."

"I've got you covered," said Geoff. He took a small aspirin tin from his pocket. "My friend Sandra is seeing this Swedish DJ. She said he has a huge cock and great molly. Want one?"

Alex popped upright and opened her mouth like a baby bird waiting to get fed. Geoff took a pill from the case and tossed it onto her tongue. She swallowed and he held the tin out to me. "Paul?" he said.

I shook my head. "I had an accident today. The cops might call me in for a drug test."

"That's sad," he said, swallowing a pill. It broke my heart to not be able to join them. I started to say something when Alex shrieked.

"No! What the fuck is this shit?"

I looked and saw that the local news station had broken into her talk show with a special report. The sound was down on the TV, so all we saw were high helicopter shots looking down on the 405 near the airport. Cars were on fire. Trucks had flipped, spilling their contents all over the road. Stuck in an endless ribbon of burning traffic, people were abandoning their vehicles and running away. By now, the room had gone quiet as everyone stared at the screen.

"Does anyone know what's going on?" said Frank. He took the remote from Alex's hand and aimed it at the TV. But when he pushed the volume control, the TV remained muted. He banged the remote against his hand. "Goddamn fucking thing."

The whole room screamed as something massive crashed through the stalled traffic. The searchlight from the news chopper stayed on it as the thing smashed its way north. When the shot pulled back, it revealed that there were several massive *things* on the road, all heading toward the city, crushing and absorbing everybody in their path. It was our first glimpse of Rollers.

We watched for a while with the sound off. Frank switched from station to station, looking for different views of the carnage. A few more people screamed when Frank found a shot of Rollers moving down Hollywood Boulevard—all spikes, blood, and blinking eyes. He headed for the front door and I followed him.

His mansion is on a high hill with a view all the way across L.A. to the ocean. We stood on his circular driveway and looked down at Hollywood. The sky buzzed with helicopters, both media and LAPD. I counted six major fires across the city. Frank grabbed my arm.

"Paul, you're going to help me keep these people under control, right?"

"What does that mean?"

"We can't let them leave. Look at that shit down there."

There was a muffled boom in the distance as a gas station or something exploded.

I said, "I take your point, Frank, but you can't make people stay."

"But you will, right? You and Macy? I can lock this place down like nobody's business."

I looked back at the choppers and the fires. "Okay. We'll stay the night. I'll help you with crowd control, but you have to let anyone leave who wants to. Otherwise, it's technically kidnapping."

"Sure," he said. "Understood. Come on."

Frank made his pitch to the crowd and, goddammit, he was a good salesman, even saving the best bit for last. After he got through explaining about how disaster-prepped he was, he took what looked like a garage door opener from his desk and pushed a button. Steel shutters slammed closed over all the outside doors and windows.

"Blast shields," he said. "You can hit those babies with an RPG and they won't budge."

It was a good speech. Still, half the crowd ran for their cars. Frank opened the gates at the end of the driveway just long enough for them to get through.

Then he locked us in.

Like a lot of heavy money types, the L.A. riots in '92 put the fear of god into Frank. That's when he started buying guns. But he turned his paranoia into art. Went full survivalist and with the kind of money he had, Frank made himself a bullet-proof Xanadu just thirty minutes from Hollywood. He had enough food, water, and medical gear to supply a small country. The mansion ran mostly on solar power, but he had a gas backup generator too. And because no one likes a boring siege, the mansion was stocked with movies and music, plus enough liquor and drugs to keep his guests high until the second coming.

After a couple of days, it was clear that whatever was happening wasn't going to end anytime soon. By then, the sky over L.A. was full of Floaters—sort of enormous jellyfish that hovered like hot air balloons and snatched up people with their long, dangling tendrils. It happened so fast you usually didn't see it, but you knew it was happening because Floaters bay like foghorns every time they snag a tasty morsel. The first Stingers had shown up in the city by then too, but we didn't know enough about them to be properly scared yet. We were preoccupied with something worse: what the freaks even *were*.

The first images were so strange it took a while to understand them. A news crew was out getting B-roll of Floaters near the Hollywood sign. One of the cameramen went into convulsions and a couple of his friends rushed over to help him.

That's when things stopped making sense.

The cameraman screamed as his chest and belly split open and what looked like tentacles coiled out. They latched onto his two friends as a translucent white *something* unfolded itself out of the guy's body and dragged his friends into the air.

That's when we knew we were fucked. The freaks weren't invaders from another planet. They were us. Maybe that's what McKee meant when he said his wife tried to eat him.

Anyway, that bit of good news was what probably inspired our first suicides: A record producer and his wife. Macy found them in one of the downstairs bathrooms, ODed on a bottle of Frank's Oxycontin. I didn't even know their names. I was just sorry Macy was the one to find them. She was hysterical when she came back upstairs and it took me a long time to calm her down. Frank opened the shields on the back doors long enough for the two of us to haul the couple outside and leave them by the pool.

That left ten people in the house. I knew Alex, Macy, Frank, and Geoff a little. They were my clients now. The rest, well, good luck.

When the world's burning, you have to make choices.

Over the next three days, I spent as much time with Alex as I could without Macy getting suspicious. By the end of the third day a few of us decided to make a run for it in one of Frank's armored limos. On TV, they were saying that the freaks were mainly over cities where the hunting was good. We wanted to see if there was a way out of L.A., maybe find somewhere with fewer freaks.

Besides, after a while, even a palace starts to feel like Alcatraz.

We left at high noon when we knew the Rollers would be asleep. That just left the Floaters to worry about, but if we kept moving we figured we could outrun them. In the limo was me, Frank, Mike (a reality TV director), and a kid who called himself Amped (one of the dead record producer's proteges—a buff Burbank white boy hip-hop kid. Really annoying).

We knew the freeways were clogged with dead cars and the main roads were the Rollers' and Floaters' favorite places to hunt, so we stuck to back streets hoping we could weave our way around the danger and out of town.

I should never have let Frank drive.

He was so busy blasting down the empty streets, showing off his shiny armored toy, that he sideswiped a sleeping Roller. Lucky for us, it was big enough and we were small enough that it didn't seem to notice the hit. But its spikes ripped a nice chunk off the limo's side and shredded one of the rear tires.

After a short screaming meltdown, I got Frank to pull into an empty gas station and park in the garage.

"I'm so sorry, guys," Frank said as we got out. "I fucked up."

I said, "Forget it. Let's change the tire and keep looking for a way out of town."

The limo was so heavy that it needed a special jack to raise it high enough to get the tire off. We finally got it working and wrestled the bad tire off and got the new one on, but it took us half an hour. Amped sat his skinny ass on a tall tool chest and smoked a spliff the whole time. We'd just gotten the wheel on and the jack stowed when my throat went dry and I smelled chalk. That's when Amped screamed and the rest of us got our first good look at a Stinger up close and personal.

The thing we didn't know at the time was that Stingers were the most dangerous freaks.

Shapeshifters.

The tool chest had unfolded around Amped and dug its barbed tentacles deep into his body. Then it began *absorbing* him. His body went soft, like a deflating balloon as the Stinger liquified him and sucked him down.

Frank, Mike, and me scrambled back into the limo. I had to elbow Frank in the gut to keep him from getting in the driver's seat, but he took it pretty well all things considered.

We needed to rethink the situation. I shot us out of the garage and back to Frank's place fast. The folks who stayed behind opened the blast shields on the front door when we got back.

Macy was the first one outside, a fist over her mouth as she stared at the torn-up car. When she saw me, she ran over and cried as she hugged me tight. I'll admit it: It was a tender moment, one of the nicest between us in a long time.

I let Frank explain what had happened to Amped. No one really knew the kid, so no one was too brokenhearted. They were a lot more interested in hearing about the Stinger.

It was another two hours before I could be alone with Alex. Once we found ourselves alone together, we crazy fucked in the room that had belonged to the ODed couple. They didn't need it anymore, and god knows we did.

Afterwards, we lay in bed and she said, "I thought I'd lost you today."

"No way, baby."

"How's Macy taking things?"

"She's fine. Let's not talk about her."

Alex got up and started putting on her clothes. "It's the end of the fucking world and we still have to sneak around."

"Don't talk like that. We'll figure a way out of this. Just you and me."

She didn't look at me as she left, just mumbled, "Sure."

Macy was at the bottom of the stairs when I came out of the room. She was looking the other way, so I don't think she saw Alex leave but we were going to have to be more careful in the future.

Everyone's phone was dropping calls so that night Frank got on a shortwave radio and started talking to people, trying to see if anyone knew a way out of town. I went into the kitchen for some food and when I got back, he'd drawn a route on a paper map from the limo's glovebox. We decided to go out again the next day.

Two more people died that night. A nice couple. Liz and Cassandra. A murder-suicide with one of Frank's guns. I checked the scene and didn't let people into their room. There was nothing anyone could do and no one else needed to see the mess. But it was clear that we needed to get out of this fucking house before we all ended up the same way.

Frank tossed me the limo keys when we went out the next day. He knew I'd never let him drive again. Two other people came with us. A couple. I couldn't remember their names and didn't ask.

We got a little over a mile from Frank's place, heading east when a shadow settled over us. I could hardly breathe, the air was so heavy with the chalk smell. And before we knew it, long serrated tendrils shot down from the sky and wrapped around the limo.

Then they lifted us into the air.

Everyone was yelling by then, even me. We knew Floaters sometimes went for cars, but none of them had ever encountered Frank's tank. We were about ten feet off the ground when a few of the tendrils snapped. It must have hurt because the Floater did its foghorn bellow and dropped us. We landed at a funny angle and ended up flipping over onto the roof. But the limo was tough enough that it held together and everybody was more or less fine and able to scramble out of the car.

The first to die was the woman whose name I didn't know.

The moment we were outside, a tendril dropped down and grabbed her in the bear trap grippers the fuckers had at the end of their appendages. A second later, she was gone. Her husband, boyfriend, or whatever he was, ran to the exact spot where she was pulled up. I tried to grab him, but another tendril hauled his dumb ass into the air a second later.

Me and Frank, we started to run.

Frank was a desk czar who paid other people to do his running for him. Between hiding and stopping to let Frank puke from exertion, it took us a couple of hours to make it back the mile or so to his house. When we got there, Alex ran out and grabbed me in a trembling hug.

"I shouldn't have let you go. I knew something bad would happen."

Macy was standing in the doorway. She just turned and went inside. I looked for her for maybe twenty minutes, but the damn mansion was the size of Houston. I couldn't find her anywhere.

I tried texting her, but it wouldn't go through. On the off chance she'd sent me a Dear John note, I checked my email, but I couldn't get into the site. I clicked some sites on Frank's computer and got the same results. The mansion's wifi was working, but it was like the whole goddamn net was down.

I went back to the living room and saw that the screen of the giant TV had gone black. Frank scrolled through the channels, but no one was broadcasting anymore. That with the net situation? Bad fucking signs. Still, we left the TV on in case something started up again.

About an hour later, I saw Macy. She opened the blast shields on the back door and went out. It was a stupid move after what had just happened with the Floater, so I went after her.

She was standing over the bodies of the ODed couple when I found her. We'd wrapped them in plastic garbage bags and duct tape, but by now in the L.A. heat they'd still gone pretty ripe.

"Are we going to end up like them?" she said.

More out of guilt than anything I said, "No way. I'll take care of you."

She scowled at me. "How, when you're so busy taking care of Alexandra?"

I didn't want to have this argument now. I didn't want to have it ever. I guess I'm a little slow. I never really had a plan on how to deal with the situation. I just hoped that things would work themselves out. But even at the end of the world, here Macy and me were, having the same old arguments.

"Come inside," I said. "It's dangerous out here."

"What do you care?"

I took a couple of steps toward her. "I care."

"Liar."

"Not now."

Macy gave me a look that somehow was wasn't all spite. She wanted to believe that we could work through this. "You mean it?" she said.

"I swear." And in that moment I did. But while I still cared about Macy, we were stuck in this endless goddamn cycle of hurt feelings and guilt. I just wanted it to be over.

I guess that's why, when one of the chaise lounges by the pool began to move, I hesitated for a fraction of a second before I said anything.

She gave me a hopeful half-smile just before the Stinger grabbed her leg. I remember it was the left one. Macy didn't scream. There was just a gasping intake of breath. She reached out for me.

"Paul?"

On TV they'd said that Stingers secreted a liquid that numbed things so they wouldn't fight and would be easier to absorb. I remembered what happened to Amped. After the initial shock of being grabbed, he didn't yell much but just sort of let it happen.

I stepped back. By then the Stinger had both of Macy's legs and another tentacle was sliding around her head, muffling her voice when she yelled my name one last time.

Even though she was the one full of Stinger juice, I was numb too. In the end, half a fucking second's hesitation was all it took.

I went back inside and closed the shields. Frank was passed out on bourbon when I got back to the living room. I found a glass, filled it to the top, and drank it straight down. After a few minutes listening to Frank snort and snore, I went to look for Alex.

Geoff had his shirt off when I found them together on the bed in the ODed couple's room. I was more puzzled than mad when I saw them kissing. Alex opened her eyes and when she saw me, she pushed Geoff off. The gun Liz and Cassandra had used to kill themselves was still sitting on the nightstand by the bed. I grabbed it and put it in my back pocket before Geoff panicked and did something stupid.

"Would you excuse us for a minute?" I said to him. He nodded and started to slink out of the room. Just before he reached the door I said, "Don't forget your shirt, tiger." I'd stepped back into the doorway so the little creep had to squeeze past me to get out.

When he was gone I closed the door.

At first, I couldn't think of anything to say. I just stood there like a moron until I mumbled, "I thought you said Geoff was gay."

"Did I say that?" said Alex like a kid caught in a lie. "He's more like… bi."

"And you two have been doing this how long?"

"Don't ask stupid questions, Paul." She started buttoning her blouse. I reached out and took one of her arms.

"I thought you loved me."

She sighed. "I *do* love you, but the Macy thing…"

"That's over. She's gone."

Alex looked puzzled. "What's that mean?"

I pulled her close and whispered, "She's gone. Dead. There's nothing stopping us from being together. I did it for you."

Alex stared at me for a moment like she was trying to figure out what I'd just said. Then she shoved me away hard. "Fuck you, Paul. Don't try to put any crazy shit you did on me."

Before I could say anything, someone screamed from the main rooms. I ran down the stairs. Geoff was pointing at Frank, who was convulsing on the sofa. Blood was already seeping through his shirt.

"Help me get him outside," I yelled. Alex had followed me downstairs. She and Geoff grabbed Frank's arms and I got his legs. Geoff opened the blast shields over the front door. We just barely got outside as the Floater burst from his guts and started into the air. Alex stumbled back a couple of steps.

"Get over here!" I shouted. She started for me, but she was way scared and froze. One of Frank's tendrils grabbed her arm and pulled her up into the sky with him.

A second later, Geoff was by my side watching Alex float away. He got a funny look on his face, one I'd seen before.

"Don't do it," I said. "Be cool and we can survive this."

Geoff was not cool.

He made a clumsy grab for the pistol. The little prick was faster than I'd counted on. The gun went off, almost hitting me in the leg. I grabbed him and pulled him in closer, the pistol between us. I'm honestly still not sure which one of us pulled the trigger when the gun went off the second time. All I know is that it was Geoff who hit the concrete and not me. I actually felt bad for a minute, but when the Floater's shadow started to move, I knew what I had to do. I left Geoff's body on the driveway, went back inside and put up the shields.

When the world's burning, you have to make choices.

That night, I heard Macy outside the house shouting my name. I opened one of the shields over a second-floor window and saw her below. She was naked and smiling.

"Come outside," she said.

I yelled at her. "You'll have to try harder than that. You're not Macy." I closed the shield and haven't been outside since.

The damn TV had gone off the air before someone could tell us that Stingers could look like people. And that they absorbed whatever information was in their lunch's brain. I guess what it got from Macy was me was our anger. Stingers must also have some psychic ability to communicate with each other because the next day there were *two* Macys outside.

Soon there were a dozen.

Another day and it was a hundred.

Now the house is surrounded and my wife, naked and furious, stretches around me for as far as I can see.

With Frank's supplies and everyone else gone, I'm set for the rest of my life in Xanadu. I talk to people on the shortwave sometimes. I watch movies. Listen to music. At night I sometimes take off the headphones and listen to Macy. She doesn't always scream. Sometimes she whispers and coos, like a sly seduction. I put the headphones on right away on those nights.

The screams I can deal with, but not the sound of Macy in love.

Eventually a Stinger got into the house. I don't know how it did it. It looked like a butcher knife and when I reached for it, it grabbed me. Fortunately, it was just a small one. I hacked it off my arm with a real knife and shoved it down the garbage disposal.

Frank had laid in a good supply of antibiotics and I'm gobbling them like popcorn. Still, the infection where the Stinger touched me is getting worse. I can feel my arm going soft, dissolving from the inside. I wrapped it in bandages and put it in a sling just so I don't have to look at it.

I wonder if, like Frank, I'll turn into a monster one day. By a lot of people's standards, I guess I already have.

There's not a lot to do around here anymore. It's harder and harder to find people to talk to on the shortwave. I've tried talking to Macy a couple of times on her cooing nights. But the sound of my voice soon gets her screaming again.

Here's the funny part, the part it took me a while to understand: There are so many Macys now that even with all the shielding over the doors and windows, if they rushed the place all at once, they'd be able to crash through. But that's not what the Stingers want. We're playing a game.

What they want is for me to open the doors and let them in.

When I dream now all I see is Macy's face disappearing under a tentacle. Alex being drawn into the sky. Frank splitting open. Geoff falling to the ground.

I know that one night when the dreams get too bad, my gamey arm starts dissolving the rest of me, or I can't stand watching *Die Hard* one more time, I'm going to call the Stingers' bluff. I'll open the doors and windows and invite them in for high tea. Will they absorb me right away?

I might be the last human in the world by then.

They might want to keep me for a while as a pet.

A memento of the early days when the world was full of people and the air wasn't always chalk.

THE FUTURE IS BLUE

CATHERYNNE M. VALENTE

Catherynne M. Valente is the *New York Times* and *USA Today* bestselling author of over two dozen works of fiction and poetry, including *Space Opera*, *Palimpsest*, *Deathless*, *Radiance*, and *The Girl Who Circumnavigated Fairyland in a Ship of Her Own Making*. She is the winner of the Andre Norton, Tiptree, Sturgeon, Prix Imaginales, Eugie Foster Memorial, Mythopoeic, Rhysling, Lambda, Locus, Sturgeon, and Hugo awards. She has been a finalist for the Nebula and World Fantasy Awards, and her story in this volume was selected for inclusion in *Best American Science Fiction and Fantasy*. She lives on an island off the coast of Maine with a small but growing menagerie of beasts, some of which are human.

1. Nihilist

My name is Tetley Abednego and I am the most hated girl in Garbagetown. I am nineteen years old. I live alone in Candle Hole, where I was born, and have no friends except for a deformed gannet bird I've named Grape Crush and a motherless elephant seal cub I've named Big Bargains, and also the hibiscus flower that has recently decided to grow out of my roof, but I haven't named it anything yet. I love encyclopedias, a cassette I found when I was eight that says *Madeline Brix's Superboss Mixtape '97* on it in very nice handwriting, plays by Mr. Shakespeare or Mr. Webster or Mr. Beckett, lipstick,

Garbagetown, and my twin brother Maruchan. Maruchan is the only thing that loves me back, but he's my twin, so it doesn't really count. We couldn't stop loving each other any more than the sea could stop being so greedy and give us back China or drive time radio or polar bears.

But he doesn't visit anymore.

When we were little, Maruchan and I always asked each other the same question before bed. Every night, we crawled into the Us-Fort together—an impregnable stronghold of a bed which we had nailed up ourselves out of the carcasses of several hacked apart bassinets, prams, and cradles. It took up the whole of our bedroom. No one could see us in there, once we closed the porthole (a manhole cover I swiped from Scrapmetal Abbey stamped with stars, a crescent moon, and the magic words *New Orleans Water Meter*), and we felt certain no one could hear us either. We lay together under our canopy of moldy green lace and shredded buggy-hoods and mobiles with only one shattered fairy fish remaining. Sometimes I asked first and sometimes he did, but we never gave the same answer twice.

"Maruchan, what do you want to be when you grow up?"

He would give it a serious think. Once, I remember, he whispered: "When I grow up I want to be the Thames!"

"Whatever for?" I giggled.

"Because the Thames got so big and so bossy and so strong that it ate London all up in one go! Nobody tells a Thames what to do or who to eat. A Thames tells *you*. Imagine having a whole city to eat, and not having to share any! Also there were millions of eels in the Thames and I only get to eat eels at Easter which isn't fair when I want to eat them all the time."

And he pretended to bite me and eat me all up. "Very well, you shall be the Thames and I shall be the Mississippi and together we shall eat up the whole world."

Then we'd go to sleep and dream the same dream. We always dreamed the same dreams, which was like living twice.

After that, whenever we were hungry, which was always all the time and forever, we'd say *we're bound for London-town!* until we drove our parents so mad that they forbade the word London in the house, but you can't forbid a word, so there.

* * *

Every morning I wake up to find words painted on my door like toadstools popping up in the night.

Today it says NIHILIST in big black letters. That's not so bad! It's almost sweet! Big Bargains flumps toward me on her fat seal-belly while I light the wicks on my beeswax door and we watch them burn together until the word melts away.

"I don't think I'm a nihilist, Big Bargains. Do you?"

She rolled over onto my matchbox stash so that I would rub her stomach. Rubbing a seal's stomach is the opposite of nihilism.

Yesterday, an old man hobbled up over a ridge of rusted bicycles and punched me so hard he broke my nose. By law, I had to let him. I had to say: *Thank you, Grandfather, for my instruction.* I had to stand there and wait in case he wanted to do something else to me. Anything but kill me, those were his rights. But he didn't want more, he just wanted to cry and ask me why I did it and the law doesn't say I have to answer that, so I just stared at him until he went away. Once a gang of schoolgirls shaved off all my hair and wrote CUNT in blue marker on the back of my skull. *Thank you, sisters, for my instruction.* The schoolboys do worse. After graduation they come round and eat my food and hold me down and try to make me cry, which I never do. It's their rite of passage. *Thank you, brothers, for my instruction.*

But other than that, I'm really a very happy person! I'm awfully lucky when you think about it. Garbagetown is the most wonderful place anybody has ever lived in the history of the world, even if you count the Pyramids and New York City and Camelot. I have Grape Crush and Big Bargains and my hibiscus flower and I can fish like I've got bait for a heart so I hardly ever go hungry and once I found a ruby ring *and* a New Mexico license plate inside a bluefin tuna. Everyone says they only hate me because I annihilated hope and butchered our future, but I know better, and anyway, it's a lie. Some people are just born to be despised. The Loathing of Tetley began small and grew bigger and bigger, like the Thames, until it swallowed me whole.

Maruchan and I were born fifty years after the Great Sorting, which is another lucky thing that's happened to me. After all, I could have been born a Fuckwit and gotten drowned with all the rest of them, or I could have grown up on a Misery Boat, sailing around hopelessly looking for land, or one of the first to realize people could live on a patch of garbage in the Pacific Ocean the size of the place that used to be called Texas, or I could have been a Sorter and spent my whole life moving rubbish from one end of the patch to the other so that a pile of crap could turn into a country and babies could be born in places like Candle Hole or Scrapmetal Abbey or Pill Hill or Toyside or Teagate.

Candle Hole is the most beautiful place in Garbagetown, which is the most beautiful place in the world. All the stubs of candles the Fuckwits threw out piled up into hills and mountains and caverns and dells, votive candles and taper candles and tea lights and birthday candles and big fat colorful pillar candles, stacked and somewhat melted into a great crumbling gorgeous warren of wicks and wax. All the houses are little cozy honeycombs melted into the hillside, with smooth round windows and low golden ceilings. At night, from far away, Candle Hole looks like a firefly palace. When the wind blows, it smells like cinnamon, and freesia, and cranberries, and lavender, and Fresh Linen Scent and New Car Smell.

2. The Terrible Power of Fuckwit Cake

Our parents' names are Life and Time. Time lay down on her Fresh Linen Scent wax bed and I came out of her first, then Maruchan. But even though I got here first, I came out blue as the ocean, not breathing, with the umbilical cord wrapped round my neck and Maruchan wailing, still squeezing onto my noose with his tiny fist, like he was trying to get me free. Doctor Pimms unstrangled and unblued me and put me in a Hawaiian Fantasies-scented wax hollow in our living room. I lay there alone, too startled by living to cry, until the sun came up and Life and Time remembered I had survived. Maruchan was so healthy and sweet natured and strong and, even though Garbagetown is the most beautiful place in the world, many children don't live past a year or two. We don't even get names until we turn ten. (Before that, we answer happily to Girl or

Boy or Child or Darling.) Better to focus on the one that will grow up rather than get attached to the sickly poor beast who hasn't got a chance.

I was born already a ghost. But I was a very noisy ghost. I screamed and wept at all hours while Life and Time waited for me to die. I only nursed when my brother was full, I only played with toys he forgot, I only spoke after he had spoken. Maruchan said his first word at the supper table: *please*. What a lovely, polite word for a lovely, polite child! After they finished cooing over him, I very calmly turned to my mother and said: *Mama, may I have a scoop of mackerel roe? It is my favorite.* I thought they would be so proud! After all, I made twelve more words than my brother. This was my moment, the wonderful moment when they would realize that they did love me and I wasn't going to die and I was special and good. But everyone got very quiet. They were not happy that the ghost could talk. I had been able to for ages, but everything in my world said to wait for my brother before I could do anything at all. *No, you may not have mackerel roe, because you are a deceitful wicked little show-off child.*

When we turned ten, we went to fetch our names. This is just the most terribly exciting thing for a Garbagetown kid. At ten, you are a real person. At ten, people want to know you. At ten, you will probably live for a good while yet. This is how you catch a name: wake up to the fabulous new world of being ten and greet your birthday Frankencake (a hodgepodge of well-preserved Fuckwit snack cakes filled with various cremes and jellies). Choose a slice, with much fanfare. Inside, your adoring and/or neglectful mother will have hidden various small objects—an aluminum pull tab, a medicine bottle cap, a broken earring, a coffee bean, a wee striped capacitor, a tiny plastic rocking horse, maybe a postage stamp. Remove item from your mouth without cutting yourself or eating it. Now, walk in the direction of your prize. Toward Aluminumopolis or Pill Hill or Spanglestoke or Teagate or Electric City or Toyside or Lost Post Gulch. Walk and walk and walk. Never once brush yourself off or wash in the ocean, even after camping on a pile of magazines or wishbones or pregnancy tests or wrapping paper with glitter reindeer on it. Walk until nobody knows you. When, finally, a stranger hollers at you to get out of the way or go back where you came from or stop stealing the good rubbish, they will, without even realizing, call you by your true name, and you can begin to pick and stumble your way home.

My brother grabbed a chocolate snack cake with a curlicue of white icing on it. I chose a pink and red tigery striped hunk of cake filled with gooshy creme de something. The sugar hit our brains like twin tsunamis. He spat out a little gold earring with the post broken off. I felt a smooth, hard gelcap lozenge in my mouth. Pill Hill it was then, and the great mountain of Fuckwit anxiety medication. But when I carefully pulled the thing out, it was a little beige capacitor with red stripes instead. Electric City! I'd never been half so far. Richies lived in Electric City. Richies and brightboys and dazzlegirls and kerosene kings. My brother was off in the opposite direction, toward Spanglestoke and the desert of engagement rings.

Maybe none of it would have happened if I'd gone to Spanglestoke for my name instead. If I'd never seen the gasoline gardens of Engine Row. If I'd gone home straightaway after finding my name. If I'd never met Goodnight Moon in the brambles of Hazmat Heath with all the garbage stars rotting gorgeously overhead. Such is the terrible power of Fuckwit Cake.

I walked cheerfully out of Candle Hole with my St. Oscar backpack strapped on tight and didn't look back once. Why should I? St. Oscar had my back. I'm not really that religious nowadays. But everyone's religious when they're ten. St. Oscar was a fuzzy green Fuckwit man who lived in a garbage can just like me, and frowned a lot just like me. He understood me and loved me and knew how to bring civilization out of trash and I loved him back even though he was a Fuckwit. Nobody chooses how they get born. Not even Oscar.

So I scrambled up over the wax ridges of my home and into the world with Oscar on my back. The Matchbox Forest rose up around me: towers of EZ Strike matchbooks and boxes from impossible, magical places like the Coronado Hotel, Becky's Diner, the Fox and Hound Pub. Garbagetowners picked through heaps and cairns of blackened, used matchsticks looking for the precious ones that still had their red and blue heads intact. But I knew all those pickers. They couldn't give me a name. I waved at the hotheads. I climbed up Flintwheel Hill, my feet slipping and sliding on the mountain of spent butane lighters, until I could see out over all of Garbagetown just as the broiling cough-drop red sun was setting over Far Boozeaway, hitting the crystal bluffs of stockpiled whiskey and gin bottles and exploding into a billion billion rubies tumbling down into the hungry sea.

I sang a song from school to the sun and the matchsticks. It's an ask-and-answer song, so I had to sing both parts myself, which feels very odd when you have always had a twin to do the asking or the answering, but I didn't mind.

> Who liked it hot and hated snow?
> The Fuckwits did! The Fuckwits did!
> Who ate up every thing that grows?
> The Fuckwits did! The Fuckwits did!
> Who drowned the world in oceans blue?
> The Fuckwits did! The Fuckwits did!
> Who took the land from me and you?
> The Fuckwits did, we know it's true!
> Are you Fuckwits, children dear?
> We're GARBAGETOWNERS, free and clear!
> But who made the garbage, rich and rank?
> The Fuckwits did, and we give thanks.

The Lawn stretched out below me, full of the grass clippings and autumn leaves and fallen branches and banana peels and weeds and gnawed bones and eggshells of the fertile Fuckwit world, slowly turning into the gold of Garbagetown: soil. Real earth. Terra bloody firma. We can already grow rice in the dells. And here and there, big, blowsy flowers bang up out of the rot: hibiscus, African tulips, bitter gourds, a couple of purple lotuses floating in the damp mucky bits. I slept next to a blue-and-white orchid that looked like my brother's face.

"Orchid, what do you want to be when you grow up?" I whispered to it. In real life, it didn't say anything back. It just fluttered a little in the moonlight and the seawind. But when I got around to dreaming, I dreamed about the orchid, and it said: *a farm*.

3. Murdercunt

In Garbagetown, you think real hard about what you're gonna eat next, where the fresh water's at, and where you're gonna sleep. Once all that's settled you can whack your mind on nicer stuff, like gannets and elephant seals and what to write next on the Bitch of Candle Hole's door. (This morning I melted MURDERCUNT off the back wall of my house. Big Bargains flopped down next to me and watched the blocky red painted letters swirl and fade into the Buttercream Birthday Cake wax. Maybe I'll name my hibiscus flower Murdercunt. It has a nice big sound.)

When I remember hunting my name, I mostly remember the places I slept. It's a real dog to find good spots. Someplace sheltered from the wind, without too much seawater seep, where no-one'll yell at you for wastreling on their patch or try to stick it in you in the middle of the night just because you're all alone and it looks like you probably don't have a knife.

I always have a knife.

So I slept with St. Oscar the Grouch for my pillow, in the shadow of a mountain of black chess pieces in Gamegrange, under a thicket of tabloids and *Wall Street Journals* and remaindered novels with their covers torn off in Bookbury, snuggled into a spaghetti-pile of unspooled cassette ribbon on the outskirts of the Sound Downs, on the lee side of a little soggy Earl Grey hillock in Teagate. In the morning I sucked on a few of the teabags and the dew on them tasted like the loveliest cuppa any Fuckwit ever poured his stupid self. I said my prayers on beds of old microwaves and moldy photographs of girls with perfect hair kissing at the camera. *St. Oscar, keep your mighty lid closed over me. Look grouchily but kindly upon me and protect me as I travel through the infinite trashcan of your world. Show me the beautiful usefulness of your Blessed Rubbish. Let me not be Taken Out before I find my destiny.*

But my destiny didn't seem to want to find me. As far as I walked, I still saw people I knew. Mr. Zhu raking his mushroom garden, nestled in a windbreak of broken milk bottles. Miss Amancharia gave me one of the coconut crabs out of her nets, which was very nice of her, but hardly a name. Even as far away as Teagate, I saw

Tropicana Sita welding a refrigerator door to a hull-metal shack. She flipped up her mask and waved at me. Dammit! She was Allsorts Sita's cousin, and Allsorts drank with my mother every Thursday at the Black Wick.

By the time I walked out of Teagate I'd been gone eight days. I was getting pretty ripe. Bits and pieces of Garbagetown were stuck all over my clothes, but no tidying up. Them's the rules. I could see the blue crackle of Electric City sparkling up out of the richie-rich Coffee Bean 'Burbs. Teetering towers of batteries rose up like desert hoodoo spires—AA, AAA, 12 Volt, DD, car, solar, lithium, anything you like. Parrots and pelicans screamed down the battery canyons, their talons kicking off sprays of AAAs that tumbled down the heights like rockslides. Sleepy banks of generators rumbled pleasantly along a river of wires and extension cords and HDMI cables. Fields of delicate lightbulbs windchimed in the breeze. Anything that had a working engine lived here. Anything that still had *juice*. If Garbagetown had a heart, it was Electric City. Electric City pumped power. Power and privilege.

In Electric City, the lights of the Fuckwit world were still on.

4. Goodnight Garbagetown

"Oi, Tetley! Fuck off back home to your darkhole! We're full up on little cunts here!"

And that's how I got my name. Barely past the battery spires of Electric City, a fat gas-huffing fucksack voltage jockey called me a little cunt. But he also called me Tetley. He brayed it down from a pyramid of telephones and his friends all laughed and drank homebrew out of a glass jug and went back to not working. I looked down—among the many scraps of rubbish clinging to my shirt and pants and backpack and hair was a bright blue teabag wrapper with TETLEY CLASSIC BLEND BLACK TEA written on it in cheerful white letters, clinging to my chest.

I tried to feel the power of my new name. The *me*-ness of it. I tried to imagine my mother and father when they were young, waking up with some torn out page of *Life* or *Time* magazine stuck to their rears, not even noticing until someone barked out their whole lives for a laugh. But I couldn't feel anything while the volt-humpers kept on staring at me like I was nothing but a used-up potato battery. I didn't even know then that the worst swear word in Electric City was *dark*. I didn't know they were waiting to see how mad I'd get 'cause they called my home a darkhole. I didn't care. They were wrong and stupid. Except for the hole part. Candle Hole never met a dark it couldn't burn down.

Maybe I should have gone home right then. I had my name! Time to hoof it back over the river and through the woods, girl. But I'd never seen Electric City and it was morning and if I stayed gone awhile longer maybe they'd miss me. Maybe they'd worry. And maybe now they'd love me, now that I was a person with a name. Maybe I could even filch a couple of batteries or a cup of gasoline and turn up at my parents' door in turbo-powered triumph. I'd tell my brother all my adventures and he'd look at me like I was magic on a stick and everything would be good forever and ever amen.

So I wandered. I gawped. It was like being in school and learning the Fuckwit song only I was walking around *inside* the Fuckwit song and it was all still happening right now everywhere. Electric City burbled and bubbled and clanged and belched and smoked just like the bad old world before it all turned blue. Everyone had such fine things! I saw a girl wearing a ballgown out of a fairy book, green and glitter and miles of ruffles and she wasn't even *going* anywhere. She was just tending her gasoline garden out the back of her little cottage, which wasn't made out of candles or picturebooks or cat food cans, but real cottage parts! Mostly doors and shutters and really rather a lot of windows, but they fit together like they never even needed the other parts of a house in the first place. And the girl in her greenglitter dress carried a big red watering can around her garden, sprinkling fuel stabilizer into her tidy rows of petrol barrels and gas cans with their graceful spouts pointed toward the sun. Why not wear that dress all the time? Just a wineglass full of what she was growing in her garden would buy almost anything else in Garbagetown. She smiled shyly at me. I hated her. And I wanted to be her.

By afternoon I was bound for London-town, so hungry I could've slurped up every eel the Thames ever had. There's no food lying around in Electric City. In Candle Hole I could've grabbed candy or a rice ball or jerky off any old midden heap. But here everybody owned their piece and kept it real neat, *mercilessly* neat, and they didn't share. I sat down on a rusty Toyota transmission and fished around in my backpack for crumbs. My engine sat on one side of a huge cyclone fence. I'd never seen one all put together before. Sure, you find torn-off shreds of wire fences, but this one was all grown up, with proper locks and chain wire all over it. It meant to Keep You Out. Inside, like hungry dogs, endless barrels and freezers and cylinders and vats went on and on, with angry writing on them that said HAZMAT or BIOHAZARD or RADIOACTIVE or WARNING or DANGER or CLASSIFIED.

"Got anything good in there?" said a boy's voice. I looked round and saw a kid my own age, with wavy black hair and big brown eyes and three little moles on his forehead. He was wearing the nicest clothes I ever saw on a boy—a blue suit that almost, *almost* fit him. With a *tie*.

"Naw," I answered. "Just a dry sweater, an empty can of Cheez Whiz, and *Madeline Brix's Superboss Mixtape '97*. It's my good luck charm." I showed him my beloved mixtape. Madeline Brix made all the dots on her *i*'s into hearts. It was a totally Fuckwit thing to do and I loved her for it even though she was dead and didn't care if I loved her or not.

"*Cool,*" the boy said, and I could tell he meant it. He didn't even call me a little cunt or anything. He pushed his thick hair out of his face. "Listen, you really shouldn't be here. No one's gonna say anything because you're not Electrified, but it's so completely dangerous. They put all that stuff in one place so it couldn't get out and hurt anyone."

"Electrified?"

"One of us. Local." He had the decency to look embarrassed. "Anyway, I saw you and I thought that if some crazy darkgirl is gonna have a picnic on Hazmat Heath, I could at least help her not die while she's doing it."

The boy held out his hand. He was holding a gas mask. He showed me how to fasten it under my hair. The sun started to set rosily behind a tangled briar of motherboards. Everything turned pink and gold and slow and sleepy. I climbed down from my engine tuffet and lay under the fence next to the boy in the suit. He'd brought a mask for himself too. We looked at each other through the eye holes.

"My name's Goodnight Moon," he said.

"Mine's…" And I did feel my new name swirling up inside me then, like good tea, like cream and sugar cubes, like the most essential me. "Tetley."

"I'm sorry I called you a darkgirl, Tetley."

"Why?"

"It's not a nice thing to call someone."

"I like it. It sounds pretty."

"It isn't. I promise. Do you forgive me?"

I tugged on the hose of my gas mask. The air coming through tasted like nickels. "Sure. I'm aces at forgiving. Been practicing all my life. Besides…" My turn to go red in the face. "At the Black Wick they'd probably call you a brightboy and that's not as pretty as it sounds, either."

Goodnight Moon's brown eyes stared out at me from behind thick glass. It was the closest I'd ever been to a boy who wasn't my twin. Goodnight Moon didn't feel like a twin. He felt like the opposite of a twin. We never shared a womb, but on the other end of it all, we might still share a grave. His tie was burgundy with green swirls in it. He hadn't tied it very well, so I could see the skin of his throat, which was very clean and probably very soft.

"Hey," he said, "do you want to hear your tape?"

"What do you mean *hear* it? It's not for hearing, it's for luck."

Goodnight Moon laughed. His laugh burst all over me like butterfly bombs. He reached into his suit jacket and pulled out a thick black rectangle. I handed him *Madeline Brix's Superboss Mixtape '97* and he hit a button on the side of the rectangle. It popped open; Goodnight Moon slotted in my tape and handed me one end of a long wire.

"Put it in your ear," he said, and I did.

A man's voice filled up my head from my jawbone up to the plates of my skull. The most beautiful and saddest voice that ever was. A voice like Candle Hole all lit up at twilight. A voice like the whole old world calling up from the bottom of the sea. The man on Madeline

Brix's tape was saying he was happy, and he hoped I was happy, too.

Goodnight Moon reached out to hold my hand just as the sky went black and starry. I was crying. He was, too. Our tears dripped out of our gas masks onto the rusty road of Electric City.

When the tape ended, I dug in my backpack for a match and a stump of candle: dark red, Holiday Memories scent. I lit it at the same moment that Goodnight Moon pulled a little flashlight out of his pocket and turned it on. We held our glowings between us. We were the same.

5. Brightbitch

Allsorts Sita came to visit me today. Clicked my knocker early in the morning, early enough that I could be sure she'd never slept in the first place. I opened for her, as I am required to do. She looked up at me with eyes like bullet holes, leaning on my waxy hinges, against the T in BRIGHTBITCH, thoughtfully scrawled in what appeared to be human shit across the front of my hut. BRIGHTBITCH smelled, but Allsorts Sita smelled worse. Her breath punched me in the nose before she did. I got a lungful of what Diet Sprite down at the Black Wick optimistically called "cognac": the thick pinkish booze you could get by extracting the fragrance oil and preservatives out of candles and mixing it with wood alcohol the kids over in Furnitureford boiled out of dining sets and china cabinets. Smells like flowers vomited all over a New Car and then killed a badger in the backseat. Allsorts Sita looked like she'd drunk so much cognac you could light one strand of her hair and she'd burn for eight days.

"You fucking whore," she slurred.

"Thank you, Auntie, for my instruction," I answered quietly.

I have a place I go to in my mind when I have visitors who aren't seals or gannet birds or hibiscus flowers. A little house made all of doors and windows, where I wear a greenglitter dress every day and water my gascan garden and read by electric light.

"I hate you. I hate you. How could you do it? We raised you and fed you and this is how you repay it all. You ungrateful bitch."

"Thank you, Auntie, for my instruction."

In my head I ran my fingers along a cyclone fence and all the barrels on the other side read LIFE and LOVE and FORGIVENESS and UNDERSTANDING.

"You've killed us all," Allsorts Sita moaned. She puked up magenta cognac on my stoop. When she was done puking she hit me over and over with closed fists. It didn't hurt too much. Allsorts is a small woman. But it hurt when she clawed my face and my breasts with her fingernails. Blood came up like wax spilling and when she finished she passed out cold, halfway in my house, halfway out.

"Thank you, Auntie, for my instruction," I said to her sleeping body. My blood dripped onto her, but in my head I was lying on my roof made of two big church doors in a gas mask listening to a man sing to me that he's never done bad things and he hopes I'm happy, he hopes I'm happy, he hopes I'm happy.

Big Bargains moaned mournfully and the lovely roof melted away like words on a door. My elephant seal friend flopped and fretted. When they've gone for my face she can't quite recognize me and it troubles her seal-soul something awful. Grape Crush, my gannet bird, never worries about silly things like facial wounds. He just brings me fish and pretty rocks. When I found him, he had a plastic six-pack round his neck with one can still stuck in the thing, dragging along behind him like a ball and chain. Big Bargains was choking on an ad insert. She'd probably smelled some ancient fish and chips grease lurking in the headlines. They only love me because I saved them. That doesn't always work. I saved everyone else, too, and all I got back was blood and shit and loneliness.

6. Revlon Super Lustrous 919: Red Ruin

I went home with my new name fastened on tight. Darkgirls can't stay in Electric City. Can't live there unless you're born there and I was only ten anyway. Goodnight Moon kissed me before I left. He still had his gas mask on so mainly our breathing hoses wound around each other like gentle elephants but I still call it a kiss. He smelled like scorched ozone and metal and paraffin and hope.

A few months later, Electric City put up a fence around the whole place. Hung up an old rusty shop sign that said EXCUSE OUR MESS WHILE WE RENOVATE. No one could go in or out except to trade and that had to get itself done on the dark side of the fence.

My mother and father didn't start loving me when I got back even though I brought six AA batteries out of the back of Goodnight Moon's tape player. My brother had got a ramen flavor packet stuck in his hair somewhere outside the Grocery Isle and was every inch of him Maruchan. A few years later I heard Life and Time telling some cousin how their marvelous and industrious and thoughtful boy had gone out in search of a name and brought back six silver batteries, enough to power anything they could dream of. What a child! What a son! So fuck them, I guess.

But Maruchan did bring something back. It just wasn't for our parents. When we crawled into the Us-Fort that first night back, we lay uncomfortably against each other. We were the same, but we weren't. We'd had separate adventures for the first time, and Maruchan could never understand why I wanted to sleep with a gas mask on now.

"Tetley, what do you want to be when you grow up?" Maruchan whispered in the dark of our pram-maze.

"Electrified," I whispered back. "What do you want to be?"

"Safe," he said. Things had happened to Maruchan, too, and I couldn't share them anymore than he could hear Madeline Brix's songs.

My twin pulled something out of his pocket and pushed it into my hand till my fingers closed round it reflexively. It was hard and plastic and warm.

"I love you, Tetley. Happy Birthday."

I opened my fist. Maruchan had stolen lipstick for me. Revlon Super Lustrous 919: Red Ruin, worn almost all the way down to the nub by some dead woman's lips.

After that, a lot of years went by but they weren't anything special.

7. If God Turned Up for Supper

I was seventeen years old when Brighton Pier came to Garbagetown. I was tall and my hair was the color of an oil spill; I sang pretty good and did figures in my head and I could make a candle out of damn near anything. People wanted to marry me here and there but I didn't want to marry them back so they thought I was stuck up. Who wouldn't want to get hitched to handsome Candyland Ocampo and ditch Candle Hole for a clean, fresh life in Soapthorpe where bubbles popped all day long like diamonds in your hair? Well, I didn't, because he had never kissed me with a gas mask on and he smelled like pine fresh cleaning solutions and not like scorched ozone at all.

Life and Time turned into little kids right in front of us. They giggled and whispered and Mum washed her hair in the sea about nine times and then soaked it in oil until it shone. Papa tucked a candle stump that had melted just right and looked like a perfect rose into her big no fancy hairdo and then, like it was a completely normal thing to do, put on a cloak sewn out of about a hundred different neckties. They looked like a prince and a princess.

"Brighton Pier came last when I was a girl, before I even had my name," Time told us, still giggling and blushing like she wasn't anyone's mother. "It's the most wonderful thing that can ever happen in the world."

"If God turned up for supper and brought all the dry land back for dessert, it wouldn't be half as good as one day on Brighton Pier," Life crowed. He picked me up in his arms and twirled me around in the air. He'd never done that before, not once, and he had his heart strapped on so tight he didn't even stop and realize what he'd done and go vacant-eyed and find something else to look at for a long while. He just squeezed me and kissed me like I came from somewhere and I didn't know what the hell a Brighton Pier was but I loved it already.

"What is it? What is it?" Maruchan and I squealed, because you can catch happiness like a plague.

"It's better the first time if you don't know," Mum assured us. "It's meant to dock in Electric City on Friday."

"So it's a ship, then?" Maruchan said. But Papa just twinkled his eyes at us and put his finger over his lips to keep the secret in.

The Pier meant to dock in Electric City. My heart fell into my stomach, got all digested up, and sizzled out into the rest of me all at once. Of course, of course it would, Electric City had the best docks, the sturdiest, the prettiest. But it seemed to me like life was happening to me on purpose, and Electric City couldn't keep a darkgirl out anymore. They had to share like the rest of us.

"What do you want to be when you grow up, Maruchan?" I said to my twin in the dark the night before we set off to see what was better than God. Maruchan's eyes gleamed with the Christmas thrill of it all.

"Brighton Pier," he whispered.

"Me, too," I sighed, and we both dreamed we were beautiful Fuckwits running through a forest of real pines, laughing and stopping to eat apples and running again and only right before we woke up did we notice that something was chasing us, something huge and electric and bound for London-town.

8. Citizens of Mutation Nation

I looked for Goodnight Moon everywhere from the moment we crossed into Electric City. The fence had gone and Garbagetown poured in and nothing was different than it had been when I got my name off the battery spires, even though the sign had said for so long that Electric City was renovating. I played a terrible game with every person that shoved past, every face in a window, every shadow juddering down an alley and the game was: *are you him?* But I lost all the hands. The only time I stopped playing was when I first saw Brighton Pier.

I couldn't get my eyes around it. It was a terrible, gorgeous whale of light and colors and music and otherness. All along a boardwalk jugglers danced and singers sang and horns horned and accordions squeezed and under it all some demonic engine screamed and wheezed. Great glass domes and towers and flags and tents glowed in the sunset but Brighton Pier made the sunset look plain-faced and unloveable. A huge wheel full of pink and emerald electric lights turned slowly in the warm wind but went nowhere. People leapt and turned somersaults and stood on each other's shoulders and they all wore such soft, vivid costumes, like they'd all been cut out of a picturebook too fine for anyone like me to read. The tumblers lashed the pier to the Electric City docks and cut the engines and after that it was nothing but music so thick and good you could eat it out of the air.

Life and Time hugged Maruchan and cheered with the rest of Garbagetown. Tears ran down their faces. Everyone's faces.

"When the ice melted and the rivers revolted and the Fuckwit world went under the seas," Papa whispered through his weeping, "a great mob hacked Brighton Pier off of Brighton and strapped engines to it and set sail across the blue. They've been going ever since. They go around the world and around again, to the places where there's still people, and trade their beauty for food and fuel. There's a place on Brighton Pier where if you look just right, it's like nothing ever drowned."

A beautiful man wearing a hat of every color and several bells stepped up on a pedestal and held a long pale cone to his mouth. The mayor of Electric City embraced him with two meaty arms and asked his terrible, stupid, unforgivable question: "Have you seen dry land?"

And the beautiful man answered him: "With my own eyes."

A roar went up like angels dying. I covered my ears. The mayor covered his mouth with his hands, speechless, weeping. The beautiful man patted him awkwardly on the back. Then he turned to us.

"Hello, Garbagetown!" he cried out and his voice sounded like everyone's most secret heart.

We screamed so loud every bird in Garbagetown fled to the heavens and we clapped like mad and some people fell onto the ground and buried their face in old batteries.

"My name is Emperor William Shakespeare the Eleventh and I am the Master of Brighton Pier! We will be performing *Twelfth Night* in the great stage tonight at seven o'clock, followed by *The Duchess of Malfi* at ten (which has werewolves) and a midnight acrobatic display! Come one, come all! Let Madame Limelight tell your FORTUNE! TEST your strength with the Hammer of the Witches! SEE the wonders of the Fuckwit World in our Memory Palace! Get letters and news from the LAST HUMAN OUTPOSTS around the globe! GASP at the citizens of Mutation Nation in the Freak Tent!

Sample a FULL MINUTE of real television, still high definition after all these years! Concerts begin in the Crystal Courtyard in fifteen minutes! Our Peep Shows feature only the FINEST actresses reading aloud from GENUINE Fuckwit historical records! Garbagetown, we are here to DAZZLE you!"

A groan went up from the crowds like each Garbagetowner was just then bedding their own great lost love and they heaved toward the lights, the colors, the horns and the voices, the silk and the electricity and the life floating down there, knotted to the edge of our little pile of trash.

Someone grabbed my hand and held me back while my parents, my twin, my world streamed away from me down to the Pier. No one looked back.

"Are you her?" said Goodnight Moon. He looked longer and leaner but not really older. He had on his tie.

"Yes," I said, and nothing was different than it had been when I got my name except now neither of us had masks and our kisses weren't like gentle elephants but like a boy and a girl and I forgot all about my strength and my fortune and the wonderful wheel of light turning around and around and going nowhere.

9. Terrorwhore

Actors are liars. Writers, too. The whole lot of them, even the horn players and the fortune tellers and the freaks and the strongmen. Even the ladies with rings in their noses and high heels on their feet playing violins all along the pier and the lie they are all singing and dancing and saying is: *we can get the old world back again.*

My door said TERRORWHORE this morning. I looked after my potato plants and my hibiscus and thought about whether or not I would ever get to have sex again. Seemed unlikely. Big Bargains concurred.

Goodnight Moon and I lost our virginities in the Peep Show tent while a lady in green fishnet stockings and a lavender garter read to us from the dinner menu of the Dorchester Hotel circa 2005.

"Whole Berkshire roasted chicken stuffed with black truffles, walnuts, duck confit, and dauphinoise potatoes," the lady purred. Goodnight Moon devoured my throat with kisses, bites, need. "Drizzled with a balsamic reduction and rosemary honey."

"What's honey?" I gasped. We could see her but she couldn't see us, which was for the best. The glass in the window only went one way.

"Beats me, kid," she shrugged, re-crossing her legs the other way. "Something you drizzle." She went on. "Sticky toffee pudding with lashings of cream and salted caramel, passionfruit soufflé topped with orbs of pistachio ice cream…"

Goodnight Moon smelled just as I remembered. Scorched ozone and metal and paraffin and hope and when he was inside me it was like hearing my name for the first time. I couldn't escape the *me*-ness of it, the *us*-ness of it, the sound and the shape of ourselves turning into our future.

"I can't believe you're here," he whispered into my breast. "I can't believe this is us."

The lady's voice drifted over my head. "Lamb cutlets on a bed of spiced butternut squash, wilted greens, and delicate hand-harvested mushrooms served with goat cheese in clouds of pastry…"

Goodnight Moon kissed my hair, my ears, my eyelids. "And now that the land's come back Electric City's gonna save us all. We can go home together, you and me, and build a house and we'll have a candle in every window so you always feel at home…"

The Dorchester dinner menu stopped abruptly. The lady dropped to her fishnetted knees and peered at us through the glass, her brilliant glossy red hair tumbling down, her spangled eyes searching for us beyond the glass.

"Whoa, sweetie, slow down," she said. "You're liable to scare a girl off that way."

All I could see in the world was Goodnight Moon's brown eyes and the sweat drying on his brown chest. Brown like the earth and all its promises. "I don't care," he said. "You scared, Tetley?" I shook my head. "Nothing can scare us now. Emperor Shakespeare said he's seen land, real dry land, and we have a plan and we're gonna get everything back again and be fat happy Fuckwits like we were always supposed to be."

The Peep Show girl's glittering eyes filled up with tears. She put her hand on the glass. "Oh... oh, baby... that's just something we say. We always say it. To everyone. It's our best show. Gives people hope, you know? But there's nothing out there, sugar. Nothing but ocean and more ocean and a handful of drifty lifeboat cities like yours circling the world like horses on a broken-down carousel. Nothing but blue."

10. We Are So Lucky

It would be nice for me if you could just say you understand. I want to hear that just once. Goodnight Moon didn't. He didn't believe her and he didn't believe me and he sold me out in the end in spite of gas masks and kissing and Madeline Brix and the man crooning in our ears that he was happy because all he could hear was Emperor William Shakespeare the Eleventh singing out his big lie. RESURRECTION! REDEMPTION! REVIVIFICATION! LAND HO!

"No, because, see," my sweetheart wept on the boardwalk while the wheel spun dizzily behind his head like an electric candy crown, "we have a plan. We've worked so hard. It *has* to happen. The mayor said as soon as we had news of dry land, the minute we knew, we'd turn it on and we'd get there first and the continents would be ours, Garbagetowners, we'd inherit the Earth. He's gonna tell everyone when the Pier leaves. At the farewell party."

"Turn what on?"

Resurrection. Redemption. Renovation. All those years behind the fence Electric City had been so busy. Disassembling all those engines they hoarded so they could make a bigger one, the biggest one. Pooling fuel in great vast stills. Practicing ignition sequences. Carving up a countryside they'd never even seen between the brightboys and brightgirls and we could have some, too, if we were good.

"You want to turn Garbagetown into a Misery Boat," I told him. "So we can just steam on ahead into nothing and go mad and use up all the gas and batteries that could keep us happy in mixtapes for another century here in one hot minute."

"The Emperor said..."

"He said his name was Duke Orsino of Illyria, too. And then Roderigo when they did the werewolf play. Do you believe that? If they'd found land, don't you think they'd have stayed there?"

But he couldn't hear me. Neither could Maruchan when I tried to tell him the truth in the Peep Show. All they could see was green. Green leafy trees and green grass and green ivy in some park that was lying at the bottom of the sea. We dreamed different dreams now, my brother and I, and all my dreams were burning.

Say you understand. I had to. I'm not a nihilist or a murdercunt or a terrorwhore. They were gonna use up every last drop of Garbagetown's power to go nowhere and do nothing and instead of measuring out teaspoons of good, honest gas, so that it lasts and we last all together, no single thing on the patch would ever turn on again, and we'd go dark, *really* dark, forever. Dark like the bottom of a hole. They had no right. *They* don't understand. This is *it*. This is the future. Garbagetown and the sea. We can't go back, not ever, not even for a minute. We are so lucky. Life is so good. We're going on and being alive and being shitty sometimes and lovely sometimes just the same as we always have, and only a Fuckwit couldn't see that.

I waited until Brighton Pier cast off, headed to the next rickety harbor of floating foolboats, filled with players and horns and glittering wheels and Dorchester menus and fresh mountains of letters we wouldn't read the answers to for another twenty years. I waited until everyone was sleeping so nobody would get hurt except the awful engine growling and panting to deliver us into the dark salt nothing of an empty hellpromise.

It isn't hard to build a bomb in Electric City. It's all just laying around behind that fence where a boy held my hand for the first time. All you need is a match.

11. What You Came For

It's such a beautiful day out. My hibiscus is just gigantic, red as the hair on a Peep Show dancer. If you want to wait, Big Bargains will be round later for her afternoon nap. Grape Crush usually brings a herring by in the evening. But I understand if you've got other places to be.

It's okay. You can hit me now. If you want to. It's what you came for. I barely feel it anymore.

Thank you for my instruction.

FRANCISCA MONTOYA'S ALMANAC OF THINGS THAT CAN KILL YOU

SHAENON K. GARRITY

Shaenon K. Garrity is a cartoonist best known for the webcomics *Narbonic* and *Skin Horse*. Her prose fiction has appeared in publications including *Strange Horizons*, *Lightspeed*, *Escape Pod*, *Drabblecast*, and the *Unidentified Funny Objects* anthologies. Her most recent book is *The Zombie Gnome Defense Guide*, written with Andrew Farago and Bryan Heemskerk. She lives in Berkeley with a cat, a man and a boy.

Allergic Reaction

If you get ill after eating or touching something that didn't make anyone else sick, you may be allergic to it. Especially if there's a rash. Allergies are caused by your body rejecting substances it doesn't like. There is no treatment but to avoid those substances. Fortunately, only a few types of allergies can kill you. Nut allergies, for instance. Bee stings. But I imagine most people with fatal allergies to common things have died by now.

I am allergic to wool, soy, peanuts, and pollen. Only my peanut allergy can kill me.

Appendicitis

There is an organ in your body called the appendix, and sometimes it goes bad and kills you. The only treatment is to cut it out of your body.

I don't recommend trying this. You'll bleed to death. On the other hand, death from appendicitis is long and excruciatingly painful. So maybe try surgery. There's something to be said for the quicker death.

Bears

Bears aren't so bad. They can kill you very easily, but mostly they leave people alone. Also, they keep wolves away. After Lauren died, I settled in Gualala because grizzly bears had been sighted in the area. Most people were afraid of the bears, but those people were idiots. Bears are so much better than wolves.

If you encounter a bear, move away slowly. If that doesn't work, drop to the ground and play dead. You want the bear to lose interest in you and go away. But if a bear wants to kill you, it'll kill you. There isn't much you can do about it. I suppose that's what scares people about bears. But if you think about it, the same thing is true of everything that can kill you.

Beriberi

This has a lot of names in different places: the shakes, the bone dance, calf legs. It starts with feeling weak and fatigued, then progresses to numbness in the arms and legs, inability to walk, facial tics, and dementia. Sufferers may also have a rapid heartbeat and shortness of breath.

As complex and frightening as these symptoms are—and I've seen them enough to know how scary they can be—the cause is a simple vitamin deficiency. Unless it's progressed too far, a diet of fresh meat, green vegetables, and brown bread (*not* anything made from the white flour or white rice found in the cities) should take care of the problem. Also, drink fresh clean water instead of beer if possible. If none of this is possible, beriberi can easily kill you.

As we traveled up the coast, back in my traveling days, Lauren and I started to see more and more stick-thin sufferers of beriberi, sometimes even in the larger settlements, and we were told more and more often that our diagnosis was useless. Where was anyone going to get fresh greens, when all the local farmland had turned poisonous and chalky, and even the trees in the woods were whitening? People got angry, they refused to pay. That was one of the things that made us think we ought to give up the traveling medicine work and settle somewhere, if we could find a healthy place that would take us.

Blood Poisoning

There are a lot of ways blood can get poisoned. Stepping on a rusty nail. Getting cut by a sharp piece of old metal. Always wear boots and gloves when foraging in the cities.

If you get an infected cut and start having spasms, especially in the jaw, you have tetanus. Tetanus can easily kill you. The only treatment we have these days is bed rest. Some people try bloodletting to release the poison, but I've never seen that work. The sickness isn't caused by poison, anyway. It's caused by bacteria that live in dirt.

You can also get blood poisoning through a tooth abscess or other dental problems. That's what got Lauren. She had a toothache and she let it go, and let it go, and one morning her whole jaw swelled up and her body was on fire. She died a few days later. That was when I had to start looking seriously for a place to settle down, because I can't travel alone, not with my allergies and my fibromyalgia. (Fibromyalgia is a painful disorder of the muscles. It's not worth going into here, because it can't kill you.) It took me three days to dig a grave in a nearby redwood grove, a safe distance from any source of water, and then I cried a little, and then I got the wagon back on the road and headed for the nearest settlement.

Keep your mouth as clean as possible, and pull rotten teeth before the rot spreads.

Botulism

Botulism causes cramps, vomiting, and breathing problems. There is no fever. You usually get it from food that's been improperly preserved. It happens sometimes with smoked and cured meats, but is most common with canned goods. If you find canned food, check the can carefully for dents or swellings. Do not eat food from damaged cans, no matter how rare and delicious it is.

There used to be a cure for botulism, if treated quickly enough, but we don't have it anymore.

When I worked at the trading post in Gualala, I threw out dozens of cans that people had salvaged from San Francisco and Berkeley. Most canned food from the old days is no good anymore. A lot of people got angry at me. Fortunately, Evan, who ran the trading post, backed me up. He'd dealt with botulism before, and he knew it can kill you.

A man once threatened to shoot me for destroying ten cans of Vienna sausages he'd found. I should have just let him eat the diseased meat. What kind of person wastes a bullet over spoiled Vienna sausages? I know how hunger grinds at you, especially if you're coming up to trade out of the dead places, but eating bacteria just makes things worse.

Gualala was a good place, though. Still healthy, but well protected from raiders. Evan gave me acrylic wool the traders brought in and I'd sit on the porch of the trading post and knit. I got a reputation as the person to talk to if you were sick or injured or were planning a big journey. People were always planning trips north, over the mountains, following rumors of healthy cropland and even operational cities up in Oregon. I don't know why they wanted to talk to me about it, since I always said the same thing: Forget it. So many things in the mountains can kill you. I advised against it every time.

Almost every time.

Childbirth

The best way to avoid dying in childbirth is to not get pregnant. If you do get pregnant, pennyroyal tea is an effective abortifacient. It can be dangerous, but the safer alternatives don't always work. If pennyroyal fails, find a woman with midwife skills and ask her to help. Do not try to perform an abortion on yourself unless all other options have been exhausted.

When Lauren and I were on the road together selling medical care, abortion was the most common service we were asked to provide. We got to be very good at it. We could usually stop a pregnancy with herbs; surgery was not often needed.

We also oversaw childbirth, of course. That was much more

difficult. With the toxins people pick up from the infected areas, a lot of women go into shock during pregnancy. They used to call that eclampsia. It will almost certainly kill you. There are many other ways childbirth can kill you, but that one is the most common right now.

If you do insist on having a baby, get to a large settlement the moment you realize you're pregnant. So many women die giving birth in the middle of nowhere, without a midwife or even another woman around. What if it's a breach birth? You and the baby will both die.

People get angry at me for talking this way about childbirth. What about our duty to carry on the human species, they say.

People are idiots.

Cholera

The colony where I grew up was wiped out by cholera. It's a stupid way to die.

It was an early colony, from before things really fell apart. Some smart people saw the trouble coming and pooled their money and bought an island, a little island off the coast of Mexico. My mother was invited to join because she was a doctor. That was a sign of how stupid these smart people were, that they thought one doctor would be enough when things got bad. One doctor and no medical resources except what she brought with her, which fortunately included a little electronic book with a whole library of books inside it.

The colony did all right for quite a few years, longer than it really should have, but some people just wouldn't dig proper outhouses. A hundred scientists and businessmen and millionaires all died because they kept using the river as a bathroom, and that's how cholera spreads. So don't poo in the river.

There, you're smarter than a scientist.

Diabetes

An old disorder of the blood. Without insulin, the only way to manage it is with a starvation diet. I doubt anyone has diabetes today.

Dysentery (Bacterial)

Don't get poo in your mouth.

Dysentery (Amoebic)

Don't drink nasty water.

Normally I don't have patience for people who lack the common sense to stick to clean water or beer, but I have to admit that accidents happen. For example, a man traveling up the coast might stop and make camp at Clearlake, not knowing that the two settlements that used to be there recently wiped each other out in a war over the last fertile fields. And they sank corpses in the lake to poison the water, and the streams in the area may look clean, but they're crawling with bacteria. It's maybe not a man's fault, under those circumstances, if he drinks the water.

For both forms of dysentery, the treatment is the same as for cholera. It's not as bad as cholera, but if you're already sick or weakened it can kill you. I've nursed a lot of people through it. I know what to do. When the patrol guards hauled Dr. Spendlove onto the porch of the trading post, I knew.

Dysentery is not a romantic disease.

Exposure

All my life, I've avoided places where the temperature drops below freezing. As far as I'm concerned, that's the best way to prevent death by exposure, just like not getting pregnant is the best way to prevent death by childbirth. Don't go north. It's so simple. Especially don't try a mountain crossing late in the year, when the air in Gualala is already crisp and cold at the height of the afternoon, and there are no stars in the night sky.

But, as with pregnancy, sometimes things happen. Sometimes you find yourself in the mountains of Oregon in December, in a shattered wagon with the snow starting to fall all around and your fibromyalgia acting up. It's not smart. Maybe it turns out you're pretty stupid after all. But it happens.

If you're caught outside in the cold, the first thing to do is build a shelter. Put pine needles or other cushioning between yourself and the ground, because the frozen earth sucks out heat. Get out of the wind and into some kind of insulation. Straw is good. I could use a pile of straw.

Share body heat.

Feral Dog Packs

Anyone who's ever gone into a city with a foraging party knows to pick up rocks to scare the dogs away. Because most dogs will slink away at the first hint of a threat, people often underestimate the danger of dog packs. People are stupid. They worry about bears and snakes and so on, but when you get down to it, truly wild animals are glad to ignore you. They don't care about humans. Dogs care. And they know us.

Not all dog packs are scared little clusters of skinny sucker dogs. Some are big and organized and know how to hunt. And I've seen normally harmless packs turn dangerous when fighting each other over territory. So play it safe. If you hear barking, turn and walk the other way.

People ask which are worse, dogs or wolves. Don't ask questions like that. If you're smart, you'll never know.

When Dr. Spendlove was a boy, he had a dog as a pet. Its name was Jacob. He talked about it while we sat around the fire at night, watching the trees for movement. Nights like this we could use a warm dog at our feet, he said. I've read books with that kind of thing, but it's hard to picture.

Foraging

Lauren and I were good at foraging. Summer and autumn up in the Berkeley Hills, foraging all day and cooking in the granite-countertop kitchen of some abandoned house at night, those were the best times. With all I'd memorized from my mother's little electronic library, I knew what to gather and what to avoid.

Without a library, it's harder. You have to be careful, because lots of things that look good can kill you. It's as true with food as it is with the rest of life.

What I ought to do here is put in some drawings of poisonous things, mushrooms and hemlock and all kinds of nightshades mostly. But I'm not much of an artist, and I've got a deadline coming up fast. Lauren could have done it. That's why you pull rotten teeth.

Frostbite

In the cold there are so many things that can kill you. Wolves, for example. And things can go wrong in too many ways. Take frostbite. As if it wasn't bad enough on its own, it can lead to gangrene, which can lead to blood poisoning, which can kill you.

There are treatments, I know. Easy ones. If the frostbite is moderate, you can chafe with snow to remove the damaged skin. If it's more severe, you have to amputate the dead parts of your body. But still, it bothers me. The skin gets so black, and it feels like fire and ice at once. It's not a good way to die.

Toes and fingers go first. If I have to amputate my fingers, I'll never finish this book.

Heatstroke

If you exert yourself out in the heat and you don't drink enough good, clean liquids, your body may become unable to handle the heat normally and go into heatstroke. A common sign is losing the ability to sweat. A person suffering from heatstroke should be moved to as cool a place as possible and kept hydrated. Cover them with damp sheets, splash them with water, make them drink.

Heatstroke can kill you, but it can also cause long-term health problems. Dr. Spendlove has a weak heart from bouts of heatstroke as a child. His family was one of the ones that stayed in Salt Lake City after the evacuation, back when the trouble started. It was a hard life of hot, dry death. But at least he escaped the worst of what was happening in the outside world, just like I did on the island off Mexico.

Still, his heart is weak. That's why I agreed to go north with him. He might have had another spell, and where would he have been without me?

Hypothermia

When you get cold enough, your body starts to freeze. If this goes on long enough, it will kill you. But don't panic. Stand too quickly, and the cold blood could rush up from your legs and give you a heart attack. Especially if you have a weak heart.

Move slowly. Try to shiver under the blankets. Blow on the little yellow fire. Keep writing.

Malnutrition

I'm sure I don't need to tell you the symptoms of malnutrition. Anyone who's ever lived around the dead places has seen it, and most places are dead places these days. Now that the white plague has spread everywhere and the cities are mostly picked clean, feeding people has gotten harder and harder. Outside of a few good places, everyone's starving to some degree or another.

The human body is funny. You can live a long, reasonably comfortable life without ever getting enough to eat, your body always eating itself a little but never too much. Or you can drop dead from the lack of a single vitamin. For most people, though, malnutrition kills sooner rather than later. There is no cure but to eat, and to eat as varied a diet as possible.

I'm sorry. That's all I have. Until there's more food, that's it.

Mites

Use only oat or wheat straw in chicken coops, and never line coops with wet straw. Keep the coops away from your house and away from your source of fresh water. This is another thing people never take seriously until they start getting sick.

Reading my mother's library when I was younger, I always thought this was the kind of thing that would kill me. Pet a chicken and pick up mites, sip a cup of cloudy water and get a tapeworm, prick your finger on a needle and the lockjaw sets in. Some tiny thing that slips into you and grinds the gears of your biology to a halt. I am a small, quiet person. I am made for a small and silly death.

And yet here I am, with my allergies and my fibromyalgia,

impossibly far from the green-and-yellow island where I used to sit in the shade and pore over my mother's library. I've made it a long way. All the way up here. Somehow, without meaning to do anything but stay alive and keep others alive if I can, it seems I've climbed to a big death after all.

Mountain Lions

They'll eat you if they're hungry, but they're usually not hungry enough, except in the most badly infected of the dead places. Not as bad as wolves, or even as bad as bears. Just avoid them, and if you see one, don't bother it. Why would you even want to bother a mountain lion? I've seen people do it. Stupid people.

A mountain lion carried off a child in Gualala. A little girl. Tell your kids to leave strange animals alone. Simple as that.

I saw mountain lion tracks this morning when I left the shelter for water and fuel. They don't worry me much. Not as much as the wolves I heard howling last night.

Pollution

I was going to have Dr. Spendlove write this section. Pollution, even if we're just talking man-made pollution, is a big topic, and it's not one I know that much about. There are just too many kinds, in the air and the water and the ground. That's why people fight so viciously for the land where crops still grow.

Dr. Spendlove knows a treatment for the white plague in the soil. Or so he says. He found a paper on it while camping in the ruins of Berkeley, collecting data from the old days. He thinks he can use it to cook a cure. That's why we risked this mountain crossing, to get this information to the lab that Dr. Spendlove is almost certain still exists in Eureka.

We could have waited for spring. Probably. If I'd been smart, I would have insisted on waiting. But he was so eager, and his heart was so weak.

I'll come back to this section later. Maybe when we reach Eureka. Maybe when Dr. Spendlove comes to.

Snakebite

Here in the northwest, there aren't many poisonous snakes. It's not worth worrying about. Anyway, they're like most animals (except the dogs, except the wolves)—leave them alone, and they're usually happy enough to leave you alone in return.

In Mexico, when I was a girl, one of my summer jobs was killing coral snakes out in the fields. They were beautiful snakes, with thick shimmering stripes the color of a campfire. Their bite could kill in twenty minutes. We stabbed them with pitchforks. Some kids saved the bodies and made the skins into belts or satchels, but I never wanted to touch anything with that much venom. For a while, before I got used to the work, I had nightmares about a coral snake brushing my foot with its fangs.

Now that I'm older, I'm a little nostalgic for coral snakes. Such a quick, warm death, and so beautiful.

Stab Wounds

People worry too much about animals. When I traveled with Lauren, and then later at the trading post in Gualala, people always asked me how to survive animal attacks. What about mountain lions, they'd say. What about snakes. What about bears.

You want the truth? Animals that can kill you are rare and mostly don't want to meet you. People that can kill you are everywhere, and they're looking for you.

Everyone knows about the raiding parties that hide in the mountain passes. Usually they'll just steal what they can and ride off. But in the winter they get hungry, just like everything else in the mountains. In the winter they get desperate. And if they've managed to scavenge, borrow, or steal a cache of weapons, maybe they'll just kill your party instead of robbing you.

It was a raiding party that took my mother's library, years ago. They rode out of the hills in Jeeps. There was gasoline back then. I was working on a sweet-potato farm near the ruins of Pasadena, and they rode out of the hills and grabbed as many of us as they could. They took my library and my boots and let me go. I guess raiding parties have hardened since then.

It used to be that gunshot wounds were the type of death you most had to fear from your fellow man. But with the old guns falling apart and bullets, even the homemade kind, getting precious, most bandits attack with knives. Clean stab wounds and bind tightly. The wound must be washed regularly, because there are many ways to die of infected wounds. Staph. Gangrene. Tetanus. It used to be uncommon for someone to die of infected wounds, but most people today were born after vaccines, so now it happens quite a lot.

I kept Dr. Spendlove's wounds as clean as I could, but the wounds were deep and the knife was filthy.

Thirst

You find out where the clean water is, and you drink that only. If there isn't enough clean water, you make beer. Lack of water will kill you long, long before lack of food. Everyone knows this, but some people still insist on working all day in the heat without enough to drink, or leaving the ice on the well uncracked until they can't break through. Fetch water. Drink. Fetch more.

I am eating snow now. It seems to be sufficient, but my lips are deeply cracked. Not bleeding. This may be a bad sign. I wish I had my library.

Typhus

Typhus! That's what I should have died of! It's common along the coast nowadays, especially as you get further up north. It's a bacterial disease spread by lice and fleas, often carried by rats. Symptoms are everything that means sickness: muscle ache, headache, vomiting, coughing, fever, chills, delirium, a pink rash that turns dull red as the typhus gets worse. A whole library of ills.

It's easy to prevent typhus with basic hygiene: Bathe regularly, keep your house clean, trap rats and feral animals, and, especially, don't let rat poo collect where you eat and sleep. But people don't do it, won't do it. We used to have many cures for typhus, but we lost them, and now there are none.

It's the perfect thing to kill me. With the wide range of symptoms,

I could keep busy observing and honing my diagnosis right up to the end. And it's such a little thing. A flea bite. A flea bite that wouldn't have happened if people had any common sense.

Instead, it looks like I'll die of hypothermia. What a personally stupid way to die. It's my own fault for going up into the mountains, fibromyalgia and all, to follow Dr. Spendlove's fluttering heart.

I've read that hypothermia is pleasant. You go numb and drift to sleep and that's the end. It may be the kindest of all the things that can kill you. If I stay here, curled against Dr. Spendlove in our makeshift shelter, it will take care of me, slow and gentle and white as the death that's creeping over the planet. It feels pleasant now, and even writing is starting to feel like too much work.

Or I could stand and walk. I won't get far. There's nowhere to go anymore. But I could stand.

Wolves
There is something to be said for the quicker death.

ACKNOWLEDGMENTS

My most heartfelt thanks and appreciation goes out to: Steve Saffel (for acquiring the book and his editorial input) and to Sam Matthews and the rest of the team at Titan Books. My agent, Seth Fishman, for being, as always, awesome and supportive. Gordon Van Gelder and Ellen Datlow, for being great mentors and friends. My wife, Christie; my stepdaughters Grace and Lotte; my mom, Marianne; and my sister, Becky—for all their love and support. My intern, Alex Puncekar. All of the writers who had stories included in this anthology, and all of my other projects. And last but not least, to everyone who bought this book, or any of my other anthologies (or subscribed to my magazines *Lightspeed* and *Nightmare*)—you're the ones who it make it all possible.

ABOUT THE EDITOR

John Joseph Adams is the series editor of *Best American Science Fiction and Fantasy*, as well as the bestselling editor of numerous anthologies, including *Wastelands*, *Brave New Worlds*, and *The Living Dead*. Recent books include *Cosmic Powers*, *What the #@&% is That?*, *Loosed Upon the World*, and The Apocalypse Triptych (consisting of *The End is Nigh*, *The End is Now*, and *The End Has Come*), and the *most* recent is *A People's Future of the United States*. Called "the reigning king of the anthology world" by Barnes & Noble, John is a two-time winner of the Hugo Award (for which he has been nominated twelve times) and an eight-time World Fantasy Award finalist. John is also the editor of John Joseph Adams Books, a science fiction and fantasy imprint from Houghton Mifflin Harcourt, where he's acquired novels by authors such as Veronica Roth, Hugh Howey, Carrie Vaughn, and Greg Bear. He is also the editor and publisher of the digital magazines *Lightspeed* and *Nightmare*, and is a producer for WIRED's *The Geek's Guide to the Galaxy* podcast. He also served as a judge for the 2015 National Book Award. Learn more at johnjosephadams.com, johnjosephadamsbooks.com, and @johnjosephadams.

WASTELANDS

AND

WASTELANDS 2

STORIES OF THE APOCALYPSE
EDITED BY JOHN JOSEPH ADAMS

Two anthologies of the best post-apocalyptic literature of the last two decades from many of today's most renowned authors of speculative fiction.

Featuring prescient tales of Armageddon and its aftermath, from today's finest writers, including: Stephen King, George R.R. Martin, Cory Doctorow, Nancy Kress, Gene Wolfe, Octavia E. Butler, Hugh Howey and many others.

Together they reveal what it will mean to survive and remain human after the end of the world...